THE LAST KINGDOM

Bernard Cornwell was born in London, raised in Essex and worked for the BBC for eleven years before meeting Judy, his American wife. Denied an American work permit he wrote a novel instead and has been writing ever since. He and Judy divide their time between Cape Cod and Charleston, South Carolina.

www.bernardcornwell.net

 /bernard.cornwell

THE LAST KINGDOM

BERNARD CORNWELL

HARPER

Harper
An imprint of HarperCollins*Publishers*
1 London Bridge Street
London SE1 9GF

www.harpercollins.co.uk

This paperback edition 2015
4

First published in Great Britain by
HarperCollins*Publishers* 2004

A catalogue record for this book is
available from the British Library

ISBN: 978-0-00-813947-6

This novel is entirely a work of fiction.
The names, characters and incidents portrayed in it,
while at times based on historical figures, are
the work of the author's imagination.

Set in Meridien by Palimpsest Book Production Limited,
Falkirk, Stirlingshire
Printed and bound in United States of America

Find out more about HarperCollins and the environment at
www.harpercollins.co.uk/green

THE LAST KINGDOM
is for Judy, with love

Wyrd bið ful āræd

CONTENTS

PLACE NAMES

The spelling of place names in Anglo-Saxon England was an uncertain business, with no consistency and no agreement even about the name itself. Thus London was variously rendered as Lundonia, Lundenberg, Lundenne, Lundene, Lundenwic, Lundenceaster and Lundres. Doubtless some readers will prefer other versions of the names listed below, but I have usually employed whatever spelling is cited in the *Oxford Dictionary of English Place-Names* for the years nearest or contained within Alfred's reign, 871–899 AD, but even that solution is not foolproof. Hayling Island, in 956, was written as both Heilincigae and Hæglingaiggæ. Nor have I been consistent myself; I have preferred the modern England to Englaland and, instead of Norðhymbralond, have used Northumbria to avoid the suggestion that the boundaries of the ancient kingdom coincide with those of the modern county. So this list, like the spellings themselves, is capricious:

Æbbanduna	Abingdon, Berkshire
Æsc's Hill	Ashdown, Berkshire
Baðum (pronounced Bathum)	Bath, Avon
Basengas	Basing, Hampshire
Beamfleot	Benfleet, Essex
Beardastopol	Barnstable, Devon
Bebbanburg	Bamburgh Castle, Northumberland
Berewic	Berwick-upon-Tweed, Northumberland
Berrocscire	Berkshire
Blaland	North Africa
Cantucton	Cannington, Somerset
Cetreht	Catterick, Yorkshire
Cippanhamm	Chippenham, Wiltshire
Cirrenceastre	Cirencester, Gloucestershire
Contwaraburg	Canterbury, Kent

Cornwalum	Cornwall
Cridianton	Crediton, Devon
Cynuit	Cynuit Hillfort, nr. Cannington, Somerset
Dalriada	Western Scotland
Defnascir	Devonshire
Deoraby	Derby, Derbyshire
Dic	Diss, Norfolk
Dunholm	Durham, County Durham
Eoferwic	York (also the Danish Jorvic, pronounced Yorvik)
Exanceaster	Exeter, Devon
Fromtun	Frampton on Severn, Gloucestershire
Gegnesburh	Gainsborough, Lincolnshire
the Gewæsc	The Wash
Gleawecestre	Gloucester, Gloucestershire
Grantaceaster	Cambridge, Cambridgeshire
Gyruum	Jarrow, County Durham
Haithabu	Hedeby, trading town in Southern Denmark
Hamanfunta	Havant, Hampshire
Hamptonscir	Hampshire
Hamtun	Southampton, Hampshire
Heilincigae	Hayling Island, Hampshire
Hreapandune	Repton, Derbyshire
Kenet	River Kennet
Ledecestre	Leicester, Leicestershire
Lindisfarena	Lindisfarne (Holy Island), Northumberland
Lundene	London
Mereton	Marten, Wiltshire
Meslach	Matlock, Derbyshire
Pedredan	River Parrett
Pictland	Eastern Scotland
the Poole	Poole Harbour, Dorset
Readingum	Reading, Berkshire
Sæfern	River Severn
Scireburnan	Sherborne, Dorset
Snotengaham	Nottingham, Nottinghamshire

Solente	Solent
Streonshall	Strensall, Yorkshire
Sumorsæte	Somerset
Suth Seaxa	Sussex (South Saxons)
Synningthwait	Swinithwaite, Yorkshire
Temes	River Thames
Thornsæta	Dorset
Tine	River Tyne
Trente	River Trent
Tuede	River Tweed
Twyfyrde	Tiverton, Devon
Uisc	River Exe
Werham	Wareham, Dorset
Wiht	Isle of Wight
Wiire	River Wear
Wiltun	Wilton, Wiltshire
Wiltunscir	Wiltshire
Winburnan	Wimborne Minster, Dorset
Wintanceaster	Winchester, Hampshire

PROLOGUE

Northumbria, 866– 867 AD

My name is Uhtred. I am the son of Uhtred, who was the son of Uhtred and his father was also called Uhtred. My father's clerk, a priest called Beocca, spelt it Utred. I do not know if that was how my father would have written it, for he could neither read nor write, but I can do both and sometimes I take the old parchments from their wooden chest and I see the name spelled Uhtred or Utred or Ughtred or Ootred. I look at those parchments which are deeds saying that Uhtred, son of Uhtred is the lawful and sole owner of the lands that are carefully marked by stones and by dykes, by oaks and by ash, by marsh and by sea, and I dream of those lands, wave-beaten and wild beneath the wind-driven sky. I dream, and know that one day I will take back the land from those who stole it from me.

I am an Ealdorman, though I call myself Earl Uhtred, which is the same thing, and the fading parchments are proof of what I own. The law says I own that land, and the law, we are told, is what makes us men under God instead of beasts in the ditch. But the law does not help me take back my land. The law wants compromise. The law thinks money will compensate for loss. The law, above all, fears the bloodfeud. But I am Uhtred, son of Uhtred, and this is the tale of a bloodfeud. It is a tale of how I will take from my enemy what the law says is mine. And it is the tale of a woman and of her father, a king.

He was my king and all that I have I owe to him. The food that

I eat, the hall where I live and the swords of my men, all came from Alfred, my king, who hated me.

This story begins long before I met Alfred. It begins when I was nine years old and first saw the Danes. It was the year 866 and I was not called Uhtred then, but Osbert, for I was my father's second son and it was the eldest who took the name Uhtred. My brother was seventeen then, tall and well-built, with our family's fair hair and my father's morose face.

The day I first saw the Danes we were riding along the sea shore with hawks on our wrists. There was my father, my father's brother, my brother, myself and a dozen retainers. It was autumn. The sea-cliffs were thick with the last growth of summer, there were seals on the rocks, and a host of seabirds wheeling and shrieking, too many to let the hawks off their leashes. We rode till we came to the criss-crossing shallows that rippled between our land and Lindisfarena, the Holy Island, and I remember staring across the water at the broken walls of the abbey. The Danes had plundered it, but that had been many years before I was born, and though the monks were living there again the monastery had never regained its former glory.

I also remember that day as beautiful and perhaps it was. Perhaps it rained, but I do not think so. The sun shone, the seas were low, the breakers gentle and the world happy. The hawk's claws gripped my wrist through the leather sleeve, her hooded head twitching because she could hear the cries of the white birds. We had left the fortress in the forenoon, riding north, and though we carried hawks we did not ride to hunt, but rather so my father could make up his mind.

We ruled this land. My father, Ealdorman Uhtred, was lord of everything south of the Tuede and north of the Tine, but we did have a king in Northumbria and his name, like mine, was Osbert. He lived to the south of us, rarely came north, and did not bother us, but now a man called Ælla wanted the throne and Ælla, who was an Ealdorman from the hills west of Eoferwic, had raised an

4

army to challenge Osbert and had sent gifts to my father to encourage his support. My father, I realise now, held the fate of the rebellion in his grip. I wanted him to support Osbert, for no other reason than the rightful king shared my name and foolishly, at nine years old, I believed any man called Osbert must be noble, good and brave. In truth Osbert was a dribbling fool, but he was the king, and my father was reluctant to abandon him. But Osbert had sent no gifts and had shown no respect, while Ælla had, and so my father worried. At a moment's notice we could lead a hundred and fifty men to war, all well armed, and given a month we could swell that force to over four hundred foemen, so whichever man we supported would be the king and grateful to us.

Or so we thought.

And then I saw them.

Three ships.

In my memory they slid from a bank of sea mist, and perhaps they did, but memory is a faulty thing and my other images of that day are of a clear, cloudless sky, so perhaps there was no mist, but it seems to me that one moment the sea was empty and the next there were three ships coming from the south.

Beautiful things. They appeared to rest weightless on the ocean, and when their oars dug into the waves they skimmed the water. Their prows and sterns curled high and were tipped with gilded beasts, serpents and dragons, and it seemed to me that on that far off summer's day the three boats danced on the water, propelled by the rise and fall of the silver wings of their oar banks. The sun flashed off the wet blades, splinters of light, then the oars dipped, were tugged and the beast-headed boats surged and I stared entranced.

'The devil's turds,' my father growled. He was not a very good Christian, but he was frightened enough at that moment to make the sign of the cross.

'And may the devil swallow them,' my uncle said. His name was Ælfric and he was a slender man; sly, dark and secretive.

The three boats had been rowing northwards, their square sails furled on their long yards, but when we turned back south to canter homewards on the sand so that our horses' manes tossed

5

like wind-blown spray and the hooded hawks mewed in alarm, the ships turned with us. Where the cliff had collapsed to leave a ramp of broken turf we rode inland, the horses heaving up the slope, and from there we galloped along the coastal path to our fortress.

To Bebbanburg. Bebba had been a queen in our land many years before, and she had given her name to my home, which is the dearest place in all the world. The fort stands on a high rock that curls out to sea. The waves beat on its eastern shore and break white on the rock's northern point, and a shallow sea-lake ripples along the western side between the fortress and the land. To reach Bebbanburg you must take the causeway to the south, a low strip of rock and sand that is guarded by a great wooden tower, the Low Gate, that is built on top of an earthen wall, and we thundered through the tower's arch, our horses white with sweat, and rode past the granaries, the smithy, the mews and the stables, all wooden buildings well thatched with rye straw, and so up the inner path to the High Gate which protected the peak of the rock that was surrounded by a wooden rampart encircling my father's hall. There we dismounted, letting slaves take our horses and hawks, and ran to the eastern rampart from where we gazed out to sea.

The three ships were now close to the islands where the puffins live and the seal-folk dance in winter. We watched them, and my stepmother, alarmed by the sound of hooves, came from the hall to join us on the rampart. 'The devil has opened his bowels,' my father greeted her.

'God and his saints preserve us,' Gytha said, crossing herself. I had never known my real mother who had been my father's second wife and, like his first, had died in childbirth, so both my brother and I, who were really half-brothers, had no mother, but I thought of Gytha as my mother and, on the whole, she was kind to me, kinder indeed than my father, who did not much like children. Gytha wanted me to be a priest, saying that my elder brother would inherit the land and become a warrior to protect it so I must find another life path. She had given my father two sons and a daughter, but none had lived beyond a year.

The three ships were coming closer now. It seemed they had come to inspect Bebbanburg, which did not worry us for the fortress was reckoned impregnable, and so the Danes could stare all they wanted. The nearest ship had twin banks of twelve oars each and, as the ship coasted a hundred paces offshore, a man leaped from the ship's side and ran down the nearer bank of oars, stepping from one shaft to the next like a dancer, and he did it wearing a mail shirt and holding a sword. We all prayed he would fall, but of course he did not. He had long fair hair, very long, and when he had pranced the full length of the oar bank he turned and ran the shafts again.

'She was trading at the mouth of the Tine a week ago,' Ælfric, my father's brother, said.

'You know that?'

'I saw her,' Ælfric said, 'I recognise that prow. See how there's a light-coloured strake on the bend?' He spat. 'She didn't have a dragon's head then.'

'They take the beast-heads off when they trade,' my father said. 'What were they buying?'

'Exchanging pelts for salt and dried fish. Said they were merchants from Haithabu.'

'They're merchants looking for a fight now,' my father said, and the Danes on the three ships were indeed challenging us by clashing their spears and swords against their painted shields, but there was little they could do against Bebbanburg and nothing we could do to hurt them, though my father ordered his wolf banner raised. The flag showed a snarling wolf's head and it was his standard in battle, but there was no wind and so the banner hung limp and its defiance was lost on the pagans who, after a while, became bored with taunting us, settled to their thwarts and rowed off to the south.

'We must pray,' my stepmother said. Gytha was much younger than my father. She was a small, plump woman with a mass of fair hair and a great reverence for Saint Cuthbert whom she worshipped because he had worked miracles. In the church beside the hall she kept an ivory comb that was said to have been Cuthbert's beard-comb, and perhaps it was.

'We must act,' my father snarled. He turned away from the battlements. 'You,' he spoke to my elder brother, Uhtred. 'Take a dozen men, ride south. Watch the pagans, but nothing more, you understand? If they land their ships on my ground I want to know where.'

'Yes, father.'

'But don't fight them,' my father ordered. 'Just watch the bastards and be back here by nightfall.'

Six other men were sent to rouse the country. Every free man owed military duty and so my father was assembling his army, and by the morrow's dusk he expected to have close to two hundred men, some armed with axes, spears or reaping hooks, while his retainers, those men who lived with us in Bebbanburg, would be equipped with well-made swords and hefty shields. 'If the Danes are outnumbered,' my father told me that night, 'they won't fight. They're like dogs, the Danes. Cowards at heart, but they're given courage by being in a pack.' It was dark and my brother had not returned, but no one was unduly anxious about that. Uhtred was capable, if sometimes reckless, and doubtless he would arrive in the small hours and so my father had ordered a beacon lit in the iron becket on top of the High Gate to guide him home.

We reckoned we were safe in Bebbanburg for it had never fallen to an enemy's assault, yet my father and uncle were still worried that the Danes had returned to Northumbria. 'They're looking for food,' my father said. 'The hungry bastards want to land, steal some cattle, then sail away.'

I remembered my uncle's words, how the ships had been at the mouth of the Tine trading furs for dried fish, so how could they be hungry? But I said nothing. I was nine years old and what did I know of Danes?

I did know that they were savages, pagans and terrible. I knew that for two generations before I was born their ships had raided our coasts. I knew that Father Beocca, my father's clerk and our mass priest, prayed every Sunday to spare us from the fury of the Northmen, but that fury had passed me by. No Danes had come to our land since I had been born, but my father had fought them often enough and that night, as we waited for my brother to return, he spoke of his old enemy. They came, he said, from northern lands where ice and mist prevailed, they worshipped the old gods, the same ones we had worshipped before the light of Christ came to bless us, and when they had first come to Northumbria, he told me, fiery dragons had whipped across the northern sky, great bolts of lightning had scarred the hills and the sea had been churned by whirlwinds.

'They are sent by God,' Gytha said timidly, 'to punish us.'

'Punish us for what?' my father demanded savagely.

'For our sins,' Gytha said, making the sign of the cross.

'Our sins be damned,' my father snarled. 'They come here because they're hungry.' He was irritated by my stepmother's piety, and he refused to give up his wolf's head banner that proclaimed our family's descent from Woden, the ancient Saxon god of battles. The wolf, Ealdwulf the smith had told me, was one of Woden's three favoured beasts, the others being the eagle and the raven. My mother wanted our banner to show the cross, but my father was proud of his ancestors, though he rarely talked about Woden. Even at nine years old I understood that a good Christian should not boast of being spawned by a pagan god, but I also liked the idea of being a god's descendant and Ealdwulf often told me tales of Woden, how he had rewarded our people by giving us the land we called England, and how he had once thrown a war spear clear around the moon, and how his shield could darken the midsummer sky and how he could reap all the corn in the world with one stroke of his great sword. I liked those tales. They were better than my stepmother's stories of Cuthbert's miracles. Christians, it seemed to me, were forever weeping and I did not think Woden's worshippers cried much.

We waited in the hall. It was, indeed it still is, a great wooden hall, strongly thatched and stout beamed, with a harp on a dais and a stone hearth in the centre of the floor. It took a dozen slaves a day to keep that great fire going, dragging the wood along the causeway and up through the gates, and at summer's end we would make a log pile bigger than the church just as a winter store. At the edges of the hall were timber platforms, filled with rammed earth and layered with woollen rugs, and it was on those

9

platforms that we lived, up above the draughts. The hounds stayed on the bracken-strewn floor below, where lesser men could eat at the year's four great feasts.

There was no feast that night, just bread and cheese and ale, and my father waited for my brother and wondered aloud if the Danes were restless again. 'They usually come for food and plunder,' he told me, 'but in some places they've stayed and taken land.'

'You think they want our land?' I asked.

'They'll take any land,' he said irritably. He was always irritated by my questions, but that night he was worried and so he talked on. 'Their own land is stone and ice, and they have giants threatening them.'

I wanted him to tell me more about the giants, but he brooded instead. 'Our ancestors,' he went on after a while, 'took this land. They took it and made it and held it. We do not give up what our ancestors gave us. They came across the sea and they fought here, and they built here and they're buried here. This is our land, mixed with our blood, strengthened with our bone. Ours.' He was angry, but he was often angry. He glowered at me, as if wondering whether I was strong enough to hold this land of Northumbria that our ancestors had won with sword and spear and blood and slaughter.

We slept after a while, or at least I slept. I think my father paced the ramparts, but by dawn he was back in the hall and it was then I was woken by the horn at the High Gate and I stumbled off the platform and out into the morning's first light. There was dew on the grass, a sea eagle circling overhead, and my father's hounds streaming from the hall door in answer to the horn's call. I saw my father running down to the Low Gate and I followed him until I could wriggle my way through the men who were crowding onto the earthen rampart to stare along the causeway.

Horsemen were coming from the south. There were a dozen of them, their horses' hooves sparkling with the dew. My brother's horse was in the lead. It was a brindled stallion, wild-eyed and with a curious gait. It threw its forelegs out as it cantered and no one could mistake that horse, but it was not Uhtred who rode it. The man bestride the saddle had long, long hair the colour of pale

10

gold, hair that tossed like the horses' tails as he rode. He wore mail, had a flapping scabbard at his side and an axe slung across one shoulder and I was certain he was the same man who had danced the oar shafts the previous day. His companions were in leather or wool and as they neared the fortress the long-haired man signalled that they should curb their horses as he rode ahead alone. He came within bowshot, though none of us on the rampart put an arrow on the string, then he pulled the horse to a stop and looked up at the gate. He stared all along the line of men, a mocking expression on his face, then he bowed, threw something on the path and wheeled the horse away. He kicked his heels and the horse sped back and his ragged men joined him to gallop south.

What he had thrown onto the path was my brother's severed head. It was brought to my father who stared at it a long time, but betrayed no feelings. He did not cry, he did not grimace, he did not scowl, he just looked at his eldest son's head and then he looked at me. 'From this day on,' he said, 'your name is Uhtred.'

Which is how I was named.

Father Beocca insisted that I should be baptised again, or else heaven would not know who I was when I arrived with the name Uhtred. I protested, but Gytha wanted it and my father cared more for her contentment than for mine, and so a barrel was carried into the church and half filled with sea water and Father Beocca stood me in the barrel and ladled water over my hair. 'Receive your servant Uhtred,' he intoned, 'into the holy company of the saints and into the ranks of the most bright angels.' I hope the saints and angels are warmer than I was that day, and after the baptism was done Gytha wept for me, though why I did not know. She might have done better to weep for my brother.

We found out what had happened to him. The three Danish ships had put into the mouth of the River Aln where there was a small settlement of fishermen and their families. Those folk had prudently fled inland, though a handful stayed and watched the

11

river mouth from woods on higher ground and they said my brother had come at nightfall and seen the Vikings torching the houses. They were called Vikings when they were raiders, but Danes or pagans when they were traders, and these men had been burning and plundering so were reckoned to be Vikings. There had seemed very few of them in the settlement, most were on their ships, and my brother decided to ride down to the cottages and kill those few, but of course it was a trap. The Danes had seen his horsemen coming and had hidden a ship's crew north of the village, and those forty men closed behind my brother's party and killed them all. My father claimed his eldest son's death must have been quick, which was a consolation to him, but of course it was not a quick death for he lived long enough for the Danes to discover who he was, or else why would they have brought his head back to Bebbanburg? The fishermen said they tried to warn my brother, but I doubt they did. Men say such things so that they are not blamed for disaster, but whether my brother was warned or not, he still died and the Danes took thirteen fine swords, thirteen good horses, a coat of mail, a helmet and my old name.

But that was not the end of it. A fleeting visit by three ships was no great event, but a week after my brother's death we heard that a great Danish fleet had rowed up the rivers to capture Eoferwic. They had won that victory on All Saints' Day, which made Gytha weep for it suggested God had abandoned us, but there was also good news for it seemed that my old namesake, King Osbert, had made an alliance with his rival, the would-be King Ælla, and they had agreed to put aside their rivalry, join forces and take Eoferwic back. That sounds simple, but of course it took time. Messengers rode, advisers confused, priests prayed, and it was not till Christmas that Osbert and Ælla sealed their peace with oaths, and then they summoned my father's men, but of course we could not march in winter. The Danes were in Eoferwic and we left them there until the early spring when news came that the Northumbrian army would gather outside the city and, to my joy, my father decreed that I would ride south with him.

'He's too young,' Gytha protested.

'He is almost ten,' my father said, 'and he must learn to fight.'

12

'He would be better served by continuing his lessons,' she said.

'A dead reader is no use to Bebbanburg,' my father said, 'and Uhtred is now the heir so he must learn to fight.'

That night he made Beocca show me the parchments kept in the church, the parchments that said we owned the land. Beocca had been teaching me to read for two years, but I was a bad pupil and, to Beocca's despair, I could make neither head nor tail of the writings. Beocca sighed, then told me what was in them. 'They describe the land,' he said, 'the land your father owns, and they say the land is his by God's law and by our own law.' And one day, it seemed, the lands would be mine for that night my father dictated a new will in which he said that if he died then Bebbanburg would belong to his son Uhtred, and I would be Ealdorman, and all the folk between the Tuede and the Tine would swear allegiance to me.

'We were kings here once,' he told me, 'and our land was called Bernicia.' He pressed his seal into the red wax, leaving the impression of a wolf's head.

'We should be kings again,' Ælfric, my uncle said.

'It doesn't matter what they call us,' my father said curtly, 'so long as they obey us,' and then he made Ælfric swear on the comb of Saint Cuthbert that he would respect the new will and acknowledge me as Uhtred of Bebbanburg. Ælfric did so swear. 'But it won't happen,' my father said. 'We shall slaughter these Danes like sheep in a fold, and we shall ride back here with plunder and honour.'

'Pray God,' Ælfric said.

Ælfric and thirty men would stay at Bebbanburg to guard the fortress and protect the women. He gave me gifts that night; a leather coat that would protect against a sword cut and, best of all, a helmet around which Ealdwulf the smith had fashioned a band of gilt bronze. 'So they will know you are a prince,' Ælfric said.

'He's not a prince,' my father said, 'but an Ealdorman's heir.' Yet he was pleased with his brother's gifts to me and added two of his own, a short sword and a horse. The sword was an old blade, cut down, with a leather scabbard lined with fleece. It had a chunky hilt, was clumsy, yet that night I slept with the blade under my blanket.

The next morning, as my stepmother wept on the ramparts of the High Gate, and under a blue, clean sky, we rode to war. Two hundred and fifty men went south, following our banner of the wolf's head.

That was in the year 867, and it was the first time I ever went to war.

And I have never ceased.

'You will not fight in the shield wall,' my father said.

'No, father.'

'Only men can stand in the shield wall,' he said, 'but you will watch, you will learn, and you will discover that the most dangerous stroke is not the sword or axe that you can see, but the one you cannot see, the blade that comes beneath the shields to bite your ankles.'

He grudgingly gave me much other advice as we followed the long road south. Of the two hundred and fifty men who went to Eoferwic from Bebbanburg, one hundred and twenty were on horseback. Those were my father's household men or else the wealthier farmers, the ones who could afford some kind of armour and had shields and swords. Most of the men were not wealthy, but they were sworn to my father's cause, and they marched with sickles, spears, reaping hooks, fish gaffs and axes. Some carried hunting bows, and all had been ordered to bring a week's food which was mostly hard bread, harder cheese and smoked fish. Many were accompanied by women. My father had ordered that no women were to march south, but he did not send them back, reckoning that the women would follow anyway, and that men fought better when their wives or lovers were watching, and he was confident that those women would see the levy of Northumbria give the Danes a terrible slaughter. He claimed we were the hardest men of England, much harder than the soft Mercians. 'Your mother was a Mercian,' he added, but said nothing more. He never talked of her. I knew they had been married less than a year, that she had died giving birth to me, and that she was an Ealdorman's daughter, but as far as my father was concerned she might never have existed. He claimed to despise the Mercians, but not as much as he scorned the coddled West Saxons. 'They don't know hardship in Wessex,' he maintained, but he reserved his severest judgment for the East Anglians. 'They live in marshes,' he once told me, 'and live like frogs.' We Northumbrians had always hated the East Anglians for long ago they had defeated us in battle, killing Æthelfrith, our king and husband to the Bebba after whom our fortress was named. I was to discover later that the East Anglians had given horses and winter shelter to the Danes who had captured Eoferwic, so my father was right to despise them. They were treacherous frogs.

Father Beocca rode south with us. My father did not much like the priest, but did not want to go to war without a man of God to say prayers. Beocca, in turn, was devoted to my father who had freed him from slavery and provided him with his education. My father could have worshipped the devil and Beocca, I think, would have turned a blind eye. He was young, clean-shaven and extraordinarily ugly, with a fearful squint, a flattened nose, unruly red hair and a palsied left hand. He was also very clever, though I did not appreciate it then, resenting that he gave me lessons. The poor man had tried so hard to teach me letters, but I mocked his efforts, preferring to get a beating from my father to concentrating on the alphabet.

We followed the Roman road, crossing their great wall at the Tine, and still going south. The Romans, my father said, had been giants who built wondrous things, but they had gone back to Rome and the giants had died and now the only Romans left were priests, but the giants' roads were still there and, as we went south, more men joined us until a horde marched on the moors either side of the stony road's broken surface. The men slept in the open, though my father and his chief retainers would bed for the night in abbeys or barns.

We also straggled. Even at nine years old I noticed how we straggled. Men had brought liquor with them, or else they stole mead or ale from the villages we passed, and they frequently got drunk and simply collapsed at the roadside and no one seemed to care. 'They'll catch up,' my father said carelessly.

'It's not good,' Father Beocca told me.

'What's not good?'

'There should be more discipline. I have read the Roman wars and know there must be discipline.'

'They'll catch up,' I said, echoing my father.

That night we were joined by men from the place called Cetreht where, long ago, we had defeated the Welsh in a great battle. The newcomers sang of the battle, chanting how we had fed the ravens with the foreigners' blood, and the words cheered my father who told me we were near Eoferwic and that next day we might expect to join Osbert and Ælla, and how the day after that we would feed the ravens again. We were sitting by a fire, one of hundreds of fires that stretched across the fields. South of us, far off across a flat land, I could see the sky glowing from the light of still more fires and knew they showed where the rest of Northumbria's army gathered.

'The raven is Woden's creature, isn't it?' I asked nervously.

My father looked at me sourly. 'Who told you that?'

I shrugged, said nothing.

'Ealdwulf?' He guessed, knowing that Bebbanburg's blacksmith, who had stayed at the fortress with Ælfric, was a secret pagan.

'I just heard it,' I said, hoping I would get away with the evasion without being hit, 'and I know we are descended from Woden.'

'We are,' my father acknowledged, 'but we have a new God now.' He stared balefully across the encampment where men were drinking. 'Do you know who wins battles, boy?'

'We do, father.'

'The side that is least drunk,' he said and then, after a pause, 'but it helps to be drunk.'

'Why?'

'Because a shield wall is an awful place.' He gazed into the fire. 'I have been in six shield walls,' he went on, 'and prayed every time it would be the last. Your brother, now, he was a man who might have loved the shield wall. He had courage.' He fell silent, thinking, then scowled. 'The man who brought his head. I want his head. I want to spit into his dead eyes then put his skull on a pole above the Low Gate.'

'You will have it,' I said.

He sneered at that. 'What do you know?' he asked. 'I brought you, boy, because you must see battle. Because our men must see that you are here. But you will not fight. You're like a young dog who watches the old dogs kill the boar, but doesn't bite. Watch and learn, watch and learn and maybe one day you'll be useful. But for now you're nothing but a pup.' He dismissed me with a wave.

Next day the Roman road ran across a flat land, crossing dykes and ditches, until at last we came to where the combined armies of Osbert and Ælla had made their shelters. Beyond them, and just visible through the scattered trees, was Eoferwic, and that was where the Danes were.

Eoferwic was, and still is, the chief city of northern England. It possesses a great abbey, an archbishop, a fortress, high walls, and a vast market. It stands beside the River Ouse, and boasts a bridge, but ships can reach Eoferwic from the distant sea, and that was how the Danes had come. They must have known that Northumbria was weakened by civil war, that Osbert, the rightful king, had marched westwards to meet the forces of the pretender Ælla, and in the absence of the king they had taken the city. It would not have been difficult for them to have discovered Osbert's absence. The trouble between Osbert and Ælla had been brewing for weeks, and Eoferwic was filled with traders, many from across the sea, who would have known of the two men's bitter rivalry. One thing I learned about the Danes was that they knew how to spy. The monks who write the chronicles tell us that they came from nowhere, their dragon-prowed ships suddenly appearing from a blue vacancy, but it was rarely like that. The Viking crews might attack unexpectedly, but the big fleets, the war fleets, went where they knew there was already trouble. They found an existing wound and filled it like maggots.

My father took me close to the city, he and a score of his men, all of us mounted and all wearing mail or leather. We could see the enemy on the wall. Some of the wall was built of stone, that was the Roman work, but much of the city was protected by an

17

earth wall, topped by a high wooden palisade, and to the east of the city part of that palisade was missing. It seemed to have been burned for we could see charred wood on top of the earthen wall where fresh stakes had been driven to hold the new palisade that would replace the burned fence.

Beyond the new stakes was a jumble of thatched roofs, the wooden bell towers of three churches and, on the river, the masts of the Danish fleet. Our scouts claimed there were thirty-four ships, which was said to mean the Danes had an army of around a thousand men. Our own army was larger, nearer to fifteen hundred, though it was difficult to count. No one seemed to be in charge. The two leaders, Osbert and Ælla, camped apart and, though they had officially made peace, they refused to speak to each other, communicating instead through messengers. My father, the third most important man in the army, could talk to both, but he was not able to persuade Osbert and Ælla to meet, let alone agree on a plan of campaign. Osbert wished to besiege the city and starve the Danes out, while Ælla urged an immediate attack. The rampart was broken, he said, and an assault would drive deep into the tangle of streets where the Danes could be hunted down and killed. I do not know which course my father preferred, for he never said, but in the end the decision was taken away from us.

Our army could not wait. We had brought some food, but that was soon exhausted, and men were going ever farther afield to find more, and some of those men did not return. They just slipped home. Other men grumbled that their farms needed work and if they did not return home they would face a hungry year. A meeting was called of every important man and they spent all day arguing. Osbert attended the meeting, which meant Ælla did not, though one of his chief supporters was there and hinted that Osbert's reluctance to assault the city was caused by cowardice. Perhaps it was, for Osbert did not respond to the jibe, proposing instead that we dug our own forts outside the city. Three or four such forts, he said, would trap the Danes. Our best fighters could man the forts, and our other men could go home to look after their fields. Another man proposed building a new bridge across the river, a bridge that would trap the Danish fleet, and he argued the point tediously, though I think everyone knew that we did not have the time to make a bridge across such a wide river. 'Besides,' King Osbert said, 'we want the Danes to take their ships away. Let them go back to the sea. Let them go and trouble someone else.' A bishop pleaded for more time, saying that Ealdorman Egbert, who held land south of Eoferwic, had yet to arrive with his men.

'Nor is Ricsig here,' a priest said, speaking of another great lord.

'He's sick,' Osbert said.

'Sickness of courage,' Ælla's spokesman sneered.

'Give them time,' the bishop suggested. 'With Egbert's and Ricsig's men we shall have enough troops to frighten the Danes with sheer numbers.'

My father said nothing at the meeting, though it was plain many men wanted him to speak, and I was perplexed that he stayed silent, but that night Beocca explained why. 'If he said we should attack,' the priest said, 'then men would assume he had sided with Ælla, while if he encouraged a siege, he would be seen to be on Osbert's side.'

'Does it matter?'

Beocca looked at me across the campfire, or one of his eyes looked at me while the other wandered somewhere in the night. 'When the Danes are beaten,' he said, 'then Osbert and Ælla's feud will start again. Your father wants none of it.'

'But whichever side he supports,' I said, 'will win.'

'But suppose they kill each other?' Beocca asked, 'who will be king then?'

I looked at him, understood, said nothing.

'And who will be king thereafter?' Beocca asked, and he pointed at me. 'You. And a king should be able to read and write.'

'A king,' I answered scornfully, 'can always hire men who can read and write.'

Then, next morning, the decision to attack or besiege was made for us, because news came that more Danish ships had appeared at the mouth of the River Humber, and that could only mean the enemy would be reinforced within a few days, and so my father, who had stayed silent for so long, finally spoke. 'We must attack,' he told both Osbert and Ælla, 'before the new boats come.'

Ælla, of course, agreed enthusiastically, and even Osbert under-stood that the new ships meant that everything was changed. Besides, the Danes inside the city had been having problems with their new wall. We woke one morning to see a whole new stretch of palisade, the wood raw and bright, but a great wind blew that day and the new work collapsed, and that caused much merri-ment in our encampments. The Danes, men said, could not even build a wall. 'But they can build ships,' Father Beocca told me.

'So?'

'A man who can build a ship,' the young priest said, 'can usually build a wall. It is not so hard as shipbuilding.'

'It fell down!'

'Perhaps it was meant to fall down,' Beocca said, and, when I just stared at him, he explained. 'Perhaps they want us to attack there?'

I do not know if he told my father of his suspicions, but if he did then I have no doubt my father dismissed them. He did not trust Beocca's opinions on war. The priest's usefulness was in encouraging God to smite the Danes and that was all and, to be fair, Beocca did pray mightily and long that God would give us the victory.

And the day after the wall collapsed we gave God his chance to fulfil Beocca's prayers.

We attacked.

I do not know if every man who assaulted Eoferwic was drunk, but they would have been had there been enough mead, ale and birch wine to go round. The drinking had gone on much of the night and I woke to find men vomiting in the dawn. Those few who, like my father, possessed mail shirts pulled them on. Most were armoured in leather, while some men had no protection other than their coats. Weapons were sharpened on whetstones. The priests walked round the camp scattering blessings, while men swore oaths of brotherhood and loyalty. Some banded together and promised to share their plunder equally, a few looked pale and more than a handful sneaked away through the dykes that crossed the flat, damp landscape.

A score of men were ordered to stay at the camp and guard the women and horses, though Father Beocca and I were both ordered to mount. 'You'll stay on horseback,' my father told me, 'and you'll stay with him,' he added to the priest.

'Of course, my lord,' Beocca said.

'If anything happens,' my father was deliberately vague, 'then ride to Bebbanburg, shut the gate and wait there.'

'God is on our side,' Beocca said.

My father looked a great warrior, which indeed he was, though he claimed to be getting too old for fighting. His greying beard jutted over his mail coat, above which he had hung a crucifix carved from ox bone that had been a gift from Gytha. His sword belt was leather studded with silver, while his great sword, Bone-Breaker, was sheathed in leather banded with gilt-bronze strappings. His boots had iron plates on either side of the ankles, reminding me of his advice about the shield wall, while his helmet was polished so that it shone, and its face-piece, with its eyeholes and snarling mouth, was inlaid with silver. His round shield was made of lime-wood, had a heavy iron boss, was covered in leather and painted with the wolf's head. Ealdorman Uhtred was going to war.

The horns summoned the army. There was little order in the array. There had been arguments about who should be on the right or left, but Beocca told me the argument had been settled when the bishop cast dice, and King Osbert was now on the right, Ælla on the left and my father in the centre, and those three chieftains' banners were advanced as the horns called. The men assembled under the banners. My father's household troops, his best warriors, were at the front, and behind them were the bands of the thegns. Thegns were important men, holders of great lands, some of them with their own fortresses, and they were the men who shared my father's platform in the feasting hall, and men who had to be watched in case their ambitions made them try to take his place, but now they loyally gathered behind him, and the ceorls, free men of the lowest rank, assembled with them. Men fought in family groups, or with friends. There were plenty of boys with the army, though I was the only one on horseback and the only one with a sword and helmet.

I could see a scatter of Danes behind the unbroken palisades on either side of the gap where their wall had fallen down, but most of their army filled that gap, making a shield barrier on top of the earthen wall, and it was a high earthen wall, at least ten or twelve feet high, and steep, so it would be a hard climb into the face of the waiting killers, but I was confident we would win. I was nine years old, almost ten.

The Danes were shouting at us, but we were too far away to hear their insults. Their shields, round like ours, were painted yellow, black, brown and blue. Our men began beating weapons on their shields and that was a fearsome sound, the first time I ever heard an army making that war music; the clashing of ash spear shafts and iron sword blades on shield-wood.

'It is a terrible thing,' Beocca said to me. 'War, it is an awful thing.'

I said nothing. I thought it was glorious and wonderful.

'The shield wall is where men die,' Beocca said, and he kissed the wooden cross that hung about his neck. 'The gates of heaven and hell will be jostling with souls before this day is done,' he went on gloomily.

'Aren't the dead carried to a feasting hall?' I asked.

He looked at me very strangely, then appeared shocked. 'Where did you hear that?'

'At Bebbanburg,' I said, sensible enough not to admit that it was Ealdwulf the smith who told me those tales as I watched him beating rods of iron into sword blades.

'That is what heathens believe,' Beocca said sternly. 'They believe dead warriors are carried to Woden's corpse-hall to feast until the world's ending, but it is a grievously wrong belief. It is an error! But the Danes are always in error. They bow down to idols, they deny the true God, they are wrong.'

'But a man must die with a sword in his hand?' I insisted.

'I can see we must teach you a proper catechism when this is done,' the priest said sternly.

I said nothing more. I was watching, trying to fix every detail of that day in my memory. The sky was summer blue, with just a few clouds off in the west, and the sunlight reflected from our army's spear points like glints of light flickering on the summer sea. Cowslips dotted the meadow where the army assembled, and a cuckoo called from the woods behind us where a crowd of our women were watching the army. There were swans on the river that was placid for there was little wind. The smoke from the cooking fires inside Eoferwic rose almost straight into the air, and that sight reminded me that there would be a feast in the city that night, a feast of roasted pork or whatever else we found in the enemy's stores. Some of our men, those in the foremost ranks, were darting forward to shout at the enemy, or else dare him to come and do private battle between the lines, one man on one man, but none of the Danes broke rank. They just stared, waited, their spears a hedge, their shields a wall, and then our horns blew again and the shouting and the shield-banging faded as our army lurched forward.

It went raggedly. Later, much later, I was to understand the reluctance of men to launch themselves against a shield wall, let alone a shield wall held at the top of a steep earthen bank, but on that day I was just impatient for our army to hurry forward and break the impudent Danes, and Beocca had to restrain me, catching hold of my bridle to stop me riding into the rearmost ranks. 'We shall wait until they break through,' he said.

'I want to kill a Dane,' I protested.

'Don't be stupid, Uhtred,' Beocca said angrily. 'You try and kill a Dane,' he went on, 'and your father will have no sons. You are his only child now, and it is your duty to live.'

So I did my duty and I hung back, and I watched as, so slowly, our army found its courage and advanced towards the city. The river was on our left, the empty encampment behind our right, and the inviting gap in the city wall was to our front and there the Danes were waiting silently, their shields overlapping.

'The bravest will go first,' Beocca said to me, 'and your father will be one of them. They will make a wedge, what the Latin authors call a *porcinum caput*. You know what that means?'

'No.' Nor did I care.

'A swine's head. Like the tusk of a boar. The bravest will go first and, if they break through, the others will follow.'

Beocca was right. Three wedges formed in front of our lines, one each from the household troops of Osbert, Ælla and my father. The men stood close together, their shields overlapping like the Danish shields, while the rearward ranks of each wedge held their shields high like a roof, and then, when they were ready, the men in the three wedges gave a great cheer and started forward. They did not run. I had expected them to run, but men cannot keep the wedge tight if they run. The wedge is war in slow time, slow enough for the men inside the wedge to wonder how strong the enemy is and to fear that the rest of the army will not follow, but they did. The three wedges had not gone more than twenty paces before the remaining mass of men moved forward.

'I want to be closer,' I said.

'You will wait,' Beocca said.

I could hear the shouts now, shouts of defiance and shouts to give a man courage, and then the archers on the city walls loosed their bows and I saw the glitter of the feathers as the arrows slashed down towards the wedges, and a moment later the throwing spears came, arching over the Danish line to fall on the upheld shields. Amazingly, at least to me, it seemed that none of our men was struck, though I could see their shields were stuck with arrows and spears like hedgehog spines, and still the three wedges advanced, and now our own bowmen were shooting at the Danes, and a handful of our men broke from the ranks behind the wedges to hurl their own spears at the enemy shield wall.

'Not long now,' Beocca said nervously. He made the sign of the cross. He was praying silently and his crippled left hand was twitching.

I was watching my father's wedge, the central wedge, the one just in front of the wolf's head banner, and I saw the closely touching shields vanish into the ditch that lay in front of the earthen wall and I knew my father was perilously close to death and I urged him to win, to kill, to give the name Uhtred of Bebbanburg even more renown, and then I saw the shield wedge emerge from the ditch and, like a monstrous beast, crawl up the face of the wall.

'The advantage they have,' Beocca said in the patient voice he used for teaching, 'is that the enemy's feet are easy targets when you come from below.' I think he was trying to reassure himself, but I believed him anyway, and it must have been true for my father's formation, first up the wall, did not seem to be checked when they met the enemy's shield wall. I could see nothing now except the flash of blades rising and falling, and I could hear that sound, the real music of battle, the chop of iron on wood, iron on iron, yet the wedge was still moving. Like a boar's razor-sharp tusk it had pierced the Danish shield wall and was moving forward, and though the Danes wrapped around the wedge, it seemed our men were winning for they pressed forward across the earthen bank, and the soldiers behind must have sensed that Ealdorman Uhtred had brought them victory for they suddenly cheered and surged to help the beleaguered wedge.

'God be praised,' Beocca said, for the Danes were fleeing. One moment they had formed a thick shield wall, bristling with weapons, and now they were vanishing into the city and our army, with the relief of men whose lives have been spared, charged after them.

'Slowly, now,' Beocca said, walking his horse forward and leading mine by the bridle.

The Danes had gone. Instead the earthen wall was black with our men who were scrambling through the gap in the city's ramparts, then down the bank's farther side into the streets and alleyways beyond. The three flags, my father's wolf head, Ælla's war axe and Osbert's cross, were inside Eoferwic. I could hear men cheering and I kicked my horse, forcing her out of Beocca's grasp. 'Come back!' he shouted, but though he followed me he did not try to drag me away. We had won, God had given us victory and I wanted to be close enough to smell the slaughter.

Neither of us could get into the city because the gap in the palisade was choked with our men, but I kicked the horse again and she forced her way into the press. Some men protested at what I was doing, then they saw the gilt-bronze circle on my helmet and knew I was nobly born and so they tried to help me

25

through, while Beocca, stranded at the back of the crowd, shouted that I should not get too far ahead of him. 'Catch up!' I called back to him.

Then he shouted again, but this time his voice was frantic, terrified, and I turned to see Danes streaming across the field where our army had advanced. It was a horde of Danes who must have sallied from the city's northern gate to cut off our retreat, and they must have known we would retreat, because it seemed they could build walls after all, and had built them across the streets inside the city, then feigned flight from the ramparts to draw us into their killing ground and now they sprang the trap. Some of the Danes who came from the city were mounted, most were on foot, and Beocca panicked. I do not blame him. The Danes like killing Christian priests and Beocca must have seen death, did not desire martyrdom, and so he turned his horse and kicked it hard and it galloped away beside the river and the Danes, not caring about the fate of one man where so many were trapped, let him go.

It is a truth that in most armies the timid men and those with the feeblest weapons are at the back. The brave go to the front, the weak seek the rear, so if you can get to the back of an enemy army you will have a massacre.

I am an old man now and it has been my fate to see panic flicker through many armies. That panic is worse than the terror of sheep penned in a cleft and being assaulted by wolves, more frantic than the writhing of salmon caught in a net and dragged to the air. The sound of it must tear the heavens apart, but to the Danes, that day, it was the sweet sound of victory and to us it was death.

I tried to escape. God knows I panicked too. I had seen Beocca racing away beside the riverside willows and I managed to turn the mare, but then one of our own men snatched at me, presumably wanting my horse, and I had the wit to draw my short sword and hack blindly at him as I kicked back my heels, but all I achieved was to ride out of the panicked mass into the path of the Danes, and all around me men were screaming and the Danish axes and swords were chopping and swinging. The grim work, the blood feast, the song of the blade, they call it, and perhaps I was

26

saved for a moment because I was the only one in our army who was on horseback and a score of the Danes were also mounted and perhaps they mistook me for one of their own, but then one of those Danes called to me in a language I did not speak and I looked at him and saw his long hair, unhelmeted, his long fair hair and his silver-coloured mail and the wide grin on his wild face and I recognised him as the man who had killed my brother and, like the fool I was, I screamed at him. A standard-bearer was just behind the long-haired Dane, flaunting an eagle's wing on a long pole. Tears were blurring my sight, and perhaps the battle madness came onto me because, despite my panic, I rode at the long-haired Dane and struck at him with my small sword, and his sword parried mine, and my feeble blade bent like a herring's spine. It just bent and he drew back his own sword for the killing stroke, saw my pathetic bent blade and began to laugh. I was pissing myself, he was laughing, and I beat at him again with the useless sword and still he laughed, and then he leaned over, plucked the weapon from my hand and threw it away. He picked me up then. I was screaming and hitting at him, but he thought it all so very funny, and he draped me belly down on the saddle in front of him and then he spurred into the chaos to continue the killing.

And that was how I met Ragnar, Ragnar the Fearless, my brother's killer and the man whose head was supposed to grace a pole on Bebbanburg's ramparts, Earl Ragnar.

PART ONE

A Pagan Childhood

One

The Danes were clever that day. They had made new walls inside the city, invited our men into the streets, trapped them between the new walls, surrounded them and killed them. They did not kill all the Northumbrian army, for even the fiercest warriors tire of slaughter and, besides, the Danes made much money from slavery. Most of the slaves taken in England were sold to farmers in the wild northern isles, or to Ireland, or sent back across the sea to the Danish lands, but some, I learned, were taken to the big slave markets in Frankia and a few were shipped south to a place where there was no winter and where men with faces the colour of scorched wood would pay good money for men and even better money for young women.

But they killed enough of us. They killed Ælla and they killed Osbert and they killed my father. Ælla and my father were fortunate, for they died in battle, swords in their hands, but Osbert was captured and he was tortured that night as the Danes feasted in a city stinking of blood. Some of the victors guarded the walls, others celebrated in the captured houses, but most gathered in the hall of Northumbria's defeated king where Ragnar took me. I did not know why he took me there, I half expected to be killed or, at best, sold into slavery, but Ragnar made me sit with his men and put a roasted goose leg, half a loaf of bread and a pot of ale in front of me, then cuffed me cheerfully round the head.

The other Danes ignored me at first. They were too busy getting drunk and cheering the fights which broke out once they were drunk, but the loudest cheers came when the captured Osbert was forced to fight against a young warrior who had extraordinary skill with a sword. He danced round the king, then chopped off his left hand before slitting his belly with a sweeping cut and, because Osbert was a heavy man, his guts spilled out like eels slithering from a ruptured sack. Some of the Danes were weak with laughter after that. The king took a long time to die, and while he cried for relief, the Danes crucified a captured priest who had fought against them in the battle. They were intrigued and repelled by our religion, and they were angry when the priest's hands pulled free of the nails and some claimed it was impossible to kill a man that way, and they argued that point drunkenly, then tried to nail the priest to the hall's timber walls a second time until, bored with it, one of their warriors slammed a spear into the priest's chest, crushing his ribs and mangling his heart.

A handful of them turned on me once the priest was dead and, because I had worn a helmet with a gilt-bronze circlet, they thought I must be a king's son and they put me in a robe and a man climbed onto the table to piss on me, and just then a huge voice bellowed at them to stop and Ragnar bullied his way through the crowd. He snatched the robe from me and harangued the men, telling them I knew not what, but whatever he said made them stop and Ragnar then put an arm round my shoulders and took me to a dais at the side of the hall and gestured I should climb up to it. An old man was eating alone there. He was blind, both eyes milky white and had a deep-lined face framed by grey hair as long as Ragnar's. He heard me clamber up and asked a question, and Ragnar answered and then walked away.

'You must be hungry, boy,' the old man said in English.

I did not answer. I was terrified of his blind eyes.

'Have you vanished?' he asked, 'did the dwarves pluck you down to the under-earth?'

'I'm hungry,' I admitted.

'So you are there after all,' he said, 'and there's pork here, and bread, and cheese, and ale. Tell me your name.'

I almost said Osbert, then remembered I was Uhtred. 'Uhtred,' I said.

'An ugly name,' the old man said, 'but my son said I was to

look after you, so I will, but you must look after me too. Could you cut me some pork?'

'Your son?' I asked.

'Earl Ragnar,' he said, 'sometimes called Ragnar the Fearless. Who were they killing in here?'

'The king,' I said, 'and a priest.'

'Which king?'

'Osbert.'

'Did he die well?'

'No.'

'Then he shouldn't have been king.'

'Are you a king?' I asked.

He laughed. 'I am Ravn,' he said, 'and once I was an earl and a warrior, but now I am blind so I am no use to anyone. They should beat me over the head with a cudgel and send me on my way to the netherworld.' I said nothing to that because I did not know what to say. 'But I try to be useful,' Ravn went on, his hands groping for bread. 'I speak your language and the language of the Britons and the tongue of the Wends and the speech of the Frisians and that of the Franks. Language is now my trade, boy, because I have become a skald.'

'A skald?'

'A scop, you would call me. A poet, a weaver of dreams, a man who makes glory from nothing and dazzles you with its making. And my job now is to tell this day's tale in such a way that men will never forget our great deeds.'

'But if you cannot see,' I asked, 'how can you tell what happened?'

Ravn laughed at that. 'Have you heard of Odin? Then you should know that Odin sacrificed one of his own eyes so that he could obtain the gift of poetry. So perhaps I am twice as good a skald as Odin, eh?'

'I am descended from Woden,' I said.

'Are you?' He seemed impressed, or perhaps he just wanted to be kind. 'So who are you, Uhtred, descendant of the great Odin?'

'I am the Ealdorman of Bebbanburg,' I said, and that reminded me I was fatherless and my defiance crumpled and, to my shame,

33

I began to cry. Ravn ignored me as he listened to the drunken shouts and the songs and the shrieks of the girls who had been captured in our camp and who now provided the warriors with the reward for their victory, and watching their antics took my mind off my sorrow because, in truth, I had never seen such things before though, God be thanked, I took plenty of such rewards myself in times to come.

'Bebbanburg?' Ravn said. 'I was there before you were born. It was twenty years ago.'

'At Bebbanburg?'

'Not in the fortress,' he admitted, 'it was far too strong. But I was to the north of it, on the island where the monks pray. I killed six men there. Not monks, men. Warriors.' He smiled to himself, remembering. 'Now tell me, Ealdorman Uhtred of Bebbanburg,' he went on, 'what is happening.'

So I became his eyes and I told him of the men dancing, and the men stripping the women of their clothes, and what they then did to the women, but Ravn had no interest in that. 'What,' he wanted to know, 'are Ivar and Ubba doing?'

'Ivar and Ubba?'

'They will be on the high platform. Ubba is the shorter and looks like a barrel with a beard, and Ivar is so skinny that he is called Ivar the Boneless. He is so thin that you could press his feet together and shoot him from a bowstring.'

I learned later that Ivar and Ubba were the two oldest of three brothers and the joint leaders of this Danish army. Ubba was asleep, his black-haired head cushioned by his arms that, in turn, were resting on the remnants of his meal, but Ivar the Boneless was awake. He had sunken eyes, a face like a skull, yellow hair drawn back to the nape of his neck, and an expression of sullen malevolence. His arms were thick with the golden rings Danes like to wear to prove their prowess in battle, while a gold chain was coiled around his neck. Two men were talking to him. One, standing just behind Ivar, seemed to whisper into his ear, while the other, a worried-looking man, sat between the two brothers. I described all this to Ravn, who wanted to know what the worried man sitting between Ivar and Ubba looked like.

'No arm rings,' I said, 'a gold circlet around his neck. Brown hair, long beard, quite old.'

'Everyone looks old to the young,' Ravn said. 'That must be King Egbert.'

'King Egbert?' I had never heard of such a person.

'He was Ealdorman Egbert,' Ravn explained, 'but he made his peace with us in the winter and we have rewarded him by making him king here in Northumbria. He is king, but we are the lords of the land.' He chuckled, and young as I was I understood the treachery involved. Ealdorman Egbert held estates to the south of our kingdom and was what my father had been in the north, a great power, and the Danes had suborned him, kept him from the fight, and now he would be called king, yet it was plain that he would be a king on a short leash. 'If you are to live,' Ravn said to me, 'then it would be wise to pay your respects to Egbert.'

'Live?' I blurted out the word. I had somehow thought that having survived the battle then of course I would live. I was a child, someone else's responsibility, but Ravn's words hammered home my reality. I should never have confessed my rank, I thought. Better to be a living slave than a dead Ealdorman.

'I think you'll live,' Ravn said. 'Ragnar likes you and Ragnar gets what he wants. He says you attacked him?'

'I did, yes.'

'He would have enjoyed that. A boy who attacks Earl Ragnar? That must be some boy, eh? Too good a boy to waste on death he says, but then my son always had a regrettably sentimental side. I would have chopped your head off, but here you are, alive, and I think it would be wise if you were to bow to Egbert.'

Now, I think, looking back so far into my past, I have probably changed that night's events. There was a feast, Ivar and Ubba were there, Egbert was trying to look like a king, Ravn was kind to me, but I am sure I was more confused and far more frightened than I have made it sound. Yet in other ways my memories of the feast are very precise. Watch and learn, my father had told me, and Ravn made me watch, and I did learn. I learned about treachery, especially when Ragnar, summoned by Ravn, took me by the collar and led me to the high dais where, after a surly gesture of permission from Ivar, I was allowed to approach the table. 'Lord King,' I squeaked, then knelt so that a surprised Egbert had to lean forward to see me. 'I am Uhtred of Bebbanburg,' I had been coached by Ravn in what I should say, 'and I seek your lordly protection.'

That produced silence, except for the mutter of the interpreter talking to Ivar. Then Ubba awoke, looked startled for a few heartbeats as if he were not sure where he was, then he stared at me and I felt my flesh shrivel for I had never seen a face so malevolent. He had dark eyes and they were full of hate and I wanted the earth to swallow me. He said nothing, just gazed at me and touched a hammer-shaped amulet hanging at his neck. Ubba had his brother's thin face, but instead of fair hair drawn back against the skull, he had bushy black hair and a thick beard that was dotted with scraps of food. Then he yawned and it was like staring into a beast's maw. The interpreter spoke to Ivar who said something and the interpreter, in turn, talked to Egbert who tried to look stern. 'Your father,' he said, 'chose to fight us.'

'And is dead,' I answered, tears in my eyes, and I wanted to say something more, but nothing would come, and instead I just snivelled like an infant and I could feel Ubba's scorn like the heat of a fire. I cuffed angrily at my nose.

'We shall decide your fate,' Egbert said loftily, and I was dismissed.

I went back to Ravn who insisted I tell him what had happened, and he smiled when I described Ubba's malevolent silence. 'He's a frightening man,' Ravn agreed, 'to my certain knowledge he's killed sixteen men in single combat, and dozens more in battle, but only when the auguries are good, otherwise he won't fight.'

'The auguries?'

'Ubba is a very superstitious young man,' Ravn said, 'but also a dangerous one. If I give you one piece of advice, young Uhtred, it is never, never, to fight Ubba. Even Ragnar would fear to do that and my son fears little.'

'And Ivar?' I asked, 'would your son fight Ivar?'

'The boneless one?' Ravn considered the question. 'He too is frightening, for he has no pity, but he does possess sense. Besides, Ragnar serves Ivar if he serves anyone, and they're friends, so they would not fight. But Ubba? Only the gods tell him what to do, and you should beware of men who take their orders from the gods. Cut me some of the crackling, boy. I particularly like pork crackling.'

I cannot remember now how long I was in Eoferwic. I was put to work, that I do remember. My fine clothes were stripped from me and given to some Danish boy, and in their place I was given a flea-ridden shift of tattered wool that I belted with a piece of rope. I cooked Ravn's meals for a few days, then the other Danish ships arrived and proved to hold mostly women and children, the families of the victorious army, and it was then I understood that these Danes had come to stay in Northumbria. Ravn's wife arrived, a big woman called Gudrun with a laugh that could have felled an ox, and she chivvied me away from the cooking fire that she now tended with Ragnar's wife, who was called Sigrid and whose hair reached to her waist and was the colour of sunlight reflecting off gold. She and Ragnar had two sons and a daughter. Sigrid had given birth to eight children, but only those three had lived. Rorik, his second son, was a year younger than me and on the very first day I met him he picked a fight, coming at me in a whirl of fists and feet, but I put him on his back and was throttling the breath out of him when Ragnar picked us both up, crashed our heads together and told us to be friends. Ragnar's eldest son, also called Ragnar, was eighteen, already a man, and I did not meet him then for he was in Ireland where he was learning to fight and to kill so he could become an Earl like his father. In time I did meet Ragnar the Younger who was very similar to his father; always cheerful, boisterously happy, enthusiastic about whatever needed to be done, and friendly to anyone who paid him respect.

Like all the other children I had work to keep me busy. There was always firewood and water to be fetched, and I spent two days helping to burn the green muck from the hull of a beached ship, and I enjoyed that even though I got into a dozen fights with Danish boys, all of them bigger than me, and I lived with black eyes, bruised knuckles, sprained wrists, and loosened teeth. My worst enemy was a boy called Sven who was two years older than me and very big for his age with a round, vacant face, a slack jaw, and a vicious temper. He was the son of one of Ragnar's ship-masters, a man called Kjartan. Ragnar owned three ships, he commanded one, Kjartan the second and a tall, weather-hardened man named Egil steered the third. Kjartan and Egil were also warriors, of course, and as shipmasters they led their crews into battle and so were reckoned important men, their arms heavy with rings, and Kjartan's son Sven took an instant dislike to me. He called me English scum, a goat-turd and dog-breath, and because he was older and bigger he could beat me fairly easily, but I was also making friends and, luckily for me, Sven disliked Rorik almost as much as he hated me, and the two of us could just thrash him together and after a while Sven avoided me unless he was sure I was alone. So apart from Sven it was a good summer. I never had quite enough to eat, I was never clean, Ragnar made us laugh and I was rarely unhappy.

Ragnar was often absent, for much of the Danish army spent that summer riding the length and breadth of Northumbria to quell the last shreds of resistance, but I heard little news, and no news of Bebbanburg. It seemed the Danes were winning, for every few days another English thegn would come to Eoferwic and kneel to Egbert, who now lived in the palace of Northumbria's king, though it was a palace that had been stripped of anything useful by the victors. The gap in the city wall had been repaired in a day, the same day that a score of us dug a great hole in the field where our army had fled in panic. We filled the hole with the rotting corpses of the Northumbrian dead. I knew some of them. I suppose my father was among them, but I did not see him. Nor, looking back, did I miss him. He had always been a morose man, expecting the worst, and not fond of children.

The worst job I was given was painting shields. We first had to boil down some cattle hides to make size, a thick glue, that we stirred into a powder we had made from crushing copper ore with big stone pestles, and the result was a viscous blue paste that had to be smeared on the newly-made shields. For days afterwards I had blue hands and arms, but our shields were hung on a ship and looked splendid. Every Danish ship had a strake running down each side from which the shields could hang, overlapping as though they were being held in the shield wall, and these shields were for Ubba's craft, the same ship I had burned and scraped clean. Ubba, it seemed, planned to leave, and wanted his ship to be beautiful. She had a beast on her prow, a prow that curved like a swan's breast from the waterline, then jutted forward. The beast, half dragon and half worm, was the topmost part, and the whole beast-head could be lifted off its stem and stowed in the bilge. 'We lift the beast-heads off,' Ragnar explained to me, 'so they don't frighten the spirits.' I had learned some of the Danish language by then.

'The spirits?'

Ragnar sighed at my ignorance. 'Every land has its spirits,' he said, 'its own little gods, and when we approach our own lands we take off the beast-heads so that the spirits aren't scared away. How many fights have you had today?'

'None.'

'They're getting frightened of you. What's that thing around your neck?'

I showed him. It was a crude iron hammer, a miniature hammer the size of a man's thumb, and the sight of it made him laugh and cuff me around the head. 'We'll make a Dane of you yet,' he said, plainly pleased. The hammer was the sign of Thor, who was a Danish god almost as important as Odin, as they called Woden, and sometimes I wondered if Thor was the more important god, but no one seemed to know or even care very much. There were no priests among the Danes, which I liked, because priests were forever telling us not to do things or trying to teach us to read or demanding that we pray, and life without them was much more pleasant. The Danes, indeed, seemed very casual about their gods, yet almost every one wore Thor's hammer. I had torn mine from the neck of a boy who had fought me, and I have it to this day.

The stern of Ubba's ship, which curved and reared as high as the prow, was decorated with a carved eagle's head, while at her masthead was a wind-vane in the shape of a dragon. The shields were hung on her flanks, though I later learned they were only displayed there for decoration and that once the ship was under way the shields were stored inboard. Just underneath the shields were the oar-holes, each rimmed with leather, fifteen holes on each side. The holes could be stopped with wooden plugs when the ship was under sail so that the craft could lean with the wind and not be swamped. I helped scrub the whole boat clean, but before we scrubbed her she was sunk in the river, just to drown the rats and discourage the fleas, and then we boys scraped every inch of wood and hammered wax-soaked wool into every seam, and at last the ship was ready and that was the day my uncle Ælfric arrived in Eoferwic.

The first I knew of Ælfric's coming was when Ragnar brought me my own helmet, the one with the gilt-bronze circlet, and a tunic edged with red embroidery, and a pair of shoes. It felt strange to walk in shoes again. 'Tidy your hair, boy,' he said, then remembered he had the helmet that he pushed onto my tousled head. 'Don't tidy your hair,' he said, grinning.

'Where are we going?' I asked him.

'To hear a lot of words, boy. To waste our time. You look like a Frankish whore in that robe.'

'That bad?'

'That's good, lad! They have great whores in Frankia; plump, pretty and cheap. Come on.' He led me from the river. The city was busy, the shops full, the streets crowded with packmules. A herd of small, dark-fleeced sheep was being driven to slaughter, and they were the only obstruction that did not part to make way for Ragnar whose reputation ensured respect, but that reputation was not grim for I saw how the Danes grinned when he greeted them. He might be called Jarl Ragnar, Earl Ragnar, but he was hugely popular, a jester and fighter who blew through fear as though it were a cobweb. He took me to the palace, which was only a large house, part-built by the Romans in stone and part-made more recently in wood and thatch. It was in the Roman part, in a vast room with stone pillars and limewashed walls, that my uncle waited and with him was Father Beocca and a dozen warriors, all of whom I knew, and all of whom had stayed to defend Bebbanburg while my father rode to war.

Beocca's crossed eyes widened when he saw me. I must have looked very different for I was long-haired, sun-darkened, skinny, taller and wilder. Then there was the hammer amulet about my neck, which he saw for he pointed to his own crucifix, then at my hammer and looked very disapproving. Ælfric and his men scowled at me as though I had let them down, but no one spoke, partly because Ivar's own guards, all of them tall men, and all of them in mail and helmets and armed with long-shafted war axes, stood across the head of the room where a simple chair, which now counted as Northumbria's throne, stood on a wooden platform.

King Egbert arrived, and with him was Ivar the Boneless and a dozen men, including Ravn who, I had learned, was a counsellor to Ivar and his brother. With Ravn was a tall man, white-haired and with a long white beard. He was wearing long robes embroidered with crosses and winged angels and I later discovered this was Wulfhere, the Archbishop of Eoferwic who, like Egbert, had given his allegiance to the Danes. The king sat, looking uncomfortable, and then the discussion began.

They were not there just to discuss me. They talked about which Northumbrian lords were to be trusted, which were to be attacked, what lands were to be granted to Ivar and Ubba, what tribute the Northumbrians must pay, how many horses were to be brought to Eoferwic, how much food was to be given to the army, which ealdormen were to yield hostages, and I sat, bored, until my name was mentioned. I perked up then and heard my uncle propose that I should be ransomed. That was the gist of it, but nothing is ever simple when a score of men decide to argue. For a long time they wrangled over my price, the Danes demanding an impossible payment of three hundred pieces of silver, and Ælfric not wanting to budge from a grudging offer of fifty. I said nothing, but just sat on the broken Roman tiles at the edge of the hall and listened. Three hundred became two seventy-five, fifty became sixty, and so it went on, the numbers edging closer, but still wide apart, and then Ravn, who had been silent, spoke for the first time. 'The Earl Uhtred,' he said in Danish, and that was the first time I heard myself described as an Earl, which was a Danish rank, 'has given his allegiance to King Egbert. In that he has an advantage over you, Ælfric.'

The words were translated and I saw Ælfric's anger when he

was given no title. But nor did he have a title, except the one he had granted to himself, and I learned about that when he spoke softly to Beocca who then spoke up for him. 'The Ealdorman Ælfric,' the young priest said, 'does not believe that a child's oath is of any significance.'

Had I made an oath? I could not remember doing so, though I had asked for Egbert's protection, and I was young enough to confuse the two things. Still, it did not much matter, what mattered was that my uncle had usurped Bebbanburg. He was calling himself Ealdorman. I stared at him, shocked, and he looked back at me with pure loathing in his face.

'It is our belief,' Ravn said, his blind eyes looking at the roof of the hall that was missing some tiles so that a light rain was spitting through the rafters, 'that we would be better served by having our own sworn Earl in Bebbanburg, loyal to us, than endure a man whose loyalty we do not know.'

Ælfric could feel the wind changing and he did the obvious thing. He walked to the dais, knelt to Egbert and kissed the king's outstretched hand and, as a reward, received a blessing from the Archbishop. 'I will offer a hundred pieces of silver,' Ælfric said, his allegiance given.

'Two hundred,' Ravn said, 'and a force of thirty Danes to garrison Bebbanburg.'

'With my allegiance given,' Ælfric said angrily, 'you will have no need of Danes in Bebbanburg.'

So Bebbanburg had not fallen and I doubted it could fall. There was no stronger fortress in all Northumbria, and perhaps in all England.

Egbert had not spoken at all, nor did he, but nor had Ivar and it was plain that the tall, thin, ghost-faced Dane was bored with the whole proceedings for he jerked his head at Ragnar who left my side and went to talk privately with his lord. The rest of us waited awkwardly. Ivar and Ragnar were friends, an unlikely friendship for they were very different men, Ivar all savage silence and grim threat, and Ragnar open and loud, yet Ragnar's eldest son served Ivar and was even now, at eighteen years old, entrusted with the leadership of some of the Danes left in Ireland who were holding onto Ivar's lands in that island. It was not unusual for eldest sons to serve another lord, Ragnar had two Earls' sons in his ships' crews and both might one day expect to inherit wealth and position if they learned how to fight. So Ragnar and Ivar now talked and Ælfric shuffled his feet and kept looking at me, Beocca prayed and King Egbert, having nothing else to do, just tried to look regal.

Ivar finally spoke. 'The boy is not for sale,' he announced.

'Ransom,' Ravn corrected him gently.

Ælfric looked furious. 'I came here . . .' he began, but Ivar interrupted him.

'The boy is not for ransom,' he snarled, then turned and walked from the big chamber. Egbert looked awkward, half rose from his throne, sat again, and Ragnar came and stood beside me.

'You're mine,' he said softly, 'I just bought you.'

'Bought me?'

'My sword's weight in silver,' he said.

'Why?'

'Perhaps I want to sacrifice you to Odin?' he suggested, then tousled my hair. 'We like you, boy,' he said, 'we like you enough to keep you. And besides, your uncle didn't offer enough silver. For five hundred pieces? I'd have sold you for that.' He laughed.

Beocca hurried across the room. 'Are you well?' he asked me.

'I'm well,' I said.

'That thing you're wearing,' he said, meaning Thor's hammer, and he reached as though to pull it from its thong.

'Touch the boy, priest,' Ragnar said harshly, 'and I'll straighten your crooked eyes before opening you from your gutless belly to your skinny throat.'

Beocca, of course, could not understand what the Dane had said, but he could not mistake the tone and his hand stopped an inch from the hammer. He looked nervous. He lowered his voice so only I could hear him. 'Your uncle will kill you,' he whispered.

'Kill me?'

'He wants to be Ealdorman. That's why he wished to ransom you. So he could kill you.'

'But,' I began to protest.

'Shh,' Beocca said. He was curious about my blue hands, but did not ask what had caused them. 'I know you are the Ealdorman,' he said instead, 'and we will meet again.' He smiled at me, glanced warily at Ragnar, and backed away.

Ælfric left. I learned later that he had been given safe passage to and from Eoferwic, which promise had been kept, but after that meeting he retreated to Bebbanburg and stayed there. Ostensibly he was loyal to Egbert, which meant he accepted the overlordship of the Danes, but they had not yet learned to trust him. That, Ragnar explained to me, was why he had kept me alive. 'I like Bebbanburg,' he told me, 'I want it.'

'It's mine,' I said stubbornly.

'And you're mine,' he said, 'which means Bebbanburg is mine. You're mine, Uhtred, because I just bought you, so I can do whatever I like with you. I can cook you, if I want, except there's not enough meat on you to feed a weasel. Now, take off that whore's tunic, give me the shoes and helmet, and go back to work.'

So I was a slave again, and happy. Sometimes, when I tell folk my story, they ask why I did not run away from the pagans, why I did not escape southwards into the lands where the Danes did not yet rule, but it never occurred to me to try. I was happy, I was alive, I was with Ragnar and it was enough.

More Danes arrived before winter. Thirty-six ships came, each with its contingent of warriors, and the ships were pulled onto the riverbank for the winter while the crews, laden with shields and weapons, marched to wherever they would spend the next few months. The Danes were casting a net over eastern Northumbria, a light one, but still a net of scattered garrisons. Yet they could not have stayed if we had not let them, but those Ealdormen and thegns who had not died at Eoferwic had bent the knee and so we were a Danish kingdom now, despite the leashed Egbert on his pathetic throne. It was only in the west, in the wilder parts of Northumbria, that no Danes ruled, but nor were there any strong forces in those wild parts to challenge them.

Ragnar took land west of Eoferwic, up in the hills. His wife and family joined him there, and Ravn and Gudrun came, plus all Ragnar's ships' crews who took over homesteads in the nearby valleys. Our first job was to make Ragnar's house larger. It had belonged to an English thegn who had died at Eoferwic, but it was no grand hall, merely a low wooden building thatched with rye straw and bracken on which grass grew so thickly that, from a distance, the house looked like a long hummock. We built a new part, not for us, but for the few cattle, sheep and goats who would survive the winter and give birth in the new year. The rest were slaughtered. Ragnar and the men did most of the killing, but as the last few beasts came to the pen, he handed an axe to Rorik, his younger son. 'One clean, quick stroke,' he ordered, and Rorik tried, but he was not strong enough and his aim was not true and the animal bellowed and bled and it took six men to restrain it while Ragnar did the job properly. The skinners moved onto the carcass and Ragnar held the axe to me. 'See if you can do better.'

A cow was pushed towards me, a man lifted her tail, she obediently lowered her head and I swung the axe, remembering exactly where Ragnar had hit each time, and the heavy blade swung true, straight into the spine just behind the skull and she went down with a crash. 'We'll make a Danish warrior of you yet,' Ragnar said, pleased.

The work lessened after the cattle slaughter. The English who still lived in the valley brought Ragnar their tribute of carcasses and grain, just as they would have delivered the supplies to their English lord. It was impossible to read from their faces what they thought of Ragnar and his Danes, but they gave no trouble, and Ragnar took care not to disturb their lives. The local priest was allowed to live and give services in his church that was a wooden shed decorated with a cross, and Ragnar sat in judgment on disputes, but always made certain he was advised by an Englishman who was knowledgeable in the local customs. 'You can't live somewhere,' he told me, 'if the people don't want you to be there. They can kill our cattle or poison our streams, and we would never know who did it. You either slaughter them all or learn to live with them.'

The sky grew paler and the wind colder. Dead leaves blew in drifts. Our main work now was to feed the surviving cattle and to keep the log pile high. A dozen of us would go up into the woods and I became proficient with an axe, learning how to bring a tree down with an economy of strokes. We would harness an ox to the bigger trunks to drag them down to the shieling, and the best trees were put aside for building, while the others were split and chopped for burning. There was also time for play and so we children made our own hall high up in the woods, a hall of unsplit logs with a thatch of bracken and a badger's skull nailed to the gable in imitation of the boar's skull that crowned Ragnar's home, and in our pretend hall Rorik and I fought over who would be king, though Thyra, his sister, who was eight years old, was always the lady of the house. She would spin wool there, because if she did not spin enough thread by winter's end she would be punished, and she would watch while we boys fought our mock battles with toy wooden swords. Most of the boys were servants' sons, or slave children, and they always insisted I was the English chief while Rorik was the Danish leader, and my war-band only received the smallest, weakest boys and so we nearly always lost, and Thyra, who had her mother's pale gold hair, would watch and spin, ever spinning, the distaff in her left hand while her right teased the thread out of the sheared fleece.

Every woman had to spin and weave. Ragnar reckoned it took five women or a dozen girls a whole winter to spin enough thread to make a new sail for a boat, and boats were always needing new sails, and so the women worked every hour the gods sent. They also cooked, boiled walnut shells to dye the new thread, picked mushrooms, tanned the skins of the slaughtered cattle, collected the moss we used for wiping our arses, rolled beeswax into candles, malted the barley and placated the gods. There were so many gods and goddesses, and some were peculiar to our own house and those the women celebrated in their own rites, while others, like Odin and Thor were mighty and ubiquitous, but they were rarely treated in the same way that the Christians worshipped their God. A man would appeal to Thor, or to Loki, or to Odin, or to Vikr, or to any of the other great beings who lived in Asgard, which seemed to be the heaven of the gods, but the Danes did not gather in a church as we had gathered every Sunday and every saint's day in Bebbanburg, and just as there were no priests among the Danes, nor were there any relics or sacred books. I missed none of it.

I wish I had missed Sven, but his father, Kjartan, had a home in the next valley and it did not take long for Sven to discover our hall in the woods and, as the first winter frosts crisped the dead leaves and the berries shone on hawthorn and holly, we found our games turning savage. We no longer split into two sides, because we now had to fight off Sven's boys who would come stalking us, but for a time no great damage was done. It was a game, after all, just a game, but one Sven won repeatedly. He stole the badger's skull from our gable, which we replaced with a fox's head and Thyra shouted at Sven's boys, skulking in the woods, that she had smeared the fox skull with poison, and we thought that very clever of her, but next morning we found our pretend hall burned to the ground.

'A hall-burning,' Rorik said bitterly.

'Hall-burning?'

'It happens at home,' Rorik explained. 'You go to an enemy's hall and burn it to the ground. But there's one thing about a hall-burning. You have to make sure everyone dies. If there are any survivors then they'll take revenge, so you attack at night, surround the hall, and kill everyone who tries to escape the flames.'

But Sven had no hall. There was his father's house, of course, and for a day we plotted revenge on that, discussing how we would burn it down and spear the family as they ran out, but it was only boastful boy talk and of course nothing came of it. Instead we built ourselves a new hall, higher in the woods. It was not as fanciful as the old, not nearly so weathertight, really nothing more than a crude shelter of branches and bracken, but we nailed a stoat's skull to its makeshift gable and assured ourselves that we still had our kingdom in the hills.

But nothing short of total victory would satisfy Sven and, a few days later, when our chores were done, just Rorik, Thyra and I went up to our new hall. Thyra span while Rorik and I argued over where the best swords were made, he saying it was Denmark and I claiming the prize for England, neither of us old enough or sensible enough to know that the best blades come from Frankia, and after a while we got tired of arguing and picked up our sharpened ash poles that served as play spears and decided to look for the wild boar that sometimes trampled through the wood at nightfall. We would not have dared try to kill a boar, they were much too big, but we pretended we were great hunters, and just as we two great hunters were readying to go into the woods, Sven attacked. Just him and two of his followers, but Sven, instead of carrying a wooden sword, swung a real blade, long as a man's arm, the steel glittering in the winter light, and he ran at us, bellowing like a madman. Rorik and I, seeing the fury in his eyes, ran away. He followed us, crashing through the wood like the wild boar we had wanted to stalk, and it was only because we were much faster that we got away from that wicked blade, and then a moment later we heard Thyra scream.

We crept back, cautious of the sword that Sven must have taken from his father's house and, when we reached our pathetic hut, found that Thyra was gone. Her distaff was on the floor and her wool was all speckled with dead leaves and pieces of twig.

Sven had always been clumsy in his strength and he had left a trail through the woods that was easy enough to follow and after a while we heard voices. We kept following, crossing the ridge-top where beeches grew, then down into our enemy's valley, and Sven did not have the sense to post a rearguard who would have seen us. Instead, revelling in his victory, he had gone to the clearing that must have been his refuge in the wood because there was a stone hearth in the centre and I remember wondering why we had never built a similar hearth for ourselves. He had tied Thyra to a tree and stripped the tunic from her upper body. There was nothing to see there, she was just a small girl, only eight years old and thus four or five years from being marriageable, but she was pretty and that was why Sven had half stripped her. I could see that Sven's two companions were unhappy. Thyra, after all, was Earl Ragnar's daughter and what had started as a game was now dangerous, but Sven had to show off. He had to prove he had no

48

fear. He had no idea Rorik and I were crouched in the under-growth, and I do not suppose he would have cared if he had known.

He had dropped the sword by the hearth and now he planted himself in front of Thyra and took down his breeches. 'Touch it,' he ordered her.

One of his companions said something I could not hear.

'She won't tell anyone,' Sven said confidently, 'and we won't hurt her.' He looked back to Thyra. 'I won't hurt you if you touch it!'

It was then I broke cover. I was not being brave. Sven's companions had lost their appetite for the game, Sven himself had his breeches around his ankles, and his sword was lying loose in the clearing's centre and I snatched it up and ran at him. He somehow kept his feet as he turned. 'I'll touch it,' I shouted, and I swung the long blade at his prick, but the sword was heavy, I had not used a man's blade before, and instead of hitting where I had aimed I sliced it down his bare thigh, opening the skin, and I swung it back, using all my strength, and the blade chopped into his waist where his clothes took most of the force. He fell over, shouting, and his two friends dragged me away as Rorik went to untie his sister.

That was all that happened. Sven was bleeding, but he managed to pull up his breeches and his friends helped him away and Rorik and I took Thyra back to the homestead where Ravn heard Thyra's sobs and our excited voices and demanded silence. 'Uhtred,' the old man said sternly, 'you will wait by the pigsties. Rorik, you will tell me what happened.'

I waited outside as Rorik told what had happened, then Rorik was sent out and I was summoned indoors to recount the after-noon's escapade. Thyra was now in her mother's arms, and her mother and grandmother were furious. 'You tell the same tale as Rorik,' Ravn said when I had finished

'Because it's the truth,' I said.

'So it would seem.'

'He raped her!' Sigrid insisted.

'No,' Ravn said firmly, 'thanks to Uhtred, he did not.'

That was the story Ragnar heard when he returned from hunting, and as it made me a hero I did not argue against its essential untruth which was that Sven would not have raped Thyra for he would not have dared. His foolishness knew few limits, but limits there were, and committing rape on the daughter of Earl Ragnar, his father's warlord, was beyond even Sven's stupidity. Yet he had made an enemy and, next day, Ragnar led six men to Kjartan's house in the neighbouring valley. Rorik and I were given horses and told to accompany the men, and I confess I was frightened. I felt I was responsible. I had, after all, started the games in the high woods, but Ragnar did not see it that way. 'You haven't offended me. Sven has.' He spoke darkly, his usual cheerfulness gone. 'You did well, Uhtred. You behaved like a Dane.' There was no higher praise he could have given me, and I sensed he was disappointed that I had charged Sven instead of Rorik, but I was older and much stronger than Ragnar's younger son so it should have been me who fought.

We rode through the cold woods and I was curious because two of Ragnar's men carried long branches of hazel that were too spindly to use as weapons, but what they were for I did not like to ask because I was nervous.

Kjartan's homestead was in a fold of the hills beside a stream that ran through pastures where he kept sheep, goats and cattle, though most had been killed now, and the few remaining animals were cropping the last of the year's grass. It was a sunny day, though cold. Dogs barked as we approached, but Kjartan and his men snarled at them and beat them back to the yard beside the house where he had planted an ash tree that did not look as though it would survive the coming winter, and then, accompanied by four men, none of them armed, he walked towards the approaching horsemen. Ragnar and his six men were armed to the hilt with shields, swords and war axes, and their broad chests were clad in mail, while Ragnar was wearing my father's helmet that he had purchased after the fighting at Eoferwic. It was a splendid helmet, its crown and face-piece decorated with silver, and I thought it looked better on Ragnar than it had on my father.

Kjartan the shipmaster was a big man, taller than Ragnar, with a flat, wide face like his son's and small, suspicious eyes and a huge beard. He glanced at the hazel branches and must have recognised their meaning for he instinctively touched the hammer-charm hanging on a silver chain about his neck. Ragnar curbed his horse and, in a gesture that showed his utter contempt, he tossed down the sword that I had carried back from the clearing where Sven had tied Thyra. By rights the sword belonged to Ragnar now, and it was a valuable weapon with silver wire wrapped around its hilt, but he tossed the blade at Kjartan's feet as though it were nothing more than a hay-knife. 'Your son left that on my land,' he said, 'and I would have words with him.'

'My son is a good boy,' Kjartan said stoutly, 'and in time he will serve at your oars and fight in your shield wall.'

'He has offended me.'

'He meant no harm, lord.'

'He has offended me,' Ragnar repeated harshly. 'He looked on my daughter's nakedness and showed her his own.'

'And he was punished for it,' Kjartan said, giving me a malevolent glance. 'Blood was shed.'

Ragnar made an abrupt gesture and the hazel branches were dropped to the ground. That was evidently Ragnar's answer, which made no sense to me, but Kjartan understood, as did Rorik who leaned over and whispered to me. 'That means he must fight for Sven now.'

'Fight for him?'

'They mark a square on the ground with the branches and they fight inside the square.'

Yet no one moved to arrange the hazel branches into a square. Instead Kjartan walked back to his house and summoned Sven who came limping from under the low lintel, his right leg bandaged. He looked sullen and terrified, and no wonder, for Ragnar and his horsemen were in their war glory, shining warriors, sword-Danes.

'Say what you have to say,' Kjartan said to his son.

Sven looked up at Ragnar. 'I am sorry,' he mumbled.

'I can't hear you,' Ragnar snarled.

'I am sorry, lord,' Sven said, shaking with fear.

'Sorry for what?' Ragnar demanded.

'For what I did.'

'And what did you do?'

Sven found no answer, or none that he cared to make, and instead he shuffled his feet and looked down at the ground. Cloud shadows raced across the far moor, and two ravens beat up to the head of the valley.

'You laid hands on my daughter,' Ragnar said, 'and you tied her to a tree, and you stripped her naked.'

'Half naked,' Sven muttered, and for his pains took a thump on the head from his father.

'A game,' Kjartan appealed to Ragnar, 'just a game, lord.'

'No boy plays such games with my daughter,' Ragnar said. I had rarely seen him angry, but he was angry now, grim and hard, no trace of the big-hearted man who could make a hall echo with laughter. He dismounted and drew his sword, his battle-blade called Heart-Breaker, and he held the tip towards Kjartan. 'Well?' he asked, 'do you dispute my right?'

'No, lord,' Kjartan said, 'but he is a good boy, strong and a hard worker, and he will serve you well.'

'And he has seen things he should not see,' Ragnar said, and he tossed Heart-Breaker into the air so that her long blade turned in the sun and he caught her by the hilt as she dropped, but now he was holding her backwards, as if she were a dagger rather than a sword. 'Uhtred!' Ragnar called, making me jump. 'He says she was only half naked. Is that true?'

'Yes, lord.'

'Then only half a punishment,' Ragnar said, and he drove the sword forward, hilt first, straight into Sven's face. The hilts of our swords are heavy, sometimes decorated with precious things, but however pretty they appear, the hilts are still brutal lumps of metal, and Heart-Breaker's hilt, banded with silver, crushed Sven's right eye. Crushed it to jelly, blinding it instantly, and Ragnar spat at him then slid his blade back into its fleece-lined scabbard.

Sven was crouching, whimpering, his hands clasped over his ruined eye.

'It is over,' Ragnar said to Kjartan.

Kjartan hesitated. He was angry, shamed and unhappy, but he

52

could not win a trial of strength with Earl Ragnar and so, at last, he nodded. 'It is over,' he agreed.

'And you no longer serve me,' Ragnar said coldly.

We rode home.

The hard winter came, the brooks froze, snow drifted to fill the streambeds, and the world was cold, silent and white. Wolves came to the edge of the woods and the midday sun was pale, as though its strength had been leeched away by the north wind.

Ragnar rewarded me with a silver arm ring, the first I ever received, while Kjartan was sent away with his family. He would no longer command one of Ragnar's ships and he would no longer receive a share of Ragnar's generosity, for now he was a man without a lord and he went to Eoferwic where he joined the garrison holding the town. It was not a prestigious job, any Dane with ambition would rather serve a lord like Ragnar who could make him rich, while the men guarding Eoferwic were denied any chance of plunder. Their task was to watch across the flat fields outside the city and to make certain that King Egbert fomented no trouble, but I was relieved that Sven was gone, and absurdly pleased with my arm ring. The Danes loved arm rings. The more a man possessed, the more he was regarded, for the rings came from success. Ragnar had rings of silver and rings of gold, rings carved as dragons and rings inlaid with glittering stones. When he moved you could hear the rings clinking. The rings could be used as money if there were no coins. I remember watching a Dane take off an arm ring and hack it to shreds with an axe, then offer a merchant scraps of the ring until the scales showed he had paid sufficient silver. That was down in the bigger valley, in a large village where most of Ragnar's younger men had settled and where traders brought goods from Eoferwic. The incoming Danes had found a small English settlement in the valley, but they needed more space for new houses and to make it they had burned down a grove of hazels, and that was what Ragnar called the place, Synningthwait, which meant the place cleared by fire. Doubtless the village had an English name, but it was already being forgotten.

'We're in England to stay now,' Ragnar told me as we went home one day after buying supplies in Synningthwait. The road was a track pounded in the snow and our horses picked a careful path between the drifts through which the black twigs of the hedge-tops just showed. I was leading the two packhorses laden with their precious bags of salt and asking Ragnar my usual questions; where swallows went in winter, why elves gave us hiccups, and why Ivar was called the Boneless. 'Because he's so thin, of course,' Ragnar said, 'so that he looks as if you could roll him up like a cloak.'

'Why doesn't Ubba have a nickname?'

'He does. He's called Ubba the Horrible.' He laughed, because he had made the nickname up, and I laughed because I was happy. Ragnar liked my company and, with my long fair hair, men mistook me for his son and I liked that. Rorik should have been with us, but he was sick that day, and the women were plucking herbs and chanting spells. 'He's often sick,' Ragnar said, 'not like Ragnar,' he meant his eldest son who helped hold onto Ivar's lands in Ireland, 'Ragnar's built like an ox,' he went on, 'never gets sick! He's like you, Uhtred.' He smiled, thinking of his eldest son, who he missed. 'He'll take land and thrive. But Rorik? Perhaps I shall have to give him this land. He can't go back to Denmark.'

'Why not?'

'Denmark is bad land,' Ragnar explained. 'It's either flat and sandy and you can't grow a fart on that sort of field, or across the water it's great steep hills with little patches of meadow where you work like a dog and starve.'

'Across the water?' I asked, and he explained that the Danes came from a country that was divided into two parts, and the two parts were surrounded by countless islands, and that the nearer part, from where he came, was very flat and very sandy, and that the other part, which lay to the east across a great sound of water, was where the mountains were. 'And there are Svear there too,' he went on.

'Svear?'

'A tribe. Like us. They worship Thor and Odin, but they speak differently.' He shrugged. 'We get along with the Svear, and with the Norse.' The Svear, the Norse and the Danes were the Northmen, the men who went on Viking expeditions, but it was the Danes who had come to take my land, though I did not say that to Ragnar. I had learned to hide my soul, or perhaps I was confused. Northumbrian or Dane? Which was I? What did I want to be?

'Suppose,' I asked, 'that the rest of the English do not want us to stay here.' I used the word 'us' deliberately.

He laughed at that. 'The English can want what they like! But you saw what happened at Yorvik.' That was how the Danes pronounced Eoferwic. For some reason they found that name difficult, so they said Yorvik instead. 'Who was the bravest English fighter at Yorvik?' Ragnar asked. 'You! A child! You charged me with that little sax! It was a gutting knife, not a sword, and you tried to kill me! I almost died laughing.' He leaned over and cuffed me affectionately. 'Of course the English don't want us here,' he went on, 'but what can they do? Next year we'll take Mercia, then East Anglia and finally Wessex.'

'My father always said Wessex was the strongest kingdom,' I said. My father had said nothing of the sort, indeed he despised the men of Wessex because he thought them effete and over-pious, but I was trying to provoke Ragnar.

I failed. 'It's the richest kingdom,' he said, 'but that doesn't make it strong. Men make a kingdom strong, not gold.' He grinned at me. 'We're the Danes. We don't lose, we win, and Wessex will fall.'

'It will?'

'It has a new weak king,' he said dismissively, 'and if he dies then his son is a mere child, so perhaps they'd put the new king's brother on the throne instead. We'd like that.'

'Why?'

'Because the brother is another weakling. He's called Alfred.'

Alfred. That was the first time I ever heard of Alfred of Wessex. I thought nothing of it at the time. Why should I have done?

'Alfred,' Ragnar continued scathingly. 'All he cares about is rutting girls, which is good! Don't tell Sigrid I said that, but there's nothing wrong with unsheathing the sword when you can, but

Alfred spends half his time rutting and the other half praying to his god to forgive him for rutting. How can a god disapprove of a good hump?'

'How do you know about Alfred?' I asked.

'Spies, Uhtred, spies. Traders, mostly. They talk to folk in Wessex, so we know all about King Æthelred and his brother Alfred. And Alfred's sick as a stoat half the time.' He paused, perhaps thinking of his younger son who was ill. 'It's a weak house,' he went on, 'and the West Saxons should get rid of them and put a real man on the throne, except they won't, and when Wessex falls there will be no more England.'

'Perhaps they'll find their strong king,' I said.

'No,' Ragnar said firmly. 'In Denmark,' he went on, 'our kings are the hard men, and if their sons are soft, then a man from another family becomes king, but in England they believe the throne passes through a woman's legs. So a feeble creature like Alfred could become king just because his father was a king.'

'You have a king in Denmark?'

'A dozen. I could call myself king if I fancied, except Ivar and Ubba might not like it, and no man offends them lightly.'

I rode in silence, listening to the horses' hooves crunching and squeaking in the snow. I was thinking of Ragnar's dream, the dream of no more England, of her land given to the Danes. 'What happens to me?' I finally blurted out.

'You?' He sounded surprised that I had asked. 'What happens to you, Uhtred, is what you make happen. You will grow, you will learn the sword, you will learn the way of the shield wall, you will learn the oar, you will learn to give honour to the gods, and then you will use what you have learned to make your life good or bad.'

'I want Bebbanburg,' I said.

'Then you must take it. Perhaps I will help you, but not yet. Before that we go south, and before we go south we must persuade Odin to look on us with favour.'

I still did not understand the Danish way of religion. They took it much less seriously than we English, but the women prayed often enough and once in a while a man would kill a good beast, dedicate it to the gods, and mount its bloody head above his door

56

to show that there would be a feast in Thor or Odin's honour in his house, but the feast, though it was an act of worship, was always the same as any other drunken feast.

I remember the Yule feast best because that was the week Weland came. He arrived on the coldest day of the winter when the snow was heaped in drifts, and he came on foot with a sword by his side, a bow on his shoulder and rags on his back and he knelt respectfully outside Ragnar's house. Sigrid made him come inside and she fed him and gave him ale, but when he had eaten he insisted on going back into the snow and waiting for Ragnar who was up in the hills, hunting.

Weland was a snake-like man, that was my very first thought on seeing him. He reminded me of my uncle Ælfric, slender, sly and secretive, and I disliked him on sight and I felt a flicker of fear as I watched him prostrate himself in the snow when Ragnar returned.

'My name is Weland,' he said, 'and I am in need of a lord.'

'You are not a youth,' Ragnar said, 'so why do you not have a lord?'

'He died, lord, when his ship sank.'

'Who was he?'

'Snorri, lord.'

'Which Snorri?'

'Son of Eric, son of Grimm, from Birka.'

'And you did not drown?' Ragnar asked as he dismounted and gave me the reins of his horse.

'I was ashore, lord, I was sick.'

'Your family? Your home?'

'I am son of Godfred, lord, from Haithabu.'

'Haithabu!' Ragnar said sourly. 'A trader?'

'I am a warrior, lord.'

'So why come to me?'

Weland shrugged. 'Men say you are a good lord, a ring-giver, but if you turn me down, lord, I shall try other men.'

'And you can use that sword, Weland Godfredson?'

'As a woman can use her tongue, lord.'

'You're that good, eh?' Ragnar asked, as ever unable to resist a jest. He gave Weland permission to stay, sending him to

Synningthwait to find shelter, and afterwards, when I said I did not like Weland, Ragnar just shrugged and said the stranger needed kindness. We were sitting in the house, half choking from the smoke that writhed about the rafters. 'There is nothing worse, Uhtred,' Ragnar said, 'than for a man to have no lord. No ring-giver,' he added, touching his own arm rings.

'I don't trust him,' Sigrid put in from the fire where she was making bannocks on a stone. Rorik, recovering from his sickness, was helping her, while Thyra, as ever, was spinning. 'I think he's an outlaw,' Sigrid said.

'He probably is,' Ragnar allowed, 'but my ship doesn't care if its oars are pulled by outlaws.' He reached for a bannock and had his hand slapped away by Sigrid who said the cakes were for Yule.

The Yule feast was the biggest celebration of the year, a whole week of food and ale and mead and fights and laughter and drunken men vomiting in the snow. Ragnar's men gathered at Synningthwait and there were horse races, wrestling matches, competitions in throwing spears, axes and rocks, and, my favourite, the tug of war where two teams of men or boys tried to pull the other into a cold stream. I saw Weland watching me as I wrestled with a boy a year older than me. Weland already looked more prosperous. His rags were gone and he wore a cloak of fox fur. I got drunk that Yule for the first time, helplessly drunk so that my legs would not work and I lay moaning with a throbbing head and Ragnar roared with laughter and made me drink more mead until I threw up. Ragnar, of course, won the drinking competition, and Ravn recited a long poem about some ancient hero who killed a monster and then the monster's mother who was even more fearsome than her son, but I was too drunk to remember much of it.

And after the Yule feast I discovered something new about the Danes and their gods, for Ragnar had ordered a great pit dug in the woods above his house, and Rorik and I helped make the pit in a clearing. We axed through tree roots, shovelled out earth, and still Ragnar wanted it deeper, and he was only satisfied when he could stand in the base of the pit and not see across its lip. A ramp led down into the hole, beside which was a great heap of exca-vated soil.

The next night all Ragnar's men, but no women, walked to the pit in the darkness. We boys carried pitch-soaked torches that flamed under the trees, casting flickering shadows that melted into the surrounding darkness. The men were all dressed and armed as though they were going to war.

Blind Ravn waited at the pit, standing at the far side from the ramp, and he chanted a great epic in praise of Odin. On and on it went, the words as hard and rhythmic as a drum beat, describing how the great god had made the world from the corpse of the giant Ymir, and how he had hurled the sun and moon into the sky, and how his spear, Gungnir, was the mightiest weapon in creation, forged by dwarves in the world's deeps, and on the poem went and the men gathered around the pit seemed to sway to the poem's pulse, sometimes repeating a phrase, and I confess I was almost as bored as when Beocca used to drone on in his stammering Latin, and I stared out into the woods, watching the shadows, wondering what things moved in the dark and thinking of the sceadugengan.

I often thought of the sceadugengan, the Shadow-Walkers. Ealdwulf, Bebbanburg's blacksmith, had first told me of them. He had warned me not to tell Beocca of the stories, and I never did, and Ealdwulf told me how, before Christ came to England, back when we English had worshipped Woden and the other gods, it had been well known that there were Shadow-Walkers who moved silent and half-seen across the land, mysterious creatures who could change their shapes. One moment they were wolves, then they were men, or perhaps eagles, and they were neither alive nor dead, but things from the shadow world, night-beasts, and I stared into the dark trees and I wanted there to be sceadugengan out there in the dark, something that would be my secret, something that would frighten the Danes, something to give Bebbanburg back to me, something as powerful as the magic which brought the Danes victory.

It was a child's dream, of course. When you are young and powerless you dream of possessing mystical strength, and once you are grown and strong you condemn lesser folk to that same dream, but as a child I wanted the power of the sceadugengan. I remember my excitement that night at the notion of harnessing the power of the Shadow-Walkers before a whinny brought my attention back to the pit and I saw that the men at the ramp had divided, and that a strange procession was coming from the dark. There was a stallion, a ram, a dog, a goose, a bull and a boar, each animal led by one of Ragnar's warriors, and at the back was an English prisoner, a man condemned for moving a field marker, and he, like the beasts, had a rope about his neck.

I knew the stallion. It was Ragnar's finest, a great black horse called Flame-Stepper, a horse Ragnar loved. Yet Flame-Stepper, like all the other beasts, was to be given to Odin that night. Ragnar did it. Stripped to his waist, his scarred chest broad in the flamelight, he used a war axe to kill the beasts one by one, and Flame-Stepper was the last animal to die and the great horse's eyes were white as it was forced down the ramp. It struggled, terrified by the stench of blood that had splashed the sides of the pit, and Ragnar went to the horse and there were tears on his face as he kissed Flame-Stepper's muzzle, and then he killed him, one blow between the eyes, straight and true, so that the stallion fell, hooves thrashing, but dead within a heartbeat. The man died last, and that was not so distressing as the horse's death, and then Ragnar stood in the mess of blood-matted fur and raised his gore-smothered axe to the sky. 'Odin!' he shouted.

'Odin!' Every man echoed the shout, and they held their swords or spears or axes towards the steaming pit. 'Odin!' they shouted again, and I saw Weland the snake staring at me across the firelit slaughter hole.

All the corpses were taken from the pit and hung from tree branches. Their blood had been given to the creatures beneath the earth and now their flesh was given to the gods above, and then we filled in the pit, we danced on it to stamp down the earth, and the jars of ale and skins of mead were handed around and we drank beneath the hanging corpses. Odin, the terrible god, had been summoned because Ragnar and his people were going to war.

I thought of the blades held over the pit of blood, I thought of the god stirring in his corpse-hall to send a blessing on these men, and I knew that all England would fall unless it found a magic as strong as the sorcery of these strong men. I was only ten years old, but on that night I knew what I would become.

I would join the sceadugengan, I would be a Shadow-Walker.

Two

Springtime, the year 868, I was eleven years old and the *Wind-Viper* was afloat.

She was afloat, but not at sea. The *Wind-Viper* was Ragnar's ship, a lovely thing with a hull of oak, a carved serpent's head at the prow, an eagle's head at the stern and a triangular wind-vane made of bronze on which a raven was painted black. The wind-vane was mounted at her masthead, though the mast was now lowered and being supported by two timber crutches so that it ran like a rafter down the centre of the long ship. Ragnar's men were rowing and their painted shields lined the ship's sides. They chanted as they rowed, pounding out the tale of how mighty Thor had fished for the dread Midgard Serpent that lies coiled about the roots of the world, and how the serpent had taken the hook baited with an ox's head, and how the giant Hymir, terrified of the vast snake, had cut the line. It is a good tale and its rhythms took us up the River Trente, which is a tributary of the Humber and flows from deep inside Mercia. We were going south, against the current, but the journey was easy, the ride placid, the sun warm and the river's margins thick with flowers. Some men rode horses, keeping pace with us on the eastern bank, while behind us was a fleet of beast-prowed ships. This was the army of Ivar the Boneless and Ubba the Horrible, a host of Northmen, sword-Danes, going to war.

All eastern Northumbria belonged to them, western Northumbria offered grudging allegiance, and now they planned to take Mercia which was the kingdom at England's heartland.

The Mercian territory stretched south to the River Temes where the lands of Wessex began, west to the mountainous country where the Welsh tribes lived, and east to the farms and marshes of East Anglia. Mercia, though not as wealthy as Wessex, was much richer than Northumbria and the River Trente ran into the kingdom's heart and the *Wind-Viper* was the tip of a Danish spear aimed at that heart.

The river was not deep, but Ragnar boasted that the *Wind-Viper* could float on a puddle, and that was almost true. From a distance she looked long, lean and knife-like, but when you were aboard you could see how the midships flared outwards so that she sat on the water like a shallow bowl rather than cut through it like a blade, and even with her belly laden with forty or fifty men, their weapons, shields, food and ale, she needed very little depth. Once in a while her long keel would scrape on gravel, but by keeping to the outside of the river's sweeping bends we were able to stay in sufficient water. That was why the mast had been lowered, so that, on the outside of the river's curves, we could slide under the overhanging trees without becoming entangled.

Rorik and I sat in the prow with his grandfather, Ravn, and our job was to tell the old man everything we could see, which was very little other than flowers, trees, reeds, waterfowl and the signs of trout rising to mayfly. Swallows had come from their winter sleep and swooped across the river while martins pecked at the banks to collect mud for their nests. Warblers were loud, pigeons clattered through new leaves and the hawks slid still and menacing across the scattered clouds. Swans watched us pass and once in a while we would see otter cubs playing beneath the pale-leaved willows and there would be a flurry of water as they fled from our coming. Sometimes we passed a riverside settlement of thatch and timber, but the folks and their livestock had already run away.

'Mercia is frightened of us,' Ravn said. He lifted his white, blind eyes to the oncoming air, 'and they are right to be frightened. We are warriors.'

'They have warriors too,' I said.

Ravn laughed. 'I think only one man in three is a warrior, and sometimes not even that many, but in our army, Uhtred, every man is a fighter. If you do not want to be a warrior you stay home in Denmark. You till the soil, herd sheep, fish the sea, but you do not take to the ships and become a fighter. But here in England? Every man is forced to the fight, yet only one in three or maybe only one in four has the belly for it. The rest are farmers who just want to run. We are wolves fighting sheep.'

Watch and learn, my father had said, and I was learning. What else can a boy with an unbroken voice do? One in three men are warriors, remember the Shadow-Walkers, beware the cut beneath the shield, a river can be an army's road to a kingdom's heart, watch and learn.

'And they have a weak king,' Ravn went on. 'Burghred, he's called, and he has no guts for a fight. He will fight, of course, because we shall force him, and he will call on his friends in Wessex to help him, but in his weak heart he knows he cannot win.'

'How do you know?' Rorik asked.

Ravn smiled. 'All winter, boy, our traders have been in Mercia. Selling pelts, selling amber, buying iron ore, buying malt, and they talk and they listen and they come back and they tell us what they heard.'

Kill the traders, I thought.

Why did I think that way? I liked Ragnar. I liked him much more than I had liked my father. I should, by rights, be dead, yet Ragnar had saved me and Ragnar spoilt me and he treated me like a son, and he called me a Dane, and I liked the Danes, yet even at that time I knew I was not a Dane. I was Uhtred of Bebbanburg and I clung to the memory of the fortress by the sea, of the birds crying over the breakers, of the puffins whirring across the whitecaps, of the seals on the rocks, of the white water shattering on the cliffs. I remembered the folk of that land, the men who had called my father 'lord', but talked to him of cousins they held in common. It was the gossip of neighbours, the comfort of knowing every family within a half-day's ride, and that was, and is, Bebbanburg to me; home. Ragnar would have given me the fortress if it could be taken, but then it would belong to the Danes and I would be nothing more than their hired man, Ealdorman at their pleasure, no better than King Egbert who was no king but a pampered dog on a short rope, and what the Dane gives, the Dane can take away, and I would hold Bebbanburg by my own effort.

Did I know all that at eleven? Some, I think. It lay in my heart, unformed, unspoken, but hard as a stone. It would be covered over in time, half forgotten and often contradicted, but it was always there. Destiny is all, Ravn liked to tell me, destiny is everything. He would even say it in English, '*wyrd bi∂ ful āræd.*'

'What are you thinking?' Rorik asked me.

'That it would be nice to swim,' I said.

The oars dipped and the *Wind-Viper* glided on into Mercia.

Next day a small force waited in our path. The Mercians had blocked the river with felled trees which did not quite bar the way, but would certainly make it hard for our oarsmen to make progress through the small gap between the tangling branches. There were about a hundred Mercians and they had a score of bowmen and spear-throwers waiting by the blockage, ready to pick off our rowers, while the rest of their men were formed into a shield wall on the eastern bank. Ragnar laughed when he saw them. That was something else I learned, the joy with which the Danes faced battle. Ragnar was whooping with joy as he leaned on the steering oar and ran the ship into the bank, and the ships behind were also grounding themselves while the horsemen who had been keeping pace with us dismounted for battle.

I watched from the *Wind-Viper*'s prow as the ships' crews hurried ashore and pulled on leather or mail. What did those Mercians see? They saw young men with wild hair, wild beards and hungry faces. Men who embraced battle like a lover. If the Danes could not fight an enemy, they fought amongst themselves. Most had nothing but monstrous pride, battle-scars and well-sharpened weapons, and with those things they would take whatever they wanted, and that Mercian shield wall did not even stay to contest the fight, but once they saw they would be outnumbered they ran away to the mocking howls of Ragnar's men who then stripped off their mail and leather and used their axes and the *Wind-Viper*'s hide-twisted ropes to clear away the fallen trees. It took a few hours to unblock the river, but then we were moving again. That night the ships clustered together on the riverbank, fires were lit ashore, men were posted as sentries and every sleeping warrior kept his weapons beside him, but no one troubled us and at dawn we moved on, soon coming to a town with thick earthen walls and a high palisade. This, Ragnar assumed, was the place the Mercians had failed to defend, but there seemed to be no sign of any soldiers on the wall so he ran the boat ashore again and led his crew towards the town.

The earth walls and timber palisade were both in good condition, and Ragnar marvelled that the town's garrison had chosen to march downriver to fight us, rather than stay behind their well-tended defences. The Mercian soldiers were plainly gone now, probably fled south, for the gates were open and a dozen townsfolk were kneeling outside the wooden arch and holding out supplicant hands for mercy. Three of the terrified people were monks, their tonsured heads bowed. 'I hate monks,' Ragnar said cheerfully. His sword, Heart-Breaker, was in his hand and he swept her naked blade in a hissing arc.

'Why?' I asked.

'Monks are like ants,' he said, 'wriggling about in black, being useless. I hate them. You'll speak for me, Uhtred. Ask them what place this is?'

I asked and learned that the town was called Gegnesburh.

'Tell them,' Ragnar instructed me, 'that my name is Earl Ragnar, I am called the Fearless and that I eat children when I'm not given food and silver.'

I duly told them. The kneeling men looked up at Ragnar who had unbound his hair which, had they known, was always a sign that he was in a mood for killing. His grinning men made a line behind him, a line heavy with axes, swords, spears, shields and war hammers.

'What food there is,' I translated a grey-bearded man's answer, 'is yours. But he says there is not much food.'

Ragnar smiled at that, stepped forward and, still smiling, swung

67

Heart-Breaker so that her blade half severed the man's head. I jumped back, not in alarm, but because I did not want my tunic spattered with his blood. 'One less mouth to feed,' Ragnar said cheerfully. 'Now ask the others how much food there is.'

The grey-bearded man was now red-bearded and he was choking and twitching as he died. His struggles slowly ended and then he just lay, dying, his eyes gazing reprovingly into mine. None of his companions tried to help him, they were too frightened. 'How much food do you have?' I demanded.

'There is food, lord,' one of the monks said.

'How much?' I demanded again.

'Enough.'

'He says there's enough,' I told Ragnar.

'A sword,' Ragnar said, 'is a great tool for discovering the truth. What about the monk's church? How much silver does it have?'

The monk gabbled that we could look for ourselves, that we could take whatever we found, that it was all ours, anything we found was ours, all was ours. I translated these panicked statements and Ragnar again smiled. 'He's not telling the truth, is he?'

'Isn't he?' I asked.

'He wants me to look because he knows I won't find, and that means they've hidden their treasure or had it taken away. Ask him if they've hidden their silver.'

I did and the monk reddened. 'We are a poor church,' he said, 'with little treasure,' and he stared wide-eyed as I translated his answer, then he tried to get up and run as Ragnar stepped forward, but he tripped over his robe and Heart-Breaker pierced his spine so that he jerked like a landed fish as he died.

There was silver, of course, and it was buried. Another of the monks told us so, and Ragnar sighed as he cleaned his sword on the dead monk's robe. 'They're such fools,' he said plaintively. 'They'd live if they answered truthfully the first time.'

'But suppose there wasn't any treasure?' I asked him.

'Then they'd tell the truth and die,' Ragnar said, and found that funny. 'But what's the point of a monk except to hoard treasure for us Danes? They're ants who hoard silver. Find the ants' nest, dig, and a man's rich.' He stepped over his victims. At first I was shocked by the ease with which he would kill a defenceless man, but Ragnar had no respect for folk who cringed and lied. He appreciated an enemy who fought, who showed spirit, but men who were weakly sly like the ones he killed at Gegnesburh's gate were beneath his contempt, no better than animals.

We emptied Gegnesburh of food, then made the monks dig up their treasure. It was not much; two silver mass cups, three silver plates, a bronze crucifix with a silver Christ, a bone carving of angels climbing a ladder and a bag of silver pennies. Ragnar distributed the coins among his men, then hacked the silver plates and cups to pieces with an axe and shared out the scraps. He had no use for the bone carving so shattered it with his sword. 'A weird religion,' he said, 'they worship just one god?'

'One god,' I said, 'but he's divided into three.'

He liked that. 'A clever trick,' he said, 'but not useful. This triple god has a mother, doesn't he?'

'Mary,' I said, following him as he explored the monastery in search of more plunder.

'I wonder if her baby came out in three bits,' he said. 'So what's this god's name?'

'Don't know.' I knew he had a name because Beocca had told me, but I could not remember it. 'The three together are the trinity,' I went on, 'but that's not God's name. Usually they just call him God.'

'Like giving a dog the name dog,' Ragnar declared, then laughed. 'So who's Jesus?'

'One of the three.'

'The one who died, yes? And he came back to life?'

'Yes,' I said, suddenly fearful that the Christian god was watching me, readying a dreadful punishment for my sins.

'Gods can do that,' Ragnar said airily. 'They die, come back to life. They're gods.' He looked at me, sensing my fear, and ruffled my hair. 'Don't you worry, Uhtred, the Christian god doesn't have power here.'

'He doesn't?'

'Of course not!' He was searching a shed at the back of the monastery and found a decent sickle that he tucked into his belt.

'Gods fight each other! Everyone knows that. Look at our gods! The Aesir and Vanir fought like cats before they made friends.' The Aesir and the Vanir were the two families of Danish gods who now shared Asgard, though at one time they had been the bitterest of enemies. 'Gods fight,' Ragnar went on earnestly, 'and some win, some lose. The Christian god is losing, otherwise why would we be here? Why would we be winning? The gods reward us if we give them respect, but the Christian god doesn't help his people, does he? They weep rivers of tears for him, they pray to him, they give him their silver, and we come along and slaughter them! Their god is pathetic. If he had any real power then we wouldn't be here, would we?'

It seemed an unassailable logic to me. What was the point of worshipping a god if he did not help you? And it was incontrovertible that the worshippers of Odin and Thor were winning, and I surreptitiously touched the hammer of Thor hanging from my neck as we returned to the *Wind-Viper*. We left Gegnesburh ravaged, its folk weeping and its store-houses emptied, and we rowed on down the wide river, the belly of our boat piled with grain, bread, salted meat and smoked fish. Later, much later, I learned that Ælswith, King Alfred's wife, had come from Gegnesburh. Her father, the man who had failed to fight us, was Ealdorman there and she had grown up in the town and always lamented that, after she had left, the Danes had sacked the place. God, she always declared, would have his revenge on the pagans who had ravaged her home town, and it seemed wise not to tell her that I had been one of the ravagers.

We ended the voyage at a town called Snotengaham, which means the home of Snot's people, and it was a much greater place than Gegnesburh, but its garrison had fled and those people who remained welcomed the Danes with piles of food and heaps of silver. There would have been time for a horseman to reach Snotengaham with news of Gegnesburh's dead, and the Danes were always happy for such messengers to spread fear of their coming, and so the larger town, with its walls, fell without a fight.

Some ships' crews were ordered to man the walls, while others raided the countryside. The first thing they sought was more horses, and when the war-bands were mounted they ranged farther afield, stealing, burning, and harrowing the land. 'We shall stay here,' Ragnar told me.

'All summer?'

'Till the world ends, Uhtred. This is Danish land now.'

At winter's end Ivar and Ubba had sent three ships back to the Danish homeland to encourage more settlers, and those new ships began arriving in ones and twos, bringing men, women and children. The newcomers were allowed to take whatever houses they wished, except for those few that belonged to the Mercian leaders who had bent the knee to Ivar and Ubba. One of those was the bishop, a young man called Æthelbrid, who preached to his congregations that God had sent the Danes. He never said why God had done this, and perhaps he did not know, but the sermons meant that his wife and children lived and his house was safe and his church was allowed to retain one silver mass cup, though Ivar insisted that the bishop's twin sons be held as hostages in case the Christian god changed his mind about the Danes.

Ragnar, like the other Danish leaders, constantly rode out into the country to bring back food and he liked me to go with him, for I could translate for him, and as the days passed we heard more and more stories of a great Mercian army gathering to the south, at Ledecestre, which Ragnar said was the greatest fortress in Mercia. It had been made by the Romans, who built better than any man could build now, and Burghred, Mercia's king, was assembling his forces there, and that was why Ragnar was so intent on gathering food. 'They'll besiege us,' he said, 'but we'll win and then Ledecestre will be ours and so will Mercia.' He spoke very calmly, as though there could be no possibility of defeat.

Rorik stayed in the town while I rode with his father. That was because Rorik was sick again, struck by cramping pains in his belly so severe that he was sometimes reduced to helpless tears. He vomited in the night, was pale, and the only relief came from a brew of herbs made for him by an old woman who was a servant of the bishop. Ragnar worried about Rorik, yet he was pleased that his son and I were such good friends. Rorik did not question his father's fondness for me, nor was he jealous. In time, he knew,

71

Ragnar planned to take me back to Bebbanburg and I would be given my patrimony and he assumed I would stay his friend and so Bebbanburg would become a Danish stronghold. I would be Earl Uhtred and Rorik and his older brother would hold other strongholds, and Ragnar would be a great lord, supported by his sons and by Bebbanburg, and we would all be Danes, and Odin would smile on us, and so the world would go on until the final conflagration when the great gods fought the monsters and the army of the dead would march from Valhalla and the underworld give up its beasts and fire would consume the great tree of life, Yggdrasil. In other words everything would stay the same until it was all no more. That was what Rorik thought, and doubtless Ragnar thought so too. Destiny, Ravn said, is everything.

News came in the high summer that the Mercian army was marching at last, and that King Æthelred of Wessex was bringing his army to support Burghred, and so we were to be faced by two of the three remaining English kingdoms. We stopped our raids into the countryside and readied Snotengaham for the inevitable siege. The palisade on the earth wall was strengthened and the ditch outside the wall was deepened. The ships were drawn up on the town's riverbank far from the walls so they could not be reduced to ash by fire-arrows shot from outside the defences, and the thatch of the buildings closest to the wall was pulled off the houses so that they could not be set ablaze.

Ivar and Ubba had decided to endure a siege because they reck-oned we were strong enough to hold what we had taken, but that if we took more territory then the Danish forces would be stretched thin and could be defeated piece by piece. It was better, they reck-oned, to let the enemy come and break himself on Snotengaham's defences.

That enemy came as the poppies bloomed. The Mercian scouts arrived first, small groups of horsemen who circled the town warily, and at midday Burghred's foot soldiers appeared, band after band of men with spears, axes, swords, sickles and hay-knives. They camped well away from the walls, using branches and turf to make a township of crude shelters that sprang up across the low hills and meadows. Snotengaham lay on the north bank of the Trente, which meant the river was between the town and the rest of Mercia, but the enemy army came from the west, having crossed the Trente somewhere to the south of the town. A few of their men stayed on the southern bank to make sure our ships did not cross the river to land men for foraging expeditions, and the presence of those men meant that the enemy surrounded us, but they made no attempt to attack us. The Mercians were waiting for the West Saxons to come and in that first week the only excitement occurred when a handful of Burghred's archers crept towards the town and loosed a few arrows at us and the missiles whacked into the palisade and stuck there, perches for birds, and that was the extent of their belligerence. After that they fortified their camp, surrounding it with a barricade of felled trees and thorn bushes. 'They're frightened that we'll make a sally and kill them all,' Ragnar said, 'so they're going to sit there and try to starve us out.'

'Will they?' I asked.

'They couldn't starve a mouse in a pot,' Ragnar said cheerfully. He had hung his shield on the outer side of the palisade, one of over twelve hundred bright-painted shields which were displayed there. We did not have twelve hundred men, but nearly all the Danes possessed more than one shield and they hung them all on the wall to make the enemy think our garrison equalled the number of shields. The great lords among the Danes hung their banners on the wall; Ubba's raven flag and Ragnar's eagle wing among them. The raven banner was a triangle of white cloth, fringed with white tassels, showing a black raven with spread wings, while Ragnar's standard was a real eagle's wing, nailed to a pole, and it was becoming so tattered that Ragnar had offered a golden arm ring to any man who could replace it. 'If they want us out of here,' he went on, 'then they'd best make an assault, and they'd best do it in the next three weeks before their men go home and cut their harvest.'

But the Mercians, instead of attacking, tried to pray us out of Snotengaham. A dozen priests, all robed and carrying cross-tipped poles, and followed by a score of monks carrying sacred banners on cross-staffs, came out from behind their barricades and paraded just beyond bowshot. The flags showed saints. One of the priests scattered holy water, and the whole group stopped every few yards to pronounce curses on us. That was the day the West Saxon forces arrived to support Burghred, whose wife was sister to Alfred and to King Æthelred of Wessex, and that was the first day I ever saw the dragon standard of Wessex. It was a huge banner of heavy green cloth on which a white dragon breathed fire, and the standard-bearer galloped to catch up with the priests and the dragon streamed behind him. 'Your turn will come,' Ragnar said quietly, talking to the rippling dragon.

'When?'

'The gods only know,' Ragnar said, still watching the standard. 'This year we should finish off Mercia, then we'll go to East Anglia, and after that, Wessex. To take all the land and treasure in England, Uhtred? Three years? Four? We need more ships though.' He meant we needed more ships' crews, more shield-Danes, more swords.

'Why not go north?' I asked him.

'To Dalriada and Pictland?' he laughed. 'There's nothing up there, Uhtred, except bare rocks, bare fields and bare arses. The land there is no better than at home.' He nodded out towards the enemy encampment. 'But this is good land. Rich and deep. You can raise children here. You can grow strong here.' He fell silent as a group of horsemen appeared from the enemy camp and followed the rider who carried the dragon standard. Even from a long way off it was possible to see that these were great men for they rode splendid horses and had mail coats glinting beneath their dark red cloaks. 'The King of Wessex?' Ragnar guessed.

'Æthelred?'

'It's probably him. We shall find out now.'

'Find out what?'

'What these West Saxons are made of. The Mercians won't attack us, so let's see if Æthelred's men are any better. Dawn, Uhtred, that's when they should come. Straight at us, ladders against the wall, lose some men, but let the rest slaughter us.' He laughed. 'That's what I'd do, but that lot?' He spat in derision.

Ivar and Ubba must have thought the same thing, for they sent two men to spy on the Mercian and West Saxon forces to see if there was any sign that ladders were being made. The two men went out at night and were supposed to skirt the besiegers' encampment and find a place to watch the enemy from outside their fortifications, but somehow they were both seen and caught. The two men were brought to the fields in front of the wall and made to kneel there with their hands tied behind their backs. A tall Englishman stood behind them with a drawn sword and I watched as he poked one of the Danes in the back, as the Dane lifted his head and then as the sword swung. The second Dane died in the same way, and the two bodies were left for the ravens to eat. 'Bastards,' Ragnar said.

Ivar and Ubba had also watched the executions. I rarely saw the brothers. Ubba stayed in his house much of the time while Ivar, so thin and wraithlike, was more evident, pacing the walls every dawn and dusk, scowling at the enemy and saying little, though now he spoke urgently to Ragnar, gesturing south to the green fields beyond the river. He never seemed to speak without a snarl, but Ragnar was not offended. 'He's angry,' he told me afterwards, 'because he needs to know if they plan to assault us. Now he wants some of my men to spy on their camp, but after that?' He nodded at the two headless bodies in the field. 'Maybe I'd better go myself.'

'They'll be watching for more spies,' I said, not wanting Ragnar to end up headless before the walls.

'A leader leads,' Ragnar said, 'and you can't ask men to risk death if you're not willing to risk it yourself.'

'Let me go,' I said.

He laughed at that. 'What kind of leader sends a boy to do a man's job, eh?'

'I'm English,' I said, 'and they won't suspect an English boy.'

Ragnar smiled at me. 'If you're English,' he said, 'then how could we trust you to tell us the truth of what you see?'

I clutched Thor's hammer. 'I will tell the truth,' I said, 'I swear it. And I'm a Dane now! You've told me that! You say I'm a Dane!'

Ragnar began to take me seriously. He knelt to look into my face. 'Are you really a Dane?' he asked.

'I'm a Dane,' I said and, at that moment I meant it. At other times I was sure I was a Northumbrian, a secret sceadugengan hidden among the Danes, and in truth I was confused. I loved Ragnar as a father, was fond of Ravn, wrestled and raced and played with Rorik when he was well enough, and all of them treated me as one of them. I was just from another tribe. There were three main tribes among the Northmen; the Danes, the Norse and the Svear, but Ragnar said there were others, like the Getes, and he was not sure where the Northmen ended and the others began, but suddenly he was worried about me. 'I'm a Dane,' I repeated forcibly, 'and who better than me to spy on them? I speak their language!'

'You're a boy,' Ragnar said, and I thought he was refusing to let me go, but instead he was getting used to the idea. 'No one will suspect a boy,' he went on. He still stared at me, then stood and glanced again at the two bodies where ravens were pecking at the severed heads. 'Are you sure, Uhtred?'

'I'm sure.'

'I'll ask the brothers,' he said, and he did, and Ivar and Ubba must have agreed for they let me go. It was after dark when the gate was opened and I slipped out. Now, I thought, I am a Shadow-Walker at last, though in truth the journey needed no supernatural skills for there was a slew of campfires in the Mercian and West Saxon lines to light the way. Ragnar had advised me to skirt the big encampment and see if there was an easy way in at the back, but instead I walked straight towards the nearest fires that lay behind the felled trees that served as the English protective wall, and beyond that black tangle I could see the dark shapes of sentries outlined by the campfires. I was nervous. For months I had been treasuring the idea of the sceadugengan, and here I was, out in the dark, and not far away there were headless bodies and my imagination invented a similar fate for myself. Why? One small part of me knew I could walk into the camp and say who I was, then demand to be taken to Burghred or to Æthelred, yet I had spoken the truth to Ragnar. I would go back, and I would tell the truth. I had promised that, and to a boy promises are solemn things, buttressed by the dread of divine revenge. I would choose my own tribe in time, but that time had not yet come, and so I crept across the field feeling very small and vulnerable, my heart thumping against my ribs, and my soul consumed by the importance of what I did.

And halfway to the Mercian camp I felt the hairs on the back of my neck prickle. I had the sensation I was being followed and I twisted, listened and stared, and saw nothing but the black shapes that shudder in the night, but like a hare I sprinted to one side, dropped suddenly and listened again, and this time I was sure I heard a footfall in the grass. I waited, watched, saw nothing and crept on until I reached the Mercian barricade and I waited again there, but heard nothing more behind me and decided I had been imagining things. I had also been worrying that I would not be able to pass the Mercian obstacles, but in the end it was simple enough because a big felled tree left plenty of space for a boy to wriggle through its branches, and I did it slowly, making no noise, then ran on into the camp and was almost immediately challenged by a sentry. 'Who are you?' the man snarled and I could see the firelight reflecting from a glittering spear head that was being run towards me.

'Osbert,' I said, using my old name.

'A boy?' The man checked, surprised.

'Needed a piss.'

'Hell, boy, what's wrong with pissing outside your shelter?'

'My master doesn't like it.'

'Who's your master?' The spear had been lifted and the man was peering at me in the small light from the fires.

'Beocca,' I said. It was the first name that came to my head.

'The priest?'

That surprised me, and I hesitated, but then nodded and that satisfied the man. 'Best get back to him then,' he said.

'I'm lost.'

'Shouldn't come all this way to piss on my sentry post then, should you?' he said, then pointed. 'It's that way, boy.'

So I walked openly through the camp, past the fires and past the small shelters where men snored. A couple of dogs barked at me. Horses whinnied. Somewhere a flute sounded and a woman sang softly. Sparks flew up from the dying fires.

The sentry had pointed me towards the West Saxon lines. I knew that because the dragon banner was hung outside a great tent that was lit by a larger fire, and I moved towards that tent for lack of anywhere else to go. I was looking for ladders, but saw none. A child cried in a shelter, a woman moaned, and some men sang near a fire. One of the singers saw me, shouted a challenge and then realised I was just a boy and waved me away. I was close to the big fire now, the one that lit the front of the bannered tent, and I skirted it, going towards the darkness behind the tent that was lit from within by candles or lanterns. Two men stood guard at the tent's front and voices murmured from inside, but no one noticed me as I slipped through the shadows, still looking for ladders. Ragnar had said the ladders would be stored together, either at the heart of the camp or close to its edge, but I saw none. Instead I heard sobbing.

I had reached the back of the big tent and was hiding beside a great stack of firewood and, judging by the stink, was close to a latrine. I crouched and saw a man kneeling in the open space between the woodpile and the big tent and it was that man who was sobbing. He was also praying and sometimes beating his chest with his fists. I was astonished, even alarmed by what he did, but I lay on my belly like a snake and wriggled in the shadows to get closer to see what else he might do.

He groaned as if in pain, raised his hands to the sky, then bent forward as if worshipping the earth. 'Spare me, God,' I heard him say, 'spare me. I am a sinner.' He vomited then, though he did not sound drunk, and after he had spewed up he moaned. I sensed he was a young man, then a flap of the tent lifted and a wash of candlelight spilled across the grass. I froze, still as a log, and saw that it was indeed a young man who was so miserable, and then also saw, to my astonishment, that the person who had lifted the tent flap was Father Beocca. I had thought it a coincidence that there should be two priests with that name, but it was no coincidence at all. It was indeed red-haired, cross-eyed Beocca and he was here, in Mercia.

'My lord,' Beocca said, dropping the flap and casting darkness over the young man.

'I am a sinner, father,' the man said. He had stopped sobbing, perhaps because he did not want Beocca to see such evidence of weakness, but his voice was full of sadness. 'I am a grievous sinner.'

'We are all sinners, my lord.'

'A grievous sinner,' the young man repeated, ignoring Beocca's solace. 'And I am married!'

'Salvation lies in remorse, my lord.'

'Then, God knows, I should be redeemed, for my remorse would fill the sky.' He lifted his head to stare at the stars. 'The flesh, father,' he groaned, 'the flesh.'

Beocca walked towards me, stopped and turned. He was almost close enough for me to touch, but he had no idea I was there. 'God sends temptation to test us, my lord,' he said quietly.

'He sends women to test us,' the young man said harshly, 'and we fail, and then he sends the Danes to punish us for our failure.'

'His way is hard,' Beocca said, 'and no one has ever doubted it.'

The young man, still kneeling, bowed his head. 'I should never have married, father. I should have joined the church. Gone to a monastery.'

'And God would have found a great servant in you, my lord, but he had other plans for you. If your brother dies . . .'

'Pray God he does not! What sort of king would I be?'

'God's king, my lord.'

So that, I thought, was Alfred. That was the very first time I ever saw him or heard his voice and he never knew. I lay in the grass, listening, as Beocca consoled the prince for yielding to temptation. It seemed Alfred had humped a servant girl and, immediately afterwards, had been overcome by physical pain and what he called spiritual torment.

'What you must do, my lord,' Beocca said, 'is bring the girl into your service.'

'No!' Alfred protested.

A harp began to play in the tent and both men checked to listen, then Beocca crouched by the unhappy prince and put a hand on his shoulder. 'Bring the girl into your service,' Beocca repeated, 'and resist her. Lay that tribute before God, let him see your strength, and he will reward you. Thank God for tempting you, lord, and praise him when you resist the temptation.'

'God will kill me,' Alfred said bitterly. 'I swore I wouldn't do it again. Not after Osferth.' Osferth? The name meant nothing to me. Later, much later, I discovered Osferth was Alfred's bastard son, whelped on another servant girl. 'I prayed to be spared the temptation,' Alfred went on, 'and to be afflicted with pain as a reminder, and as a distraction, and God in his mercy made me sick, but still I yielded. I am the most miserable of sinners.'

'We are all sinners,' Beocca said, his good hand still on Alfred's shoulder, 'and we are all fallen short of the glory of God.'

'None has fallen as far as me,' Alfred moaned.

'God sees your remorse,' Beocca said, 'and he will lift you up. Welcome the temptation, lord,' he went on urgently, 'welcome it, resist it, and give thanks to God when you succeed. And God will reward you, lord, he will reward you.'

'By removing the Danes?' Alfred asked bitterly.

'He will, my lord, he will.'

'But not by waiting,' Alfred said, and now there was a sudden hardness in his voice that made Beocca draw away from him. Alfred stood, towering over the priest. 'We should attack them!'

'Burghred knows his business,' Beocca said soothingly, 'and so does your brother. The pagans will starve, my lord, if that is God's will.'

So I had my answer, and it was that the English were not planning an assault, but rather hoped to starve Snotengaham into surrender. I dared not carry that answer straight back to the town, not while Beocca and Alfred were so close to me, and so I stayed and listened as Beocca prayed with the prince and then, when Alfred was calm, the two moved back to the tent and went inside.

And I went back. It took a long time, but no one saw me. I was a true sceadugengan that night, moving among the shadows like a spectre, climbing the hill to the town until I could run the last hundred paces and I called Ragnar's name and the gate creaked open and I was back in Snotengaham.

Ragnar took me to see Ubba when the sun rose and, to my

surprise, Weland was there, Weland the snake, and he gave me a sour look, though not so sour as the scowl on Ubba's dark face. 'So what did you do?' he growled.

'I saw no ladders . . .' I began.

'What did you do?' Ubba snarled, and so I told my tale from the beginning, how I had crossed the fields and had thought I was being followed, and had dodged like a hare, then gone through the barricade and spoken to the sentry. Ubba stopped me there and looked at Weland. 'Well?'

Weland nodded. 'I saw him through the barricade, lord, heard him speak to a man.'

So Weland had followed me? I looked at Ragnar who shrugged. 'My lord Ubba wanted a second man to go,' he explained, 'and Weland offered.'

Weland gave me a smile, the kind of smile the devil might give a bishop entering hell. 'I could not get through the barrier, lord,' he told Ubba.

'But you saw the boy go through?'

'And heard him speak to the sentry, lord, though what he said I could not tell.'

'Did you see ladders?' Ubba asked Weland.

'No, lord, but I only skirted the fence.'

Ubba stared at Weland, making him uncomfortable, then transferred his dark eyes to me and made me uncomfortable. 'So you got through the barrier,' he said, 'so what did you see?' I told him how I had found the large tent, and of the conversation I had overheard, how Alfred had wept because he had sinned, and how he had wanted to attack the town and how the priest had said that God would starve the Danes if that was his will, and Ubba believed me because he reckoned a boy could not make up the story of the servant girl and the prince.

Besides, I was amused, and it showed. Alfred, I thought, was a pious weakling, a weeping penitent, a pathetic nothing, and even Ubba smiled as I described the sobbing prince and the earnest priest. 'So,' Ubba asked me, 'no ladders?'

'I saw none, lord.'

He stared at me with that fearsomely bearded face and then, to

81

my astonishment, he took off one of his arm rings and tossed it to me. 'You're right,' he told Ragnar, 'he is a Dane.'

'He's a good boy,' Ragnar said.

'Sometimes the mongrel you find in the field turns out to be useful,' Ubba said, then beckoned to an old man who had been sitting on a stool in the room's corner.

The old man was called Storri and, like Ravn, he was a skald, but also a sorcerer and Ubba would do nothing without his advice, and now, without saying a word, Storri took a sheaf of thin white sticks, each the length of a man's hand, and he held them just above the floor, muttered a prayer to Odin, then let them go. They made a small clattering noise as they fell, and then Storri leaned forward to look at the pattern they made.

They were runesticks. Many Danes consulted the runesticks, but Storri's skill at reading the signs was famous, and Ubba was a man so riddled with superstition that he would do nothing unless he believed the gods were on his side. 'Well?' he asked impatiently.

Storri ignored Ubba, instead he stared at the score of sticks, seeing if he could detect a rune letter or a significant pattern in their random scatter. He moved around the small pile, still peering, then nodded slowly. 'It could not be better,' he said.

'The boy told the truth?'

'The boy told the truth,' Storri said, 'but the sticks talk of today, not of last night, and they tell me all is well.'

'Good.' Ubba stood and took his sword from a peg on the wall. 'No ladders,' he said to Ragnar, 'so no assault. We shall go.'

They had been worried that the Mercians and West Saxons would launch an attack on the walls while they made a raid across the river. The southern bank was lightly garrisoned by the besiegers, holding little more than a cordon of men to deter forage parties crossing the Trente, but that afternoon Ubba led six ships across the river and attacked those Mercians, and the runesticks had not lied, for no Danes died and they brought back horses, weapons, armour and prisoners.

Twenty prisoners.

The Mercians had beheaded two of our men, so now Ubba killed twenty of theirs, and did it in their sight so they could see his revenge. The headless bodies were thrown into the ditch in front of the wall and the twenty heads were stuck on spears and mounted above the northern gate.

'In war,' Ragnar told me, 'be ruthless.'

'Why did you send Weland to follow me?' I asked him, hurt.

'Because Ubba insisted on it,' he said.

'Because you didn't trust me?'

'Because Ubba trusts no one except Storri,' he said. 'And I trust you, Uhtred.'

The heads above Snotengaham's gate were pecked by birds till they were nothing but skulls with hanks of hair that stirred in the summer wind. The Mercians and the West Saxons still did not attack. The sun shone. The river rippled prettily past the town where the ships were drawn up on the bank.

Ravn, though he was blind, liked to come to the ramparts where he would demand that I describe all I could see. Nothing changes, I would say, the enemy are still behind their hedge of felled trees, there are clouds above the distant hills, a hawk hunts, the wind ripples the grass, the swifts are gathering in groups, nothing changes, and tell me about the runesticks, I begged him.

'The sticks!' he laughed.

'Do they work?'

He thought about it. 'If you can read them, yes. I was good at reading the runes before I lost my eyes.'

'So they do work,' I said eagerly.

Ravn gestured towards the landscape he could not see. 'Out there, Uhtred,' he said, 'there are a dozen signs from the gods, and if you know the signs then you know what the gods want. The runesticks give the same message, but I have noticed one thing.' He paused and I had to prompt him, and he sighed as though he knew he should not say more. But he did. 'The signs are best read by a clever man,' he went on, 'and Storri is clever. I dare say I am no fool.'

I did not really understand what he was saying. 'But Storri is always right?'

'Storri is cautious. He won't take risks, and Ubba, though he doesn't know it, likes that.'

'But the sticks are messages from the gods?'

'The wind is a message from the gods,' Ravn said, 'as is the flight of a bird, the fall of a feather, the rise of a fish, the shape of a cloud, the cry of a vixen, all are messages, but in the end, Uhtred, the gods speak in only one place.' He tapped my head. 'There.'

I still did not understand and was obscurely disappointed. 'Could I read the sticks?'

'Of course,' he said, 'but it would be sensible to wait till you're older. What are you now?'

'Eleven,' I said, tempted to say twelve.

'Maybe you'd best wait a year or two before reading the sticks. Wait till you're old enough to marry, four or five years from now?'

That seemed an unlikely proposition for I had no interest in marriage back then. I was not even interested in girls, though that would change soon enough.

'Thyra, perhaps?' Ravn suggested.

'Thyra!' I thought of Ragnar's daughter as a playmate, not as a wife. Indeed, the very idea of it made me laugh.

Ravn smiled at my amusement. 'Tell me, Uhtred, why we let you live.'

'I don't know.'

'When Ragnar captured you,' he said, 'he thought you could be ransomed, but he decided to keep you. I thought he was a fool, but he was right.'

'I'm glad,' I said, meaning it.

'Because we need the English,' Ravn went on. 'We are few, the English are many, despite which we shall take their land, but we can only hold it with the help of Englishmen. A man cannot live in a home that is forever besieged. He needs peace to grow crops and raise cattle, and we need you. When men see that Earl Uhtred is on our side then they won't fight us. And you must marry a Danish girl so that when your children grow they will be both Dane and English and see no difference.' He paused, contemplating that distant future, then chuckled. 'Just make sure they're not Christians, Uhtred.'

'They will worship Odin,' I said, again meaning it.

'Christianity is a soft religion,' Ravn said savagely, 'a woman's creed. It doesn't ennoble men, it makes them into worms. I hear birds.'

'Two ravens,' I said, 'flying north.'

'A real message!' he said delightedly, 'Huginn and Muminn are going to Odin.'

Huginn and Muminn were the twin ravens that perched on the god's shoulders where they whispered into his ear. They did for Odin what I did for Ravn, they watched and told him what they saw. He sent them to fly all over the world and to bring back news, and the news they carried back that day was that the smoke from the Mercian encampment was less thick. Fewer fires were lit at night. Men were leaving that army.

'Harvest time,' Ravn said in disgust.

'Does that matter?'

'They call their army the fyrd,' he explained, forgetting for a moment that I was English, 'and every able man is supposed to serve in the fyrd, but when the harvest ripens they fear hunger in the winter so they go home to cut their rye and barley.'

'Which we then take?'

He laughed. 'You're learning, Uhtred.'

Yet the Mercians and West Saxons still hoped they could starve us and, though they were losing men every day, they did not give up until Ivar loaded a cart with food. He piled cheeses, smoked fish, newly baked bread, salted pork and a vat of ale onto the cart and, at dawn, a dozen men dragged it towards the English camp. They stopped just out of bowshot and shouted to the enemy sentries that the food was a gift from Ivar the Boneless to King Burghred.

Next day a Mercian horseman rode towards the town carrying a leafy branch as a sign of truce. The English wanted to talk. 'Which means,' Ravn told me, 'that we have won.'

'It does?'

'When an enemy wants to talk,' he said, 'it means he does not want to fight. So we have won.'

And he was right.

Three

Next day we made a pavilion in the valley between the town and the English encampment, stretching two ships' sails between timber poles, the whole thing supported by seal-hide ropes lashed to pegs, and there the English placed three high-backed chairs for King Burghred, King Æthelred and for Prince Alfred, and draped the chairs with rich red cloths. Ivar and Ubba sat on milking stools.

Both sides brought thirty or forty men to witness the discussions, which began with an agreement that all weapons were to be piled twenty paces behind the two delegations. I helped carry swords, axes, shields and spears, then went back to listen.

Beocca was there and he spotted me. He smiled. I smiled back. He was standing just behind the young man I took to be Alfred, for though I had heard him in the night I had not seen him clearly. He alone among the three English leaders was not crowned with a circlet of gold, though he did have a large, jewelled cloak brooch which Ivar eyed rapaciously. I saw, as Alfred took his seat, that the prince was thin, long-legged, restless, pale and tall. His face was long, his nose long, his beard short, his cheeks hollow and his mouth pursed. His hair was a nondescript brown, his eyes worried, his brow creased, his hands fidgety and his face frowning. He was only nineteen, I later learned, but he looked ten years older. His brother, King Æthelred, was much older, over thirty, and he was also long-faced, but burlier and even more anxious-looking, while Burghred, King of Mercia, was a stubby man, heavy-bearded, with a bulging belly and a balding pate.

Alfred said something to Beocca who produced a sheet of parchment and a quill which he gave to the prince. Beocca then held a small vial of ink so that Alfred could dip the quill and write.

'What is he doing?' Ivar asked.

'He is making notes of our talks,' the English interpreter answered.

'Notes?'

'So there is a record, of course.'

'He has lost his memory?' Ivar asked, while Ubba produced a very small knife and began to clean his fingernails. Ragnar pretended to write on his hand, which amused the Danes.

'You are Ivar and Ubba?' Alfred asked through his interpreter.

'They are,' our translator answered. Alfred's pen scratched, while his brother and brother-in-law, both kings, seemed content to allow the young prince to question the Danes.

'You are sons of Lothbrok?' Alfred continued.

'Indeed,' the interpreter answered.

'And you have a brother? Halfdan?'

'Tell the bastard to shove his writing up his arse,' Ivar snarled, 'and to shove the quill up after it, and then the ink until he shits black feathers.'

'My lord says we are not here to discuss family,' the interpreter said suavely, 'but to decide your fate.'

'And to decide yours,' Burghred spoke for the first time.

'Our fate?' Ivar retorted, making the Mercian king quail from the force of his skull-gaze, 'our fate is to water the fields of Mercia with your blood, dung the soil with your flesh, pave it with your bones, and rid it of your filthy stink.'

The discussion carried on like that for a long time, both sides threatening, neither yielding, but it had been the English who called for the meeting and the English who wanted to make peace and so the terms were slowly hammered out. It took two days, and most of us who were listening became bored and lay on the grass in the sunlight. Both sides ate in the field, and it was during one such meal that Beocca cautiously came across to the Danish side and greeted me warily. 'You're getting tall, Uhtred,' he said.

'It is good to see you, father,' I answered dutifully. Ragnar was watching, but without any sign of worry on his face.

'You're still a prisoner, then?' Beocca asked.

'I am,' I lied.

He looked at my two silver arm rings which, being too big for me, rattled at my wrist. 'A privileged prisoner,' he said wryly.

'They know I am an Ealdorman,' I said.

'Which you are, God knows, though your uncle denies it.'

'I have heard nothing of him,' I said truthfully.

Beocca shrugged. 'He holds Bebbanburg. He married your father's wife and now she is pregnant.'

'Gytha!' I was surprised. 'Pregnant?'

'They want a son,' Beocca said, 'and if they have one . . .' he did not finish the thought, but nor did he need to. I was the Ealdorman, and Ælfric had usurped my place, yet I was still his heir and would be until he had a son. 'The child must be born any day now,' Beocca said, 'but you need not worry.' He smiled and leaned towards me so he could speak in a conspiratorial whisper. 'I brought the parchments.'

I looked at him with utter incomprehension. 'You brought the parchments?'

'Your father's will! The land-charters!' He was shocked that I did not immediately understand what he had done. 'I have the proof that you are the Ealdorman!'

'I am the Ealdorman,' I said, as if proof did not matter. 'And always will be.'

'Not if Ælfric has his way,' Beocca said, 'and if he has a son then he will want the boy to inherit.'

'Gytha's children always die,' I said.

'You must pray that every child lives,' Beocca said crossly, 'but you are still the Ealdorman. I owe that to your father, God rest his soul.'

'So you abandoned my uncle?' I asked.

'Yes, I did!' he said eagerly, plainly proud that he had fled Bebbanburg. 'I am English,' he went on, his crossed eyes blinking in the sun, 'so I came south, Uhtred, to find Englishmen willing to fight the pagans, Englishmen able to do God's will and I found them in Wessex. They are good men, godly men, stalwart men!'

'Ælfric doesn't fight the Danes?' I asked. I knew he did not, but I wanted to hear it confirmed.

'Your uncle wants no trouble,' Beocca said, 'and so the pagans thrive in Northumbria and the light of our Lord Jesus Christ grows dimmer every day.' He put his hands together as if in prayer, his palsied left hand quivering against his ink-stained right. 'And it is not just Ælfric who succumbs. Ricsig of Dunholm gives them feasts, Egbert sits on their throne, and for that betrayal there must be weeping in heaven. It must be stopped, Uhtred, and I went to Wessex because the king is a godly man and knows it is only with God's help that we can defeat the pagans. I shall see if Wessex is willing to ransom you.' That last sentence took me by surprise so that instead of looking pleased I looked puzzled, and Beocca frowned. 'You didn't hear me?' he asked.

'You want to ransom me?'

'Of course! You are noble, Uhtred, and you must be rescued! Alfred can be generous about such things.'

'I would like that,' I said, knowing it was what I was supposed to say.

'You should meet Alfred,' he said enthusiastically. 'You'll enjoy that!'

I had no wish to meet Alfred, certainly not after listening to him whimper about a servant girl he had humped, but Beocca was insistent and so I went to Ragnar and asked his permission. Ragnar was amused. 'Why does the squinty bastard want you to meet Alfred?' he asked, looking at Beocca.

'He wants me to be ransomed. He thinks Alfred might pay.'

'Pay good money for you!' Ragnar laughed. 'Go on,' he said carelessly, 'it never hurts to see the enemy close up.'

Alfred was with his brother, some distance away, and Beocca talked to me as he led me towards the royal group. 'Alfred is his brother's chief helper,' he explained. 'King Æthelred is a good man, but nervous. He has sons, of course, but both are very young . . .' his voice tailed away.

'So if he dies,' I said, 'the eldest son becomes king?'

'No, no!' Beocca sounded shocked, 'Æthelwold's much too young. He's no older than you!'

'But he's the king's son,' I insisted.

'When Alfred was a small boy,' Beocca leaned down and lowered

90

his voice, though not its intensity, 'his father took him to Rome. To see the Pope! And the Pope, Uhtred, invested him as the future king!' He stared at me as if he had proved his point.

'But he's not the heir,' I said, puzzled.

'The Pope made him heir!' Beocca hissed at me. Later, much later, I met a priest who had been in the old king's entourage and he said Alfred had never been invested as the future king, but instead had been given some meaningless Roman honour, but Alfred, to his dying day, insisted the Pope had conferred the succession on him, and so justified his usurpation of the throne that by rights should have gone to Æthelred's eldest son.

'But if Æthelwold grows up,' I began.

'Then of course he might become king,' Beocca interrupted me impatiently, 'but if his father dies before Æthelwold grows up then Alfred will be king.'

'Then Alfred will have to kill him,' I said, 'him and his brother.'

Beocca gazed at me in shocked amazement. 'Why do you say that?' he asked.

'He has to kill them,' I said, 'just like my uncle wanted to kill me.'

'He did want to kill you. He probably still does!' Beocca made the sign of the cross, 'but Alfred is not Ælfric! No, no. Alfred will treat his nephews with Christian mercy, of course he will, which is another reason he should become king. He is a good Christian, Uhtred, as I pray you are, and it is God's will that Alfred should become king. The Pope proved that! And we have to obey God's will. It is only by obedience to God that we can hope to defeat the Danes.'

'Only by obedience?' I asked. I thought swords might help.

'Only by obedience,' Beocca said firmly, 'and by faith. God will give us victory if we worship him with all our hearts, and if we mend our ways and give him the glory. And Alfred will do that! With him at our head the very hosts of heaven will come to our aid. Æthelwold can't do that. He's a lazy, arrogant, tiresome child.' Beocca seized my hand and pulled me through the entourage of West Saxon and Mercian lords. 'Now remember to kneel to him, boy, he is a prince.' He led me to where Alfred was sitting and I duly knelt as Beocca introduced me. 'This is the boy I spoke of, lord,' he said, 'he is the Ealdorman Uhtred of Northumbria, a prisoner of the Danes since Eoferwic fell, but a good boy.'

Alfred gave me an intense look which, to be honest, made me uncomfortable. I was to discover in time that he was a clever man, very clever, and thought twice as fast as most others, and he was also a serious man, so serious that he understood everything except jokes. Alfred took everything heavily, even a small boy, and his inspection of me was long and searching as if he tried to plumb the depths of my unfledged soul. 'Are you a good boy?' he finally asked me.

'I try to be, lord,' I said.

'Look at me,' he ordered, for I had lowered my eyes. He smiled when I met his gaze. There was no sign of the sickness he had complained of when I eavesdropped on him and I wondered if, after all, he had been drunk that night. It would have explained his pathetic words, but now he was all earnestness. 'How do you try to be good?' he asked.

'I try to resist temptation, lord,' I said, remembering Beocca's words to him behind the tent.

'That's good,' he said, 'very good, and do you resist it?'

'Not always,' I said, then hesitated, tempted to mischief, and then, as ever, yielded to temptation. 'But I try, lord,' I said earnestly, 'and I tell myself I should thank God for tempting me and I praise him when he gives me the strength to resist the temptation.'

Both Beocca and Alfred stared at me as if I had sprouted angel's wings. I was only repeating the nonsense I had heard Beocca advise Alfred in the dark, but they thought it revealed my great holiness, and I encouraged them by trying to look meek, innocent and pious. 'You are a sign from God, Uhtred,' Alfred said fervently. 'Do you say your prayers?'

'Every day, lord,' I said, and did not add that those prayers were addressed to Odin.

'And what is that about your neck? A crucifix?' He had seen the leather thong and, when I did not answer, he leaned forward and plucked out Thor's hammer that had been hidden behind my shirt. 'Dear God,' he said, and made the sign of the cross. 'And you wear those too,' he added, grimacing at my two arm rings which were cut with Danish rune-letters. I must have looked a proper little heathen.

'They make me wear them, lord,' I said, and felt his impulse to tear the pagan symbol off the thong, 'and beat me if I don't,' I added hastily.

'Do they beat you often?' he asked.

'All the time, lord,' I lied.

He shook his head sadly, then let the hammer fall. 'A graven image,' he said, 'must be a heavy burden for a small boy.'

'I was hoping, lord,' Beocca intervened, 'that we could ransom him.'

'Us?' Alfred asked, 'ransom him?'

'He is the true Ealdorman of Bebbanburg,' Beocca explained, 'though his uncle has taken the title, but the uncle will not fight the Danes.'

Alfred gazed at me, thinking, then frowned. 'Can you read, Uhtred?' he asked.

'He has begun his lessons,' Beocca answered for me. 'I taught him, lord, though in all honesty he was ever a reluctant pupil. Not good with his letters, I fear. His thorns were prickly and his ashes spindly.'

I said that Alfred did not understand jokes, but he loved that one, even though it was feeble as watered milk and stale as old cheese. But it was beloved of all who taught reading, and both Beocca and Alfred laughed as though the jest were fresh as dew at sunrise. The thorn, ð and the ash, æ were two letters of our alphabet. 'His thorns are prickly,' Alfred echoed, almost incoherent with laughter, 'and his ashes spindly. His *b*'s don't buzz and his *i*'s,' he stopped, suddenly embarrassed. He had been about to say my *i*'s were crossed, then he remembered Beocca and he looked contrite. 'My dear Beocca.'

'No offence, my lord, no offence.' Beocca was still happy, as happy as when he was immersed in some tedious text about how Saint Cuthbert baptised puffins or preached the gospel to the seals. He had tried to make me read that stuff, but I had never got beyond the shortest words.

'You are fortunate to have started your studies early,' Alfred said to me, recovering his seriousness. 'I was not given a chance to read until I was twelve years old!' His tone suggested I should be shocked and surprised by this news so I dutifully looked appalled. 'That was grievously wrong of my father and step-mother,' Alfred went on sternly, 'they should have started me much earlier.'

'Yet now you read as well as any scholar, my lord,' Beocca said.

'I do try,' Alfred said modestly, but he was plainly delighted with the compliment.

'And in Latin too!' Beocca said, 'and his Latin is much better than mine!'

'I think that's true,' Alfred said, giving the priest a smile.

'And he writes a clear hand,' Beocca told me, 'such a clear, fine hand!'

'As must you,' Alfred told me firmly, 'to which end, young Uhtred, we shall indeed offer to ransom you, and if God helps us in that endeavour then you shall serve in my household and the first thing you will do is become a master of reading and writing. You'll like that!'

'I will, lord,' I said, meaning it to sound as a question, though it came out as dull agreement.

'You will learn to read well,' Alfred promised me, 'and learn to pray well, and learn to be a good honest Christian, and when you are of age you can decide what to be!'

'I will want to serve you, lord,' I lied, thinking that he was a pale, boring, priest-ridden weakling.

'That is commendable,' he said, 'and how will you serve me, do you think?'

'As a soldier, lord, to fight the Danes.'

'If God wishes it,' he said, evidently disappointed in my answer, 'and God knows we shall need soldiers, though I pray daily that the Danes will come to a knowledge of Christ and so discover their sins and be led to end their wicked ways. Prayer is the answer,' he said vehemently, 'prayer and fasting and obedience, and if God answers our prayers, Uhtred, then we shall need no soldiers, but a kingdom always has need of good priests. I wanted that office for myself, but God disposed otherwise. There is no higher calling than the priestly service. I might be a prince, but in God's eyes I am a worm while Beocca is a jewel beyond price!'

'Yes, lord,' I said, for want of anything else to say. Beocca tried to look modest.

Alfred leaned forward, hid Thor's hammer behind my shirt, then laid a hand on my head. 'God's blessing on you, child,' he said, 'and may his face shine upon you and release you from your thraldom and bring you into the blessed light of freedom.'

'Amen,' I said.

They let me go then and I went back to Ragnar. 'Hit me,' I said.

'What?'

'Thump me around the head.'

He glanced up and saw that Alfred was still watching me, so he cuffed me harder than I expected. I fell down, grinning. 'So why did I just do that?' Ragnar asked.

'Because I said you were cruel to me,' I said, 'and beat me constantly.' I knew that would amuse Ragnar and it did. He hit me again, just for luck. 'So what did the bastards want?' he asked.

'They want to ransom me,' I said, 'so they can teach me to read and write, and then make me into a priest.'

'A priest? Like the squinty little bastard with the red hair?'

'Just like him.'

Ragnar laughed. 'Maybe I should ransom you. It would be a punishment for telling lies about me.'

'Please don't,' I said fervently, and at that moment I wondered why I had ever wanted to go back to the English side. To exchange Ragnar's freedom for Alfred's earnest piety seemed a miserable fate to me. Besides, I was learning to despise the English. They would not fight, they prayed instead of sharpening their swords, and it was no wonder the Danes were taking their land.

Alfred did offer to ransom me, but balked at Ragnar's price that was ludicrously high, though not nearly so steep as the price Ivar and Ubba extracted from Burghred.

Mercia was to be swallowed. Burghred had no fire in his big belly, no desire to go on fighting the Danes who got stronger as he grew weaker. Perhaps he was fooled by all those shields on Snotengaham's walls, but he must have decided he could not beat the Danes and instead he surrendered. It was not just our forces in Snotengaham that persuaded him to do this. Other Danes were raiding across the Northumbrian border, ravaging Mercian lands, burning churches, slaughtering monks and nuns, and those horsemen were now close to Burghred's army and were forever harassing his forage parties, and so Burghred, weary of unending defeat, weakly agreed to every outrageous demand, and in return he was allowed to stay as King of Mercia, but that was all. The Danes were to take his fortresses and garrison them, and they were free to take Mercian estates as they wished, and Burghred's fyrd was to fight for the Danes if they demanded it, and Burghred, moreover, was to pay a vast price in silver for this privilege of losing his kingdom while keeping his throne. Æthelred and Alfred, having no part to play in the discussions, and seeing that their ally had collapsed like a pricked bladder, left on the second day, riding south with what remained of their army, and thus Mercia fell.

First Northumbria, then Mercia. In just two years half of England was gone and the Danes were only just beginning.

We ravaged the land again. Bands of Danes rode into every part of Mercia and slaughtered whoever resisted, took whatever they wished, then garrisoned the principal fortresses before sending messages to Denmark for more ships to come. More ships, more men, more families and more Danes to fill the great land that had fallen into their laps.

I had begun to think I would never fight for England because by the time I was old enough to fight there would be no England. So I decided I would be a Dane. Of course I was confused, but I did not spend much time worrying about my confusion. Instead, as I approached twelve years old, I began my proper education. I was made to stand for hours holding a sword and shield stretched out in front of me until my arms ached, I was taught the strokes of the blade, made to practise with throwing spears, and given a pig to slaughter with a war spear. I learned to fend with a shield, how to drop it to stop the lunge beneath the rim, and how to shove the heavy shield boss into an enemy's face to smash his nose and blind him with tears. I learned to pull an oar. I grew, put on muscle, began to speak in a man's voice and was slapped by my first girl. I looked like a Dane. Strangers still mistook me for Ragnar's son for I had the same fair hair that I wore long and tied with a strip of leather at the nape of my neck, and Ragnar was pleased when that happened though he made it plain that I would not replace Ragnar the Younger or Rorik. 'If Rorik lives,' he said sadly, for Rorik was still sickly. 'You will have to fight for your inheritance,' Ragnar told me, and so I learned to fight and, that winter, to kill.

We returned to Northumbria. Ragnar liked it there and, though he could have taken better land in Mercia, he liked the northern hills and the deep vales and the dark hanging woods where, as the first frosts crisped the morning, he took me hunting. A score of men and twice as many dogs beat through the woods, trying to trap boar. I stayed with Ragnar, both of us armed with heavy boar spears. 'A boar can kill you, Uhtred,' he warned me, 'he can rip you from the crotch to the neck unless you place the spear just right.'

The spear, I knew, must be placed in the beast's chest or, if you were lucky, down its throat. I knew I could not kill a boar, but if one came, I would have to try. A full-grown boar can be twice the weight of a man and I did not have the strength to drive one back, but Ragnar was determined to give me first strike and he would be close behind to help. And so it happened. I have killed hundreds of boar since, but I will always remember that first beast; the small eyes, the sheer anger, the determination, the stench, the bristling hairs flecked with mud, and the sweet thud of the spear going deep into the chest, and I was hurled back as if I had been kicked by Odin's eight-legged horse, and Ragnar drove his own spear through the thick hide and the beast squealed and roared, legs scrabbling, and the pursuing dogs howled, and I found my feet, gritted my teeth, and put my weight on the spear and felt the boar's life pulsing up the ash shaft. Ragnar gave me a tusk from that carcass and I hung it next to Thor's hammer and in the days that followed I wanted to do nothing except hunt, though I was not allowed to pursue boar unless Ragnar was with me, but when Rorik was well enough he and I would take our bows into the woods to look for deer.

It was on one of those expeditions, high up at the edge of the woods, just beneath the moors that were dappled by melting snow, that the arrow almost took my life. Rorik and I were creeping through undergrowth and the arrow missed me by inches, sizzling past my head to thump into an ash tree. I turned, putting an arrow on my own string, but saw no one, then we heard feet racing away downhill through the trees and we followed, but whoever had shot the arrow ran too fast for us.

'An accident,' Ragnar said. 'He saw movement, thought you were a deer, and loosed. It happens.' He looked at the arrow which we had retrieved, but it had no marks of ownership. It was just a goose-fledged shaft of hornbeam tipped with an iron head. 'An accident,' he decreed.

Later that winter we moved back to Eoferwic and spent days repairing the boats. I learned to split oak trunks with wedge and mallet, cleaving out the long pale planks that patched the rotted hulls. Spring brought more ships, more men, and with them was Halfdan, youngest brother of Ivar and Ubba. He came ashore roaring with energy, a tall man with a big beard and scowling eyes. He embraced Ragnar, thumped me on the shoulder, punched Rorik in the head, swore he would kill every Christian in England, then went to see his brothers. The three of them planned the new war which, they promised, would strip East Anglia of its treasures and, as the days warmed, we readied for it.

Half the army would march by land, while the other half, which included Ragnar's men, would go by sea and so I anticipated my first proper voyage, but before we left Kjartan came to see Ragnar, and trailing him was his son Sven, his missing eye a red hole in his angry face. Kjartan knelt to Ragnar and bowed his head. 'I would come with you, lord,' he said.

Kjartan had made a mistake by letting Sven follow him, for Ragnar, usually so generous, gave the boy a sour look. I call him a boy, but in truth Sven was almost a man now and promised to be a big one, broad in the chest, tall and strong. 'You would come with me,' Ragnar echoed flatly.

'I beg you, lord,' Kjartan said, and it must have taken a great effort to say those words, for Kjartan was a proud man, but in Eoferwic he had found no plunder, earned no arm rings, and made no reputation for himself.

'My ships are full,' Ragnar said coldly, and turned away. I saw the look of hatred on Kjartan's face.

'Why doesn't he sail with someone else?' I asked Ravn.

'Because everyone knows he offended Ragnar, so to give him a place at the oars is to risk my son's dislike.' Ravn shrugged. 'Kjartan should go back to Denmark. If a man loses his lord's trust then he has lost everything.'

But Kjartan and his one-eyed son stayed in Eoferwic instead of going back to Denmark, and we sailed, first flowing with the current back down the Ouse and so into the Humber where we spent the night. Next morning we took the shields off the ships' sides, then waited till the tide lifted their hulls and we could row eastwards into the first great seas.

I had been offshore at Bebbanburg, going with fishermen to cast nets about the Farne Islands, but this was a different sensation. The *Wind-Viper* rode those waves like a bird instead of thrashing through like a swimmer. We rowed out of the river, then took advantage of a north-west wind to hoist the great sail and the oars were fiddled out of their holes, the holes were covered with wooden plugs and the great sweeps stored inboard as the sail cracked, bellied, trapped the wind and drove us southwards. There were eighty-nine ships altogether, a fleet of dragon-headed killers, and they raced each other, calling insults whenever they travelled faster than some other boat. Ragnar leaned on the steering oar, his hair flying in the wind and a smile as broad as the ocean on his face. Seal-hide ropes creaked, the boat seemed to leap up the seas, seethe through their tops and slide in flying spray down their faces. I was frightened at first, for the *Wind-Viper* bent to that wind, almost dropping her leeward side beneath the great green sea, but then I saw no fear on the other men's faces and I learned to enjoy the wild ride, whooping with delight when the bow smashed into a heavy sea and the green water flew like an arrow shower down the deck.

'I love this!' Ragnar called to me. 'In Valhalla I hope to find a ship, a sea and a wind!'

The shore was ever in sight, a low green line to our right, sometimes broken by dunes, but never by trees or hills, and as the sun sank we turned towards that land and Ragnar ordered the sail furled and the oars out.

We rowed into a water land, a place of marsh and reed, of bird cries and long-legged herons, of eel traps and ditches, of shallow channels and long meres, and I remembered my father saying the East Anglians were frogs. We were on the edge of their country now, at the place where Mercia ended and East Anglia began in a tangle of water, mud and salt flats. 'They call it the Gewæsc,' Ragnar said.

'You've been here?'

'Two years ago,' he said. 'Good country to raid, Uhtred, but treacherous water. Too shallow.'

The Gewæsc was very shallow and Weland was in the *Wind-Viper*'s bow, weighing the depth with a lump of iron tied to a rope. The oars only dipped if Weland said there was sufficient water and so we crept westwards into the dying light followed by the rest of the fleet. The shadows were long now, the red sun slicing into the open jaws of the dragon, serpent and eagle heads on the ships' prows. The oars worked slowly, their blades dripping water as they swept forward for the next stroke, and our wake spread in long slow ripples touched red by dying sun-fire.

We anchored that night and slept aboard the ships and in the dawn Ragnar made Rorik and me climb his mast. Ubba's ship was nearby and he too had men clambering up towards the painted wind-vane at the masthead.

'What can you see?' Ragnar called up to us.

'Three men on horseback,' Rorik answered, pointing south, 'watching us.'

'And a village,' I added, also pointing south.

To the men on shore we were something from their darkest fears. All they could see was a thicket of masts and the savage carved beasts at the high prows and sterns of our ships. We were an army, brought here by our dragon boats, and they knew what would follow and, as I watched, the three horsemen turned and galloped south.

We went on. Ubba's ship led the way now, following a twisting shallow channel and I could see Ubba's sorcerer, Storri, standing in the bows and I guessed he had cast the runes and predicted success. 'Today,' Ragnar told me wolfishly, 'you will learn the Viking way.'

To be a Viking was to be a raider, and Ragnar had not conducted a shipborne raid in many years. He had become an invader instead, a settler, but Ubba's fleet had come to ravage the coastline and draw the East Anglian army towards the sea while his brother, Ivar, led the land army south from Mercia, and so that early summer I learned the Viking ways. We took the ships to the mainland where Ubba found a stretch of land with a thin neck that could easily be defended and, once our ships were safely drawn onto the beach, we dug an earthwork across the neck as a rampart. Then large parties of men disappeared into the countryside, returning next morning with captured horses and the horses were used to mount another war-band that rode inland as Ragnar led his men on foot along the tangled shoreline.

We came to a village, I never did learn its name, and we burned it to the ground. There was no one there. We burned farmsteads, a church, and marched on, following a road that angled away from the shore, and at dusk we saw a larger village and we hid in a wood, lit no fires, and attacked at dawn.

We came shrieking from the half-light. We were a nightmare in the dawn; men in leather with iron helmets, men with round painted shields, men with axes, swords and spears. The folk in that place had no weapons and no armour, and perhaps they had not even known there were Danes in their countryside for they were not ready for us. They died. A few brave men tried to make a stand by their church, but Ragnar led a charge against them and they were slaughtered where they stood, and Ragnar pushed open the church door to find the small building filled with women and children. The priest was in front of the altar and he cursed Ragnar in Latin as the Dane stalked up the small nave, and the priest was still cursing when Ragnar disembowelled him.

We took a bronze crucifix, a dented silver plate and some coins from the church. We found a dozen good cooking pots in the houses and some shears, sickles and iron spits. We captured cattle, goats, sheep, oxen, eight horses, and sixteen young women. One woman screamed that she could not leave her child and I watched Weland spit the small boy on a spear, then thrust the bloodied corpse into the woman's arms. Ragnar sent her away, not because he pitied her, but because one person was always spared to carry news of the horror to other places. Folk must fear the Danes, Ragnar said, and then they would be ready to surrender. He gave me a piece of burning wood he had taken from a fire. 'Burn the thatch, Uhtred,' he ordered, so I went from house to house, putting fire to the reed thatch. I burned the church and then, just as I approached the last house, a man burst from the door with a three-pronged eel spear that he lunged at me. I twisted aside, avoiding his thrust by luck rather than judgement, and I hurled the burning wood at the man's face and the flames made him duck as I backed away, and Ragnar threw me a spear, a heavy war spear made for thrusting rather than throwing, and it skidded in the dust in front of me and I understood he was letting me fight as I plucked it up. He would not have let me die, for he had two of his bowmen standing ready with arrows on their strings, but he did not interfere as the man ran at me and lunged again.

I parried, knocking the rusted eel spear aside and stepping back again to give myself room. The man was twice my size and more than twice my weight. He was cursing me, calling me a devil's bastard, a worm of hell, and he rushed me again and I did what I had learned hunting the boar. I stepped to my left, waited till he levelled the spear, stepped back to the right and thrust.

It was not a clean thrust, nor did I have the weight to hurl him back, but the spear point punctured his belly and then his weight pushed me back as he half snarled and half gasped, and I fell, and he fell on top of me, forced sideways because the spear was in his guts, and he tried to take a grip of my throat, but I wriggled out from beneath him, picked up his own eel spear and rammed it at his throat. There were rivulets of blood on the earth, droplets spraying in the air, and he was jerking and choking, blood bubbling at his ripped throat, and I tried to pull the eel spear back, but the barbs on the points were caught in his gullet, so I ripped the war spear from his belly and tried to stop him jerking by thrusting it down hard into his chest, but it only glanced off his ribs. He was making a terrible noise, and I suppose I was in a panic, and I was unaware that Ragnar and his men were almost helpless with laughter as they watched me try to kill the East Anglian. I did, in the end, or else he just bled to death, but by then I had poked and stabbed and torn him until he looked as though a pack of wolves had set on him.

But I got a third arm ring, and there were grown warriors in Ragnar's band who only wore three. Rorik was jealous, but he was younger and his father consoled him that his time would come. 'How does it feel?' Ragnar asked me.

'Good,' I said, and God help me, it did.

It was then that I first saw Brida. She was my age, black-haired, thin as a twig, with big dark eyes and a spirit as wild as a hawk in spring, and she was among the captured women and, as the Danes began dividing those captives amongst themselves, an older woman pushed the child forward as if giving her to the Vikings. Brida snatched up a piece of wood and turned on the woman and beat at her, driving her back, screaming that she was a sour-faced bitch, a dried-up hank of gristle, and the older woman tripped and fell into a patch of nettles where Brida went on thrashing her. Ragnar was laughing, but eventually pulled the child away and, because he loved anyone with spirit, gave her to me. 'Keep her safe,' he said, 'and burn that last house.'

So I did.

And I learned another thing.

Start your killers young, before their consciences are grown. Start them young and they will be lethal.

We took our plunder back to the ships and that night, as I drank my ale, I thought of myself as a Dane. Not English, not any more. I was a Dane and I had been given a perfect childhood, perfect, at least, to the ideas of a boy. I was raised among men, I was free, I ran wild, I was encumbered by no laws, was troubled by no priests, was encouraged to violence, and I was rarely alone.

And it was that, that I was rarely alone, which kept me alive.

Every raid brought more horses, and more horses meant more men could go farther afield and waste more places, steal more silver and take more captives. We had scouts out now, watching for the approach of King Edmund's army. Edmund ruled East Anglia and, unless he wished to collapse as feebly as Burghred of Mercia, he had to send men against us to preserve his kingdom, and so we watched the roads and waited.

Brida stayed close to me. Ragnar had taken a strong liking to her, probably because she treated him defiantly and because she alone did not weep when she was captured. She was an orphan and had been living in the house of her aunt, the woman whom she had beaten and whom she hated, and within days Brida was happier among the Danes than she had ever been among her own people. She was a slave now, a slave who was supposed to stay in the camp and cook, but one dawn as we went raiding she ran after us and hauled herself up behind my saddle and Ragnar was amused by that and let her come along.

We went far south that day, out of the flat lands where the marshes stretched, and into low wooded hills amongst which were fat farms and a fatter monastery. Brida laughed when Ragnar killed the abbot, and afterwards, as the Danes collected their plunder, she took my hand and led me over a low rise to a farm which had already been plundered by Ragnar's men. The farm belonged to the monastery and Brida knew the place because her aunt had frequently gone to the monastery to pray. 'She wanted children,' Brida said, 'and only had me.' Then she pointed at the farm and watched for my reaction.

It was a Roman farm, she told me, though like me she had little idea who the Romans really were, only that they had once lived in England and then had gone. I had seen plenty of their buildings before, there were some in Eoferwic, but those other buildings had crumbled, then been patched with mud and reroofed with thatch, while this farm looked as though the Romans had only just left.

It was astonishing. The walls were of stone, perfectly cut, square and close-mortared, and the roof was of tile, patterned and tight-fitting, and inside the gate was a courtyard surrounded with a pillared walkway and in the largest room was an amazing picture on the floor, made up of thousands of small coloured stones, and I gaped at the leaping fish that were pulling a chariot in which a bearded man stood holding an eel spear like the one I had faced in Brida's village. Hares surrounded the picture, chasing each other through looping strands of leaves. There had been other pictures painted on the walls, but they had faded or else been discoloured by water that had leaked through the old roof. 'It was the abbot's house,' Brida told me, and she took me into a small room where there was a cot beside which one of the abbot's servants lay dead in his own blood. 'He brought me in here,' she said.

'The abbot did?'

'And told me to take my clothes off.'

'The abbot did?' I asked again.

'I ran away,' she said in a very matter-of-fact tone, 'and my aunt beat me. She said I should have pleased him and he'd have rewarded us.'

We wandered through the house and I felt a wonder that we could no longer build like this. We knew how to sink posts in the ground and make beams and rafters and roof them with thatch from rye or reed, but the posts rotted, the thatch mouldered, and the houses sagged. In summer our houses were winter dark, and all year they were choked with smoke, and in winter they stank of cattle, yet this house was light and clean and I doubted any cow had ever dunged on the man in his fish-drawn chariot. It was an unsettling thought, that somehow we were sliding back into the smoky dark and that never again would man make something so perfect as this small building. 'Were the Romans Christians?' I asked Brida.

'Don't know,' she said. 'Why?'

'Nothing,' I said, but I had been thinking that the gods reward those they love and it would have been nice to know which gods had looked after the Romans. I hoped they had worshipped Odin, though these days, I knew, they were Christians because the Pope lived in Rome and Beocca had taught me that the Pope was the chief of all the Christians, and was a very holy man. His name, I remembered, was Nicholas. Brida could not have cared less about the gods of the Romans, instead she knelt to explore a hole in the floor that seemed to lead only to a cellar so shallow that no person could ever get inside. 'Maybe elves lived there?' I suggested.

'Elves live in the woods,' she insisted. She decided the abbot might have hidden treasures in the space and borrowed my sword so she could widen the hole. It was not a real sword, merely a sax, a very long knife, but Ragnar had given it to me and I wore it proudly.

'Don't break the blade,' I told her, and she stuck her tongue out at me, then began prising the mortar at the hole's edge while I went back to the courtyard to look at the raised pond that was green and scummy now, but somehow I knew it had once been filled with clear water. A frog crawled onto the small stone island in the centre and I again remembered my father's verdict on the East Anglians; mere frogs.

Weland came through the gate. He stopped just inside and licked his lips, tongue flickering, then half smiled. 'Lost your sax, Uhtred?'

'No,' I said.

'Ragnar sent me,' he said, 'we're leaving.'

I nodded, said nothing, but knew that Ragnar would have sounded a horn if we were truly ready to leave.

'So come on, boy,' he said.

I nodded again, still said nothing.

His dark eyes glanced at the building's empty windows, then at the pool. 'Is that a frog,' he asked, 'or a toad?'

'A frog.'

'In Frankia,' he said, 'men say you can eat frogs.' He walked towards the pool and I moved to stay on the far side from him, keeping the raised stone structure between us. 'Have you eaten a frog, Uhtred?'

'No.'

'Would you like to?'

'No.'

He put a hand into a leather bag which hung from his sword belt that was strapped over a torn mail coat. He had money now, two arm rings, proper boots, an iron helmet, a long sword and the mail coat which needed mending, but was far better protection than the rags he had worn when he first came to Ragnar's house. 'This coin if you catch a frog,' he said, spinning a silver penny in the air.

'I don't want to catch a frog,' I said sullenly.

'I do,' he said, grinning, and he drew the sword, its blade hissing on the scabbard's wooden throat, and he stepped into the pool, the water not reaching the tops of his boots, and the frog leaped away, plopping into the green scum, and Weland was not looking at the frog, but at me, and I knew he was going to kill me, but for some reason I could not move. I was astonished, and yet I was not astonished. I had never liked him, never trusted him, and I understood that he had been sent to kill me and had only failed because I had always been in company until this moment when I had let Brida lead me away from Ragnar's band. So Weland had his chance now. He smiled at me, reached the centre of the pool, came closer, raised the sword and I found my feet at last and raced back into the pillared walkway. I did not want to go into the house, for Brida was there, and I knew he would kill her if he found her. He jumped out of the pond and chased me, and I raced down the walkway, around the corner, and he cut me off, and I dodged back, wanting to reach the gateway, but he knew that was what I wanted and he took care to keep between me and my escape. His boots left wet footprints on the Roman flagstones.

'What's the matter, Uhtred?' he asked, 'frightened of frogs?'

'What do you want?' I asked.

'Not so cocky now, eh? Ealdorman?' He stalked towards me, sword flashing from side to side. 'Your uncle sends his regards and trusts you will burn in hell while he lives in Bebbanburg.'

'You come from . . .' I began, but it was obvious Weland was serving Ælfric so I did not bother to finish the question, but instead edged backwards.

'The reward for your death will be the weight of his newborn child in silver,' Weland said, 'and the child should be born by now. And he's impatient for your death, your uncle is. I almost managed to track you down that night outside Snotengaham, and almost hit you with an arrow last winter, but you ducked. Not this time, but it will be quick, boy. Your uncle said to make it quick, so kneel down, boy, just kneel.' He swept the blade left and right, his wrist whippy so the sword hissed. 'I haven't given her a name yet,' he said. 'Perhaps after this she'll be known as Orphan-Killer.'

I feinted right, went left, but he was quick as a stoat and he blocked me, and I knew I was cornered, and he knew it too and smiled. 'I'll make it quick,' he said, 'I promise.'

Then the first roof tile hit his helmet. It could not have hurt much, but the unexpected blow jarred him backwards and confused him, and the second tile hit his waist and the third smacked him on the shoulder, and Brida shouted from the roof. 'Back through the house!' I ran, the lunging sword missing me by inches, and I twisted through the door, ran over the fish-drawn chariot, through a second door, another door, saw an open window and dove through, and Brida jumped down from the roof and together we ran for the nearby woods.

Weland followed me, but he abandoned the pursuit when we vanished in the trees. Instead he went south, on his own, fleeing what he knew Ragnar would do to him, and for some reason I was in tears by the time I found Ragnar again. Why did I cry? I do not know, unless it was the confirmation that Bebbanburg was gone, that my beloved refuge was occupied by an enemy, and an enemy who, by now, might have a son.

Brida received an arm ring, and Ragnar let it be known that if any man touched her he, Ragnar, would personally geld that man with a mallet and a plank-splitter. She rode home on Weland's horse.

And next day the enemy came.

*   *   *

Ravn had sailed with us, blind though he was, and I was required to be his eyes so I described how the East Anglian army was forming on a low ridge of dry land to the south of our camp. 'How many banners?' he asked me.

'Twenty-three,' I said, after a pause to count them.

'Showing?'

'Mostly crosses,' I said, 'and some saints.'

'He's a very pious man, King Edmund,' Ravn said, 'he even tried to persuade me to become a Christian.' He chuckled at the memory. We were sitting on the prow of one of the beached ships, Ravn in a chair, Brida and I at his feet, and the Mercian twins, Ceolnoth and Ceolberht on his far side. They were the sons of Bishop Æthelbrid of Snotengaham and they were hostages even though their father had welcomed the Danish army, but, as Ravn said, taking the bishop's sons hostage would keep the man honest. There were dozens of other such hostages from Mercia and Northumbria, all sons of prominent men, and all under sentence of death if their fathers caused trouble. There were other Englishmen in the army, serving as soldiers and, if it were not for the language they spoke, they would have been indistinguishable from the Danes. Most of them were either outlaws or masterless men, but all were savage fighters, exactly the kind of men the English needed to face their enemy, but now those men were fighting for the Danes against King Edmund. 'And he's a fool,' Ravn said scornfully.

'A fool?' I asked.

'He gave us shelter during the winter before we attacked Eoferwic,' Ravn explained, 'and we had to promise not to kill any of his churchmen.' He laughed softly. 'What a very silly condition. If their god was any use then we couldn't have killed them anyway.'

'Why did he give you shelter?'

'Because it was easier than fighting us,' Ravn said. He was using English because the other three children did not understand Danish, though Brida was learning quickly. She had a mind like a fox, quick and sly. Ravn smiled. 'The silly King Edmund believed we would go away in the springtime and not come back, yet here we are.'

'He shouldn't have done it,' one of the twins put in. I could not tell them apart, but was annoyed by them for they were fierce Mercian patriots, despite their father's change of allegiance. They were ten years old and forever upbraiding me for loving the Danes.

'Of course he shouldn't have done it,' Ravn agreed mildly.

'He should have attacked you!' Ceolnoth or Ceolberht said.

'He would have lost if he had,' Ravn said, 'we made a camp, protected it with walls, and stayed there. And he paid us money to make no trouble.'

'I saw King Edmund once,' Brida put in.

'Where was that, child?' Ravn asked.

'He came to the monastery to pray,' she said, 'and he farted when he knelt down.'

'No doubt their god appreciated the tribute,' Ravn said loftily, frowning because the twins were now making farting noises.

'Were the Romans Christians?' I asked him, remembering my curiosity at the Roman farm.

'Not always,' Ravn said. 'They had their own gods once, but they gave them up to become Christians and after that they knew nothing but defeat. Where are our men?'

'Still in the marsh,' I said.

Ubba had hoped to stay in the camp and so force Edmund's army to attack along the narrow neck of land and die on our short earthen wall, but instead the English had remained south of the treacherous lowland and were inviting us to attack them. Ubba was tempted. He had made Storri cast the runesticks and rumour said that the result was uncertain, and that fed Ubba's caution. He was a fearsome fighter, but always wary when it came to picking a fight, but the runesticks had not predicted disaster and so he had taken the army out into the marsh where it now stood on whatever patches of drier land it could find, and from where two tracks led up to the low ridge. Ubba's banner, the famous raven on its three-sided cloth, was midway between the two paths, both of which were strongly guarded by East Anglian shield walls, and any attack up either path would mean that a few of our men would have to attack a lot of theirs, and Ubba must have been having second thoughts for he was hesitating. I described all that to Ravn.

'It doesn't do,' he told me, 'to lose men, even if we win.'

'But if we kill lots of theirs?' I asked.

'They have more men, we have few. If we kill a thousand of theirs then they will have another thousand tomorrow, but if we lose a hundred men then we must wait for more ships to replace them.'

'More ships are coming,' Brida said.

'I doubt there will be any more this year,' Ravn said.

'No,' she insisted, 'now,' and she pointed and I saw four ships nosing their way through the tangle of low islands and shallow creeks.

'Tell me,' Ravn said urgently.

'Four ships,' I said, 'coming from the west.'

'From the west? Not the east?'

'From the west,' I insisted, which meant they were not coming from the sea, but from one of the four rivers which flowed into the Gewæsc.

'Prows?' Ravn demanded.

'No beasts on the prows,' I said, 'just plain wooden posts.'

'Oars?'

'Ten a side, I think, maybe eleven. But there are far more men than rowers.'

'English ships!' Ravn sounded amazed, for other than small fishing craft and some tubby cargo vessels the English had few ships, yet these four were warships, built long and sleek like the Danish ships, and they were creeping through the mazy water-ways to attack Ubba's beached fleet. I could see smoke trickling from the foremost ship and knew they must have a brazier on board and so were planning to burn the Danish boats and thus trap Ubba.

But Ubba had also seen them, and already the Danish army was streaming back towards the camp. The leading English ship began to shoot fire-arrows at the closest Danish boat and, though there was a guard on the boats, that guard was composed of the sick and the lame, and they were not strong enough to defend the ships against a seaborne attack. 'Boys!' one of the guards bellowed.

'Go,' Ravn told us, 'go,' and Brida, who considered herself as good as any boy, came with the twins and me. We jumped down to the beach and ran along the water's edge to where smoke was thickening above the beached Danish boat. Two English ships were shooting fire-arrows now, while the last two attackers were trying to edge past their companions to reach more of our craft.

Our job was to extinguish the fire while the guards hurled spears at the English crews. I used a shield to scoop up sand that I dumped onto the fire. The English ships were close and I could see they were made of new raw wood. A spear thumped close to me and I picked it up and threw it back, though feebly because it clattered against an oar and fell into the sea. The twins were not trying to put out the fire and I hit one of them and threatened to hit him harder if they did not make an effort, but we were too late to save the first Danish ship which was well ablaze, so we abandoned it and tried to rescue the next one, but a score of fire-arrows slammed into the rowers' benches, another landed on the furled sail, and two of the boys were dead at the water's edge. The leading English ship turned to the beach then, its prow thick with men bristling with spears, axes and swords. 'Edmund!' they shouted, 'Edmund!' The bow grated on the beach and the warriors jumped off to begin slaughtering the Danish ships' guard. The big axes slammed down and blood spattered up the beach or was sluiced away by the tiny waves which washed the sand. I grabbed Brida's hand and pulled her away, splashing through a shallow creek where tiny silver fish scattered in alarm. 'We have to save Ravn!' I told her.

She was laughing. Brida always enjoyed chaos.

Three of the English ships had beached themselves and their crews were ashore, finishing off the Danish guards. The last ship glided on the falling tide, shooting fire-arrows, but then Ubba's men were back in the camp and they advanced on the English with a roar. Some men had stayed with the raven banner at the earthen wall to make sure King Edmund's forces could not swarm over the neck of land to take the camp, but the rest came screaming and vengeful. The Danes love their ships. A ship, they say, is like a woman or a sword, sharp and beautiful, worth dying for, and certainly worth fighting for, and the East Anglians, who had done so well, had now made a mistake for the tide was ebbing and they could not shove their boats off into the small waves. Some of the Danes protected their own unharmed boats by raining throwing axes, spears and arrows at the crew of the single enemy boat afloat, while the rest attacked the Englishmen ashore.

That was a slaughter. That was Danish work. That was a fit fight for the skalds to celebrate. Blood was thick on the tideline, blood slurping with the rise and fall of the small waves, men screaming and falling, and all about them the smoke of the burning boats was whirling so that the hazed sun was red above a sand turned red, and in that smoke the rage of the Danes was terrible. It was then I first saw Ubba fight and marvelled at him, for he was a bringer of death, a grim warrior, a sword-lover. He did not fight in a shield wall, but ran into his enemies, shield slamming one way as his war axe gave death in the other, and it seemed he was indestructible for, at one moment, he was surrounded by East Anglian fighters, but there was a scream of hate, a clash of blade on blade, and Ubba came out of the tangle of men, his blade red, blood in his beard, trampling his enemies into the blood-rich tide, and looking for more men to kill. Ragnar joined him, and Ragnar's men followed, harvesting an enemy beside the sea, screaming hate at men who had burned their ships, and when the screaming and killing were done we counted sixty-eight English bodies, and some we could not count for they had run into the sea and drowned there, dragged down by the weight of weapons and armour. The sole East Anglian ship to escape was a ship of the dying, its new wooden flanks running with blood. The victorious Danes danced over the corpses they had made, then made a heap of captured weapons. There were thirty Danish dead, and those men were burned on a half-burned ship, another six Danish craft had been destroyed, but Ubba captured the three beached English boats which Ragnar declared to be pieces of shit. 'It's astonishing they even floated,' he said, kicking at a badly caulked strake.

Yet the East Anglians had done well, I thought. They had made mistakes, but they had hurt Danish pride by burning dragon ships, and if King Edmund had attacked the wall protecting the camp he might have turned the slaughter into a massacre of Danes, but

King Edmund had not attacked. Instead, as his shipmen died beneath the smoke, he had marched away.

He thought he was facing the Danish army by the sea, only to find that the real attack had come by land. He had just learned that Ivar the Boneless was invading his land.

And Ubba was enraged. The few English prisoners were sacrificed to Odin, their screams a call to the god that we needed his help. And next morning, leaving the burned boats like smoking black skeletons on the beach, we rowed the dragon fleet west.

Four

King Edmund of East Anglia is now remembered as a saint, as one of those blessed souls who live for ever in the shadow of God. Or so the priests tell me. In heaven, they say, the saints occupy a privileged place, living on the high platform of God's great hall where they spend their time singing God's praises. For ever. Just singing. Beocca always told me that it would be an ecstatic existence, but to me it seems very dull. The Danes reckon their dead warriors are carried to Valhalla, the corpse-hall of Odin, where they spend their days fighting and their nights feasting and swiving, and I dare not tell the priests that this seems a far better way to endure the afterlife than singing to the sound of golden harps. I once asked a bishop whether there were any women in heaven. 'Of course there are, my lord,' he answered, happy that I was taking an interest in doctrine, 'many of the most blessed saints are women.'

'I mean women we can hump, bishop.'

He said he would pray for me. Perhaps he did.

I do not know if King Edmund was a saint. He was a fool, that was for sure. He had given the Danes refuge before they attacked Eoferwic, and given them more than refuge. He had paid them coin, provided them with food and supplied their army with horses, all on the two promises that they would leave East Anglia in the spring and that they would not harm a single churchman. They kept their promises, but now, two years later and much stronger, the Danes were back, and King Edmund had decided to fight them. He had seen what had happened to Mercia and Northumbria, and must have known his own kingdom would suffer the same fate, and so he gathered his fyrd and prayed to his god and marched to do battle. First he faced us by the sea, then, hearing that Ivar was marching around the edge of the great watery wastes west of the Gewæsc, he turned about to confront him. Ubba then led our fleet up the Gewæsc and we nosed into one of the rivers until the channel was so narrow our oars could not be used, and then men towed the boats, wading through waist-deep water until we could go no farther and there we left the ships under guard while the rest of us followed soggy paths through endless marshland until, at long last, we came to higher ground. No one knew where we were, only that if we went south we had to reach the road along which Edmund had marched to confront Ivar. Cut that road and we would trap him between our forces and Ivar's army.

Which is precisely what happened. Ivar fought him, shield wall against shield wall, and we knew none of it until the first East Anglian fugitives came streaming eastwards to find another shield wall waiting for them. They scattered rather than fight us, we advanced, and from the few prisoners we took we discovered that Ivar had beaten them easily. That was confirmed next day when the first horsemen from Ivar's forces reached us.

King Edmund fled southwards. East Anglia was a big country, he could easily have found refuge in a fortress, or else he could have gone to Wessex, but instead he put his faith in God and took shelter in a small monastery at Dic. The monastery was lost in the wetlands and perhaps he believed he would never be found there, or else, as I heard, one of the monks promised him that God would shroud the monastery in a perpetual fog in which the pagans would get lost, but the fog never came and the Danes arrived instead.

Ivar, Ubba and their brother Halfdan rode to Dic, taking half their army while the other half set about pacifying East Anglia, which meant raping, burning and killing until the people submitted, which most did swiftly enough. East Anglia, in short, fell as easily as Mercia, and the only bad news for the Danes was that there had been unrest in Northumbria. Rumours spoke of some kind of revolt, Danes had been killed, and Ivar wanted that rising quenched, but he dared not leave East Anglia so soon after capturing it, so at Dic he made a proposal to King Edmund that would leave Edmund as king just as Burghred still ruled over Mercia.

The meeting was held in the monastery's church that was a surprisingly large hall made of timber and thatch, but with great leather panels hanging on the walls. The panels were painted with gaudy scenes. One of the pictures showed naked folk tumbling down to hell where a massive serpent with a fanged mouth swallowed them up. 'Corpse-Ripper,' Ragnar said with a shudder.

'Corpse-Ripper?'

'A serpent that waits in Niflheim,' he explained, touching his hammer amulet. Niflheim, I knew, was a kind of Norse hell, but unlike the Christian hell, Niflheim was icy cold. 'Corpse-Ripper feeds on the dead,' Ragnar went on, 'but he also gnaws at the tree of life. He wants to kill the whole world and bring time to an end.' He touched his hammer again.

Another panel, behind the altar, showed Christ on the cross, and next to it was a third painted leather panel that fascinated Ivar. A man, naked but for a loincloth, had been tied to a stake and was being used as a target by archers. At least a score of arrows had punctured his white flesh, but he still had a saintly expression and a secret smile as though, despite his troubles, he was quite enjoying himself. 'Who is that?' Ivar wanted to know.

'The blessed Saint Sebastian,' King Edmund was seated in front of the altar, and his interpreter provided the answer. Ivar, skull eyes staring at the painting, wanted to know the whole story, and Edmund recounted how the blessed Saint Sebastian, a Roman soldier, had refused to renounce his faith and so the emperor had ordered him shot to death with arrows. 'Yet he lived!' Edmund said eagerly, 'he lived because God protected him and God be praised for that mercy.'

'He lived?' Ivar asked suspiciously.

'So the emperor had him clubbed to death instead,' the interpreter finished the tale.

'So he didn't live?'

'He went to heaven,' King Edmund said, 'so he lived.'

Ubba intervened, wanting to have the concept of heaven explained to him, and Edmund eagerly sketched its delights, but

Ubba spat in derision when he realised that the Christian heaven was Valhalla without any of the amusements. 'And Christians want to go to heaven?' he asked in disbelief.

'Of course,' the interpreter said.

Ubba sneered. He and his two brothers were attended by as many Danish warriors as could cram themselves into the church, while King Edmund had an entourage of two priests and six monks who all listened as Ivar proposed his settlement. King Edmund could live, he could rule in East Anglia, but the chief fortresses were to be garrisoned by Danes, and Danes were to be granted whatever land they required, except for royal land. Edmund would be expected to provide horses for the Danish army, coin and food for the Danish warriors, and his fyrd, what was left of it, would march under Danish orders. Edmund had no sons, but his chief men, those who lived, had sons who would become hostages to ensure that the East Anglians kept the terms Ivar proposed.

'And if I say no?' Edmund asked.

Ivar was amused by that. 'We take the land anyway.'

The king consulted his priests and monks. Edmund was a tall, spare man, bald as an egg though he was only about thirty years old. He had protruding eyes, a pursed mouth and a perpetual frown. He was wearing a white tunic which made him look like a priest himself. 'What of God's church?' he finally asked Ivar.

'What of it?'

'Your men have desecrated God's altars, slaughtered his servants, defiled his image and stolen his tribute!' The king was angry now. One of his hands was clenched on the arm of his chair that was set in front of the altar, while the other hand was a fist which beat time with his accusations.

'Your god cannot look after himself?' Ubba enquired.

'Our God is a mighty God,' Edmund declared, 'the creator of the world, yet he also allows evil to exist to test us.'

'Amen,' one of the priests murmured as Ivar's interpreter translated the words.

'He brought you!' the king spat, 'pagans from the north! Jeremiah foretold this!'

'Jeremiah?' Ivar asked, quite lost now.

118

One of the monks had a book, the first I had seen in many years, and he unwrapped its leather cover, paged through the stiff leaves and gave it to the king who reached into a pocket and took out a small ivory pointer that he used to indicate the words he wanted. *'Quia malum ego,'* he thundered, the pale pointer moving along the lines, *'adduco ab aquilone et contritionem magnam!'*

He stopped there, glaring at Ivar, and some of the Danes, impressed by the forcefulness of the king's words, even though none of them understood a single one of them, touched their hammer charms. The priests around Edmund looked reproachfully at us. A sparrow flew in through a high window and perched for a moment on an arm of the high wooden cross that stood on the altar.

Ivar's dread face showed no reaction to Jeremiah's words and it finally dawned on the East Anglian interpreter, who was one of the priests, that the king's impassioned reading had meant nothing to any of us. 'For I will bring evil from the north,' he translated, 'and great destruction.'

'It is in the book!' Edmund said fiercely, giving the volume back to the monk.

'You can keep your church,' Ivar said carelessly.

'It is not enough,' Edmund said. He stood up to give his next words more force. 'I will rule here,' he went on, 'and I will suffer your presence if I must, and I will provide you with horses, food, coin and hostages, but only if you, and all of your men, submit to God. You must be baptised!'

That word was lost on the Danish interpreter, and on the king's, and finally Ubba looked to me for help. 'You have to stand in a barrel of water,' I said, remembering how Beocca had baptised me after my brother's death, 'and they pour more water over you.'

'They want to wash me?' Ubba asked, astonished.

I shrugged. 'That's what they do, lord.'

'You will become Christians!' Edmund said, then shot me an irritated look. 'We can baptise in the river, boy. Barrels are not necessary.'

'They want to wash you in the river,' I explained to Ivar and Ubba, and the Danes laughed.

Ivar thought about it. Standing in a river for a few minutes was not such a bad thing, especially if it meant he could hurry back to quell whatever trouble afflicted Northumbria. 'I can go on worshipping Odin once I'm washed?' he asked.

'Of course not!' Edmund said angrily. 'There is only one God!'

'There are many gods,' Ivar snapped back, 'many! Everyone knows that.'

'There is only one God, and you must serve him.'

'But we're winning,' Ivar explained patiently, almost as if he talked to a child, 'which means our gods are beating your one god.'

The king shuddered at this awful heresy. 'Your gods are false gods,' he said, 'they are turds of the devil, they are evil things who will bring darkness to the world, while our God is great, he is all powerful, he is magnificent.'

'Show me,' Ivar said.

Those two words brought silence. The king, his priests and monks all stared at Ivar in evident puzzlement.

'Prove it,' Ivar said, and his Danes murmured their support of the idea.

King Edmund blinked, evidently lost for inspiration, then had a sudden idea and pointed at the leather panel on which was painted Saint Sebastian's experience of being an archers' target. 'Our God spared the blessed Saint Sebastian from death by arrows!' Edmund said, 'which is proof enough, is it not?'

'But the man still died,' Ivar pointed out.

'Only because that was God's will.'

Ivar thought about that. 'So would your god protect you from my arrows?' he asked.

'If it is his will, yes.'

'So let's try,' Ivar proposed. 'We shall shoot arrows at you, and if you survive then we'll all be washed.'

Edmund stared at the Dane, wondering if he was serious, then looked nervous when he saw that Ivar was not joking. The king opened his mouth, found he had nothing to say and closed it again, then one of his tonsured monks murmured to him and he must have been trying to persuade the king that God was suggesting this ordeal in order to extend his church, and that a miracle would result, and the Danes would become Christians and we would all be friends and end up singing together on the high platform in heaven. The king did not look entirely convinced by this argument, if that was indeed what the monk was proposing, but the Danes wanted to attempt the miracle now and it was no longer up to Edmund to accept or refuse the trial.

A dozen men shoved the monks and priests aside while more went outside to find bows and arrows. The king, trapped in his defence of God, was kneeling at the altar, praying as hard as any man has ever prayed. The Danes were grinning. I was enjoying it. I think I rather hoped to see a miracle, not because I was a Christian, but because I just wanted to see a miracle. Beocca had often told me about miracles, stressing that they were the real proof of Christianity's truths, but I had never seen one. No one had ever walked on the water at Bebbanburg and no lepers were healed there and no angels had filled our night skies with blazing glory, but now, perhaps, I would see the power of God that Beocca had forever preached to me. Brida just wanted to see Edmund dead.

'Are you ready?' Ivar demanded of the king.

Edmund looked at his priests and monks and I wondered if he was about to suggest that one of them should replace him in this test of God's power. Then he frowned and looked back to Ivar. 'I will accept your proposal,' he said.

'That we shoot arrows at you?'

'That I remain king here.'

'But you want to wash me first.'

'We can dispense with that,' Edmund said.

'No,' Ivar said. 'You have claimed your god is all powerful, that he is the only god, so I want it proved. If you are right then all of us will be washed. Are we agreed?' This question was asked of the Danes who roared their approval.

'Not me,' Ravn said, 'I won't be washed.'

'We will all be washed!' Ivar snarled, and I realised he truly was interested in the outcome of the test, more interested, indeed, than he was in making a quick and convenient peace with Edmund. All men need the support of their god and Ivar was trying to discover whether he had, all these years, been worshipping at the wrong shrine. 'Are you wearing armour?' he asked Edmund.

'No.'

'Best to be sure,' Ubba intervened and glanced at the fatal painting. 'Strip him,' he ordered.

The king and the churchmen protested, but the Danes would not be denied and King Edmund was stripped stark naked. Brida enjoyed that. 'He's puny,' she said. Edmund, the butt of laughter now, did his best to look dignified. The priests and monks were on their knees, praying, while six archers took their stance a dozen paces from Edmund.

'We are going to find out,' Ivar told us, stilling the laughter, 'whether the English god is as powerful as our Danish gods. If he is, and if the king lives, then we shall become Christians, all of us!'

'Not me,' Ravn said again, but quietly so that Ivar could not hear. 'Tell me what happens, Uhtred.'

It was soon told. Six arrows hit, the king screamed, blood spattered the altar, he fell down, he twitched like a gaffed salmon, and six more arrows thumped home. Edmund twitched some more, and the archers kept on shooting, though their aim was bad because they were half helpless with laughter, and they went on shooting until the king was as full of feathered shafts as a hedgehog has spikes. And he was quite dead by then. He was bloodied, his white skin red-laced, open-mouthed and dead. His god had failed him miserably. Nowadays, of course, that story is never told, instead children learn how brave Saint Edmund stood up to the Danes, demanded their conversion and was murdered. So now he is a martyr and saint, warbling happily in heaven, but the truth is that he was a fool and talked himself into martyrdom.

The priests and monks wailed, so Ivar ordered them killed as well, then he decreed that Earl Godrim, one of his chiefs, would rule in East Anglia and that Halfdan would savage the country to quench the last sparks of resistance. Godrim and Halfdan would be given a third of the army to keep East Anglia quiet, while the rest of us would return to subdue the unrest in Northumbria.

So now East Anglia was gone.

And Wessex was the last kingdom of England.

We returned to Northumbria, half rowing and half sailing the *Wind-Viper* up the gentle coast, then rowing against the rivers' currents as we travelled up the Humber, then the Ouse until Eoferwic's walls came in sight, and there we hauled the ship onto dry land so she would not rot through the winter. Ivar and Ubba returned with us, so that a whole fleet skimmed the river, oars dripping, beastless prows bearing branches of green oak to show we came home victorious. We brought home much treasure. The Danes set much store by treasure. Their men follow their leaders because they know they will be rewarded with silver, and in the taking of three of England's four kingdoms the Danes had amassed a fortune which was shared among the men and some, a few, decided to take their money back home to Denmark. Most stayed, for the richest kingdom remained undefeated and men reckoned they would all become as wealthy as gods once Wessex fell.

Ivar and Ubba had come to Eoferwic expecting trouble. They had their shields displayed on the flanks of their ships, but whatever unrest had disturbed Northumbria had not affected the city and King Egbert, who ruled at the pleasure of the Danes, sulkily denied there had been any rising at all. Archbishop Wulfhere said the same. 'There is always banditry,' he declared loftily, 'and perhaps you heard rumours of it?'

'Or perhaps you are deaf,' Ivar snarled, and Ivar was right to be suspicious for, once it was known that the army had returned, messengers came from Ealdorman Ricsig of Dunholm. Dunholm was a great fortress on a high crag that was almost surrounded by the River Wiire, and the crag and the river made Dunholm almost as strong as Bebbanburg. It was ruled by Ricsig who had never drawn his sword against the Danes. When we attacked Eoferwic and my father was killed, Ricsig had claimed to be sick and his men had stayed home, but now he sent servants to tell Ivar that a band of Danes had been slaughtered at Gyruum. That was the

123

site of a famous monastery where a man called Bede wrote a history of the English church which Beocca had always praised to me, saying that when I learned to read properly I could give myself the treat of reading it. I have yet to do so, but I have been to Gyruum and seen where the book was written for Ragnar was asked to take his men there and discover what had happened.

It seemed six Danes, all of them masterless men, had gone to Gyruum and demanded to see the monastery's treasury and, when the monks claimed to be penniless, the six had started killing, but the monks had fought back and, as there were over a score of monks, and as they were helped by some men from the town, they succeeded in killing the six Danes who had then been spitted on posts and left to rot on the foreshore. Thus far, as Ragnar admitted, the fault lay with the Danes, but the monks, encouraged by this slaughter, had marched west up the River Tine, and attacked a Danish settlement where there were only a few men, those too old or too sick to travel south with the army, and there they had raped and killed at least a score of women and children, proclaiming that this was now a holy war. More men had joined the makeshift army, but Ealdorman Ricsig, fearing the revenge of the Danes, had sent his own troops to disperse them. He had captured a good number of the rebels, including a dozen monks, who were now held at his fortress above the river at Dunholm.

All this we heard from Ricsig's messengers, then from folk who had survived the massacre, and one of those was a girl the same age as Ragnar's daughter, and she said the monks had raped her one at a time, and afterwards they had forcibly baptised her. She said there had been nuns present as well, women who had urged the men on and had taken part in the slaughter afterwards. 'Nests of vipers,' Ragnar said. I had never seen him so angry, not even when Sven had exposed himself to Thyra. We dug up some of the Danish dead and all were naked and all were blood-spattered. They had all been tortured.

A priest was found and made to tell us the names of the chief monasteries and nunneries in Northumbria. Gyruum was one, of course, and just across the river was a large nunnery, while to the south, where the Wiire met the sea, was a second monastery. The house at Streonshall was close to Eoferwic, and that held many nuns, while close to Bebbanburg, on the island that Beocca had always told me was sacred, was the monastery of Lindisfarena. There were many others, but Ragnar was content with the chief places, and he sent men to Ivar and Ubba suggesting that the nuns of Streonshall should be dispersed, and any found to have joined the revolt should be killed, then he set about Gyruum. Every monk was killed, the buildings that were not made of stone were burned, the treasures, for they did indeed have silver and gold hidden beneath their church, were taken. I remember we discovered a great pile of writings, sheet upon sheet of parchments, all smothered in tight black writing, and I have no idea what the writings were, and now I never will, for they were all burned, and once Gyruum was no more we went south to the monastery at the mouth of the Wiire and we did the same there, and afterwards crossed the Tine and obliterated the nunnery on the northern bank. The nuns there, led by their abbess, deliberately scarred their own faces. They knew we were coming and so, to deter rape, cut their cheeks and foreheads and so met us all bloody, screaming and ugly. Why they did not run away I do not know, but instead they waited for us, cursed us, prayed for heaven's revenge on us, and died.

I never told Alfred that I took part in that famous harrowing of the northern houses. The tale is still told as evidence of Danish ferocity and untrustworthiness, indeed every English child is told the story of the nuns who cut their faces to the bone so that they would be too ugly to rape, though that did not work any more than King Edmund's prayers had saved him from arrows. I remember one Easter listening to a sermon about the nuns, and it was all I could do not to interrupt and say that it had not happened as the priest described. The priest claimed that the Danes had promised that no monk or nun would ever be hurt in Northumbria, and that was not true, and he claimed that there was no cause for the massacres, which was equally false, and then he told a marvellous tale of how the nuns had prayed and God had placed an invisible curtain at the nunnery gate, and the Danes had pushed against the curtain and could not pierce it, and I was wondering why, if the nuns had this invisible shield, they had bothered to scar themselves, but they must have known how the story would end, because the Danes were supposed to have fetched a score of small children from the nearby village and threatened to cut their throats unless the curtain was lifted, which it was.

None of that happened. We arrived, they screamed, the young ones were raped and then they died. But not all of them, despite the famous tales. At least two were pretty and not at all scarred, and both of them stayed with Ragnar's men and one of them gave birth to a child who grew up to become a famous Danish warrior. Still, priests have never been great men for the truth and I kept quiet which was just as well. In truth we never killed everybody because Ravn drove it home to me that you always left one person alive to tell the tale so that news of the horror would spread.

Once the nunnery was burned we went to Dunholm where Ragnar thanked the Ealdorman Ricsig, though Ricsig was plainly shocked by the revenge the Danes had taken. 'Not every monk and nun took part in the slaughter,' he pointed out reprovingly.

'They are all evil,' Ragnar insisted.

'Their houses,' Ricsig said, 'are places of prayer and of contemplation, places of learning.'

'Tell me,' Ragnar demanded, 'what use is prayer, contemplation or learning? Does prayer grow rye? Does contemplation fill a fishing net? Does learning build a house or plough a field?'

Ricsig had no answer to those questions, nor indeed did the Bishop of Dunholm, a timid man who made no protest at the slaughter, not even when Ricsig meekly handed over his prisoners who were put to death in various imaginative ways. Ragnar had become convinced that the Christian monasteries and nunneries were sources of evil, places where sinister rites were performed to encourage folk to attack the Danes and he saw no point in letting such places exist. The most famous monastery of all, though, was that at Lindisfarena, the house where Saint Cuthbert had lived, and the house that had first been sacked by the Danes two generations before. It had been that attack which had been portended by dragons in the sky and whirlwinds churning the sea and lightning storms savaging the hills, but I saw no such strange wonders as we marched north.

I was excited. We were going close to Bebbanburg and I wondered whether my uncle, the false Ealdorman Ælfric, would dare come out of his fortress to protect the monks of Lindisfarena who had always looked to our family for their safety. We all rode horses, three ships' crews, over a hundred men, for it was late in the year and the Danes did not like taking their ships into hard weather. We skirted Bebbanburg, riding in the hills, catching occasional glimpses of the fortress's wooden walls between the trees. I stared at it, seeing the fretting sea beyond, dreaming.

We crossed the flat coastal fields and came to the sandy beach where a track led to Lindisfarena, but at high tide the track was flooded and we were forced to wait. We could see the monks watching us on the farther shore. 'The rest of the bastards will be burying their treasures,' Ragnar said.

'If they have any left,' I said.

'They always have some left,' Ragnar said grimly.

'When I was last here,' Ravn put in, 'we took a chest of gold! Pure gold!'

'A big chest?' Brida asked. She was mounted behind Ravn, serving as his eyes this day. She came everywhere with us, spoke good Danish by now and was regarded as bringing luck by the men, who adored her.

'As big as your chest,' Ravn said.

'Not much gold then,' Brida said, disappointed.

'Gold and silver,' Ravn reminisced, 'and some walrus tusks. Where did they get those?'

The sea relented, the bickering waves slunk back down the long sands and we rode through the shallows, past the withies that marked the track, and the monks ran off. Small flickers of smoke marked where farmsteads dotted the island and I had no doubt those folk were burying what few possessions they owned.

'Will any of these monks know you?' Ragnar asked me.

'Probably.'

'Does that worry you?'

It did, but I said it did not, and I touched Thor's hammer and somewhere in my thoughts there was a tendril of worry that God, the Christian god, was watching me. Beocca always said that everything we did was watched and recorded, and I had to remind myself that the Christian god was failing and that Odin, Thor and the Danish gods were winning the war in heaven. Edmund's death had proved that and so I consoled myself that I was safe.

The monastery lay on the south of the island from where I could see Bebbanburg on its crag of rock. The monks lived in a scatter of small timber buildings, thatched with rye and moss, and built about a small stone church. The abbot, a man called Egfrith, came to meet us carrying a wooden cross. He spoke Danish, which was unusual, and he showed no fear. 'You are most welcome to our small island,' he greeted us enthusiastically, 'and you should know that I have one of your countrymen in our sick chamber.'

Ragnar rested his hands on the fleece-covered pommel of his saddle. 'What is that to me?' he asked.

'It is an earnest of our peaceful intentions, lord,' Egfrith said. He was elderly, grey-haired, thin and missing most of his teeth so that his words came out sibilant and distorted. 'We are a humble house,' he went on, 'we tend the sick, we help the poor and we serve God.' He looked along the line of Danes, grim helmeted men with their shields hanging by their left knees, swords and axes and spears bristling. The sky was low that day, heavy and sullen, and a small rain was darkening the grass. Two monks came from the church carrying a wooden box that they placed behind Egfrith, then backed away. 'That is all the treasure we have,' Egfrith said, 'and you are welcome to it.'

Ragnar jerked his head at me and I dismounted, walked past the abbot and opened the box to find it was half full of silver pennies, most of them clipped, and all of them dull because they were of bad quality. I shrugged at Ragnar as if to suggest they were poor reward.

'You are Uhtred!' Egfrith said. He had been staring at me.

'So?' I answered belligerently.

'I heard you were dead, lord,' he said, 'and I praise God you are not.'

'You heard I was dead?'

'That a Dane killed you.'

128

We had been talking in English and Ragnar wanted to know what had been said, so I translated. 'Was the Dane called Weland?' Ragnar asked Egfrith.

'He is called that,' Egfrith said.

'Is?'

'Weland is the man lying here recovering from his wounds, lord,' Egfrith looked at me again as though he could not believe I was alive.

'His wounds?' Ragnar wanted to know.

'He was attacked, lord, by a man from the fortress. From Bebbanburg.'

Ragnar, of course, wanted to hear the whole tale. It seemed Weland had made his way back to Bebbanburg where he claimed to have killed me, and so received his reward in silver coins, and he was escorted from the fortress by a half dozen men who included Ealdwulf, the blacksmith who had told me stories in his forge, and Ealdwulf had attacked Weland, hacking an axe down into his shoulder before the other men dragged him off. Weland had been brought here, while Ealdwulf, if he still lived, was back in Bebbanburg.

If Abbot Egfrith thought Weland was his safeguard, he had miscalculated. Ragnar scowled at him. 'You gave Weland shelter even though you thought he had killed Uhtred?' he demanded.

'This is a house of God,' Egfrith said, 'so we give every man shelter.'

'Including murderers?' Ragnar asked, and he reached behind his head and untied the leather lace which bound his hair. 'So tell me, monk, how many of your men went south to help their comrades murder Danes?'

Egfrith hesitated, which was answer enough, and then Ragnar drew his sword and the abbot found his voice. 'Some did, lord,' he admitted, 'I could not stop them.'

'You could not stop them?' Ragnar asked, shaking his head so that his wet unbound hair fell around his face. 'Yet you rule here?'

'I am the abbot, yes.'

'Then you could stop them.' Ragnar was looking angry now and I suspected he was remembering the bodies we had disinterred near Gyruum, the little Danish girls with blood still on their thighs. 'Kill them,' he told his men.

I took no part in that killing. I stood by the shore and listened to the birds cry and I watched Bebbanburg and heard the blades doing their work, and Brida came to stand beside me and she took my hand and stared south across the white-flecked grey to the great fortress on its crag. 'Is that your house?' she asked.

'That is my house.'

'He called you lord.'

'I am a lord.'

She leaned against me. 'You think the Christian god is watching us.'

'No,' I said, wondering how she knew that I had been thinking about that very question.

'He was never our god,' she said fiercely. 'We worshipped Woden and Thor and Eostre and all the other gods and goddesses, and then the Christians came and we forgot our gods, and now the Danes have come to lead us back to them.' She stopped abruptly.

'Did Ravn tell you that?'

'He told me some,' she said, 'but the rest I worked out. There's war between the gods, Uhtred, war between the Christian god and our gods, and when there is war in Asgard the gods make us fight for them on earth.'

'And we're winning?' I asked.

Her answer was to point to the dead monks, scattered on the wet grass, their robes bloodied, and now that their killing was done Ragnar dragged Weland out of his sickbed. The man was plainly dying, for he was shivering and his wound stank, but he was conscious of what was happening to him. His reward for killing me had been a heavy bag of good silver coins that weighed as much as a new-born babe, and that we found beneath his bed and we added it to the monastery's small hoard to be divided among our men.

Weland himself lay on the bloodied grass, looking from me to Ragnar. 'You want to kill him?' Ragnar asked me.

'Yes,' I said, for no other response was expected. Then I remembered the beginning of my tale, the day when I had seen Ragnar oar-dancing just off this coast and how, next morning, he had brought my brother's head to Bebbanburg. 'I want to cut off his head,' I said.

Weland tried to speak, but could only manage a guttural groan. His eyes were on Ragnar's sword.

Ragnar offered the blade to me. 'It's sharp enough,' he said, 'but you'll be surprised by how much force is needed. An axe would be better.'

Weland looked at me now. His teeth chattered and he twitched. I hated him. I had disliked him from the first, but now I hated him, yet I was still oddly nervous of killing him even though he was already half dead. I have learned that it is one thing to kill in battle, to send a brave man's soul to the corpse-hall of the gods, but quite another to take a helpless man's life, and he must have sensed my hesitation for he managed a pitiful plea for his life. 'I will serve you,' he said.

'Make the bastard suffer,' Ragnar answered for me, 'send him to the corpse-goddess, but let her know he's coming by making him suffer.'

I do not think he suffered much. He was already so feeble that even my puny blows drove him to swift unconsciousness, but even so it took a long time to kill him. I hacked away. I have always been surprised by how much effort is needed to kill a man. The skalds make it sound easy, but it rarely is. We are stubborn creatures, we cling to life and are very hard to kill, but Weland's soul finally went to its fate as I chopped and sawed and stabbed and at last succeeded in severing his bloody head. His mouth was twisted into a rictus of agony, and that was some consolation.

Now I asked more favours of Ragnar, knowing he would give them to me. I took some of the poorer coins from the hoard, then went to one of the larger monastery buildings and found the writing place where the monks copied books. They used to paint beautiful letters on the books and, before my life was changed at Eoferwic, I used to go there with Beocca and sometimes the monks would let me daub scraps of parchment with their wonderful colours.

I wanted the colours now. They were in bowls, mostly as powder, a few mixed with gum, and I needed a piece of cloth which I found in the church; a square of white linen that had been used to cover the sacraments. Back in the writing place I drew a wolf's head in charcoal on the white cloth and then I found some ink and began to fill in the outline. Brida helped me and she proved to be much better at making pictures than I was, and she gave the wolf a red eye and a red tongue, and flecked the black ink with white and blue that somehow suggested fur, and once the banner was made we tied it to the staff of the dead abbot's cross. Ragnar was rummaging through the monastery's small collection of sacred books, tearing off the jewel-studded metal plates that decorated their front covers, and once he had all the plates, and once my banner was made, we burned all the timber buildings.

The rain stopped as we left. We trotted across the causeway, turned south, and Ragnar, at my request, went down the coastal track until we reached the place where the road crossed the sands to Bebbanburg.

We stopped there and I untied my hair so that it hung loose. I gave the banner to Brida who would ride Ravn's horse while the old man waited with his son. And then, a borrowed sword at my side, I rode home.

Brida came with me as standard-bearer and the two of us cantered along the track. The sea broke white to my right and slithered across the sands to my left. I could see men on the walls and up on the Low Gate, watching, and I kicked the horse, making it gallop, and Brida kept pace, her banner flying above, and I curbed the horse where the track turned north to the gate and now I could see my uncle. He was there, Ælfric the Treacherous, thin-faced, dark-haired, gazing at me from the Low Gate and I stared up at him so he would know who I was, and then I threw Weland's severed head onto the ground where my brother's head had once been thrown. I followed it with the silver coins.

I threw thirty coins. The Judas price. I remembered that church tale. It was one of the few that I had liked.

There were archers on the wall, but none drew. They just watched. I gave my uncle the evil sign, the devil's horns made with the two outer fingers, and then I spat at him, turned and trotted away. He knew I was alive now, knew I was his enemy, and knew I would kill him like a dog if ever I had the chance.

'Uhtred!' Brida called. She had been looking behind and I twisted in the saddle to see that one warrior had jumped over the wall, had fallen heavily, but was now running towards us. He was a big man, heavily bearded, and I thought I could never fight such a man, and then I saw the archers loose their arrows and they flecked the ground about the man who I now saw was Ealdwulf, the smith.

'Lord Uhtred!' Ealdwulf called, 'Lord Uhtred!' I turned the horse and went to him, shielding him from the arrows with my horse's bulk, but none of the arrows came close and I suspect, looking back on that distant day, that the bowmen were deliberately missing. 'You live, lord!' Ealdwulf beamed up at me.

'I live.'

'Then I come with you,' he said firmly.

'But your wife, your son?' I asked.

'My wife died, lord, last year, and my son was drowned while fishing.'

'I am sorry,' I said. An arrow skidded through the dune grass, but it was yards away.

'Woden gives, and Woden takes away,' Ealdwulf said, 'and he has given me back my lord.' He saw Thor's hammer about my neck and, because he was a pagan, he smiled.

And I had my first follower. Ealdwulf the smith.

'He's a gloomy man, your uncle,' Ealdwulf told me as we journeyed south, 'miserable as shit, he is. Even his new son don't cheer him up.'

'He has a son?'

'Ælfric the Younger, he's called, and he's a bonny wee thing. Healthy as you like. Gytha's sick though. She won't last long. And you, lord? You look well.'

'I am well.'

'You'd be twelve now?'

'Thirteen.'

133

'A man, then. Is that your woman?' He nodded at Brida.

'My friend.'

'No meat on her,' Ealdwulf said, 'so better as a friend.' The smith was a big man, almost forty years old, with hands, forearms and face black-scarred from countless small burns from his forge. He walked beside my horse, his pace apparently effortless despite his advanced years. 'So tell me about these Danes,' he said, casting a dubious look at Ragnar's warriors.

'They're led by Earl Ragnar,' I said, 'who is the man who killed my brother. He's a good man.'

'He's the one who killed your brother?' Ealdwulf seemed shocked.

'Destiny is everything,' I said, which might have been true but also avoided having to make a longer answer.

'You like him?'

'He's like a father to me. You'll like him.'

'He's still a Dane, though, isn't he, lord? They might worship the right gods,' Ealdwulf said grudgingly, 'but I'd still like to see them gone.'

'Why?'

'Why?' Ealdwulf seemed shocked that I had asked. 'Because this isn't their land, lord, that's why. I want to walk without being afraid. I don't want to touch my forelock to a man just because he has a sword. There's one law for them and another for us.'

'There's no law for them,' I said.

'If a Dane kills a Northumbrian,' Ealdwulf said indignantly, 'what can a man do? There's no wergild, no reeve to see, no lord to seek justice.'

That was true. Wergild was the blood price of a man's life, and every person had a wergild. A man's was more than a woman's, unless she was a great woman, and a warrior's was greater than a farmer's, but the price was always there, and a murderer could escape being put to death if the family of the murdered man would accept the wergild. The reeve was the man who enforced the law, reporting to his Ealdorman, but that whole careful system of justice had vanished since the Danes had come. There was no law now except what the Danes said it was, and that was what they wanted it to be, and I knew that I revelled in that chaos, but then I was privileged. I was Ragnar's man, and Ragnar protected me, but without Ragnar I would be no better than an outlaw or a slave.

'Your uncle doesn't protest,' Ealdwulf went on, 'but Beocca did. You remember him? Red-haired priest with a shrivelled hand and crossed eyes?'

'I met him last year,' I said.

'You did? Where?'

'He was with Alfred of Wessex.'

'Wessex!' Ealdwulf said, surprised. 'Long way to go. But he was a good man, Beocca, despite being a priest. He ran off because he couldn't stand the Danes. Your uncle was furious. Said Beocca deserved to be killed.'

Doubtless, I thought, because Beocca had taken the parchments that proved me to be the rightful Ealdorman. 'My uncle wanted me killed too,' I said, 'and I never thanked you for attacking Weland.'

'Your uncle was going to give me to the Danes for that,' he said, 'only no Dane complained, so he did nothing.'

'You're with the Danes now,' I said, 'and you'd better get used to it.'

Ealdwulf thought about that for a moment. 'Why not go to Wessex?' he asked.

'Because the West Saxons want to turn me into a priest,' I said, 'and I want to be a warrior.'

'Go to Mercia then,' Ealdwulf suggested.

'That's ruled by the Danes.'

'But your uncle lives there.'

'My uncle?'

'Your mother's brother!' He was astonished that I did not know my own family. 'He's Ealdorman Æthelwulf, if he still lives.'

'My father never talked about my mother,' I said.

'Because he loved her. She was a beauty, your mother, a piece of gold, and she died giving birth to you.'

'Æthelwulf,' I said.

'If he lives.'

135

But why go to Æthelwulf when I had Ragnar? Æthelwulf was family, of course, but I had never met him and I doubted he even remembered my existence, and I had no desire to find him, and even less desire to learn my letters in Wessex, so I would stay with Ragnar. I said as much to Ealdwulf. 'He's teaching me to fight,' I said.

'Learn from the best, eh?' Ealdwulf said grudgingly. 'That's how you become a good smith. Learn from the best.'

Ealdwulf was a good smith and, despite himself, he came to like Ragnar for Ragnar was generous and he appreciated good workmanship. A smithy was added onto our home near Synningthwait and Ragnar paid good silver for a forge, an anvil, and for the great hammers, tongs and files that Ealdwulf needed. It was late winter before all was ready, and then ore was purchased from Eoferwic and our valley echoed to the clang of iron on iron, and even on the coldest days the smithy was warm and men gathered there to exchange stories or to tell riddles. Ealdwulf was a great man for riddles and I would translate for him as he baffled Ragnar's Danes. Most of his riddles were about men and women and what they did together and those were easy enough to guess, but I liked the complicated ones. My father and mother gave me up for dead, one riddle began, then a loyal kinswoman wrapped and protected me, and I killed all her children, but she still loved me and fed me until I rose above the dwelling houses of men and so left her. I could not guess that one, nor could any of the Danes, and Ealdwulf refused to give me the answer even when I begged him and it was only when I told the riddle to Brida that I learned the solution. 'A cuckoo, of course,' she said instantly. She was right, of course.

By spring the forge needed to be larger, and all that summer Ealdwulf made metal for swords, spears, axes and spades. I asked him once if he minded working for the Danes and he just shrugged. 'I worked for them in Bebbanburg,' he said, 'because your uncle does their bidding.'

'But there are no Danes in Bebbanburg?'

'None,' he admitted, 'but they visit and are made welcome. Your uncle pays them tribute.' He stopped suddenly, interrupted by a shout of what I thought was pure rage.

I ran out of the smithy to see Ragnar standing in front of the house while, approaching up the track, was a crowd of men led by a mounted warrior. And such a warrior. He had a mail coat, a fine helmet hanging from the saddle, a bright-painted shield, a long sword and arms thick with rings. He was a young man with long fair hair and a thick gold beard, and he roared back at Ragnar like a rutting stag, then Ragnar ran towards him and I half thought the young man would draw the sword and kick at his horse, but instead he dismounted and ran uphill and, when the two met, they embraced and thumped each other's backs and Ragnar, when he turned towards us, had a smile that would have lit the darkest crypt of hell. 'My son!' he shouted up at me, 'my son!'

It was Ragnar the Younger, come from Ireland with a ship's crew and, though he did not know me, he embraced me, lifting me off the ground, whirled his sister around, thumped Rorik, kissed his mother, shouted at the servants, scattered gifts of silver chain links, and petted the hounds. A feast was ordered, and that night he gave us his news, saying he now commanded his own ship, that he had come for a few months only and that Ivar wanted him back in Ireland by the spring. He was so like his father, and I liked him immediately, and the house was always happy when Ragnar the Younger was there. Some of his men lodged with us, and that autumn they cut trees and added a proper hall to the house, a hall fit for an earl with big beams and a high gable on which a boar's skull was nailed.

'You were lucky,' he told me one day. We were thatching the new roof, laying down the thick rye straw and combing it flat.

'Lucky?'

'That my father didn't kill you at Eoferwic.'

'I was lucky,' I agreed.

'But he was always a good judge of men,' he said, passing me a pot of ale. He perched on the roof ridge and gazed across the valley. 'He likes it here.'

'It's a good place. What about Ireland?'

He grinned. 'Bog and rock, Uhtred, and the skraelings are vicious.' The skraelings were the natives. 'But they fight well! And there's silver there, and the more they fight the more silver we get. Are you going to drink all that ale, or do I get some?'

I handed him back the pot and watched as the ale ran down his beard as he drained it. 'I like Ireland well enough,' he said when he had finished, 'but I won't stay there. I'll come back here. Find land in Wessex. Raise a family. Get fat.'

'Why don't you come back now?'

'Because Ivar wants me there, and Ivar's a good lord.'

'He frightens me.'

'A good lord should be frightening.'

'Your father isn't.'

'Not to you, but what about the men he kills? Would you want to face Earl Ragnar the Fearless in a shield wall?'

'No.'

'So he is frightening,' he said, grinning. 'Go and take Wessex,' he said, 'and find the land that will make me fat.'

We finished the thatch, and then I had to go up into the woods because Ealdwulf had an insatiable appetite for charcoal which is the only substance that burns hot enough to melt iron. He had shown a dozen of Ragnar's men how to produce it, but Brida and I were his best workers and we spent much time among the trees. The charcoal heaps needed constant attention and, as each would burn for at least three days, Brida and I would often spend all night beside such a pile, watching for a tell-tale wisp of smoke coming from the bracken and turf covering the burn. Such smoke betrayed that the fire inside was too hot and we would have to scramble over the warm heap to stuff the crack with earth and so cool the fire deep inside the pile.

We burned alder when we could get it, for that was the wood Ealdwulf preferred, and the art of it was to char the alder logs, but not let them burst into flame. For every four logs we put into a pile we would get one back, while the rest vanished to leave the lightweight, deep black, dirty charcoal. It could take a week to make the pile. The alder was carefully stacked in a shallow pit, and a hole was left in the stack's centre which we filled with charcoal from the previous burn. Then we would put a layer of bracken over the whole thing, cover that with thick turves and, when all was done, put fire down the central hole and, when we were sure the charcoal was alight, stuff the hole tight. Now the silent, dark fire had to be controlled. We would open gaps at the base of the pit to let a little air in, but if the wind changed then the air holes had to be stuffed and others made. It was tedious work, and Ealdwulf's appetite for charcoal seemed unlimited, but I enjoyed it. To be all night in the dark, beside the warm burn, was to be a sceadugengan, and besides, I was with Brida and we had become more than friends.

She lost her first baby up beside the charcoal burn. She had not even known she was pregnant, but one night she was assailed with cramps and spear-like pains, and I wanted to go and fetch Sigrid, but Brida would not let me. She told me she knew what was happening, but I was scared helpless by her agony and I shuddered in fear throughout the dark until, just before dawn, she gave birth to a tiny dead baby boy. We buried it with its afterbirth, and Brida stumbled back to the homestead where Sigrid was alarmed by her appearance and gave her a broth of leeks and sheep brains and made her stay at home. Sigrid must have suspected what had happened for she was sharp with me for a few days and she told Ragnar it was time Brida was married. Brida was certainly of age, being thirteen, and there were a dozen young Danish warriors in Synningthwait who were in need of wives, but Ragnar declared that Brida brought his men luck and he wanted her to ride with us when we attacked Wessex.

'And when will that be?' Sigrid asked.

'Next year,' Ragnar suggested, 'or the year after. No longer.'

'And then?'

'Then England is no more,' Ragnar said. 'It will all be ours.' The last of the four kingdoms would have fallen and England would be Daneland and we would all be Danes or slaves or dead.

We celebrated the Yule feast and Ragnar the Younger won every competition in Synningthwait, he hurled rocks farther than anyone, wrestled men to the ground and even drank his father into insensibility. Then followed the dark months, the long winter, and in spring, when the gales had subsided, Ragnar the Younger had to leave and we had a melancholy feast on the eve of his going, and next morning he led his men away from the hall, going down the track in a grey drizzle. Ragnar watched his son all the way down into the valley and when he turned back to his newly-built hall he had tears in his eyes. 'He's a good man,' he told me.

'I liked him,' I said truthfully, and I did, and many years later, when I met him again, I still liked him.

There was an empty feeling after Ragnar the Younger had left, but I remember that spring and summer fondly for it was in those long days that Ealdwulf made me a sword. 'I hope it's better than my last one,' I said ungraciously.

'Your last one?'

'The one I carried when we attacked Eoferwic,' I said.

'That thing! That wasn't mine. Your father bought it in Berewic, and I told him it was crap, but it was only a short sword. Good for killing ducks, maybe, but not for fighting. What happened to it?'

'It bent,' I said, remembering Ragnar laughing at the feeble weapon.

'Soft iron, boy, soft iron.'

There were two sorts of iron, he told me, the soft and the hard. The hard made the best cutting edge, but it was brittle and a sword made of such iron would snap at the first brutal stroke, while a sword made of the softer metal would bend as my short sword had done. 'So what we do is use both,' he told me, and I watched as he made seven iron rods. Three were of the hard iron, and he was not really sure how he made the iron hard, only that the glowing metal had to be laid in the burning charcoal, and if he got it just right then the cooled metal would be hard and unbending. The other four rods were longer, much longer, and they were not exposed to the charcoal for the same length of time, and those four he twisted until each had been turned into a spiral. They were still straight rods, but tightly twisted until they were the same length as the hard iron rods. 'Why do you do that?' I asked.

'You'll see,' he said mysteriously, 'you'll see.'

He finished with seven rods, each as thick as my thumb. Three were of the hard metal, which Ragnar called steel, while the four softer rods were prettily twisted into their tight spirals. One of the hard rods was longer and slightly thicker than the others, and that one was the sword's spine and the extra length was the tang onto which the hilt would eventually be riveted. Ealdwulf began by hammering that rod flat so that it looked like a very thin and feeble sword, then he placed the four twisted rods either side of it, two to each side so that they sheathed it, and he welded the last two steel rods on the outside to become the sword's edges, and it looked grotesque then, a bundle of mismatched rods, but this was when the real work began, the work of heating and hammering, metal glowing red, the black dross twisting as it burned away from the iron, the hammer swinging, sparks flying in the dark forge, the hiss of burning metal plunged into water, the patience as the emerging blade was cooled in a trough of ash shavings. It took days, yet as the hammering and cooling and heating went on I saw how the four twisted rods of soft iron, which were now all melded into the harder steel, had been smoothed into wondrous patterns, repetitive curling patterns that made flat, smoky wisps in the blade. In some lights you could not see the patterns, but in the dusk, or when, in winter, you breathed on the blade, they showed. Serpent breath, Brida called the patterns, and I decided to give the sword that name; Serpent-Breath. Ealdwulf finished the blade by hammering grooves which ran down the centre of each side. He said they helped stop the sword being trapped in an enemy's flesh. 'Blood channels,' he grunted.

The boss of the hilt was of iron, as was the heavy crosspiece, and both were simple, undecorated and big, and when all was done, I shaped two pieces of ash to make the handle. I wanted the sword decorated with silver or gilt bronze, but Ealdwulf refused. 'It's a tool, lord,' he said, 'just a tool. Something to make your work easier, and no better than my hammer.' He held the blade up so that it caught the sunlight. 'And one day,' he went on, leaning towards me, 'you will kill Danes with her.'

She was heavy, Serpent-Breath, too heavy for a fourteen-year-old, but I would grow into her. Her point tapered more than Ragnar liked, but that made her well-balanced for it meant there was not much weight at the blade's outer end. Ragnar liked weight there, for it helped break down enemy shields, but I preferred Serpent-Breath's agility, given her by Ealdwulf's skill, and that skill meant she never bent nor cracked, not ever, for I still have her. The ash handles have been replaced, the edges have been nicked by enemy blades, and she is slimmer now because she has been sharpened so often, but she is still beautiful, and sometimes I breathe on her flanks and see the patterns emerge in the blade, the curls and wisps, the blue and silver appearing in the metal like magic, and I remember that spring and summer in the woods of Northumbria and I think of Brida staring at her reflection in the newly-made blade.

And there is magic in Serpent-Breath. Ealdwulf had his own spells that he would not tell me, the spells of the smith, and Brida took the blade into the woods for a whole night and never told me what she did with it, and those were the spells of a woman, and when we made the sacrifice of the pit slaughter, and killed a man, a horse, a ram, a bull and a drake, I asked Ragnar to use Serpent-Breath on the doomed man so that Odin would know she existed and would look well on her. Those are the spells of a pagan and a warrior.

And I think Odin did see her, for she has killed more men than I can ever remember.

It was late summer before Serpent-Breath was finished and then, before autumn brought its sea-churning storms, we went south. It was time to obliterate England, so we sailed towards Wessex.

Five

We gathered at Eoferwic where the pathetic King Egbert was forced to inspect the Danes and wish them well. He rode down the riverbank where the boats waited and where the ragged crews lined on the shore and gazed at him scornfully, knowing he was not a real king, and behind him rode Kjartan and Sven, now part of his Danish bodyguard, though I assumed their job was as much to keep Egbert a prisoner as to keep him alive. Sven, a man now, wore a scarf over his missing eye, and he and his father looked far more prosperous. Kjartan wore mail and had a huge war axe slung on his shoulder, while Sven had a long sword, a coat of fox pelts, and two arm rings. 'They took part in the massacre at Streonshall,' Ragnar told me. That was the large nunnery near Eoferwic, and it was evident that the men who had taken their revenge on the nuns had made good plunder.

Kjartan, a dozen rings on his arms, looked Ragnar in the eye. 'I would still serve you,' he said, though without the humility of the last time he had asked.

'I have a new shipmaster,' Ragnar said, and said no more, and Kjartan and Sven rode on, though Sven gave me the evil sign with his left hand.

The new shipmaster was called Toki, a nickname for Thorbjorn, and he was a splendid sailor and a better warrior who told tales of rowing with the Svear into strange lands where no trees grew except birch and where winter covered the land for months. He claimed the folk there ate their own young, worshipped giants and had a third eye at the back of their heads, and some of us believed his tales.

We rowed south on the last of the summer tides, hugging the coast as we always did and spending the nights ashore on East Anglia's barren coast. We were going towards the River Temes which Ragnar said would take us deep inland to the northern boundary of Wessex.

Ragnar now commanded the fleet. Ivar the Boneless had returned to the lands he had conquered in Ireland, taking a gift of gold from Ragnar to his eldest son, while Ubba was ravaging Dalriada, the land north of Northumbria. 'Small pickings up there,' Ragnar said scornfully, but Ubba, like Ivar, had amassed so much treasure in his invasions of Northumbria, Mercia and East Anglia that he was not minded to gather more from Wessex, though, as I shall tell you in its proper place, Ubba was to change his mind later and come south.

But for the moment Ivar and Ubba were absent and so the main assault on Wessex would be led by Halfdan, the third brother, who was marching his land army out of East Anglia and would meet us somewhere on the Temes. Ragnar was not happy about the change of command, Halfdan, he muttered, was an impetuous fool, too hotheaded, but he cheered up when he remembered my tales of Alfred which confirmed that Wessex was led by men who put their hopes in the Christian god who had been shown to possess no power at all. We had Odin, we had Thor, we had our ships, we were warriors.

After four days we came to the Temes and rowed against its great current as the river slowly narrowed on us. On the first morning that we came to the river only the northern shore, which was East Anglian territory, was visible, but by midday the southern bank, that used to be the Kingdom of Kent and was now a part of Wessex, was a dim line on the horizon. By evening the banks were a half-mile apart, but there was little to see for the river flowed through flat, dull marshland. We used the tide when we could, blistered our hands on the oars when we could not, and so pulled upstream until, for the very first time, I came to Lundene.

I thought Eoferwic was a city, but Eoferwic was a village compared to Lundene. It was a vast place, thick with smoke from cooking fires, and built where Mercia, East Anglia and Wessex met. Burghred of Mercia was Lundene's lord, so it was Danish land now, and no one opposed us as we came to the astonishing bridge which stretched so far across the wide Temes.

Lundene. I came to love that place. Not as I love Bebbanburg, but there was a life to Lundene that I found nowhere else, because the city was like nowhere else. Alfred once told me that every wickedness under the sun was practised there, and I am glad to say he was right. He prayed for the place, I revelled in it, and I can still remember gawking at the city's two hills as Ragnar's ship ghosted against the current to come close to the bridge. It was a grey day and a spiteful rain was pitting the river, yet to me the city seemed to glow with sorcerous light.

It was really two cities built on two hills. The first, to the east, was the old city that the Romans had made, and it was there that the bridge began its span across the wide river and over the marshes on the southern bank. That first city was a place of stone buildings and had a stone wall, a real wall, not earth and wood, but masonry, high and wide, skirted by a ditch. The ditch had filled with rubbish and the wall was broken in places where it had been patched with timber, but so had the city itself where huge Roman buildings were buttressed by thatched wooden shacks where a few Mercians lived, though most were reluctant to make their homes in the old city. One of their kings had built himself a palace within the stone wall, and a great church, its lower half of masonry and upper parts of wood, had been made atop the hill, but most of the folk, as if fearing the Roman ghosts, lived outside the walls, in a new city of wood and thatch that stretched out to the west.

The old city once had wharves and quays, but they had long rotted so that the waterfront east of the bridge was a treacherous place of rotted pilings and broken piers that stabbed the river like shattered teeth. The new city, like the old, was on the river's northern bank, but was built on a low hill to the west, a half-mile upstream from the old, and had a shingle beach sloping up to the houses that ran along the riverside road. I have never seen a beach so foul, so stinking of carcasses and shit, so covered in rubbish, so stark with the slimy ribs of abandoned ships and loud with squalling gulls, but that was where our boats had to go and that meant we first had to negotiate the bridge.

The gods alone know how the Romans had built such a thing. A man could walk from one side of Eoferwic to the other and he would still not have walked the length of Lundene's bridge, though in that year of 871 the bridge was broken and it was no longer possible to walk its full length. Two arches in the centre had long fallen in, though the old Roman piers that had supported the missing roadway were still there and the river foamed treacherously as its water seethed past the broken piers. To make the bridge the Romans had sunk pilings into the Temes's bed, then into the tangle of foetid marshes on the southern bank, and the pilings were so close together that the water heaped up on their farther side, then fell through the gaps in a glistening rush. To reach the dirty beach by the new city we would have to shoot one of the two gaps, but neither was wide enough to let a ship through with its oars extended. 'It will be interesting,' Ragnar said drily.

'Can we do it?' I asked.

'They did it,' he said, pointing at ships beached upstream of the bridge, 'so we can.' We had anchored, waiting for the rest of the fleet to catch up. 'The Franks,' Ragnar went on, 'have been making bridges like this on all their rivers. You know why they do it?'

'To get across?' I guessed. It seemed an obvious answer.

'To stop us getting upriver,' Ragnar said. 'If I ruled Lundene I'd repair that bridge, so let's be grateful the English couldn't be bothered.'

We shot the gap in the bridge by waiting for the heart of the rising tide. The tide flows strongest halfway between its ebb and the flood, and that brought a surge of water that diminished the flow of the current cascading between the piers. In that short time we might get seven or eight ships through the gap and it was done by rowing at full speed towards the gap and, at the very last minute, raising the oar blades so they would clear the rotted piers, and the momentum of the ship should then carry her through. Not every ship made it on the first try. I watched two slew back, thump against a pier with the crash of breaking blades, then drift back downstream with crews of cursing men, but the *Wind-Viper* made it, almost coming to a stop just beyond the bridge, but we managed to get the frontmost oars in the water, hauled, and inch by inch we crept away from the sucking gap, then men from two ships anchored upstream managed to cast us lines and they hauled us away from the bridge until suddenly we were in slack water and could row her to the beach.

On the southern bank, beyond the dark marshes, where trees grew on low hills, horsemen watched us. They were West Saxons, and they would be counting ships to estimate the size of the Great Army. That was what Halfdan called it, the Great Army of the Danes come to take all of England, but so far we were anything but great. We would wait in Lundene to let more ships come and for more men to march down the long Roman roads from the north. Wessex could wait awhile as the Danes assembled.

And, as we waited, Brida, Rorik and I explored Lundene. Rorik had been sick again, and Sigrid had been reluctant to let him travel with his father, but Rorik pleaded with his mother to let him go, Ragnar assured her that the sea voyage would mend all the boy's ills, and so he was here. He was pale, but not sickly, and he was as excited as I was to see the city. Ragnar made me leave my arm rings and Serpent-Breath behind for, he said, the city was full of thieves. We wandered the newer part first, going through malodorous alleys where the houses were full of men working leather, beating at bronze or forging iron. Women sat at looms, a flock of sheep was being slaughtered in a yard, and there were shops selling pottery, salt, live eels, bread, cloth, weapons, any imaginable thing. Church bells set up a hideous clamour at every prayer time or whenever a corpse was carried for burial in the city's graveyards. Packs of dogs roamed the streets, red kites roosted everywhere, and smoke lay like a fog over the thatch that had all turned a dull black. I saw a wagon so loaded with thatching reed that the wagon itself was hidden by its heap of sagging reeds that scraped on the road and ripped and tore against the buildings on either side of the street as two slaves goaded and whipped the bleeding oxen. Men shouted at the slaves that the load was too big, but they went on whipping, and then a fight broke out when the wagon tore down a great piece of rotted roof. There were beggars everywhere; blind children, women without legs, a man with a weeping ulcer on his cheek. There were folk speaking languages I had never heard, folk in strange costumes who had come across the sea, and in the old city, which we explored the next day, I saw two men with skin the colour of chestnuts and Ravn told me later they came from Blaland, though he was not certain where that was. They wore thick robes, had curved swords, and were talking to a slave dealer whose premises were full of captured English folk who would be shipped to the mysterious Blaland. The dealer called to us. 'You three belong to anyone?' He was only half joking.

'To Earl Ragnar,' Brida said, 'who would love to pay you a visit.'

'Give his lordship my respects,' the dealer said, then spat, and eyed us as we walked away.

The buildings of the old city were extraordinary. They were Roman work, high and stout, and even though their walls were broken and their roofs had fallen in they still astonished. Some were three or even four floors high and we chased each other up and down their abandoned stairways. Few English folk lived here, though many Danes were now occupying the houses as the army assembled. Brida said that sensible people would not live in a Roman town because of the ghosts that haunted the old buildings, and maybe she was right though I had seen no ghosts in Eoferwic, but her mention of spectres made us all nervous as we peered down a flight of steps into a dark, pillared cellar.

We stayed in Lundene for weeks and even when Halfdan's army reached us we did not move west. Mounted bands did ride out to forage, but the Great Army still gathered and some men grumbled we were waiting too long, that the West Saxons were being given precious time to ready themselves, but Halfdan insisted on lingering. The West Saxons sometimes rode close to the city, and twice there were fights between our horsemen and their horsemen, but after a while, as Yule approached, the West Saxons must have decided we would do nothing till winter's end and their patrols stopped coming close to the city.

'We're not waiting for spring,' Ragnar told me, 'but for deep winter.'

'Why?'

'Because no army marches in winter,' he said wolfishly, 'so the West Saxons will all be at home, sitting around their fires and praying to their feeble god. By spring, Uhtred, all England will be ours.'

We all worked that early winter. I hauled firewood, and when I was not hauling logs from the wooded hills north of the city, I was learning the skills of the sword. Ragnar had asked Toki, his new shipmaster, to be my teacher and he was a good one. He watched me rehearse the basic cuts, then told me to forget them. 'In a shield wall,' he said, 'it's savagery that wins. Skill helps, and cunning is good, but savagery wins. Get one of these,' he held out a sax with a thick blade, much thicker than my old sax. I despised the sax for it was much shorter than Serpent-Breath and far less beautiful, but Toki wore one beside his proper sword, and he persuaded me that in the shield wall the short, stout blade was better. 'You've no room to swing or hack in a shield wall,' he said, 'but you can thrust, and a short blade uses less room in a crowded fight. Crouch and stab, bring it up into their groins.' He made Brida hold a shield and pretend to be the enemy, and then, with me on his left, he cut at her from above and she instinctively raised the shield. 'Stop!' he said, and she froze into stillness. 'See?' he told me, pointing at the raised shield, 'your partner makes the enemy raise their shield, then you can slice into their groin.' He taught me a dozen other moves, and I practised because I liked it and the more I practised the more muscle I grew and the more skilful I became.

We usually practised in the Roman arena. That is what Toki called it, the arena, though what the word meant neither he nor I had any idea, but it was, in a place of extraordinary things, astonishing. Imagine an open space as large as a field surrounded by a great circle of tiered stone where weeds now grew from the crumbling mortar. The Mercians, I later learned, had held their folkmoots here, but Toki said the Romans had used it for displays of fighting in which men died. Maybe that was another of his fantastic stories, but the arena was huge, unimaginably huge, a thing of mystery, the work of giants, dwarfing us, so big that all the Great Army could have collected inside and there would still have been room for two more armies just as big on the tiered seats.

Yule came, and the winter feast was held and the army vomited in the streets and still we did not march, but shortly afterwards the leaders of the Great Army met in the palace next to the arena. Brida and I, as usual, were required to be Ravn's eyes and he, as usual, told us what we were seeing.

The meeting was held in the church of the palace, a Roman building with a roof shaped like a half-barrel on which the moon and stars were painted, though the blue and golden paint was peeling and discoloured now. A great fire had been lit in the centre of the church and it was filling the high roof with swirling smoke. Halfdan presided from the altar, and around him were the chief Earls. One was an ugly man with a blunt face, a big brown beard and a finger missing from his left hand. 'That is Bagseg,' Ravn told us, 'and he calls himself a king, though he's no better than anyone else.' Bagseg, it seemed, had come from Denmark in the summer, bringing eighteen ships and nearly six hundred men. Next to him was a tall, gloomy man with white hair and a twitching face. 'Earl Sidroc,' Ravn told us, 'and his son must be with him?'

'Thin man,' Brida said, 'with a dripping nose.'

'Earl Sidroc the Younger. He's always sniffing. My son is there?'

'Yes,' I said, 'next to a very fat man who keeps whispering to him and grinning.'

'Harald!' Ravn said. 'I wondered if he would turn up. He's another king.'

'Really?' Brida asked.

'Well, he calls himself king, and he certainly rules over a few muddy fields and a herd of smelly pigs.'

All those men had come from Denmark, and there were others besides. Earl Fraena had brought men from Ireland, and Earl Osbern who had provided the garrison for Lundene while the army gathered, and together these kings and Earls had assembled well over two thousand men.

Osbern and Sidroc proposed crossing the river and striking directly south. This, they argued, would cut Wessex in two and the eastern part, which used to be the Kingdom of Kent, could then be taken quickly. 'There has to be much treasure in Contwaraburg,' Sidroc insisted, 'it's the central shrine of their religion.'

'And while we march on their shrine,' Ragnar said, 'they will come up behind us. Their power is not in the east, but in the west. Defeat the west and all Wessex falls. We can take Contwaraburg once we've beaten the west.'

This was the argument. Either take the easy part of Wessex or else attack their major strongholds that lay to the west, and two merchants were asked to speak. Both men were Danes who had been trading in Readingum only two weeks before. Readingum lay a few miles upriver and was on the edge of Wessex, and they claimed to have heard that King Æthelred and his brother, Alfred, were gathering the shire forces from the west and the two merchants reckoned the enemy army would number at least three thousand.

'Of whom only three hundred will be proper fighting men,' Halfdan interjected sarcastically, and was rewarded by the sound of men banging swords or spears against their shields. It was while this noise echoed under the church's barrel roof that a new group of warriors entered, led by a very tall and very burly man in a black tunic. He looked formidable, clean-shaven, angry and very rich for his black cloak had an enormous brooch of amber mounted in gold, his arms were heavy with golden rings and he wore a golden hammer on a thick golden chain about his neck. The warriors made way for him, his arrival causing silence among the crowd nearest to him, and the silence spread as he walked up the church until the mood, that had been of celebration, suddenly seemed wary.

'Who is it?' Ravn whispered to me.

'Very tall,' I said, 'many arm rings.'

'Gloomy,' Brida put in, 'dressed in black.'

'Ah! The Earl Guthrum,' Ravn said

'Guthrum?'

'Guthrum the Unlucky,' Ravn said.

'With all those arm rings?'

'You could give Guthrum the world,' Ravn said, 'and he would still believe you had cheated him.'

'He has a bone hanging in his hair,' Brida said.

'You must ask him about that,' Ravn said, evidently amused, but he would say no more about the bone, which was evidently a rib and was tipped with gold.

I learned Guthrum the Unlucky was an Earl from Denmark who had been wintering at Beamfleot, a place that lay a good distance east of Lundene on the northern side of the Temes estuary, and once he had greeted the men bunched about the altar he announced that he had brought fourteen ships upriver. No one applauded. Guthrum, who had the saddest, sourest face I had ever seen, stared at the assembly like a man standing trial and expecting a dire verdict. 'We had decided,' Ragnar broke the uncomfortable silence, 'to go west.' No such decision had been made, but nor did anyone contradict Ragnar. 'Those ships that are already through the bridge,' Ragnar went on, 'will take their crews upstream and the rest of the army will march on foot or horseback.'

'My ships must go upstream,' Guthrum said.

'They are through the bridge?'

'They will still go upstream,' Guthrum insisted, thus letting us know that his fleet was below the bridge.

'It would be better,' Ragnar said, 'if we went tomorrow.' In the last few days the whole of the Great Army had assembled in Lundene, marching in from the settlements east and north where some had been quartered, and the longer we waited, the more of the precious food supply would be consumed.

'My ships go upstream,' Guthrum said flatly.

'He's worried,' Ravn whispered to me, 'that he can't carry away the plunder on horseback. He wants his ships so he can fill them with treasure.'

'Why let him come?' I asked. It was plain no one liked Earl Guthrum, and his arrival seemed as unwelcome as it was inconvenient, but Ravn just shrugged the question off. Guthrum, it seemed, was here, and if he was here he must take part. That still seems incomprehensible to me, just as I still did not understand why Ivar and Ubba were not joining the attack on Wessex.

It was true that both men were rich and scarcely needed more riches, but for years they had talked of conquering the West Saxons and now both had simply turned away. Guthrum did not need land or wealth either, but he thought he did, so he came. That was the Danish way. Men served in a campaign if they wished, or else they stayed at home, and there was no single authority among the Danes. Halfdan was the Great Army's ostensible leader, but he did not frighten men as his two older brothers did and so he could do nothing without the agreement of the other chieftains. An army, I learned in time, needs a head. It needs one man to lead it, but give an army two leaders and you halve its strength.

It took two days to get Guthrum's ships past the bridge. They were beautiful things, those ships, larger than most Danish boats, and each decorated at prow and stern with black painted serpent heads. His men, and there were many of them, all wore black. Even their shields were painted black, and while I thought Guthrum to be one of the most miserable men I had ever seen, I had to confess his troops were impressive. We might have lost two days, but we had gained the black warriors.

And what was there to fear? The Great Army had gathered, it was midwinter when no one fought so the enemy should not be expecting us, and that enemy was led by a king and a prince more interested in prayer than in fighting. All Wessex lay before us and common report said that Wessex was as rich a country as any in all the world, rivalling Frankia for its treasures, and inhabited by monks and nuns whose houses were stuffed with gold, spilling over with silver and ripe for slaughter. We would all be rich.

So we went to war.

Ships on the winter Temes. Ships sliding past brittle reeds and leafless willows and bare alders. Wet oar blades shining in the pale sunlight. The prows of our ships bore their beasts to quell the spirits of the land we invaded, and it was good land with rich fields, though all were deserted. There was almost a celebratory air to that brief

153

voyage, a celebration unspoiled by the presence of Guthrum's dark ships. Men oar-walked, the same feat I had watched Ragnar perform on that far off day when his three ships had appeared off Bebbanburg. I tried it myself and raised a huge cheer when I fell in. It looked easy to run along the oar bank, leaping from shaft to shaft, but a rower only had to twitch an oar to cause a man to slip and the river water was bitterly cold so that Ragnar made me strip off my wet clothes and wear his bearskin cloak until I was warm. Men sang, the ships forged against the current, the far hills to north and south slowly closed on the river's banks and, as evening came, we saw the first horsemen on the southern skyline. Watching us.

We reached Readingum at dusk. Each of Ragnar's three ships was loaded with spades, many of them forged by Ealdwulf, and our first task was to start making a wall. As more ships came, more men helped, and by nightfall our camp was protected by a long, straggling earth wall which would have been hardly any obstacle to an attacking force for it was merely a low mound that was easy to cross, but no one did come and assault us, and no Wessex army appeared next morning and so we were free to make the wall higher and more formidable.

Readingum was built where the River Kenet flows into the Temes, and so our wall was built between the two rivers. It enclosed the small town which had been abandoned by its inhabitants and provided shelter for most of the ships' crews. The land army was still out of sight for they had marched along the north bank of the Temes, in Mercian territory, and were seeking a ford which they found further upstream so that our wall was virtually finished by the time they marched in. At first we thought it was the West Saxon army coming, but it was Halfdan's men, marching out of enemy territory which they had found deserted.

The wall was high now, and because there were deep woods to the south, we had cut trees to make a palisade along its whole length that was about eight hundred paces. In front of the wall we dug a ditch that flooded when we broke through the two rivers' banks, and across the ditch we were making four bridges guarded by wooden forts. This was our base. From here we could march deep into Wessex, and we needed to, for, with so many men and now horses inside the wall, there was a risk of hunger unless we found supplies of grain, hay and cattle. We had brought barrels of ale and a large amount of flour, salt meat and dried fish in the ships, but it was astonishing how fast those great heaps diminished.

The poets, when they speak of war, talk of the shield wall, they talk of the spears and arrows flying, of the blade beating on the shield, of the heroes who fall and the spoils of the victors, but I was to discover that war was really about food. About feeding men and horses. About finding food. The army that eats wins. And, if you keep horses in a fortress, it is about shovelling dung. Just two days after the land army came to Readingum, we were short of food and the two Sidrocs, father and son, led a large force west into enemy territory to find stores of food for men and horses, and instead they found the fyrd of Berrocscire.

We learned later that the whole idea of attacking in winter was no surprise to the West Saxons after all. The Danes were good at spying, their merchants exploring the places the warriors would go, but the West Saxons had their own men in Lundene and they knew how many men we were, and when we would march, and they had assembled an army to meet us. They had also sought help from the men of southern Mercia, where Danish rule was lightest, and Berrocscire lay immediately north of the West Saxon border and the men of Berrocscire had crossed the river to help their neighbours and their fyrd was led by an Ealdorman called Æthelwulf.

Was it my uncle? There were many men called Æthelwulf, but how many were Ealdormen in Mercia? I admit I felt strange when I heard the name, and I thought of the mother I had never met. In my mind she was the woman who was ever kind, ever gentle, ever loving and I thought she must be watching me from somewhere, heaven or Asgard or wherever our souls go in the long darkness, and I knew she would hate that I was with the army that marched against her brother, and so that night I was in a black mood.

But so was the Great Army for my uncle, if Æthelwulf was indeed my uncle, had trounced the two Earls. Their foraging party had walked into an ambush and the men of Berrocscire had killed twenty-one Danes and taken another eight prisoner. The Englishmen had lost a few men themselves, and yielded one prisoner, but they had gained the victory, and it made no difference that the Danes had been outnumbered. The Danes expected to win, and instead they had been chased home without the food we needed. They felt shamed and a shudder went through the army because they did not think mere Englishmen could beat them.

We were not starving yet, but the horses were desperately short of hay which, anyway, was not the best food for them, but we had no oats and so forage parties simply cut whatever winter grass we could find beyond our growing wall and the day after Æthelwulf's victory Rorik, Brida and I were in one of those groups, slashing at grass with long knives and stuffing sacks with the poor feed, when the army of Wessex came.

They must have been encouraged by Æthelwulf's victory, for now the whole enemy army attacked Readingum. The first I knew of it was the sound of screaming from farther west, then I saw horsemen galloping among our forage parties, hacking down with swords or skewering men with spears, and the three of us just ran, and I heard the hooves behind and snatched a look and saw a man riding at us with a spear and knew one of us must die and I took Brida's hand to drag her out of his path and just then an arrow shot from Readingum's wall slapped into the horseman's face and he twisted away, blood pouring from his cheek, and meanwhile panicking men were piling around the two central bridges and the West Saxon horsemen, seeing it, galloped towards them. The three of us half waded and half swam the ditch, and two men hauled us, wet, muddy and shivering, up across the wall.

It was chaos outside now. The foragers crowding at the ditch's far side were being hacked down, and then the Wessex infantry appeared, band after band of them emerging from the far woods to fill the fields. I ran back to the house where Ragnar was lodging and found Serpent-Breath beneath the cloaks where I hid her, and I strapped her on and ran out to find Ragnar. He had gone north, to the bridge close beside the Temes, and Brida and I caught up with his men there. 'You shouldn't come,' I told Brida. 'Stay with Rorik.' Rorik was younger than us and, after getting soaked in the ditch he had started shivering and feeling sick and I had made him stay behind.

Brida ignored me. She had equipped herself with a spear and looked excited, though nothing was happening yet. Ragnar was staring over the wall, and more men were assembling at the gate, but Ragnar did not open it to cross the bridge. He did glance back to see how many men he had. 'Shields!' he shouted, for, in their haste, some men had come with nothing but swords or axes, and those men now ran to fetch their shields. I had no shield, but nor was I supposed to be there and Ragnar did not see me.

What he saw was the end of a slaughter as the West Saxon horsemen chopped into the last of the foragers. A few of the enemy were put down by our arrows, but neither the Danes nor the English had many bowmen. I like bowmen. They can kill at a great distance and, even if their arrows do not kill, they make an enemy nervous. Advancing into arrows is a blind business, for you must keep your head beneath the rim of the shield, but shooting a bow is a great skill. It looks easy, and every child has a bow and some arrows, but a man's bow, a bow capable of killing a stag at a hundred paces, is a huge thing, carved from yew, and needing immense strength to haul, and the arrows fly wild unless a man has practised constantly, and so we never had more than a handful of archers. I never mastered the bow. With a spear, an axe or a sword I was lethal, but with a bow I was like most men, useless.

I sometimes wonder why we did not stay behind our wall. It was virtually finished, and to reach it the enemy must cross the ditch or file over the four bridges, and they would have been forced to do that under a hail of arrows, spears and throwing axes. They would surely have failed, but then they might have besieged us behind that wall and so Ragnar decided to attack them. Not just Ragnar. While Ragnar was gathering men at the northern gate, Halfdan had been doing the same at the southern end, and when both believed they had enough men, and while the enemy infantry was still some two hundred paces away, Ragnar ordered the gate opened and led his men through.

The West Saxon army, under its great dragon banner, was advancing towards the central bridges, evidently thinking that the slaughter there was a foretaste of more slaughter to come. They had no ladders, so how they thought they would cross the newly-made wall I do not know, but sometimes in battle a kind of madness descends and men do things without reason. The men of Wessex had no reason to concentrate on the centre of our wall, especially as they could not hope to cross it, but they did, and now our men swarmed from the two flanking gates to attack them from north and south.

'Shield wall!' Ragnar roared, 'shield wall!'

You can hear a shield wall being made. The best shields are made of lime, or else of willow, and the wood knocks together as men overlap the shields. Left side of the shield in front of your neighbour's right side, that way the enemy, most of whom are right-handed, must try to thrust through two layers of wood.

'Make it tight!' Ragnar called. He was in the centre of the shield wall, in front of his ragged eagle wing standard, and he was one of the few men with an expensive helmet which would mark him to the enemy as a chieftain, a man to be killed. Ragnar still used my father's helmet, the beautiful one made by Ealdwulf with the face-piece and the inlay of silver. He also wore a mail shirt, again one of the few men to possess such a treasure. Most men were armoured in leather.

The enemy was turning outwards to meet us, making their own shield wall, and I saw a group of horsemen galloping up their centre behind the dragon banner. I thought I saw Beocca's red hair among them and that made me certain Alfred was there, probably among a gaggle of black-robed priests who were doubt-less praying for our deaths.

The West Saxon shield wall was longer than ours. It was not only longer, but thicker, because while our wall was backed by three ranks of men, theirs had five or six. Good sense would have dictated that we either stayed where we were and let them attack us, or that we should have retreated back across the bridge and ditch, but more Danes were coming to thicken Ragnar's ranks and Ragnar himself was in no mood to be sensible. 'Just kill them!' he screamed, 'just kill them! Kill them!' And he led the line forward and, without any pause, the Danes gave a great war shout and surged with him. Usually the shield walls spend hours staring at each other, calling out insults, threatening, and working up the courage to that most awful of moments when wood meets wood and blade meets blade, but Ragnar's blood was fired and he did not care. He just charged.

That attack made no sense, but Ragnar was furious. He had been offended by Æthelwulf's victory, and insulted by the way their horsemen had cut down our foragers, and all he wanted to do was hack into the Wessex ranks, and somehow his passion spread through his men so that they howled as they ran forward. There is something terrible about men eager for battle.

A heartbeat before the shields clashed, our rearmost men threw their spears. Some had three or four spears that they hurled one after the other, launching them over the heads of our front ranks. There were spears coming back, and I plucked one from the turf and hurled it back as hard as I could.

I was in the rearmost rank, pushed back there by men who told me to get out of their way, but I advanced with them and Brida, grinning with mischief, came with me. I told her to go back to the town, but she just stuck her tongue out at me and then I heard the hammering crash, the wooden thunder, of shields meeting shields. That was followed by the sound of spears striking lime-wood, the ringing of blade on blade, but I saw nothing of it because I was not then tall enough, but the shock of the shield walls made the men in front of me reel back, then they were pushing forward again, trying to force their own front rank through the West Saxon shields. The right-hand side of our wall was bending back where the enemy outflanked us, but our reinforcements were hurrying to that place, and the West Saxons lacked the courage to charge home. Those West Saxons had been at the rear of their advancing army, and the rear is always where the timid men congregate. The real fight was to my front and the noise there was of blows, iron shield boss on shield-wood, blades on shields, men's feet shuffling, the clangour of weapons, and few voices except those wailing in pain or in a sudden scream. Brida dropped onto all fours and wrig-

159

gled between the legs of the men in front of her, and I saw she was lancing her spear forward to give the blow that comes beneath the shield's rim. She lunged into a man's ankle, he stumbled, an axe fell and there was a gap in the enemy line and our line bulged forward, and I followed, using Serpent-Breath as a spear, jabbing at men's boots, then Ragnar gave a mighty roar, a shout to stir the gods in the great sky halls of Asgard, and the shout asked for one more great effort. Swords chopped, axes swung, and I could sense the enemy retreating from the fury of the Northmen.

Good Lord deliver us.

Blood on the grass now, so much blood that the ground was slick, and there were bodies that had to be stepped over as our shield wall thrust forward, leaving Brida and me behind, and I saw her hands were red because blood had seeped down the long ash shaft of her spear. She licked the blood and gave me a sly smile. Halfdan's men were fighting on the enemy's farther side now, their battle noise suddenly louder than ours because the West Saxons were retreating from Ragnar's attack, but one man, tall and well-built, resisted us. He had a mail coat belted with a red leather sword belt and a helmet even more glorious than Ragnar's, for the Englishman's helmet had a silver boar modelled on its crown, and I thought for a moment it could be King Æthelred himself, but this man was too tall, and Ragnar shouted at his men to stand aside and he swung his sword at the boar-helmeted enemy who parried with his shield, lunged with his sword, and Ragnar took the blow on his own shield and rammed it forward to crash against the man who stepped back, tripped on a corpse and Ragnar swung his sword overhand, as if he were killing an ox, and the blade chopped down onto the mail coat as a rush of enemy came to save their lord.

A charge of Danes met them, shield on shield, and Ragnar was roaring his victory and stabbing down into the fallen man, and suddenly there were no more Wessex men resisting us, unless they were dead or wounded, and their army was running, their king and their prince both spurring away on horseback surrounded by priests, and we jeered and cursed them, told them they were women, that they fought like girls, that they were cowards.

160

And then we rested, catching breath on a field of blood, our own corpses among the enemy dead, and Ragnar saw me then, and saw Brida, and laughed. 'What are you two doing here?'

For answer Brida held up her bloodied spear and Ragnar glanced at Serpent-Breath and saw her reddened tip. 'Fools,' he said, but fondly, and then one of our men brought a West Saxon prisoner and made him inspect the lord whom Ragnar had killed. 'Who is he?' Ragnar demanded.

I translated for him.

The man made the sign of the cross. 'It is the Lord Æthelwulf,' he said.

And I said nothing.

'What did he say?' Ragnar asked.

'It is my uncle,' I said.

'Ælfric?' Ragnar was astonished. 'Ælfric from Northumbria?'

I shook my head. 'He is my mother's brother,' I explained, 'Æthelwulf of Mercia.' I did not know that he was my mother's brother, perhaps there was another Æthelwulf in Mercia, but I felt certain all the same that this was Æthelwulf, my kin, and the man who had won the victory over the Earls Sidroc. Ragnar, the previous day's defeat revenged, whooped for joy while I stared into the dead man's face. I had never known him, so why was I sad? He had a long face with a fair beard and a trimmed moustache. A good-looking man, I thought, and he was family, and that seemed strange for I knew no family except Ragnar, Ravn, Rorik and Brida.

Ragnar had his men strip Æthelwulf of his armour and take his precious helmet, and then, because the Ealdorman had fought so bravely, Ragnar left the corpse its other clothes and put a sword into its hand so that the gods could take the Mercian's soul to the great hall where brave warriors feast with Odin.

And perhaps the Valkyries did take his soul, because next morning, when we went out to bury the dead, Ealdorman Æthelwulf's body was gone.

I heard later, much later, that he was indeed my uncle. I also heard that some of his own men had crept back to the field that night and somehow found their lord's body and taken it to his own country for a Christian burial.

And perhaps that is true too. Or perhaps Æthelwulf is in Odin's corpse-hall.

But we had seen the West Saxons off. And we were still hungry. So it was time to fetch the enemy's food.

Why did I fight for the Danes? All lives have questions, and that one still haunts me, though in truth there was no mystery. To my young mind the alternative was to be sitting in some monastery learning to read, and give a boy a choice like that and he would fight for the devil rather than scratch on a tile or make marks on a clay tablet. And there was Ragnar, whom I loved, and who sent his three ships across the Temes to find hay and oats stored in Mercian villages and he found just enough so that by the time the army marched westwards our horses were in reasonable condition.

We were marching on Æbbanduna, another frontier town on the Temes between Wessex and Mercia, and, according to our prisoner, a place where the West Saxons had amassed their supplies. Take Æbbanduna and Æthelred's army would be short of food, Wessex would fall, England would vanish and Odin would triumph.

There was the small matter of defeating the West Saxon army first, but we marched just four days after routing them in front of the walls of Readingum, so we were blissfully confident that they were doomed. Rorik stayed behind, for he was sick again, and the many hostages, like the Mercian twins Ceolberht and Ceolnoth, also stayed in Readingum, guarded there by the small garrison we left to watch over the precious ships.

The rest of us marched or rode. I was among the older of the boys who accompanied the army, our job in battle was to carry the spare shields that could be pushed forward through the ranks in battle. Shields got chopped to pieces in fighting. I have often seen warriors fighting with a sword or axe in one hand, and nothing but the iron shield boss hung with scraps of wood in the other. Brida also came with us, mounted behind Ravn on his horse, and for a time I walked with them, listening as Ravn rehearsed the opening lines of a poem called the Fall of the West Saxons. He had got as far as listing our heroes, and describing how they readied themselves for battle, when one of those heroes, the gloomy Earl Guthrum, rode alongside us. 'You look well,' he greeted Ravn in a tone which suggested that was a condition unlikely to last.

'I cannot look at all,' Ravn said. He liked puns.

Guthrum, swathed in a black cloak, looked down at the river. We were advancing along a low range of hills and, even in the winter sunlight, the river valley looked lush. 'Who will be King of Wessex?' he asked.

'Halfdan?' Ravn suggested mischievously.

'Big kingdom,' Guthrum said gloomily. 'Could do with an older man.' He looked at me sourly. 'Who's that?'

'You forget I am blind,' Ravn said, 'so who is who? Or are you asking me which older man you think should be made king? Me, perhaps?'

'No, no! The boy leading your horse. Who is he?'

'That is the Earl Uhtred,' Ravn said grandly, 'who understands that poets are of such importance that their horses must be led by mere Earls.'

'Uhtred? A Saxon?'

'Are you a Saxon, Uhtred?'

'I'm a Dane,' I said.

'And a Dane,' Ravn went on, 'who wet his sword at Readingum. Wet it, Guthrum, with Saxon blood.' That was a barbed comment, for Guthrum's black-clothed men had not fought outside the walls.

'And who's the girl behind you?'

'Brida,' Ravn said, 'who will one day be a skald and a sorceress.'

Guthrum did not know what to say to that. He glowered at his horse's mane for a few strides, then returned to his original subject. 'Does Ragnar want to be king?'

'Ragnar wants to kill people,' Ravn said. 'My son's ambitions are very few; merely to hear jokes, solve riddles, get drunk, give rings, lie belly to belly with women, eat well and go to Odin.'

'Wessex needs a strong man,' Guthrum said obscurely. 'A man who understands how to govern.'

'Sounds like a husband,' Ravn said.

'We take their strongholds,' Guthrum said, 'but we leave half their land untouched! Even Northumbria is only half garrisoned. Mercia has sent men to Wessex, and they're supposed to be on our side. We win, Ravn, but we don't finish the job.'

'And how do we do that?' Ravn asked.

'More men, more ships, more deaths.'

'Deaths?'

'Kill them all!' Guthrum said with a sudden vehemence, 'every last one! Not a Saxon alive.'

'Even the women?' Ravn asked.

'We could leave some young ones,' Guthrum said grudgingly, then scowled at me. 'What are you looking at, boy?'

'Your bone, lord,' I said, nodding at the gold-tipped bone hanging in his hair.

He touched the bone. 'It's one of my mother's ribs,' he said. 'She was a good woman, a wonderful woman, and she goes with me wherever I go. You could do worse, Ravn, than make a song for my mother. You knew her, didn't you?'

'I did indeed,' Ravn said blandly. 'I knew her well enough, Guthrum, to worry that I lack the poetic skills to make a song worthy of such an illustrious woman.'

The mockery flew straight past Guthrum the Unlucky. 'You could try,' he said. 'You could try, and I would pay much gold for a good song about her.'

He was mad, I thought, mad as an owl at midday, and then I forgot him because the army of Wessex was ahead, barring our road and offering battle.

The dragon banner of Wessex was flying on the summit of a long low hill that lay athwart our road. To reach Æbbanduna, which evidently lay a short way beyond the hill and was hidden by it, we would need to attack up the slope and across that ridge of open grassland, but to the north, where the hills fell away to the River Temes, there was a track along the river which suggested we might skirt the enemy position. To stop us he would need to come down the hill and give battle on level ground.

Halfdan called the Danish leaders together and they talked for a long time, evidently disagreeing about what should be done. Some men wanted to attack uphill and scatter the enemy where they were, but others advised fighting the West Saxons in the flat river meadows, and in the end Earl Guthrum the Unlucky persuaded them to do both. That, of course, meant splitting our army into two, but even so I thought it was a clever idea. Ragnar, Guthrum and the two Earls Sidroc would go down to the lower ground, thus threatening to pass by the enemy-held hill, while Halfdan, with Harald and Bagseg, would stay on the high ground and advance towards the dragon banner on the ridge. That way the enemy might hesitate to attack Ragnar for fear that Halfdan's troops would fall on their rear. Most likely, Ragnar said, the enemy would decide not to fight at all, but instead retreat to Æbbanduna where we could besiege them. 'Better to have them penned in a fortress than roaming around,' he said cheerfully.

'Better still,' Ravn commented drily, 'not to divide the army.'

'They're only West Saxons,' Ragnar said dismissively.

It was already afternoon and, because it was winter, the day was short so there was not much time, though Ragnar thought there was more than enough daylight remaining to finish off Æthelred's troops. Men touched their charms, kissed sword hilts, hefted shields, then we were marching down the hill, going off the chalk grasslands into the river valley. Once there, we were half hidden by the leafless trees, but now and again I could glimpse Halfdan's men advancing along the hill crests and I could see there were West Saxon troops waiting for them, which suggested that Guthrum's plan was working and that we could march clear around the enemy's northern flank. 'What we do then,' Ragnar said, 'is climb up behind them, and the bastards will be trapped. We'll kill them all!'

'One of them has to stay alive,' Ravn said.

'One? Why?'

'To tell the tale, of course. Look for their poet. He'll be handsome. Find him and let him live.'

Ragnar laughed. There were, I suppose, about eight hundred of us, slightly fewer than the contingent that had stayed with Halfdan, and the enemy army was probably slightly larger than our two forces combined, but we were all warriors and many of the West Saxon fyrd were farmers forced to war and so we saw nothing but victory.

Then, as our leading troops marched out of an oakwood, we saw the enemy had followed our example and divided their own army into two. One half was waiting on the hill for Halfdan while the other half had come to meet us.

Alfred led our opponents. I knew that because I could see Beocca's red hair and, later on, I glimpsed Alfred's long anxious face in the fighting. His brother, King Æthelred, had stayed on the heights where, instead of waiting for Halfdan to assault him, he was advancing to make his own attack. The Saxons, it seemed, were avid for battle.

So we gave it to them.

Our forces made shield wedges to attack their shield wall. We called on Odin, we howled our war cries, we charged, and the West Saxon line did not break, it did not buckle, but instead held fast and so the slaughterwork began.

Ravn told me time and again that destiny was everything. Fate rules. The three spinners sit at the foot of the tree of life and they make our lives and we are their playthings, and though we think we make our own choices, all our fates are in the spinners' threads. Destiny is everything, and that day, though I did not know it, my destiny was spun. *Wyrd biđ ful ãræd*, fate is unstoppable.

What is there to say of the battle that the West Saxons said happened at a place they called Æsc's Hill? I assume Æsc was the thegn who had once owned the land, and his fields received a rich tilth of blood and bone that day. The poets could fill a thousand lines telling what happened, but battle is battle. Men die. In the shield wall it is sweat, terror, cramp, half blows, full blows, screaming and cruel death.

There were really two battles at Æsc's Hill, the one above and the other below, and the deaths came swiftly. Harald and Bagseg died, Sidroc the Older watched his son die and then was cut down himself, and with him died Earl Osbern and Earl Fraena, and so many other good warriors, and the Christian priests were calling on their god to give the West Saxon swords strength, and that day Odin was sleeping and the Christian god was awake.

We were driven back. On top of the hill and in the valley we were driven back, and it was only the weariness of the enemy that stopped a full slaughter and let our survivors retreat from the fight, leaving their companions behind in their death blood. Toki was one of them. The shipmaster, so full of sword skill, died in the ditch behind which Alfred's shield wall had waited for us. Ragnar, blood all over his face and with enemy's blood matted in his unbound hair, could not believe it. The West Saxons were jeering.

The West Saxons had fought like fiends, like men inspired, like men who know their whole future rested on a winter afternoon's work, and they had beaten us.

Destiny is all. We were defeated and went back to Readingum.

Six

These days, whenever Englishmen talk of the battle of Æsc's Hill, they speak of God giving the West Saxons the victory because King Æthelred and his brother Alfred were praying when the Danes appeared.

Maybe they are right. I can well believe that Alfred was praying, but it helped that he chose his position well. His shield wall was just beyond a deep, winter-flooded ditch and the Danes had to fight their way up from that mud-bottomed trough and they died as they came, and men who would rather have been farmers than warriors beat off an assault of sword-Danes, and Alfred led the farmers, encouraged them, told them they could win, and put his faith in God. I think the ditch was the reason that he won, but he would doubtless have said that God dug the ditch.

Halfdan lost as well. He was attacking uphill, climbing a smooth gentle slope, but it was late in the day and the sun was in his men's eyes, or so they said afterwards, and King Æthelred, like Alfred, encouraged his men so well that they launched a howling downhill attack that bit deep into Halfdan's ranks, who became discouraged when they saw the lower army retreating from Alfred's stubborn defence. There were no angels with fiery swords present, despite what the priests now say. At least I saw none. There was a waterlogged ditch, there was a battle, the Danes lost and destiny changed.

I did not know the Danes could lose, but at fourteen years old I learned that lesson and, for the first time I heard Saxon cheers and jeers, and something hidden in my soul stirred.

And we went back to Readingum.

There was plenty more fighting as winter turned to spring and spring to summer. New Danes came with the new year, and our ranks were thus restored, and we won all our subsequent encounters with the West Saxons, twice fighting them at Basengas in Hamptonscir, then at Mereton, which was in Wiltunscir and thus deep inside their territory, and again in Wiltunscir at Wiltun, and each time we won, which meant we held the battlefield at day's end, but at none of those clashes did we destroy the enemy. Instead we wore each other out, fought each other to a bloody standstill, and as summer caressed the land we were no nearer conquering Wessex than we had been at Yule.

But we did manage to kill King Æthelred. That happened at Wiltun where the king received a deep axe wound to his left shoulder and, though he was hurried from the field, and though priests and monks prayed over his sickbed, and though cunning men treated him with herbs and leeches, he died after a few days.

And he left an heir, an ætheling, Æthelwold. He was Prince Æthelwold, eldest son of Æthelred, but he was not old enough to be his own master for, like me, he was only fifteen, yet even so some men proclaimed his right to be named the King of Wessex, but Alfred had far more powerful friends and he deployed the legend of the Pope having invested him as the future king. The legend must have worked its magic for, sure enough, at the meeting of the Wessex witan, which was the assembly of nobles, bishops and powerful men, Alfred was acclaimed as the new king. Perhaps the witan had no choice. Wessex, after all, was desperately fighting off Halfdan's forces and it would have been a bad time to make a boy into a king. Wessex needed a leader and so the witan chose Alfred, and Æthelwold and his younger brother were whisked off to an abbey where they were told to get on with their lessons. 'Alfred should have murdered the little bastards,' Ragnar told me cheerfully, and he was probably right.

So Alfred, the youngest of six brothers, was now the King of Wessex. The year was 871. I did not know it then, but Alfred's wife had just given birth to a daughter he named Æthelflaed. Æthelflaed was fifteen years younger than me and even if I had known of her birth I would have dismissed it as unimportant. But destiny is all. The spinners work and we do their will whether we will or not.

Alfred's first act as king, other than to bury his brother and put his nephews away in a monastery and have himself crowned and go to church a hundred times and weary God's ears with unceasing prayers, was to send messengers to Halfdan proposing a conference. He wanted peace, it seemed, and as it was midsummer and we were no nearer to victory than we had been at midwinter, Halfdan agreed to the meeting, and so, with his army's leaders and a bodyguard of picked men, he went to Baðum.

I went too, with Ragnar, Ravn and Brida. Rorik, still sick, stayed in Readingum and I was sorry he did not see Baðum for, though it was only a small town, it was almost as marvellous as Lundene. There was a bath in the town's centre, not a small tub, but an enormous building with pillars and a crumbling roof above a great stone hollow that was filled with hot water. The water came from the underworld and Ragnar was certain that it was heated by the forges of the dwarves. The bath, of course, had been built by the Romans, as had all the other extraordinary buildings in Baðum's valley. Not many men wanted to get into the bath because they feared water even though they loved their ships, but Brida and I went in and I discovered she could swim like a fish. I clung to the edge and marvelled at the strange experience of having hot water all over my naked skin.

Beocca found us there. The centre of Baðum was covered by a truce which meant no man could carry weapons there, and West Saxons and Danes mixed amicably enough in the streets so there was nothing to stop Beocca searching for me. He came to the bath with two other priests, both gloomy-looking men with running noses, and they watched as Beocca leaned down to me. 'I saw you come in here,' he said, then he noticed Brida who was swimming underwater, her long black hair streaming, then she reared up and

171

he could not miss her small breasts and he recoiled as though she were the devil's handmaid. 'She's a girl, Uhtred!'

'I know,' I said.

'Naked!'

'God is good,' I said.

He stepped forward to slap me, but I pushed myself away from the edge of the bath and he nearly fell in. The other two priests were staring at Brida. God knows why. They probably had wives, but priests, I have found, get very excited about women. So do warriors, but we do not shake like aspens just because a girl shows us her tits. Beocca tried to ignore her, though that was difficult because Brida swam up behind me and put her arms around my waist. 'You must slip away,' Beocca whispered to me.

'Slip away?'

'From the pagans! Come to our quarters, we'll hide you.'

'Who is he?' Brida asked me. She spoke in Danish.

'He was a priest I knew at home,' I said.

'Ugly, isn't he?' she said.

'You have to come,' Beocca hissed at me. 'We need you!'

'You need me?'

He leaned even closer. 'There's unrest in Northumbria, Uhtred. You must have heard what happened.' He paused to make the sign of the cross. 'All those monks and nuns slaughtered! They were murdered! A terrible thing, Uhtred, but God will not be mocked. There is to be a rising in Northumbria and Alfred will encourage it. If we can say that Uhtred of Bebbanburg is on our side it will help!'

I doubted it would help at all. I was fifteen and hardly old enough to inspire men into making suicidal attacks on Danish strongholds. 'She's not a Dane,' I told Beocca, who I did not think would have said these things if he believed Brida could understand them, 'she's from East Anglia.'

He stared at her. 'East Anglia?'

I nodded, then let mischief have its way. 'She's the niece of King Edmund,' I lied, and Brida giggled and ran a hand down my body to try to make me laugh.

Beocca made the sign of the cross again. 'Poor man! A martyr! Poor girl.' Then he frowned. 'But . . .' he began, then stopped,

172

quite incapable of understanding why the dreaded Danes allowed two of their prisoners to frolic naked in a bath of hot water, then he closed his squinty eyes because he saw where Brida's hand had come to rest. 'We must get you both out of here,' he said urgently, 'to a place where you can learn God's ways.'

'I should like that,' I said and Brida squeezed so hard that I almost cried out in pain.

'Our quarters are to the south of here,' Beocca said, 'across the river and on top of the hill. Go there, Uhtred, and we shall take you away. Both of you.'

Of course I did no such thing. I told Ragnar, who laughed at my invention that Brida was King Edmund's niece and shrugged at the news that there would be an uprising in Northumbria. 'There are always rumours of revolts,' he said, 'and they all end the same way.'

'He was very certain,' I said.

'All it means is that they've sent monks to stir up trouble. I doubt it will amount to much. Anyway, once we've settled with Alfred we can go back. Go home, eh?'

But settling with Alfred was not as easy as Halfdan or Ragnar had supposed. It was true that Alfred was the supplicant and that he wanted peace because the Danish forces had been raiding deep into Wessex, but he was not ready to collapse as Burghred had yielded in Mercia. When Halfdan proposed that Alfred stay king, but that the Danes occupy the chief West Saxon forts, Alfred threatened to walk out and continue the war. 'You insult me,' he said calmly. 'If you wish to take the fortresses, then come and take them.'

'We will,' Halfdan threatened and Alfred merely shrugged as if to say the Danes were welcome to try, but Halfdan knew, as all the Danes knew, that their campaign had failed. It was true that we had scoured large swathes of Wessex, we had taken much treasure, slaughtered or captured livestock, burned mills and homes and churches, but the price had been high. Many of our best men were dead or else so badly wounded that they would be forced to live off their lords' charity for the rest of their days. We had also failed to take a single West Saxon fortress, which meant that when winter came we would be forced to withdraw to the safety of Lundene or Mercia.

Yet if the Danes were exhausted by the campaign, so were the West Saxons. They had also lost many of their best men, they had lost treasure and Alfred was worried that the Britons, the ancient enemy who had been defeated by his ancestors, might flood out of their fastnesses in Wales and Cornwalum. Yet Alfred would not succumb to his fears, he would not meekly give in to Halfdan's demands, though he knew he must meet some of them, and so the bargaining went on for a week and I was surprised by Alfred's stubbornness.

He was not an impressive man to look at. There was something spindly about him, and his long face had a weak cast, but that was a deception. He never smiled as he faced Halfdan, he rarely took those clever brown eyes off his enemy's face, he pressed his point tediously and he was always calm, never raising his voice even when the Danes were screaming at him. 'What we want,' he explained again and again, 'is peace. You need it, and it is my duty to give it to my country. So you will leave my country.' His priests, Beocca among them, wrote down every word, filling precious sheets of parchment with endless lines of script. They must have used every drop of ink in Wessex to record that meeting and I doubt anyone ever read the whole account.

Not that the meetings went on all day. Alfred insisted they could not start until he had attended church, and he broke at midday for more prayer, and he finished before sundown so that he could return to the church. How that man prayed! But his patient bargaining was just as remorseless, and in the end Halfdan agreed to evacuate Wessex, but only on payment of six thousand pieces of silver and, to make sure it was paid, he insisted that his forces must remain in Readingum where Alfred was required to deliver three wagons of fodder daily and five wagons of rye grain. When the silver was paid, Halfdan promised, the ships would slide back down the Temes and Wessex would be free of pagans. Alfred argued against allowing the Danes to stay in Readingum, insisting that they withdraw east of Lundene, but in the end, desperate for peace, he accepted that they could remain in the town and so, with solemn oaths on both sides, the peace was made.

I was not there when the conference ended, nor was Brida. We had been there most days, serving as Ravn's eyes in the big Roman hall where the talking went on, but when we got bored, or rather when Ravn was tired of our boredom, we would go to the bath and swim. I loved that water.

We were swimming on the day before the talking finished. There were just the two of us in the great echoing chamber. I liked to stand where the water gushed in from a hole in a stone, letting it cascade over my long hair, and I was standing there, eyes closed, when I heard Brida squeal. I opened my eyes and just then a pair of strong hands gripped my shoulders. My skin was slippery and I twisted away, but a man in a leather coat jumped into the bath, told me to be quiet, and seized me again. Two other men were wading across the pool, using long staves to shepherd Brida to the water's edge. 'What are you . . .' I began to ask, using Danish.

'Quiet, boy,' one of the men answered. He was a West Saxon and there were a dozen of them, and when they had pulled our wet naked bodies out of the water they wrapped us in big, stinking cloaks, scooped up our clothes and hurried us away. I shouted for help and was rewarded by a thump on my head that might have stunned an ox.

We were pushed over the saddles of two horses and then we travelled for some time with men mounted behind us, and the cloaks were only taken off at the top of the big hill that overlooks Baðum from the south. And there, beaming at us, was Beocca. 'You are rescued, lord,' he said to me, 'praise Almighty God, you are rescued! As are you, my lady,' he added to Brida.

I could only stare at him. Rescued? Kidnapped, more like. Brida looked at me, and I at her, and she gave the smallest shake of her head as if to suggest we should keep silent, at least I took it to mean that, and did so, then Beocca told us to get dressed.

I had slipped my hammer amulet and my arm rings into my belt pouch when I undressed and I left them there as Beocca hurried us into a nearby church, little more than a wood and straw shack that was no bigger than a peasant's pigsty, and there he gave thanks to God for our deliverance. Afterwards he took us to a nearby hall where we were introduced to Ælswith, Alfred's wife, who was attended by a dozen women, three of them nuns, and guarded by a score of heavily armed men.

Ælswith was a small woman with mouse-brown hair, small eyes, a small mouth and a very determined chin. She was wearing a blue dress which had angels embroidered in silver thread about its skirt and about the hem of its wide sleeves, and she wore a heavy crucifix of gold. A baby was in a wooden cradle beside her and later, much later, I realised that the baby must have been Æthelflaed, so that was the very first time I ever saw her, though I thought nothing of it at the time. Ælswith welcomed me, speaking in the distinctive tones of a Mercian, and after she had enquired about my parentage, she told me we had to be related because her father was Æthelred who had been an Ealdorman in Mercia, and he was first cousin to the late lamented Æthelwulf whose body I had seen outside Readingum. 'And now you,' she turned to Brida, 'Father Beocca tells me you are niece to the holy King Edmund?'

Brida just nodded.

'But who are your parents?' Ælswith demanded, frowning. 'Edmund had no brothers, and his two sisters are nuns.'

'Hild,' Brida said. I knew that had been the name of her aunt, whom Brida had hated.

'Hild?' Ælswith was puzzled, more than puzzled, suspicious. 'Neither of good King Edmund's sisters are called Hild.'

'I'm not his niece,' Brida confessed in a small voice.

'Ah.' Ælswith leaned back in her chair, her sharp face showing the look of satisfaction some people assume when they have caught a liar telling an untruth.

'But I was taught to call him uncle,' Brida went on, surprising me, for I thought she had found herself in an impossible quandary and was confessing the lie, but instead, I realised, she was embroidering it. 'My mother was called Hild and she had no husband but she insisted I call King Edmund uncle,' she spoke in a small, frightened voice, 'and he liked that.'

'He liked it?' Ælswith snapped. 'Why?'

'Because,' Brida said, and then blushed, and how she made herself blush I do not know, but she lowered her eyes, reddened and looked as if she were about to burst into tears.

'Ah,' Ælswith said again, catching on to the girl's meaning and blushing herself. 'So he was your . . .' she did not finish, not wanting to accuse the dead and holy King Edmund of having fathered a bastard on some woman called Hild.

'Yes,' Brida said, and actually started crying. I stared up at the hall's smoke-blackened rafters and tried not to laugh. 'He was ever so kind to me,' Brida sobbed, 'and the nasty Danes killed him!'

Ælswith plainly believed Brida. Folk usually do believe the worst in other folk, and the saintly King Edmund was now revealed as a secret womaniser, though that did not stop him eventually becoming a saint, but it did condemn Brida because Ælswith now proposed that she be sent to some nunnery in southern Wessex. Brida might have royal blood, but it was plainly tainted by sin, so Ælswith wanted her locked away for life. 'Yes,' Brida agreed meekly, and I had to pretend I was choking in the smoke. Then Ælswith presented us both with crucifixes. She had two ready, both of silver, but she whispered to one of the nuns and a small wooden one was substituted for one of the silver crucifixes and that one was presented to Brida while I received a silver one, which I obediently hung about my neck. I kissed mine, which impressed Ælswith, and Brida hurriedly imitated me, but nothing she could do now would impress Alfred's wife. Brida was a self-condemned bastard.

Alfred returned from Baðum after nightfall and I had to accompany him to church where the prayers and praises went on forever. Four monks chanted, their droning voices half sending me to sleep, and afterwards, for it did eventually end, I was invited to join Alfred for a meal. Beocca impressed on me that this was an honour, that not many folk were asked to eat with the king, but I had eaten with Danish chieftains who never seemed to mind who shared their table so long as they did not spit in the gruel, so I was not flattered. I was hungry, though. I could have eaten a whole roasted ox and I was impatient as we ceremonially washed our hands in basins of water held by the servants and then as we stood by our stools and chairs as Alfred and Ælswith were conducted to the table. A bishop allowed the food to cool as he said an interminable prayer asking God to bless what we were about to eat, and then at last we sat, but what a disappointment that supper was! No pork, no beef, no mutton, not a thing a man might want to eat, but only curds, leeks, soft eggs, bread, diluted ale and barley boiled into a gelid broth as palatable as frogspawn. Alfred kept saying how good it was, but in the end he did confess that he was afflicted with terrible pains in his belly and that this pap-like diet kept the agony at bay.

'The king is a martyr to meat,' Beocca explained to me. He was one of the three priests at the high table, another of whom was a bishop who had no teeth and mashed his bread into the broth with a candle stick, and there were also two Ealdormen and, of course, Ælswith who did much of the talking. She was opposing the notion of allowing the Danes to stay in Readingum, but in the end Alfred said he had no choice and that it was a small concession to make for peace, and that ended the discussion. Ælswith did rejoice that her husband had negotiated the release of all the young hostages held by Halfdan's army, which Alfred had insisted on for he feared those young ones would be led away from the true church. He looked at me as he spoke about that, but I took little notice, being far more interested in one of the servants who was a young girl, perhaps four or five years older than me, who was startlingly pretty with a mass of black-ringleted hair and I wondered if she was the girl who Alfred kept close so he could thank God for giving him the strength to resist temptation. Later, much later, I discovered she was the same girl. Her name was Merewenna and I thanked God, in time, for not resisting temptation with her, but that lies far ahead in my tale, and for now I was at Alfred's disposal or, rather, at Ælswith's.

'Uhtred must learn to read,' she said. What business it was of hers I did not know, but no one disputed her statement.

'Amen,' Beocca said.

'The monks at Winburnan can teach him,' she suggested.

'A very good idea, my lady,' Beocca said, and the toothless bishop nodded and dribbled his approval.

'Abbot Hewald is a very diligent teacher,' Ælswith said. In truth Abbot Hewald was one of those bastards who would rather whip the young than teach them, but doubtless that was what Ælswith meant.

'I rather think,' Alfred put in, 'that young Uhtred's ambition is to be a warrior.'

'In time, if God wills it, he will be,' Ælswith said, 'but what use is a soldier who cannot read God's word?'

'Amen,' Beocca said.

'No use at all,' Alfred agreed. I thought teaching a soldier to read was about as much use as teaching a dog to dance, but said nothing, though Alfred sensed my scepticism. 'Why is it good for a soldier to read, Uhtred?' he demanded of me.

'It is good for everyone to read,' I said dutifully, earning a smile from Beocca.

'A soldier who reads,' Alfred said patiently, 'is a soldier who can read orders, a soldier who will know what his king wants. Suppose you are in Northumbria, Uhtred, and I am in Wessex, how else will you know my will?'

That was breathtaking, though I was too young to realise it at the time. If I was in Northumbria and he was in Wessex then I was none of his damned business, but of course Alfred was already thinking ahead, far ahead, to a time when there would be one English kingdom and one English king. I just gaped at him and he smiled at me. 'So Winburnan it is, young man,' he said, 'and the sooner you are there, the better.'

'The sooner?' Ælswith knew nothing of this suggested haste and was sharply suspicious.

'The Danes, my dear,' Alfred explained, 'will look for both children. If they discover they are here they may well demand their return.'

'But all hostages are to be freed,' Ælswith objected, 'you said so yourself.'

'Was Uhtred a hostage?' Alfred asked softly, staring at me. 'Or was he in danger of becoming a Dane?' He left the questions hanging, and I did not try to answer them. 'We must make you into a true Englishman,' Alfred said, 'so you must go south in the morning. You and the girl.'

'The girl doesn't matter,' Ælswith said dismissively. Brida had been sent to eat with the kitchen slaves.

'If the Danes discover she's Edmund's bastard,' one of the Ealdormen observed, 'they'll use her to destroy his reputation.'

'She never told them that,' I piped up, 'because she thought they might mock him.'

'There's some good in her then,' Ælswith said grudgingly. She helped herself to one of the soft-boiled eggs. 'But what will you do,' she demanded of her husband, 'if the Danes accuse you of rescuing the children?'

'I shall lie, of course,' Alfred said. Ælswith blinked at him, but the bishop mumbled that the lie would be for God and so forgivable.

I had no intention of going to Winburnan. That was not because I was suddenly avid to be a Dane, but it had everything to do with Serpent-Breath. I loved that sword, and I had left it with Ragnar's servants, and I wanted her back before my life took whatever path the spinners required of me and, to be sure, I had no wish to give up life with Ragnar for the scant joys of a monastery and a teacher. Brida, I knew, wished to go back to the Danes, and it was Alfred's sensible insistence that we be removed from Baðum as soon as possible that gave us our opportunity.

We were sent away next morning, before dawn, going south into a hilly country and escorted by a dozen warriors who resented the job of taking two children deep into the heartland of Wessex. I was given a horse, Brida was provided with a mule, and a young priest called Willibald was officially put in charge of delivering Brida to a nunnery and me to Abbot Hewald. Father Willibald was a nice man with an easy smile and a kind manner. He could imitate bird calls and made us laugh by inventing a conversation between a quarrelsome fieldfare with its chack-chack call and a soaring skylark, then he made us guess what birds he was imitating, and that entertainment, mixed in with some harmless riddles, took us to a settlement high above a soft-flowing river in the heavily wooded countryside. The soldiers insisted on stopping there because they said the horses needed a rest. 'They really need ale,' Willibald told us, and shrugged as if it was understandable.

It was a warm day. The horses were hobbled outside the hall, the soldiers got their ale, bread and cheese, then sat in a circle and threw dice and grumbled, leaving us to Willibald's supervision, but the young priest stretched out on a half-collapsed haystack and fell asleep in the sunlight. I looked at Brida, she looked at me, and it was as simple as that. We crept along the side of the hall, circled an enormous dungheap, dodged through some pigs that rooted in a field, wriggled through a hedge and then we were in woodland where we both started to laugh. 'My mother insisted I call him uncle,' Brida said in her small voice, 'and the nasty Danes killed him,' and we both thought that was the funniest thing we had ever heard, and then we came to our senses and hurried northwards.

It was a long time before the soldiers searched for us, and later they brought hunting dogs from the hall where they had purchased ale, but by then we had waded up a stream, changed direction again, found higher ground, and hidden ourselves. They did not find us, though all afternoon we could hear the hounds baying in the valley. They must have been searching the riverbank, thinking we had gone there, but we were safe and alone and high.

They searched for two days, never coming close, and on the third day we saw Alfred's royal cavalcade riding south on the road under the hill. The meeting at Baðum was over, and that meant the Danes were retreating to Readingum and neither of us had any idea how to reach Readingum, but we knew we had travelled west to reach Baðum, so that was a start, and we knew we had to find the River Temes, and our only two problems were food and the need to avoid being caught.

That was a good time. We stole milk from the udders of cows and goats. We had no weapons, but we fashioned cudgels from fallen branches and used them to threaten some poor old man who was patiently digging a ditch and had a small sack with bread and pease pudding for his meal, and we stole that, and we caught fish with our hands, a trick that Brida taught me, and we lived in the woods. I wore my hammer amulet again. Brida had thrown away her wooden crucifix, but I kept the silver one for it was valuable.

After a few days we began travelling by night. We were both frightened at first, for the night is when the sceadugengan stir from their hiding places, but we became good at traversing the darkness. We skirted farms, following the stars, and we learned how to move without noise, how to be shadows. One night something large and growling came close and we heard it shifting, pawing the ground, and we both beat at the leaf mould with our cudgels and yelped and the thing went away. A boar? Perhaps. Or perhaps one of the shapeless, nameless sceadugengan that curdle dreams.

We had to cross a range of high, bare hills where we managed to steal a lamb before the shepherd's dogs even knew we were there. We lit a fire in the woods north of the hills and cooked the meat, and next night we found the river. We did not know what river, but it was wide, it flowed beneath deep trees, and nearby was a settlement where we saw a small round boat made of bent willow sticks covered with goatskin, and that night we stole the boat and let it carry us downstream, past settlements, under bridges, ever going east.

We did not know it, but the river was the Temes, and so we came safe to Readingum.

Rorik had died. He had been sick for so long, but there were times when he had seemed to recover, but whatever illness carried him away had done so swiftly and Brida and I reached Readingum on the day that his body was burned. Ragnar, in tears, stood by the pyre and watched as the flames consumed his son. A sword, a bridle, a hammer amulet and a model ship had been placed on the fire, and after it was done the melted metal was placed with the ashes in a great pot that Ragnar buried close to the Temes. 'You are my second son now,' he told me that night, and then remembered Brida, 'and you are my daughter.' He embraced us both, then got drunk. Next morning he wanted to ride out and kill West Saxons, but Ravn and Halfdan restrained him.

The truce was holding. Brida and I had only been gone a little over three weeks and already the first silver was coming to Readingum, along with fodder and food. Alfred, it seemed, was a man of his word and Ragnar was a man of grief. 'How will I tell Sigrid?' he wanted to know.

'It is bad for a man to have only one son,' Ravn told me, 'almost as bad as having none. I had three, but only Ragnar lives. Now only his eldest lives.' Ragnar the Younger was still in Ireland.

'He can have another son,' Brida said.

'Not from Sigrid,' Ravn said, 'but he could take a second wife, I suppose. It is sometimes done.'

Ragnar had given me back Serpent-Breath, and another arm ring. He gave a ring to Brida too, and he took some consolation from the story of our escape. We had to tell it to Halfdan and to Guthrum the Unlucky, who stared at us dark-eyed as we described the meal with Alfred, and Alfred's plans to educate me, and even grief-stricken Ragnar laughed when Brida retold the story of how she had claimed to be King Edmund's bastard.

'This Queen Ælswith,' Halfdan wanted to know, 'what is she like?'

'No queen,' I said, 'the West Saxons won't have queens.' Beocca had told me that. 'She is merely the king's wife.'

'She is a weasel pretending to be a thrush,' Brida said.

'Is she pretty?' Guthrum asked.

'A pinched face,' Brida said, 'and piggy eyes and a pursed mouth.'

'He'll get no joy there then,' Halfdan said, 'why did he marry her?'

'Because she's from Mercia,' Ravn said, 'and Alfred would have Mercia on his side.'

'Mercia belongs to us,' Halfdan growled.

'But Alfred would take it back,' Ravn said, 'and what we should do is send ships with rich gifts for the Britons. If they attack from Wales and Cornwalum then he must divide his army.'

That was an unfortunate thing to say, for Halfdan still smarted from the memory of dividing his own army at Æsc's Hill, and he just scowled into his ale. So far as I know he never did send gifts to the Britons, and it would have been a good idea if he had, but he was distracted by his failure to take Wessex, and there were rumours of unrest in both Northumbria and Mercia. The Danes had captured so much of England so quickly that they had never really subdued their conquest, nor did they hold all the fortresses in the conquered land and so revolts flared like heathland fires. They were easily put down, but untended they would spread and become dangerous. It was time, Halfdan said, to stamp on the fires and to cow the conquered English into terrified submission. Once that was done, once Northumbria, Mercia and East Anglia were quiet, the attack on Wessex could be resumed.

The last of Alfred's silver came and the Danish army released the young hostages, including the Mercian twins, and the rest of us went back to Lundene. Ragnar dug up the pot with his younger son's ashes and carried it downstream on *Wind-Viper*. 'I shall take it home,' he told me, 'and bury him with his own people.'

We could not travel north that year. It was autumn when we reached Lundene and so we had to wait through the winter, and it was not till spring that Ragnar's three ships left the Temes and sailed north. I was almost sixteen then, and growing fast so that I was suddenly a head taller than most men, and Ragnar made me take the steering oar. He taught me to guide a ship, how to anticipate the buffet of wind or wave and how to heave on the steering oar before the ship veered. I learned the subtle touch, though at first the ship swayed drunkenly as I put too much pressure on the oar, but in time I came to feel the ship's will in the long oar's shaft and learned to love the quiver in the ash as the sleek hull gained her full speed.

'I shall make you my second son,' Ragnar told me on that voyage.

I did not know what to say.

'I shall always favour my eldest,' he went on, meaning Ragnar the Younger, 'but you shall still be as a son to me.'

'I would like that,' I said awkwardly. I gazed at the distant shore

184

that was flecked by the little dun sails of the fishing boats that were fleeing from our ships. 'I am honoured,' I said.

'Uhtred Ragnarson,' he said, trying it out, and he must have liked the sound of it for he smiled, but then he thought of Rorik again and the tears came to his eyes and he just stared eastwards into the empty sea.

That night we slept in the mouth of the Humber.

And two days later came back to Eoferwic.

The king's palace had been repaired. It had new shutters on its high windows and the roof was freshly thatched with golden rye straw. The palace's old Roman walls had been scrubbed so that the lichen was gone from the joints between the stones. Guards stood at the outer gate and, when Ragnar demanded entry, they curtly told him to wait and I thought he would draw his sword, but before his anger could erupt Kjartan appeared. 'My lord Ragnar,' he said sourly.

'Since when does a Dane wait at this gate?' Ragnar demanded.

'Since I ordered it,' Kjartan retorted, and there was insolence in his voice. He, like the palace, looked prosperous. He wore a cloak of black bear fur, had tall boots, a chain-mail tunic, a red leather sword belt and almost as many arm rings as Ragnar. 'No one enters here without my permission,' Kjartan went on, 'but of course you are welcome, Earl Ragnar.' He stepped aside to let Ragnar, myself and three of Ragnar's men into the big hall where, five years before, my uncle had tried to buy me from Ivar. 'I see you still have your English pet,' Kjartan said, looking at me.

'Go on seeing while you have eyes,' Ragnar said carelessly. 'Is the king here?'

'He only grants audience to those people who arrange to see him,' Kjartan said.

Ragnar sighed and turned on his erstwhile shipmaster. 'You itch me like a louse,' he said, 'and if it pleases you, Kjartan, we shall lay the hazel rods and meet man to man. And if that does not please you, then fetch the king because I would speak with him.'

185

Kjartan bridled, but decided he did not want to face Ragnar's sword in a fighting space marked by hazel branches and so, with an ill grace, he went into the palace's back rooms. He made us wait long enough, but eventually King Egbert appeared, and with him were six guards who included one-eyed Sven who now looked as wealthy as his father. Big too, almost as tall as I was, with a broad chest and hugely muscled arms.

Egbert looked nervous but did his best to appear regal. Ragnar bowed to him, then said there were tales of unrest in Northumbria and that Halfdan had sent him north to quell any such disturbances. 'There is no unrest,' Egbert said, but in such a frightened voice that I thought he would piss his breeches.

'There were disturbances in the inland hills,' Kjartan said dismissively, 'but they ended.' He patted his sword to show what had ended them.

Ragnar persevered, but learned nothing more. A few men had evidently risen against the Danes, there had been ambushes on the road leading to the west coast, the perpetrators had been hunted down and killed, and that was all Kjartan would say. 'Northumbria is safe,' he finished, 'so you can return to Halfdan, my lord, and keep on trying to defeat Wessex.'

Ragnar ignored that last barb. 'I shall go to my home,' he said, 'bury my son and live in peace.'

Sven was fingering his sword hilt and looking at me sourly with his one eye, but while the enmity between us, and between Ragnar and Kjartan, was obvious, no one made trouble and we left. The ships were hauled onto shore, the silver fetched from Readingum was shared out among the crews, and we went home carrying Rorik's ashes.

Sigrid wailed at the news. She tore her dress and tangled her hair and screamed, and the other women joined her, and a procession carried Rorik's ashes to the top of the nearest hill where the pot was buried, and afterwards Ragnar stayed there, looking across the hills and watching the white clouds sail across the western sky.

We stayed home all the rest of that year. There were crops to grow, hay to cut, a harvest to reap and to grind. We made cheese and butter. Merchants and travellers brought news, but none from Wessex where, it seemed, Alfred still ruled and had his peace, and so that kingdom remained, the last one of England. Ragnar sometimes spoke of returning there, carrying his sword to gain more riches, but the fight seemed to have gone from him that summer. He sent a message to Ireland, asking that his eldest son come home, but such messages were not reliable and Ragnar the Younger did not come that year. Ragnar also thought of Thyra, his daughter. 'He says it's time I married,' she said to me one day as we churned butter.

'You?' I laughed.

'I'm nearly fourteen!' she said defiantly.

'So you are. Who'll marry you?'

She shrugged. 'Mother likes Anwend.' Anwend was one of Ragnar's warriors, a young man not much older than me, strong and cheerful, but Ragnar had an idea she should marry one of Ubba's sons, but that would mean she would go away and Sigrid hated that thought and Ragnar slowly came around to Sigrid's way of thinking. I liked Anwend and thought he would make a good husband for Thyra who was growing ever more beautiful. She had long golden hair, wide-set eyes, a straight nose, unscarred skin, and a laugh that was like a ripple of sunshine. 'Mother says I must have many sons,' she said.

'I hope you do.'

'I'd like a daughter too,' she said, straining with the churn because the butter was solidifying and the work getting harder. 'Mother says Brida should marry as well.'

'Brida might have different ideas,' I said.

'She wants to marry you,' Thyra said.

I laughed at that. I thought of Brida as a friend, my closest friend, and just because we slept with each other, or we did when Sigrid was not watching, did not make me want to marry her. I did not want to marry at all, I thought only of swords and shields and battles, and Brida thought of herbs.

She was like a cat. She came and went secretly, and she learned all that Sigrid could teach her about herbs and their uses. Bindweed as a purgative, toadflax for ulcers, marsh marigold to keep elves away from the milk pails, chickweed for coughs, cornflower for fevers, and she learned other spells she would not tell me, women's spells, and said that if you stayed silent in the night, unmoving, scarce breathing, the spirits would come, and Ravn taught her how to dream with the gods, which meant drinking ale in which pounded redcap mushrooms had been steeped, and she was often ill for she drank it too strong, but she would not stop, and she made her first songs then, songs about birds and about beasts, and Ravn said she was a true skald. Some nights, when we watched the charcoal burn, she would recite to me, her voice soft and rhythmic. She had a dog now that followed her everywhere. She had found him in Lundene on our homeward journey and he was black and white, as clever as Brida herself, and she called him Nihtgenga, which means night-walker, or goblin. He would sit with us by the charcoal pyre and I swear he listened to her songs. Brida made pipes from straw and played melancholy tunes and Nihtgenga would watch her with big sad eyes until the music overcame him and then he would raise his muzzle and howl, and we would both laugh and Nihtgenga would be offended and Brida would have to pet him back to happiness.

We forgot the war until, when the summer was at its height and a pall of heat lay over the hills, we had an unexpected visitor. Earl Guthrum the Unlucky came to our remote valley. He came with twenty horsemen, all dressed in black, and he bowed respectfully to Sigrid who chided him for not sending warning. 'I would have made a feast,' she said.

'I brought food,' Guthrum said, pointing to some packhorses, 'I did not want to empty your stores.'

He had come from distant Lundene, wanting to talk with Ragnar and Ravn, and Ragnar invited me to sit with them because, he said, I knew more than most men about Wessex, and Wessex was what Guthrum wished to talk about, though my contribution was small. I described Alfred, described his piety, and warned Guthrum that though the West Saxon king was not an impressive man to look at, he was undeniably clever. Guthrum shrugged at that. 'Cleverness is overrated,' he said gloomily. 'Clever doesn't win battles.'

'Stupidity loses them,' Ravn put in, 'like dividing the army when we fought outside Æbbanduna?'

Guthrum scowled, but decided not to pick a fight with Ravn, and instead asked Ragnar's advice on how to defeat the West Saxons, and demanded Ragnar's assurance that, come the new year, Ragnar would bring his men to Lundene and join the next assault. 'If it is next year,' Guthrum said gloomily. He scratched at the back of his neck, jiggling his mother's gold-tipped bone that still hung from his hair. 'We may not have sufficient men.'

'Then we will attack the year after,' Ragnar said.

'Or the one after that,' Guthrum said, then frowned. 'But how do we finish the pious bastard?'

'Split his forces,' Ragnar said, 'because otherwise we'll always be outnumbered.'

'Always? Outnumbered?' Guthrum looked dubious at that assertion.

'When we fought here,' Ragnar said, 'some Northumbrians decided not to fight us and they took refuge in Mercia. When we fought in Mercia and East Anglia the same thing happened, and men fled from us to find sanctuary in Wessex. But when we fight in Wessex they have nowhere to go. No place is safe for them. So they must fight, all of them. Fight in Wessex and the enemy is cornered.'

'And a cornered enemy,' Ravn put in, 'is dangerous.'

'Split them,' Guthrum said pensively, ignoring Ravn again.

'Ships on the south coast,' Ragnar suggested, 'an army on the Temes, and British warriors coming from Brycheinog, Glywysing and Gwent.' Those were the southern Welsh kingdoms where the Britons lurked beyond Mercia's western border. 'Three attacks,' Ragnar went on, 'and Alfred will have to deal with them all and he won't be able to do it.'

'And you will be there?' Guthrum asked.

'You have my word,' Ragnar said, and then the conversation turned to what Guthrum had seen on his journey, and admittedly he was a pessimistic man and prone to see the worst in everything, but he despaired of England. There was trouble in Mercia, he said, and the East Anglians were restless, and now there was talk that King Egbert in Eoferwic was encouraging revolt.

'Egbert!' Ragnar was surprised at the news, 'he couldn't encourage a piss out of a drunk man!'

'It's what I'm told,' Guthrum said, 'may not be true. Fellow called Kjartan told me.'

'Then it's almost certainly not true.'

'Not true at all,' Ravn agreed.

'He seemed a good man to me,' Guthrum said, obviously unaware of Ragnar's history with Kjartan, and Ragnar did not enlighten him, and probably forgot the conversation once Guthrum had travelled on.

Yet Guthrum had been right. Plotting was going on in Eoferwic, though I doubt it was Egbert who did it. Kjartan did it, and he started by spreading rumours that King Egbert was secretly organising a rebellion, and the rumours became so loud and the king's reputation so poisoned that one night Egbert, fearing for his life, managed to evade his Danish guards and flee south with a dozen companions. He took shelter with King Burghred of Mercia who, though his country was occupied by Danes, had been allowed to keep his own household guard that was sufficient to protect his new guest. Ricsig of Dunholm, the man who had handed the captured monks to Ragnar, was declared the new king of Northumbria, and he rewarded Kjartan by allowing him to ravage any place that might have harboured rebels in league with Egbert. There had been no rebellion, of course, but Kjartan had invented one, and he savaged the few remaining monasteries and nunneries in Northumbria, thus becoming even wealthier, and he stayed as Ricsig's chief warrior and tax collector.

All this passed us by. We brought in the harvest, feasted, and it was announced that at Yule there would be a wedding between Thyra and Anwend. Ragnar asked Ealdwulf the smith to make Anwend a sword as fine as Serpent-Breath, and Ealdwulf said he would and, at the same time, make me a short sword of the kind Toki had recommended for fighting in the shield wall, and he made me help him beat out the twisted rods. All that autumn we worked until Ealdwulf had made Anwend's sword and I had helped make my own sax. I called her Wasp-Sting because she was short and I could not wait to try her out on an enemy, which Ealdwulf said was foolishness. 'Enemies come soon enough in a man's life,' he told me, 'you don't need to seek them out.'

I made my first shield in the early winter, cutting the limewood, forging the great boss with its handle that was held through a hole in the wood, painting it black and rimming it with an iron strip. It was much too heavy, that shield, and later I learned how to make them lighter, but as the autumn came I carried shield, sword and sax everywhere, accustoming myself to their weight, practising the strokes and parries, dreaming. I half feared and half longed for my first shield wall, for no man was a warrior until he had fought in the shield wall, and no man was a real warrior until he had fought in the front rank of the shield wall, and that was death's kingdom, the place of horror, but like a fool I aspired to it.

And we readied ourselves for war. Ragnar had promised his support to Guthrum and so Brida and I made more charcoal and Ealdwulf hammered out spear points and axe heads and spades, while Sigrid found joy in the preparations for Thyra's wedding. There was a betrothal ceremony at the beginning of winter when Anwend, dressed in his best clothes that were neatly darned, came to our hall with six of his friends and he shyly proposed himself to Ragnar as Thyra's husband. Everyone knew he was going to be her husband, but the formalities were important, and Thyra sat between her mother and father as Anwend promised Ragnar that he would love, cherish and protect Thyra, and then proposed a bride price of twenty pieces of silver which was much too high, but which, I suppose, meant he really loved Thyra.

'Make it ten, Anwend,' Ragnar said, generous as ever, 'and spend the rest on a new coat.'

'Twenty is good,' Sigrid said firmly, for the bride price, though given to Ragnar, would become Thyra's property once she was married.

'Then have Thyra give you a new coat,' Ragnar said, taking the money, and then he embraced Anwend and there was a feast and Ragnar was happier that night than he had been since Rorik's death. Thyra watched the dancing, sometimes blushing as she met

191

Anwend's eyes. Anwend's six friends, all warriors of Ragnar, would come back with him for the wedding and they would be the men who would watch Anwend take Thyra to his bed and only when they reported that she was a proper woman would the marriage be deemed to have taken place.

But those ceremonies would have to wait until Yule. Thyra would be wedded then, we would have our feast, the winter would be endured, we would go to war. In other words we thought the world would go on as it ever did.

And at the foot of Yggdrasil, the tree of life, the three spinners mocked us.

I have spent many Christmases at the West Saxon court. Christmas is Yule with religion, and the West Saxons managed to spoil the midwinter feast with chanting monks, droning priests and savagely long sermons. Yule is supposed to be a celebration and a consolation, a moment of warm brightness in the heart of winter, a time to eat because you know that the lean times are coming when food will be scarce and ice locks the land, and a time to be happy and get drunk and behave irresponsibly and wake up next morning wondering if you will ever feel well again, but the West Saxons handed the feast to the priests who made it as joyous as a funeral. I have never really understood why people think religion has a place in the midwinter feast, though of course the Danes remembered their gods at that time, and sacrificed to them, but they also believed Odin, Thor and the other gods were all feasting in Asgard and had no wish to spoil the feasts in Midgard, our world. That seems sensible, but I have learned that most Christians are fearfully suspicious of enjoyment and Yule offered far too much of that for their taste. Some folk in Wessex knew how to celebrate it, and I always did my best, but if Alfred was anywhere close then you could be sure that we were required to fast, pray and repent through the whole twelve days of Christmas.

Which is all by way of saying that the Yule feast where Thyra would be married was to be the greatest in Danish memory. We worked hard as it approached. We kept more animals alive than usual, and slaughtered them just before the feast so that their meat would not need to be salted, and we dug great pits where the pigs and cows would be cooked on huge gridirons that Ealdwulf made. He grumbled about it, saying that forging cooking implements took him away from his real work, but he secretly enjoyed it because he loved his food. As well as pork and beef we planned to have herring, salmon, mutton, pike, freshly baked bread, cheese, ale, mead, and, best of all, the puddings that were made by stuffing sheep intestines with blood, offal, oats, horseradish, wild garlic and juniper berries. I loved those puddings, and still do, all crisp on the outside, but bursting with warm blood when you bite into them. I remember Alfred grimacing with distaste as I ate one and as the bloody juices ran into my beard, but then he was sucking on a boiled leek at the time.

We planned sports and games. The lake in the heart of the valley had frozen and I was fascinated by the way the Danes strapped bones to their feet and glided on the ice, a pastime that lasted until the ice broke and a young man drowned, but Ragnar reckoned the lake would be hard frozen again after Yule and I was determined to learn the skill of ice-gliding. For the moment, though, Brida and I were still making charcoal for Ealdwulf who had decided to make Ragnar a sword, the finest he had ever made, and we were charged with turning two wagonloads of alderwood into the best possible fuel.

We planned to break the pile the day before the feast, but it was bigger than any we had made before and it was still not cool enough, and if you break a pile before it is ready then the fire will flare up with terrible force and burn all the half-made charcoal into ash, and so we made certain every vent was properly sealed and reckoned we would have time to break it on Yule morning before the celebrations began. Most of Ragnar's men and their families were already at the hall, sleeping wherever they could find shelter and ready for the first meal of the day and for the games that would take place in the meadow before the marriage ceremony, but Brida and I spent that last night up at the pile for fear that some animal would scratch through the turf and so start

193

a draught that would revive the burn. I had Serpent-Breath and Wasp-Sting, for I would go nowhere without them, and Brida had Nihtgenga, for she would go nowhere without him, and we were both swathed in furs because the night was cold. When a pile was burning you could rest on the turf and feel the heat, but not that night because the fire was almost gone.

'If you go very still,' Brida said after dark, 'you can feel the spirits.'

I think I fell asleep instead, but sometime towards dawn I woke and found Brida was also asleep. I sat up carefully, so as not to wake her, and I stared into the dark and I went very still and listened for the sceadugengan. Goblins and elves and sprites and spectres and dwarves, all those things come to Midgard at night and prowl among the trees, and when we guarded the charcoal piles both Brida and I put out food for them so they would leave us in peace. So I woke, I listened, and I heard the small sounds of a wood at night, the things moving, the claws in the dead leaves, the wind's soft sighs.

And then I heard the voices.

I woke Brida and we were both still. Nihtgenga growled softly until Brida whispered that he should be quiet.

Men were moving in the dark, and some were coming to the charcoal pile and we slipped away into the blackness under the trees. We could both move like shadows and Nihtgenga would make no sound without Brida's permission. We had gone uphill because the voices were downhill, and we crouched in utter darkness and heard men moving around the charcoal pile, and then there was the crack of flint and iron and a small flame sprung up. Whoever it was searched for the folk they reckoned would be watching the charcoal, but they did not find us, and after a while they moved downhill and we followed.

Dawn was just leeching the eastern sky with a wolf-grey edge. There was frost on the leaves and a small wind. 'We should get to Ragnar,' I whispered.

'We can't,' Brida said, and she was right, for there were scores of men in the trees and they were between us and the hall, and we were much too far away to shout a warning to Ragnar, and so we tried to go around the strangers, hurrying along the hill's ridge so we could drop down to the forge where Ealdwulf slept, but before we had gone halfway the fires burst into life.

That dawn is seared on my memory, burned there by the flames of a hall-burning. There was nothing we could do except watch. Kjartan and Sven had come to our valley with over a hundred men and now they attacked Ragnar by setting fire to the thatch of his hall. I could see Kjartan and his son, standing amidst the flaming torches that lit the space in front of the door, and as folk came from the hall they were struck by spears or arrows so that a pile of bodies grew in the firelight which became ever brighter as the thatch flared and finally burst into a tumultuous blaze that outshone the light of the grey dawn. We could hear people and animals screaming inside. Some men burst from the hall with weapons in hand, but they were cut down by the soldiers who surrounded the hall, men at every door or window, men who killed the fugitives, though not all of them. The younger women were pushed aside under guard, and Thyra was given to Sven who struck her hard on the head and left her huddled at his feet as he helped kill her family.

I did not see Ravn, Ragnar or Sigrid die, though die they did, and I suspect they were burned in the hall when the roof collapsed in a roaring gout of flame, smoke and wild sparks. Ealdwulf also died and I was in tears. I wanted to draw Serpent-Breath and rush into those men around the flames, but Brida held me down, and then she whispered to me that Kjartan and Sven would surely search the nearby woods for any survivors, and she persuaded me to pull back into the lightening trees. Dawn was a sullen iron band across the sky and the sun cloud-hidden in shame as we stumbled uphill to find shelter among some fallen rocks deep in the high wood.

All that day the smoke rose from Ragnar's hall, and next night there was a glow above the tangled black branches of the trees, and next morning there were still wisps of smoke coming from the valley where we had been happy. We crept closer, both of us hungry, to see Kjartan and his men raking through the embers.

They pulled out lumps and twists of melted iron, a mail coat fused into a crumpled horror, silver welded into chunks, and they took whatever they found that could be sold or used again. At times they appeared frustrated, as if they had not found enough treasure, though they took enough. A wagon carried Ealdwulf's tools and anvil down the valley. Thyra had a rope put around her neck, was placed on a horse and led away by one-eyed Sven. Kjartan pissed on a heap of glowing cinders, then laughed as one of his men said something. By afternoon they were gone.

I was sixteen and no longer a child.

And Ragnar, my lord, who had made me his son, was dead.

The bodies were still in the ashes, though it was impossible to tell who was who, or even to tell men from women for the heat had shrunk the dead so they all looked like children and the children like babies. Those who had died outside the hall were recognisable and I found Ealdwulf there, and Anwend, both stripped naked. I looked for Ragnar, but could not identify him. I wondered why he had not burst from the hall, sword in hand, and decided he knew he was going to die and did not want to give his enemy the satisfaction of seeing it.

We found food in one of the storage pits that Kjartan's men had missed as they searched the hall. We had to shift hot charred pieces of timber to uncover the pit, and the bread, cheese and meat had all been soured by smoke and ash, but we ate. Neither of us spoke. At dusk some English folk came cautiously to the hall and stared at the destruction. They were wary of me, thinking of me as a Dane, and they dropped to their knees as I approached. They were the lucky ones, for Kjartan had slaughtered every Northumbrian in Synningthwait, down to the last baby, and had loudly blamed them for the hall-burning. Men must have known it was his doing, but his savagery at Synningthwait confused things and, in time, many folk came to believe that the English had attacked Ragnar, and Kjartan had taken revenge for their attack. But these English had escaped his swords. 'You will come back in the morning,' I told them, 'and bury the dead.'

'Yes, lord.'

'You will be rewarded,' I promised them, thinking I would have to surrender one of my precious arm rings.

'Yes, lord,' one of them repeated, and then I asked them if they knew why this had happened and they looked nervous, but finally one said he had been told that Earl Ragnar was planning a revolt against Ricsig. One of the Englishmen who served Kjartan had told him that when he went down to their hovels to find ale. He had also told them to hide themselves before Kjartan slaughtered the valley's inhabitants.

'You know who I am?' I asked the man.

'The Lord Uhtred, lord.'

'Tell no man I'm alive,' I said and he just stared at me. Kjartan, I decided, must think that I was dead, that I was one of the shrunken charred bodies in the hall, and while Kjartan did not care about me, Sven did, and I did not want him hunting me. 'And return in the morning,' I went on, 'and you will have silver.'

There is a thing called the bloodfeud. All societies have them, even the West Saxons have them, despite their vaunted piety. Kill a member of my family and I shall kill one of yours, and so it goes on, generation after generation or until one family is all dead, and Kjartan had just wished a bloodfeud on himself. I did not know how, I did not know where, I could not know when, but I would revenge Ragnar. I swore it that night.

And I became rich that night. Brida waited until the English folk were gone and then she led me to the burned remnants of Ealdwulf's forge and she showed me the vast piece of scorched elm, a section of a tree's trunk, that had held Ealdwulf's anvil. 'We must move that,' she said.

It took both of us to tip over that monstrous piece of elm, and beneath it was nothing but earth, but Brida told me to dig there and, for want of other tools, I used Wasp-Sting and had only gone down a hand's breadth when I struck metal. Gold. Real gold. Coins and small lumps. The coins were strange, incised with a writing I had never seen before, neither Danish runes nor English letters, but something weird which I later learned came from the people far away who live in the desert and worship a god called

197

Allah who I think must be a god of fire because *al*, in our English tongue, means burning. There are so many gods, but those folk who worshipped Allah made good coin and that night we unearthed forty-eight of them, and as much again in loose gold, and Brida told me she had watched Ragnar and Ealdwulf bury the hoard one night. There was gold, silver pennies, and four pieces of jet, and doubtless this was the treasure Kjartan had expected to find, for he knew Ragnar was wealthy, but Ragnar had hidden it well. All men hide a reserve of wealth for the day when disaster comes. I have buried hoards in my time, and even forgotten where one was and perhaps, years from now, some lucky man will find it. That hoard, Ragnar's hoard, belonged to his eldest son, but Ragnar, it was strange to think he was just Ragnar now, no longer Ragnar the Younger, was far away in Ireland and I doubted he was even alive, for Kjartan would surely have sent men to kill him. But alive or dead he was not here and so we took the hoard.

'What do we do?' Brida asked that night. We were back in the woods.

I already knew what we would do, perhaps I had always known. I am an Englishman of England, but I had been a Dane while Ragnar was alive for Ragnar loved me and cared for me and called me his son, but Ragnar was dead and I had no other friends among the Danes. I had no friends among the English, for that matter, except for Brida of course, and unless I counted Beocca who was certainly fond of me in a complicated way, but the English were my folk and I think I had known that ever since the moment at Æsc's Hill where for the first time I saw Englishmen beat Danes. I had felt pride then. Destiny is all, and the spinners touched me at Æsc's Hill and now, at last, I would respond to their touch.

'We go south,' I said.

'To a nunnery?' Brida asked, thinking of Ælswith and her bitter ambitions.

'No.' I had no wish to join Alfred and learn to read and bruise my knees with praying. 'I have relatives in Mercia,' I said. I had never met them, knew nothing of them, but they were family and family has its obligations, and the Danish hold on Mercia was looser than elsewhere and perhaps I could find a home and I would not be a burden because I carried gold.

I had said I knew what I would do, but that is not wholly true. The truth is that I was in a well of misery, tempted to despair and with tears ever close to my eyes. I wanted life to go on as before, to have Ragnar as my father, to feast and to laugh. But destiny grips us and, next morning, in a soft winter rain, we buried the dead, paid silver coins, and then walked southwards. We were a boy on the edge of being a grown man, a girl and a dog, and we were going to nowhere.

PART TWO

The Last Kingdom

Seven

I settled in southern Mercia. I found another uncle, this one called Ealdorman Æthelred, son of Æthelred, brother of Æthelwulf, father of Æthelred, and brother to another Æthelred who had been the father of Ælswith who was married to Alfred, and Ealdorman Æthelred, with his confusing family, grudgingly acknowledged me as a nephew, though the welcome became slightly warmer when I presented him with two gold coins and swore on a crucifix that it was all the money I possessed. He assumed Brida was my lover, in which he was right, and thereafter he ignored her.

The journey south was wearisome, as all winter journeys are. For a time we sheltered at an upland homestead near Meslach and the folk there took us for outlaws. We arrived at their hovel in an evening of sleet and wind, both of us half frozen, and we paid for food and shelter with a few links from the chain of the silver crucifix Ælswith had given me, and in the night the two eldest sons came to collect the rest of our silver, but Brida and I were awake, half expecting such an attempt, and I had Serpent-Breath and Brida had Wasp-Sting and we threatened to geld both boys. The family was friendly after that, or at least scared into docility, believing me when I told them that Brida was a sorceress. They were pagans, some of the many English heretics left in the high hills, and they had no idea that the Danes were swarming over England. They lived far from any village, grunted prayers to Thor and Odin, and sheltered us for six weeks and we worked for our keep by chopping wood, helping their ewes give birth and then standing guard over the sheep pens to keep the wolves at bay.

In early spring we moved on. We avoided Hreapandune, for that was where Burghred kept his court, the same court to which the hapless Egbert of Northumbria had fled, and there were many Danes settled around the town. I did not fear Danes, I could talk to them in their own tongue, knew their jests and even liked them, but if word got back to Eoferwic that Uhtred of Bebbanburg still lived then I feared Kjartan would put a reward on my head. So I asked at every settlement about Ealdorman Æthelwulf who had died fighting the Danes at Readingum, and I learned he had lived at a place called Deoraby, but that the Danes had taken his lands, and his younger brother had gone to Cirrenceastre that lay in the far southern parts of Mercia, very close to the West Saxon border, and that was good because the Danes were thickest in Mercia's north, and so we went to Cirrenceastre and found it was another Roman town, well walled with stone and timber, and that Æthelwulf's brother, Æthelred, was now Ealdorman and lord of the place.

We arrived when he sat in court and we waited in his hall among the petitioners and oath-takers. We watched as two men were flogged and a third branded on the face and sent into outlawry for cattle-thieving, and then a steward brought us forward, thinking we had come to seek redress for a grievance, and the steward told us to bow, and I refused and the man tried to make me bend at the waist and I struck him in the face, and that got Æthelred's attention. He was a tall man, well over forty years old, almost hairless except for a huge beard, and as gloomy as Guthrum. When I struck the steward he beckoned to his guards who were lolling at the hall's edges. 'Who are you?' he growled at me.

'I am the Ealdorman Uhtred,' I said, and the title stilled the guards and made the steward back nervously away. 'I am the son of Uhtred of Bebbanburg,' I went on, 'and of Æthelgifu, his wife. I am your nephew.'

He stared at me. I must have looked a wreck for I was travel-stained and long-haired and ragged, but I had two swords and monstrous pride. 'You are Æthelgifu's boy?' he asked.

'Your sister's son,' I said, and even then I was not certain this was the right family, but it was, and Ealdorman Æthelred made the sign of the cross in memory of his younger sister, whom he hardly remembered, and waved the guards back to the hall's sides and asked me what I wanted.

'Shelter,' I said, and he nodded grudgingly. I told him I had been a prisoner of the Danes ever since my father's death, and he accepted that willingly enough, but in truth he was not very interested in me, indeed my arrival was a nuisance for we were two more mouths to feed, but family imposes obligation, and Ealdorman Æthelred met his. He also tried to have me killed.

His lands, which stretched to the River Sæfern in the west, were being raided by Britons from Wales. The Welsh were old enemies, the ones who had tried to stop our ancestors from taking England, indeed their name for England is Lloegyr, which means the Lost Lands, and they were forever raiding or thinking of raiding or singing songs about raiding, and they had a great hero called Arthur who was supposed to be sleeping in his grave and one day he was going to rise up and lead the Welsh to a great victory over the English and so take back the Lost Lands, though so far that has not happened.

About a month after I arrived Æthelred heard that a Welsh warband had crossed the Sæfern and were taking cattle from his lands near Fromtun and he rode to clear them out. He went westwards with fifty men, but ordered the chief of his household troops, a warrior called Tatwine, to block their retreat near the ancient Roman town of Gleawecestre. He gave Tatwine a force of twenty men that included me. 'You're a big lad,' Æthelred said to me before he left, 'have you ever fought in a shield wall?'

I hesitated, wanting to lie, but decided that poking a sword between men's legs at Readingum was not the same thing. 'No, lord,' I said.

'Time you learned. That sword must be good for something, where did you get it?'

'It was my father's, lord,' I lied, for I did not want to explain that I had not been a prisoner of the Danes, nor that the sword had been a gift, for Æthelred would have expected me to give it to him. 'It is the only thing of my father's I have,' I added pathetically, and he grunted, waved me away, and told Tatwine to put me in the shield wall if it came to a fight.

I know that because Tatwine told me so when everything was over. Tatwine was a huge man, as tall as me, with a chest like a blacksmith and thick arms on which he made marks with ink and a needle. The marks were just blotches, but he boasted that each one was a man he had killed in battle, and I once tried to count them, but gave up at thirty-eight. His sleeves hid the rest. He was not happy to have me in his band of warriors, and even less happy when Brida insisted on accompanying me, but I told him she had sworn an oath to my father never to leave my side and that she was a cunning woman who knew spells that would confuse the enemy, and he believed both lies and probably thought that once I was dead his men could have their joy of Brida while he took Serpent-Breath back to Æthelred.

The Welsh had crossed the Sæfern high up, then turned south into the lush water meadows where cattle grew fat. They liked to come in fast and go out fast, before the Mercians could gather forces, but Æthelred had heard of their coming in good time and, as he rode west, Tatwine led us north to the bridge across the Sæfern that was the quickest route home to Wales.

The raiders came straight into that trap. We arrived at the bridge at dusk, slept in a field, were awake before dawn and, just as the sun rose, saw the Welshmen and their stolen cattle coming towards us. They made an effort to ride further north, but their horses were tired, ours were fresh, and they realised there was no escape and so they returned to the bridge. We did the same and, dismounted, formed the shield wall. The Welsh made their wall. There were twenty-eight of them, all savage-looking men with shaggy hair and long beards and tattered coats, but their weapons looked well cared for and their shields were stout.

Tatwine spoke some of their language and he told them that if they surrendered now they would be treated mercifully by his lord. Their only response was to howl at us, and one of them turned around, lowered his breeches, and showed us his dirty backside, which passed as a Welsh insult.

Nothing happened then. They were in their shield wall on the road, and our shield wall blocked the bridge, and they shouted insults and Tatwine forbade our men to shout back, and once or twice it seemed as if the Welsh were going to run to their horses and try to escape by galloping northwards, but every time they hinted at such a move, Tatwine ordered the servants to bring up our horses, and the Welsh understood that we would pursue and overtake them and so they went back to the shield wall and jeered at us for not assaulting them. Tatwine was not such a fool. The Welshmen outnumbered us which meant that they could overlap us, but by staying on the bridge our flanks were protected by its Roman parapets and he wanted them to come at us there. He placed me in the centre of the line, and then stood behind me. I understood later that he was ready to step into my place when I fell. I had an old shield with a loose handle loaned to me by my uncle.

Tatwine again tried to persuade them to surrender, promising that only half of them would be put to death, but as the other half would all lose a hand and an eye, it was not a tempting offer. Still they waited, and might have waited until nightfall had not some local people come along and one of them had a bow and some arrows, and he began shooting at the Welsh who, by now, had been drinking steadily through the morning. Tatwine had given us all some ale, but not much.

I was nervous. More than nervous, I was terrified. I had no armour, while the rest of Tatwine's men were in mail or good leather. Tatwine had a helmet, I had hair. I expected to die, but I remembered my lessons and slung Serpent-Breath on my back, strapping her sword belt around my throat. A sword is much quicker to draw over the shoulder, and I expected to begin the fight with Wasp-Sting. My throat was dry, a muscle in my right leg quivered, my belly felt sour, but entwined with that fear was excitement. This was what life had led to, a shield wall, and if I survived this then I would be a warrior.

The arrows flew one after the other, mostly thumping into shields, but one lucky shaft slid past a shield and sank into a man's chest and he fell back, and suddenly the Welsh leader lost patience and gave a great scream. And they charged.

It was a small shield wall, not a great battle. A cattle skirmish, not a clash of armies, but it was my first shield wall, and I instinctively rattled my shield against my neighbours' shields, to make sure they touched, and I lowered Wasp-Sting, meaning to bring her up under the rim, and I crouched slightly to receive the charge, and the Welsh were howling like madmen, a noise meant to scare us, but I was too intent on doing what I had been taught to be distracted by the howls.

'Now!' Tatwine shouted and we all lunged our shields forward and there was a blow on mine like Ealdwulf's hammer thumping the anvil, and I was aware of an axe swinging overhead to split my skull and I ducked, raising the shield, and stabbed Wasp-Sting up into the man's groin. She went smooth and true, just as Toki had taught me, and that groin-stroke is a wicked blow, one of the killer strikes, and the man screamed a terrible scream, just like a woman in childbirth, and the short sword was stuck in his body, blood pouring down her hilt and the axe tumbled down my back as I straightened. I drew Serpent-Breath across my left shoulder and swung at the man attacking my right-hand neighbour. It was a good stroke, straight into the skull, and I ripped her back, letting Ealdwulf's edge do its work, and the man with Wasp-Sting in his crotch was under my feet so I stamped on his face. I was shouting now, shouting in Danish, shouting their deaths, and it was all suddenly easy, and I stepped over my first victim to finish off the second, and that meant I had broken our shield wall, which did not matter because Tatwine was there to guard the space. I was in the Welsh space now, but with two dead men beside me, and a third man turned on me, sword coming in a great scything stroke that I met with the shield boss and, as he tried to cover his body with his own shield, I lunged Serpent-Breath into his throat, ripped her out, swung her all the way around and she clanged against a shield behind me, and I turned, all savagery and anger now, and I charged a fourth man, throwing him down with my weight, and he began to shout for mercy and received none.

The joy of it. The sword joy. I was dancing with joy, joy seething in me, the battle joy that Ragnar had so often spoken of, the warrior joy. If a man has not known it, then he is no man. It was no battle, that, no proper slaughter, just a thief-killing, but it was my first fight and the gods had moved in me, had given my arm speed and my shield strength, and when it was done, and when

I danced in the blood of the dead, I knew I was good. Knew I was more than good. I could have conquered the world at that moment and my only regret was that Ragnar had not seen me, but then I thought he might be watching from Valhalla and I raised Serpent-Breath to the clouds and shouted his name. I have seen other young men come from their first fights with that same joy, and I have buried them after their next battle. The young are fools and I was young. But I was good.

The cattle thieves were finished. Twelve were dead or so badly wounded as to be near death and the others had fled. We caught them easily enough and, one by one, we killed them, and afterwards I went back to the man whose shield had kissed mine when the walls clashed and I had to put my right foot into his bloody crotch to drag Wasp-Sting free of his clinging flesh, and at that moment all I wanted was more enemies to kill.

'Where did you learn to fight, boy?' Tatwine asked me.

I turned on him as though he were an enemy, pride flaring in my face and Wasp-Sting twitching as if she were hungry for blood. 'I am an Ealdorman of Northumbria,' I told him.

He paused, wary of me, then nodded. 'Yes, lord,' he said, then reached forward and felt the muscles of my right arm. 'Where did you learn to fight?' he asked, leaving off the insulting 'boy'.

'I watched the Danes.'

'Watched,' he said tonelessly. He looked into my eyes, then grinned and embraced me. 'God love me,' he said, 'but you're a savage one. Your first shield wall?'

'My first,' I admitted.

'But not your last, I dare say, not your last.'

He was right about that.

I have sounded immodest, but I have told the truth. These days I employ poets to sing my praises, but only because that is what a lord is supposed to do, though I often wonder why a man should get paid for mere words. These word-stringers make nothing, grow nothing, kill no enemies, catch no fish and raise no cattle. They just take silver in exchange for words, which are free anyway. It is a clever trick, but in truth they are about as much use as priests.

I did fight well, that is no lie, but I had spent my growing years dreaming of little else, and I was young, and the young are reckless in battle, and I was strong and quick, and the enemy were tired. We left their severed heads on the bridge parapets as a greeting for other Britons coming to visit their Lost Lands, then we rode south to meet Æthelred who was doubtless disappointed to find me alive and still hungry, but he accepted Tatwine's verdict that I could be useful as a fighter.

Not that there would be much battle, except against outlaws and cattle thieves. Æthelred would have liked to fight the Danes because he fretted under their rule, but he feared their revenge and so took care not to offend them. That was easy enough, for Danish rule was light in our part of Mercia, but every few weeks some Danes would come to Cirrenceastre and demand cattle or food or silver and he had little choice but to pay. In truth he did not look north to the impotent King Burghred as his lord, but south to Wessex, and had I possessed any intelligence in those days I would have understood that Alfred was extending his influence over those southern parts of Mercia. The influence was not obvious, no West Saxon soldiers patrolled the country, but Alfred's messengers were forever riding and talking to the chief men, persuading them to bring their warriors south if the Danes attacked Wessex again.

I should have been wary of those West Saxon envoys, but I was too caught up in the intrigues of Æthelred's household to pay them any notice. The Ealdorman did not like me much, but his eldest son, also called Æthelred, detested me. He was a year younger than I, but very conscious of his dignity and a great hater of the Danes. He was also a great hater of Brida, mainly because he tried to hump her and got a knee in the groin for his trouble, and after that she was put to work in Ealdorman Æthelred's kitchens and she warned me, the very first day, not to touch the gruel. I did not, but the rest of the table all suffered from liquid bowels for the next two days thanks to the elderberries and iris root she had added to the pot. The younger Æthelred and I were forever quarrelling, though he was more careful after I beat him with my fists the day I found him whipping Brida's dog.

I was a nuisance to my uncle. I was too young, too big, too loud, too proud, too undisciplined, but I was also a family member and a lord, and so Ealdorman Æthelred endured me and was happy to let me chase Welsh raiders with Tatwine. We almost always failed to catch them.

I came back from one such pursuit late at night and let a servant rub down the horse while I went to find food and instead, of all people, discovered Father Willibald in the hall where he was sitting close to the embers of the fire. I did not recognise him at first, nor did he know me when I walked in all sweaty with a leather coat, long boots, a shield and two swords. I just saw a figure by the fire. 'Anything to eat there?' I asked, hoping I would not have to light a tallow candle and grope through the servants sleeping in the kitchen.

'Uhtred,' he said, and I turned and peered through the gloom. Then he whistled like a blackbird and I recognised him. 'Is that Brida with you?' the young priest asked.

She was also in leather, with a Welsh sword strapped to her waist. Nihtgenga ran to Willibald, whom he had never met, and allowed himself to be stroked. Tatwine and the other warriors all tramped in, but Willibald ignored them. 'I hope you're well, Uhtred?'

'I'm well, father,' I said, 'and you?'

'I'm very well,' he said.

He smiled, obviously wanting me to ask why he had come to Æthelred's hall, but I pretended to be uninterested. 'You didn't get into trouble for losing us?' I asked him instead.

'The Lady Ælswith was very angry,' he admitted, 'but Alfred seemed not to mind. He did chide Father Beocca though.'

'Beocca? Why?'

'Because Beocca had persuaded him you wanted to escape the Danes, and Beocca was wrong. Still, no harm done.' He smiled. 'And now Alfred has sent me to find you.'

I squatted close to him. It was late summer, but the night was surprisingly chill so I threw another log onto the fire so that sparks flew up and a puff of smoke drifted into the high beams. 'Alfred sent you,' I said flatly. 'He still wants to teach me to read?'

'He wants to see you, lord.'

I looked at him suspiciously. I called myself a lord, and so I was by birthright, but I was well imbued with the Danish idea that lordship was earned, not given, and I had not earned it yet. Still, Willibald was showing respect. 'Why does he want to see me?' I asked.

'He would talk with you,' Willibald said, 'and when the talk is done you are free to come back here or, indeed, go anywhere else you wish.'

Brida brought me some hard bread and cheese. I ate, thinking. 'What does he want to talk to me about?' I asked Willibald, 'God?'

The priest sighed. 'Alfred has been king for two years, Uhtred, and in those years he has had only two things on his mind. God and the Danes, but I think he knows you cannot help him with the first.' I smiled. Æthelred's hounds had woken as Tatwine and his men settled on the high platforms where they would sleep. One of the hounds came to me, hoping for food and I stroked his rough fur and I thought how Ragnar had loved his hounds. Ragnar was in Valhalla now, feasting and roaring and fighting and whoring and drinking, and I hoped there were hounds in the Northmen's heaven, and boars the size of oxen, and spears sharp as razors. 'There is only one condition attached to your journey,' Willibald went on, 'and that is that Brida is not to come.'

'Brida's not to come, eh?' I repeated.

'The Lady Ælswith insists on it,' Willibald said.

'Insists?'

'She has a son now,' Willibald said, 'God be praised, a fine boy called Edward.'

'If I were Alfred,' I said, 'I'd keep her busy too.'

Willibald smiled. 'So will you come?'

I touched Brida, who had settled beside me. 'We'll come,' I promised him, and Willibald shook his head at my obstinacy, but did not try to persuade me to leave Brida behind.

Why did I go? Because I was bored. Because my cousin Æthelred disliked me. Because Willibald's words had suggested that Alfred did not want me to become a scholar, but a warrior. I went because fate determines our lives.

We left in the morning. It was a late summer's day, a soft rain falling on trees heavy with leaf. At first we rode through Æthelred's fields, thick with rye and barley and loud with the rattling noise of corncrakes, but after a few miles we were in the wasteland that was the frontier region between Wessex and Mercia. There had been a time when these fields were fertile, when the villages were full and sheep roamed the higher hills, but the Danes had ravaged the area in the summer after their defeat at Æsc's Hill, and few men had come back to settle the land. Alfred, I knew, wanted folk to come here to plant crops and rear cattle, but the Danes had threatened to kill any man who used the land for they knew as well as Alfred that such men would look to Wessex for protection, that they would become West Saxons and increase the strength of Wessex, and Wessex, as far as the Danes were concerned, existed only because they had yet to take it.

Yet that land was not entirely deserted. A few folk still lived in the villages, and the woods were full of outlaws. We saw none, and that was good for we still had a fair amount of Ragnar's hoard that Brida carried. Each coin was now wrapped in a scrap of rag so that the frayed leather bag did not clink as she moved.

By day's end we were well south of that region and into Wessex and the fields were lush again and the villages full. No wonder the Danes yearned for this land.

Alfred was at Wintanceaster, which was the West Saxon capital and a fine town in a rich countryside. The Romans had made Wintanceaster, of course, and Alfred's palace was mostly Roman, though his father had added a great hall with beautifully carved beams, and Alfred was building a church that was even bigger than the hall, making its walls from stone that were covered with a spider's web of timber scaffolding when I arrived. There was a market beside the new building and I remember thinking how odd it was to see so many folk without a single Dane among them. The Danes looked like us, but when Danes walked through a market in northern England the crowds parted, men bowed, and there was a hint of fear. None here. Women haggled over apples and

213

bread and cheese and fish, and the only language I heard was the raw accents of Wessex.

Brida and I were given quarters in the Roman part of the palace. No one tried to part us this time. We had a small room, lime-washed, with a straw mattress, and Willibald said we should wait there, and we did until we got bored with waiting, after which we explored the palace, finding it full of priests and monks. They looked at us strangely, for both of us wore arm rings cut with Danish runes. I was a fool in those days, a clumsy fool, and did not have the courtesy to take the arm rings off. True, some English wore them, especially the warriors, but not in Alfred's palace. There were plenty of warriors in his household, many of them the great Ealdormen who were Alfred's courtiers, led his retainers and were rewarded by land, but such men were far outnumbered by priests, and only a handful of men, the trusted bodyguard of the king's household, were permitted to carry weapons in the palace. In truth it was more like a monastery than a king's court. In one room there were a dozen monks copying books, their pens scratching busily, and there were three chapels, one of them beside a courtyard that was full of flowers. It was beautiful, that court-yard, buzzing with bees and thick with fragrance. Nihtgenga was just pissing on one of the flowering bushes when a voice spoke behind us. 'The Romans made the courtyard.'

I turned and saw Alfred. I went on one knee, as a man should when he sees a king, and he waved me up. He was wearing woollen breeches, long boots and a simple linen shirt, and he had no escort, neither guard nor priest. His right sleeve was ink-stained. 'You are welcome, Uhtred,' he said.

'Thank you, lord,' I said, wondering where his entourage was. I had never seen him without a slew of priests within fawning distance, but he was quite alone that day.

'And Brida,' he said, 'is that your dog?'

'He is,' she said defiantly.

'He looks a fine beast. Come,' he ushered us through a door into what was evidently his own private chamber. It had a tall desk at which he could stand and write. The desk had four candleholders, though as it was daylight the candles were not lit. A small table held a bowl of water so he could wash the ink off his hands. There was a low bed covered in sheepskins, a stool on which were piled six books and a sheaf of parchments, and a low altar on which was an ivory crucifix and two jewelled reliquaries. The remains of a meal were on the window ledge. He moved the plates, bent to kiss the altar, then sat on the ledge and began sharpening some quills for writing. 'It is kind of you to come,' he said mildly. 'I was going to talk with you after supper tonight, but I saw you in the garden, so thought we could talk now.' He smiled and I, lout that I was, scowled. Brida squatted by the door with Nihtgenga close to her.

'Ealdorman Æthelred tells me you are a considerable warrior, Uhtred,' Alfred said.

'I've been lucky, lord.'

'Luck is good, or so my own warriors tell me. I have not yet worked out a theology of luck, and perhaps I never will. Can there be luck if God disposes?' He frowned at me for a few heartbeats, evidently thinking about the apparent contradiction, but then dismissed the problem as an amusement for another day. 'So I suppose I was wrong to try and encourage you to the priesthood?'

'There's nothing wrong with encouragement, lord,' I said, 'but I had no wish to be a priest.'

'So you ran away from me. Why?'

I think he expected me to be embarrassed and to evade his question, but I told him the truth. 'I went back to fetch my sword,' I told him. I wished I had Serpent-Breath at that moment, because I hated being without her, but the palace doorkeeper had insisted I give up all my weapons, even the small knife I used for eating.

He nodded seriously, as if that were a good reason. 'It's a special sword?'

'The best in the world, lord.'

He smiled at that, recognising a boy's misplaced enthusiasm. 'So you went back to Earl Ragnar?'

I nodded this time, but said nothing.

'Who did not hold you prisoner, Uhtred,' he said sternly, 'indeed he never did, did he? He treated you like a son.'

'I loved him,' I blurted out.

He stared at me and I became uncomfortable under his gaze.

215

He had very light eyes that gave you the sense of being judged. 'Yet in Eoferwic,' Alfred went on mildly, 'they are saying you killed him.'

Now it was my time to stare at him. I was angry, confused, astonished and surprised, so confused that I did not know what to say. But why was I so surprised? What else would Kjartan claim? Except, I thought, Kjartan must have thought me dead, or I hoped he thought me dead.

'They lie,' Brida said flatly.

'Do they?' Alfred asked me, still in a mild voice.

'They lie,' I said angrily.

'I never doubted it,' he said. He put down his quills and knife and leaned over to the heap of stiff parchments that rested on his pile of books and sifted through them until he found the one he was looking for. He read for a few moments. 'Kjartan? Is that how it is pronounced?'

'Kjartan,' I corrected him, making the 'j' sound like a 'y'.

'Earl Kjartan now,' Alfred said, 'and reckoned to be a great lord. Owner of four ships.'

'That's all written down?' I asked.

'Whatever I discover of my enemies is written down,' Alfred said, 'which is why you are here. To tell me more. Did you know Ivar the Boneless is dead?'

My hand instinctively went to Thor's hammer, which I wore under my jerkin. 'No. Dead?' It astonished me. Such was my awe of Ivar that I suppose I had thought he would live for ever, but Alfred spoke the truth. Ivar the Boneless was dead.

'He was killed fighting against the Irish,' Alfred said, 'and Ragnar's son has returned to Northumbria with his men. Will he fight Kjartan?'

'If he knows Kjartan killed his father,' I said, 'he'll disembowel him.'

'Earl Kjartan has sworn an oath of innocence in the matter,' Alfred said.

'Then he lies.'

'He's a Dane,' Alfred said, 'and the truth is not in them.' He gave me a sharp look, doubtless for the many lies I had fed him

216

over the years. He stood then and paced the small room. He had said that I was there to tell him about the Danes, but in the next few moments he was the one who did the telling. King Burghred of Mercia, he said, was tired of his Danish overlords and had decided to flee to Rome.

'Rome?'

'I was taken there twice as a child,' he said, 'and I remember the city as a very untidy place,' that was said very sternly, 'but a man feels close to God there, so it is a good place to pray. Burghred is a weak man, but he did his small best to alleviate Danish rule, and once he is gone then we can expect the Danes to fill his land. They will be on our frontier. They will be in Cirrenceastre.' He looked at me. 'Kjartan knows you're alive.'

'He does?'

'Of course he does. The Danes have spies, just as we do.' And Alfred's spies, I realised, had to be efficient for he knew so much. 'Does Kjartan care about your life?' he went on. 'If you tell the truth about Ragnar's death, Uhtred, then he does care because you can contradict his lies and if Ragnar learns that truth from you then Kjartan will certainly fear for his life. It is in Kjartan's interest, therefore, to kill you. I tell you this only so that you may consider whether you wish to return to Cirrenceastre where the Danes have,' he paused, 'influence. You will be safer in Wessex, but how long will Wessex last?' He evidently did not expect an answer, but kept pacing. 'Ubba has sent men to Mercia, which suggests he will follow. Have you met Ubba?'

'Many times.'

'Tell me of him.'

I told him what I knew, told him that Ubba was a great warrior, though very superstitious and that intrigued Alfred who wanted to know all about Storri the sorcerer and about the runesticks, and I told him how Ubba never picked battles for the joy of fighting, but only when the runes said he could win, but that once he fought he did so with a terrible savagery. Alfred wrote it all down, then asked if I had met Halfdan, the youngest brother, and I said I had, but very briefly.

'Halfdan speaks of avenging Ivar,' Alfred said, 'so it's possible he will not come back to Wessex. Not soon, anyway. But even with Halfdan in Ireland there will be plenty of pagans left to attack us.' He explained how he had anticipated an attack this year, but the Danes had been disorganised and he did not expect that to last. 'They will come next year,' he said, 'and we think Ubba will lead them.'

'Or Guthrum,' I said.

'I had not forgotten him. He is in East Anglia now.' He glanced reproachfully at Brida, remembering her tales of Edmund. Brida, quite unworried, just watched him with half-closed eyes. He looked back to me. 'What do you know of Guthrum?'

Again I talked and again he wrote. He was intrigued about the bone in Guthrum's hair, and shuddered when I repeated Guthrum's insistence that every Englishman be killed. 'A harder job than he thinks,' Alfred said drily. He laid the pen down and began pacing again. 'There are different kinds of men,' he said, 'and some are to be more feared than others. I feared Ivar the Boneless, for he was cold and thought carefully. Ubba? I don't know, but I suspect he is dangerous. Halfdan? A brave fool, but with no thoughts in his head. Guthrum? He is the least to be feared.'

'The least?' I sounded dubious. Guthrum might be called the Unlucky, but he was a considerable chieftain and led a large force of warriors.

'He thinks with his heart, Uhtred,' Alfred said, 'not his head. You can change a man's heart, but not his head.' I remember staring at Alfred then, thinking that he spouted foolishness like a horse pissing, but he was right. Or almost right because he tried to change me, but never succeeded.

A bee drifted through the door, Nihtgenga snapped impotently at it and the bee droned out again. 'But Guthrum will attack us?' Alfred asked.

'He wants to split you,' I said. 'One army by land, another by sea, and the Britons from Wales.'

Alfred looked at me gravely. 'How do you know that?'

So I told him about Guthrum's visit to Ragnar and the long conversation which I had witnessed, and Alfred's pen scratched, little flecks of ink spattering from the quill at rough spots on the parchment. 'What this suggests,' he spoke as he wrote, 'is that

Ubba will come from Mercia by land and Guthrum by sea from East Anglia.' He was wrong about that, but it seemed likely at the time. 'How many ships can Guthrum bring?'

I had no idea. 'Seventy?' I suggested, 'a hundred?'

'Far more than that,' Alfred said severely, 'and I cannot build even twenty ships to oppose them. Have you sailed, Uhtred?'

'Many times.'

'With the Danes?' he asked pedantically.

'With the Danes,' I confirmed.

'What I would like you to do,' he said, but at that moment a bell tolled somewhere in the palace and he immediately broke off from what he was saying. 'Prayers,' he said, putting down his quill, 'you will come.' It was not a question, but a command.

'I have things to do,' I said, waited a heartbeat, 'lord.'

He blinked at me in surprise for he was not used to men opposing his wishes, especially when it came to saying prayers, but I kept a stubborn face and he did not force the issue. There was the slap of sandalled feet on the paved path outside his chamber and he dismissed us as he hurried to join the monks going to their service. A moment later the drone of a chant began, and Brida and I abandoned the palace, going into the town where we discovered a tavern that sold decent ale. I had been offered none by Alfred. The folk there were suspicious of us, partly because of the arm rings with their Danish runes, and partly because of our strange accents, mine from the north and Brida's from the east, but a sliver of our silver was weighed and trusted, and the wary atmosphere subsided when Father Beocca came in, saw us, and raised his inky hands in welcome. 'I have been searching high and low for you,' he said, 'Alfred wanted you.'

'He wanted to pray,' I said.

'He would have you eat with him.'

I drank some ale. 'If I live to be a hundred, father,' I began.

'I pray you live longer than that,' Beocca said, 'I pray you live as long as Methuselah.'

I wondered who that was. 'If I live to be a hundred,' I said again, 'I hope never to eat with Alfred again.'

He shook his head sadly, but agreed to sit with us and take a pot of ale. He reached over and pulled at the leather thong half hidden by my jerkin and so revealed the hammer. He tutted. 'You lied to me, Uhtred,' he said sadly. 'When you ran away from Father Willibald we made enquiries. You were never a prisoner! You were treated as a son!'

'I was,' I agreed.

'But why did you not come to us then? Why did you stay with the Danes?'

I smiled. 'What would I have learned here?' I asked. He began to answer, but I stilled him. 'You would have made me a scholar, father,' I said, 'and the Danes made me a warrior. And you will need warriors when they come back.'

Beocca understood that, but he was still sad. He looked at Brida. 'And you, young lady, I hope you did not lie?'

'I always tell the truth, father,' she said in a small voice, 'always.'

'That is good,' he said, then reached over again to hide my amulet. 'Are you a Christian, Uhtred?' he asked.

'You baptised me yourself, father,' I said evasively.

'We will not defeat the Danes unless we hold the faith,' he said earnestly, then smiled, 'but will you do what Alfred wants?'

'I don't know what he wants. He ran off to wear out his knees before he could tell me.'

'He wants you to serve on one of the ships he's building,' he said. I just gaped at him. 'We're building ships, Uhtred,' Beocca went on enthusiastically, 'ships to fight the Danes, but our sailors are not fighters. They're, well, sailors! And they're fishermen, of course, and traders, but we need men who can teach them what the Danes do. Their ships raid our shores incessantly. Two ships come? Three ships? Sometimes more. They land, burn, kill, take slaves and vanish. But with ships we can fight them.' He punched his withered left hand with his right and winced with the pain. 'That's what Alfred wants.'

I glanced at Brida who gave a small shrug as if to say that she thought Beocca was telling the truth.

I thought of the two Æthelreds, younger and older, and their dislike of me. I remembered the joy of a ship on the seas, of the wind tearing at the rigging, of the oars bending and flashing back the sun, of the songs of the rowers, of the heartbeat of the steering-oar, of the seethe of the long green water against the hull. 'Of course I'll do it,' I said.

'Praise God,' Beocca said. And why not?

I met Æthelflaed before I left Wintanceaster. She was three or four years old, I suppose, and full of words. She had bright gold hair. She was playing in the garden outside Alfred's study and I remember she had a rag doll and Alfred played with her and Ælswith worried he was making her too excited. I remember her laugh. She never lost that laugh. Alfred was good with her for he loved his children. Most of the time he was solemn, pious and very self-disciplined, but with small children he became playful and I almost liked him as he teased Æthelflaed by hiding her rag doll behind his back. I also remember how Æthelflaed ran over to Nihtgenga and fondled him and Ælswith called her back. 'Dirty dog,' she told her daughter, 'you'll get fleas or worse. Come here!' She gave Brida a very sour look and muttered, 'Scrætte!' That means prostitute and Brida pretended not to have heard, as did Alfred. Ælswith ignored me, but I did not mind because Alfred had summoned a palace slave who laid a helmet and a mail coat on the grass. 'For you, Uhtred,' Alfred said.

The helmet was bright iron, dented on the crown by the blow of a weapon, polished with sand and vinegar, and with a face-piece in which two eyeholes stared like the pits of a skull. The mail was good, though it had been pierced by a spear or sword where the owner's heart had been, but it had been expertly repaired by a good smith and it was worth many pieces of silver. 'They were both taken from a Dane at Æsc's Hill,' Alfred told me. Ælswith watched disapprovingly.

'Lord,' I said, and went on one knee and kissed his hand.

'A year's service,' he said, 'is all I ask of you.'

'You have it, lord,' I said, and sealed that promise with another kiss on his ink-stained knuckles.

I was dazzled. The two pieces of armour were rare and valuable, and I had done nothing to deserve such generosity, unless to behave boorishly is to deserve favours. And Alfred had been generous, though a lord should be generous. That is what a lord is, a giver of rings, and a lord who does not distribute wealth is a lord who will lose the allegiance of his men, yet even so I had not earned the gifts, though I was grateful for them. I was dazzled by them and, for a moment, I thought Alfred a great and good and admirable man.

I should have thought a moment longer. He was generous, of course, but Alfred, unlike his wife, was never grudging with gifts, but why give such valuable armour to a half-fledged youth? Because I was useful to him. Not very useful, but still of use. Alfred sometimes played chess, a game for which I have small patience, but in chess there are pieces of great value and pieces of little worth, and I was one of those. The pieces of great value were the lords of Mercia who, if he could bind them to him, would help Wessex fight the Danes, but he was already looking beyond Mercia into East Anglia and Northumbria and he had no Northumbrian lords in exile except me, and he foresaw a time when he would need a Northumbrian to persuade the northern folk to accept a southern king. If I had been really valuable, if I could have brought him the allegiance of folk nearer his frontier, then he would have given me a noble West Saxon wife, for a woman of high birth is the greatest gift a lord can bestow, but a helmet and a coat of mail were sufficient for the distant idea of Northumbria. I doubt he thought I could deliver that country to him, but he did see that one day I might be useful in its delivery and so he bound me to him with gifts and made the bonds acceptable with flattery. 'None of my men has fought on shipboard,' he told me, 'so they must learn. You might be young, Uhtred, but you have experience which means you know more than they do. So go and teach them.'

Me? Know more than his men? I had sailed in *Wind-Viper*, that was all, but I had never fought from a ship, though I was not going to tell Alfred that. Instead I accepted his gifts and went south to the coast, and thus he had tucked away a pawn that might one day be useful. To Alfred, of course, the most valuable pieces on the board were his bishops who were supposed to pray the Danes out of England, and no bishop ever went unfed in Wessex, but I could not complain for I had a coat of mail, a helmet of iron, and looked like a warrior. Alfred loaned us horses for our journey and he sent Father Willibald with us, not as a guardian this time, but because he insisted that his new ships' crews must have a priest to look after their spiritual needs. Poor Willibald. He used to get sick as a dog every time a ripple touched a ship, but he never abandoned his responsibilities, especially towards me. If prayers could make a man into a Christian then I would be a saint ten times over by now.

Destiny is all. And now, looking back, I see the pattern of my life's journey. It began in Bebbanburg and took me south, ever southwards, until I reached the farthest coast of England and could go no further and still hear my own language. That was my childhood's journey. As a man I have gone the other way, ever northwards, carrying sword and spear and axe to clear the path back to where I began. Destiny. The spinners favour me, or at least they have spared me, and for a time they made me a sailor.

I took my mail coat and helmet in the year 874, the same year that King Burghred fled to Rome, and Alfred expected Guthrum to come in the following spring, but he did not, nor in the summer, and so Wessex was spared an invasion in 875. Guthrum should have come, but he was a cautious man, ever expecting the worst, and he spent a full eighteen months raising the greatest army of Danes that had ever been seen in England. It dwarfed the Great Army that had marched to Readingum, and it was an army that should have finished Wessex and granted Guthrum's dream of slaughtering the last Englishman in England. Guthrum's host did come in time and when that time came the three spinners cut England's threads one by one until she dangled by a wisp, but that story must wait and I mention it now only to explain why we were given time to prepare ourselves.

And I was given to *Heahengel*. So help me, that was the ship's name. It means Archangel. She was not mine, of course, she had a shipmaster called Werferth who had commanded a tubby boat that had traded across the sea before he was persuaded to steer

Heahengel, and her warriors were led by a grim old beast called Leofric. And me? I was the turd in the butter-churn.

I was not needed. All Alfred's flattering words about me teaching his sailors how to fight were just that, mere words. But he had persuaded me to join his fleet, and I had promised him a year, and here I was in Hamtun which was a fine port at the head of a long arm of the sea. Alfred had ordered twelve ships made, and their maker was a shipwright who had been an oarsman on a Danish boat before escaping in Frankia and making his way back to England. There was not much about ship fighting that he did not know, and nothing I could teach anyone, but ship fighting is a very simple affair. A ship is a scrap of land afloat. So a ship fight is a land fight at sea. Bang your boat alongside the enemy, make a shield wall, and kill the other crew. But our shipwright, who was a cunning man, had worked out that a larger ship gave its crew an advantage because it could hold more men and its sides, being higher, would serve as a wall, and so he had built twelve big ships which at first looked odd to me for they had no beast-heads at their prows or sterns, though they did all have crucifixes nailed to their masts. The whole fleet was commanded by Ealdorman Hacca, who was brother to the Ealdorman of Hamptonscir, and the only thing he said when I arrived was to advise me to wrap my mail coat in an oiled sack so it would not rust. After that he gave me to Leofric.

'Show me your hands,' Leofric ordered. I did and he sneered. 'You'll have blisters soon, Earsling.'

That was his favourite word, earsling. It means arseling. That was me, though sometimes he called me Endwerc, which means a pain in the arse, and he made me an oarsman, one of the sixteen on the bæcbord, which is the left-hand side of the ship as you look forward. The other side is the steorbord, for it is on that side that the steering oar is rigged. We had sixty warriors aboard, thirty-two rowed at a time unless the sail could be hoisted, and we had Werferth at the steering oar and Leofric snarling up and down telling us to pull harder.

All autumn and winter we rowed up and down Hamtun's wide channel and beyond in the Solente, which is the sea south of the island called Wiht, and we fought the tide and wind, hammering *Heahengel* through short, cold waves until we had become a crew and could make her leap across the sea and, to my surprise, I found that *Heahengel* was a fast ship. I had thought that, being so much bigger, she would be slower than the Danish ships, but she was fast, very fast, and Leofric was turning her into a lethal weapon.

He did not like me and though he called me Earsling and Endwerc I did not face him down because I would have died. He was a short, wide man, muscled like an ox, with a scarred face, a quick temper and a sword so battered that its blade was slim as a knife. Not that he cared, for his preferred weapon was the axe. He knew I was an Ealdorman, but did not care, nor did he care that I had once served on a Danish boat. 'The only thing the Danes can teach us, Earsling,' he told me, 'is how to die.'

He did not like me, but I liked him. At night, when we filled one of Hamtun's taverns, I would sit near him to listen to his few words which were usually scornful, even about our own ships. 'Twelve,' he snarled, 'and how many can the Danes bring?'

No one answered.

'Two hundred?' he suggested. 'And we have twelve?'

Brida beguiled him one night into talking about his fights, all of them ashore, and he talked of Æsc's Hill, how the Danish shield wall had been broken by a man with an axe, and it was obviously Leofric himself who had done that, and he told how the man had held the axe halfway up its shaft because that made it quicker to recover from the blow, though it diminished the force of the weapon, and how the man had used his shield to hold off the enemy on his left, killed the one in front then the one to the right, and then had slipped his hand down the axe handle to start swinging it in terrible, flashing strokes that carved through the Danish lines. He saw me listening and gave me his usual sneer. 'Been in a shield wall, Earsling?'

I held up one finger.

'He broke the enemy shield wall,' Brida said. She and I lived in the tavern stables and Leofric liked Brida though he refused to allow her on board *Heahengel* because he reckoned a woman brought ill-luck to a ship. 'He broke the wall,' Brida said, 'I saw it.'

He gazed at me, not sure whether to believe her. I said nothing. 'Who were you fighting,' he asked after a pause, 'nuns?'

'Welshmen,' Brida said.

'Oh, Welshmen! Hell, they die easy,' he said, which was not true, but it let him keep his scorn of me, and next day, when we had a practice fight with wooden staves instead of real weapons, he made sure he opposed me and he beat me to the ground as if I were a yapping dog, opening a cut on my skull and leaving me dazed. 'I'm not a Welshman, Earsling,' he said. I liked Leofric a lot.

The year turned. I became eighteen years old. The great Danish army did not come, but their ships did. The Danes were being Vikings again, and their dragon ships came in ones and twos to harry the West Saxon coast, to raid and to rape and to burn and to kill, but this year Alfred had his own ships ready.

So we went to sea.

Eight

We spent the spring, summer and autumn of the year 875 rowing up and down Wessex's south coast. We were divided into four flotillas, and Leofric commanded *Heahengel*, *Ceruphin* and *Cristenlic* which meant Archangel, Cherubim and Christian. Alfred had chosen the names. Hacca, who led the whole fleet, sailed in the *Evangelista* which soon acquired the reputation of being an unlucky ship, though her real ill fortune was to have Hacca on board. He was a nice enough man, generous with his silver, but he hated ships, hated the sea, and wanted nothing more than to be a warrior on dry land, which meant that *Evangelista* was always on Hamtun's hard undergoing repairs.

But not the *Heahengel*. I tugged that oar till my body ached and my hands were hard as oak, but the rowing put muscle on me, so much muscle. I was big now, big, tall and strong, and cocky and belligerent as well. I wanted nothing more than to try *Heahengel* against some Danish ship, yet our first encounter was a disaster. We were off the coast of Suth Seaxa, a marvellous coast of rearing white cliffs, and *Ceruphin* and *Cristenlic* had gone far out to sea while we slid inshore hoping to attract a Viking ship that would pursue us into an ambush sprung by the other two craft. The trap worked, only the Viking was better than us. He was smaller, much smaller, and we pursued him against the falling tide, gaining on him with every dip of our oars, but then he saw *Ceruphin* and *Cristenlic* slamming in from the south, their oar blades flashing back the sunlight and their bow waves seething white, and the Danish shipmaster turned his craft as if she had been mounted on a spindle and, with the strong tide now helping him, dashed back at us.

'Turn into him!' Leofric roared at Werferth who was at the steering oar, but instead Werferth turned away, not wanting to bring on a collision, and I saw the oars of the Danish ship slide into their holes as she neared us and then she ran down our steor-bord flank, snapping our oars one by one, the impact throwing the oar shafts back into our rowers with enough force to break some men's ribs, and then the Danish archers, they had four or five aboard, began loosing their arrows. One went into Werferth's neck and there was blood pouring down the steering deck and Leofric was bellowing in impotent rage as the Danes, oars slid out again, sped safely away down the fast ebbing tide. They jeered as we wallowed in the waves.

'Have you steered a boat, Earsling?' Leofric asked me, pulling the dying Werferth aside.

'Yes.'

'Then steer this one.' We limped home with only half our proper oars, and we learned two lessons. One was to carry spare oars and the second was to carry archers, except that Ealdorman Freola, who commanded the fyrd of Hamptonscir, said he could spare no bowmen, that he had too few as it was, and that the ships had already consumed too many of his other warriors, and besides, he said, we should not need archers. Hacca, his brother, told us not to make a fuss. 'Just throw spears,' he advised Leofric.

'I want archers,' Leofric insisted.

'There are none!' Hacca said, spreading his hands.

Father Willibald wanted to write a letter to Alfred. 'He will listen to me,' he said.

'So you write to him,' Leofric said sourly, 'and what happens then?'

'He will send archers, of course!' Father Willibald said brightly.

'The letter,' Leofric said, 'goes to his damn clerks, who are all priests, and they put it in a pile, and the pile gets read slowly, and when Alfred finally sees it he asks for advice, and two damned bishops have their say, and Alfred writes back wanting to know more, and by then it's Candlemas and we're all dead with Danish arrows in our backs.' He glared at Willibald and I began to like

Leofric even more. He saw me grinning. 'What's so funny, Endwerc?' he demanded.

'I can get you archers,' I said.

'How?'

With one piece of Ragnar's gold, which we displayed in Hamtun's marketplace and said that the gold coin, with its weird writing, would go to the best archer to win a competition that would be held one week hence. That coin was worth more than most men could earn in a year and Leofric was curious how I had come by it, but I refused to tell him. Instead I set up targets and word spread through the countryside that rich gold was to be had with cheap arrows, and over forty men arrived to test their skill and we simply marched the best twelve on board *Heahengel* and another ten each to *Ceruphin* and *Cristenlic*, then took them to sea. Our twelve protested, of course, but Leofric snarled at them and they all suddenly decided they wanted nothing better than to sail the Wessex coast with him. 'For something that dribbled out of a goat's backside,' Leofric told me, 'you're not completely useless.'

'There'll be trouble when we get back,' I warned him.

'Of course there'll be trouble,' he agreed, 'trouble from the shire reeve, from the Ealdorman, from the bishop and from the whole damned lot of them.' He laughed suddenly, a very rare occurrence. 'So let's kill some Danes first.'

We did. And by chance it was the same ship that had shamed us, and she tried the same trick again, but this time I turned *Heahengel* into her and our bows smashed into her quarter and our twelve archers were loosing shafts into her crew. *Heahengel* had ridden up over the other ship, half sinking her and pinning her down, and Leofric led a charge over the prow, and there was blood thickening the water in the Viking bilge. Two of our men managed to tie the ships together which meant I could leave the steering oar and, without bothering to put on either helmet or mail coat, I jumped aboard with Serpent-Breath and joined the fight. There were shields clashing in the wide midships, spears jabbing, swords and axes swinging, arrows flighting overhead, men screaming, men dying, the rage of battle, the joy of blade song and it was all over before *Ceruphin* or *Cristenlic* could join us.

How I did love it. To be young, to be strong, to have a good sword and to survive. The Danish crew had been forty-six strong and all but one died, and he only lived because Leofric bellowed that we must take a prisoner. Three of our men died, and six were foully wounded and they probably all died once we got them ashore, but we bailed out the Viking ship and went back to Hamtun with her in tow, and in her blood-drenched belly we found a chest of silver that she had stolen from a monastery on Wiht. Leofric presented a generous amount to the bowmen, so that when we went ashore and were confronted by the reeve, who demanded that we give up the archers, only two of them wanted to go. The rest could see their way to becoming wealthy, and so they stayed.

The prisoner was called Hroi. His lord, whom we had killed in the battle, had been called Thurkil and he served Guthrum, who was in East Anglia where he now called himself king of that country. 'Does he still wear the bone in his hair?' I asked.

'Yes, lord,' Hroi said. He did not call me lord because I was an Ealdorman, for he did not know that. He called me lord because he did not want me to kill him when the questioning was done.

Hroi did not think Guthrum would attack this year. 'He waits for Halfdan,' he told me.

'And Halfdan's where?'

'In Ireland, lord.'

'Avenging Ivar?'

'Yes, lord.'

'You know Kjartan?'

'I know three men so called, lord.'

'Kjartan of Northumbria,' I said, 'father of Sven.'

'Earl Kjartan, you mean?'

'He calls himself Earl now?' I asked.

'Yes, lord, and he is still in Northumbria.'

'And Ragnar? Son of Ragnar the Fearless?'

'Earl Ragnar is with Guthrum, lord, in East Anglia. He has four boats.'

We chained Hroi and sent him under guard to Wintanceaster for Alfred liked to talk with Danish prisoners. I do not know what

230

happened to him. He was probably hanged or beheaded, for Alfred did not extend Christian mercy to pagan pirates.

And I thought of Ragnar the Younger, Earl Ragnar now, and wondered if I would meet his boats on the Wessex coast, and wondered too whether Hroi had lied and that Guthrum would invade that summer. I thought he would, for there was much fighting across the island of Britain. The Danes of Mercia had attacked the Britons in north Wales, I never did discover why, and other Danish bands raided across the West Saxon frontier, and I suspected those raids were meant to discover West Saxon weaknesses before Guthrum launched his Great Army, but no army came and, as the summer reached its height, Alfred felt safe enough to leave his forces in North Wessex to visit the fleet.

His arrival coincided with news that seven Danish ships had been seen off Heilincigae, an island which lay in shallow waters not far to Hamtun's east, and the news was confirmed when we saw smoke rising from a pillaged settlement. Only half our ships were in Hamtun, the others were at sea, and one of the six in port, the *Evangelista*, was on the hard having her bottom scraped. Hacca was nowhere near Hamtun, gone to his brother's house probably, and he would doubtless be annoyed that he had missed the king's visit, but Alfred had given us no warning of his arrival, probably because he wanted to see us as we really were, rather than as we would have been had we known he was coming. As soon as he heard about the Danes off Heilincigae he ordered us all to sea and boarded *Heahengel* along with two of his guards and three priests, one of whom was Beocca who came to stand beside the steering oar.

'You've got bigger, Uhtred,' he said to me, almost reproachfully. I was a good head taller than him now, and much broader in the chest.

'If you rowed, father,' I said, 'you'd get bigger.'

He giggled. 'I can't imagine myself rowing,' he said, then pointed at my steering oar. 'Is that difficult to manage?' he asked.

I let him take it and suggested he turned the boat slightly to the steorbord and his crossed eyes widened in astonishment as he tried to push the oar and the water fought against him. 'It needs strength,' I said, taking the oar back.

'You're happy, aren't you?' He made it sound like an accusation.

'I am, yes.'

'You weren't meant to be,' he said.

'No?'

'Alfred thought this experience would humble you.'

I stared at the king who was up in the bows with Leofric, and I remembered the king's honeyed words about me having something to teach these crews, and I realised he had known I had nothing to contribute, yet he had still given me the helmet and armour. That, I assumed, was so I would give him a year of my life in which he hoped Leofric would knock the arrogance out of my bumptious youthfulness. 'Didn't work, did it?' I said, grinning.

'He said you must be broken like a horse.'

'But I'm not a horse, father, I'm a lord of Northumbria. What did he think? That after a year I'd be a meek Christian ready to do his bidding?'

'Is that such a bad thing?'

'It's a bad thing,' I said. 'He needs proper men to fight the Danes, not praying lickspittles.'

Beocca sighed, then made the sign of the cross because poor Father Willibald was feeding the gulls with his vomit. 'It's time you were married, Uhtred,' Beocca said sternly.

I looked at him in astonishment. 'Married! Why do you say that?'

'You're old enough,' Beocca said.

'So are you,' I retorted, 'and you're not married, so why should I be?'

'I live in hope,' Beocca said. Poor man, he had a squint, a palsied hand and a face like a sick weasel, which really did not make him a great favourite with women. 'But there is a young woman in Defnascir you should look at,' he told me enthusiastically, 'a very well born young lady! A charming creature, and,' he paused, evidently having run out of the girl's qualities, or else because he could not invent any new ones, 'her father was the shire reeve, rest his soul. A lovely girl. Mildrith, she's called.' He smiled at me expectantly.

'A reeve's daughter,' I said flatly. 'The king's reeve? The shire reeve?'

'Her father was reeve of southern Defnascir,' Beocca said, sliding the man down the social ladder, 'but he left Mildrith property. A fair piece of land near Exanceaster.'

'A reeve's daughter,' I repeated, 'not an Ealdorman's daughter?'

'She's sixteen, I believe,' Beocca said, gazing at the shingled beach sliding away to our east.

'Sixteen,' I said scathingly, 'and unmarried, which suggests she has a face like a bag of maggots.'

'That is hardly relevant,' he said crossly.

'You don't have to sleep with her,' I said, 'and no doubt she's pious?'

'She is a devoted Christian, I'm happy to say.'

'You've seen her?' I asked.

'No,' he admitted, 'but Alfred has talked of her.'

'This is Alfred's idea?'

'He likes to see his men settled, to have their roots in the land.'

'I'm not his man, father. I'm Uhtred of Bebbanburg, and the lords of Bebbanburg don't marry pious maggot-faced bitches of low birth.'

'You should meet her,' he persisted, frowning at me. 'Marriage is a wonderful thing, Uhtred, ordained by God for our happiness.'

'How would you know?'

'It is,' he insisted weakly.

'I'm already happy,' I said. 'I hump Brida and I kill Danes. Find another man for Mildrith. Why don't you marry her? Good God, father, you must be near thirty! If you don't marry soon you'll go to your grave a virgin. Are you a virgin?'

He blushed, but did not answer because Leofric came back to the steering deck with a black scowl. He never looked happy, but he appeared grimmer than ever at that moment and I had an idea that he had been arguing with Alfred, an argument he had plainly lost. Alfred himself followed, a serene look of indifference on his long face. Two of his priests trailed him, carrying parchment, ink

233

and quills and I realised notes were being taken. 'What would you say, Uhtred, was the most crucial equipment for a ship?' Alfred asked me. One of the priests dipped his quill in the ink in readiness for my answer, then staggered as the ship hit a wave. God knows what his writing looked like that day. 'The sail?' Alfred prompted me. 'Spears? Archers? Shields? Oars?'

'Buckets,' I said.

'Buckets?' He looked at me with disapproval, suspecting I was mocking him.

'Buckets to bail the ship, lord,' I said, nodding down into *Heahengel*'s belly where four men scooped out sea water and chucked it over the side, though a good deal landed on the rowers. 'What we need, lord, is a better way of caulking ships.'

'Write that down,' Alfred instructed the priests, then stood on tiptoe to look across the intervening low land into the sea-lake where the enemy ships had been sighted.

'They'll be long gone,' Leofric growled.

'I pray not,' Alfred said.

'The Danes don't wait for us,' Leofric said. He was in a terrible mood, so terrible that he was willing to snarl at his king. 'They aren't fools,' he went on, 'they land, they raid and they go. They'll have sailed on the ebb.' The tide had just turned and was flooding against us now, though I never did quite understand the tides in the long waters from the sea to Hamtun for there were twice as many high tides there as anywhere else. Hamtun's tides had a mind of their own, or else were confused by the channels.

'The pagans were there at dawn,' Alfred said.

'And they'll be miles away by now,' Leofric said. He spoke to Alfred as if he were another crewman, using no respect, but Alfred was always patient with such insolence. He knew Leofric's worth.

But Leofric was wrong that day about the enemy. The Viking ships were not gone, but still off Heilincigae, all seven of them, having been trapped there by the falling tide. They were waiting for the rising water to float them free, but we arrived first, coming into the sea-lake through the narrow entrance which leads from the northern bank of the Solente. Once through the entrance a ship is in a world of marshes, sandbanks, islands and fish traps, not unlike the waters of the Gewæsc. We had a man aboard who had grown up on those waters, and he guided us, but the Danes had lacked any such expertise and they had been misled by a line of withies, stuck into the sand at low tide to mark a channel, which had been deliberately moved to entice them onto a mudbank on which they were now firmly stuck.

Which was splendid. We had them trapped like foxes in a one-hole earth and all we had to do was anchor in the sea-lake entrance, hope our anchors held against the strong currents, wait for them to float off and then slaughter them, but Alfred was in a hurry. He wanted to get back to his land forces and insisted we return him to Hamtun before nightfall, and so, against Leofric's advice, we were ordered to an immediate attack.

That too was splendid, except that we could not approach the mudbank directly for the channel was narrow and it would mean going in single file and the lead ship would face seven Danish ships on its own, and so we had to row a long way to approach them from the south, which meant that they could escape to the sea-lake's entrance if the tide floated them off, which it might very well do, and Leofric muttered into his beard that we were going about the battle all wrong. He was furious with Alfred.

Alfred, meanwhile, was fascinated by the enemy ships, which he had never seen so clearly before. 'Are the beasts representations of their gods?' he asked me, referring to the finely carved prows and sterns that flaunted their monsters, dragons and serpents.

'No, lord, just beasts,' I said. I was beside him, having relinquished the steering oar to the man who knew these waters, and I told the king how the carved heads could be lifted off their posts so that they did not terrify the spirits of the land.

'Write that down,' he ordered a priest. 'And the wind-vanes at the mastheads?' he asked me, looking at the nearer one which was painted with an eagle, 'are they designed to frighten the spirits?'

I did not answer. Instead I was staring at the seven ships across the slick hump of the mudbank and I recognised one. *Wind-Viper*. The light-coloured strake in the bow was clear enough, but even so I would have recognised her. *Wind-Viper*, lovely *Wind-Viper*, ship of dreams, here at Heilincigae.

'Uhtred?' Alfred prompted me.

'They're just wind-vanes, lord,' I said. And if *Wind-Viper* was here, was Ragnar here too? Or had Kjartan taken the ship and leased it to a shipmaster?

'It seems a deal of trouble,' Alfred said pettishly, 'to decorate a ship.'

'Men love their ships,' I said, 'and fight for them. You honour what you fight for, lord. We should decorate our ships.' I spoke harshly, thinking we would love our ships more if they had beasts on their prows, and had proper names like *Blood-Spiller*, *Sea-Wolf* or *Widow-Maker*. Instead the *Heahengel* led the *Ceruphin* and *Cristenlic* through the tangled waters, and behind us were the *Apostol* and the *Eftwyrd*, which meant Judgment Day and was probably the best named of our fleet because she sent more than one Dane to the sea's embrace.

The Danes were digging, trying to deepen the treacherous channel and so float their ships, but as we came nearer they realised they would never complete such a huge task and went back to their stranded boats to fetch armour, helmets, shields and weapons. I pulled on my coat of mail, its leather lining stinking of old sweat, and I pulled on the helmet, then strapped Serpent-Breath on my back and Wasp-Sting to my waist. This was not going to be a sea-fight, but a land battle, shield wall against shield wall, a maul in the mud, and the Danes had the advantage because they could mass where we must land and they could meet us as we came off the ships, and I did not like it. I could see Leofric hated it, but Alfred was calm enough as he pulled on his helmet. 'God is with us,' he said.

'He needs to be,' Leofric muttered, then raised his voice to shout at the steersman. 'Hold her there!' It was tricky to keep *Heahengel* still in the swirling current, but we backed oars and she slewed around as Leofric peered at the shore. I assumed he was waiting for the other ships to catch up so that we could all land together, but he had seen a spit of muddy sand projecting from the shore and had worked out that if we beached *Heahengel* there then our first men off the prow would not have to face a shield wall composed of seven Viking crews. The spit was narrow, only wide enough for three or four men to stand abreast and a fight there would be between equal numbers. 'It's a good enough place to die, Earsling,' he told me, and led me forward. Alfred hurried behind us. 'Wait,' Leofric snapped at the king so savagely that Alfred actually obeyed. 'Put her on the spit!' Leofric yelled back to the steersman, 'now!'

Ragnar was there. I could see the eagle wing on its pole, and then I saw him, looking so like his father that for a moment I thought I was a boy again.

'Ready, Earsling?' Leofric said. He had assembled his half-dozen best warriors, all of us in the prow, while behind us the bowmen readied to launch their arrows at the Danes who were hurrying towards the narrow stretch of muddy sand. Then we lurched forward as *Heahengel*'s bow scraped aground. 'Now!' Leofric shouted, and we jumped overboard into water that came up to our knees, and then we instinctively touched shields, made the wall, and I was gripping Wasp-Sting as the first Danes ran at us.

'Kill them!' Leofric shouted, and I thrust the shield forward and there was the great clash of iron boss on limewood, and an axe whirled overhead, but a man behind me caught it on his shield and I was stabbing under my shield, bringing the short sword up, but she rammed into a Danish shield. I wrenched her free, stabbed again, and felt a pain in my ankle as a blade sliced through water and boot. Blood swirled in the sea, but I was still standing, and I heaved forward, smelling the Danes, gulls screaming overhead, and more of the Danes were coming, but more of our men were joining us, some up to their waists in the tide, and the front of the battle was a shoving match now because no one had room to swing a weapon. It was a grunting, cursing shield battle, and Leofric, beside me, gave a shout and we heaved up and they stepped back a half-pace and our arrows slashed over our helmets and I slammed Wasp-Sting forward, felt her break through leather or mail, twisted her in flesh, pulled her back, pushed with the shield, kept my head down under the rim, pushed again, stabbed again, brute force, stout shield and good steel, nothing else. A man was drowning, blood streaming in the ripples from his twitching body, and I suppose we were shouting, but I never remember much about that. You remember the pushing, the smell, the snarling bearded faces, the anger, and then *Cristenlic* rammed her bows into the flank of the Danish line, crumpling men into the water, drowning and crushing them, and her crew jumped into the small waves with spears, swords and axes. A third boat arrived, more men landed, and I heard Alfred behind me, shouting at us to break their line, to kill them. I was ramming Wasp-Sting down at a man's ankles, jabbing again and again, pushing with the shield, and then he stumbled and our line surged forward and he tried to stab up into my groin, but Leofric slammed his axe head down, turning the man's face into a mask of blood and broken teeth. 'Push!' Leofric yelled, and we heaved at the enemy, and suddenly they were breaking away and running.

We had not beaten them. They were not running from our swords and spears, but rather because the rising tide was floating their ships and they ran to rescue them, and we stumbled after them, or rather I stumbled because my right ankle was bleeding and hurting, and we still did not have enough men ashore to overwhelm their crews and they were hurling themselves on board their ships, but one crew, brave men all, stayed on the sand to hold us back.

'Are you wounded, Earsling?' Leofric asked me.

'It's nothing.'

'Stay back,' he ordered me. He was forming *Heahengel*'s men into a new shield wall, a wall to thump into that one brave crew, and Alfred was there now, mail armour shining bright, and the Danes must have known he was a great lord, but they did not abandon their ships for the honour of killing him. I think that if Alfred had brought the dragon banner and fought beneath it, so that the Danes could recognise him as the king, they would have stayed and fought us and might very well have killed or captured Alfred, but the Danes were always wary of taking too many casualties and they hated losing their beloved ships, and so they just wanted to be away from that place. To which end they were willing to pay the price of the one ship to save the others, and that one ship was not *Wind-Viper*. I could see her being pushed into the channel, could see her creeping away backwards, see her oars striking against sand rather than water, and I splashed through

238

the small waves, skirting our shield wall and leaving the fight to my right as I bellowed at the ship. 'Ragnar! Ragnar!'

Arrows were flicking past me. One struck my shield, another glanced off my helmet with a click and that reminded me that he would not recognise me with the helmet on and so I dropped Wasp-Sting and bared my head. 'Ragnar!'

The arrows stopped. The shield walls were crashing, men were dying, most of the Danes were escaping, and Earl Ragnar stared at me across the widening gap and I could not tell from his face what he was thinking, but he had stopped his handful of bowmen from shooting at me, and then he cupped his hands to his mouth. 'Here!' he shouted at me, 'tomorrow's dusk!' Then his oars bit water, the *Wind-Viper* turned like a dancer, the blades dragged the sea and she was gone.

I retrieved Wasp-Sting and went to join the fight, but it was over. Our crews had massacred that one Danish crew, all except a handful of men who had been spared on Alfred's orders. The rest were a bloody pile on the tideline and we stripped them of their armour and weapons, took off their clothes and left their white bodies to the gulls. Their ship, an old and leaking vessel, was towed back to Hamtun.

Alfred was pleased. In truth he had let six ships escape, but it had still been a victory and news of it would encourage his troops fighting in the north. One of his priests questioned the prisoners, noting their answers on parchment. Alfred asked some questions of his own, which the priest translated, and when he had learned all that he could he came back to where I was steering and looked at the blood staining the deck by my right foot. 'You fight well, Uhtred.'

'We fought badly, lord,' I said, and that was true. Their shield wall had held, and if they had not retreated to rescue their ships they might even have beaten us back into the sea. I had not done well. There are days when the sword and shield seem clumsy, when the enemy seems quicker, and this had been one such day. I was angry with myself.

'You were talking to one of them,' Alfred said accusingly. 'I saw you. You were talking to one of the pagans.'

'I was telling him, lord,' I said, 'that his mother was a whore, his father a turd of hell and that his children are pieces of weasel shit.'

He flinched at that. He was no coward, Alfred, and he knew the anger of battle, but he never liked the insults that men shouted. I think he would have liked war to be decorous. He looked behind *Heahengel* where the dying sun's light was rippling our long wake red. 'The year you promised to give me will soon be finished,' he said.

'True, lord.'

'I pray you will stay with us.'

'When Guthrum comes, lord,' I said, 'he will come with a fleet to darken the sea and our twelve ships will be crushed.' I thought perhaps that was what Leofric had been arguing about, about the futility of trying to stem a seaborne invasion with twelve ill-named ships. 'If I stay,' I asked, 'what use will I be if the fleet dares not put to sea?'

'What you say is true,' Alfred said, suggesting that his argument with Leofric had been about something else, 'but the crews can fight ashore. Leofric tells me you are as good a warrior as any he has seen.'

'Then he has never seen himself, lord.'

'Come to me when your time is up,' he said, 'and I will find a place for you.'

'Yes, lord,' I said, but in a tone which only acknowledged that I understood what he wanted, not that I would obey him.

'But you should know one thing, Uhtred,' his voice was stern, 'if any man commands my troops that man must know how to read and write.'

I almost laughed at that. 'So he can read the Psalms, lord?' I asked sarcastically.

'So he can read my orders,' Alfred said coldly, 'and send me news.'

'Yes, lord,' I said again.

They had lit beacons in Hamtun's waters so we could find our way home, and the night wind stirred the liquid reflections of moon and stars as we slid to our anchorage. There were lights

240

ashore, and fires, and ale, and food and laughter, and best of all the promise of meeting Ragnar next day.

Ragnar took a huge risk, of course, in going back to Heilincigae, though perhaps he reckoned, truthfully as it turned out, that our ships would need a day to recover from the fight. There were injured men to tend, weapons to sharpen, and so none of our fleet put to sea that day.

Brida and I rode horses to Hamanfunta, a village that lived off trapping eels, fishing and making salt, and a sliver of a coin found stabling for our horses and a fisherman willing to take us out to Heilincigae where no one now lived, for the Danes had slaughtered them all. The fisherman would not wait for us, too frightened of the coming night and the ghosts that would be moaning and screeching on the island, but he promised to return in the morning.

Brida, Nihtgenga and I wandered that low place, going past the previous day's Danish dead that had already been pecked ragged by the gulls, past burned-out huts where folk had made a poor living from the sea and the marsh before the Vikings came and then, as the sun sank, we carried charred timbers to the shore and I used flint and steel to make a fire. The flames flared up in the dusk and Brida touched my arm to show me *Wind-Viper*, dark against the darkening sky, coming through the sea-lake's entrance. The last of the daylight touched the sea red and caught the gilding on *Wind-Viper*'s beast-head.

I watched her, thinking of all the fear that such a sight brought on England. Wherever there was a creek, a harbour or a river mouth, men feared to see the Danish ships. They feared those beasts at the prow, feared the men behind the beasts and prayed to be spared the Northmen's fury. I loved the sight. Loved *Wind-Viper*. Her oars rose and fell, I could hear the shafts creaking in their leather-lined holes, and I could see mailed men at her prow, and then the bows scrunched on the sand and the long oars went still.

Ragnar put the ladder against the prow. All Danish ships have a short ladder to let them climb down to a beach, and he came down the rungs slowly and alone. He was in full mail coat, helmeted, with a sword at his side and once ashore he paced to the small flames of our fire like a warrior come for vengeance. He stopped a spear's length away and then stared at me through the black eyeholes of his helmet. 'Did you kill my father?' he asked harshly.

'On my life,' I said, 'on Thor,' I pulled out the hammer amulet and clutched it, 'on my soul,' I went on, 'I did not.'

He pulled off his helmet, stepped forward and we embraced. 'I knew you did not,' he said.

'Kjartan did it,' I said, 'and we watched him.' We told him the whole story, how we had been in the high woods watching the charcoal cool, and how we had been cut off from the hall, and how it had been fired, and how the folk had been slaughtered.

'If I could have killed one of them,' I said, 'I would, and I would have died doing it, but Ravn always said there should be at least one survivor to tell the tale.'

'What did Kjartan say?' Brida asked.

Ragnar was sitting now, and two of his men had brought bread and dried herrings and cheese and ale. 'Kjartan said,' Ragnar spoke softly, 'that the English rose against the hall, encouraged by Uhtred, and that he revenged himself on the killers.'

'And you believed him?' I asked.

'No,' he admitted. 'Too many men said he did it, but he is Earl Kjartan now, he leads three times more men than I do.'

'And Thyra?' I asked, 'what does she say?'

'Thyra?' He stared at me, puzzled.

'Thyra lived,' I told him. 'She was taken away by Sven.'

He just stared at me. He had not known that his sister lived and I saw the anger come on his face, and then he raised his eyes to the stars and he howled like a wolf.

'It is true,' Brida said softly, 'your sister lived.'

Ragnar drew his sword and laid it on the sand and touched the blade with his right hand. 'If it is the last thing I do,' he swore, 'I shall kill Kjartan, kill his son, and all his followers. All of them!'

'I would help,' I said. He looked at me through the flames. 'I loved your father,' I said, 'and he treated me like a son.'

'I will welcome your help, Uhtred,' Ragnar said formally. He wiped the sand from the blade and slid it back into its fleece-lined scabbard. 'You will sail with us now?'

I was tempted. I was even surprised at how strongly I was tempted. I wanted to go with Ragnar, I wanted the life I had lived with his father, but fate rules us. I was sworn to Alfred for a few more weeks, and I had fought alongside Leofric for all these months, and fighting next to a man in the shield wall makes a bond as tight as love. 'I cannot come,' I said, and wished I could have said the opposite.

'I can,' Brida said, and somehow I was not surprised by that. She had not liked being left ashore in Hamtun as we sailed to fight, she felt trammelled and useless, unwanted, and I think she yearned after the Danish ways. She hated Wessex. She hated its priests, hated their disapproval and hated their denial of all that was joy.

'You are a witness of my father's death,' Ragnar said to her, still formal.

'I am.'

'Then I would welcome you,' he said, and looked at me again.

I shook my head. 'I am sworn to Alfred for the moment. By winter I shall be free of the oath.'

'Then come to us in the winter,' Ragnar said, 'and we shall go to Dunholm.'

'Dunholm?'

'It is Kjartan's fortress now. Ricsig lets him live there.'

I thought of Dunholm's stronghold on its soaring crag, wrapped by its river, protected by its sheer rock and its high walls and strong garrison. 'What if Kjartan marches on Wessex?' I asked.

Ragnar shook his head. 'He will not, because he does not go where I go, so I must go to him.'

'He fears you then?'

Ragnar smiled, and if Kjartan had seen that smile he would have shivered. 'He fears me,' Ragnar said. 'I hear he sent men to kill me in Ireland, but their boat was driven ashore and the skraelings killed the crew. So he lives in fear. He denies my father's

243

death, but he still fears me.'

'There is one last thing,' I said, and nodded at Brida who brought out the leather bag with its gold, jet and silver. 'It was your father's,' I said, 'and Kjartan never found it, and we did, and we have spent some of it, but what remains is yours.' I pushed the bag towards him and made myself instantly poor.

Ragnar pushed it back without a thought, making me rich again. 'My father loved you too,' he said, 'and I am wealthy enough.'

We ate, we drank, we slept, and in the dawn, when a light mist shimmered over the reed beds, the *Wind-Viper* went. The last thing Ragnar said to me was a question. 'Thyra lives?'

'She survived,' I said, 'so I think she must still live.'

We embraced, they went and I was alone.

I wept for Brida. I felt hurt. I was too young to know how to take abandonment. During the night I had tried to persuade her to stay, but she had a will as strong as Ealdwulf's iron, and she had gone with Ragnar into the dawn mist and left me weeping. I hated the three spinners at that moment, for they wove cruel jests into their vulnerable threads, and then the fisherman came to fetch me and I went back home.

Autumn gales tore at the coast and Alfred's fleet was laid up for the winter, dragged ashore by horses and oxen, and Leofric and I rode to Wintanceaster, only to discover that Alfred was at his estate at Cippanhamm. We were permitted into the Wintanceaster palace by the doorkeeper, who either recognised me or was terrified of Leofric, and we slept there, but the place was still haunted by monks, despite Alfred's absence, and so we spent the day in a nearby tavern. 'So what will you do, Earsling?' Leofric asked me, 'renew your oath to Alfred?'

'Don't know.'

'Don't know,' he repeated sarcastically. 'Lost your decision with your girl?'

'I could go back to the Danes,' I said.

'That would give me a chance to kill you,' he said happily.

'Or stay with Alfred.'

'Why not do that?'

'Because I don't like him,' I said.

'You don't have to like him. He's your king.'

'He's not my king,' I said, 'I'm a Northumbrian.'

'So you are, Earsling, a Northumbrian Ealdorman, eh?'

I nodded, demanded more ale, tore a piece of bread in two and pushed one piece towards Leofric. 'What I should do,' I said, 'is go back to Northumbria. There is a man I have to kill.'

'A feud?'

I nodded again.

'There is one thing I know about bloodfeuds,' Leofric said, 'which is that they last a lifetime. You will have years to make your killing, but only if you live.'

'I'll live,' I said lightly.

'Not if the Danes take Wessex, you won't. Or maybe you will live, Earsling, but you'll live under their rule, under their law and under their swords. If you want to be a free man, then stay here and fight for Wessex.'

'For Alfred?'

Leofric leaned back, stretched, belched and took a long drink. 'I don't like him either,' he admitted, 'and I didn't like his brothers when they were kings here, and I didn't like his father when he was king, but Alfred's different.'

'Different?'

He tapped his scarred forehead. 'The bastard thinks, Earsling, which is more than you or I ever do. He knows what has to be done, and don't underestimate him. He can be ruthless.'

'He's a king,' I said, 'he should be ruthless.'

'Ruthless, generous, pious, boring, that's Alfred,' Leofric spoke gloomily. 'When he was a child his father gave him toy warriors. You know, carved out of wood? Just little things. He used to line them up and there wasn't one out of place, not one, and not even a speck of dust on any of them!' He seemed to find that appalling, for he scowled. 'Then when he was fifteen or so he went wild for a time. Humped every slave girl in the palace, and I've no doubt he lined them up too and made sure they didn't have any dust

245

before he rammed them.'

'He had a bastard too, I hear,' I said.

'Osferth,' Leofric said, surprising me with his knowledge, 'hidden away in Winburnan. Poor little bastard must be six, seven years old now? You're not supposed to know he exists.'

'Nor are you.'

'It was my sister he whelped him on,' Leofric said, then saw my surprise. 'I'm not the only good-looking one in my family, Earsling.' He poured more ale. 'Eadgyth was a palace servant and Alfred claimed to love her.' He sneered, then shrugged. 'But he looks after her now. Gives her money, sends priests to preach to her. His wife knows all about the poor little bastard, but won't let Alfred go near him.'

'I hate Ælswith,' I said.

'A bitch from hell,' he agreed happily.

'And I like the Danes,' I said.

'You do? So why do you kill them?'

'I like them,' I said, ignoring his question, 'because they're not frightened of life.'

'They're not Christians, you mean.'

'They're not Christians,' I agreed. 'Are you?'

Leofric thought for a few heartbeats. 'I suppose so,' he said grudgingly, 'but you're not, are you?' I shook my head, showed him Thor's hammer and he laughed. 'So what will you do, Earsling,' he asked me, 'if you go back to the pagans? Other than follow your bloodfeud?'

That was a good question and I thought about it as much as the ale allowed me. 'I'd serve a man called Ragnar,' I said, 'as I served his father.'

'So why did you leave his father?'

'Because he was killed.'

Leofric frowned. 'So you can stay there so long as your Danish lord lives, is that right? And without a lord you're nothing?'

'I'm nothing,' I admitted. 'But I want to be in Northumbria to take back my father's fortress.'

'Ragnar will do that for you?'

'He might do. His father would have done, I think.'

'And if you get back your fortress,' he asked, 'will you be lord of it? Lord of your own land? Or will the Danes rule you?'

'The Danes will rule.'

'So you settle to be a slave, eh? Yes, lord, no, lord, let me hold your prick while you piss all over me, lord?'

'And what happens if I stay here?' I asked sourly.

'You'll lead men,' he said.

I laughed at that. 'Alfred has lords enough to serve him.'

Leofric shook his head. 'He doesn't. He has some good warlords, true, but he needs more. I told him, that day on the boat when he let the bastards escape, I told him to send me ashore and give me men. He refused.' He beat the table with a massive fist. 'I told him I'm a proper warrior, but still the bastard refused me!'

So that, I thought, was what the argument had been about. 'Why did he refuse you?' I asked.

'Because I can't read,' Leofric snarled, 'and I'm not learning now! I tried once, and it makes no damn sense to me. And I'm not a lord, am I? Not even a thegn. I'm just a slave's son who happens to know how to kill the king's enemies, but that's not good enough for Alfred. He says I can assist,' he said that word as if it soured his tongue, 'one of his Ealdormen, but I can't lead men because I can't read, and I can't learn to read.'

'I can,' I said, or the drink said.

'You take a long time to understand things, Earsling,' Leofric said with a grin. 'You're a damned lord, and you can read, can't you?'

'No, not really. A bit. Short words.'

'But you can learn?'

I thought about it. 'I can learn.'

'And we have twelve ships' crews,' he said, 'looking for employment, so we give them to Alfred and we say that Lord Earsling is their leader and he gives you a book and you read out the pretty words, then you and I take the bastards to war and do some proper damage to your beloved Danes.'

I did not say yes, nor did I say no, because I was not sure what I wanted. What worried me was that I found myself agreeing with whatever the last person suggested I did; when I had been with Ragnar I had wanted to follow him and now I was seduced by

Leofric's vision of the future. I had no certainty, so instead of saying yes or no I went back to the palace and I found Merewenna, and discovered she was indeed the maid who had caused Alfred's tears on the night that I had eavesdropped on him in the Mercian camp outside Snotengaham, and I did know what I wanted to do with her, and I did not cry afterwards.

And next day, at Leofric's urging, we rode to Cippanhamm.

Nine

I suppose, if you are reading this, that you have learned your letters, which probably means that some damned monk or priest rapped your knuckles, cuffed you around the head or worse. Not that they did that to me, of course, for I was no longer a child, but I endured their sniggers as I struggled with letters. It was mostly Beocca who taught me, complaining all the while that I was taking him from his real work which was the making of a life of Swithun, who had been Bishop of Wintanceaster when Alfred was a child, and Beocca was writing the bishop's life. Another priest was translating the book into Latin, Beocca's mastery of that tongue not being good enough for the task, and the pages were being sent to Rome in hopes that Swithun would be named a saint. Alfred took a great interest in the book, forever coming to Beocca's room and asking whether he knew that Swithun had once preached the gospel to a trout or chanted a psalm to a seagull, and Beocca would write the stories in a state of great excitement, and then, when Alfred was gone, reluctantly return to whatever text he was forcing me to decipher. 'Read it aloud,' he would say, then protest wildly. 'No, no, no! Forliðan is to suffer shipwreck! This is a life of Saint Paul, Uhtred, and the apostle suffered shipwreck! Not the word you read at all!'

I looked at it again. 'It's not forlegnis?'

'Of course it's not!' he said, going red with indignation. 'That word means . . .' he paused, realising that he was not teaching me English, but how to read it.

'Prostitute,' I said, 'I know what it means. I even know what they charge. There's a redhead in Chad's tavern who . . .'

'Forliðan,' he interrupted me, 'the word is forliðan. Read on.'

Those weeks were strange. I was a warrior now, a man, yet in Beocca's room it seemed I was a child again as I struggled with the black letters crawling across the cracked parchments. I learned from the lives of the saints, and in the end Beocca could not resist letting me read some of his own growing life of Swithun. He waited for my praise, but instead I shuddered. 'Couldn't we find something more interesting?' I asked him.

'More interesting?' Beocca's good eye stared at me reproach-fully.

'Something about war,' I suggested, 'about the Danes. About shields and spears and swords.'

He grimaced. 'I dread to think of such writings! There are some poems,' he grimaced again and evidently decided against telling me about the belligerent poems, 'but this,' he tapped the parch-ment, 'this will give you inspiration.'

'Inspiration! How Swithun mended some broken eggs?'

'It was a saintly act,' Beocca chided me. 'The woman was old and poor, the eggs were all she had to sell, and she tripped and broke them. She faced starvation! The saint made the eggs whole again and, God be praised, she sold them.'

'But why didn't Swithun just give her money?' I demanded, 'or take her back to his house and give her a proper meal?'

'It is a miracle!' Beocca insisted, 'a demonstration of God's power.'

'I'd like to see a miracle,' I said, remembering King Edmund's death.

'That is a weakness in you,' Beocca said sternly. 'You must have faith. Miracles make belief easy, which is why you should never pray for one. Much better to find God through faith than through miracles.'

'Then why have miracles?'

'Oh, read on, Uhtred,' the poor man said tiredly, 'for God's sake, read on.'

I read on. But life in Cippanhamm was not all reading. Alfred hunted at least twice a week, though it was not hunting as I had known it in the north. He never pursued boar, preferring to shoot at stags with a bow. The prey was driven to him by beaters, and if a stag did not appear swiftly he would get bored and go back to his books. In truth I think he only went hunting because it was expected of a king, not because he enjoyed it, but he did endure it. I loved it, of course. I killed wolves, stags, foxes and boars and it was on one of those boar hunts that I met Æthelwold.

Æthelwold was Alfred's oldest nephew, the boy who should have succeeded his father, King Æthelred, though he was no longer a boy for he was only a month or so younger than me, and in many ways he was like me, except that he had been sheltered by his father and by Alfred and so had never killed a man or even fought in a battle. He was tall, well-built, strong and as wild as an unbroken colt. He had long dark hair, his family's narrow face, and strong eyes that caught the attention of serving girls. All girls, really. He hunted with me and with Leofric, drank with us, whored with us when he could escape the priests who were his guardians, and constantly complained about his uncle, though those complaints were only spoken to me, never to Leofric whom Æthelwold feared. 'He stole the crown,' Æthelwold said of Alfred.

'The witan thought you were too young,' I pointed out.

'I'm not young now, am I?' he asked indignantly, 'so Alfred should step aside.'

I toasted that idea with a pot of ale, but said nothing.

'They won't even let me fight!' Æthelwold said bitterly. 'He says I ought to become a priest. The stupid bastard.' He drank some ale before giving me a serious look. 'Talk to him, Uhtred.'

'What am I to say? That you don't want to be a priest?'

'He knows that. No, tell him I'll fight with you and Leofric.'

I thought about that for a short while, then shook my head. 'It won't do any good.'

'Why not?'

'Because,' I said, 'he fears you making a name for yourself.'

Æthelwold frowned at me. 'A name?' he asked, puzzled.

'If you become a famous warrior,' I said, knowing I was right, 'men will follow you. You're already a prince, which is dangerous

251

enough, but Alfred won't want you to become a famous warrior prince, will he?'

'The pious bastard,' Æthelwold said. He pushed his long black hair off his face and gazed moodily at Eanflæd, the redhead who was given a room in the tavern and brought it a deal of business. 'God, she's pretty,' he said. 'He was caught humping a nun once.'

'Alfred was? A nun?'

'That's what I was told. And he was always after girls. Couldn't keep his breeches buttoned! Now the priests have got hold of him. What I ought to do,' he went on gloomily, 'is slit the bastard's gizzard.'

'Say that to anyone but me,' I said, 'and you'll be hanged.'

'I could run off and join the Danes,' he suggested.

'You could,' I said, 'and they'd welcome you.'

'Then use me?' he asked, showing that he was not entirely a fool.

I nodded. 'You'll be like Egbert or Burghred, or that new man in Mercia.'

'Ceolwulf.'

'King at their pleasure,' I said. Ceolwulf, a Mercian Ealdorman, had been named king of his country now that Burghred was on his knees in Rome, but Ceolwulf was no more a real king than Burghred had been. He issued coins, of course, and he administered justice, but everyone knew there were Danes in his council chamber and he dared do nothing that would earn their wrath. 'So is that what you want?' I asked. 'To run off to the Danes and be useful to them?'

He shook his head. 'No.' He traced a pattern on the table with spilt ale. 'Better to do nothing,' he suggested.

'Nothing?'

'If I do nothing,' he said earnestly, 'then the bastard might die. He's always ill! He can't live long, can he? And his son is just a baby. So if he dies I'll be king! Oh, sweet Jesus!' This blasphemy was uttered because two priests had entered the tavern, both of them in Æthelwold's entourage, though they were more like jailers than courtiers and they had come to find him and take him off to his bed.

252

Beocca did not approve of my friendship with Æthelwold. 'He's a foolish creature,' he warned me.

'So am I, or so you tell me.'

'Then you don't need your foolishness encouraged, do you? Now let us read about how the holy Swithun built the town's East Gate.'

By the Feast of the Epiphany I could read as well as a clever twelve-year-old, or so Beocca said, and that was good enough for Alfred who did not, after all, require me to read theological texts, but only to decipher his orders, should he ever decide to give me any, and that, of course, was the heart of the matter. Leofric and I wanted to command troops, to which end I had endured Beocca's teaching and had come to appreciate the holy Swithun's skill with trout, seagulls and broken eggs, but the granting of those troops depended on the king, and in truth there were not many troops to command.

The West Saxon army was in two parts. The first and smaller part was composed of the king's own men, his retainers who guarded him and his family. They did nothing else because they were professional warriors, but they were not many and neither Leofric nor I wanted anything to do with them because joining the household guard would mean staying in close proximity to Alfred which, in turn, would mean going to church.

The second part of the army, and by far the largest, was the fyrd, and that, in turn, was divided among the shires. Each shire, under its Ealdorman and reeve, was responsible for raising the fyrd that was supposedly composed of every able-bodied man within the shire boundary. That could raise a vast number of men. Hamptonscir, for example, could easily put three thousand men under arms, and there were nine shires in Wessex capable of summoning similar numbers. Yet, apart from the troops who served the Ealdormen, the fyrd was mostly composed of farmers. Some had a shield of sorts, spears and axes were plentiful enough, but swords and armour were in short supply, and worse, the fyrd was always reluctant to march beyond its shire borders, and even more reluctant to serve when there was work to be done on the farm. At Æsc's Hill, the one battle the West Saxons had won against the

Danes, it had been the household troops who had gained the victory. Divided between Alfred and his brother they had spearheaded the fighting while the fyrd, as it usually did, looked menacing, but only became engaged when the real soldiers had already won the fight. The fyrd, in brief, was about as much use as a hole in a boat's bottom, but that was where Leofric could expect to find men.

Except there were those ships' crews getting drunk in Hamtun's winter taverns and those were the men Leofric wanted, and to get them he had to persuade Alfred to relieve Hacca of their command, and luckily for us Hacca himself came to Cippanhamm and pleaded to be released from the fleet. He prayed daily, he told Alfred, never to see the ocean again. 'I get seasick, lord.'

Alfred was always sympathetic to men who suffered sickness because he was so often ill himself, and he must have known that Hacca was an inadequate commander of ships, but Alfred's problem was how to replace him. To which end he summoned four bishops, two abbots and a priest to advise him, and I learned from Beocca that they were all praying about the new appointment. 'Do something!' Leofric snarled at me.

'What the devil am I supposed to do?'

'You have friends who are priests! Talk to them. Talk to Alfred, Earsling.' He rarely called me that any more, only when he was angry.

'He doesn't like me,' I said. 'If I ask him to put us in charge of the fleet he'll give it to anyone but us. He'll give it to a bishop, probably.'

'Hell!' Leofric said.

In the end it was Eanflæd who saved us. The redhead was a merry soul and had a particular fondness for Leofric, and she heard us arguing and sat down, slapped her hands on the table to silence us, and then asked what we were fighting about. Then she sneezed because she had a cold.

'I want this useless earsling,' Leofric jerked his thumb at me, 'to be named commander of the fleet, only he's too young, too ugly, too horrible and too pagan, and Alfred's listening to a pack of bishops who'll end up naming some wizened old fart who doesn't know his prow from his prick.'

'Which bishops?' Eanflæd wanted to know.

'Scireburnan, Wintanceaster, Winburnan and Exanceaster,' I said.

She smiled, sneezed again, and two days later I was summoned to Alfred's presence. It turned out that the Bishop of Exanceaster was partial to redheads.

Alfred greeted me in his hall; a fine building with beams, rafters and a central stone hearth. His guards watched us from the doorway where a group of petitioners waited to see the king, and a huddle of priests prayed at the hall's other end, but the two of us were alone by the hearth where Alfred paced up and down as he talked. He said he was thinking of appointing me to command the fleet. Just thinking, he stressed. God, he went on, was guiding his choice, but now he must talk with me to see whether God's advice chimed with his own intuition. He put great store by intuition. He once lectured me about a man's inner eye, and how it could lead us to a higher wisdom, and I dare say he was right, but appointing a fleet commander did not need mystical wisdom, it needed finding a raw fighter willing to kill some Danes. 'Tell me,' he went on, 'has learning to read bolstered your faith?'

'Yes, lord,' I said with feigned eagerness.

'It has?' He sounded dubious.

'The life of Saint Swithun,' I said, waving a hand as if to suggest it had overwhelmed me, 'and the stories of Chad!' I fell silent as if I could not think of praise sufficient for that tedious man.

'The blessed Chad!' Alfred said happily. 'You know men and cattle were cured by the dust of his corpse?'

'A miracle, lord,' I said.

'It is good to hear you say as much, Uhtred,' Alfred said, 'and I rejoice in your faith.'

'It gives me great happiness, lord,' I replied with a straight face.

'Because it is only with faith in God that we shall prevail against the Danes.'

'Indeed, lord,' I said with as much enthusiasm as I could muster, wondering why he did not just name me commander of the fleet and be done with it.

But he was in a discursive mood. 'I remember when I first met

255

you,' he said, 'and I was struck by your childlike faith. It was an inspiration to me, Uhtred.'

'I am glad of it, lord.'

'And then,' he turned and frowned at me, 'I detected a lessening of faith in you.'

'God tries us, lord,' I said.

'He does! He does!' He winced suddenly. He was always a sick man. He had collapsed in pain at his wedding, though that might have been the horror of realising what he was marrying, but in truth he was prone to bouts of sudden griping agony. That, he had told me, was better than his first illness, which had been an affliction of ficus, which is a real endwerc, so painful and bloody that at times he had been unable to sit, and sometimes that ficus came back, but most of the time he suffered from the pains in his belly. 'God does try us,' he went on, 'and I think God was testing you. I would like to think you have survived the trial.'

'I believe I have, lord,' I said gravely, wishing he would just end this ridiculous conversation.

'But I still hesitate to name you,' he admitted. 'You are young! It is true you have proved your diligence by learning to read and that you are nobly born, but you are more likely to be found in a tavern than in a church. Is that not true?'

That silenced me, at least for a heartbeat or two, but then I remembered something Beocca had said to me during his interminable lessons and, without thinking, without even really knowing what they meant, I said the words aloud. '"The son of man is come eating and drinking",' I said, '"and . . ."'

'"You say, look, a greedy man and a drinker!"' Alfred finished the words for me. 'You are right, Uhtred, right to chide me. Glory to God! Christ was accused of spending his time in taverns, and I forgot it. It is in the scriptures!'

The gods help me, I thought. The man was drunk on God, but he was no fool, for now he turned on me like a snake. 'And I hear you spend time with my nephew. They say you distract him from his lessons.'

I put my hand on my heart. 'I will swear an oath, lord,' I said, 'that I have done nothing except dissuade him from rashness.'

And that was true, or true enough. I had never encouraged Æthelwold in his wilder flights of fancy that involved cutting Alfred's throat or running away to join the Danes. I did encourage him to ale, whores and blasphemy, but I did not count those things as rash. 'My oath on it, lord,' I said.

The word oath was powerful. All our laws depend on oaths. Life, loyalty and allegiance depend on oaths, and my use of the word persuaded him. 'I thank you,' he said earnestly, 'and I should tell you, Uhtred, that to my surprise the Bishop of Exanceaster had a dream in which a messenger of God appeared to him and said that you should be made commander of the fleet.'

'A messenger of God?' I asked.

'An angel, Uhtred.'

'Praise God,' I said gravely, thinking how Eanflæd would enjoy discovering that she was now an angel.

'Yet,' Alfred said, and winced again as pain flared in his arse or belly, 'yet,' he said again, and I knew something unexpected was coming. 'I worry,' he went on, 'that you are of Northumbria, and that your commitment to Wessex is not of the heart.'

'I am here, lord,' I said.

'But for how long?'

'Till the Danes are gone, lord.'

He ignored that. 'I need men bound to me by God,' he said, 'by God, by love, by duty, by passion and by land.' He paused, looking at me, and I knew the sting was in that last word.

'I have land in Northumbria,' I said, thinking of Bebbanburg.

'West Saxon land,' he said, 'land that you will own, land that you will defend, land that you will fight for.'

'A blessed thought,' I said, my heart sinking at what I suspected was coming.

Only it did not come immediately, instead he abruptly changed the subject and talked, very sensibly, about the Danish threat. The fleet, he said, had succeeded in reducing the Viking raids, but he expected the new year to bring a Danish fleet, and one much too large for our twelve ships to oppose. 'I dare not lose the fleet,' he said, 'so I doubt we should fight their ships. I'm expecting a land army of pagans to come down the Temes and for their fleet to assault our south coast. I can hold one, but not the other, so the fleet commander's job will be to follow their ships and harry them. Distract them. Keep them looking one way while I destroy their land army.'

I said I thought that was a good idea, which it probably was, though I wondered how twelve ships were supposed to distract a whole fleet, but that was a problem which would have to wait until the enemy fleet arrived. Alfred then returned to the matter of the land and that, of course, was the deciding factor which would give me or deny me the fleet. 'I would tie you to me, Uhtred,' he said earnestly.

'I shall give you an oath, lord,' I said.

'You will indeed,' he responded tartly, 'but I still want you to be of Wessex.'

'A high honour, lord,' I said. What else could I say?

'You must belong to Wessex,' he said, then smiled as though he did me a favour. 'There is an orphan in Defnascir,' he went on, and here it came, 'a girl, who I would see married.'

I said nothing. What is the point of protesting when the executioner's sword is in mid swing?

'Her name is Mildrith,' he went on, 'and she is dear to me. A pious girl, modest and faithful. Her father was reeve to Ealdorman Odda, and she will bring land to her husband, good land, and I would have a good man hold that good land.'

I offered a smile that I hoped was not too sickly. 'He would be a fortunate man, lord,' I said, 'to marry a girl who is dear to you.'

'So go to her,' he commanded me, 'and marry her,' the sword struck, 'and then I shall name you commander of the fleet.'

'Yes, lord,' I said.

Leofric, of course, laughed like a demented jackdaw. 'He's no fool, is he?' he said when he had recovered. 'He's making you into a West Saxon. So what do you know about this Miltewærc.' Miltewærc is a pain in the spleen.

'Mildrith,' I said, 'and she's pious.'

'Of course she's pious. He wouldn't want you to marry her if she was a leg-spreader.'

'She's an orphan,' I said, 'and aged about sixteen or seventeen.'

'Christ! That old? She must be an ugly sow! But poor thing, she must be wearing out her knees praying to be spared a rutting from an earsling like you. But that's her fate! So let's get you married, then we can kill some Danes.'

It was winter. We had spent the Christmas feast at Cippanhamm, and that was no Yule, and now we rode south through frost and rain and wind. Father Willibald accompanied us, for he was still priest to the fleet, and my plan was to reach Defnascir, do what was grimly necessary, and then ride straight to Hamtun to make certain the winter work on the twelve boats was being done properly. It is in winter that ships are caulked, scraped, cleaned, and made tight for the spring, and the thought of ships made me dream of the Danes, and of Brida, and I wondered where she was, what she did, and whether we would meet again. And I thought of Ragnar. Had he found Thyra? Did Kjartan live? Theirs was another world now, and I knew I drifted away from it and was being entangled in the threads of Alfred's tidy life. He was trying to make me into a West Saxon, and he was half succeeding. I was sworn now to fight for Wessex and it seemed I must marry into it, but I still clung to that ancient dream of retaking Bebbanburg.

I loved Bebbanburg and I almost loved Defnascir as much. When the world was made by Thor from the carcass of Ymir he did well when he fashioned Defnascir and its shire next door, Thornsæta. Both were beautiful lands of soft hills and quick streams, of rich fields and thick soil, of high heaths and good harbours. A man could live well in either shire, and I could have been happy in Defnascir had I not loved Bebbanburg more. We rode down the valley of the River Uisc, through well-tended fields of red earth, past plump villages and high halls until we came to Exanceaster which was the shire's chief town. It had been made by the Romans who had built a fortress on a hill above the Uisc and surrounded it with a wall of flint, stone and brick, and the wall was still there and guards challenged us as we reached the northern gate.

'We come to see Ealdorman Odda,' Willibald said.

'On whose business?'

'The king's,' Willibald said proudly, flourishing a letter that bore

Alfred's seal, though I doubt the guards would have recognised it, but they seemed properly impressed and let us through into a town of decaying Roman buildings amidst which a timber church reared tall next to Ealdorman Odda's hall.

The Ealdorman made us wait, but at last he came with his son and a dozen retainers, and one of his priests read the king's letter aloud. It was Alfred's pleasure that Mildrith should be married to his loyal servant, the Ealdorman Uhtred, and Odda was commanded to arrange the ceremony with as little delay as possible. Odda was not pleased at the news. He was an elderly man, at least forty years old, with grey hair and a face made grotesque by bulbous wens. His son, Odda the Younger, was even less pleased, for he scowled at the news. 'It isn't seemly, father,' he complained.

'It is the king's wish.'

'But . . .'

'It is the king's wish!'

Odda the Younger fell silent. He was about my age, almost nineteen, good-looking, black-haired, and elegant in a black tunic that was as clean as a woman's dress and edged with gold thread. A golden crucifix hung at his neck. He gave me a grim look, and I must have appeared travel-stained and ragged to him, and after inspecting me and finding me about as appealing as a wet mongrel, he turned on his heel and stalked from the hall.

'Tomorrow morning,' Odda announced unhappily, 'the bishop can marry you. But you must pay the bride price first.'

'The bride price?' I asked. Alfred had mentioned no such thing, though of course it was customary.

'Thirty-three shillings,' Odda said flatly, and with the hint of a smirk.

Thirty-three shillings was a fortune. A hoard. The price of a good war horse or a ship. It took me aback and I heard Leofric give a gasp behind me. 'Is that what Alfred says?' I demanded.

'It is what I say,' Odda said, 'for Mildrith is my goddaughter.'

No wonder he smirked. The price was huge and he doubted I could pay it, and if I could not pay it then the girl was not mine and, though Odda did not know it, the fleet would not be mine either. Nor, of course, was the price merely thirty-three shillings, or 396 silver pence, it was double that, for it was also customary for a husband to give his new wife an equivalent sum after the marriage was consummated. That second gift was none of Odda's business and I doubted very much whether I would want to pay it, just as Ealdorman Odda was now certain, from my hesitation, that I would not be paying him the bride price without which there could be no marriage contract.

'I can meet the lady?' I asked.

'You may meet her at the ceremony tomorrow morning,' Odda said firmly, 'but only if you pay the bride price. Otherwise, no.'

He looked disappointed as I opened my pouch and gave him one gold coin and thirty-six silver pennies. He looked even more disappointed when he saw that was not all the coin I possessed, but he was trapped now. 'You may meet her,' he told me, 'in the cathedral tomorrow.'

'Why not now?' I asked.

'Because she is at her prayers,' the Ealdorman said, and with that he dismissed us.

Leofric and I found a place to sleep in a tavern close to the cathedral, which was the bishop's church, and that night I got drunk as a spring hare. I picked a fight with someone, I have no idea who, and only remember that Leofric, who was not quite as drunk as me, pulled us apart and flattened my opponent, and after that I went into the stable yard and threw up all the ale I had just drunk. I drank some more, slept badly, woke to hear rain seething on the stable roof and then vomited again.

'Why don't we just ride to Mercia?' I suggested to Leofric. The king had lent us horses and I did not mind stealing them.

'What do we do there?'

'Find men?' I suggested. 'Fight?'

'Don't be daft, Earsling,' Leofric said. 'We want the fleet. And if you don't marry the ugly sow, I don't get to command it.'

'I command it,' I said.

'But only if you marry,' Leofric said, 'and then you'll command the fleet and I'll command you.'

Father Willibald arrived then. He had slept in the monastery next door to the tavern and had come to make sure I was ready, and looked alarmed at my ragged condition. 'What's that mark on your face?' he asked.

'Bastard hit me last night,' I said, 'I was drunk. So was he, but I was more drunk. Take my advice, father, never get into a fight when you're badly drunk.'

I drank more ale for breakfast. Willibald insisted I wear my best tunic, which was not saying much for it was stained, crumpled and torn. I would have preferred to wear my coat of mail, but Willibald said that was inappropriate for a church, and I suppose he was right, and I let him brush me down and try to dab the worst stains out of the wool. I tied my hair with a leather lace, strapped on Serpent-Breath and Wasp-Sting, which again Willibald said I should not wear in a holy place, but I insisted on keeping the weapons, and then, a doomed man, I went to the cathedral with Willibald and Leofric.

It was raining as if the heavens were being drained of all their water. Rain bounced in the streets, flowed in streams down the gutters and leaked through the cathedral's thatch. A brisk cold wind was coming from the east and it found every crack in the cathedral's wooden walls so that the candles on the altars flickered and some blew out. It was a small church, not much bigger than Ragnar's burned hall, and it must have been built on a Roman foundation for the floor was made of flagstones that were now being puddled by rainwater. The bishop was already there, two other priests fussed with the guttering candles on the high altar, and then Ealdorman Odda arrived with my bride.

Who took one look at me and burst into tears.

What was I expecting? A woman who looked like a sow, I suppose, a woman with a pox-scarred face and a sour expression and haunches like an ox. No one expects to love a wife, not if they marry for land or position, and I was marrying for land and she was marrying because she had no choice, and there really is no point in making too much of a fuss about it, because that is the way the world works. My job was to take her land, work it, make money, and Mildrith's duty was to give me sons and make sure there was food and ale on my table. Such is the holy sacrament of marriage.

I did not want to marry her. By rights, as an Ealdorman of Northumbria, I could expect to marry a daughter of the nobility, a daughter who would bring much more land than twelve hilly hides in Defnascir. I might have expected to marry a daughter who could increase Bebbanburg's holdings and power, but that was plainly not going to happen, so I was marrying a girl of ignoble birth who would now be known as the Lady Mildrith and she might have shown some gratitude for that, but instead she cried and even tried to pull away from Ealdorman Odda.

He probably sympathised with her, but the bride price had been paid, and so she was brought to the altar and the bishop, who had come back from Cippanhamm with a streaming cold, duly made us man and wife. 'And may the blessing of God the Father,' he said, 'God the Son and God the Holy Ghost be on your union.' He was about to say amen, but instead sneezed mightily.

'Amen,' Willibald said. No one else spoke.

So Mildrith was mine.

Odda the Younger watched as we left the church and he probably thought I did not see him, but I did, and I marked him down. I knew why he was watching.

For the truth of it, which surprised me, was that Mildrith was desirable. That word does not do her justice, but it is so very hard to remember a face from long ago. Sometimes, in a dream, I see her, and she is real then, but when I am awake and try to summon her face I cannot do it. I remember she had clear, pale skin, that her lower lip jutted out too much, that her eyes were very blue and her hair the same gold as mine. She was tall, which she disliked, thinking it made her unwomanly, and had a nervous expression, as though she constantly feared disaster, and that can be very attractive in a woman and I confess I found her attractive. That did surprise me, indeed it astonished me, for such a woman should have long been married. She was almost seventeen years old, and by that age most women have already given birth to three or four

263

children or else been killed in the attempt, but as we rode to her holdings that lay to the west of the River Uisc's mouth I heard some of her tale. She was being drawn in a cart by two oxen that Willibald had insisted garlanding with flowers. Leofric, Willibald and I rode alongside the cart, and Willibald asked her questions and she answered him readily enough for he was a priest and a kind man.

Her father, she said, had left her land and debts, and the debts were greater than the value of the land. Leofric sniggered when he heard the word debts. I said nothing, but just stared doggedly ahead.

The trouble, Mildrith said, had begun when her father had granted a tenth of his holdings as ælmesæcer, which is land devoted to the church. The church does not own it, but has the right to all that the land yields, whether in crops or cattle, and her father had made the grant, Mildrith explained, because all his children except her had died and he wanted to find favour with God. I suspected he had wanted to find favour with Alfred, for in Wessex an ambitious man was well advised to look after the church if he wanted the king to look after him.

But then the Danes had raided, cattle had been slaughtered, a harvest failed, and the church took her father to law for failing to provide the land's promised yield. Wessex, I discovered, was very devoted to the law, and all the men of law are priests, every last one of them, which means that the law is the church, and when Mildrith's father died the law had decreed that he owed the church a huge sum, quite beyond his ability to pay, and Alfred, who had the power to lift the debt, refused to do so. What this meant was that any man who married Mildrith married the debt, and no man had been willing to take that burden until a Northumbrian fool wandered into the trap like a drunk staggering downhill.

Leofric was laughing. Willibald looked worried.

'So what is the debt?' I asked.

'Two thousand shillings, lord,' Mildrith said in a very small voice.

Leofric almost choked laughing and I could have cheerfully killed him on the spot.

'And it increases yearly?' Willibald asked shrewdly.

'Yes,' Mildrith said, refusing to meet my eyes. A more sensible man would have explored Mildrith's circumstances before the marriage contract was made, but I had just seen marriage as a route to the fleet. So now I had the fleet, I had the debt and I had the girl, and I also had a new enemy, Odda the Younger, who had plainly wanted Mildrith for himself, though his father, wisely, had refused to saddle his family with the crippling debt, nor, I suspected, did he want his son to marry beneath him.

There is a hierarchy among men. Beocca liked to tell me it reflected the hierarchy of heaven, and perhaps it does, but I know nothing of that, but I do know how men are ranked. At the top is the king, and beneath him are his sons, and then come the Ealdormen who are the chief nobles of the land and without land a man cannot be noble, though I was, because I have never abandoned my claim to Bebbanburg. The king and his Ealdormen are the power of a kingdom, the men who hold great lands and raise the armies, and beneath them are the lesser nobles, usually called reeves, and they are responsible for law in a lord's land, though a man can cease to be a reeve if he displeases his lord. The reeves are drawn from the ranks of thegns, who are wealthy men who can lead followers to war, but who lack the wide holdings of noblemen like Odda or my father. Beneath the thegns are the ceorls, who are all free men, but if a ceorl loses his livelihood then he could well become a slave, which is the bottom of the dungheap. Slaves can be, and often are, freed, though unless a slave's lord gives him land or money he will soon be a slave again. Mildrith's father had been a thegn, and Odda had made him a reeve, responsible for keeping the peace in a wide swathe of southern Defnascir, but he had also been a thegn of insufficient land, whose foolishness had diminished the little he possessed, and so he had left Mildrith impoverished which made her unsuitable as a wife for an Ealdorman's son, though she was reckoned good enough for an exiled lord from Northumbria. In truth she was just another pawn on Alfred's chessboard and he had only given her to me so that I became responsible for paying the church a vast sum.

He was a spider, I thought sourly, a priestly-black spider spinning sticky webs, and I thought I had been so clever when I talked to him in the hall at Cippanhamm. In truth I could have prayed openly to Thor before pissing on the relics of Alfred's altar and he would still have given me the fleet because he knew the fleet would have little to do in the coming war, and he had only wanted to trap me for his future ambitions in the north of England. So now I was trapped, and the bastard Ealdorman Odda had carefully let me walk into the trap.

The thought of Defnascir's Ealdorman prompted a question from me. 'What bride price did Odda give you?' I asked Mildrith.

'Fifteen shillings, lord.'

'Fifteen shillings?' I asked, shocked.

'Yes, lord.'

'The cheap bastard,' I said.

'Cut the rest out of him,' Leofric snarled. A pair of very blue eyes looked at him, then at me, then vanished under the cloak again.

Her twelve hides of land, that were now mine, lay in the hills above the River Uisc's sea-reach, in a place called Oxton which simply means a farm where oxen are kept. It was a shieling, as the Danes would say, a farmstead, and the house had a thatch so overgrown with moss and grass that it looked like an earth mound. There was no hall, and a nobleman needs a hall in which to feed his followers, but it did have a cattle shed and a pig shed and land enough to support sixteen slaves and five families of tenants, all of whom were summoned to greet me, as well as half a dozen household servants, most of whom were also slaves, and they welcomed Mildrith fondly for, since her father's death, she had been living in the household of Ealdorman Odda's wife while the farmstead was managed by a man called Oswald who looked about as trustworthy as a stoat.

That night we made a meal of peas, leeks, stale bread and sour ale, and that was my first marriage feast in my own house which was also a house under threat of debt. Next morning it had stopped raining and I breakfasted on more stale bread and sour ale, and then walked with Mildrith to a hilltop from where I could stare down at the wide sea-reach that lay across the land like the flattened grey blade of an axe. 'Where do these folk go,' I asked, meaning her slaves and tenants, 'when the Danes come?'

'Into the hills, lord.'

'My name is Uhtred.'

'Into the hills, Uhtred.'

'You won't go into the hills,' I said firmly.

'I won't?' Her eyes widened in alarm.

'You will come with me to Hamtun,' I said, 'and we shall have a house there so long as I command the fleet.'

She nodded, plainly nervous, and then I took her hand, opened it, and poured in thirty-three shillings, so many coins that they spilt onto her lap. 'Yours, wife,' I said.

And so she was. My wife. And that same day we left, going eastwards, man and wife.

The story hurries now. It quickens like a stream coming to a fall in the hills and, like a cascade foaming down jumbled rocks, it gets angry and violent, confused even. For it was in that year, 876, that the Danes made their greatest effort yet to rid England of its last kingdom, and the onslaught was huge, savage and sudden.

Guthrum the Unlucky led the assault. He had been living in Grantaceaster, calling himself King of East Anglia, and Alfred, I think, assumed he would have good warning if Guthrum's army left that place, but the West Saxon spies failed and the warnings did not come, and the Danish army was all mounted on horses, and Alfred's troops were in the wrong place and Guthrum led his men south across the Temes and clear across all Wessex to capture a great fortress on the south coast. That fortress was called Werham and it lay not very far west of Hamtun, though between us and it lay a vast stretch of inland sea called the Poole. Guthrum's army assaulted Werham, captured it, raped the nuns in Werham's nunnery, and did it all before Alfred could react. Once inside the fortress Guthrum was protected by two rivers, one to the north of the town and the other to the south. To the east was the wide placid Poole and a massive wall and ditch guarded the only approach from the west.

There was nothing the fleet could do. As soon as we heard that the Danes were in Werham we readied ourselves for sea, but no sooner had we reached the open water than we saw their fleet and that ended our ambitions.

I have never seen so many ships. Guthrum had marched across Wessex with close to a thousand horsemen, but now the rest of his army came by sea and their ships darkened the water. There were hundreds of boats. Men later said three hundred and fifty, though I think there were fewer, but certainly there were more than two hundred. Ship after ship, dragon prow after serpent head, oars churning the dark sea white, a fleet going to battle, and all we could do was slink back into Hamtun and pray that the Danes did not sail up Hamtun Water to slaughter us.

They did not. The fleet sailed on to join Guthrum in Werham, so now a huge Danish army was lodged in southern Wessex, and I remembered Ragnar's advice to Guthrum. Split their forces, Ragnar had said, and that surely meant another Danish army lay some-where to the north, just waiting to attack, and when Alfred went to meet that second army, Guthrum would erupt from behind Werham's walls to attack him in the rear.

'It's the end of England,' Leofric said darkly. He was not much given to gloom, but that day he was downcast. Mildrith and I had taken a house in Hamtun, one close to the water, and he ate with us most nights we were in the town. We were still taking the ships out, now in a flotilla of twelve, always in hope of catching some Danish ships unawares, but their raiders only sallied out of the Poole in large numbers, never fewer than thirty ships, and I dared not lose Alfred's navy in a suicidal attack on such large forces. In the height of the summer a Danish force came to Hamtun's water, rowing almost to our anchorage, and we lashed our ships together, donned armour, sharpened weapons and waited for their attack. But they were no more minded for battle than we were. To reach us they would have to negotiate a mud-bordered channel and they could only put two ships abreast in that place and so they were content to jeer at us from the open water and then leave.

Guthrum waited in Werham and what he waited for, we later learned, was for Halfdan to lead a mixed force of Northmen and Britons out of Wales. Halfdan had been in Ireland, avenging Ivar's death, and now he was supposed to bring his fleet and army to Wales, assemble a great army there and lead it across the Sæfern sea and attack Wessex. But, according to Beocca, God intervened. God or the three spinners. Fate is everything, for news came that Halfdan had died in Ireland, and of the three brothers only Ubba now lived, though he was still in the far wild north. Halfdan had been killed by the Irish, slaughtered along with scores of his men in a vicious battle, and so the Irish saved Wessex that year.

We knew none of that in Hamtun. We made our impotent forays and waited for news of the second blow that must fall on Wessex, and still it did not come, and then, as the first autumn gales fretted the coast, a messenger came from Alfred, whose army was camped to the west of Werham, demanding that I go to the king. The messenger was Beocca and I was surprisingly pleased to see him, though annoyed that he gave me the command verbally. 'Why did I learn to read?' I demanded of him, 'if you don't bring written orders?'

'You learned to read, Uhtred,' he said happily, 'to improve your mind, of course,' then he saw Mildrith and his mouth began to open and close like a landed fish. 'Is this?' he began, and was struck dumb as a stick.

'The Lady Mildrith,' I said.

'Dear lady,' Beocca said, then gulped for air and twitched like a puppy wanting a pat. 'I have known Uhtred,' he managed to say to her, 'since he was a little child! Since he was just a little child.'

'He's a big one now,' Mildrith said, which Beocca thought was a wonderful jest for he giggled immoderately.

'Why,' I managed to stem his mirth, 'am I going to Alfred?'

'Because Halfdan is dead, God be praised, and no army will come from the north, God be praised, and so Guthrum seeks terms! The discussions have already started, and God be praised for that too.' He beamed at me as though he was responsible for this rush of good news, and perhaps he was because he went on

269

to say that Halfdan's death was the result of prayers. 'So many prayers, Uhtred. You see the power of prayer?'

'God be praised indeed,' Mildrith answered instead of me. She was indeed very pious, but no one is perfect. She was also pregnant, but Beocca did not notice and I did not tell him.

I left Mildrith in Hamtun, and rode with Beocca to the West Saxon army. A dozen of the king's household troops served as our escort, for the route took us close to the northern shore of the Poole and Danish boats had been raiding that shore before the truce talks opened. 'What does Alfred want of me?' I asked Beocca constantly, insisting, despite his denials, that he must have some idea, but he claimed ignorance and in the end I stopped asking.

We arrived outside Werham on a chill autumn evening. Alfred was at his prayers in a tent that was serving as his royal chapel and Ealdorman Odda and his son waited outside and the Ealdorman gave me a guarded nod while his son ignored me. Beocca went into the tent to join the prayers while I squatted, drew Serpent-Breath and sharpened her with the whetstone I carried in my pouch.

'Expecting to fight?' Ealdorman Odda asked me sourly.

I looked at his son. 'Maybe,' I said, then looked back to the father. 'You owe my wife money,' I said, 'eighteen shillings.' He reddened, said nothing, though the son put a hand to his sword hilt and that made me smile and stand, Serpent-Breath's naked blade already in my grip. Ealdorman Odda pulled his son angrily away. 'Eighteen shillings!' I called after them, then squatted again and ran the stone down the sword's long edge.

Women. Men fight for them, and that was another lesson to learn. As a child I thought men struggled for land or for mastery, but they fight for women just as much. Mildrith and I were unexpectedly content together, but it was clear that Odda the Younger hated me because I had married her, and I wondered if he would dare do anything about that hatred. Beocca once told me the tale of a prince from a far away land who stole a king's daughter and the king led his army to the prince's land and thousands of great warriors died in the struggle to get her back. Thousands! And all for a woman. Indeed the argument that began this tale, the rivalry between King Osbert of Northumbria and Ælla, the man who wanted to be king, all began because Ælla stole Osbert's wife. I have heard some women complain that they have no power and that men control the world, and so they do, but women still have the power to drive men to battle and to the grave beyond.

I was thinking of these things as Alfred came from the tent. He had the look of beatific pleasure he usually wore when he had just said his prayers, but he was also walking stiffly, which probably meant the ficus was troubling him again, and he looked distinctly uncomfortable when we sat down to supper that night. The meal was an unspeakable gruel I would hesitate to serve to pigs, but there was bread and cheese enough so I did not starve. I did note that Alfred was distant with me, hardly acknowledging my presence, and I put that down to the fleet's failure to achieve any real victory during that summer, yet he had still summoned me and I wondered why if all he intended to do was ignore me.

Yet, next morning, he summoned me after prayers and we walked up and down outside the royal tent where the dragon banner flew in the autumn sun. 'The fleet,' Alfred said, frowning, 'can it prevent the Danes leaving the Poole?'

'No, lord.'

'No?' That was said sharply. 'Why not?'

'Because, lord,' I said, 'we have twelve ships and they have over two hundred. We could kill a few of them, but in the end they'll overwhelm us and you won't have any fleet left and they'll still have more than two hundred ships.'

I think Alfred knew that, but he still did not like my answer. He grimaced, then walked in silence for a few more paces. 'I am glad you married,' he said abruptly.

'To a debt,' I said sharply.

He did not like my tone, but allowed it. 'The debt, Uhtred,' he said reprovingly, 'is to the church, so you must welcome it. Besides, you're young, you have time to pay. The Lord, remember, loves a cheerful giver.' That was one of his favourite sayings and if I heard it once I heard it a thousand times. He turned on his heel, then looked back. 'I shall expect your presence at the negotiations,' he said, but did not explain why, nor wait for any response, but just walked on.

He and Guthrum were talking. A canopy had been raised between Alfred's camp and Werham's western wall, and it was beneath that shelter that a truce was being hammered out. Alfred would have liked to assault Werham, but the approach was narrow, the wall high and in very good repair, and the Danes were numerous. It would have been a very risky fight, and one that the Danes could expect to win, and so Alfred had abandoned the idea. As for the Danes, they were trapped. They had been relying on Halfdan coming to attack Alfred in the rear, but Halfdan was dead in Ireland, and Guthrum's men were too many to be carried away on their ships, big as their fleet was, and if they tried to break out by land they would be forced to fight Alfred on the narrow strip of land between the two rivers, and that would cause a great slaughter. I remembered Ravn telling me how the Danes feared to lose too many men for they could not replace them quickly. Guthrum could stay where he was, of course, but then Alfred would besiege him and Alfred had already ordered that every barn, granary or store-house within raiding distance of the Poole was to be emptied. The Danes would starve in the coming winter.

Which meant that both sides wanted peace, and Alfred and Guthrum had been discussing terms, and I arrived just as they were finishing the discussions. It was already too late in the year for the Danish fleet to risk a long journey around Wessex's southern coast, and so Alfred had agreed that Guthrum could remain in Werham through the winter. He also agreed to supply them with food on condition that they made no raids, and he agreed to give them silver because he knew the Danes always wanted silver, and in return they promised that they would stay peaceably in Werham and leave peaceably in the spring when their fleet would go back to East Anglia and the rest of their army would march north through Wessex, guarded by our men, until they reached Mercia.

No one, on either side, believed the promises, so they had to be secured, and for that each side demanded hostages, and the hostages had to be of rank, or else their lives would be security for nothing. A dozen Danish Earls, none of whom I knew, were to be delivered to Alfred, and an equivalent number of English nobles given to Guthrum.

Which was why I had been summoned. Which was why Alfred had been so distant with me, for he knew all along that I was to be one of the hostages. My use to him had lessened that year, because of the fleet's impotence, but my rank still had bargaining power, and so I was among the chosen. I was Ealdorman Uhtred, and only useful because I was a noble, and I saw Odda the Younger smiling broadly as my name was accepted by the Danes.

Guthrum and Alfred then swore oaths. Alfred insisted that the Danish leader made his oath with one hand on the relics that Alfred always carried in his baggage. There was a feather from the dove that Noah had released from the ark, a glove that had belonged to Saint Cedd and, most sacred of all, a toe-ring that had belonged to Mary Magdalene. The holy ring, Alfred called it, and a bemused Guthrum put his hand on the scrap of gold and swore he would keep his promises, then insisted that Alfred put a hand on the bone he hung in his hair and he made the King of Wessex swear on a dead Danish mother that the West Saxons would keep the treaty. Only when those oaths were made, sanctified by the gold of a saint and the bone of a mother, were the hostages exchanged, and as I walked across the space between the two sides Guthrum must have recognised me for he gave me a long, contemplative look, and then we were escorted, with ceremony, to Werham.

Where Earl Ragnar, son of Ragnar, welcomed me.

There was joy in that meeting. Ragnar and I embraced like brothers, and I thought of him as a brother, and he thumped my back, poured ale, and gave me news. Kjartan and Sven still lived and were still in Dunholm. Ragnar had confronted them in a formal meeting where both sides were forbidden to carry weapons, and Kjartan had sworn that he was innocent of the hall-burning and declared he knew nothing of Thyra. 'The bastard lied,' Ragnar told me, 'and I know he lied. And he knows he will die.'

'But not yet?'

'How can I take Dunholm?'

Brida was there, sharing Ragnar's bed, and she greeted me

warmly, though not as hotly as Nihtgenga who leaped all over me and washed my face with his tongue. Brida was amused that I was going to be a father. 'But it will be good for you,' she said.

'Good for me? Why?'

'Because you'll be a proper man.'

I thought I was that already, yet there was still one thing lacking, one thing I had never confessed to anyone, not to Mildrith, not to Leofric, and not now to Ragnar or Brida. I had fought the Danes, I had seen ships burn and watched men drown, but I had never fought in a great shield wall. I had fought in small ones, I had fought ship's crew against ship's crew, but I had never stood on a wide battlefield and watched the enemy's banners hide the sun, and known the fear that comes when hundreds or thousands of men are coming to the slaughter. I had been at Eoferwic and at Æsc's Hill and I had seen the shield walls clash, but I had not been in the front rank. I had been in fights, but they had all been small and small fights end quickly. I had never endured the long blood-letting, the terrible fights when thirst and weariness weaken a man and the enemy, no matter how many you kill, keeps on coming. Only when I had done that, I thought, could I call myself a proper man.

I missed Mildrith, and that surprised me. I also missed Leofric, though there was huge pleasure in Ragnar's company, and the life of a hostage was not hard. We lived in Werham, received enough food and watched the grey of winter shorten the days. One of the hostages was a cousin of Alfred's, a priest called Wælla, who fretted and sometimes wept, but the rest of us were content enough. Hacca, who had once commanded Alfred's fleet, was among the hostages, and he was the only one I knew well, but I spent my time with Ragnar and his men who accepted me as one of them and even tried to make me a Dane again. 'I have a wife,' I told them.

'So bring her!' Ragnar said. 'We never have enough women.'

But I was English now. I did not hate the Danes, indeed I preferred their company to the company of the other hostages, but I was English. That journey was done. Alfred had not changed my allegiance, but Leofric and Mildrith had, or else the three spinners had become bored with teasing me, though Bebbanburg still haunted me and I did not know how, if I was to keep my loyalty to Alfred, I would ever see that lovely place again.

Ragnar accepted my choice. 'But if there's peace,' he said, 'will you help me fight Kjartan?'

'If?' I repeated the word.

He shrugged. 'Guthrum still wants Wessex. We all do.'

'If there's peace,' I promised, 'I will come north.'

Yet I doubted there would be peace. In the spring Guthrum would leave Wessex, the hostages would be freed, and then what? The Danish army still existed and Ubba yet lived, so the onslaught on Wessex must begin again, and Guthrum must have been thinking the same for he talked with all the hostages in an effort to discover Alfred's strength. 'It is a great strength,' I told him, 'you may kill his army and another will spring up.' It was all nonsense, of course, but what else did he expect me to say?

I doubt I convinced Guthrum, but Wælla, the priest who was Alfred's cousin, put the fear of God into him. Guthrum spent hours talking with Wælla, and I often interpreted for him, and Guthrum was not asking about troops or ships, but about God. Who was the Christian god? What did he offer? He was fascinated by the tale of the crucifixion and I think, had we been given time enough, Wælla could even have persuaded Guthrum to convert. Wælla certainly thought so himself for he enjoined me to pray for such a conversion. 'It's close, Uhtred,' he told me excitedly, 'and once he has been baptised then there will be peace!'

Such are the dreams of priests. My dreams were of Mildrith and the child she carried. Ragnar dreamed of revenge. And Guthrum?

Despite his fascination with Christianity, Guthrum dreamed of just one thing.

He dreamed of war.

PART THREE

The Shield Wall

Ten

Alfred's army withdrew from Werham. Some West Saxons stayed to watch Guthrum, but very few, for armies are expensive to maintain and, once gathered, they always seem to fall sick, so Alfred took advantage of the truce to send the men of the fyrds back to their farms while he and his household troops went to Scireburnan that lay a half-day's march north-west of Werham and, happily for Alfred, was home to a bishop and a monastery. Beocca told me that Alfred spent that winter reading the ancient law codes from Kent, Mercia and Wessex, and doubtless he was readying himself to compile his own laws, which he eventually did. I am certain he was happy that winter, criticising his ancestors' rules and dreaming of the perfect society where the church told us what not to do and the king punished us for doing it.

Huppa, Ealdorman of Thornsæta, commanded the few men who were left facing Werham's ramparts, while Odda the Younger led a troop of horsemen who patrolled the shores of the Poole, but the two bands made only a small force and they could do little except keep an eye on the Danes, and why should they do more? There was a truce, Guthrum had sworn on the holy ring, and Wessex was at peace.

The Yule feast was a thin affair in Werham, though the Danes did their best and at least there was plenty of ale so men got drunk, but my chief memory of that Yule is of Guthrum crying. The tears poured down his face as a harpist played a sad tune and a skald recited a poem about Guthrum's mother. Her beauty, the skald said, was rivalled only by the stars, while her kindness was such that flowers sprang up in winter to pay her homage. 'She was a rancid bitch,' Ragnar whispered to me, 'and ugly as a bucket of shit.'

'You knew her?'

'Ravn knew her. He always said she had a voice that could cut down a tree.'

Guthrum was living up to his name 'the Unlucky'. He had come so close to destroying Wessex and it had only been Halfdan's death that had cheated him of the prize, and that was not Guthrum's fault, yet there was a simmering resentment among the trapped army. Men muttered that nothing could ever prosper under Guthrum's leadership, and perhaps that distrust had made him gloomier than ever, or perhaps it was hunger.

For the Danes were hungry. Alfred kept his word and sent food, but there was never quite enough, and I did not understand why the Danes did not eat their horses that were left to graze on the winter marshes between the fortress and the Poole. Those horses grew desperately thin, their pathetic grazing supplemented by what little hay the Danes had discovered in the town and when that was gone they pulled the thatch from some of Werham's houses, and that poor diet kept the horses alive until the first glimmerings of spring. I welcomed those new signs of the turning year; the song of a missel thrush, the dog violets showing in sheltered spots, the lambs' tails on the hazel trees and the first frogs croaking in the marsh. Spring was coming, and when the land was green Guthrum would leave and we hostages would be freed.

We received little news other than what the Danes told us, but sometimes a message was delivered to one or other of the hostages, usually nailed to a willow tree outside the gate, and one such message was addressed to me and, for the first time, I was grateful that Beocca had taught me to read for Father Willibald had written and told me I had a son. Mildrith had given birth before Yule and the boy was healthy and she was also healthy and the boy was called Uhtred. I wept when I read that. I had not expected to feel so much, but I did, and Ragnar asked why I was crying and I told him and he produced a barrel of ale and we gave ourselves a feast, or as much of a feast as we could make, and he gave me a tiny silver arm ring as a gift for the boy. I had a son. Uhtred.

Next day I helped Ragnar relaunch *Wind-Viper*. She had been dragged ashore so her timbers could be caulked, and we stowed her bilges with the stones that served as ballast and rigged her mast and afterwards killed a hare that we had trapped in the fields where the horses tried to graze, and Ragnar poured the hare's blood on the *Wind-Viper*'s stem and called on Thor to send her fair winds and for Odin to send her great victories. We ate the hare that night and drank the last of the ale, and next morning a dragon boat arrived, coming from the sea, and I was amazed that Alfred had not ordered our fleet to patrol the waters off the Poole's mouth, but none of our boats was there, and so that single Danish ship came upriver and brought a message for Guthrum.

Ragnar was vague about the ship. It came from East Anglia, he said, which turned out to be untrue, and merely brought news of that kingdom, which was equally untrue. It had come from the west, around Cornwalum, from the lands of the Welsh, but I only learned that later and, at the time, I did not care, because Ragnar also told me that we should be leaving soon, very soon, and I only had thoughts for the son I had not seen. Uhtred Uhtredson.

That night Guthrum gave the hostages a feast, a good feast too, with food and ale that had been brought on the newly arrived dragon ship, and Guthrum praised us for being good guests and he gave each of us an arm ring, and promised we would all be free soon. 'When?' I asked.

'Soon!' His long face glistened in the firelight as he raised a horn of ale to me. 'Soon! Now drink!'

We all drank, and after the feast we hostages went to the nunnery's hall where Guthrum insisted we slept. In the daytime we were free to roam wherever we wanted inside the Danish lines, and free to carry weapons if we chose, but at night he wanted all the hostages in one place so that his black-cloaked guards could keep an eye on us, and it was those guards who came for us in the night's dark heart. They carried flaming torches and they kicked us awake, ordering us outside, and one of them kicked Serpent-Breath away when I reached for her. 'Get outside,' he snarled, and when I reached for the sword again a spear stave cracked across my skull and two more spears jabbed my arse, and I had no choice but to stumble out of the door into a gusting wind that was bringing a cold, spitting rain, and the wind tore at the flaming torches which lit the street where at least a hundred Danes waited, all armed, and I could see they had saddled and bridled their thin horses and my first thought was that these were the men who would escort us back to the West Saxon lines.

Then Guthrum, cloaked in black, pushed through the helmeted men. No words were spoken. Guthrum, grim-faced, the white bone in his hair, just nodded, and his black-cloaked men drew their swords and poor Wælla, Alfred's cousin, was the first hostage to die. Guthrum winced slightly at the priest's death, for I think he had liked Wælla, but by then I was turning, ready to fight the men behind me even though I had no weapon and knew that fight could only end with my death. A sword was already coming for me, held by a Dane in a leather jerkin that was studded with metal rivets, and he was grinning as he ran the blade towards my unprotected belly and he was still grinning as the throwing axe buried its blade between his eyes. I remember the thump of that blade striking home, the spurt of blood in the flamelight, the noise as the man fell onto the flint and shingle street, and all the while the frantic protests from the other hostages as they were murdered, but I lived. Ragnar had hurled the axe and now stood beside me, sword drawn. He was in his war gear, in polished chain mail, in high boots and a helmet which he had decorated with a pair of eagle wings, and in the raw light of the wind-fretted fires he looked like a god come down to Midgard.

'They must all die,' Guthrum insisted. The other hostages were dead or dying, their hands bloodied from their hopeless attempts to ward off the blades, and a dozen war Danes, swords red, now edged towards me to finish the job.

'Kill this one,' Ragnar shouted, 'and you must kill me first.' His men came out of the crowd to stand beside their lord. They were outnumbered by at least five to one, but they were Danes and they showed no fear.

Guthrum stared at Ragnar. Hacca was still not dead and he twitched in his agony and Guthrum, irritated that the man lived, drew his sword and rammed it into Hacca's throat. Guthrum's men were stripping the arm rings from the dead, rings that had been gifts from their master just hours before. 'They all must die,' Guthrum said when Hacca was still. 'Alfred will kill our hostages now, so it must be man for man.'

'Uhtred is my brother,' Ragnar said, 'and you are welcome to kill him, lord, but you must first kill me.'

Guthrum stepped back. 'This is no time for Dane to fight Dane,' he said grudgingly, and sheathed his sword to show that I could live. I stepped across the street to find the man who had stolen Serpent-Breath, Wasp-Sting and my armour, and he gave them to me without protest.

Guthrum's men were mounting their horses. 'What's happening?' I asked Ragnar.

'What do you think?' he asked truculently.

'I think you're breaking the truce.'

'We did not come this far,' he said, 'to march away like beaten dogs.' He watched as I buckled Serpent-Breath's belt. 'Come with us,' he said.

'Come with you where?'

'To take Wessex, of course.'

I do not deny that there was a tug on my heart strings, a temptation to join the wild Danes in their romp across Wessex, but the tug was easily resisted. 'I have a wife,' I told him, 'a child.'

He grimaced. 'Alfred has trapped you, Uhtred.'

'No,' I said, 'the spinners did that.' Urðr, Verðandi and Skuld, the three women who spin our threads at the foot of Yggdrasil, had decided my fate. Destiny is all. 'I shall go to my woman,' I said.

'But not yet,' Ragnar said with a half-smile, and he took me to the river where a small boat carried us to where the newly launched *Wind-Viper* was anchored. A half-crew was already aboard, as was Brida, who gave me a breakfast of bread and ale. At first light, when there was just enough grey in the sky to reveal the glistening mud of the river's banks, Ragnar ordered the anchor raised and we drifted downstream on current and tide, gliding past the dark shapes of other Danish ships until we came to a reach wide enough to turn *Wind-Viper* and there the oars were fitted, men

283

tugged and she swivelled gracefully, both oar banks began to pull and she shot out into the Poole where most of the Danish fleet rode at anchor. We did not go far, just to the barren shore of a big island that sits in the centre of the Poole, a place of squirrels, seabirds and foxes. Ragnar let the ship glide towards the shore and, when her prow touched the beach, he embraced me. 'You are free,' he said.

'Thank you,' I said fervently, remembering those bloodied corpses by Werham's nunnery.

He held onto my shoulders. 'You and I,' he said, 'are tied as brothers. Don't forget that. Now go.'

I splashed through the shallows as the *Wind-Viper*, a ghostly grey in the dawn, backed away. Brida called a farewell, I heard the oars bite and the ship was gone.

That island was a forbidding place. Fishermen and fowlers had lived there once, and an anchorite, a monk who lives by himself, had occupied a hollow tree in the island's centre, but the coming of the Danes had driven them all away and the remnants of the fishermen's houses were nothing but charred timbers on blackened ground. I had the island to myself, and it was from its shore that I watched the vast Danish fleet row towards the Poole's entrance, though they stopped there rather than go to sea because the wind, already brisk, had freshened even more and now it was a half-gale blowing from the south and the breakers were shattering wild and white above the spit of sand that protected their new anchorage. The Danish fleet had moved there, I surmised, because to stay in the river would have exposed their crews to the West Saxon bowmen who would be among the troops re-occupying Werham.

Guthrum had led his horsemen out of Werham, that much was obvious, and all the Danes who had remained in the town were now crammed onto the ships where they waited for the weather to calm so they could sail away, but to where, I had no idea.

All day that south wind blew, getting harder and bringing a slashing rain, and I became bored of watching the Danish fleet fret at its anchors and so I explored the island's shore and found the remnants of a small boat half hidden in a thicket and I hauled the wreck down to the water and discovered it floated well enough, and the wind would take me away from the Danes and so I waited for the tide to turn and then, half swamped in the broken craft, I floated free. I used a piece of wood as a crude paddle, but the wind was howling now and it drove me wet and cold across that wide water until, as night fell, I came to the Poole's northern shore and there I became one of the sceadugengan again, picking my way through reeds and marshes until I found higher ground where bushes gave me shelter for a broken sleep. In the morning I walked eastwards, still buffeted by wind and rain, and so came to Hamtun that evening.

Where I found that Mildrith and my son were gone.

Taken by Odda the Younger.

Father Willibald told me the tale. Odda had come that morning, while Leofric was down at the shore securing the boats against the bruising wind, and Odda had said that the Danes had broken out, that they would have killed their hostages, that they might come to Hamtun at any moment, and that Mildrith should flee. 'She did not want to go, lord,' Willibald said, and I could hear the timidity in his voice. My anger was frightening him. 'They had horses, lord,' he said, as if that explained it.

'You didn't send for Leofric?'

'They wouldn't let me, lord.' He paused. 'But we were scared, lord. The Danes had broken the truce and we thought you were dead.'

Leofric had set off in pursuit, but by the time he learned Mildrith was gone Odda had at least a half-morning's start and Leofric did not even know where he would have gone. 'West,' I said, 'back to Defnascir.'

'And the Danes?' Leofric asked, 'where are they going?'

'Back to Mercia?' I guessed.

Leofric shrugged. 'Across Wessex? With Alfred waiting? And you say they went on horseback? How fit were the horses?'

'They weren't fit. They were half starved.'

'Then they haven't gone to Mercia,' he said firmly.

'Perhaps they've gone to meet Ubba,' Willibald suggested.

'Ubba!' I had not heard that name in a long time.

'There were stories, lord,' Willibald said nervously, 'that he was among the Britons in Wales. That he had a fleet on the Sæfern.'

That made sense. Ubba was replacing his dead brother, Halfdan, and evidently leading another force of Danes against Wessex, but where? If he crossed the Sæfern's wide sea then he would be in Defnascir, or perhaps he was marching around the river, heading into Alfred's heartland from the north, but for the moment I did not care. I only wanted to find my wife and child. There was pride in that desire, of course, but more than pride. Mildrith and I were suited to each other, I had missed her, I wanted to see my child. That ceremony in the rain-dripping cathedral had worked its magic and I wanted her back and I wanted to punish Odda the Younger for taking her away. 'Defnascir,' I said again, 'that's where the bastard's gone. And that's where we go tomorrow.' Odda, I was certain, would head for the safety of home. Not that he feared my revenge, for he surely assumed I was dead, but he would be worried about the Danes, and I was worried that they might have found him on his westward flight.

'You and me?' Leofric asked.

I shook my head. 'We take *Heahengel* and a full fighting crew.'

Leofric looked sceptical. 'In this weather?'

'The wind's dropping,' I said, and it was, though it still tugged at the thatch and rattled the shutters, but it was calmer next morning, but not by much for Hamtun's water was still flecked white as the small waves ran angrily ashore, suggesting that the seas beyond the Solente would be huge and furious. But there were breaks in the cloud, the wind had gone into the east, and I was in no mood to wait. Two of the crew, both seamen all their lives, tried to dissuade me from the voyage. They had seen this weather before, they said, and the storm would come back, but I refused to believe them and they, to their credit, came willingly as did Father Willibald, which was brave of him for he hated the sea and was facing rougher water than any he had seen before.

We rowed up Hamtun's water, hoisted the sail in the Solente, brought the oars inboard and ran before that east wind as though the serpent Corpse-Ripper was at our stern. *Heahengel* hammered through the short seas, threw the white water high, raced, and that was while we were still in sheltered waters. Then we passed the white stacks at Wiht's end, the rocks that are called the Nædles, and the first tumultuous seas hit us and the *Heahengel* bent to them. Yet still we flew, and the wind was dropping and the sun shone through rents in the dark clouds to glitter on the churning sea, and Leofric suddenly roared a warning and pointed ahead.

He was pointing to the Danish fleet. Like me they believed the weather was improving, and they must have been in a hurry to join Guthrum, for the whole fleet was coming out of the Poole and was now sailing south to round the rocky headland, which meant, like us, they were going west. Which could mean they were going to Defnascir or perhaps planning to sail clear about Cornwalum to join Ubba in Wales.

'You want to tangle with them?' Leofric asked me grimly.

I heaved on the steering oar, driving us south. 'We'll go outside them,' I said, meaning we would head out to sea and I doubted any of their ships would bother with us. They were in a hurry to get wherever they were going and with luck, I thought, *Heahengel* would outrun them for she was a fast ship and they were still well short of the headland.

We flew downwind and there was joy in it, the joy of steering a boat through angry seas, though I doubt there was much joy for the men who had to bail *Heahengel*, chucking the water over the side, and it was one of those men who looked astern and called a sudden warning to me. I turned to see a black squall seething across the broken seas. It was an angry patch of darkness and rain, coming fast, so fast that Willibald, who had been clutching the ship's side as he vomited overboard, fell to his knees, made the sign of the cross and began to pray. 'Get the sail down!' I shouted at Leofric, and he staggered forward, but too late, much too late, for the squall struck.

One moment the sun had shone, then we were abruptly thrust into the devil's playground as the squall hit us like a shield wall. The ship shuddered, water and wind and gloom smashing us in sudden turmoil and *Heahengel* swung to the blow, going broadside to the sea and nothing I could do would hold her straight, and I saw Leofric stagger across the deck as the stærbord side went under water. 'Bail!' I shouted desperately, 'bail!' And then, with a noise like thunder, the great sail split into tatters that whipped off the yard, and the ship came slowly upright, but she was low in the water, and I was using all my strength to keep her coming round, creeping round, reversing our course so that I could put her bows into that turmoil of sea and wind, and the men were praying, making the sign of the cross, bailing water, and the remnants of the sail and the broken lines were mad things, ragged demons, and the sudden gale was howling like the furies in the rigging and I thought how futile it would be to die at sea so soon after Ragnar had saved my life.

Somehow we got six oars into the water and then, with two men to an oar, we pulled into that seething chaos. Twelve men pulled six oars, three men tried to cut the rigging's wreckage away, and the others threw water over the side. No orders were given, for no voice could be heard above that shrieking wind that was flensing the skin from the sea and whipping it in white spindrift. Huge swells rolled, but they were no danger for the *Heahengel* rode them, but their broken tops threatened to swamp us, and then I saw the mast sway, its shrouds parting, and I shouted uselessly, for no one could hear me, and the great spruce spar broke and fell. It fell across the ship's side and the water flowed in again, but Leofric and a dozen men somehow managed to heave the mast overboard and it banged down our flank, then jerked because it was still held to the ship by a tangle of seal-hide ropes. I saw Leofric pluck an axe from the swamped bilge and start to slash at that tangle of lines, but I screamed at him with all my breath to put the axe down.

Because the mast, tied to us and floating behind us, seemed to steady the ship. It held *Heahengel* into the waves and wind, and let the great seas go rolling beneath us, and we could catch our breath at last. Men looked at each other as if amazed to find themselves alive, and I could even let go of the steering oar because the mast, with the big yard and the remnants of its sail still attached, was holding us steady. I found my body aching. I was soaked through, must have been cold, but did not notice.

Leofric came to stand beside me. *Heahengel*'s prow was facing eastwards, but we were travelling westwards, driven backwards by the tide and wind, and I turned to make certain we had sea room, and then touched Leofric's shoulder and pointed towards the shore.

Where we saw a fleet dying.

The Danes had been sailing south, following the shore from the Poole's entrance to the rearing headland, and that meant they were on a lee shore, and in that sudden resurgence of the storm they stood no chance. Ship after ship was being driven ashore. A few had made it past the headland, and another handful were trying to row clear of the cliffs, but most were doomed. We could not see their deaths, but I could imagine them. The crash of hulls against rocks, the churning water breaking through the planks, the pounding of sea and wind and timber on drowning men, dragon prows splintering and the halls of the sea god filling with the souls of warriors and, though they were the enemy, I doubt any of us felt anything but pity. The sea gives a cold and lonely death.

Ragnar and Brida. I just gazed, but could not distinguish one ship from another through the rain and broken sea. We did watch one ship, which seemed to have escaped, suddenly sink. One moment she was on a wave, spray flying from her hull, oars pulling her free, and next she was just gone. She vanished. Other ships were banging each other, oars tangling and splintering. Some tried to turn and run back to the Poole and many of those were driven ashore, some on the sands and some on the cliffs. A few ships, pitifully few, beat their way clear, men hauling on the oars in a frenzy, but all the Danish ships were overloaded, carrying men whose horses had died, carrying an army we knew not where, and that army now died.

We were south of the headland now, being driven fast to the west, and a Danish ship, smaller than ours, came close and the steersman looked across and gave a grim smile as if to acknowledge there was only one enemy now, the sea. The Dane drifted ahead of us, not slowed, as we were, by trailing wreckage. The rain hissed down, a malevolent rain, stinging on the wind, and the sea was full of planks, broken spars, dragon prows, long oars, shields and corpses. I saw a dog swimming frantically, eyes white, and for a moment I thought it was Nihtgenga, then saw this dog had black ears while Nihtgenga had white. The clouds were the colour of iron, ragged and low, and the water was being shredded into streams of white and green-black, and the *Heahengel* reared to each sea, crashed down into the troughs and shook like a live thing with every blow, but she lived. She was well-built, she kept us alive, and all the while we watched the Danish ships die and Father Willibald prayed.

Oddly his sickness had passed. He looked pale, and doubtless felt wretched, but as the storm pummelled us his vomiting ended and he even came to stand beside me, steadying himself by holding onto the steering oar. 'Who is the Danish god of the sea?' he asked me over the wind's noise.

'Njor∂!' I shouted back.

He grinned. 'You pray to him and I'll pray to God.'

I laughed. 'If Alfred knew you'd said that you'd never become a bishop!'

'I won't become a bishop unless we survive this! So pray!'

I did pray, and slowly, reluctantly, the storm eased. Low clouds raced over the angry water, but the wind died and we could cut away the wreckage of mast and yard and unship the oars and turn *Heahengel* to the west and row through the flotsam of a shattered war fleet. A score of Danish ships were in front of us, and there were others behind us, but I guessed that at least half their fleet had sunk, perhaps more, and I felt an immense fear for Ragnar and Brida. We caught up with the smaller Danish ships and I steered close to as many as I could and shouted across the broken seas. 'Did you see *Wind-Viper*?'

'No,' they called back. No, came the answer, again and again. They knew we were an enemy ship, but did not care for there was no enemy out in that water except the water itself, and so we rowed on, a mastless ship, and left the Danes behind us and as night fell, and as a streak of sunlight leaked like seeping blood into a rift of the western clouds, I steered *Heahengel* into the crooked reach of the River Uisc, and once we were behind the headland the sea calmed and we rowed, suddenly safe, past the long spit of sand and turned into the river and I could look up into the darkening hills to where Oxton stood, and I saw no light there.

We beached *Heahengel* and staggered ashore and some men knelt and kissed the ground while others made the sign of the cross. There was a small harbour in the wide river reach and some houses by the harbour and we filled them, demanded that fires were lit and food brought, and then, in the darkness, I went back outside and saw the sparks of light flickering upriver. I realised they were torches being burned on the remaining Danish boats that had somehow found their way into the Uisc and now rowed inland, going north towards Exanceaster, and I knew that was where Guthrum must have ridden and that the Danes were there, and the fleet's survivors would thicken his army and Odda the Younger, if he lived, might well have tried to go there too.

With Mildrith and my son. I touched Thor's hammer and prayed they were alive.

And then, as the dark boats passed upstream, I slept.

In the morning we pulled *Heahengel* into the small harbour where she could rest on the mud when the tide fell. We were forty-eight men, tired but alive. The sky was ribbed with clouds, high and grey-pink, scudding before the storm's dying wind.

We walked to Oxton through woods full of bluebells. Did I expect to find Mildrith there? I think I did, but of course she was not. There was only Oswald the steward and the slaves and none of them knew what was happening.

Leofric insisted on a day to dry clothes, sharpen weapons and fill bellies, but I was in no mood to rest so I took two men, Cenwulf and Ida, and walked north towards Exanceaster that lay on the far side of the Uisc. The river settlements were empty, for the folk had heard of the Danes coming and had fled into the hills, and so we walked the higher paths and asked them what had happened, but they knew nothing except that there were dragon ships in the river, and we could see those for ourselves. There was a storm-battered fleet drawn up on the riverbank beneath Exanceaster's stone walls. There were more ships than I had suspected, suggesting that a good part of Guthrum's fleet had survived by staying in the Poole when the storm struck, and a few of those ships were still arriving, their crews rowing up the narrow river. We counted hulls and reckoned there were close to ninety boats, which meant that almost half of Guthrum's fleet had survived, and I tried to distinguish *Wind-Viper*'s hull among the others, but we were too far away.

Guthrum the Unlucky. How well he deserved that name, though in time he came close to earning a better, but for now he had been unfortunate indeed. He had broken out of Werham, had doubtless hoped to resupply his army in Exanceaster and then strike north, but the gods of sea and wind had struck him down and he was left with a crippled army. Yet it was still a strong army and, for the moment, safe behind Exanceaster's Roman walls.

I wanted to cross the river, but there were too many Danes by their ships, so we walked further north and saw armed men on the road which led west from Exanceaster, a road which crossed the bridge beneath the city and led over the moors towards Cornwalum, and I stared a long time at those men, fearing they might be Danes, but they were staring east, suggesting that they watched the Danes and I guessed they were English and so we went down from the woods, shields slung on our backs to show we meant no harm.

There were eighteen men, led by a thegn named Withgil who had been the commander of Exanceaster's garrison and who had lost most of his men when Guthrum attacked. He was reluctant to tell the story, but it was plain he had expected no trouble and had posted only a few guards on the eastern gate, and when they had seen the approaching horsemen the guards had thought they were English and so the Danes had been able to capture the gate and then pierce the town. Withgil claimed to have made a fight at the fort in the town's centre, but it was obvious from his men's embarrassment that it had been a pathetic resistance, if it amounted to any resistance at all, and the probable truth was that Withgil had simply run away.

'Was Odda there?' I asked.

'Ealdorman Odda?' Withgil asked. 'Of course not.'

'Where was he?'

Withgil frowned at me as if I had just come from the moon. 'In the north, of course.'

'The north of Defnascir?'

'He marched a week ago. He led the fyrd.'

'Against Ubba?'

'That's what the king ordered,' Withgil said.

'So where's Ubba?' I demanded.

It seemed that Ubba had brought his ships across the wide Sæfern sea and had landed far to the west in Defnascir. He had travelled before the storm struck, which suggested his army was intact, and Odda had been ordered north to block Ubba's advance into the rest of Wessex, and if Odda had marched a week ago then surely Odda the Younger would know that and would have ridden to join his father? Which suggested that Mildrith was there, wherever there was. I asked Withgil if he had seen Odda the Younger, but he said he had neither seen nor heard of him since Christmas.

'How many men does Ubba have?' I asked.

'Many,' Withgil said, which was not helpful, but all he knew.

'Lord,' Cenwulf touched my arm and pointed east and I saw horsemen appearing on the low fields which stretched from the river towards the hill on which Exanceaster is built. A lot of horsemen, and behind them came a standard-bearer and, though we were too far away to see the badge on the flag, the green and white proclaimed that it was the West Saxon banner. So Alfred had come here? It seemed likely, but I was in no mind to cross the river and find out. I was only interested in searching for Mildrith.

War is fought in mystery. The truth can take days to travel, and ahead of truth flies rumour, and it is ever hard to know what is really happening, and the art of it is to pluck the clean bone of fact from the rotting flesh of fear and lies.

So what did I know? That Guthrum had broken the truce and had taken Exanceaster, and that Ubba was in the north of Defnascir. Which suggested that the Danes were trying to do what they had failed to do the previous year, split the West Saxon forces, and while Alfred faced one army the other would ravage the land or, perhaps, descend on Alfred's rear, and to prevent that the fyrd of

Defnascir had been ordered to block Ubba. Had that battle been fought? Was Odda alive? Was his son alive? Were Mildrith and my son alive? In any clash between Ubba and Odda I would have reckoned on Ubba. He was a great warrior, a man of legend among the Danes, and Odda was a fussy, worried, greying and ageing man.

'We go north,' I told Leofric when we were back at Oxton. I had no wish to see Alfred. He would be besieging Guthrum, and if I walked into his camp he would doubtless order me to join the troops ringing the city and I would sit there, wait, and worry. Better to go north and find Ubba.

So next morning, under a spring sun, the *Heahengel*'s crew marched north.

The war was between the Danes and Wessex. My war was with Odda the Younger, and I knew I was driven by pride. The preachers tell us that pride is a great sin, but the preachers are wrong. Pride makes a man, it drives him, it is the shield wall around his reputation and the Danes understood that. Men die, they said, but reputation does not die.

What do we look for in a lord? Strength, generosity, hardness and success, and why should a man not be proud of those things? Show me a humble warrior and I will see a corpse. Alfred preached humility, he even pretended to it, loving to appear in church with bare feet and prostrating himself before the altar, but he never possessed true humility. He was proud, and men feared him because of it, and men should fear a lord. They should fear his displeasure and fear that his generosity will cease. Reputation makes fear, and pride protects reputation, and I marched north because my pride was endangered. My woman and child had been taken from me, and I would take them back, and if they had been harmed then I would take my revenge and the stink of that man's blood would make other men fear me. Wessex could fall for all I cared, my reputation was more important and so we marched, skirting Exanceaster, following a twisting cattle track into the hills until we reached Twyfyrde, a small place crammed with refugees from Exanceaster, and none of them had seen or heard news of Odda the Younger, nor had they heard of any battle to the north, though a priest claimed that lightning had struck thrice in the previous night which he swore was a sign that God had struck down the pagans.

From Twyfyrde we took paths that edged the great moor, walking through country that was deep-wooded, hilly and lovely. We would have made better time if we had possessed horses, but we had none, and the few we saw were old, sick and there were never enough for all our men and so we walked, sleeping that night in a deep combe bright with blossom and sifted with blue-bells, and a nightingale sang us to sleep and the dawn chorus woke us and we walked on beneath the white mayflower, and that afternoon we came to the hills above the northern shore and we met folk who had fled the coastal lands, bringing with them their families and livestock, and their presence told us we must soon see the Danes.

I did not know it but the three spinners were making my fate. They were thickening the threads, twisting them tighter, making me into what I am, but staring down from that high hill I only felt a flicker of fear, for there was Ubba's fleet, rowing east, keeping pace with the horsemen and infantry who marched along the shore.

The folk who had fled their homes told us that the Danes had come from the Welsh lands across the wide Sæfern sea, and that they had landed at a place called Beardastopol which lies far in Defnascir's west, and there they had collected horses and supplies, but then their attack eastwards into the West Saxon heartland had been delayed by the great storm which had wrecked Guthrum's fleet. Ubba's ships had stayed in Beardastopol's harbour until the storm passed and then, inexplicably, they had still waited even when the weather improved and I guessed that Ubba, who would do nothing without the consent of the gods, had cast the rune-sticks, found them unfavourable, and so waited until the auguries were better. Now the runes must have been good for Ubba's army was on the move. I counted thirty-six ships which suggested an army of at least twelve or thirteen hundred men.

'Where are they going?' one of my men asked.

'East,' I grunted, what else could I say? East into Wessex. East

295

into the rich heartland of England's last kingdom. East to Wintanceaster or to any of the other plump towns where the churches, monasteries and nunneries were brimming with treasure, east to where the plunder waited, east to where there was food and more horses, east to invite more Danes to come south across Mercia's frontier, and Alfred would be forced to turn around and face them, and then Guthrum's army would come from Exanceaster and the army of Wessex would be caught between two hosts of Danes, except that the fyrd of Defnascir was somewhere on this coast and it was their duty to stop Ubba's men.

We walked east, passing from Defnascir into Sumorsæte, and shadowing the Danes by staying on the higher ground, and that night I watched as Ubba's ships came inshore and the fires were lit in the Danish camp, and we lit our own fires deep in a wood and were marching again before dawn and thus got ahead of our enemies and by midday we could see the first West Saxon forces. They were horsemen, presumably sent to scout the enemy, and they were now retreating from the Danish threat, and we walked until the hills dropped away to where a river flowed into the Sæfern sea, and it was there that we discovered that Ealdorman Odda had decided to make his stand, in a fort built by the old people on a hill near the river.

The river was called the Pedredan and close to its mouth was a small place called Cantucton, and near Cantucton was the ancient earth-walled fort that the locals said was named Cynuit. It was old, that fort, Father Willibald said it was older than the Romans, that it had been old when the world was young, and the fort had been made by throwing up earth walls on a hilltop and digging a ditch outside the walls. Time had worked on those walls, wearing them down and making the ditch shallower, and grass had overgrown the ramparts, and on one side the wall had been ploughed almost to nothing, ploughed until it was a mere shadow on the turf, but it was a fortress and the place where Ealdorman Odda had taken his forces and where he would die if he could not defeat Ubba, whose ships were already showing in the river's mouth.

I did not go straight to the fort, but stopped in the shelter of some trees and dressed for war. I became Ealdorman Uhtred in his battle glory. The slaves at Oxton had polished my mail coat with sand and I pulled it on, and over it I buckled a leather sword belt for Serpent-Breath and Wasp-Sting. I pulled on tall boots, put on the shining helmet and picked up my iron-bossed shield and, when all the straps were tight and the buckles firm, I felt like a god dressed for war, dressed to kill. My men buckled their own straps, laced their boots, tested their weapons' edges and even Father Willibald cut himself a stave, a great piece of ash that could break a man's skull. 'You won't need to fight, father,' I told him.

'We all have to fight now, lord,' he said. He took a step back and looked me up and down, and a small smile came to his face. 'You've grown up,' he said.

'It's what we do, father,' I said.

'I remember when I first saw you. A child. Now I fear you.'

'Let's hope the enemy does,' I said, not quite sure what enemy I meant, whether Odda or Ubba, and I wished I had Bebbanburg's standard, the snarling wolf's head, but I had my swords and my shield and I led my men out of the wood and across the fields to where the fyrd of Defnascir would make its stand.

The Danes were a mile or so to our left, spilling from the coast road and hurrying to surround the hill called Cynuit, though they would be too late to bar our path. To my right were more Danes, ship-Danes, bringing their dragon-headed boats up the Pedredan.

'They outnumber us,' Willibald said.

'They do,' I agreed. There were swans on the river, corncrakes in the uncut hay and crimson orchids in the meadows. This was the time of year when men should be haymaking or shearing their sheep. I need not be here, I thought to myself. I need not go to this hilltop where the Danes will come to kill us. I looked at my men and wondered if they thought the same, but when they caught my eye they only grinned, or nodded, and I suddenly realised that they trusted me. I was leading them and they were not questioning me, though Leofric understood the danger. He caught up with me.

'There's only one way off that hilltop,' he said softly.

'I know.'

'And if we can't fight our way out,' he said, 'then we'll stay there. Buried.'

'I know,' I said again, and I thought of the spinners and knew they were tightening the threads, and I looked up Cynuit's slope and saw there were some women at the very top, women being sheltered by their men, and I thought Mildrith might be among them, and that was why I climbed the hill because I did not know where else to seek her.

But the spinners were sending me to that old earth fort for another reason. I had yet to stand in the big shield wall, in the line of warriors, in the heave and horror of a proper battle where to kill once is merely to invite another enemy to come. The hill of Cynuit was the road to full manhood and I climbed it because I had no choice, the spinners sent me.

Then a roar sounded to our right, down in the Pedredan's valley, and I saw a banner being raised beside a beached ship. It was the banner of the raven. Ubba's banner. Ubba, last and strongest and most frightening of the sons of Lothbrok, had brought his blades to Cynuit. 'You see that boat?' I said to Willibald, pointing to where the banner flew. 'Ten years ago,' I said, 'I cleaned that ship. I scoured it, scrubbed it, cleaned it.' Danes were taking their shields from the shield-strake and the sun glinted on their myriad spear blades. 'I was ten years old,' I told Willibald.

'The same boat?' he asked.

'Maybe. Maybe not.' Perhaps it was a new ship. It did not matter, really, all that mattered was that it had brought Ubba.

To Cynuit.

The men of Defnascir had made a line where the old fort's wall had eroded away. Some, a few, had spades and were trying to remake the earth barrier, but they would not be given time to finish, not if Ubba assaulted the hill, and I pushed through them, using my shield to thrust men out of my way, ignoring all those who questioned who we were, and so we made our way to the hill's summit where Odda's banner of a black stag flew.

I pulled off my helmet as I neared him. I tossed the helmet to Father Willibald, then drew Serpent-Breath for I had seen Odda the Younger standing beside his father, and he was staring at me as though I were a ghost, and to him I must have appeared just that. 'Where is she?' I shouted, and I pointed Serpent-Breath at him. 'Where is she?'

Odda's retainers drew swords or levelled spears, and Leofric drew his battle-thinned blade, Dane-Killer.

'No!' Father Willibald shouted and he ran forward, his staff raised in one hand and my helmet in the other. 'No!' He tried to head me off, but I pushed him aside, only to find three of Odda's priests barring my way. That was one thing about Wessex, there were always priests. They appeared like mice out of a burning thatch, but I thrust the priests aside and confronted Odda the Younger. 'Where is she?' I demanded.

Odda the Younger was in mail. Mail so brightly polished that it hurt the eye. He had a helmet inlaid with silver, boots to which iron plates were strapped and a blue cloak held about his neck by a great brooch of gold and amber.

'Where is she?' I asked a fourth time, and this time Serpent-Breath was a hand's length from his throat.

'Your wife is at Cridianton,' Ealdorman Odda answered. His son was too scared to open his mouth.

I had no idea where Cridianton was. 'And my son?' I stared into Odda the Younger's frightened eyes. 'Where is my son?'

'They are both with my wife at Cridianton!' Ealdorman Odda answered, 'and they are safe.'

'You swear to that?' I asked.

'Swear?' The Ealdorman was angry now, his ugly, bulbous face red. 'You dare ask me to swear?' He drew his own sword. 'We can cut you down like a dog,' he said and his men's swords twitched.

I swept my own sword around till it pointed down to the river. 'You know whose banner that is?' I asked, raising my voice so that a good portion of the men on Cynuit's hill could hear me. 'That is the raven banner of Ubba Lothbrokson. I have watched Ubba Lothbrokson kill. I have seen him trample men into the sea, cut their bellies open, take off their heads, wade in their blood and make his sword screech with their death-song, and you would kill me who is ready to fight him alongside you? Then do it.' I spread my arms, baring my body to the Ealdorman's sword. 'Do it,' I spat at him, 'but first swear my wife and child are safe.'

He paused a long time, then lowered his blade. 'They are safe,' he said, 'I swear it.'

'And that thing,' I pointed Serpent-Breath at his son, 'did not touch her?'

The Ealdorman looked at his son who shook his head. 'I swear I did not,' Odda the Younger said, finding his voice. 'I only wanted her to be safe. We thought you were dead and I wanted her to be safe. That is all, I swear it.'

I sheathed Serpent-Breath. 'You owe my wife eighteen shillings,' I said to the Ealdorman, then turned away.

I had come to Cynuit. I had no need to be on that hilltop. But I was there. Because destiny is everything.

Eleven

Ealdorman Odda did not want to kill Danes. He wanted to stay where he was and let Ubba's forces besiege him. That, he reckoned, would be enough. 'Keep their army here,' he said heavily, 'and Alfred can march to attack them.'

'Alfred,' I pointed out, 'is besieging Exanceaster.'

'He will leave men there to watch Guthrum,' Odda said loftily, 'and march here.' He did not like talking to me, but I was an Ealdorman and he could not bar me from his council of war that was attended by his son, the priests and a dozen thegns, all of whom were becoming irritated by my comments. I insisted Alfred would not come to our relief, and Ealdorman Odda was refusing to move from the hilltop because he was sure Alfred would come. His thegns, all of them big men with heavy coats of mail and grim, weather-hardened faces, agreed with him. One muttered that the women had to be protected.

'There shouldn't be any women here,' I said.

'But they are here,' the man said flatly. At least a hundred women had followed their men and were now on the hilltop where there was no shelter for them or their children.

'And even if Alfred comes,' I asked, 'how long will it take?'

'Two days?' Odda suggested. 'Three?'

'And what will we drink while he's coming?' I asked. 'Bird piss?'

They all just stared at me, hating me, but I was right for there was no spring on Cynuit. The nearest water was the river, and between us and the river were Danes, and Odda understood well

301

enough that we would be assailed by thirst, but he still insisted we stay. Perhaps his priests were praying for a miracle.

The Danes were just as cautious. They outnumbered us, but not by many, and we held the high ground which meant they would have to fight up Cynuit's steep slope, and so Ubba chose to surround the hill rather than assault it. The Danes hated losing men, and I remembered Ubba's caution at the Gewæsc where he had hesitated to attack Edmund's forces up the two paths from the marsh, and perhaps that caution was reinforced by Storri, his sorcerer, if Storri still lived. Whatever the reason, instead of forming his men into the shield wall to assault the ancient fort, Ubba posted them in a ring about Cynuit and then, with five of his shipmasters, climbed the hill. He carried no sword or shield which showed he wanted to talk.

Ealdorman Odda, his son, two thegns and three priests went to meet Ubba and, because I was an Ealdorman, I followed them. Odda gave me a malevolent look, but again he was unable to deny me, and so we met halfway down the slope where Ubba offered no greeting and did not even waste time on the usual ritual insults, but pointed out that we were trapped and that our wisest course was to surrender. 'You will give up your weapons,' he said, 'I shall take hostages, and you will all live.'

One of Odda's priests translated the demands to the Ealdorman. I watched Ubba. He looked older than I remembered, with grey hairs among the black tangle of his beard, but he was still a frightening man; huge chested, confident and harsh.

Ealdorman Odda was plainly frightened. Ubba, after all, was a renowned Danish chieftain, a man who had ranged across long seas to give great slaughter, and now Odda was forced to confront him. He did his best to sound defiant, retorting that he would stay where he was and put his faith in the one true God.

'Then I shall kill you,' Ubba answered.

'You may try,' Odda said.

It was a feeble response and Ubba spat in scorn. He was about to turn away, but then I spoke and needed no interpreter. 'Guthrum's fleet is gone,' I said. 'Njorð reached from the deep, Ubba Lothbrokson, and he snatched Guthrum's fleet down to the seabed. All those brave men are gone to Ran and Ægir.' Ran was

302

Njorð's wife and Ægir, the giant who guarded the souls of drowned men. I brought out my hammer charm and held it up. 'I speak the truth, Lord Ubba,' I said. 'I watched that fleet die and I saw its men go under the waves.'

He stared at me with his flat, hard eyes and the violence in his heart was like the heat of a forge. I could feel it, but I could also sense his fear, not of us, but of the gods. He was a man who did nothing without a sign from the gods, and that was why I had talked of the gods when I spoke about the fleet's drowning. 'I know you,' he growled, pointing at me with two fingers to avert the evil of my words.

'And I know you, Ubba Lothbrokson,' I said, and I let go of the charm and held up three fingers. 'Ivar dead,' I folded one finger down, 'Halfdan dead,' the second finger, 'and only you are left. What did the runes say? That by the new moon there will be no Lothbrok brother left in Midgard?'

I had touched a nerve, as I intended to, for Ubba instinctively felt for his own hammer charm. Odda's priest was translating, his voice a low murmur, and the Ealdorman was staring at me with wide astonished eyes.

'Is that why you want us to surrender?' I asked Ubba. 'Because the runesticks tell you we cannot be killed in battle?'

'I shall kill you,' Ubba said. 'I shall cut you from your crotch to your gullet. I shall spill you like offal.'

I made myself smile, though that was hard when Ubba was making threats. 'You may try, Ubba Lothbrokson,' I said, 'but you will fail. And I know. I cast the runes, Ubba, I cast the runes under last night's moon, and I know.'

He hated it, for he believed my lie. He wanted to be defiant, but for a moment he could only stare at me in fear because his own runesticks, I guessed, had told him what I was telling him, that any attack on Cynuit would end in failure. 'You're Ragnar's boy,' he said, placing me at last.

'And Ragnar the Fearless speaks to me,' I said, 'he calls from the corpse-hall, he wants vengeance, Ubba, vengeance on the Danes, for Ragnar was killed treacherously by his own folk. I'm his messenger now, a thing from the corpse-hall, and I have come for you.'

'I didn't kill him!' Ubba snarled.

'Why should Ragnar care?' I asked. 'He just wants vengeance and to him one Danish life is as good as another, so cast your runes again and then offer us your sword. You are doomed, Ubba.'

'And you're a piece of weasel shit,' he said and said no more, but just turned and hurried away.

Ealdorman Odda was still staring at me. 'You know him?' he asked.

'I've known Ubba since I was ten years old,' I said, watching the Danish chieftain walk away. I was thinking that if I had a choice, that if I could follow my warrior's heart, I would rather fight alongside Ubba than against him, but the spinners had decreed otherwise. 'Since I was ten,' I went on, 'and the one thing I know about Ubba is that he fears the gods. He's terrified now. You can attack him and his heart will let him down because he thinks he will lose.'

'Alfred will come,' Odda said.

'Alfred watches Guthrum,' I said. I was not certain of that, of course. For all I knew Alfred could be watching us now from the hills, but I doubted he would leave Guthrum free to plunder Wessex. 'He watches Guthrum,' I said, 'because Guthrum's army is twice as large as Ubba's. Even with his fleet half drowned, Guthrum has more men, and why would Alfred let them loose from Exanceaster? Alfred won't come,' I finished, 'and we shall all die of thirst before Ubba attacks us.'

'We have water,' his son said sulkily, 'and ale.' He had been watching me resentfully, awed that I had spoken so familiarly with Ubba.

'You have ale and water for a day,' I said scornfully and saw from the Ealdorman's expression that I was right.

Odda turned and stared south down the Pedredan's valley. He was hoping to see Alfred's troops, yearning for a glimpse of sunlight on spear heads, but of course there was nothing there except the trees stirring in the wind.

Odda the Younger sensed his father's uncertainty. 'We can wait for two days,' he urged.

'Death will be no better after two days,' Odda said heavily. I admired him then. He had been hoping not to fight, hoping that

304

his king would rescue him, but in his heart he knew I was right and knew that these Danes were his responsibility and that the men of Defnascir held England in their hands and must preserve it. 'Dawn,' he said, not looking at me. 'We shall attack at dawn.'

We slept in war gear. Or rather men tried to sleep when they were wearing leather or mail, with sword belts buckled, helmets and weapons close, and we lit no fires for Odda did not want the enemy to see that we were readied for battle, but the enemy had fires, and our sentries could watch down the slopes and use the enemy's light to look for infiltrators. None came. There was a waning moon sliding in and out of ragged clouds. The Danish fires ringed us, heaviest to the south by Cantucton where Ubba camped. More fires burned to the east, beside the Danish ships, the flames reflecting off the gilded beast-heads and painted dragon prows. Between us and the river was a meadow at the far side of which the Danes watched the hill, and beyond them was a wide stretch of marsh and at the marsh's far side was a strip of firmer land beside the river where some hovels offered the Danish ship-guards shelter. The hovels had belonged to fishermen, long fled, and fires were lit between them. A handful of Danes paced the bank beside those fires, walking beneath the carved prows and I stood on the ramparts and gazed at those long, graceful ships and prayed that *Wind-Viper* still lived.

I could not sleep. I was thinking of shields and Danes and swords and fear. I was thinking of my child that I had never seen and of Ragnar the Fearless, wondering if he watched me from Valhalla. I was worrying that I would fail next day when, at last, I came to the life-gate of a shield wall, and I was not the only one denied sleep for, at the heart of the night, a man climbed the grassy rampart to stand beside me and I saw it was Ealdorman Odda. 'How do you know Ubba?' he asked.

'I was captured by the Danes,' I said, 'and was raised by them. The Danes taught me to fight.' I touched one of my arm rings. 'Ubba gave me this one.'

'You fought for him?' Odda asked, not accusingly, but with curiosity.

'I fought to survive,' I said evasively.

He looked back to the moon-touched river. 'When it comes to a fight,' he said, 'the Danes are no fools. They will be expecting an attack at dawn.' I said nothing, wondering whether Odda's fears were changing his mind. 'And they outnumber us,' he went on.

I still said nothing. Fear works on a man, and there is no fear like the prospect of confronting a shield wall. I was filled with fear that night, for I had never fought man to man in the clash of armies. I had been at Æsc's Hill, and at the other battles of that far off summer, but I had not fought in the shield wall. Tomorrow, I thought, tomorrow, and like Odda I wanted to see Alfred's army rescue us, but I knew there would be no rescue. 'They outnumber us,' Odda said again, 'and some of my men have nothing but reaping hooks as weapons.'

'A reaping hook can kill,' I said, though it was a stupid thing to say. I would not want to face a Dane if I carried nothing but a reaping hook. 'How many have proper weapons?' I asked.

'Half?' he guessed.

'Then those men are our front ranks,' I said, 'and the rest pick up weapons from the enemy dead.' I had no idea what I was speaking of, but only knew I must sound confident. Fear might work on a man, but confidence fights against fear.

Odda paused again, gazing at the dark ships below. 'Your wife and son are well,' he said after a while.

'Good.'

'My son merely rescued her.'

'And prayed I was dead,' I said.

He shrugged. 'Mildrith lived with us after her father's death and my son became fond of her. He meant no harm and he gave none.' He held a hand out to me and I saw, in the small moonlight, that he offered me a leather purse. 'The rest of the bride price,' he said.

'Keep it, lord,' I said, 'and give it to me after the battle, and if I die, give it to Mildrith.'

An owl went overhead, pale and fast, and I wondered what augury that was. Far off to the east, up the coast, far beyond the Pedredan, a tiny fire flickered and that too was an augury, but I could not read it.

'My men are good men,' Odda said, 'but if they are outflanked?' Fear was still haunting him. 'It would be better,' he went on, 'if Ubba were to attack us.'

'It would be better,' I agreed, 'but Ubba will do nothing unless the runesticks tell him to do it.'

Fate is all. Ubba knew that, which is why he read the signs from the gods, and I knew the owl had been a sign, and it had flown over our heads, across the Danish ships and gone towards that distant fire burning along the Sæfern's shore, and I suddenly remembered King Edmund's four boats coming to the East Anglian beach and the fire-arrows thumping into the beached Danish ships and I realised I could read the auguries after all. 'If your men are outflanked,' I said, 'they will die. But if the Danes are outflanked, they will die. So we must outflank them.'

'How?' Odda asked bitterly. All he could see was slaughter in the dawn; an attack, a fight and a defeat, but I had seen the owl. The owl had flown from the ships to the fire, and that was the sign. Burn the ships. 'How do we outflank them?' Odda asked.

And still I remained silent, wondering if I should tell him. If I followed the augury it would mean splitting our forces, and that was the mistake the Danes had made at Æsc's Hill, and so I hesitated, but Odda had not come to me because he suddenly liked me, but because I had been defiant with Ubba. I alone on Cynuit was confident of victory, or seemed to be, and that, despite my age, made me the leader on this hill. Ealdorman Odda, old enough to be my father, wanted my support. He wanted me to tell him what to do, me who had never been in a great shield wall, but I was young and I was arrogant and the auguries had told me what must be done, and so I told Odda.

'Have you ever seen the sceadugengan?' I asked him.

His response was to make the sign of the cross.

'When I was a child,' I said, 'I dreamed of the sceadugengan. I

307

went out at night to find them and I learned the ways of the night so I could join them.'

'What has that to do with the dawn?' he asked.

'Give me fifty men,' I said, 'and they will join my men and at dawn they will attack there.' I pointed towards the ships. 'We'll start by burning their ships.'

Odda looked down the hill at the nearer fires which marked where the enemy sentries were posted in the meadow to our east. 'They'll know you're coming,' he said, 'and be ready for you.' He meant that a hundred men could not cross Cynuit's skyline, go downhill, break through the sentries and cross the marsh in silence. He was right. Before we had gone ten paces the sentries would have seen us and the alarm would be sounded and Ubba's army, that was surely as ready for battle as our own, would stream from its southern encampment to confront my men in the meadow before they reached the marsh.

'But when the Danes see their ships burning,' I said, 'they will go to the river's bank, not to the meadow. And the riverbank is hemmed by marsh. They can't outflank us there.' They could, of course, but the marsh would give them uncertain footing so it would not be so dangerous as being outflanked in the meadow.

'But you will never reach the riverbank,' he said, disappointed in my idea.

'A Shadow-Walker can reach it,' I said.

He looked at me, said nothing.

'I can reach it,' I said, 'and when the first ship burns every Dane will run to the bank, and that's when the hundred men make their charge. The Danes will be running to save their ships, and that will give the hundred men time to cross the marsh. They go as fast as they can, they join me, we burn more ships, and the Danes will be trying to kill us.' I pointed to the riverbank, showing where the Danes would go from their camp along the strip of firm ground to where the ships were beached, 'and when the Danes are all on that bank,' I went on, 'between the river and the marsh, you lead the fyrd to take them in the rear.'

He brooded, watching the ships. If we attacked at all then the obvious place was down the southern slope, straight into the heart of Ubba's

308

forces, and that would be a battle of shield wall against shield wall, our nine hundred men against his twelve hundred, and at the beginning we would have the advantage for many of Ubba's men were posted around the hill and it would take time for those men to hurry back and join the Danish ranks, and in that time we would drive deep into their camp, but their numbers would grow and we might well be stopped, outflanked and then would come the hard slaughter. And in that hard slaughter they would have the advantage of numbers and they would wrap around our ranks and our rearmost men, those with sickles instead of weapons, would begin to die.

But if I went down the hill and began to burn the boats then the Danes would race down the riverbank to stop me, and that would put them on the narrow strip of riverside land, and if the hundred men under Leofric joined me, then we might hold them long enough for Odda to reach their rear and then it would be the Danes who would die, trapped between Odda, my men, the marsh and the river. They would be trapped like the Northumbrian army had been trapped at Eoferwic.

But at Æsc's Hill disaster had come to the side which first split its forces.

'It could work,' Odda said tentatively.

'Give me fifty men,' I urged him, 'young ones.'

'Young?'

'They have to run down the hill,' I said. 'They have to go fast. They have to reach the ships before the Danes, and they must do it in the dawn.' I spoke with a confidence I did not feel and I paused for his agreement, but he said nothing. 'Win this, lord,' I said, and I did not call him 'lord' because he outranked me, but because he was older than me, 'then you will have saved Wessex. Alfred will reward you.'

He thought for a while and maybe it was the thought of a reward that persuaded him, for he nodded. 'I will give you fifty men,' he said.

Ravn had given me much advice and all of it was good, but now, in the night wind, I remembered just one thing he had said to me on the night we first met, something I had never forgotten.

Never, he had said, never fight Ubba.

* * *

The fifty men were led by the shire reeve, Edor, a man who looked as hard as Leofric and, like Leofric, had fought in the big shield walls. He carried a cut-off boar spear as his favourite weapon, though a sword was strapped to his side. The spear, he said, had the weight and strength to punch through mail and could even break through a shield.

Edor, like Leofric, had simply accepted my idea. It never occurred to me that they might not accept it, yet looking back I am astonished that the battle of Cynuit was fought according to the idea of a twenty-year-old who had never stood in a slaughter wall. Yet I was tall, I was a lord, I had grown up among warriors, and I had the arrogant confidence of a man born to battle. I am Uhtred, son of Uhtred, son of another Uhtred, and we had not held Bebbanburg and its lands by whimpering at altars. We are warriors.

Edor's men and mine assembled behind Cynuit's eastern rampart where they would wait until the first ship burned in the dawn. Leofric was on the right with the *Heahengel*'s crew, and I wanted him there because that was where the blow would fall when Ubba led his men to attack us at the river's edge. Edor and the men of Defnascir were on the left and their chief job, apart from killing whoever they first met on the riverbank, was to snatch up flaming timbers from the Danish fires and hurl them into more ships. 'We're not trying to burn all the ships,' I said, 'just get four or five ablaze. That'll bring the Danes like a swarm of bees.'

'Stinging bees,' a voice said from the dark.

'You're frightened?' I asked scornfully. 'They're frightened! Their auguries are bad, they think they're going to lose and the last thing they want is to face men of Defnascir in a grey dawn. We'll make them scream like women, we'll kill them, and we'll send them to their Danish hell.' That was the extent of my battle speech. I should have talked more, but I was nervous because I had to go down the hill first, first and alone. I had to live my childhood dream of shadow-walking, and Leofric and Edor would not lead the hundred men down to the river until they saw the Danes go to rescue their ships,

310

and if I could not touch fire to the ships then there would be no attack and Odda's fears would come back and the Danes would win and Wessex would die and there would be no more England. 'So rest now,' I finished lamely. 'It will be three or four hours till dawn.'

I went back to the rampart and Father Willibald joined me there, holding out his crucifix that had been carved from an ox's thigh bone. 'You want God's blessing?' he asked me.

'What I want, father,' I said, 'is your cloak.' He had a fine woollen cloak, hooded and dyed a dark brown. He gave it me and I tied the cords around my neck, hiding the sheen of my mail coat. 'And in the dawn, father,' I said, 'I want you to stay up here. The riverbank will be no place for priests.'

'If men die there,' he said, 'then it is my place.'

'You want to go to heaven in the morning?'

'No.'

'Then stay here,' I spoke more savagely than I intended, but that was nervousness, and then it was time to go for, though the night was still dark and the dawn a long way off, I needed time to slink through the Danish lines. Leofric saw me off, walking with me to the northern flank of Cynuit that was in mooncast shadow. It was also the least guarded side of the hill, for the northern slope led to nothing except marshes and the Sæfern sea. I gave Leofric my shield. 'I don't need it,' I said. 'It will just make me clumsy.'

He touched my arm. 'You're a cocky bastard, Earsling, aren't you?'

'Is that a fault?'

'No, lord,' he said, and that last word was high praise. 'God go with you,' he added, 'whichever god it is.'

I touched Thor's hammer, then tucked it under my mail. 'Bring the men fast when you see the Danes go to the ships,' I said.

'We'll come fast,' he promised me, 'if the marsh lets us.'

I had seen Danes cross the marsh in the daylight and had noted that it was soft ground, but not rank bogland. 'You can cross it fast,' I said, then pulled the cloak's hood over my helmet. 'Time to go,' I said.

Leofric said nothing and I dropped down from the rampart into the shallow ditch. So now I would become what I had always

311

wanted to be, a Shadow-Walker. Childhood's dream had become life and death, and touching Serpent-Breath's hilt for luck, I crossed the ditch's lip. I went at a crouch, and halfway down the hill I dropped to my belly and slithered like a serpent, black against the grass, inching my way towards a space between two dying fires.

The Danes were sleeping, or close to sleep. I could see them sitting by the dying fires, and once I was out of the hill's shadow there was enough moonlight to reveal me and there was no cover for the meadow had been cropped by sheep, but I moved like a ghost, a belly-crawling ghost, inching my way, making no noise, a shadow on the grass, and all they had to do was look, or walk between the fires, but they heard nothing, suspected nothing and so saw nothing. It took an age, but I slipped through them, never going closer to an enemy than twenty paces, and once past them I was in the marsh and there the tussocks offered shadow and I could move faster, wriggling through slime and shallow water, and the only scare came when I startled a bird from its nest and it leaped into the air with a cry of alarm and a swift whirr of wings. I sensed the Danes staring towards the marsh, but I was motionless, black and unmoving in the broken shadow, and after a while there was only silence. I waited, water seeping through my mail, and I prayed to Hoder, blind son of Odin and god of the night. Look after me, I prayed, and I wished I had made a sacrifice to Hoder, but I had not, and I thought that Ealdwulf would be looking down at me and I vowed to make him proud. I was doing what he had always wanted me to do, carrying Serpent-Breath against the Danes.

I worked my way eastwards, behind the sentries, going to where the ships were beached. No grey showed in the eastern sky. I still went slowly, staying on my belly, going slowly enough for the fears to work on me. I was aware of a muscle quivering in my right thigh, of a thirst that could not be quenched, of a sourness in the bowels. I kept touching Serpent-Breath's hilt, remembering the charms that Ealdwulf and Brida had worked on the blade. Never, Ravn had said, never fight Ubba.

The east was still dark. I crept on, close to the sea now so I could gaze up the wide Sæfern and see nothing except the shimmer of the sinking moon on the rippled water that looked like a sheet of hammered silver. The tide was flooding, the muddy shore narrowing as the sea rose. There would be salmon in the Pedredan, I thought, salmon swimming with the tide, going back to the sea, and I touched the sword hilt for I was close to the strip of firm land where the hovels stood and the ship-guards waited. My thigh shivered. I felt sick.

But blind Hoder was watching over me. The ship-guards were no more alert than their comrades at the hill's foot, and why should they be? They were further from Odda's forces, and they expected no trouble, indeed they were there only because the Danes never left their ships unguarded, and these ship-guards had mostly gone into the fishermen's hovels to sleep, leaving just a handful of men sitting by the small fires. Those men were motionless, probably half asleep, though one was pacing up and down beneath the high prows of the beached ships.

I stood.

I had shadow-walked, but now I was on Danish ground, behind their sentries, and I undid the cloak's cords, took it off and wiped the mud from my mail and then walked openly towards the ships, my boots squelching in the last yards of marshland, and then I just stood by the northernmost boat, threw my helmet down in the shadow of the ship, and waited for the one Dane who was on his feet to discover me.

And what would he see? A man in mail, a lord, a shipmaster, a Dane, and I leaned on the ship's prow and stared up at the stars. My heart thumped, my thigh quivered, and I thought that if I died this morning at least I would be with Ragnar again. I would be with him in Valhalla's hall of the dead, except some men believed that those who did not die in battle went instead to Niflheim, that dreadful cold hell of the Northmen where the corpse goddess Hel stalks through the mists and the serpent Corpse-Ripper slithers across the frost to gnaw the dead, but surely, I thought, a man who died in a hall-burning would go to Valhalla, not to grey Niflheim? Surely Ragnar was with Odin, and then I heard the Dane's footsteps and I glanced at him with a smile. 'A chill morning,' I said.

'It is.' He was an older man with a grizzled beard and he was plainly puzzled by my sudden appearance, but he was not suspicious.

'All quiet,' I said, jerking my head to the north to suggest I had been visiting the sentries on the Sæfern's side of the hill.

'They're frightened of us,' he said.

'So they should be.' I faked a huge yawn, then pushed myself away from the ship and walked a couple of paces north as though I was stretching tired limbs, then pretended to notice my helmet at the water's edge. 'What's that?'

He took the bait, going into the ship's shadow to bend over the helmet and I drew my knife, stepped close to him and drove the blade up into his throat. I did not slit his throat, but stabbed it, plunged the blade straight in and twisted it and at the same time I pushed him forward, driving his face into the water and I held him there so that if he did not bleed to death he would drown, and it took a long time, longer than I expected, but men are hard to kill. He struggled for a time and I thought the noise he made might bring the men from the nearest fire, but that fire was forty or fifty paces down the beach and the small waves of the river were loud enough to cover the Dane's death throes, and so I killed him and no one knew of it, none but the gods saw it, and when his soul was gone I pulled the knife from his throat, retrieved my helmet, and went back to the ship's prow.

And waited there until dawn lightened the eastern horizon. Waited till there was a rim of grey at the edge of England.

And it was time.

I strolled towards the nearest fire. Two men sat there. 'Kill one,' I sang softly, 'and two then three, kill four and five, and then some more.' It was a Danish rowing chant, one that I had heard so often on the *Wind-Viper*. 'You'll be relieved soon,' I greeted them cheerfully.

They just stared at me. They did not know who I was, but just like the man I had killed, they were not suspicious even though I spoke their tongue with an English twist. There were plenty of English in the Danish armies.

'A quiet night,' I said, and leaned down and took the unburned end of a piece of flaming wood from the fire. 'Egil left a knife on his ship,' I explained, and Egil was a common enough name among the Danes to arouse no suspicion, and they just watched as I walked north, presuming I needed the flame to light my way onto the ships. I passed the hovels, nodded to three men resting beside another fire, and kept walking until I had reached the centre of the line of beached ships and there, whistling softly as though I did not have a care in the world, I climbed the short ladder left leaning on the ship's prow and jumped down into the hull and made my way between the rowers' benches. I had half expected to find men asleep in the ships, but the boat was deserted except for the scrabble of rats' feet in the bilge.

I crouched in the ship's belly where I thrust the burning wood beneath the stacked oars, but I doubted it would be sufficient to set those oars aflame and so I used my knife to shave kindling off a rowers' bench and, when I had enough scraps of wood, I piled them over the flame and saw the fire spring up. I cut more, then hacked at the oar shafts to give the flames purchase, and no one shouted at me from the bank. Anyone watching must have thought I merely searched the bilge and the flames were still not high enough to cause alarm, but they were spreading and I knew I had very little time and so I sheathed the knife and slid over the boat's side. I lowered myself into the Pedredan, careless what the water would do to my mail and weapons, and once in the river I waded northwards from ship's stern to ship's stern, until at last I had cleared the last boat and had come to where the grey-bearded corpse was thumping softly in the river's small waves, and there I waited.

And waited. The fire, I thought, must have gone out. I was cold.

And still I waited. The grey on the world's rim lightened, and then, suddenly, there was an angry shout and I moved out of the shadow and saw the Danes running towards the flames that were bright and high on the ship I had fired, and so I went to their abandoned fire and took another burning brand and hurled that into a second ship, and the Danes were scrambling onto the burning boat that was sixty paces away and none saw me. Then a horn sounded, sounded again and again, sounding the alarm and I knew Ubba's men would be coming from their camp at

Cantucton, and I carried a last piece of fiery wood to the ships, burned my hand as I thrust it under a pile of oars, then I waded back into the river to hide beneath the shadowed belly of a boat.

The horn still sounded. Men were scrambling from the fisher-men's hovels, going to save their fleet, and more men were running from their camp to the south, and so Ubba's Danes fell into our trap. They saw their ships burning and went to save them. They streamed from the camp in disorder, many without weapons, intent only on quenching the flames that flickered up the rigging and threw lurid shadows on the bank. I was hidden, but knew Leofric would be coming, and now it was all timing. Timing and the blessing of the spinners, the blessing of the gods, and the Danes were using their shields to scoop water into the first burning ship, but then another shout sounded and I knew they had seen Leofric, and he had surely burst past the first line of sentries, slaughtering them as he went, and was now in the marsh. I waded out of the shadow, out from beneath the ship's overhanging hull, and saw Leofric's men coming, saw thirty or forty Danes running north to meet his charge, but then those Danes saw the new fires in the northernmost ships and they were assailed by panic because there was fire behind them and warriors in front of them, and most of the other Danes were still a hundred paces away and I knew that so far the gods were fighting for us.

I waded from the water. Leofric's men were coming from the marsh and the first swords and spears clashed, but Leofric had the advantage of numbers and *Heahengel*'s crew overran the handful of Danes, chopping them with axe and sword, and one crewman turned fast, panic in his face when he saw me coming, and I shouted my name, stooped to pick up a Danish shield, and Edor's men were behind us and I called to them to feed the ship-fires while the men of *Heahengel* formed a shield wall across the strip of firm land. Then we walked forward. Walked towards Ubba's army that was only just realising that they were being attacked.

We marched forward. A woman scrambled from a hovel, screamed when she saw us and fled up the bank towards the Danes where a man was roaring at men to form a shield wall. 'Edor!' I shouted, knowing we would need his men now, and he

316

brought them to thicken our line so that we made a solid shield wall across the strip of firm land, and we were a hundred strong and in front of us was the whole Danish army, though it was an army in panicked disorder, and I glanced up at Cynuit and saw no sign of Odda's men. They would come, I thought, they would surely come, and then Leofric bellowed that we were to touch shields, and the limewood rattled on limewood and I sheathed Serpent-Breath and drew Wasp-Sting.

Shield wall. It is an awful place, my father had said, and he had fought in seven shield walls and was killed in the last one. Never fight Ubba, Ravn had said.

Behind us the northernmost ships burned and in front of us a rush of maddened Danes came for revenge and that was their undoing, for they did not form a proper shield wall, but came at us like mad dogs, intent only on killing us, sure they could beat us for they were Danes and we were West Saxons, and we braced and I watched a scar-faced man, spittle flying from his mouth as he screamed, charge at me and it was then that the battle-calm came. Suddenly there was no more sourness in my bowels, no dry mouth, no shaking muscles, but only the magical battle-calm. I was happy.

I was tired too. I had not slept. I was soaking wet. I was cold, yet suddenly I felt invincible. It is a wondrous thing, that battle-calm. The nerves go, the fear wings off into the void, and all is clear as precious crystal and the enemy has no chance because he is so slow, and I swept the shield left, taking the scar-faced man's spear thrust, lunged Wasp-Sting forward and the Dane ran onto her point. I felt the impact run up my arm as her tip punctured his belly muscles, and I was already twisting her, ripping her up and free, sawing through leather, skin, muscle and guts, and his blood was warm on my cold hand, and he screamed, ale breath in my face, and I punched him down with the shield's heavy boss, stamped on his groin, killed him with Wasp-Sting's tip in his throat, and a second man was on my right, beating at my neighbour's shield with an axe, and he was easy to kill, point into the throat, and then we were going forward. A woman, hair unbound, came at me with a spear and I kicked her brutally hard, then smashed her face with the shield's iron rim so that she fell screaming

317

into a dying fire and her unbound hair flared up bright as burning kindling, and *Heahengel*'s crew was with me, and Leofric was bellowing at them to kill and to kill fast. This was our chance to slaughter Danes who had made a foolish attack on us, who had not formed a proper shield wall, and it was axe work and sword work, butchers' work with good iron, and already there were thirty or more Danish dead and seven ships were burning, their flames spreading with astonishing speed.

'Shield wall!' I heard the cry from the Danes. The world was light now, the sun just beneath the horizon. The northernmost ships had become a furnace. A dragon's head reared in the smoke, its gold eyes bright. Gulls screamed above the beach. A dog chased along the ships, yelping. A mast fell, spewing sparks high into the silver air, and then I saw the Danes make their shield wall, saw them organise themselves for our deaths and saw the raven banner, the triangle of cloth which proclaimed that Ubba was here and coming to give us slaughter.

'Shield wall!' I shouted, and that was the first time I ever gave that order. 'Shield wall!' We had grown ragged, but now it was time to be tight. To be shield to shield. There were hundreds of Danes in front of us and they came to overwhelm us, and I banged Wasp-Sting against the metal rim of my shield. 'They're coming to die!' I shouted, 'they're coming to bleed! They're coming to our blades!'

My men cheered. We had started a hundred strong, but had lost half a dozen men in the early fighting, but the remaining men cheered even though five or six times their number came to kill them, and Leofric began the battle chant of Hegga, an English rowers' chant, rhythmic and harsh, telling of a battle fought by our ancestors against the men who had held Britain before we came, and now we fought for our land again, and behind me a lone voice uttered a prayer and I turned to see Father Willibald holding a spear. I laughed at his disobedience.

Laughter in battle. That was what Ragnar had taught me, to take joy from the fight. Joy in the morning, for the sun was touching the east now, filling the sky with light, driving darkness beyond the world's western rim and I hammered Wasp-Sting against my shield, making a noise to drown the shouts of the Danes, and I knew we would be hard hit and that we must hold until Odda came, but I was relying on Leofric to be the bastion on our right flank where the Danes were sure to try and lap around us by going through the marsh. Our left was safe, for that was by the ships, and the right was where we would be broken if we could not hold.

'Shields!' I bellowed, and we touched shields again for the Danes were coming and I knew they would not hesitate in their attack. We were too few to frighten them, they would not need to work up courage for this battle, they would just come.

And come they did. A thick line of men, shield to shield, new morning light touching axe heads and spear heads and swords.

The spears and throwing axes came first, but in the front rank we crouched behind shields and the second rank held their shields above ours and the missiles thumped home, banging hard, but doing no injury, and then I heard the wild war shout of the Danes, felt a last flutter of fear and then they were there.

The thunder of shield hitting shield, my shield knocked back against my chest, shouts of rage, a spear between my ankles, Wasp-Sting lunging forward and blocked by a shield, a scream to my left, an axe flailing overhead. I ducked, lunged again, hit shield again, pushed back with my own shield, twisted the sax free, stamped on the spear, stabbed Wasp-Sting over my shield into a bearded face and he twisted away, blood filling his mouth from his torn cheek and I took a half-pace forward, stabbed again, and a sword glanced off my helmet and thumped my shoulder and a man pulled me hard backwards because I was ahead of our line and the Danes were shouting, pushing, stabbing, and the first shield wall to break would be the shield wall to die and I knew Leofric was hard pressed on the right, but I had no time to look or help because the man with the torn cheek was thrashing at my shield with a short axe, trying to splinter it. I lowered the shield suddenly, spoiling his stroke, and slashed Wasp-Sting at his face a second time and she grated on skull-bone, drew blood and I hammered his shield with my own and he staggered back, was pushed forward by the men behind him and this time Wasp-Sting took his throat and he was bubbling blood and air from a slit gullet. He fell to his knees, and the man behind him slammed a spear forward that broke through

319

my shield, but stuck there, and the Danes were still heaving, but their own dying man obstructed them and the spearman tripped on him, and the man to my right chopped his shield edge onto his head and I kicked him in the face then slashed Wasp-Sting down. A Dane pulled the spear from my shield, stabbed with it, was cut down by the man on my left. More Danes came and we were stepping back, bending back because there were Danes in the marshland who were turning our right flank, but Leofric brought the men steadily around till our backs were to the burning ships, and I could feel the heat of their burning and I thought we must die here. We would die with swords in our hands and flames at our backs and I hacked frantically at a red-bearded Dane, trying to shatter his shield, and Ida, the man to my right, was on the ground, guts spilling through torn leather, and a Dane came at me from that side and I flicked Wasp-Sting at his face, ducked, took his axe blow on my breaking shield, shouted at the men behind to fill the gap, and stabbed Wasp-Sting at the axeman's feet, slicing into an ankle, and a spear took him in the side of the head and I gave a great shout and heaved at the oncoming Danes, but there was no space to fight, no space to see, just a grunting mass of men hacking and stabbing and dying and bleeding, and then Odda came.

The Ealdorman had waited till the Danes were crowded on the riverbank, waited till they were pushing each other in their eagerness to reach and to kill us, and then he launched his men across Cynuit's brow and they came like thunder with swords and axes and sickles and spears. The Danes saw them and there were shouts of warning and almost immediately I felt the pressure lessen to my front as the rearward Danes turned to meet the new threat, and I rammed Wasp-Sting out to pierce a man's shoulder, and she went deep in, grating against bone, but the man twisted away, snatching the blade out of my hand so I drew Serpent-Breath and shouted at my men to kill the bastards. This was our day, I shouted, and Odin was giving us victory.

Forward now. Forward to battle-slaughter. Beware the man who loves battle. Ravn had told me that only one man in three or perhaps one man in four is a real warrior and the rest are reluctant fighters, but I was to learn that only one man in twenty is a lover of battle. Such men were the most dangerous, the most skilful, the ones who reaped the souls and the ones to fear. I was such a one, and that day, beside the river where the blood flowed into the rising tide, and beside the burning boats, I let Serpent-Breath sing her song of death. I remember little except a rage, an exultation, a massacre. This was the moment the skalds celebrate, the heart of the battle that leads to victory, and the courage had gone from those Danes in a heartbeat. They had thought they were winning, thought they had trapped us by the burning ships and thought to send our miserable souls to the afterworld, and instead the fyrd of Defnascir came on them like a storm.

'Forward!' I shouted.

'Wessex!' Leofric bellowed, 'Wessex!' He was hacking with his axe, chopping men to the ground, leading the *Heahengel*'s crew away from the fiery ships.

The Danes were going backwards, trying to escape us, and we could choose our victims and Serpent-Breath was lethal that day. Hammer a shield forward, strike a man off balance, thrust the blade forward, push him down, stab into the throat, find the next man. I pushed a Dane into the smouldering remnants of a campfire, killed him while he screamed, and some Danes were now fleeing to their unburned ships, pushing them into the flooding tide, but Ubba was still fighting. Ubba was shouting at his men to form a new shield wall, to protect the boats, and such was Ubba's hard will, such his searing anger, that the new shield wall held. We hit it hard, hammered it with sword and axe and spear, but again there was no space, just the heaving, grunting, breath-stinking struggle, only this time it was the Danes who stepped back, pace by pace, as Odda's men joined mine to wrap around the Danes and hammer them with iron.

But Ubba was holding. Holding his rearguard firm, holding them under the raven banner, and in every moment that he held us off another ship was pushed away from the river's bank. All he wanted to achieve now was to save men and ships, to let a part of his army escape, to let them get away from this press of shield and blade, and six Danish ships were already rowing out to the Sæfern sea, and more were filling with men and I screamed

321

at my troops to break through, to kill them, but there was no space to kill, only blood-slicked ground and blades stabbing under shields, and men heaving at the opposing wall, and the wounded crawling away from the back of our line.

And then, with a roar of fury, Ubba hacked into our line with his great war axe. I remembered how he had done that in the fight beside the Gewæsc, how he had seemed to disappear into the ranks of the enemy only to kill them, and his huge blade was whirling again, making space, and our line went back and the Danes followed Ubba who seemed determined to win this battle on his own and to make a name that would never be forgotten among the annals of the Northmen. The battle-madness was on him, the runesticks were forgotten, and Ubba Lothbrokson was making his legend and another man went down, crushed by the axe, and Ubba bellowed defiance, the Danes stepped forward behind him, and now Ubba threatened to pierce our line clean through, and I shoved backwards, going through my men and went to where Ubba fought and there I shouted his name, called him the son of a goat, a turd of men, and he turned, eyes wild, and saw me.

'You bastard whelp,' he snarled, and the men in front of me ducked aside as he came forward, mail coat drenched in blood, a part of his shield missing, his helmet dented and his axe blade red.

'Yesterday,' I said, 'I saw a raven fall.'

'You bastard liar,' he said and the axe came around and I caught it on the shield and it was like being struck by a charging bull. He wrenched the axe free and a great sliver of wood was torn away to let the new daylight through the broken shield.

'A raven,' I said, 'fell from a clear sky.'

'You whore's pup,' he said and the axe came again, and again the shield took it and I staggered back, the rent in the shield widening.

'It called your name as it fell,' I said.

'English filth,' he shouted and swung a third time, but this time I stepped back and flicked Serpent-Breath out in an attempt to cut off his axe hand, but he was fast, snake fast, and he pulled back just in time.

'Ravn told me I would kill you,' I said. 'He foretold it. In a dream by Odin's pit, among the blood, he saw the raven banner fall.'

'Liar!' he screamed and came at me, trying to throw me down with weight and brute force, and I met him, shield boss to shield boss, and I held him, swinging Serpent-Breath at his head, but the blow glanced off his helmet and I leaped back a heartbeat before the axe swung where my legs had been, lunged forward, took him clean on the chest with Serpent-Breath's point, but I did not have any force in the blow and his mail took the lunge and stopped it, and he swung the axe up, trying to gut me from crotch to chest, but my ragged shield stopped his blow, and we both stepped back.

'Three brothers,' I said, 'and you alone of them live. Give my regards to Ivar and to Halfdan. Say that Uhtred Ragnarson sent you to join them.'

'Bastard,' he said, and he stepped forward, swinging the axe in a massive sideways blow that was intended to crush my chest, but the battle-calm had come on me, and the fear had flown and the joy was there and I rammed the shield sideways to take his axe strike, felt the heavy blade plunge into what was left of the wood and I let go of the shield's handle so that the half-broken tangle of metal and wood dangled from his blade, and then I struck at him. Once, twice, both of them huge blows using both hands on Serpent-Breath's hilt and using all the strength I had taken from the long days at *Heahengel*'s oar, and I drove him back, cracked his shield, and he lifted his axe, my shield still cumbering it, and then slipped. He had stepped on the spilt guts of a corpse, and his left foot slid sideways and, while he was unbalanced, I stabbed Serpent-Breath forward and the blade pierced the mail above the hollow of his elbow and his axe arm dropped, all strength stolen from it. Serpent-Breath flicked back to slash across his mouth, and I was shouting, and there was blood in his beard and he knew then, knew he would die, knew he would see his brothers in the corpse-hall. He did not give up. He saw death coming and fought it by trying to hammer me with his shield again, but I was too quick, too exultant, and the next stroke was in his neck and he staggered, blood pouring onto his shoulder, more blood trickling between the links of his chain mail, and he looked at me as he tried to stay upright.

'Wait for me in Valhalla, lord,' I said.

He dropped to his knees, still staring at me. He tried to speak, but nothing came and I gave him the killing stroke.

'Now finish them!' Ealdorman Odda shouted, and the men who had been watching the duel screamed in triumph and rushed at the enemy and there was panic now as the Danes tried to reach their boats, and some were throwing down weapons and the cleverest were lying flat, pretending to be dead, and men with sickles were killing men with swords. The women from Cynuit's summit were in the Danish camp now, killing and plundering.

I knelt by Ubba and closed his nerveless right fist about the handle of his war axe. 'Go to Valhalla, lord,' I said. He was not dead yet, but he was dying for my last stroke had pierced deep into his neck, and then he gave a great shudder and there was a croaking noise in his throat and I kept on holding his hand tight to the axe as he died.

A dozen more boats escaped, all crowded with Danes, but the rest of Ubba's fleet was ours, and while a handful of the enemy fled into the woods where they were hunted down, the remaining Danes were either dead or prisoners, and the raven banner fell into Odda's hands, and we had the victory that day, and Willibald, spear point reddened, was dancing with delight.

We took horses, gold, silver, prisoners, women, ships, weapons and mail. I had fought in the shield wall.

Ealdorman Odda had been wounded, struck on the head by an axe that had pierced his helmet and driven into his skull. He lived, but his eyes were white, his skin pale, his breath shallow and his head matted with blood. Priests prayed over him in one of the small village houses and I saw him there, but he could not see me, could not speak, perhaps could not hear, but I shoved two of the priests aside, knelt by his bed and thanked him for taking the fight to the Danes. His son, unwounded, his armour apparently unscratched in the battle, watched me from the darkness of the room's far corner.

I straightened from his father's low bed. My back ached and my arms were burning with weariness. 'I am going to Cridianton,' I told young Odda.

He shrugged as if he did not care where I went. I ducked under the low door where Leofric waited for me. 'Don't go to Cridianton,' he told me.

'My wife is there,' I said. 'My child is there.'

'Alfred is at Exanceaster,' he said.

'So?'

'So the man who takes news of this battle to Exanceaster gets the credit for it,' he said.

'Then you go,' I said.

The Danish prisoners wanted to bury Ubba, but Odda the Younger had ordered the body to be dismembered and its pieces given to the beasts and birds. That had not been done yet, though the great battle-axe that I had put in Ubba's dying hand was gone, and I regretted that, for I had wanted it, but I wanted Ubba treated decently as well and so I let the prisoners dig their grave. Odda the Younger did not confront me, but let the Danes bury their leader and make a mound over his corpse and thus send Ubba to his brothers in the corpse-hall.

And when it was done I rode south with a score of my men, all of us mounted on horses we had taken from the Danes.

I went to my family.

These days, so long after that battle at Cynuit, I employ a harpist. He is an old Welshman, blind, but very skilful, and he often sings tales of his ancestors. He likes to sing of Arthur and Guinevere, of how Arthur slaughtered the English, but he takes care not to let me hear those songs, instead praising me and my battles with outrageous flattery by singing the words of my poets who describe me as Uhtred Strong-Sword or Uhtred Death-Giver or Uhtred the Beneficent. I sometimes see the old blind man smiling to himself as his hands pluck the strings and I have more sympathy with his scepticism than I do with the poets who are a pack of snivelling sycophants.

But in the year 877 I employed no poets and had no harpist. I was a young man who had come dazed and dazzled from the shield wall, and who stank of blood as I rode south and yet, for some reason, as we threaded the hills and woods of Defnascir, I thought of a harp.

Every lord has a harp in the hall. As a child, before I went to Ragnar, I would sometimes sit by the harp in Bebbanburg's hall and I was intrigued by how the strings would play themselves. Pluck one string and the others would shiver to give off a tiny music. 'Wasting your time, boy?' my father had snarled as I crouched by the harp one day, and I suppose I had been wasting it, but on that spring day in 877 I remembered my childhood's harp and how its strings would quiver if just one was touched. It was not music, of course, just noise, and scarcely audible noise at that, but after the battle in Pedredan's valley it seemed to me that my life was made of strings and if I touched one then the others, though separate, would make their sound. I thought of Ragnar the Younger and wondered if he lived, and whether his father's killer, Kjartan, still lived, and how he would die if he did, and thinking of Ragnar made me remember Brida, and her memory slid on to an image of Mildrith, and that brought to mind Alfred and his bitter wife Ælswith, and all those separate people were a part of my life, strings strung on the frame of Uhtred, and though they were separate they affected each other and together they would make the music of my life.

Daft thoughts, I told myself. Life is just life. We live, we die, we go to the corpse-hall. There is no music, just chance. Fate is relentless.

'What are you thinking?' Leofric asked me. We were riding through a valley that was pink with flowers.

'I thought you were going to Exanceaster?' I said.

'I am, but I'm going to Cridianton first, then taking you on to Exanceaster. So what are you thinking? You look gloomy as a priest.'

'I'm thinking about a harp.'

'A harp!' He laughed. 'Your head's full of rubbish.'

'Touch a harp,' I said, 'and it just makes noise, but play it and it makes music.'

'Sweet Christ!' He looked at me with a worried expression. 'You're as bad as Alfred. You think too much.'

He was right. Alfred was obsessed by order, obsessed by the task of marshalling life's chaos into something that could be controlled. He would do it by the church and by the law, which are much the same thing, but I wanted to see a pattern in the strands of life. In the end I found one, and it had nothing to do with any god, but with people. With the people we love. My harpist is right to smile when he chants that I am Uhtred the Gift-Giver or Uhtred the Avenger or Uhtred the Widow-Maker, for he is old and he has learned what I have learned, that I am really Uhtred the Lonely. We are all lonely and all seek a hand to hold in the darkness. It is not the harp, but the hand that plays it.

'It will give you a headache,' Leofric said, 'thinking too much.'

'Earsling,' I said to him.

Mildrith was well. She was safe. She had not been raped. She wept when she saw me, and I took her in my arms and wondered that I was so fond of her, and she said she had thought I was dead and told me she had prayed to her god to spare me, and she took me to the room where our son was in his swaddling clothes and, for the first time, I looked at Uhtred, son of Uhtred, and I prayed that one day he would be the lawful and sole owner of lands that are carefully marked by stones and by dykes, by oaks and by ash, by marsh and by sea. I am still the owner of those lands that were purchased with our family's blood, and I will take those lands back from the man who stole them from me and I will give them to my sons. For I am Uhtred, Earl Uhtred, Uhtred of Bebbanburg, and destiny is everything.

Historical Note

Alfred, famously, is the only monarch in English history to be accorded the honour of being called 'the Great' and this novel, with the ones that follow, will try to show why he gained that title. I do not want to anticipate those other novels, but broadly, Alfred was responsible for saving Wessex and, ultimately, English society from the Danish assaults, and his son Edward, daughter Æthelflaed and grandson Æthelstan finished what he began to create which was, for the first time, a political entity they called 'Englaland'. I intend Uhtred to be involved in the whole story.

But the tale begins with Alfred who was, indeed, a very pious man and frequently sick. A recent theory suggests that he suffered from Crohn's Disease, which causes acute abdominal pains, and from chronic piles, details we can glean from a book written by a man who knew him very well, Bishop Asser, who came into Alfred's life after the events described in this novel. Currently there is a debate whether Bishop Asser did write that life, or whether it was forged a hundred years after Alfred's death, and I am utterly unqualified to judge the arguments of the contending academics, but even if it is a forgery it contains much that has the smack of truth, suggesting that whoever wrote it knew a great deal about Alfred. The author, to be sure, wanted to present Alfred in a glowing light, as warrior, scholar and Christian, but he does not shy away from his hero's youthful sins. Alfred, he tells us, 'was unable to abstain from carnal desire' until God generously made him sick enough to resist temptation. Whether Alfred did have an illegitimate son, Osferth, is debatable, but it seems very possible.

The biggest challenge Alfred faced was an invasion of England by the Danes. Some readers may be disappointed that those Danes are called Northmen or pagans in the novel, but are rarely described as Vikings. In this I follow the early English writers who suffered from the Danes, and who rarely used the word Viking which, anyway, describes an activity rather than a people or a tribe. To go viking meant to go raiding, and the Danes who fought against England in the ninth century, though undoubtedly raiders, were pre-eminently invaders and occupiers. Much fanciful imagery has been attached to them, chief of which are the horned helmet, the berserker and the ghastly execution called the spread-eagle, by which a victim's ribs were splayed apart to expose the lungs and heart. That seems to have been a later invention, as does the existence of the berserker, the crazed naked warrior who attacked in a mad frenzy. Doubtless there were insanely frenzied warriors, but there is no evidence that lunatic nudists made regular appearances on the battlefield. The same is true of the horned helmet for which there is not a scrap of contemporary evidence. Viking warriors were much too sensible to place a pair of protuberances on their helmets so ideally positioned as to enable an enemy to knock the helmet off. It is a pity to abandon the iconic horned helmets, but alas, they did not exist.

The assault on the church by the Danes is well recorded. The invaders were not Christians and saw no reason to spare churches, monasteries and nunneries from their attacks, especially as those places often contained considerable treasures. Whether the concerted attack on the northern monastic houses happened is debatable. The source is extremely late, a thirteenth-century chronicle written by Roger of Wendover, but what is certain is that many bishoprics and monasteries did disappear during the Danish assault, and that assault was not a great raid, but a deliberate attempt to eradicate English society and replace it with a Danish state.

Ivar the Boneless, Ubba, Halfdan, Guthrum, the various kings, Alfred's nephew Æthelwold, Ealdorman Odda and the Ealdormen whose names begin with Æ (a vanished letter, called the ash), all existed. Alfred should properly be spelt Ælfred, but I preferred the usage by which he is known today. It is not certain how King Edmund of East Anglia died, though he was certainly killed by the Danes and in one ancient version the future saint was indeed riddled with arrows like Saint Sebastian. Ragnar and Uhtred are fictional, though a family with Uhtred's name did hold Bebbanburg (now Bamburgh Castle) later in the Anglo-Saxon period, and as that family are my ancestors I decided to give them that magical place a little earlier than the records suggest. Most of the major events happened; the assault on York, the siege of Nottingham, the attacks on the four kingdoms, all are recorded in the Anglo-Saxon Chronicle or in Asser's life of King Alfred which together are the major sources for the period.

I used both those sources and also consulted a host of secondary works. Alfred's life is remarkably well documented for the period, some of that documentation written by Alfred himself, but even so, as Professor James Campbell wrote in an essay on the king, 'arrows of insight have to be winged by the feathers of specula- tion'. I have feathered lavishly, as historical novelists must, yet as much of the novel as possible is based on real events. Guthrum's occupation of Wareham, the exchange of hostages and his breaking of the truce, his murder of the hostages and occupation of Exeter all happened, as did the loss of most of his fleet in a great storm off Durlston Head near Swanage. The one large change I have made was to bring Ubba's death forward by a year, so that, in the next book, Uhtred can be elsewhere, and, persuaded by the argu- ments in John Peddie's book, *Alfred, Warrior King*, I placed that action at Cannington in Somerset rather than at the more tradi- tional site of Countisbury Head in north Devon.

Alfred was the king who preserved the idea of England, which his son, daughter and grandson made explicit. At a time of great danger, when the English kingdoms were perilously near to extinc- tion, he provided a bulwark which allowed the Anglo-Saxon culture to survive. His achievements were greater than that, but his story is far from over, so Uhtred will campaign again.

The STARBUCK Chronicles
Rebel
Copperhead
Battle Flag
The Bloody Ground

The WARLORD Chronicles
The Winter King
The Enemy of God
Excalibur

By Bernard Cornwell and Susannah Kells

A Crowning Mercy
Fallen Angels

Non-Fiction

Waterloo: The History of Four Days, Three Armies
and Three Battles

THE SHARPE SERIES
(IN CHRONOLOGICAL ORDER)

THE PALE
HORSEMAN

BERNARD CORNWELL

HARPER

Harper

An imprint of HarperCollins*Publishers*
1 London Bridge Street
London SE1 9GF

www.harpercollins.co.uk

This paperback edition 2015
2

First published in Great Britain by
HarperCollins*Publishers* 2005

A catalogue record for this book is
available from the British Library

ISBN: 978-0-00-813948-3

This novel is entirely a work of fiction.
The names, characters and incidents portrayed in it,
while at times based on historical figures, are
the work of the author's imagination.

Set in Meridien by Palimpsest Book Production Limited,
Falkirk, Stirlingshire
Printed and bound in the U.S.A. by
RR Donnelley

THE PALE HORSEMAN
is for
George MacDonald Fraser,
in admiration

Ac her forþ berað; fugelas singað,
gylleð grǽghama.

For here starts war, carrion birds sing,
and grey wolves howl.

From The Fight at Finnsburh

CONTENTS

PLACE NAMES

The spelling of place names in Anglo-Saxon England was an uncertain business, with no consistency and no agreement even about the name itself. Thus London was variously rendered as Lundonia, Lundenberg, Lundenne, Lundene, Lundenwic, Lundenceaster and Lundres. Doubtless some readers will prefer other versions of the names listed below, but I have usually employed whichever spelling is cited in the *Oxford Dictionary of English Place-Names* for the years nearest or contained within Alfred's reign, 871–899 AD, but even that solution is not foolproof. Hayling Island, in 956, was written as both Heilincigae and Hæglingaiggæ. Nor have I been consistent myself; I use England instead of Englaland, and have preferred the modern form Northumbria to Norðhymbralond to avoid the suggestion that the boundaries of the ancient kingdom coincide with those of the modern county. So this list, like the spellings themselves, is capricious.

Æsc's Hill	Ashdown, Berkshire
Æthelingæg	Athelney, Somerset
Afen	River Avon, Wiltshire
Andefera	Andover, Wiltshire
Baðum (pronounced Bathum)	Bath, Avon
Bebbanburg	Bamburgh Castle, Northumberland
Brant	Brent Knoll, Somerset

Bru	River Brue, Somerset
Cippanhamm	Chippenham, Wiltshire
Contwaraburg	Canterbury, Kent
Cornwalum	Cornwall
Cracgelad	Cricklade, Wiltshire
Cridianton	Crediton, Devon
Cynuit	Cynuit Hillfort, nr. Cannington, Somerset
Dærentmora	Dartmoor, Devon
Defereal	Kingston Deverill, Wiltshire
Defnascir	Devonshire
Dornwaraceaster	Dorchester, Dorset
Dreyndynas	'Fort of thorns', fictional, set in Cornwall
Dunholm	Durham, County Durham
Dyfed	South-west Wales, mostly now Pembrokeshire
Dyflin	Dublin, Eire
Eoferwic	York (also the Danish Jorvic, pronounced Yorvik)
Ethandun	Edington, Wiltshire
Exanceaster	Exeter, Devon
Exanmynster	Exminster, Devon
Gewæsc	The Wash
Gifle	Yeovil, Somerset
Gleawecestre	Gloucester, Gloucestershire
Glwysing	Welsh kingdom, approximately Glamorgan and Gwent
Hamptonscir	Hampshire
Hamtun	Southampton, Hampshire

Lindisfarena	Lindisfarne (Holy Island), Northumberland
Lundene	London
Lundi	Lundy Island, Devon
Mærlebeorg	Marlborough, Wiltshire
Ocmundtun	Okehampton, Devon
Palfleot	Pawlett, Somerset
Pedredan	River Parrett
Penwith	Land's End, Cornwall
Readingum	Reading, Berkshire
Sæfern	River Severn
Sceapig	Isle of Sheppey, Kent
Scireburnan	Sherborne, Dorset
Sillans	The Scilly Isles
Soppan Byrg	Chipping Sodbury, Gloucestershire
Sumorsæte	Somerset
Suth Seaxa	Sussex (South Saxons)
Tamur	River Tamar
Temes	River Thames
Thon	River Tone, Somerset
Thornsæta	Dorset
Uisc	River Exe
Werham	Wareham, Dorset
Wilig	River Wylye
Wiltunscir	Wiltshire
Winburnan	Wimborne Minster, Dorset
Wintanceaster	Winchester, Hampshire

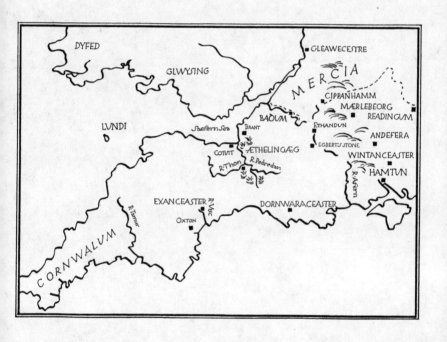

PART ONE

Viking

One

These days I look at twenty-year-olds and think they are pathetically young, scarcely weaned from their mothers' tits, but when I was twenty I considered myself a full-grown man. I had fathered a child, fought in the shield wall, and was loath to take advice from anyone. In short I was arrogant, stupid and headstrong. Which is why, after our victory at Cynuit, I did the wrong thing.

We had fought the Danes beside the ocean, where the river runs from the great swamp and the Sæfern Sea slaps on a muddy shore, and there we had beaten them. We had made a great slaughter and I, Uhtred of Bebbanburg, had done my part. More than my part, for at the battle's end, when the great Ubba Lothbrokson, most feared of all the Danish leaders, had carved into our shield wall with his great war axe, I had faced him, beaten him and sent him to join the *einherjar*, that army of the dead who feast and swive in Odin's corpse-hall.

What I should have done then, what Leofric told me to do, was ride hard to Exanceaster where Alfred, King of the West Saxons, was besieging Guthrum. I should have arrived deep in the night, woken the king from his sleep and laid Ubba's battle banner of the black raven and Ubba's great war axe, its blade still crusted with blood, at Alfred's feet.

3

I should have given the king the good news that the Danish army was beaten, that the few survivors had taken to their dragon-headed ships, that Wessex was safe and that I, Uhtred of Bebbanburg, had achieved all of those things.

Instead I rode to find my wife and child.

At twenty years old I would rather have been ploughing Mildrith than reaping the reward of my good fortune, and that is what I did wrong, but, looking back, I have few regrets. Fate is inexorable, and Mildrith, though I had not wanted to marry her and though I came to detest her, was a lovely field to plough.

So, in that late spring of the year 877, I spent the Saturday riding to Cridianton instead of going to Alfred. I took twenty men with me and I promised Leofric that we would be at Exanceaster by midday on Sunday and I would make certain Alfred knew we had won his battle and saved his kingdom.

'Odda the Younger will be there by now,' Leofric warned me. Leofric was almost twice my age, a warrior hardened by years of fighting the Danes. 'Did you hear me?' he asked when I said nothing. 'Odda the Younger will be there by now,' he said again, 'and he's a piece of goose shit who'll take all the credit.'

'The truth cannot be hidden,' I said loftily.

Leofric mocked that. He was a bearded squat brute of a man who should have been the commander of Alfred's fleet, but he was not well-born and Alfred had reluctantly given me charge of the twelve ships because I was an ealdorman, a noble, and it was only fitting that a high-born man should command the West Saxon fleet even though it had been much too puny to confront the massive array of Danish ships that had come to Wessex's south coast. 'There are times,' Leofric grumbled, 'when you are an earsling.' An earsling was something that had dropped out of a creature's backside and was one of Leofric's favourite insults. We were friends.

'We'll see Alfred tomorrow,' I said.

'And Odda the Younger,' Leofric said patiently, 'has seen him today.'

Odda the Younger was the son of Odda the Elder who had given my wife shelter, and the son did not like me. He did not like me because he wanted to plough Mildrith, which was reason enough for him to dislike me. He was also, as Leofric said, a piece of goose shit, slippery and slick, which was reason enough for me to dislike him.

'We shall see Alfred tomorrow,' I said again, and next morning we all rode to Exanceaster, my men escorting Mildrith, our son and his nurse, and we found Alfred on the northern side of Exanceaster where his green and white dragon banner flew above his tents. Other banners snapped in the damp wind, a colourful array of beasts, crosses, saints and weapons announcing that the great men of Wessex were with their king. One of those banners showed a black stag, which confirmed that Leofric had been right and that Odda the Younger was here in south Defnascir. Outside the camp, between its southern margin and the city walls, was a great pavilion made of sail-cloth stretched across guyed poles, and that told me that Alfred, instead of fighting Guthrum, was talking to him. They were negotiating a truce, though not on that day, for it was a Sunday and Alfred would do no work on a Sunday if he could help it. I found him on his knees in a makeshift church made from another poled sail-cloth, and all his nobles and thegns were arrayed behind him, and some of those men turned as they heard our horses' hooves. Odda the Younger was one of those who turned and I saw the apprehension show on his narrow face.

The bishop who was conducting the service paused to let the congregation make a response, and that gave Odda an excuse to look away from me. He was kneeling close to Alfred, very close, suggesting that he was high in the king's

5

favour, and I did not doubt that he had brought the dead Ubba's raven banner and war axe to Exanceaster and claimed the credit for the fight beside the sea. 'One day,' I said to Leofric, 'I shall slit that bastard from the crotch to the gullet and dance on his offal.'

'You should have done it yesterday.'

A priest had been kneeling close to the altar, one of the many priests who always accompanied Alfred, and he saw me and slid backwards as unobtrusively as he could until he was able to stand and hurry towards me. He had red hair, a squint, a palsied left hand and an expression of astonished joy on his ugly face. 'Uhtred!' he called as he ran towards our horses, 'Uhtred! We thought you were dead!'

'Me?' I grinned at the priest. 'Dead?'

'You were a hostage!'

I had been one of the dozen English hostages in Werham, but while the others had been murdered by Guthrum, I had been spared because of Earl Ragnar who was a Danish warchief and as close to me as a brother. 'I didn't die, father,' I said to the priest, whose name was Beocca, 'and I'm surprised you did not know that.'

'How could I know it?'

'Because I was at Cynuit, father, and Odda the Younger could have told you that I was there and that I lived.'

I was staring at Odda as I spoke and Beocca caught the grimness in my voice. 'You were at Cynuit?' he asked nervously.

'Odda the Younger didn't tell you?'

'He said nothing.'

'Nothing!' I kicked my horse forward, forcing it between the kneeling men and thus closer to Odda. Beocca tried to stop me, but I pushed his hand away from my bridle. Leofric, wiser than me, held back, but I pushed the horse into the back rows of the congregation until the press of worshippers made it impossible to advance further, and then I stared at Odda as I spoke to Beocca. 'He didn't describe Ubba's death?' I asked.

'He says Ubba died in the shield wall,' Beocca said, his voice a hiss so that he did not disturb the liturgy, 'and that many men contributed to his death.'

'Is that all he told you?'

'He says he faced Ubba himself,' Beocca said.

'So who do men think killed Ubba Lothbrokson?' I asked.

Beocca could sense trouble coming and he tried to calm me. 'We can talk of these things later,' he said, 'but for now, Uhtred, join us in prayer.' He used my name rather than calling me lord because he had known me since I was a child. Beocca, like me, was a Northumbrian, and he had been my father's priest, but when the Danes took our country he had come to Wessex to join those Saxons who still resisted the invaders. 'This is a time for prayer,' he insisted, 'not for quarrels.'

But I was in a mood for quarrels. 'Who do men say killed Ubba Lothbrokson?' I asked again.

'They give thanks to God that the pagan is dead,' Beocca evaded my question, and tried to hush my voice with frantic gestures from his palsied left hand.

'Who do you think killed Ubba?' I asked, and when Beocca did not answer, I provided the answer for him. 'You think Odda the Younger killed him?' I could see that Beocca did believe that, and the anger surged in me. 'Ubba fought me man on man,' I said, too loudly now, 'one on one, just me and him. My sword against his axe. And he was unwounded when the fight began, father, and at the end of it he was dead. He had gone to his brothers in the corpse-hall.' I was furious now and my voice had risen until I was shouting, and the distracted congregation all turned to stare at me. The bishop, whom I recognised as the bishop of

7

Exanceaster, the same man who had married me to Mildrith, frowned nervously. Only Alfred seemed unmoved by the interruption, but then, reluctantly, he stood and turned towards me as his wife, the pinch-faced Ælswith, hissed into his ear.

'Is there any man here,' I was still shouting, 'who will deny that I, Uhtred of Bebbanburg, killed Ubba Lothbrokson in single combat?'

There was silence. I had not intended to disrupt the service, but monstrous pride and ungovernable rage had driven me to defiance. The faces gazed at me, the banners flapped in the desultory wind and the small rain dripped from the edges of the sail-cloth awning. Still no one answered me, but men saw that I was staring at Odda the Younger and some looked to him for a response, but he was struck dumb. 'Who killed Ubba?' I shouted at him.

'This is not seemly,' Alfred said angrily.

'This killed Ubba!' I declared, and I drew Serpent-Breath.

And that was my next mistake.

In the winter, while I was mewed up in Werham as one of the hostages given to Guthrum, a new law had been passed in Wessex, a law which decreed that no man other than the royal bodyguards was to draw a weapon in the presence of the king. The law was not just to protect Alfred, but also to prevent the quarrels between his great men becoming lethal and, by drawing Serpent-Breath, I had unwittingly broken the law so that his household troops were suddenly converging on me with spears and drawn swords until Alfred, red-cloaked and bare-headed, shouted for every man to be still.

Then he walked towards me and I could see the anger

on his face. He had a narrow face with a long nose and chin, a high forehead, and a thin-lipped mouth. He normally went clean-shaven, but he had grown a short beard that made him look older. He had not lived thirty years yet, but looked closer to forty. He was painfully thin, and his frequent illnesses had given his face a crabbed look. He looked more like a priest than the king of the West Saxons, for he had the irritated, pale face of a man who spends too much time out of the sun and poring over books, but there was an undoubted authority in his eyes. They were very light eyes, as grey as mail, unforgiving. 'You have broken my peace,' he said, 'and offended the peace of Christ.'

I sheathed Serpent-Breath, mainly because Beocca had muttered at me to stop being a damned fool and to put my sword away, and now the priest was tugging my right leg, trying to make me dismount and kneel to Alfred, whom he adored. Ælswith, Alfred's wife, was staring at me with pure scorn. 'He should be punished,' she called out.

'You will go there,' the king said, pointing towards one of his tents, 'and wait for my judgment.'

I had no choice but to obey, for his household troops, all of them in mail and helmets, pressed about me and so I was taken to the tent where I dismounted and ducked inside. The air smelled of yellowed, crushed grass. The rain pattered on the linen roof and some leaked through onto an altar that held a crucifix and two empty candle-holders. The tent was evidently the king's private chapel and Alfred made me wait there a long time. The congregation dispersed, the rain ended and a watery sunlight emerged between the clouds. A harp played somewhere, perhaps serenading Alfred and his wife as they ate. A dog came into the tent, looked at me, lifted its leg against the altar and went out again. The sun vanished behind cloud and more rain pattered on the canvas, then there was a flurry at the tent's opening and two men entered. One was Æthelwold, the king's nephew, and the man who should have inherited Wessex's throne from his father except he had been reckoned too young and so the crown had gone to his uncle instead. He gave me a sheepish grin, deferring to the second man who was heavy-set, full-bearded and ten years older than Æthelwold. He introduced himself by sneezing, then blew his nose into his hand and wiped the snot onto his leather coat. 'Call it spring-time,' he grumbled, then stared at me with a truculent expression. 'Damned rain never stops. You know who I am?'

'Wulfhere,' I said, 'Ealdorman of Wiltunscir.' He was a cousin to the king and a leading power in Wessex.

He nodded. 'And you know who this damn fool is?' he asked, gesturing at Æthelwold who was holding a bundle of white cloth.

'We know each other,' I said. Æthelwold was only a month or so younger than I, and he was fortunate, I suppose, that his Uncle Alfred was such a good Christian or else he could have expected a knife in the night. He was much better looking than Alfred, but foolish, flippant and usually drunk, though he appeared sober enough on that Sunday morning.

'I'm in charge of Æthelwold now,' Wulfhere said, 'and of you. And the king sent me to punish you.' He brooded on that for a heartbeat. 'What his wife wants me to do,' he went on, 'is pull the guts out of your smelly arse and feed them to the pigs.' He glared at me. 'You know what the penalty is for drawing a sword in the king's presence?'

'A fine?' I guessed.

'Death, you fool, death. They made a new law last winter.'

'How was I supposed to know?'

'But Alfred's feeling merciful,' Wulfhere ignored my question. 'So you're not to dangle off a gallows. Not today, anyhow. But he wants your assurance you'll keep the peace.'

'What peace?'

'His damned peace, you fool. He wants us to fight the Danes, not slice each other up. So for the moment you have to swear to keep the peace.'

'For the moment?'

'For the moment,' he said tonelessly, and I just shrugged. He took that for acceptance. 'So you killed Ubba?' he asked.

'I did.'

'That's what I hear.' He sneezed again. 'You know Edor?'

'I know him,' I said. Edor was one of Ealdorman Odda's battle chiefs, a warrior of the men of Defnascir, and he had fought beside us at Cynuit.

'Edor told me what happened,' Wulfhere said, 'but only because he trusts me. For God's sake stop fidgeting!' This last shout was directed at Æthelwold who was poking beneath the altar's linen cover, presumably in search of something valuable. Alfred, rather than murder his nephew, seemed intent on boring him to death. Æthelwold had never been allowed to fight, lest he make a reputation for himself, instead he had been forced to learn his letters, which he hated, and so he idled his time away, hunting, drinking, whoring and filled with resentment that he was not the king. 'Just stand still, boy,' Wulfhere snarled.

'Edor told you,' I said, unable to keep the outrage from my voice, 'because he trusts you? You mean what happened at Cynuit is a secret? A thousand men saw me kill Ubba!'

'But Odda the Younger took the credit,' Wulfhere said, 'and his father is badly wounded and if he dies then Odda the Younger will become one of the richest men in Wessex, and he'll lead more troops and pay more priests than you can ever hope to do, so men won't want to offend him, will they? They'll pretend to believe him, to keep him generous. And the king already believes him, and why shouldn't he? Odda arrived here with Ubba Lothbrokson's banner and war

11

axe. He dropped them at Alfred's feet, then knelt and gave the praise to God, and promised to build a church and monastery at Cynuit, and what did you do? Ride a damned horse into the middle of mass and wave your sword about. Not a clever thing to do with Alfred.'

I half smiled at that, for Wulfhere was right. Alfred was uncommonly pious, and a sure way to succeed in Wessex was to flatter that piety, imitate it and ascribe all good fortune to God.

'Odda's a prick,' Wulfhere growled, surprising me, 'but he's Alfred's prick now, and you're not going to change that.'

'But I killed . . .'

'I know what you did!' Wulfhere interrupted me. 'And Alfred probably suspects you're telling the truth, but he believes Odda made it possible. He thinks Odda and you both fought Ubba. He may not even care if neither of you did, except that Ubba's dead and that's good news, and Odda brought that news and so the sun shines out of Odda's arse, and if you want the king's troops to hang you off a high branch then you'll make a feud with Odda. Do you understand me?'

'Yes.'

Wulfhere sighed. 'Leofric said you'd see sense if I beat you over the head long enough.'

'I want to see Leofric,' I said.

'You can't,' Wulfhere said sharply. 'He's being sent back to Hamtun where he belongs. But you're not going back. The fleet will be put in someone else's charge. You're to do penance.'

For a moment I thought I had misheard. 'I'm to do what?' I asked.

'You're to grovel,' Æthelwold spoke for the first time. He grinned at me. We were not exactly friends, but we had drunk together often enough and he seemed to like me.

12

'You're to dress like a girl,' Æthelwold continued, 'go on your knees and be humiliated.'

'And you're to do it right now,' Wulfhere added.

'I'll be damned . . .'

'You'll be damned anyway,' Wulfhere snarled at me, then snatched the white bundle from Æthelwold's grasp and tossed it at my feet. It was a penitent's robe, and I left it on the ground. 'For God's sake, lad,' Wulfhere said, 'have some sense. You've got a wife and land here, don't you? So what happens if you don't do the king's bidding? You want to be outlawed? You want your wife in a nunnery? You want the church to take your land?'

I stared at him. 'All I did was kill Ubba and tell the truth.'

Wulfhere sighed. 'You're a Northumbrian,' he said, 'and I don't know how they did things up there, but this is Alfred's Wessex. You can do anything in Wessex except piss all over his church, and that's what you just did. You pissed, son, and now the church is going to piss all over you.' He grimaced as the rain beat harder on the tent, then he frowned, staring at the puddle spreading just outside the entrance. He was silent a long time, before turning and giving me a strange look. 'You think any of this is important?'

I did, but I was so astonished by his question, which had been asked in a soft, bitter voice, that I had nothing to say.

'You think Ubba's death makes any difference?' he asked, and again I thought I had misheard. 'And even if Guthrum makes peace,' he went on, 'you think we've won?' His heavy face was suddenly savage. 'How long will Alfred be king? How long before the Danes rule here?'

I still had nothing to say. Æthelwold, I saw, was listening intently. He longed to be king, but he had no following, and Wulfhere had plainly been appointed as his guardian to keep him from making trouble. But Wulfhere's words suggested the trouble would come anyway. 'Just do what Alfred

13

wants,' the ealdorman advised me, 'and afterwards find a way to keep living. That's all any of us can do. If Wessex falls we'll all be looking for a way to stay alive, but in the meantime put on that damned robe and get it over with.'

'Both of us,' Æthelwold said, and he picked up the robe and I saw he had fetched two of them, folded together.

'You?' Wulfhere snarled at him. 'Are you drunk?'

'I'm penitent for being drunk. Or I was drunk, now I'm penitent.' He grinned at me, then pulled the robe over his head. 'I shall go to the altar with Uhtred,' he said, his voice muffled by the linen.

Wulfhere could not stop him, but Wulfhere knew, as I knew, that Æthelwold was making a mockery of the rite. And I knew Æthelwold was doing it as a favour to me, though as far as I knew he owed me no favour. But I was grateful to him, so I put on the damned frock and, side by side with the king's nephew, went to my humiliation.

I meant little to Alfred. He had a score of great lords in Wessex, while across the frontier in Mercia there were other lords and thegns who lived under Danish rule but who would fight for Wessex if Alfred gave them an opportunity. All of those great men could bring him soldiers, could rally swords and spears to the dragon banner of Wessex, while I could bring him nothing except my sword, Serpent-Breath. True, I was a lord, but I was from far off Northumbria and I led no men and so my only value to him was far in the future. I did not understand that yet. In time, as the rule of Wessex spread northwards, my value grew, but back then, in 877, when I was an angry twenty-year-old, I knew nothing except my own ambitions.

And I learned humiliation. Even today, a lifetime later,

I remember the bitterness of that penitential grovel. Why did Alfred make me do it? I had won him a great victory, yet he insisted on shaming me, and for what? Because I had disturbed a church service? It was partly that, but only partly. He loved his god, loved the church and passionately believed that the survival of Wessex lay in obedience to the church and so he would protect the church as fiercely as he would fight for his country. And he loved order. There was a place for everything and I did not fit and he genuinely believed that if I could be brought to God's heel then I would become part of his beloved order. In short he saw me as an unruly young hound that needed a good whipping before it could join the disciplined pack.

So he made me grovel.

And Æthelwold made a fool of himself.

Not at first. At first it was all solemnity. Every man in Alfred's army was there to watch, and they made two lines in the rain. The lines stretched to the altar under the guyed sail-cloth where Alfred and his wife waited with the bishop and a gaggle of priests. 'On your knees,' Wulfhere said to me. 'You have to go on your knees,' he insisted tonelessly, 'and crawl up to the altar. Kiss the altar cloth, then lie flat.'

'Then what?'

'Then God and the king forgive you,' he said, and waited. 'Just do it,' he snarled.

So I did it. I went down on my knees and I shuffled through the mud, and the silent lines of men watched me, and then Æthelwold, close beside me, began to wail that he was a sinner. He threw his arms in the air, fell flat on his face, howled that he was penitent, shrieked that he was a sinner, and at first men were embarrassed and then they were amused. 'I've known women!' Æthelwold shouted at the rain, 'and they were bad women! Forgive me!'

Alfred was furious, but he could not stop a man making

15

a fool of himself before God. Perhaps he thought Æthelwold's remorse was genuine? 'I've lost count of the women!' Æthelwold shouted, then beat his fists in the mud. 'Oh God, I love tits! God, I love naked women, God, forgive me for that!' The laughter spread, and every man must have remembered that Alfred, before piety caught him in its clammy grip, had been notorious for the women he had pursued. 'You must help me, God!' Æthelwold cried as we shuffled a few feet farther. 'Send me an angel!'

'So you can hump her?' a voice called from the crowd and the laughter became a roar.

Ælswith was hurried away, lest she hear something unseemly. The priests whispered together, but Æthelwold's penitence, though extravagant, seemed real enough. He was weeping. I knew he was really laughing, but he howled as though his soul was in agony. 'No more tits, God!' he called, 'no more tits!' He made a fool of himself, but, as men already thought him a fool, he did not mind. 'Keep me from tits, God!' he shouted, and now Alfred left, knowing that the solemnity of the day was ruined, and most of the priests left with him, so that Æthelwold and I crawled to an abandoned altar where Æthelwold turned in his mud-spattered robe and leaned against the table. 'I hate him,' he said softly, and I knew he referred to his uncle. 'I hate him,' he went on, 'and now you owe me a favour, Uhtred.'

'I do,' I said.

'I'll think of one,' he said.

Odda the Younger had not left with Alfred. He seemed bemused. My humiliation, which he had surely thought to enjoy, had turned into laughter and he was aware that men were watching him, judging his truthfulness, and he moved closer to a huge man who was evidently one of his bodyguards. That man was tall and very broad about the chest, but it was his face that commanded attention for it looked as

16

though his skin had been stretched too tight across his skull, leaving his face incapable of making any expression other than one of pure hatred and wolfish hunger. Violence came off the man like the stench of a wet hound and when he looked at me it was like a beast's soulless stare, and I instinctively understood that this was the man who would kill me if Odda found a chance to commit murder. Odda was nothing, a rich man's spoiled son, but his money gave him the means to command men who were killers. Then Odda plucked at the tall man's sleeve and they both turned and walked away.

Father Beocca had stayed by the altar. 'Kiss it,' he ordered me, 'then lie flat.'

I stood up instead. 'You can kiss my arse, father,' I said. I was angry, and my anger frightened Beocca who backed away.

But I had done what the king wanted. I had been penitent.

The tall man beside Odda the Younger was named Steapa. Steapa Snotor, men called him, or Steapa the Clever. 'It's a joke,' Wulfhere told me as I ripped off the penitent's frock and pulled on my mail coat.

'A joke?'

'Because he's dumb as an ox,' Wulfhere said. 'He's got frog spawn instead of a brain. He's stupid, but he's not a stupid fighter. You didn't see him at Cynuit?'

'No,' I said curtly.

'So what's Steapa to you?' Wulfhere asked.

'Nothing,' I said. I had asked the ealdorman who Odda's bodyguard was so that I could learn the name of the man who might try to kill me, but that possible murder was none of Wulfhere's business.

Wulfhere hesitated, wanting to ask more, then deciding he would fetch no better answer. 'When the Danes come,' he said, 'you'll be welcome to join my men.'

Æthelwold, Alfred's nephew, was holding my two swords and he drew Serpent-Breath from her scabbard and stared at the wispy patterns in her blade. 'If the Danes come,' he spoke to Wulfhere, 'you must let me fight.'

'You don't know how to fight.'

'Then you must teach me.' He slid Serpent-Breath back into the scabbard. 'Wessex needs a king who can fight,' he said, 'instead of pray.'

'You should watch your tongue, lad,' Wulfhere said, 'in case it gets cut out.' He snatched the swords from Æthelwold and gave them to me. 'The Danes will come,' he said, 'so join me when they do.'

I nodded, but said nothing. When the Danes came, I thought, I planned to be with them. I had been raised by Danes after being captured at the age of ten and they could have killed me, but instead they had treated me well. I had learned their language and worshipped their gods until I no longer knew whether I was Danish or English. Had Earl Ragnar the Elder lived I would never have left them, but he had died, murdered in a night of treachery and fire, and I had fled south to Wessex. But now I would go back. Just as soon as the Danes left Exanceaster I would join Ragnar's son, Ragnar the Younger, if he lived. Ragnar the Younger's ship had been in the fleet which had been hammered in the great storm. Scores of ships had sunk, and the remnants of the fleet had limped to Exanceaster where the boats were now burned to ash on the riverbank beneath the town. I did not know if Ragnar lived. I hoped he lived, and I prayed he would escape Exanceaster and then I would go to him, offer him my sword, and carry that blade against Alfred of Wessex. Then, one day, I would dress Alfred in a frock and make him crawl on his knees to an altar of Thor. Then kill him.

Those were my thoughts as we rode to Oxton. That was the estate Mildrith had brought me in marriage and it was a beautiful place, but so saddled with debt that it was more of a burden than a pleasure. The farmland was on the slopes of hills facing east towards the broad sea-reach of the Uisc and above the house were thick woods of oak and ash from which flowed small clear streams that cut across the fields where rye, wheat and barley grew. The house, it was not a hall, was a smoke-filled building made from mud, dung, oak and rye-straw, and so long and low that it looked like a green, moss-covered mound from which smoke escaped through the roof's central hole. In the attached yard were pigs, chickens and mounds of manure as big as the house. Mildrith's father had farmed it, helped by a steward named Oswald who was a weasel, and he caused me still more trouble on that rainy Sunday as we rode back to the farm.

I was furious, resentful and vengeful. Alfred had humiliated me which made it unfortunate for Oswald that he had chosen that Sunday afternoon to drag an oak tree down from the high woods. I was brooding on the pleasures of revenge as I let my horse pick its way up the track through the trees and saw eight oxen hauling the great trunk towards the river. Three men were goading the oxen, while a fourth, Oswald, rode the trunk with a whip. He saw me and jumped off and, for a heartbeat, it looked as if he wanted to run into the trees, but then he realised he could not evade me and so he just stood and waited as I rode up to the great oak log.

'Lord,' Oswald greeted me. He was surprised to see me. He probably thought I had been killed with the other hostages, and that belief had made him careless.

My horse was nervous because of the stink of blood from

the oxen's flanks and he stepped backwards and forwards in small steps until I calmed him by patting his neck. Then I looked at the oak trunk that must have been forty feet long and as thick about as a man is tall. 'A fine tree,' I said to Oswald.

He glanced towards Mildrith who was twenty paces away. 'Good day, lady,' he said, clawing off the woollen hat he wore over his springy red hair.

'A wet day, Oswald,' she said. Her father had appointed the steward and Mildrith had an innocent faith in his reliability.

'I said,' I spoke loudly, 'a fine tree. So where was it felled?'

Oswald tucked the hat into his belt. 'On the top ridge, lord,' he said vaguely.

'The top ridge on my land?'

He hesitated. He was doubtless tempted to claim it came from a neighbour's land, but that lie could easily have been exposed and so he said nothing.

'From my land?' I asked again.

'Yes, lord,' he admitted.

'And where is it going?'

He hesitated again, but had to answer. 'Wigulf's mill.'

'Wigulf buys it?'

'He'll split it, lord.'

'I didn't ask what he will do with it,' I said, 'but whether he will buy it.'

Mildrith, hearing the harshness in my voice, intervened to say that her father had sometimes sent timber to Wigulf's mill, but I waved her to silence. 'Will he buy it?' I asked Oswald.

'We need the timber, lord, to make repairs,' the steward said, 'and Wigulf takes his fee in split wood.'

'And you drag the tree on a Sunday?' He had nothing to say to that. 'Tell me,' I went on, 'if we need planks for

20

repairs, then why don't we split the trunk ourselves? Do we lack men? Or wedges? Or mauls?'

'Wigulf has always done it,' Oswald said in a surly tone.

'Always?' I repeated and Oswald said nothing. 'Wigulf lives in Exanmynster?' I guessed. Exanmynster lay a mile or so northwards and was the nearest settlement to Oxton.

'Yes, lord,' Oswald said.

'So if I ride to Exanmynster now,' I said, 'Wigulf will tell me how many similar trees you've delivered to him in the last year?'

There was silence, except for the rain dripping from leaves and the intermittent burst of birdsong. I edged my horse a few steps closer to Oswald, who gripped his whip's handle as if readying it to lash out at me. 'How many?' I asked.

Oswald said nothing.

'How many?' I demanded, louder.

'Husband,' Mildrith called.

'Quiet!' I shouted at her and Oswald looked from me to her and back to me. 'And how much has Wigulf paid you?' I asked. 'What does a tree like this fetch? Eight shillings? Nine?'

The anger that had made me act so impetuously at the king's church service rose again. It was plain that Oswald was stealing the timber and being paid for it, and what I should have done was charge him with theft and have him arraigned before a court where a jury of men would decide his guilt or innocence, but I was in no mood for such a process. I just drew Serpent-Breath and kicked my horse forward. Mildrith screamed a protest, but I ignored her. Oswald ran, and that was a mistake, because I caught him easily, and Serpent-Breath swung once and opened up the back of his skull so I could see brains and blood as he fell. He twisted in the leaf mould and I wheeled the horse back and stabbed down into his throat.

21

'That was murder!' Mildrith shouted at me.

'That was justice,' I snarled at her, 'something lacking in Wessex.' I spat on Oswald's body, which was still twitching. 'The bastard's been stealing from us.'

Mildrith kicked her horse, leading the nurse who carried our child uphill. I let her go. 'Take the trunk up to the house,' I ordered the slaves who had been goading the oxen. 'If it's too big to drag uphill then split it here and take the planks to the house.'

I searched Oswald's house that evening and discovered fifty-three shillings buried in the floor. I took the silver, confiscated his cooking pots, spit, knives, buckles and a deer-skin cloak, then drove his wife and three children off my land. I had come home.

Two

My anger was not slaked by Oswald's killing. The death of a dishonest steward was no consolation for what I perceived as a monstrous injustice. For the moment Wessex was safe from the Danes, but it was only safe because I had killed Ubba Lothbrokson and my reward had been humiliation.

Poor Mildrith. She was a peaceable woman who thought well of everyone she met, and now she found herself married to a resentful, angry warrior. She was frightened of Alfred's wrath, terrified that the church would punish me for disturbing its peace, and worried that Oswald's relatives would demand a wergild from me. And so they would. A wergild was the blood price that every man, woman and child possessed. Kill a man and you must pay his price or else die yourself, and I had no doubt that Oswald's family would go to Odda the Younger, who had been named the Ealdorman of Defnascir because his father was too badly wounded to continue as ealdorman, and Odda would instruct the shire reeve to pursue me and place me on trial, but I did not care. I hunted boar and deer, I brooded and waited for news of the negotiations at Exanceaster. I was expecting Alfred to do what he always did which was to make peace with the Danes and so release them, and when he did I would go to Ragnar.

And as I waited I found my first retainer. He was a slave and I discovered him in Exanmynster on a fine spring day. There was a hiring-fair where men looked for employment through the busy days of hay-making and harvest, and like all fairs there were jugglers, storytellers, stiltwalkers, musicians and acrobats. There was also a tall, white-haired man with a lined, serious face, who was selling enchanted leather bags that turned iron into silver. He showed us how it was done, and I saw him place two common nails into the bag and a moment later they were pure silver. He said we had to place a silver crucifix in the bag and then sleep one night with it tied around our necks before the magic worked and I paid him three silver shillings for one bag, and it never worked. I spent months searching for the man, but never found him. Even these days I come across such men and women, selling sorcerous pouches or boxes, and now I have them whipped and run off my land, but I was only twenty then and I believed my own eyes. That man had attracted a large crowd, but there were even more people gathered by the church gate where shouts erupted every few minutes. I pushed my horse into their rear ranks, getting dirty looks from folk who knew I had killed Oswald, but none dared accuse me of the murder for I carried both Serpent-Breath and Wasp-Sting.

A young man was by the church gate. He was stripped to the waist, barefooted and had a rope around his neck, and the rope was tied to the gatepost. In his hand was a short, stout stave. He had long unbound fair hair, blue eyes, a stubborn face and blood all over his chest, belly and arms. Three men guarded him. They too were fair-haired and blue-eyed, and they shouted in a strange accent. 'Come and fight the heathen! Three pennies to make the bastard bleed! Come and fight!'

'Who is he?' I asked.

'A Dane, lord, a pagan Dane.' The man tugged off his hat when he spoke to me, then turned back to the crowd. 'Come and fight him! Get your revenge! Make a Dane bleed! Be a good Christian! Hurt a pagan!'

The three men were Frisians. I suspected they had been in Alfred's army and, now that he was talking to the Danes rather than fighting them, the three had deserted. Frisians come from across the sea and they come for one reason only, money, and this trio had somehow captured the young Dane and were profiting from him so long as he lasted. And that could have been some time, for he was good. A strong young Saxon paid his three pence and was given a sword with which he hacked wildly at the prisoner, but the Dane parried every blow, wood chips flying from his stave, and when he saw an opening he cracked his opponent around the head hard enough to draw blood from his ear. The Saxon staggered away, half stunned, and the Dane rammed the stave into his belly and, as the Saxon bent to gasp for breath, the stave whistled around in a blow that would have cracked his skull open like an egg, but the Frisians dragged on the rope so that the Dane fell backwards. 'Do we have another hero?' a Frisian shouted as the young Saxon was helped away. 'Come on, lads! Show your strength! Beat a Dane bloody!'

'I'll beat him,' I said. I dismounted and pushed through the crowd. I gave my horse's reins to a boy, then drew Serpent-Breath. 'Three pence?' I asked the Frisians.

'No, lord,' one of them said.

'Why not?'

'We don't want a dead Dane, do we?' the man answered.

'We do!' someone shouted from the crowd. The folk in the Uisc valley did not like me, but they liked the Danes even less and they relished the prospect of watching a prisoner being slaughtered.

25

'You can only wound him, lord,' the Frisian said. 'And you must use our sword.' He held out the weapon. I glanced at it, saw its blunt edge, and spat.

'Must?' I asked.

The Frisian did not want to argue. 'You can only draw blood, lord,' he said.

The Dane flicked hair from his eyes and watched me. He held the stave low. I could see he was nervous, but there was no fear in his eyes. He had probably fought a hundred battles since the Frisians captured him, but those fights had been against men who were not soldiers, and he must have known, from my two swords, that I was a warrior. His skin was blotched with bruises and laced by blood and scars, and he surely expected another wound from Serpent-Breath, but he was determined to give me a fight.

'What's your name?' I asked in Danish.

He blinked at me, surprised.

'Your name, boy,' I said. I called him 'boy', though he was not much younger than me.

'Haesten,' he said.

'Haesten who?'

'Haesten Storrison,' he said, giving me his father's name.

'Fight him! Don't talk to him!' a voice shouted from the crowd.

I turned to stare at the man who had shouted and he could not meet my gaze, then I turned fast, very fast, and whipped Serpent-Breath in a quick sweep that Haesten instinctively parried so that Serpent-Breath cut through the stave as if it was rotten. Haesten was left with a stub of wood, while the rest of his weapon, a yard of thick ash, lay on the ground.

'Kill him!' someone shouted.

'Just draw blood, lord,' a Frisian said, 'please, lord. He's not a bad lad, for a Dane. Just make him bleed and we'll pay you.'

I kicked the ash stave away from Haesten. 'Pick it up,' I said.

He looked at me nervously. To pick it up he would have to go to the end of his tether, then stoop, and at that moment he would expose his back to Serpent-Breath. He watched me, his eyes bitter beneath the fringe of dirty hair, then decided I would not attack him as he bent over. He went to the stave and, as he leaned down, I kicked it a few inches further away. 'Pick it up,' I ordered him again.

He still held the stub of ash and, as he took a further step, straining against the rope, he suddenly whipped around and tried to ram the broken end into my belly. He was fast, but I had half expected the move and caught his wrist in my left hand. I squeezed hard, hurting him. 'Pick it up,' I said a third time.

This time he obeyed, stooping to the stave, and to reach it he stretched his tether tight and I slashed Serpent-Breath onto the taut rope, severing it. Haesten, who had been straining forward, fell onto his face as the hide rope was cut. I put my left foot onto his back and let the tip of Serpent-Breath rest on his spine. 'Alfred,' I said to the Frisians, 'has ordered that all Danish prisoners are to be taken to him.'

The three looked at me, said nothing.

'So why have you not taken this man to the king?' I demanded.

'We didn't know, lord,' one of them said, 'no one told us,' which was not surprising because Alfred had given no such order.

'We'll take him to the king now, lord,' another reassured me.

'I'll save you the trouble,' I said. I took my foot off Haesten. 'Get up,' I told him in Danish. I threw a coin to the boy holding my horse and hauled myself into the saddle where I offered Haesten a hand. 'Get up behind me,' I ordered him.

27

The Frisians protested, coming at me with their swords drawn, so I pulled Wasp-Sting from her scabbard and gave it to Haesten who had still not mounted. Then I turned the horse towards the Frisians and smiled at them. 'These people,' I waved Serpent-Breath at the crowd, 'already think I am a murderer. I'm also the man who met Ubba Lothbrokson beside the sea and killed him there. I tell you this so you may boast that you killed Uhtred of Bebbanburg.'

I lowered the sword so it pointed at the nearest man and he backed away. The others, no more eager to fight than the first, went with him. Haesten then pulled himself up behind me and I spurred the horse into the crowd, which parted reluctantly.

Once free of them I made Haesten dismount and give me back Wasp-Sting. 'How did you get captured?' I asked him.

He told me he had been on one of Guthrum's ships caught in the storm, and his ship had sunk, but he had clung to some wreckage and been washed ashore where the Frisians had found him. 'There were two of us, lord,' he said, 'but the other died.'

'You're a free man now,' I told him.

'Free?'

'You're my man,' I said, 'and you'll give me an oath, and I'll give you a sword.'

'Why?' he wanted to know.

'Because a Dane saved me once,' I said, 'and I like the Danes.'

I also wanted Haesten because I needed men. I did not trust Odda the Younger, and I feared Steapa Snotor, Odda's warrior, and so I would have swords at Oxton. Mildrith, of course, did not want sword-Danes at her house. She wanted ploughmen and peasants, milkmaids and servants, but I told her I was a lord, and a lord has swords.

I am indeed a lord, a lord of Northumbria. I am Uhtred

of Bebbanburg. My ancestors, who can trace their lineage back to the god Woden, the Danish Odin, were once kings in northern England, and if my uncle had not stolen Bebbanburg from me when I was just ten years old I would have lived there still as a Northumbrian lord safe in his sea-washed fastness. The Danes had captured Northumbria, and their puppet king, Ricsig, ruled in Eoferwic, but Bebbanburg was too strong for any Dane and my uncle Ælfric ruled there, calling himself Ealdorman Ælfric, and the Danes left him in peace so long as he did not trouble them, and I often dreamed of going back to Northumbria to claim my birthright. But how? To capture Bebbanburg I would need an army, and all I had was one young Dane, Haesten.

And I had other enemies in Northumbria. There was Earl Kjartan and his son Sven, who had lost an eye because of me, and they would kill me gladly, and my uncle would pay them to do it, and so I had no future in Northumbria, not then. But I would go back. That was my soul's wish, and I would go back with Ragnar the Younger, my friend, who still lived because his ship had weathered the storm. I heard that from a priest who had listened to the negotiations outside Exanceaster and he was certain that Earl Ragnar had been one of the Danish lords in Guthrum's delegation. 'A big man,' the priest told me, 'and very loud.' That description convinced me that Ragnar lived and my heart was glad for it, for I knew that my future lay with him, not with Alfred. When the negotiations were finished and a truce made, the Danes would doubtless leave Exanceaster and I would give my sword to Ragnar and carry it against Alfred, who hated me. And I hated him.

I told Mildrith that we would leave Defnascir and go to Ragnar, that I would be his man and that I would pursue my bloodfeud against Kjartan and against my uncle under

29

Ragnar's eagle banner, and Mildrith responded with tears and more tears.

I cannot bear a woman's crying. Mildrith was hurt and she was confused and I was angry and we snarled at each other like wildcats and the rain kept falling and I raged like a beast in a cage and wished Alfred and Guthrum would finish their talking because everyone knew that Alfred would let Guthrum go, and once Guthrum left Exanceaster then I could join the Danes and I did not care whether Mildrith came or not, so long as my son, who bore my name, went with me. So by day I hunted, at night I drank and dreamed of revenge and then one evening I came home to find Father Willibald waiting in the house.

Willibald was a good man. He had been chaplain to Alfred's fleet when I commanded those twelve ships, and he told me he was on his way back to Hamtun, but he thought I would like to know what had unfolded in the long talks between Alfred and Guthrum. 'There is peace, lord,' he told me, 'thanks be to God, there is peace.'

'Thanks be to God,' Mildrith echoed.

I was cleaning the blood from the blade of a boar spear and said nothing. I was thinking that Ragnar was released from the siege now and I could join him.

'The treaty was sealed with solemn oaths yesterday,' Willibald said, 'and so we have peace.'

'They gave each other solemn oaths last year,' I said sourly. Alfred and Guthrum had made peace at Werham, but Guthrum had broken the truce and murdered the hostages he had been holding. Eleven of the twelve had died, and only I had lived because Ragnar was there to protect me. 'So what have they agreed?' I asked.

'The Danes are to give up all their horses,' Willibald said, 'and march back into Mercia.'

Good, I thought, because that was where I would go.

I did not say that to Willibald, but instead sneered that Alfred was just letting them march away. 'Why doesn't he fight them?' I asked.

'Because there are too many, lord. Because too many men would die on both sides.'

'He should kill them all.'

'Peace is better than war,' Willibald said.

'Amen,' Mildrith said.

I began sharpening the spear, stroking the whetstone down the long blade. It seemed to me that Alfred had been absurdly generous. Guthrum, after all, was the one remaining leader of any stature on the Danish side, and he had been trapped, and if I had been Alfred there would have been no terms, only a siege, and at its end the Danish power in southern England would have been broken. Instead Guthrum was to be allowed to leave Exanceaster. 'It is the hand of God,' Willibald said.

I looked at him. He was a few years older than I was, but always seemed younger. He was earnest, enthusiastic and kind. He had been a good chaplain to the twelve ships, though the poor man was ever seasick and blanched at the sight of blood. 'God made the peace?' I asked sceptically.

'Who sent the storm that sank Guthrum's ships?' Willibald retorted fervently, 'who delivered Ubba into our hands?'

'I did,' I said.

He ignored that. 'We have a godly king, lord,' he said, 'and God rewards those that serve him faithfully. Alfred has defeated the Danes! And they see it! Guthrum can recognise divine intervention! He has been making enquiries about Christ.'

I said nothing.

'Our king believes,' the priest went on, 'that Guthrum is not far from seeing the true light of Christ.' He leaned forward and touched my knee. 'We have fasted, lord,' he

31

said, 'we have prayed, and the king believes that the Danes will be brought to Christ and when that happens there will be a permanent peace.'

He meant every word of that nonsense and, of course, it was sweet music to Mildrith's ears. She was a good Christian and had great faith in Alfred, and if the king believed that his god would bring victory then she would believe it too. It seemed madness to me, but I said nothing as a servant brought us barley ale, bread, smoked mackerel and cheese. 'We shall have a Christian peace,' Willibald said, making the sign of the cross above the bread before he ate, 'sealed by hostages.'

'We've given Guthrum hostages again?' I asked, astonished.

'No,' Willibald said. 'But he has agreed to give us hostages. Including six earls!'

I stopped sharpening the spear and looked at Willibald. 'Six earls?'

'Including your friend, Ragnar!' Willibald seemed pleased by this news, but I was appalled. If Ragnar was not with the Danes then I could not go to them. He was my friend and his enemies were my enemies, but without Ragnar to protect me I would be horribly vulnerable to Kjartan and Sven, the father and son who had murdered Ragnar's father and who wanted me dead. Without Ragnar, I knew, I could not leave Wessex.

'Ragnar's one of the hostages?' I asked. 'You're sure?'

'Of course I'm sure. He will be held by Ealdorman Wulfhere. All the hostages are to be held by Wulfhere.'

'For how long?'

'For as long as Alfred wishes, or until Guthrum is baptised. And Guthrum has agreed that our priests can talk to his men.' Willibald gave me a pleading look. 'We must have faith in God,' he said. 'We must give God time to work on

32

the hearts of the Danes. Guthrum understands now that our god has power!'

I stood and went to the door, pulling aside the leather curtain and staring down at the wide sea-reach of the Uisc. I was sick at heart. I hated Alfred, did not want to be in Wessex, but now it seemed I was doomed to stay there. 'And what do I do?' I asked.

'The king will forgive you, lord,' Willibald said nervously.

'Forgive me?' I turned on him. 'And what does the king believe happened at Cynuit? You were there, father,' I said, 'so did you tell him?'

'I told him.'

'And?'

'He knows you are a brave warrior, lord,' Willibald said, 'and that your sword is an asset to Wessex. He will receive you again, I'm sure, and he will receive you joyfully. Go to church, pay your debts and show that you are a good man of Wessex.'

'I'm not a West Saxon,' I snarled at him, 'I'm a Northumbrian!'

And that was part of the problem. I was an outsider. I spoke a different English. The men of Wessex were tied by family, and I came from the strange north and folk believed I was a pagan, and they called me a murderer because of Oswald's death, and sometimes, when I rode about the estate, men would make the sign of the cross to avert the evil they saw in me. They called me Uhtredærwe, which means Uhtred the Wicked, and I was not unhappy with the insult, but Mildrith was. She assured them I was a Christian, but she lied, and our unhappiness festered all that summer. She prayed for my soul, I fretted for my freedom, and when she begged me to go with her to the church at Exanmynster I growled at her that I would never set foot in another church all my days. She would weep when I said that and

her tears drove me out of the house to hunt, and sometimes the chase would take me down to the water's edge
where I would stare at *Heahengel*.

She lay canted on the muddy foreshore, lifted and
dropped repeatedly by the tides, abandoned. She was one
of Alfred's fleet, one of the twelve large warships he had
built to harry the Danish boats that raided Wessex's coast,
and Leofric and I had brought *Heahengel* up from Hamtun
in pursuit of Guthrum's fleet and we had survived the storm
that sent so many Danes to their deaths and we had beached
Heahengel here, left her mastless and without a sail, and she
was still on the Uisc's foreshore, rotting and apparently
forgotten.

Archangel. That was what her name meant. Alfred had
named her and I had always hated the name. A ship should
have a proud name, not a snivelling religious word, and she
should have a beast on her prow, high and defiant, a dragon's
head to challenge the sea or a snarling wolf to terrify an
enemy. I sometimes climbed on board *Heahengel* and saw
how the local villagers had plundered some of her upper
strakes, and how there was water in her belly, and I remembered her proud days at sea and the wind whipping through
her seal-hide rigging and the crash as we had rammed a
Danish boat.

Now, like me, *Heahengel* had been left to decay, and sometimes I dreamed of repairing her, of finding new rigging and
a new sail, of finding men and taking her long hull to sea.
I wanted to be anywhere but where I was, I wanted to be
with the Danes, and every time I said that Mildrith would
weep again. 'You can't make me live among the Danes!'

'Why not? I did.'

'They're pagans! My son won't grow up a pagan!'

'He's my son too,' I said, 'and he will worship the gods
I worship.' There would be more tears then, and I would

34

storm out of the house and take the hounds up to the high woods and wonder why love soured like milk. After Cynuit I had so wanted to see Mildrith, yet now I could not abide her misery and piety and she could not endure my anger. All she wanted me to do was till my fields, milk my cows and gather my harvest to pay the great debt she had brought me in marriage. That debt came from a pledge made by Mildrith's father, a pledge to give the church the yield of almost half his land. That pledge was for all time, binding on his heirs, but Danish raids and bad harvests had ruined him. Yet the church, venomous as serpents, still insisted that the debt be paid, and said that if I could not pay then our land would be taken by monks, and every time I went to Exanceaster I could sense the priests and monks watching me and enjoying the prospect of their enrichment. Exanceaster was English again, for Guthrum had handed over the hostages and gone north so that peace of a sort had come to Wessex. The fyrds, the armies of each shire, had been disbanded and sent back to their farms. Psalms were being sung in all the churches and Alfred, to mark his victory, was sending gifts to every monastery and nunnery. Odda the Younger, who was being celebrated as the champion of Wessex, had been given all the land about the place where the battle had been fought at Cynuit and he had ordered a church to be built there, and it was rumoured that the church would have an altar of gold as thanks to God for allowing Wessex to survive.

Though how long would it survive? Guthrum lived and I did not share the Christian belief that God had sent Wessex peace. Nor was I the only one, for in midsummer Alfred returned to Exanceaster where he summoned his Witan, a council of the kingdom's leading thegns and churchmen, and Wulfhere of Wiltunscir was one of the men summoned and I went into the city one evening and was told the

35

ealdorman and his followers had lodgings in The Swan, a tavern by the east gate. He was not there, but Æthelwold, Alfred's nephew, was doing his best to drain the tavern of ale. 'Don't tell me the bastard summoned you to the Witan?' he greeted me sourly. The 'bastard' was Alfred who had snatched the throne from the young Æthelwold.

'No,' I said. 'I came to see Wulfhere.'

'The ealdorman is in church,' Æthelwold said, 'and I am not.' He grinned and waved to the bench opposite him. 'Sit and drink. Get drunk. Then we'll find two girls. Three, if you like. Four, if you want?'

'You forget I'm married,' I said.

'As if that ever stopped anyone.'

I sat and one of the maids brought me ale. 'Are you in the Witan?' I asked Æthelwold.

'What do you think? You think that bastard wants my advice? "Lord king," I'd say, "why don't you jump off a high cliff and pray that God gives you wings."' He pushed a plate of pork ribs towards me. 'I'm here so they can keep an eye on me. They're making sure I'm not plotting treason.'

'Are you?'

'Of course I am.' He grinned. 'Are you going to join me? You do owe me a favour.'

'You want my sword at your service?' I asked.

'Yes.' He was serious.

'So it's you and me,' I said, 'against all Wessex. Who else will fight with us?'

He frowned, thinking, but came up with no names. He stared down at the table and I felt sorry for him. I had always liked Æthelwold, but no one would ever trust him for he was as careless as he was irresponsible. Alfred, I thought, had judged him right. Let him be free and he would drink and whore himself into irrelevance. 'What I should do,' he said, 'is go and join Guthrum.'

36

'Why don't you?'

He looked up at me, but had no answer. Maybe he knew the answer, that Guthrum would welcome him, honour him, use him and eventually kill him. But maybe that was a better prospect than his present life. He shrugged and leaned back, pushing hair off his face. He was a startlingly handsome young man, and that too distracted him, for girls were attracted to him like priests to gold. 'What Wulfhere thinks,' he said, his voice slurring slightly, 'is that Guthrum is going to come and kill us all.'

'Probably,' I said.

'And if my uncle dies,' he said, not bothering to lower his voice even though there were a score of men in the tavern, 'his son is much too young to be king.'

'True.'

'So it'll be my turn!' He smiled.

'Or Guthrum's turn,' I said.

'So drink, my friend,' he said, 'because we're all in the cesspit.' He grinned at me, his charm suddenly evident. 'So if you won't fight for me,' he asked, 'how do you propose to pay back the favour?'

'How would you like it paid?'

'You could kill Abbot Hewald? Very nastily? Slowly?'

'I could do that,' I said. Hewald was abbot at Winburnan and famous for the harshness with which he taught boys to read.

'On the other hand,' Æthelwold went on, 'I'd like to kill that scrawny bastard myself, so don't do it for me, I'll think of something that won't make my uncle happy. You don't like him, do you?'

'No.'

'Then we'll brew up some mischief. Oh God,' this last imprecation was because Wulfhere's voice was suddenly loud just outside the door. 'He's angry at me.'

'Why?'

'One of the dairymaids is pregnant. I think he wanted to do it himself, but I churned her first.' He drained his ale. 'I'm going to the Three Bells. Want to come?'

'I have to speak to Wulfhere.'

Æthelwold left by the back door as the ealdorman ducked through the front. Wulfhere was accompanied by a dozen thegns, but he saw me and crossed the room. 'They've been reconsecrating the bishop's church,' he grumbled. 'Hours upon damned hours! Nothing but chanting and prayers, hours of prayers just to get the taint of the Danes out of the place.' He sat heavily. 'Did I see Æthelwold here?'

'Yes.'

'Wanted you to join his rebellion, did he?'

'Yes.'

'Damned fool. So why are you here? Come to offer me your sword?' He meant swear my allegiance to him and so become his warrior.

'I want to see one of the hostages,' I said, 'so I seek your permission.'

'Hostages,' he snapped his fingers for ale. 'Damned hostages. I've had to make new buildings to house them. And who pays for that?'

'You do?'

'Of course I do. And I'm supposed to feed them too? Feed them? Guard them? Wall them in? And does Alfred pay anything?'

'Tell him you're building a monastery,' I suggested.

He looked at me as if I were mad, then saw the jest and laughed. 'True enough, he'd pay me then, wouldn't he? Have you heard about the monastery they're building at Cynuit?'

'I hear it's to have an altar of gold.'

He laughed again. 'That's what I hear. I don't believe it,

but I hear it.' He watched one of the tavern girls cross the floor. 'It's not my permission you need to see the hostages,' he said, 'but Alfred's, and he won't give it to you.'

'Alfred's permission?' I asked.

'They're not just hostages,' he said, 'but prisoners. I have to wall them in and watch them day and night. Alfred's orders. He might think God brought us peace, but he's made damn sure he's got high-born hostages. Six earls! You know how many retainers they have? How many women? How many mouths to feed?'

'If I go to Wiltunscir,' I said, 'can I see Earl Ragnar?'

Wulfhere frowned at me. 'Earl Ragnar? The noisy one? I like him. No, lad, you can't, because no one's allowed to see them except a damned priest who talks their language. Alfred sent him and he's trying to make them into Christians, and if you go without my permission then Alfred will hear you've been there and he'll want an explanation from me. No one can see the poor bastards.' He paused to scratch at a louse under his collar. 'I have to feed the priest too, and Alfred doesn't pay for that either. He doesn't even pay me to feed that lout Æthelwold!'

'When I was a hostage in Werham,' I explained, 'Earl Ragnar saved my life. Guthrum killed the others, but Ragnar guarded me. He said they'd have to kill him before they killed me.'

'And he looks like a hard man to kill,' Wulfhere said, 'but if Guthrum attacks Wessex that's what I'm supposed to do. Kill the lot of them. Maybe not the women.' He stared gloomily into the tavern's yard where a group of his men were playing dice in the moonlight. 'And Guthrum will attack,' he added in a low voice.

'That's not what I hear.'

He looked at me suspiciously 'And what do you hear, young man?'

39

'That God has sent us peace.'

Wulfhere laughed at my mockery. 'Guthrum's in Gleawecestre,' he said, 'and that's just a half day's march from our frontier. And they say more Danish ships arrive every day. They're in Lundene, they're in the Humber, they're in the Gewæsc.' He scowled. 'More ships, more men, and Alfred's building churches! And there's this fellow Svein.'

'Svein?'

'Brought his ships from Ireland. Bastard's in Wales now, but he won't stay there, will he? He'll come to Wessex. And they say more Danes are joining him from Ireland.' He brooded on this bad news. I did not know whether it was true, for such rumours were ever current, but Wulfhere plainly believed it. 'We should march on Gleawecestre,' he said, 'and slaughter the lot of them before they slaughter us, but we've got a kingdom ruled by priests.'

That was true, I thought, just as it was certain that Wulfhere would not make it easy for me to see Ragnar. 'Will you give a message to Ragnar?' I asked.

'How? I don't speak Danish. I could ask the priest, but he'll tell Alfred.'

'Does Ragnar have a woman with him?' I asked.

'They all do.'

'A thin girl,' I said, 'black hair. Face like a hawk.'

He nodded cautiously. 'Sounds right. Has a dog, yes?'

'She has a dog,' I said, 'and its name is Nihtgenga.'

He shrugged as if he did not care what the dog was called, then he understood the significance of the name. 'An English name?' he asked. 'A Danish girl calls her dog Goblin?'

'She isn't Danish,' I said. 'Her name is Brida, and she's a Saxon.'

He stared at me, then laughed. 'The cunning little bitch. She's been listening to us, hasn't she?'

40

Brida was indeed cunning. She had been my first lover, an East Anglian girl who had been raised by Ragnar's father and who now slept with Ragnar. 'Talk to her,' I said, 'and give her my greetings, and say that if it comes to war . . .' I paused, not sure what to say. There was no point in promising to do my best to rescue Ragnar, for if war came then the hostages would be slaughtered long before I could reach them.

'If it comes to war?' Wulfhere prompted me.

'If it comes to war,' I said, repeating the words he had spoken to me before my penance, 'we'll all be looking for a way to stay alive.'

Wulfhere stared at me for a long time and his silence told me that though I had failed to find a message for Ragnar I had given a message to Wulfhere. He drank ale. 'So the bitch speaks English, does she?'

'She's a Saxon.'

As was I, but I hated Alfred and I would join Ragnar when I could, if I could, whatever Mildrith wanted, or so I thought. But deep under the earth, where the corpse serpent gnaws at the roots of Yggdrasil, the tree of life, there are three spinners. Three women who make our fate. We might believe we make choices, but in truth our lives are in the spinners' fingers. They make our lives, and destiny is everything. The Danes know that, and even the Christians know it. *Wyrd bið ful aræd*, we Saxons say, fate is inexorable, and the spinners had decided my fate because, a week after the Witan had met, when Exanceaster was quiet again, they sent me a ship.

The first I knew of it was when a slave came running from Oxton's fields saying that there was a Danish ship in the estuary of the Uisc and I pulled on boots and mail, snatched my swords from their peg, shouted for a horse to be saddled and rode to the foreshore where *Heahengel* rotted.

And where, standing in from the long sandspit that protects the Uisc from the greater sea, another ship approached. Her sail was furled on the long yard and her dripping oars rose and fell like wings and her long hull left a spreading wake that glittered silver under the rising sun. Her prow was high, and standing there was a man in full mail, a man with a helmet and spear, and behind me, where a few fisherfolk lived in hovels beside the mud, people were hurrying towards the hills and taking with them whatever few possessions they could snatch. I called to one of them. 'It's not a Dane!'

'Lord?'

'It's a West Saxon ship,' I called, though they did not believe me and hurried away with their livestock. For years they had done this. They would see a ship and they would run, for ships brought Danes and Danes brought death, but this ship had no dragon or wolf or eagle's head on its prow. I knew the ship. It was the *Eftwyrd*, the best named of all Alfred's ships which otherwise bore pious names like *Heahengel* or *Apostol* or *Cristenlic*. *Eftwyrd* meant judgement day which, though Christian in inspiration, accurately described what she had brought to many Danes.

The man in the prow waved and, for the first time since I had crawled on my knees to Alfred's altar, my spirits lifted. It was Leofric, and then the *Eftwyrd*'s bows slid onto the mud and the long hull juddered to a halt. Leofric cupped his hands. 'How deep is this mud?'

'It's nothing!' I shouted back, 'a hand's depth, no more!'

'Can I walk on it?'

'Of course you can!' I shouted back.

He jumped and, as I had known he would, sank up to

42

his thighs in the thick black slime, and I bent over my saddle's pommel in laughter, and the *Eftwyrd*'s crew laughed with me as Leofric cursed, and it took ten minutes to extricate him from the muck, by which time a score of us were plastered in the stinking stuff, but then the crew, who were mostly my old oarsmen and warriors, brought ale ashore, and bread and salted pork, and we made a midday meal beside the rising tide.

'You're an earsling,' Leofric grumbled, looking at the mud clogging up the links of his mail coat.

'I'm a bored earsling,' I said.

'You're bored?' Leofric said, 'so are we.' It seemed the fleet was not sailing. It had been given into the charge of a man named Burgweard who was a dull, worthy soldier whose brother was bishop of Scireburnan, and Burgweard had orders not to disturb the peace. 'If the Danes aren't off the coast,' Leofric said, 'then we aren't.'

'So what are you doing here?'

'He sent us to rescue that piece of shit,' he nodded at *Heahengel*. 'He wants twelve ships again, see?'

'I thought they were building more?'

'They were building more, only it all stopped because some thieving bastards stole the timber while we were fighting at Cynuit, and then someone remembered *Heahengel* and here we are. Burgweard can't manage with just eleven.'

'If he isn't sailing,' I asked, 'why does he want another ship?'

'In case he has to sail,' Leofric explained, 'and if he does then he wants twelve. Not eleven, twelve.'

'Twelve? Why?'

'Because,' Leofric paused to bite off a piece of bread, 'because it says in the gospel book that Christ sent out his disciples two by two, and that's how we have to go, two ships together, all holy, and if we've only got eleven then that means we've only got ten, if you follow me.'

I stared at him, not sure whether he was jesting. 'Burgweard insists you sail two by two?'

Leofric nodded. 'Because it says so in Father Willibald's book.'

'In the gospel book?'

'That's what Father Willibald tells us,' Leofric said with a straight face, then saw my expression and shrugged. 'Honest! And Alfred approves.'

'Of course he does.'

'And if you do what the gospel book tells you,' Leofric said, still with a straight face, 'then nothing can go wrong, can it?'

'Nothing,' I said. 'So you're here to rebuild *Heahengel*?'

'New mast,' Leofric said, 'new sail, new rigging, patch up those timbers, caulk her, then tow her back to Hamtun. It could take a month!'

'At least.'

'And I never was much good at making things. Good at fighting, I am, and I can drink ale as well as any man, but I was never much good with a mallet and wedge or with adzes. They are.' He nodded at a group of a dozen men who were strangers to me.

'Who are they?'

'Shipwrights.'

'So they do the work?'

'Can't expect me to do it!' Leofric protested. 'I'm in command of the *Eftwyrd*!'

'So,' I said, 'you're planning to drink my ale and eat my food for a month while those dozen men do the work?'

'You have any better ideas?'

I gazed at the *Eftwyrd*. She was a well-made ship, longer than most Danish boats and with high sides that made her

44

a good fighting platform. 'What did Burgweard tell you to do?' I asked.

'Pray,' Leofric said sourly, 'and help repair *Heahengel*.'

'I hear there's a new Danish leader in the Sæfern Sea,' I said, 'and I'd like to know if it's true. A man called Svein. And I hear more ships are joining him from Ireland.'

'He's in Wales, this Svein?'

'That's what I hear.'

'He'll be coming to Wessex then,' Leofric said.

'If it's true.'

'So you're thinking . . .' Leofric said, then stopped when he realised just what I was thinking.

'I'm thinking that it doesn't do a ship or crew any good to sit around for a month,' I said, 'and I'm thinking that there might be plunder to be had in the Sæfern Sea.'

'And if Alfred hears we've been fighting up there,' Leofric said, 'he'll gut us.'

I nodded up river towards Exanceaster. 'They burned a hundred Danish ships up there,' I said, 'and their wreckage is still on the riverbank. We should be able to find at least one dragon's head to put on her prow.'

Leofric stared at the *Eftwyrd*. 'Disguise her?'

'Disguise her,' I said, because if I put a dragon head on *Eftwyrd* no one would know she was a Saxon ship. She would be taken for a Danish boat, a sea raider, part of England's nightmare.

Leofric smiled. 'I don't need orders to go on a patrol, do I?'

'Of course not.'

'And we haven't fought since Cynuit,' he said wistfully, 'and no fighting means no plunder.'

'What about the crew?' I asked.

He turned and looked at them. 'Most of them are evil bastards,' he said, 'they won't mind. And they all need plunder.'

'And between us and the Sæfern Sea,' I said, 'there are the Britons.'

'And they're all thieving bastards, the lot of them,' Leofric said. He looked at me and grinned. 'So if Alfred won't go to war, we will?'

'You have any better ideas?' I asked.

Leofric did not answer for a long time. Instead, idly, as if he was just thinking, he tossed pebbles towards a puddle. I said nothing, just watched the small splashes, watched the pattern the fallen pebbles made, and knew he was seeking guidance from fate. The Danes cast rune sticks, we all watched for the flight of birds, we tried to hear the whispers of the gods, and Leofric was watching the pebbles fall to find his fate. The last one clicked on another and skidded off into the mud and the trail it left pointed south towards the sea. 'No,' he said, 'I don't have any better ideas.'

And I was bored no longer, because we were going to be Vikings.

We found a score of carved beasts' heads beside the river beneath Exanceaster's walls, all of them part of the sodden, tangled wreckage that showed where Guthrum's fleet had been burned and we chose two of the least scorched carvings and carried them aboard *Eftwyrd*. Her prow and stern culminated in simple posts and we had to cut the posts down until the sockets of the two carved heads fitted. The creature at the stern, the smaller of the two, was a gape-mouthed serpent, probably intended to represent Corpse-Ripper, the monster that tore at the dead in the Danish underworld, while the beast we placed at the bow was a dragon's head, though it was so blackened and disfigured by fire that it looked more like a horse's head. We dug into the scorched eyes until we

46

found unburned wood, and did the same with the open mouth and when we were finished the thing looked dramatic and fierce. 'Looks like a fyrdraca now,' Leofric said happily. A fire-dragon.

The Danes could always remove the dragon or beast-heads from the bows and sterns of their ships because they did not want the horrid-looking creatures to frighten the spirits of friendly land and so they only displayed the carved monsters when they were in enemy waters. We did the same, hiding our fyrdraca and serpent head in *Eftwyrd*'s bilges as we went back down river to where the shipwrights were beginning their work on *Heahengel*. We hid the beast-heads because Leofric did not want the shipwrights to know he planned mischief. 'That one,' he jerked his head towards a tall, lean, grey-haired man who was in charge of the work, 'is more Christian than the Pope. He'd bleat to the local priests if he thought we were going off to fight someone, and the priests will tell Alfred and then Burgweard will take *Eftwyrd* away from me.'

'You don't like Burgweard?'

Leofric spat for answer. 'It's a good thing there are no Danes on the coast.'

'He's a coward?'

'No coward. He just thinks God will fight the battles. We spend more time on our knees than at the oars. When you commanded the fleet we made money. Now even the rats on board are begging for crumbs.'

We had made money by capturing Danish ships and taking their plunder, and though none of us had become rich we had all possessed silver to spare. I was still wealthy enough because I had a hoard hidden at Oxton, a hoard that was the legacy of Ragnar the Elder, and a hoard that the church and Oswald's relatives would make their own if they could, but a man can never have enough silver. Silver buys land, it buys the loyalty of warriors, it is the power of a lord, and without silver a man must bend the knee or else become a slave. The Danes led men by the lure of silver, and we were no different. If I was to be a lord, if I was to storm the walls of Bebbanburg, then I would need men and I would need a great hoard to buy the swords and shields and spears and hearts of warriors, and so we would go to sea and look for silver, though we told the shipwrights that we merely planned to patrol the coast. We shipped barrels of ale, boxes of hard-baked bread, cheeses, kegs of smoked mackerel and flitches of bacon. I told Mildrith the same story, that we would be sailing back and forth along the shores of Defnascir and Thornsæta. 'Which is what we should be doing anyway,' Leofric said, 'just in case a Dane arrives.'

'The Danes are lying low,' I said.

Leofric nodded. 'And when a Dane lies low you know there's trouble coming.'

I believed he was right. Guthrum was not far from Wessex, and Svein, if he existed, was just a day's voyage from her north coast. Alfred might believe his truce would hold and that the hostages would secure it, but I knew from my childhood how land-hungry the Danes were, and how they lusted after the lush fields and rich pastures of Wessex. They would come, and if Guthrum did not lead them then another Danish chieftain would gather ships and men and bring his swords and axes to Alfred's kingdom. The Danes, after all, ruled the other three English kingdoms. They held my own Northumbria, they were bringing settlers to East Anglia and their language was spreading southwards through Mercia, and they would not want the last English kingdom flourishing to their south. They were like wolves, shadow-skulking for the moment, but watching a flock of sheep fatten.

I recruited eleven young men from my land and took them on board *Eftwyrd*, and brought Haesten too, and he was useful for he had spent much of his young life at the oars. Then, one misty morning, as the strong tide ebbed westwards, we slid *Eftwyrd* away from the river's bank, rowed her past the low sandspit that guards the Uisc and so out to the long swells of the sea. The oars creaked in their leather-lined holes, the bow's breast split the waves to shatter water white along the hull, and the steering oar fought against my touch and I felt my spirits rise to the small wind and I looked up into the pearly sky and said a prayer of thanks to Thor, Odin, Njord and Hoder.

A few small fishing boats dotted the inshore waters, but as we went south and west, away from the land, the sea emptied. I looked back at the low dun hills slashed brighter green where rivers pierced the coast, and then the green faded to grey, the land became a shadow and we were alone with the white birds crying and it was then we heaved the serpent's head and the fyrdraca from the bilge and slotted them over the posts at stem and stern, pegged them into place and turned our bows westwards.

The *Eftwyrd* was no more. Now the *Fyrdraca* sailed, and she was hunting trouble.

Three

The crew of the *Eftwyrd* turned *Fyrdraca* had been at Cynuit with me. They were fighting men and they were offended that Odda the Younger had taken credit for a battle they had won. They had also been bored since the battle. Once in a while, Leofric told me, Burgweard exercised his fleet by taking it to sea, but most of the time they waited in Hamtun. 'We did go fishing once, though,' Leofric admitted.

'Fishing?'

'Father Willibald preached a sermon about feeding five thousand folk with two scraps of bread and a basket of herring,' he said, 'so Burgweard said we should take nets out and fish. He wanted to feed the town, see? Lots of hungry folk.'

'Did you catch anything?'

'Mackerel. Lots of mackerel.'

'But no Danes?'

'No Danes,' Leofric said, 'and no herring, only mackerel. The bastard Danes have vanished.'

We learned later that Guthrum had given orders that no Danish ships were to raid the Wessex coast and so break the truce. Alfred was to be lulled into a conviction that peace had come, and that meant there were no pirates roaming the seas between Kent and Cornwalum and their absence encouraged traders to come from the lands to the south to sell wine or to buy fleeces. The *Fyrdraca* took two such ships in the first four days. They were both Frankish ships, tubby in their hulls, and neither with more than six oars a side, and both believed the *Fyrdraca* was a Viking ship for they saw her beast-heads, and they heard Haesten and I talk Danish and they saw my arm rings. We did not kill the crews, but just stole their coins, weapons and as much of their cargo as we could carry. One ship was heaped with bales of wool, for the folk across the water prized Saxon fleeces, but we could take only three of the bales for fear of cluttering the *Fyrdraca*'s benches.

At night we found a cove or river's mouth, and by day we rowed to sea and looked for prey, and each day we went further westwards until I was sure we were off the coast of Cornwalum, and that was enemy country. It was the old enemy that had confronted our ancestors when they first came across the North Sea to make England. That enemy spoke a strange language, and some Britons lived north of Northumbria and others lived in Wales or in Cornwalum, all places on the wild edges of the isle of Britain where they had been pushed by our coming. They were Christians, indeed Father Beocca had told me they had been Christians before we were and he claimed that no one who was a Christian could be a real enemy of another Christian, but nevertheless the Britons hated us. Sometimes they allied themselves with the Northmen to attack us, and sometimes the Northmen raided them, and sometimes they made war against us on their own, and in the past the men of Cornwalum had made much trouble for Wessex, though Leofric claimed they had been punished so badly that they now pissed themselves whenever they saw a Saxon.

Not that we saw any Britons at first. The places we sheltered were deserted, all except one river mouth where a skin boat pushed off shore and a half naked man paddled out to us and held up some crabs which he wanted to sell to us. We took a basketful of the beasts and paid him two pennies. Next night we grounded *Fyrdraca* on a rising tide and collected fresh water from a stream, and Leofric and I climbed a hill and stared inland. Smoke rose from distant valleys, but there was no one in sight, not even a shepherd. 'What are you expecting,' Leofric asked, 'enemies?'

'A monastery,' I said.

'A monastery!' He was amused. 'You want to pray?'

'Monasteries have silver,' I said.

'Not down here, they don't. They're poor as stoats. Besides.'

'Besides what?'

He jerked his head towards the crew. 'You've got a dozen good Christians aboard. Lot of bad ones too, of course, but at least a dozen good ones. They won't raid a monastery with you.' He was right. A few of the men had showed some scruples about piracy, but I assured them that the Danes used trading ships to spy on their enemies. That was true enough, though I doubt either of our victims had been serving the Danes, but both ships had been crewed by foreigners and, like all Saxons, the crew of the *Fyrdraca* had a healthy dislike of foreigners, though they made an exception for Haesten and the dozen crewmen who were Frisians. The Frisians were natural pirates, bad as the Danes, and these twelve had come to Wessex to get rich from war and so were glad that the *Fyrdraca* was seeking plunder.

As we went west we began to see coastal settlements, and some were surprisingly large. Cenwulf, who had fought with us at Cynuit and was a good man, told us that the Britons of Cornwalum dug tin out of the ground and sold it to strangers. He knew that because his father had been a trader and had frequently sailed this coast. 'If they sell tin,' I said, 'then they must have money.'

'And men to guard it,' Cenwulf said drily.

'Do they have a king?'

No one knew. It seemed probable, though where the king lived or who he was we could not know, and perhaps, as Haesten suggested, there was more than one king. They did have weapons because, one night, as the *Fyrdraca* crept into a bay, an arrow flew from a clifftop to be swallowed in the sea beside our oars. We might never have known that arrow had been shot except I happened to be looking up and saw it, fledged with dirty grey feathers, flickering down from the sky to vanish with a plop. One arrow, and no others followed, so perhaps it was a warning, and that night we let the ship lie at its anchor and in the dawn we saw two cows grazing close to a stream and Leofric fetched his axe. 'The cows are there to kill us,' Haesten warned us in his new and not very good English.

'The cows will kill us?' I asked in amusement.

'I have seen it before, lord. They put cows to bring us on land, then they attack.'

We granted the cows mercy, hauled the anchor and pulled towards the bay's mouth and a howl sounded behind us and I saw a crowd of men appear from behind bushes and trees, and I took one of the silver rings from my left arm and gave it to Haesten. It was his first arm ring and, being a Dane, he was inordinately proud of it. He polished it all morning.

The coast became wilder and refuge more difficult to find, but the weather was placid. We captured a small eight-oared ship that was returning to Ireland and relieved it of sixteen pieces of silver, three knives, a heap of tin ingots, a sack of goose feathers and six goatskins. We were hardly becoming rich, though *Fyrdraca*'s belly was becoming cluttered with pelts, fleeces and ingots of tin. 'We need to sell it all,' Leofric said.

But to whom? We knew no one who traded here. What

I needed to do, I thought, was land close to one of the larger settlements and steal everything. Burn the houses, kill the men, plunder the headman's hall and go back to sea, but the Britons kept lookouts on the headlands and they always saw us coming, and whenever we were close to one of their towns we would see armed men waiting. They had learned how to deal with Vikings, which was why, Haesten told me, the Northmen now sailed in fleets of five or six ships.

'Things will be better,' I said, 'when we turn the coast.' I knew Cornwalum ended somewhere to the west and we could then sail up into the Sæfern Sea where we might find a Danish ship on its voyage from Ireland, but Cornwalum seemed to be without end. Whenever we saw a headland that I thought must mark the end of the land it turned out to be a false hope, for another cliff would lie beyond, and then another, and sometimes the tide flowed so strongly that even when we sailed due west we were driven back east. Being a Viking was more difficult than I thought, and then one day the wind freshened from the west and the waves heaved higher and their tops were torn ragged and rain squalls hissed dark from a low sky and we ran north-wards to seek shelter in the lee of a headland. We dropped our anchor there and felt *Fyrdraca* jerk and tug like a fretful horse at her long rope of twisted hide.

All night and all next day the weather raged past the headland. Water shattered white on high cliffs. We were safe enough, but our food was getting low, and I had half decided we must abandon our plans to make ourselves rich and sail back to the Uisc where we could pretend we had only been patrolling the coast, but on our second dawn under the lee of that high cliff, as the wind subsided and the rain dropped to a chill drizzle, a ship appeared about the eastern spit of land.

'Shields!' Leofric shouted, and the men, cold and unhappy, found their weapons and lined the ship's side.

The ship was smaller than ours, much smaller. She was squat, high-bowed, with a stumpy mast holding a wide yard on which a dirty sail was furled. A half-dozen oarsmen manned her, and the steersman was bringing her directly towards *Fyrdraca*, and then, as she came closer and as her small bows broke the water white, I saw a green bough had been tied to her short mast.

'They want to talk,' I said.

'Let's hope they want to buy,' Leofric grumbled.

There was a priest in the small ship. I did not know he was a priest at first, for he looked as ragged as any of the crewmen, but he shouted that he wished to speak with us, and he spoke Danish, though not well, and I let the boat come up on the flank protected from the wind where her crewmen gazed up at a row of armed men holding shields. Cenwulf and I pulled the priest over our side. Two other men wanted to follow, but Leofric threatened them with a spear and they dropped back and the smaller ship drew away to wait while the priest spoke with us.

He was called Father Mardoc and, once he was aboard and sitting wetly on one of *Fyrdraca*'s rowing benches, I saw the crucifix about his neck. 'I hate Christians,' I said, 'so why should we not feed you to Njord?'

He ignored that, or perhaps he did not know that Njord was one of the sea gods. 'I bring you a gift,' he said, 'from my master,' and he produced, from beneath his cloak, two battered arm rings.

I took them. They were poor things, mere ringlets of copper, old, filthy with verdigris and of almost no value, and for a moment I was tempted to toss them scornfully into the sea, but reckoned our voyage had made such small profit that even those scabby treasures must be kept. 'Who is your master?' I asked.

'King Peredur.'

I almost laughed. King Peredur? A man can expect a king to be famous, but I had never heard of Peredur which suggested he was little more than a local chieftain with a high-sounding title. 'And why does this Peredur,' I asked, 'send me miserable gifts?'

Father Mardoc still did not know my name and was too frightened to ask it. He was surrounded by men in leather, men in mail, and by shields and swords, axes and spears, and he believed all of us were Danes for I had ordered any of *Fyrdraca*'s crew who wore crosses or crucifixes to hide them beneath their clothes. Only Haesten and I spoke, and if Father Mardoc thought that strange he did not say anything of it, instead he told me how his lord, King Peredur, had been treacherously attacked by a neighbour called Callyn, and Callyn's forces had taken a high fort close to the sea and Peredur would pay us well if we were to help him recapture the fort that was called Dreyndynas.

I sent Father Mardoc to sit in the *Fyrdraca*'s bow while we talked about his request. Some things were obvious. Being paid well did not mean we would become rich, but that Peredur would try to fob us off with as little as possible and, most likely, having given it to us he would then try to take it back by killing us all. 'What we should do,' Leofric advised, 'is find this man Callyn and see what he'll pay us.'

Which was good enough advice except none of us knew how to find Callyn, whom we later learned was King Callyn, which did not mean much for any man with a following of more than fifty armed men called himself a king in Cornwalum, and so I went to the *Fyrdraca*'s bows and talked with Father Mardoc again, and he told me that Dreyndynas was a high fort, built by the old people, and that it guarded the road eastwards, and so long as Callyn held the fort, so long were Peredur's people trapped in their lands.

'You have ships,' I pointed out.

57

'And Callyn has ships,' he said, 'and we cannot take cattle in ships.'

'Cattle?'

'We need to sell cattle to live,' he said.

So Callyn had surrounded Peredur and we represented a chance to tip the balance in this little war. 'So how much will your king pay us?' I asked.

'A hundred pieces of silver,' he said.

I drew Serpent-Breath. 'I worship the real gods,' I told him, 'and I am a particular servant of Hoder, and Hoder likes blood and I have given him none in many days.'

Father Mardoc looked terrified, which was sensible of him. He was a young man, though it was hard to tell for his hair and beard were so thick that most of the time he was just a broken nose and pair of eyes surrounded by a greasy black tangle. He told me he had learned to speak Danish when he had been enslaved by a chieftain called Godfred, but that he had managed to escape when Godfred raided the Sillans, islands that lay well out in the western sea-wastes. 'Is there any wealth in the Sillans?' I asked him. I had heard of the islands, though some men claimed they were mythical and others said the islands came and went with the moons, but Father Mardoc said they existed and were called the Isles of the Dead.

'So no one lives there?' I asked.

'Some folk do,' he said, 'but the dead have their houses there.'

'Do they have wealth as well?'

'Your ships have taken it all,' he said. This was after he had promised me that Peredur would be more generous, though he did not know how generous, but he said the king was willing to pay far more than a hundred silver coins for our help, and so we had him shout to his ship that they were to lead us around the coast to Peredur's settlement.

I did not let Father Mardoc go back to his ship for he would serve as a hostage if the tale he had told us was false and Peredur was merely luring us to an ambush.

He was not. Peredur's home was a huddle of buildings built on a steep hill beside a bay and protected by a wall of thorn bushes. His people lived within the wall and some were fishermen and some were cattle herders and none was wealthy, though the king himself had a high hall where he welcomed us, though not before we had taken more hostages. Three young men, all of whom we were assured were Peredur's sons, were delivered to *Fyrdraca* and I gave the crew orders that the three were to be killed if I did not return, and then I went ashore with Haesten and Cenwulf. I went dressed for war, with mail coat and helmet polished, and Peredur's folk watched the three of us pass with frightened eyes. The place stank of fish and shit. The people were ragged and their houses mere hovels that were built up the side of the steep hill that was crowned with Peredur's hall. There was a church beside the hall, its thatch thick with moss and its gable decorated with a cross made from sea-whitened driftwood.

Peredur was twice my age, a squat man with a sly face and a forked black beard. He greeted us from a throne, which was just a chair with a high back, and he waited for us to bow to him, but none of us did and that made him scowl. A dozen men were with him, evidently his courtiers, though none looked wealthy and all were elderly except for one much younger man who was in the robes of a Christian monk, and he stood out in that smoke-darkened hall like a raven in a clutch of gulls for his black robes were clean, his face close-shaven and his hair and tonsure neatly trimmed. He was scarcely older than I, was thin and stern-faced, and that face looked clever, and it also carried an expression of marked distaste for us. We were pagans, or at least Haesten and I were pagans and I had told Cenwulf to keep his mouth shut and his crucifix hidden, and so the monk assumed all three of us were heathen Danes. The monk spoke Danish, far better Danish than Father Mardoc. 'The king greets you,' he said. He had a voice as thin as his lips and as unfriendly as his pale green eyes. 'He greets you and would know who you are.'

'My name is Uhtred Ragnarson,' I said.

'Why are you here, Uhtred Ragnarson?' the priest asked.

I contemplated him. I did not just look at him, but I studied him as a man might study an ox before killing it. I gave him a look which suggested I was wondering where to make the cuts, and he got my meaning and did not wait for an answer to his question, an answer which was obvious if we were Danes. We were here to thieve and kill, of course, what else did he think a Viking ship would be doing?

Peredur spoke to the monk and they muttered for some time and I looked around the hall, searching for any evidence of wealth. I saw almost nothing except for three whalebones stacked in a corner, but Peredur plainly had some treasure for he wore a great heavy torque of bronze about his neck and there were silver rings on his grubby fingers, an amber brooch at the neck of his cloak and a golden crucifix hidden in the cloak's lice-ridden folds. He would keep his hoard buried, I thought, and I doubted any of us would become rich from this alliance, but in truth we were not becoming rich from our voyage either, and at least Peredur would have to feed us while we haggled.

'The king,' the monk interrupted my thoughts, 'wishes to know how many men you can lead against the enemy.'

'Enough,' I said flatly.

'Does that not depend,' the monk observed slyly, 'on how many enemy there are?'

'No,' I said. 'It depends on this,' and I slapped Serpent-Breath's hilt. It was a good, arrogant reply, and probably what the monk expected. And, in truth, it was convincing for I was broad in the chest and a giant in this hall where I was a full head taller than any other man. 'And who are you, monk?' I demanded.

'My name is Asser,' he said. It was a British name, of course, and in the English tongue it meant a he-ass, and ever after I thought of him as the Ass. And there was to be a lot of the ever after for, though I did not know it, I had just met a man who would haunt my life like a louse. I had met another enemy, though on that day in Peredur's hall he was just a strange British monk who stood out from his companions because he washed. He invited me to follow him to a small door at the side of the hall and, motioning Haesten and Cenwulf to stay where they were, I ducked through the door to find myself standing beside a dung-heap, but the point of taking me outside had been to show me the view eastwards.

I stared across a valley. On the nearer slope were the smoke-blackened roofs of Peredur's settlement, then came the thorn fence that had been made along the stream which flowed to the sea. On the stream's far side the hills rose gently to a far off crest and there, breaking the skyline like a boil, was Dreyndynas. 'The enemy,' Asser said.

A small fort, I noted. 'How many men are there?'

'Does it matter to you?' Asser asked sourly, paying me back for my refusal to tell him how many men I led, though I assumed Father Mardoc had made a count of the crew while he was on board *Fyrdraca*, so my defiance had been pointless.

'You Christians,' I said, 'believe that at death you go to heaven. Isn't that right?'

'What of it?'

'You must surely welcome such a fate?' I asked. 'To be near your god?'

'Are you threatening me?'

'I don't threaten vermin,' I said, enjoying myself. 'How many men are in that fort?'

'Forty? Fifty?' He plainly did not know. 'We can assemble forty.'

'So tomorrow,' I said, 'your king can have his fort back.'

'He is not my king,' Asser said, irritated by the assumption.

'Your king or not,' I said, 'he can have his fort back so long as he pays us properly.'

That negotiation lasted until dark. Peredur, as Father Mardoc had said, was willing to pay more than a hundred shillings, but he feared we would take the money and leave without fighting and so he wanted some kind of surety from me. He wanted hostages, which I refused to give, and after an hour or more of argument we had still not reached an agreement, and it was then that Peredur summoned his queen. That meant nothing to me, but I saw the Ass stiffen as though he were offended, then sensed that every other man in the hall was strangely apprehensive. Asser made a protest, but the king cut him off with an abrupt slice of his hand and then a door at the back of the hall was opened and Iseult came to my life.

Iseult. Finding her there was like discovering a jewel of gold in a midden. I saw her and I forgot Mildrith. Dark Iseult, black-haired Iseult, huge-eyed Iseult. She was small, thin as an elf, with a luminous face and hair as black as a raven's feathers. She wore a black cloak and had silver bands about her neck and silver bracelets at her wrists and silver rings at her ankles and the jewellery clinked gently as she walked towards us. She was maybe two or three years younger than me, but somehow, despite her youth, she managed to scare Peredur's courtiers who backed away from her. The king looked nervous, while Asser, standing beside me, made the sign of the cross, then spat to ward off evil.

I just stared at her, entranced. There was pain on her face, as if she found life unbearable, and there was fear on her husband's face when he spoke to her in a quiet, respectful voice. She shuddered when he talked and I thought that perhaps she was mad, for the grimace on her face was awful, disfiguring her beauty, but then she calmed and looked at me and the king spoke to Asser.

'You will tell the queen who you are and what you will do for King Peredur,' Asser told me in a distant, disapproving voice.

'She speaks Danish?' I asked.

'Of course not,' he snapped. 'Just tell her and get this farce over.'

I looked into her eyes, those big, dark eyes, and had the uncanny suspicion that she could see right through my gaze and decipher my innermost thoughts. But at least she did not grimace when she saw me as she had when her husband spoke. 'My name is Uhtred Ragnarson,' I said, 'and I am here to fight for your husband if he pays what I am worth. And if he doesn't pay, we go.'

I thought Asser would translate, but the monk stayed silent.

Iseult still stared at me and I stared back. She had a flaw-less skin, untouched by illness, and a strong face, but sad. Sad and beautiful. Fierce and beautiful. She reminded me of Brida, the East Anglian who had been my lover and who was now with Ragnar, my friend. Brida was as full of fury as a scabbard is filled with blade, and I sensed the same in this queen who was so young and strange and dark and lovely.

'I am Uhtred Ragnarson,' I heard myself speaking again, though I had scarcely been aware of any urge to talk, 'and I work miracles.'

Why I said that I do not know. I later learned that she had no idea what I had said, for at that time the only tongue she spoke was that of the Britons, but nevertheless she seemed to understand me and she smiled. Asser caught his breath. 'Be careful, Dane,' he hissed, 'she is a queen.'

'A queen?' I asked, still staring at her, 'or the queen?'

'The king is blessed with three wives,' the monk said disapprovingly.

Iseult turned away and spoke to the king. He nodded, then gestured respectfully towards the door through which Iseult had come. She was evidently dismissed and she obediently went to the door, but paused there and gave me a last, speculative look. Then she was gone.

And suddenly it was easy. Peredur agreed to pay us a hoard of silver. He showed us the hoard that had been hidden in a back room. There were coins, broken jewellery, battered cups and three candleholders which had been taken from the church, and when I weighed the silver, using a balance fetched from the market place, I discovered there was three hundred and sixteen shillings' worth, which was not negligible. Asser divided it into two piles, one only half the size of the other. 'We shall give you the smaller portion tonight,' the monk said, 'and the rest you will get when Dreyndynas is recovered.'

'You think I am a fool?' I asked, knowing that after the fight it would be hard to get the rest of the silver.

'You take me for one?' he retorted, knowing that if he gave us all the silver then *Fyrdraca* would vanish in the dawn.

We agreed in the end that we would take the one third now and that the other two thirds would be carried to the battlefield so that it was easily accessible. Peredur had hoped I would leave that larger portion in his hall, and then I would have faced an uphill fight through his dung-spattered streets, and that was a fight I would have lost, and it was probably the prospect of such a battle that had stopped Callyn's men attacking Peredur's hall. They hoped to starve him, or at least Asser believed that.

'Tell me about Iseult,' I demanded of the monk when the bargaining was done.

He sneered at that. 'I can read you like a missal,' he said.

'Whatever a missal is,' I said, pretending ignorance.

'A book of prayers,' he said, 'and you will need prayers if you touch her.' He made the sign of the cross. 'She is evil,' he said vehemently.

'She's a queen, a young queen,' I said, 'so how can she be evil?'

'What do you know of the Britons?'

'That they stink like stoats,' I said, 'and thieve like jackdaws.'

He gave me a sour look and, for a moment, I thought he would refuse to say more, but he swallowed his British pride. 'We are Christians,' he said, 'and God be thanked for that great mercy, but among our people there are still some old superstitions. Pagan ways. Iseult is part of that.'

'What part?'

He did not like talking about it, but he had raised the subject of Iseult's evil and so he reluctantly explained. 'She was born in the springtime,' he said, 'eighteen years ago, and at her birth there was an eclipse of the sun, and the folk here are credulous fools and they believe a dark child born at the sun's death has power. They have made her into a,' he paused, not knowing the Danish word, 'a *gwrach*,' he said, a word that meant nothing to me. '*Dewines*,' he said irritably and, when I still showed incomprehension, he at last found a word. 'A sorceress.'

'A witch?'

'And Peredur married her. Made her his shadow queen.

That is what kings did with such girls. They take them into their households so they may use their power.'

'What power?'

'The skills the devil gives to shadow queens, of course,' he said irritably. 'Peredur believes she can see the future. But it is a skill she will retain only so long as she is a virgin.'

I laughed at that. 'If you disapprove of her, monk, then I would be doing you a favour if I raped her.' He ignored that, or at least he made no reply other than to give me a harsh scowl. 'Can she see the future?' I asked.

'She saw you victorious,' he said, 'and told the king he could trust you, so you tell me?'

'Then assuredly she can see the future,' I said.

Brother Asser sneered at that answer. 'They should have strangled her with her own birth-cord,' he snarled. 'She is a pagan bitch, a devil's thing, evil.'

There was a feast that night, a feast to celebrate our pact and I hoped Iseult would be there, but she was not. Peredur's older wife was present, but she was a sullen, grubby creature with two weeping boils on her neck and she hardly spoke. Yet it was a surprisingly good feast. There was fish, beef, mutton, bread, ale, mead and cheese, and while we ate Asser told me he had come from the kingdom of Dyfed, which lay north of the Sæfern Sea, and that his king, who had an impossible British name which sounded like a man coughing and spluttering, had sent him to Cornwalum to dissuade the British kings from supporting the Danes.

I was surprised by that, so surprised that I looked away from the girls serving the food. A harpist played at the hall's end and two of the girls swayed in time to the music as they walked. 'You don't like Danes,' I said.

'You are pagans,' Asser said scornfully.

'So how come you speak the pagan tongue?' I asked.

66

'Because my abbot would have us send missionaries to the Danes.'

'You should go,' I said. 'It would be a quick route to heaven for you.'

He ignored that. 'I learned Danish among many other tongues,' he said loftily, 'and I speak the language of the Saxons too. And you, I think, were not born in Denmark?'

'How do you know?'

'Your voice,' he said. 'You are from Northumbria?'

'I am from the sea,' I said.

He shrugged. 'In Northumbria,' he said severely, 'the Danes have corrupted the Saxons so that they think of themselves as Danes.' He was wrong, but I was scarcely in a position to correct him. 'Worse,' he went on, 'they have extinguished the light of Christ.'

'Is the light of Thor too bright for you?'

'The West Saxons are Christians,' he said, 'and it is our duty to support them, not because of a love for them, but because of our fellow love for Christ.'

'You have met Alfred of Wessex?' I asked sourly.

'I look forward to meeting him,' he said fervently, 'for I hear he is a good Christian.'

'I hear the same.'

'And Christ rewards him,' Asser went on.

'Rewards him?'

'Christ sent the storm that destroyed the Danish fleet,' Asser said, 'and Christ's angels destroyed Ubba. That is proof of God's power. If we fight against Alfred then we range ourselves against Christ, so we must not do it. That is my message to the kings of Cornwalum.'

I was impressed that a British monk at the end of the land of Britain knew so much of what happened in Wessex, and I reckoned Alfred would have been pleased to hear Asser's nonsense, though of course Alfred had sent many messengers to the British. His messengers had all been priests or monks and they had preached the gospel of their god slaughtering the Danes, and Asser had evidently taken up their message enthusiastically. 'So why are you fighting Callyn?' I asked.

'He would join the Danes,' Asser said.

'And we're going to win,' I said, 'so Callyn is sensible.'

Asser shook his head. 'God will prevail.'

'You hope,' I said, touching the small amulet of Thor's hammer I wore on a thong around my neck. 'But if you are wrong, monk, then we'll take Wessex and Callyn will share the spoils.'

'Callyn will share nothing,' Asser said spitefully, 'because you will kill him tomorrow.'

The Britons have never learned to love the Saxons. Indeed they hate us, and in those years when the last English kingdom was on the edge of destruction, they could have tipped the balance by joining Guthrum. Instead they held back their sword arms, and for that the Saxons can thank the church. Men like Asser had decided that the Danish heretics were a worse enemy than English Christians, and if I were a Briton I would resent that, because the Britons might have taken back much of their lost lands if they had allied themselves with the pagan Northmen. Religion makes strange bedfellows.

So does war, and Peredur offered Haesten and myself two of the serving girls to seal our bargain. I had sent Cenwulf back to *Fyrdraca* with a message for Leofric, warning him to be ready to fight in the morning, and I thought perhaps Haesten and I should retreat to the ship, but the serving girls were pretty and so we stayed, and I need not have worried for no one tried to kill us in the night, and no one even tried when Haesten and I carried the first third of the silver down to the water's edge where a small boat carried us to our ship. 'There's twice as much as that waiting for us,' I told Leofric.

He stirred the sack of silver with his foot. 'And where were you last night?'

'In bed with a Briton.'

'Earsling,' he said. 'So who are we fighting?'

'A pack of savages.'

We left ten men as ship guards. If Peredur's men made a real effort to capture *Fyrdraca* then those ten would have had a hard fight, and probably a losing fight, but they had the three hostages who may or may not have been Peredur's sons, so that was a risk we had to take, and it seemed safe enough because Peredur had assembled his army on the eastern side of the town. I say army, though it was only forty men, and I brought thirty more, and my thirty were well armed and looked ferocious in their leather. Leofric, like me, wore mail, as did half a dozen of my crewmen, and I had my fine helmet with its face-plate so I, at least, looked like a lord of battles.

Peredur was in leather, and he had woven black horse-tails into his hair and onto the twin forks of his beard so that the horsetails hung down wild and long and scary. His men were mostly armed with spears, though Peredur himself possessed a fine sword. Some of his men had shields and a few had helmets, and though I did not doubt their bravery I did not reckon them formidable. My crewmen were formidable. They had fought Danish ships off the Wessex coast and they had fought in the shield wall at Cynuit and I had no doubt that we could destroy whatever troops Callyn had placed in Dreyndynas.

It was afternoon before we climbed the hill. We should have gone in the morning, but some of Peredur's men were recovering from their night's drinking, and the women of his settlement kept pulling others away, not wanting them to die, and then Peredur and his advisers huddled and talked about how they should fight the battle, though what there was to talk about I did not know. Callyn's men were in the fort, we were outside it, so we had to assault the bastards. Nothing clever, just an attack, but they talked for a long time, and Father Mardoc said a prayer, or rather he shouted it, and then I refused to advance because the rest of the silver had not been fetched.

It came, carried in a chest by two men, and so at last, under the afternoon sun, we climbed the eastern hill. Some women followed us, shrieking their battle-screams, which was a waste of breath because the enemy was still too far away to hear them.

'So what do we do?' Leofric asked me.

'Form a wedge,' I guessed. 'Our best men in the front rank and you and me in front of them, then kill the bastards.'

He grimaced. 'Have you ever assaulted one of the old people's forts?'

'Never.'

'It can be hard,' he warned me.

'If it's too hard,' I said, 'we'll just kill Peredur and his men and take their silver anyway.'

Brother Asser, his neat black robes muddied about their skirts, hurried over to me. 'Your men are Saxons!' he said accusingly.

'I hate monks,' I snarled at him. 'I hate them more than I hate priests. I like killing them. I like slitting their bellies. I like watching the bastards die. Now run off and die before I cut your throat.'

He ran off to Peredur with his news that we were Saxons. The king stared at us morosely. He had thought he had recruited a crew of Danish Vikings, and now he discovered we were West Saxons and he was not happy, so I drew Serpent-Breath and banged her blade against my limewood shield. 'You want to fight this battle or not?' I asked him through Asser.

Peredur decided he wanted to fight, or rather he wanted us to fight the battle for him, and so we slogged on up the hill which had a couple of false crests so it was well into the afternoon before we emerged onto the long, shallow summit and could see Dreyndynas's green turf walls on the skyline. A banner flew there. It was a triangle of cloth, supported on its pole by a small cross-staff, and the banner showed a white horse prancing on a green field.

I stopped then. Peredur's banner was a wolf's tail hung from a pole, I carried none, though, like most Saxons, mine would have been a rectangular flag. I only knew one people who flew triangular banners and I turned on Brother Asser as he sweated up the hill. 'They're Danes,' I accused him.

'So?' he demanded. 'I thought you were a Dane, and all the world knows the Danes will fight anyone for silver, even other Danes. But are you frightened of them, Saxon?'

'Your mother didn't give birth to you,' I told him, 'but farted you out of her shrivelled arsehole.'

'Frightened or not,' Asser said, 'you've taken Peredur's silver, so you must fight them now.'

'Say one more word, monk,' I said, 'and I'll cut off your scrawny balls.' I was gazing uphill, trying to estimate numbers. Everything had changed since I had seen the white horse banner because instead of fighting against half-armed British savages we would have to take on a crew of lethal Danes, but if I was surprised by that, then the Danes were equally surprised to see us. They were crowding Dreyndynas's wall, which was made of earth fronted with a ditch and topped with a thorn fence. It would be a hard wall to attack, I thought, especially if it was defended by Danes. I counted over forty men on the skyline and knew there would be others I could not see, and the numbers

71

alone told me this assault would fail. We could attack, and we might well get as far as the thorn palisade, but I doubted we could hack our way through, and the Danes would kill a score of us as we tried, and we would be lucky to retreat down the hill without greater loss.

'We're in a cesspit,' Leofric said to me.

'Up to our necks.'

'So what do we do? Turn on them and take the money?'

I did not answer because the Danes had dragged a section of the thorn fence aside and three of them now jumped down from the ramparts and strolled towards us. They wanted to talk.

'Who the hell is that?' Leofric asked.

He was staring at the Danish leader. He was a huge man, big as Steapa Snotor, and dressed in a mail coat that had been polished with sand until it shone. His helmet, as highly polished as his mail, had a face-plate modelled as a boar's mask with a squat, broad snout, and from the helmet's crown there flew a white horsetail. He wore arm rings over his mail, rings of silver and gold that proclaimed him to be a warrior chief, a sword-Dane, a lord of war. He walked the hillside as if he owned it, and in truth, he did own it because he possessed the fort.

Asser hurried to meet the Danes, going with Peredur and two of his courtiers. I went after them and found Asser trying to convert the Danes. He told them that God had brought us and we would slaughter them all and their best course was to surrender now and yield their heathen souls to God. 'We shall baptise you,' Asser said, 'and there will be much rejoicing in heaven.'

The Danish leader slowly pulled off his helmet and his face was almost as frightening as the boar-snouted mask. It was a broad face, hardened by sun and wind, with the blank, expressionless eyes of a killer. He was around thirty years

72

old, had a tightly-cropped beard and a scar running from the corner of his left eye down across his cheek. He gave the helmet to one of his men and, without saying a word, hauled up the skirt of his mail coat and began pissing on Asser's robe. The monk leaped back.

The Dane, still pissing, looked at me. 'Who are you?'

'Uhtred Ragnarson. And you?'

'Svein of the White Horse,' he said it defiantly, as though I would know his reputation, and for a heartbeat I said nothing. Was this the same Svein who was said to be gathering troops in Wales? Then what was he doing here?

'You're Svein of Ireland?' I asked.

'Svein of Denmark,' he said. He let the mail coat drop and glared at Asser who was threatening the Danes with heaven's vengeance. 'If you want to live,' he told Asser, 'shut your filthy mouth.' Asser shut his mouth. 'Ragnarson,' Svein looked back to me. 'Earl Ragnar? Ragnar Ravnson? The Ragnar who served Ivar?'

'The same,' I said.

'Then you are the Saxon son?'

'I am. And you?' I asked. 'You're the Svein who has brought men from Ireland?'

'I have brought men from Ireland,' he admitted.

'And gather forces in Wales?'

'I do what I do,' he said vaguely. He looked at my men, judging how well they would fight, then he looked me up and down, noting my mail and helmet, and noting especially my arm rings, and when the inspection was done he jerked his head to indicate that he and I should walk away a few paces and talk privately.

Asser objected, saying anything that was spoken should be heard by all, but I ignored him and followed Svein uphill. 'You can't take this fort,' Svein told me.

'True.'

'So what do you do?'

'Go back to Peredur's settlement, of course.'

He nodded. 'And if I attack the settlement?'

'You'll take it,' I said, 'but you'll lose men. Maybe a dozen?'

'Which will mean a dozen fewer oarsmen,' he said, thinking, and then he looked past Peredur to where two men carried the box. 'Is that your battle price?'

'It is.'

'Split it?' he suggested.

I hesitated a heartbeat. 'And we'll split what's in the town?' I asked.

'Agreed,' he said, then looked at Asser who was hissing urgently at Peredur. 'He knows what we're doing,' he said grimly, 'so a necessary deception is about to happen.' I was still trying to understand what he meant when he struck me in the face. He struck hard, and my hand went to Serpent-Breath and his two men ran to him, swords in hand.

'I'll come out of the fort and join you,' Svein said to me softly. Then, louder, 'You bastard piece of goat-dropping.'

I spat at him as his two men pretended to drag him away, then I stalked back to Asser. 'We kill them all,' I said savagely. 'We kill them all!'

'What did he say to you?' Asser asked. He had feared, rightly as it happened, that Svein and I had made our own alliance, but Svein's quick display had put doubts in the monk's mind, and I fed the doubts by raging like a madman, screaming at the retreating Svein that I would send his miserable soul to Hel who was the goddess of the dead. 'Are you going to fight?' Asser demanded.

'Of course we're going to fight!' I shouted at him, then I crossed to Leofric. 'We're on the same side as the Danes,' I told him quietly. 'We kill these Britons, capture their settle-

74

ment and split everything with the Danes. Tell the men, but tell them quietly.'

Svein, true to his word, brought his men out of Dreyndynas. That should have warned Asser and Peredur of treachery, for no sensible man would abandon a fine defensive position like a thorn-topped earth wall to fight a battle on open ground, but they put it down to Danish arrogance. They assumed Svein believed he could destroy us all in open battle, and he made that assumption more likely by parading a score of his men on horseback, suggesting that he intended to tear our shield wall open with his swords and axes and then pursue the survivors with spear-armed cavalry. He made his own shield wall in front of the horsemen, and I made another shield wall on the left of Peredur's line, and once we were in the proper array we shouted insults at each other. Leofric was going down our line, whispering to the men, and I sent Cenwulf and two others to the rear with their own orders, and just then Asser ran across to us.

'Attack,' the monk demanded, pointing at Svein.

'When we're ready,' I said, for Leofric had not yet given every man his orders.

'Attack now!' Asser spat at me, and I almost gutted the bastard on the spot and would have saved myself a good deal of future trouble if I had, but I kept my patience and Asser went back to Peredur where he began praying, both hands held high in the air, demanding that God send fire from heaven to consume the pagans.

'You trust Svein?' Leofric had come back to my side.

'I trust Svein,' I said. Why? Only because he was a Dane and I liked the Danes. These days, of course, we are all agreed that they are the spawn of Satan, untrustworthy pagans, savages, and anything else we care to call them, but in truth the Danes are warriors and they like other warriors,

75

and though it is true that Svein might have persuaded me to attack Peredur so that he could then attack us, I did not believe it. Besides, there was something I wanted in Peredur's hall and, to get her, I needed to change sides.

'*Fyrdraca*!' I shouted, and that was our signal, and we swung our shield wall around to the right and went at it.

It was, of course, an easy slaughter. Peredur's men had no belly for a fight. They had been hoping that we would take the brunt of the Danish assault and that they could then scavenge for plunder among Svein's wounded, but instead we turned on them, attacked them, and cut them down, and Svein came on their right, and Peredur's men fled. That was when Svein's horsemen kicked back their heels, levelled their spears and charged.

It was not a fight, it was a massacre. Two of Peredur's men put up some resistance, but Leofric swatted their spears aside with his axe and they died screaming, and Peredur went down to my sword, and he put up no fight at all, but seemed resigned to his death that I gave him quickly enough. Cenwulf and his two companions did what I had ordered them to do, which was to intercept the chest of silver, and we rallied around them as Svein's riders chased down the fugitives. The only man to escape was Asser, the monk, which he managed by running north instead of west. Svein's horsemen were ranging down the hill, spearing Peredur's men in the backs, and Asser saw that only death lay that way and so, with surprising quickness, he changed direction and sprinted past my men, his skirts clutched up about his knees, and I shouted at the men on the right of the line to kill the bastard, but they simply looked at me and let him go. 'I said kill him!' I snarled.

'He's a monk!' One of them answered. 'You want me to go to hell?'

I watched Asser run slantwise into the valley and, in

truth, I did not much care whether he lived or died. I thought Svein's horsemen would catch him, but perhaps they did not see him. They did catch Father Mardoc and one of them took off the priest's head with a single swing of his sword which made some of my men cross themselves.

The horsemen made their killing, but Svein's other Danes made a shield wall that faced us, and in its centre, beneath the white horse banner, was Svein himself in his boar-mask helmet. His shield had a white horse painted on its boards and his weapon was an axe, the largest war axe I had ever seen. My men shifted nervously. 'Stand still!' I snarled at them.

'Up to our necks in it,' Leofric said quietly.

Svein was staring at us and I could see the death light in his eyes. He was in a killing mood, and we were Saxons, and there was a knocking sound as his men hefted shields to make the wall, and so I tossed Serpent-Breath into the air. Tossed her high so that the big blade whirled about in the sun, and of course they were all wondering whether I would catch her or whether she would thump onto the grass.

I caught her, winked at Svein and slid the blade into her scabbard. He laughed and the killing mood passed as he realised he could not afford the casualties he would inevitably take in fighting us. 'Did you really think I was going to attack you?' he called across the springy turf.

'I was hoping you would attack me,' I called back, 'so I wouldn't have to split the plunder with you.'

He dropped the axe and walked towards us, and I walked towards him and we embraced. Men on both sides lowered weapons. 'Shall we take the bastard's miserable village?' Svein asked.

So we all went back down the hill, past the bodies of Peredur's men, and there was no one defending the thorn wall about the settlement so it was an easy matter to get inside, and a few men tried to protect their homes, but very few. Most of the folk fled to the beach, but there were not enough boats to take them away, and so Svein's Danes rounded them up and began sorting them into the useful and the dead. The useful were the young women and those who could be sold as slaves, the dead were the rest.

I took no part in that. Instead, with all of my men, I went straight to Peredur's hall. Some Danes, reckoning that was where the silver would be, were also climbing the hill, but I reached the hall first, pushed open the door and saw Iseult waiting there.

I swear she was expecting me for her face showed no fear and no surprise. She was sitting in the king's throne, but stood as if welcoming me as I walked up the hall. Then she took the silver from her neck and her wrists and her ankles and held it mutely out as an offering and I took it all and tossed it to Leofric. 'We divide it with Svein,' I said.

'And her?' He sounded amused. 'Do we share her too?'

For answer I took the cloak from about Iseult's neck. Beneath it she wore a black dress. I still had Serpent-Breath drawn and I used the bloodied blade to slash at the cloak until I could tear a strip from its hem. Iseult watched me, her face showing nothing. When the strip was torn away I gave her back the cloak, then tied one end of the cloth strip about her neck and tied the other end to my belt. 'She's mine,' I said.

More Danes were coming into the hall and some stared wolfishly at Iseult, and then Svein arrived and snarled at his men to start digging up the hall floor to search for hidden coins or silver. He grinned when he saw Iseult's leash. 'You can have her, Saxon,' he said. 'She's pretty, but I like them with more meat on the bone.'

I kept Iseult with me as we feasted that night. There was

78

a good deal of ale and mead in the settlement and so I ordered my men not to fight with the Danes, and Svein told his men not to fight with us, and on the whole we were obeyed, though inevitably some men quarrelled over the captured women and one of the boys I had brought from my estate got a knife in his belly and died in the morning.

Svein was amused that we were a West Saxon ship. 'Alfred sent you?' he asked me.

'No.'

'He doesn't want to fight, does he?'

'He'll fight,' I said, 'except he thinks his god will do the fighting for him.'

'Then he's an idiot,' Svein said, 'the gods don't do our bidding. I wish they did.' He sucked on a pork bone. 'So what are you doing here?' he asked.

'Looking for money,' I said, 'the same as you.'

'I'm looking for allies,' he said.

'Allies?'

He was drunk enough to speak more freely than he had when we first met, and I realised this was indeed the Svein who was said to be gathering men in Wales. He admitted as much, but added he did not have enough warriors. 'Guthrum can lead two thousand men to battle, maybe more! I have to match that.'

So he was a rival to Guthrum. I tucked that knowledge away. 'You think the Cornishmen will fight with you?'

'They promised they would,' he said, spitting out a shred of gristle. 'That's why I came here. But the bastards lied. Callyn isn't a proper king, he's a village chief! I'm wasting my time here.'

'Could the two of us beat Callyn?' I asked.

Svein thought about it, then nodded. 'We could.' He frowned suddenly, staring into the hall's shadows, and I saw he was looking at one of his men who had a girl on his lap.

79

He evidently liked the girl for he slapped the table, pointed to her, beckoned, and the man reluctantly brought her. Svein sat her down, pulled her tunic open so he could see her breasts, then gave her his pot of ale. 'I'll think about it,' he told me.

'Or are you thinking of attacking me?' I asked.

He grinned. 'You are Uhtred Ragnarson,' he said, 'and I heard about the fight on the river where you killed Ubba.'

I evidently had more of a reputation among my enemies than I did among my so-called friends. Svein insisted I tell the tale of Ubba's death, which I did, and I told him the truth which was that Ubba had slipped and fallen, and that had let me take his life.

'But men say you fought well,' Svein said.

Iseult listened to all this. She did not speak our language, but her big eyes seemed to follow every word. When the feast was over I took her to the small rooms at the back of the hall and she used my makeshift leash to pull me into her wood-walled chamber. I made a bed from our cloaks. 'When this is done,' I told her in words she could not understand, 'you'll have lost your power.'

She touched a finger to my lips to silence me and she was a queen so I obeyed her.

In the morning we finished ravaging the town. Iseult showed me which houses might have something of value and generally she was right though the search meant demolishing the houses, for folk hide their small treasures in their thatch, so we scattered rats and mice as we hauled down the mouldy straw and sifted through it, and afterwards we dug under every hearth, or wherever else a man might bury silver, and we collected every scrap of metal, every cooking pot or fish-hook, and the search took all day. That night we divided the hoard on the beach.

Svein had evidently thought about Callyn and, being sober by the time he did his thinking, he had decided that the king was too strong. 'We can easily beat him,' he said, 'but we'll lose men.'

A ship's crew can only endure so many losses. We had lost none in the fight against Peredur, but Callyn was a stronger king and he was bound to be suspicious of Svein which meant that he would have his household troops ready and armed. 'And he's got little enough to take,' Svein said scornfully.

'He's paying you?'

'He's paying me,' Svein said, 'just as Peredur paid you.'

'I split that with you,' I said.

'Not the money he paid you before the fight,' Svein said with a grin, 'you didn't split that.'

'What money?' I asked.

'So we're even,' he said, and we had both done well enough out of Peredur's death, for Svein had slaves and we each now possessed over nine hundred shillings' worth of silver and metal, which was not a fortune, especially once it was divided among the men, but it was better than I had done so far on the voyage. I also had Iseult. She was no longer leashed to me, but she stayed beside me and I sensed that she was happy about that. She had taken a vicious pleasure in seeing her home destroyed and I decided she must have hated Peredur. He had feared her and she had hated him, and if it was true that she had been able to see the future then she had seen me and given her husband bad advice to make that future come true.

'So where do you go now?' Svein asked. We were walking along the beach, past the huddled slaves who watched us with dark, resentful eyes.

'I have a mind,' I said, 'to go into the Sæfern Sea.'

'There's nothing left there,' he said scornfully.

'Nothing?'

'It's been scoured,' he said, meaning that Danish and Norse ships had bled the coasts dry of any treasure. 'All you'll find in the Sæfern Sea,' he went on, 'are our ships bringing men from Ireland.'

'To attack Wessex?'

'No!' He grinned at me. 'I've a mind to start trading with the Welsh kingdoms.'

'And I have a mind,' I said, 'to take my ship to the moon and build a feasting hall there.'

He laughed. 'But speaking of Wessex,' he said, 'I hear they're building a church where you killed Ubba?'

'I hear the same.'

'A church with an altar of gold?'

'I've heard that too,' I allowed. I hid my surprise that he knew of Odda the Younger's plans, but I should not have been surprised. A rumour of gold would spread like couch grass. 'I've heard it,' I said again, 'but I don't believe it.'

'Churches have money,' he said thoughtfully, then frowned, 'but that's a strange place to build a church.'

'Strange, why?'

'So close to the sea? An easy place to attack?'

'Or perhaps they want you to attack,' I said, 'and have men ready to defend it?'

'A lure, you mean?' He thought about that.

'And hasn't Guthrum given orders that the West Saxons aren't to be provoked,' I said.

'Guthrum can order what he wants,' Svein said harshly, 'but I am Svein of the White Horse and I don't take orders from Guthrum.' He walked on, frowning as he threaded the fishing nets that men now dead had hung to dry. 'Men say Alfred is not a fool.'

'Nor is he.'

'If he has put valuables beside the sea,' he said, 'he will not leave them unguarded.' He was a warrior, but like the best warriors he was no madman. When folk speak of the Danes these days they have an idea that they were all savage pagans, unthinking in their terrible violence, but most were like Svein and feared losing men. That was always the great Danish fear, and the Danish weakness. Svein's ship was called the *White Horse* and had a crew of fifty-three men, and if a dozen of those men were to be killed or gravely wounded, then the *White Horse* would be fatally weakened. Once in a fight, of course, he was like all Danes, terrifying, but there was always a good deal of thinking before there was any fighting. He scratched at a louse, then gestured towards the slaves his men had taken. 'Besides, I have these.'

He meant he would not go to Cynuit. The slaves, once they were sold, would bring him silver and he must have reckoned Cynuit was not worth the casualties.

Svein needed my help next morning. His own ship was in Callyn's harbour and he asked me to take him and a score of his men to fetch it. We left the rest of his crew at Peredur's settlement. They guarded the slaves he would take away, and they also burned the place as we carried Svein east up the coast to Callyn's settlement. We waited a day there as Svein settled his accounts with Callyn, and we used the time to sell fleeces and tin to Callyn's traders and, though we received a poor enough price, it was better to travel with silver than with bulky cargo. The *Fyrdraca* was glittering with silver now and the crewmen, knowing they would receive their proper share, were happy. Haesten wanted to go with Svein, but I refused his request. 'I saved your life,' I told him, 'and you have to serve me longer to pay for that.' He accepted that and was pleased when I gave him a second arm ring as a reward for the men he had killed at Dreyndynas.

Svein's *White Horse* was smaller than *Fyrdraca*. Her prow had a carved horse's head and her stern a wolf's head, while at her masthead was a wind-vane decorated with a white horse. I asked Svein about the horse and he laughed. 'When I was sixteen,' he said, 'I wagered my father's stallion against our king's white horse. I had to beat the king's champion at wrestling and swordplay. My father beat me for making the wager, but I won! So the white horse is lucky. I ride only white horses.' And so his ship was the *White Horse* and I followed her back up the coast to where a thick plume of smoke marked where Peredur had ruled.

'Are we staying with him?' Leofric asked, puzzled that we were going back west rather than turning towards Defnascir.

'I have a mind to see where Britain ends,' I said, and I had no wish to return to the Uisc and to Mildrith's misery.

Svein put the slaves into the belly of his boat. We spent one last night in the bay, under the thick smoke, and in the morning, as the rising sun flickered across the sea, we rowed away. As we passed the western headland, going into the wide ocean, I saw a man watching us from the cliff's top and I saw he was robed in black and, though he was a long way off, I thought I recognised Asser. Iseult saw him too and she hissed like a cat, made a fist and threw it at him, opening her fingers at the last moment as if casting a spell at the monk.

Then I forgot him because *Fyrdraca* was back in the open sea and we were going to the place where the world ended.

And I had a shadow queen for company.

PART TWO

The Swamp King

Four

I love the sea. I grew up beside it, though in my memories the seas off Bebbanburg are grey, usually sullen, and rarely sunlit. They are nothing like the great waters that roll from beyond the Isles of the Dead to thunder and shatter against the rocks at the west of Britain. The sea heaves there, as if the ocean gods flexed their muscles, and the white birds cry endlessly, and the wind rattles the spray against the cliffs and *Fyrdraca*, running before that bright wind, left a path in the sea and the steering oar fought me, pulsing with the life of the water and the flexing of the ship and the joy of the passage. Iseult stared at me, astonished by my happiness, but then I gave her the oar and watched her thin body heave against the sea's strength until she understood the power of the oar and could move the ship, and then she laughed. 'I would live on the sea,' I told her, though she did not understand me. I had given her an arm ring from Peredur's hoard and a silver toe ring and a necklace of monster's teeth, all sharp and long and white, strung on a silver wire.

I turned and watched Svein's *White Horse* cut through the water. Her bows would sometimes break from a wave so that the forepart of her hull, all green and dark with growth, would rear skywards with her horse's head snarling at the sun, and then she would crash down and the seas would explode white about her timbers. Her oars, like ours, were inboard and the oar-holes plugged, and we both ran under sail and *Fyrdraca* was the faster ship, which was not because she was more cunningly built, but because her hull was longer.

There is such joy in a good ship, and a greater joy to have the ship's belly fat with other men's silver. It is the Viking joy, driving a dragon-headed hull through a wind-driven sea towards a future full of feasts and laughter. The Danes taught me that and I love them for it, pagan swine though they might be. At that moment, running before Svein's *White Horse*, I was as happy as a man could be, free of all the churchmen and laws and duties of Alfred's Wessex, but then I gave orders that the sail was to be lowered and a dozen men uncleated the lines and the big yard scraped down the mast. We had come to Britain's ending and I would turn about, and I waved to Svein as the *White Horse* swept past us. He waved back, watching the *Fyrdraca* wallow in the long ocean swells.

'Seen enough?' Leofric asked me.

I was staring at the end of Britain where the rocks endured the sea's assault. 'Penwith,' Iseult said, giving me the British name for the headland.

'You want to go home?' I asked Leofric.

He shrugged. The crew was turning the yard, lining it fore and aft so it could be stowed on its crutches while other men were binding the sail so it did not flap. The oars were being readied to take us eastwards and the *White Horse* was getting smaller as it swept up into the Sæfern Sea.

I stared after Svein, envying him. 'I need to be rich,' I said to Leofric.

He laughed at that.

'I have a path to follow,' I said, 'and it goes north. North back to Bebbanburg. And Bebbanburg has never been captured, so I need many men to take it. Many good men and many sharp swords.'

'We have silver,' he said, gesturing into the boat's bilge.

'Not enough,' I answered sourly. My enemies had money and Alfred claimed that I owed the church money, and the courts of Defnascir would be chasing me for wergild. I could only go home if I had enough silver to pay off the church, to bribe the courts and to attract men to my banner. I stared at the *White Horse*, which was now little more than a sail above the wind-fretted sea and I felt the old temptation to go with the Danes. Wait till Ragnar was free and give him my sword arm, but then I would be fighting against Leofric and I would still need to make money, raise men, go north and fight for my birthright. I touched Thor's hammer and prayed for a sign.

Iseult spat. That was not quite true. She said a word which sounded like someone clearing their throat, spitting and choking all at the same time, and she was pointing over the ship's side and I saw a strange fish arching out of the water. The fish was as big as a deerhound and had a triangular fin. 'Porpoise,' Leofric said.

'*Llamhydydd*,' Iseult said again, giving the fish its British name.

'They bring sailors luck,' Leofric said.

I had never seen a porpoise before, but suddenly there were a dozen of the creatures. They were grey and their backs glistened in the sun and they were all going north.

'Put the sail back up,' I told Leofric.

He stared at me. The crew was unlashing the oars and taking the plugs from the oar-holes. 'You want the sail up?' Leofric asked.

'We're going north.' I had prayed for a sign and Thor had sent me the porpoise.

89

'There's nothing in the Sæfern Sea,' Leofric said. 'Svein told you that.'

'Svein told me there was no plunder in the Sæfern Sea,' I said, 'because the Danes have taken it all, so that means the Danes have the plunder.' I felt a surge of happiness so intense that I punched Leofric's shoulder and gave Iseult a hug. 'And he told me that their ships are coming from Ireland.'

'So?' Leofric rubbed his shoulder.

'Men from Ireland!' I told Leofric. 'Danes coming from Ireland to attack Wessex. And if you brought a ship's crew from Ireland, what would you bring with you?'

'Everything you possess,' Leofric said flatly.

'And they don't know we're here! They're sheep, and we are a fire-dragon.'

He grinned. 'You're right,' he said.

'Of course I'm right! I'm a lord! I'm right and I'm going to be rich! We're all going to be rich! We shall eat off gold plates, piss down our enemies' throats and make their wives into our whores.' I was shouting this nonsense as I walked down the boat's centre, casting off the sail's lashings. 'We'll all be rich with silver shoes and golden bonnets. We'll be richer than kings! We'll wallow in silver, shower our whores with gold and shit lumps of amber! Tie those oars up! Plug the holes, we're going north, we're going to be rich as bishops, every man of us!' The men were grinning, pleased because I was roaring my enthusiasm, and men like to be led.

They did have qualms about going north, for that would take us out of sight of land, and I had never been that far from the shore, and I was frightened too, for Ragnar the Elder had often told me tales of Norsemen who had been tempted out into the sea-wastes, to sail ever farther westwards, and he said there were lands out there, lands beyond the Isles of the Dead, lands where ghosts walked, but I am not sure if he told the truth. I am sure, though, that he told me that many of those ships never returned. They voyage into the dying sun and they go onwards because they cannot bear to turn back and so they sail to where the lost ships die at the world's dark ending.

Yet the world did not end to the north. I knew that, though I was not certain what did lie northwards. Dyfed was there, somewhere, and Ireland, and there were other places with barbarous names and savage people who lived like hungry dogs on the wild edges of the land, but there was also a waste of sea, a wilderness of empty waves and so, once the sail was hoisted and the wind was thrusting the *Fyrdraca* northwards, I leaned on the oar to take her somewhat to the east for fear we would otherwise be lost in the ocean's vastness.

'You know where you're going?' Leofric asked me.

'No.'

'Do you care?'

I grinned at him for answer. The wind, which had been southerly, came more from the west, and the tide took us eastwards, so that by the afternoon I could see land, and I thought it must be the land of the Britons on the north side of the Sæfern, but as we came closer I saw it was an island. I later discovered it was the place the Northmen call Lundi, because that is their word for the puffin, and the island's high cliffs were thick with the birds, which shrieked at us when we came into a cove on the western side of the island. It was an uncomfortable place to anchor for the night because the big seas rolled in and so we dropped the sail, took out the oars, and rowed around the cliffs until we found shelter on the eastern side.

I went ashore with Iseult and we dug some puffin burrows to find eggs, though all were hatched so we contented

91

ourselves with killing a pair of goats for the evening meal. There was no one living on the island, though there had been because there were the remains of a small church and a field of graves. The Danes had burned everything, pulled down the church and dug up the graves in search of gold. We climbed to a high place and I searched the evening sea for ships, but saw none, though I wondered if I could see land to the south. It was hard to be sure for the southern horizon was thick with dark cloud, but a darker strip within the cloud could have been hills and I assumed I was looking at Cornwalum or the western part of Wessex. Iseult sang to herself.

I watched her. She was gutting one of the dead goats, doing it clumsily for she was not accustomed to such work. She was thin, so thin that she looked like the ælfcynn, the elf-kind, but she was happy. In time I would learn just how much she had hated Peredur. He had valued her and made her a queen, but he had also kept her a prisoner in his hall so that he alone could profit from her powers. Folk would pay Peredur to hear Iseult's prophecies and one of the reasons Callyn had fought his neighbour was to take Iseult for himself. Shadow queens were valued among the Britons for they were part of the old mysteries, the powers that had brooded over the land before the monks arrived, and Iseult was one of the last shadow queens. She had been born in the sun's darkness, but now she was free and I was to find she had a soul as wild as a falcon. Mildrith, poor Mildrith, wanted order and routine. She wanted the hall swept, the clothes clean, the cows milked, the sun to rise, the sun to set and for nothing to change, but Iseult was different. She was strange, shadow-born, and full of mystery. Nothing she said to me those first days made any sense, for we had no language in common, but on the island, as the sun set and I took the knife to finish cutting the entrails from the goat, she plucked twigs and wove a small cage. She showed me the cage, broke it and then, with her long white fingers, mimed a bird flying free. She pointed to herself, tossed the twig scraps away and laughed.

Next morning, still ashore, I saw boats. There were two of them and they were sailing to the west of the island, going northwards. They were small craft, probably traders from Cornwalum, and they were running before the south-west wind towards the hidden shore where I assumed Svein had taken the *White Horse*.

We followed the two small ships. By the time we had waded out to *Fyrdraca*, raised her anchor and rowed her from the lee of the island both boats were almost out of sight, but once our sail was hoisted we began to overhaul them. They must have been terrified to see a dragon ship shoot out from behind the island, but I lowered the sail a little to slow us down and so followed them for much of the day until, at last, a blue-grey line showed at the sea's edge. Land. We hoisted the sail fully and seethed past the two small, tubby boats and so, for the first time, I came to the shore of Wales. The Britons had another name for it, but we simply called it Wales which means 'foreigners', and much later I worked out that we must have made that land-fall in Dyfed, which is the name of the churchman who converted the Britons of Wales to Christianity and had the westernmost kingdom of the Welsh named for him.

We found a deep inlet for shelter. Rocks guarded the entrance, but once inside we were safe from wind and sea. We turned the ship so that her bows faced the open sea, and the cove was so narrow that our stern scraped stone as we slewed *Fyrdraca* about, and then we slept on board, men and their women sprawled under the rowers' benches. There were a dozen women aboard, all captured from Peredur's tribe, and one of them managed to escape that night,

93

presumably sliding over the side and swimming to shore. It was not Iseult. She and I slept in the small black space beneath the steering platform, a hole screened by a cloak, and Leofric woke me there in the dawn, worried that the missing woman would raise the country against us. I shrugged. 'We won't be here long.'

But we stayed in the cove all day. I wanted to ambush ships coming around the coast and we saw two, but they travelled together and I could not attack more than one ship at a time. Both ships were under sail, riding the south-west wind, and both were Danish, or perhaps Norse, and both were laden with warriors. They must have come from Ireland, or perhaps from the east coast of Northumbria, and doubtless they travelled to join Svein, lured by the prospect of capturing good West Saxon land. 'Burgweard should have the whole fleet up here,' I said. 'He could tear through these bastards.'

Two horsemen came to look at us in the afternoon. One had a glinting chain about his neck, suggesting he was of high rank, but neither man came down to the shingle beach. They watched from the head of the small valley that fell to the cove and after a while they went away. The sun was low now, but it was summer so the days were long. 'If they bring men,' Leofric said as the two horsemen rode away, but he did not finish the thought.

I looked up at the high bluffs on either side of the cove. Men could rain rocks down from those heights and the *Fyrdraca* would be crushed like an egg. 'We could put sentries up there,' I suggested, but just then Eadric, who led the men who occupied the forward steorbord benches, shouted that there was a ship in sight. I ran forward and there she was.

The perfect prey.

She was a large ship, not so big as *Fyrdraca*, but large all

94

the same, and she was riding low in the water for she was so heavily laden. Indeed, she carried so many people that her crew had not dared raise the sail for, though the wind was not heavy, it would have bent her leeward side dangerously close to the water. So she was being rowed and now she was close inshore, evidently looking for a place where she could spend the night and her crew had plainly been tempted by our cove and only now realised that we already filled it. I could see a man in her bows pointing further up the coast and meanwhile my men were arming themselves, and I shouted at Haesten to take the steering oar. He knew what to do and I was confident he would do it well, even though it might mean the death of fellow Danes. We cut the lines that had tethered us to the shore as Leofric brought me my mail coat, helmet and shield. I dressed for battle as the oars were shipped, then pulled on my helmet so that suddenly the edges of my vision were darkened by its faceplate.

'Go!' I shouted, and the oars bit and the *Fyrdraca* surged out. Some of the oar blades struck rock as we pulled, but none broke, and I was staring at the ship ahead, so close now, and her prow was a snarling wolf, and I could see men and women staring at us, not believing what they saw. They thought they saw a Danish ship, one of their own, yet we were armed and we were coming for them. A man shouted a warning and they scrambled for their weapons, and Leofric yelled at our men to put their hearts into the oars, and the long shafts bent under the strain as *Fyrdraca* leaped across the small waves and I yelled at the men to leave the oars, to come to the bows, and Cenwulf and the twelve men he commanded were already there as our big bows slammed through the enemy oars, snapping them.

Haesten had done well. I had told him to steer for the forward part of the ship, where her freeboard was low, and our bows rode up across her strakes, plunging her low in the water, and we staggered with the impact, but then I jumped down into the wolf-headed ship's belly. Cenwulf and his men were behind me, and there we began the killing.

The enemy ship was so loaded with men that they probably outnumbered us, but they were bone weary from a long day's rowing, they had not expected an attack, and we were hungry for wealth. We had done this before and the crew was well trained, and they chopped their way down the boat, swords and axes swinging, and the sea was slopping over the side so that we waded through water as we clambered over the rowers' benches. The water about our feet grew red. Some of our victims jumped overboard and clung to shattered oars in an attempt to escape us. One man, big-bearded and wild-eyed, came at us with a great sword and Eadric drove a spear into his chest and Leofric struck the man's head with his axe, struck again, and blood sprayed up to the sail that was furled fore and aft on its long yard. The man sank to his knees and Eadric ground the spear deeper so that blood spilled down to the water. I almost fell as a wave tilted the half-swamped ship. A man screamed and lunged a spear at me, I took it on my shield, knocked it aside and rammed Serpent-Breath at his face. He half fell, trying to escape the lunge, and I knocked him over the side with my shield's heavy boss. I sensed movement to my right and swung Serpent-Breath like a reaping scythe and struck a woman in the head. She went down like a felled calf, a sword in her hand. I kicked the sword away and stamped on the woman's belly. A child screamed and I shoved her aside, lunged at a man in a leather jerkin, raised my shield to block his axe blow and then spitted him on Serpent-Breath. The sword went deep into his belly, so deep that the blade stuck and I had to stand on him to tug it free. Cenwulf went past me, his snarling face covered in blood, sword swinging. The water was up to my knees, and then I staggered and almost fell as the whole ship lurched and I realised we had drifted ashore and struck rocks. Two horses were tethered in the ship's belly and the beasts screamed at the smell of blood. One broke its tether and jumped overboard, swimming white-eyed towards the open sea.

'Kill them! Kill them!' I heard myself shouting. It was the only way to take a ship, to empty her of fighting men, but she was now emptying herself as the survivors jumped onto the rocks and clambered away through the sucking backwash of blood-touched water. A half-dozen men had been left aboard *Fyrdraca* and they were fending her off the rocks with oars. A blade stabbed the back of my right ankle and I turned to see a wounded man trying to hamstring me with a short knife and I stabbed down again and again, butchering him in the weltering water, and I think he was the last man to die on board, though a few Danes were still clinging to the ship's side and those we cut away.

The *Fyrdraca* was seaward of the doomed ship now, and I shouted at the men aboard to bring her close. She heaved up and down, much higher than the half-sunk ship, and we threw our plunder up and over the side. There were sacks, boxes and barrels. Many were heavy, and some clinked with coin. We stripped the enemy dead of their valuables, taking six coats of mail and a dozen helmets and we found another three coats of mail in the flooded bilge. I took eight arm rings off dead men. We tossed weapons aboard *Fyrdraca*, then cut away the captured ship's rigging. I loosed the remaining horse that stood shivering as the water rose. We took the ship's yard and sail, and all the time her survivors watched from the shore where some had found a precarious refuge above the sea-washed rocks. I went to the space beneath her sleeping platform and found a great war-helm there, a beautiful thing with a decorated face-plate and a wolf's head moulded in silver on the crown, and I tossed my old helmet onto *Fyrdraca* and donned the new one, and then passed out sacks of coin. Beneath the sacks was what I thought must be a small shield wrapped in black cloth and I half thought of leaving it where it was, then threw it into *Fyrdraca* anyway. We were rich.

'Who are you?' a man shouted from onshore.

'Uhtred,' I called back.

He spat at me and I laughed. Our men were climbing back on board *Fyrdraca* now. Some were retrieving oars from the water, and Leofric was pushing *Fyrdraca* away, fearful that she would be caught on the rocks. 'Get on board!' he shouted at me, and I saw I was the last man, and so I took hold of *Fyrdraca*'s stern, put a foot on an oar, and heaved myself over her side. 'Row!' Leofric shouted, and so we pulled away from the wreck.

Two young women had been thrown up with the plunder and I found them weeping by *Fyrdraca*'s mast. One spoke no language that I recognised and later we discovered she was from Ireland, but the other was Danish and, as soon as I squatted beside her, she lashed out at me and spat in my face. I slapped her back, and that made her lash out again. She was a tall girl, strong, with a tangled mass of fair hair and bright blue eyes. She tried to claw her fingers through the eye-holes of my new helmet and I had to slap her again, which made my men laugh. Some were shouting at her to keep fighting me, but instead she suddenly burst into tears and leaned back against the mast root. I took off the helmet and asked her name, and her only answer was to wail that she wanted to die, but when I said she was free to throw herself off the ship she did not move. Her name was Freyja, she was fifteen years old, and her father had been the owner of the ship we had sunk. He had been the big man with the sword, and his name had been Ivar and he had held

98

land at Dyflin, wherever that was, and Freyja began to weep again when she looked at my new helmet which had belonged to her father. 'He died without cutting his nails,' she said accusingly, as if I were responsible for that ill luck, and it was bad fortune indeed because now the grim things of the underworld would use Ivar's nails to build the ship that would bring chaos at the world's end.

'Where were you going?' I asked her.

To Svein, of course. Ivar had been unhappy in Dyflin, which was in Ireland and had more Norsemen than Danes and also possessed savagely unfriendly native tribes, and he had been lured by the prospect of land in Wessex and so he had abandoned his Irish steading, put all his goods and wealth aboard his ships, and sailed eastwards.

'Ships?' I asked her.

'There were three when we left,' Freyja said, 'but we lost the others in the night.'

I guessed they were the two ships we had seen earlier, but the gods had been good to me for Freyja confirmed that her father had put his most valuable possessions into his own ship, and that was the one we had captured, and we had struck lucky for there were barrels of coin and boxes of silver. There was amber, jet and ivory. There were weapons and armour. We made a rough count as the *Fyrdraca* wallowed offshore and we could scarce believe our fortune. One box contained small lumps of gold, roughly shaped as bricks, but best of all was the wrapped bundle which I had thought was a small shield, but which, when we unwrapped the cloth, proved to be a great silver plate on which was modelled a crucifixion. All about the death scene, ringing the plate's heavy rim, were saints. Twelve of them. I assumed they were the apostles and that the plate had been the treasure of some Irish church or monastery before Ivar had captured it. I showed the plate to my men.

'This,' I said reverently, 'is not part of the plunder. This must go back to the church.'

Leofric caught my eye, but did not laugh.

'It goes back to the church,' I said again, and some of my men, the more pious ones, muttered that I was doing the right thing. I wrapped the plate and put it under the steering platform.

'How much is your debt to the church?' Leofric asked me.

'You have a mind like a goat's arsehole,' I told him.

He laughed, then looked past me. 'Now what do we do?' he asked.

I thought he was asking what we should do with the rest of our charmed lives, but instead he was gazing at the shore where, in the evening light, I could see armed men lining the clifftop. The Britons of Dyfed had come for us, but too late. Yet their presence meant we could not go back into our cove, and so I ordered the oars to be manned and for the ship to row eastwards. The Britons followed us along the shore. The woman who had escaped in the night must have told them we were Saxons and they must have been praying we would seek refuge on land so they could kill us. Few ships stayed at sea overnight, not unless they were forced to, but I dared not seek shelter and so I turned south and rowed away from the shore, while in the west the sun leaked red fire through rifts in the cloud so that the whole sky glowed as if a god had bled across the heavens.

'What will you do with the girl?' Leofric asked me.

'Freyja?'

'Is that her name? You want her?'

'No,' I said.

'I do.'

'She'll eat you alive,' I warned him. She was probably a head taller than Leofric.

'I like them like that,' he said.

'All yours,' I said, and such is life. One day Freyja was the pampered daughter of an earl and the next she was a slave.

I gave the coats of mail to those who deserved them. We had lost two men, and another three were badly injured, but that was a light cost. We had, after all, killed twenty or thirty Danes and the survivors were ashore where the Britons might or might not treat them well. Best of all we had become rich and that knowledge was a consolation as night fell.

Hoder is the god of the night and I prayed to him. I threw my old helmet overboard as a gift to him, because all of us were scared of the dark that swallowed us, and it was a complete dark because clouds had come from the west to smother the sky. No moon, no stars. For a time there was the gleam of firelight on the northern shore, but that vanished and we were blind. The wind rose, the seas heaved us, and we brought the oars inboard and let the air and water carry us for we could neither see nor steer. I stayed on deck, peering into the dark, and Iseult stayed with me, under my cloak, and I remembered the look of delight on her face when we had gone into battle.

Dawn was grey and the sea was white-streaked grey and the wind was cold, and there was no land in sight, but two white birds flew over us and I took them for a sign and rowed in the direction they had gone, and late that day, in a bitter sea and cold rain, we saw land and it was the Isle of Puffins again where we found shelter in the cove and made fires ashore.

'When the Danes know what we've done,' Leofric said.

'They'll look for us,' I finished the sentence for him.

'Lots of them will look for us.'

'Then it's time to go home,' I said.

101

The gods had been good to us and, next dawn, in a calming sea, we rowed south to the land and followed the coast towards the west. We would go around the wild headlands where the porpoises swam, turn east and so find home.

Much later I discovered what Svein had done after we parted company and, because what he did affected my life and made the enmity between me and Alfred worse, I shall tell it here.

I suspect that the thought of a gold altar at Cynuit had gnawed into his heart, for he carried the dream back to Glwysing where his men gathered. Glwysing was another kingdom of the Britons in the south of Wales, a place where there were good harbours and where the king welcomed the Danes for their presence prevented Guthrum's men from raiding across the Mercian border.

Svein ordered a second ship and its crew to accompany him and together they attacked Cynuit. They came in the dawn, hidden by a mist, and I can imagine their beast-headed ships appearing in the early greyness like monsters from a nightmare. They went up river, oars splashing, then grounded the boats and the crews streamed ashore, men in mail and helmets, spear-Danes, sword-Danes, and they found the half-built church and monastery.

Odda the Younger was making the place, but he knew it was too close to the sea and so he had decided to make it a fortified building. The church's tower was to be of stone, and high enough for men to keep a watch from its summit, and the priests and monks were to be surrounded by a palisade and a flooded ditch, but when Svein came ashore none of the work was finished and so it was indefensible, and besides, there were scarce forty troops there and those

102

all died or fled within minutes of the Danes landing. The Danes then burned what work had been done and cut down the high wooden cross which customarily marked a monastery and which had been the first thing the builders had made.

The builders were monks, many of them novices, and Svein herded them together and demanded they show him where the valuables were hidden and promised them mercy if they told the truth. Which they did. There was not much of value, certainly no altar of gold, but supplies and timber needed to be purchased and so the monks had a chest of silver pennies which was reward enough for the Danes, who then pulled down the half-constructed church tower, wrecked the unfinished palisade and slaughtered some cattle. Then Svein asked the monks where Ubba was buried and was met by sullen silence, and the swords were drawn again and the question asked a second time, and the monks were forced to confess that the church was being built directly over the dead chieftain's grave. That grave had been an earth mound, but the monks had dug it up and thrown the body into the river, and when the Danes heard that story the mercy fled from their souls.

The monks were made to wade in the river until some bones were found, and those bones were placed on a funeral pyre made from the timbers of the half-constructed buildings. It was, by all accounts, a huge pyre, and when it was lit, and when the bones were at the heart of a furnace blaze, the monks were thrown onto the flames. While their bodies burned the Danes selected two girls, captured from the soldiers' shelters, raped them and then strangled them, sending their souls to be company for Ubba in Valhalla. We heard all this from two children who survived by hiding in a nettle patch, and some folk from the nearby town who were dragged to see the end of the funeral pyre. 'Svein of the White Horse did this,' they were told, and made to repeat the words. It was a Danish custom to leave some witnesses to their horror, so that the tales would spread fear and make cowards of other folk who might be attacked, and sure enough the story of the burned monks and murdered girls went through Wessex like a high wind through dry grass. It became exaggerated as such tales do. The number of dead monks went from sixteen to sixty, the raped girls from two to twenty, and the stolen silver from a chest of pennies to a hoard worthy of the gods. Alfred sent a message to Guthrum, demanding to know why he should not slaughter the hostages he held, and Guthrum sent him a present of gold, two captured gospel books and a grovelling letter in which he claimed that the two ships had not been from his forces, but were pirates from beyond the sea. Alfred believed him and so the hostages lived and the peace prevailed, but Alfred commanded that a curse should be pronounced on Svein in every church of Wessex. The Danish chieftain was to be damned through all eternity, his men were to burn in the fires of hell and his children, and his children's children, were all to bear the mark of Cain. I asked a priest what the mark was, and he explained that Cain was the son of Adam and Eve and the first murderer, but he did not know what mark he had carried. He thought God would recognise it.

So Svein's two ships sailed away, leaving a pillar of smoke on the Wessex shore, and I knew none of it. In time I would know all of it, but for now I was going home.

We went slowly, sheltering each night, retracing our steps that took us past the blackened hillside where Peredur's settlement had stood, and on we went, under a summer's sun and rain, until we had returned to the Uisc.

The *Heahengel* was afloat now and her mast was stepped, which meant Leofric could take her and the *Eftwyrd*, for the *Fyrdraca* was no more, back to Hamtun. We divided the plunder first and, though Leofric and I took the greater share, every man went away wealthy. I was left with Haesten and Iseult, and I took them up to Oxton where Mildrith wept with relief because she had thought I might be dead. I told her we had been patrolling the coast, which was true enough, and that we had captured a Danish ship laden with wealth, and I spilled the coins and gold bricks onto the floor and gave her a bracelet of amber and a necklace of jet, and the gifts distracted her from Iseult who watched her with wide, dark eyes, and if Mildrith saw the British girl's jewellery she said nothing.

We had come back in time for the harvest, though it was poor for there had been much rain that summer. There was a black growth on the rye which meant it could not even be fed to the animals, though the straw was good enough to thatch the hall I built. I have always enjoyed building. I made the hall from clay, gravel and straw, all packed together to make thick walls. Oak beams straddled the walls, and oak rafters held a high, long roof that looked golden when the thatch was first combed into place. The walls were painted with powdered lime in water, and one of the local men poured ox-blood into the mix so that the walls were the colour of a summer sky at sunset. The hall's great door faced east towards the Uisc and I paid a man from Exanceaster to carve the doorposts and lintels with writhing wolves, for the banner of Bebbanburg, my banner, is a wolf's head. Mildrith wanted the carving to show saints, but she got wolves. I paid the builders well, and when other men heard that I had silver they came looking for employment, and though they were there to build my hall I took only those who had experience of fighting. I equipped them with spades, axes, adzes, weapons and shields.

'You are making an army,' Mildrith accused me. Her relief at my homecoming had soured quickly when it was apparent that I was no more a Christian than when I had left her.

'Seventeen men? An army?'

'We are at peace,' she said. She believed that because the priests preached it, and the priests only said what they were told to say by the bishops, and the bishops took their orders from Alfred. A travelling priest sought shelter with us one night and he insisted that the war with the Danes was over.

'We still have Danes on the border,' I said.

'God has calmed their hearts,' the priest insisted and told me that God had killed the Lothbrok brothers, Ubba, Ivar and Halfdan, and that the rest of the Danes were so shocked by the deaths that they no longer dared to fight against Christians. 'It is true, lord,' the priest said earnestly, 'I heard it preached in Cippanhamm, and the king was there and he praised God for the truth of it. We are to beat our swords into ard points and our spear blades into reaping hooks.'

I laughed at the thought of melting Serpent-Breath into a tool to plough Oxton's fields, but then I did not believe the priest's nonsense. The Danes were biding their time, that was all, yet it did seem peaceful as the summer slid imperceptibly into autumn. No enemies crossed the frontier of Wessex and no ships harried our coasts. We threshed the corn, netted partridges, hunted deer on the hill, staked nets in the river and practised with our weapons. The women span thread, gathered nuts, and picked mushrooms and blackberries. There were apples and pears, for this was the time of plenty, the time when the livestock was fattened before the winter slaughter. We ate like kings and, when my hall was finished, I gave a feast and Mildrith saw the ox head over the door and knew it was an offering to Thor, but said nothing.

Mildrith hated Iseult, which was hardly surprising, for

I had told Mildrith that Iseult was a queen of the Britons and that I held her for the ransom that the Britons would offer. I knew no such ransom would ever come, but the story went some way to explaining Iseult's presence, but Mildrith resented that the British girl was given her own house. 'She is a queen,' I said.

'You take her hunting,' Mildrith said resentfully.

I did more than that, but Mildrith chose to be blind to much of it. Mildrith wanted little more than her church, her baby and an unvarying routine. She had charge of the women who milked the cows, churned the butter, span wool and collected honey, and she took immense pride that those things were done well. If a neighbour visited there would be a flurry of panic as the hall was cleaned, and she worried much about those neighbours' opinions. She wanted me to pay Oswald's wergild. It did not matter to Mildrith that the man had been caught thieving, because to pay the wergild would make peace in the valley of the Uisc. She even wanted me to visit Odda the Younger. 'You could be friends,' she pleaded.

'With that snake?'

'And Wirken says you have not paid the tithe.'

Wirken was the priest in Exanmynster, and I hated him. 'He eats and drinks the tithe,' I snarled. The tithe was the payment all landholders were supposed to make to the church, and by rights I should have sent Wirken part of my harvest, but I had not. Yet the priest was often at Oxton, coming when he thought I was hunting, and he ate my food and drank my ale and was growing fat on them.

'He comes to pray with us,' Mildrith said.

'He comes to eat,' I said.

'And he says the bishop will take the land if we don't pay the debt.'

'The debt will be paid,' I said.

'When? We have the money!' She gestured at the new hall. 'When?' she insisted.

'When I want to,' I snarled. I did not tell her when, or how, because if I had, then Wirken the priest would know, and the bishop would know. It was not enough to pay the debt. Mildrith's father had foolishly donated part of our land's future produce to the church, and I wanted that burden taken away so the debt would not go on through eternity, and to do that I needed to surprise the bishop, and so I kept Mildrith ignorant, and inevitably those arguments would end with her tears. I was bored with her and she knew it. I found her beating Iseult's maid one day. The girl was a Saxon I had given to Iseult as a servant, but she also worked in the dairy and Mildrith was beating her because some cheeses had not been turned. I dragged Mildrith away, and that, of course, provoked another argument and Mildrith proved not to be so blind after all for she accused me of trying to whelp bastards on Iseult, which was true enough, but I reminded her that her own father had sired enough bastards, half a dozen of whom now worked for us. 'You leave Iseult and her maid alone,' I said, causing more tears. They were not happy days.

It was the time when Iseult learned to speak English, or at least the Northumbrian version of English for she learned it mostly from me. 'You're my mon,' she said. I was Mildrith's man and Iseult's mon. She said she had been born again on the day I came into Peredur's hall. 'I had dreamed of you,' she said, 'tall and golden haired.'

'Now you don't dream?' I asked, knowing that her powers of scrying came from dreams.

'I do still dream,' she said earnestly, 'my brother speaks to me.'

'Your brother?' I asked, surprised.

'I was born a twin,' she told me, 'and my brother came

first and then, as I was born, he died. He went to the shadow world and he speaks to me of what he sees there.'

'What does he see?'

'He sees your king.'

'Alfred,' I said sourly, 'is that good or bad?'

'I don't know. The dreams are shadowy.'

She was no Christian. Instead she believed that every place and every thing had its own god or goddess; a nymph for a stream, a dryad for a wood, a spirit for a tree, a god for the fire and another for the sea. The Christian god, like Thor or Odin, was just one more deity among this unseen throng of powers, and her dreams, she said, were like eavesdropping on the gods. One day, as she rode beside me on the hills above the empty sea, she suddenly said that Alfred would give me power.

'He hates me,' I told her, 'he'll give me nothing.'

'He will give you power,' she said flatly. I stared at her and she gazed to where the clouds met the waves. Her black hair was unbound and the sea wind stirred it. 'My brother told me,' she said. 'Alfred will give you power and you will take back your northern home and your woman will be a creature of gold.'

'My woman?'

She looked at me and there was sadness in her face. 'There,' she said, 'now you know,' and she kicked back her heels and made the horse run along the ridge top, her hair streaming, her eyes wet with tears. I wanted to know more, but she said she had told me what she had dreamed and I must be content.

At summer's end we drove the swine into the forests to feed on the fallen beechnuts and acorns. I bought bags of salt because the killing time was coming and the meat of our pigs and cattle would have to be salted into barrels to feed us through the winter. Some of that food would come from the men who rented land at the edge of the estate, and I visited them all so they would know I expected payment of wheat, barley and livestock, and, to show them what would happen if they tried to cheat me, I bought a dozen good swords from a smith in Exanceaster. I gave the swords to my men, and in the shortening days we practised with them. Mildrith might not believe war was coming, but I did not think God had changed Danish hearts.

The late autumn brought heavy rain and the shire-reeve to Oxton. The reeve was called Harald and he was charged with keeping the peace of Defnascir, and he came on horse-back and with him were six other horsemen, all in mail coats and helmets, and all with swords or spears. I waited for him in the hall, making him dismount and come into the smoky shadows. He came cautiously, expecting an ambush, then his eyes became accustomed to the gloom and he saw me standing by the central hearth. 'You are summoned to the shire court,' he told me.

His men had followed Harald into the hall. 'You bring swords into my house?' I asked.

Harald looked around the hall and he saw my men armed with their spears and axes. I had seen the horsemen approaching and summoned my men and ordered them to arm themselves.

Harald had the reputation of being a decent man, sensible and fair, and he knew how weapons in a hall could lead to slaughter. 'You will wait outside,' he told his men, and I gestured for my men to put their weapons down. 'You are summoned . . .' Harald began again.

'I heard you,' I said.

'There is a debt to be paid,' he said, 'and a man's death to make good.'

I said nothing. One of my hounds growled softly and I put a hand into its fur to silence it.

110

'The court will meet on All Saints' Day,' Harald said, 'at the cathedral.'

'I shall be there,' I said.

He took off his helmet to reveal a balding pate fringed with brown hair. He was at least ten years older than I, a big man, with two fingers missing from his shield hand. He limped slightly as he walked towards me. I calmed the hounds, waited.

'I was at Cynuit,' he said to me, speaking softly.

'So was I,' I said, 'though men pretend I was not.'

'I know what you did,' he said.

'So do I.'

He ignored my surliness. He was showing me sympathy, though I was too proud to show I appreciated it. 'The ealdorman has sent men,' he warned me, 'to take this place once judgment is given.'

There was a gasp behind me and I realised Mildrith had come into the hall. Harald bowed to her.

'The hall will be taken?' Mildrith asked.

'If the debt is not paid,' Harald said, 'the land will be given to the church.' He stared up at the newly hewn rafters as if wondering why I would build a hall on land doomed to be given to God.

Mildrith came to stand beside me. She was plainly distressed by Harald's summons, but she made a great effort to compose herself. 'I am sorry,' she said, 'about your wife.'

A flicker of pain crossed Harald's face as he made the sign of the cross. 'She was sick a long time, lady. It was merciful of God, I think, to take her.'

I had not known he was a widower, nor did I care much. 'She was a good woman,' Mildrith said.

'She was,' Harald said.

'And I pray for her.'

'I thank you for that,' Harald said.

111

'As I pray for Odda the Elder,' Mildrith went on.

'God be praised, he lives,' Harald made the sign of the cross again. 'But he is feeble and in pain.' He touched his scalp showing where Odda the Elder had been wounded.

'So who is the judge?' I asked harshly, interrupting the two.

'The bishop,' Harald said.

'Not the ealdorman?'

'He is at Cippanhamm.'

Mildrith insisted on giving Harald and his men ale and food. She and Harald talked a long time, sharing news of neighbours and family. They were both from Defnascir and I was not, and so I knew few of the folk they talked about, but I pricked up my ears when Harald said that Odda the Younger was marrying a girl from Mercia. 'She's in exile here,' he said, 'with her family.'

'Well born?' Mildrith asked.

'Exceedingly,' Harald said.

'I wish them much joy,' Mildrith said with evident sincerity. She was happy that day, warmed by Harald's company, though when he had gone she chided me for being churlish. 'Harald is a good man,' she insisted, 'a kind man. He would have given you advice. He would have helped you!'

I ignored her, but two days later I went into Exanceaster with Iseult and all my men. Including Haesten I now had eighteen warriors and I had armed them, given them shields and leather coats, and I led them through the market that always accompanied the court's sittings. There were stilt-walkers and jugglers, a man who ate fire, and a dancing bear. There were singers, harpists, storytellers, beggars, and pens of sheep, goats, cattle, pigs, geese, ducks and hens. There were fine cheeses, smoked fish, bladders of lard, pots of honey, trays of apples and baskets of pears. Iseult, who

112

had not been to Exanceaster before, was amazed at the size of the city, and the life of it, and the seething closeness of its houses, and I saw folk make the sign of the cross when they saw her for they had heard of the shadow queen held at Oxton and they knew her for a foreigner and a pagan.

Beggars crowded at the bishop's gate. There was a crippled woman with a blind child, men who had lost arms or legs in the wars, a score of them, and I threw them some pence, then, because I was on horseback, ducked under the archway of the courtyard beside the cathedral where a dozen chained felons were awaiting their fate. A group of young monks, nervous of the chained men, were plaiting beehives, while a score of armed men were clustered around three fires. They eyed my followers suspiciously as a young priest, his hands flapping, hurried across the puddles. 'Weapons are not to be brought into the precinct!' he told me sternly.

'They've got weapons,' I nodded at the men warming themselves by the flames.

'They are the reeve's men.'

'Then the sooner you deal with my business,' I said, 'the sooner my weapons will be gone.'

He looked up at me, his face anxious. 'Your business?'

'Is with the bishop.'

'The bishop is at prayer,' the priest said reprovingly, as though I should have known that. 'And he cannot see every man who comes here. You can talk to me.'

I smiled and raised my voice a little. 'In Cippanhamm, two years ago,' I said, 'your bishop was friends with Eanflæd. She has red hair and works her trade out of the Corncrake tavern. Her trade is whoring.'

The priest's hands were flapping again in an attempt to persuade me to lower my voice.

'I've been with Eanflæd,' I said, 'and she told me about the bishop. She said . . .'

The monks had stopped making beehives and were listening, but the priest cut me off by half shouting. 'The bishop might have a moment free.'

'Then tell him I'm here,' I said pleasantly.

'You are Uhtred of Oxton?' he asked.

'No,' I said. 'I am the Lord Uhtred of Bebbanburg.'

'Yes, lord.'

'Sometimes known as Uhtredærwe,' I added mischievously. Uhtred the Wicked.

'Yes, lord,' the priest said again and hurried away.

The bishop was called Alewold and he was really the bishop of Cridianton, but that place had not been thought as safe as Exanceaster and so for years the bishops of Cridianton had lived in the larger town which, as Guthrum had shown, was not the wisest decision. Guthrum's Danes had pillaged the cathedral and the bishop's house, which was still scantily furnished and I discovered Alewold sitting behind a table that looked as if it had once belonged to a butcher, for its hefty top was scored with knife cuts and stained with old blood. He looked at me indignantly. 'You should not be here,' he said.

'Why not?'

'You have business before the court tomorrow.'

'Tomorrow,' I said, 'you sit as a judge. Today you are a bishop.'

He acknowledged that with a small nod. He was an elderly man with a heavy jowled face and a reputation as a severe judge. He had been with Alfred in Scireburnan when the Danes arrived in Exanceaster, which is why he was still alive, and, like all the bishops in Wessex, he was a fervent supporter of the king, and I had no doubt that Alfred's dislike of me was known to Alewold, which meant I could expect little clemency when the court sat.

'I am busy,' Alewold said, gesturing at the parchments on

114

the stained table. Two clerks shared the table and a half-dozen resentful priests had gathered behind the bishop's chair.

'My wife,' I said, 'inherited a debt to the church.'

Alewold looked at Iseult who alone had come into the house with me. She looked beautiful, proud and wealthy. There was silver at her throat and in her hair, and her cloak was fastened with two brooches, one of jet and the other of amber. 'Your wife?' the bishop asked snidely.

'I would discharge the debt,' I said, ignoring his question, and I tipped a bag onto his butcher's table and the big silver plate we had taken from Ivar slid out. The silver made a satisfying noise as it thumped down and suddenly, in that small dark room ill-lit by three rush lights and a small, wood-barred window, it seemed as if the sun had come out. The heavy silver glowed and Alewold just stared at it.

There are good priests. Beocca is one and Willibald another, but I have discovered in my long life that most churchmen preach the merits of poverty while they lust after wealth. They love money and the church attracts money like a candle brings moths. I knew Alewold was a greedy man, as greedy for wealth as he was for the delights of a red-haired whore in Cippanhamm, and he could not take his eyes from that plate. He reached out and caressed the thick rim as if he scarce believed what he was seeing, and then he pulled the plate towards him and examined the twelve apostles. 'A pyx,' he said reverently.

'A plate,' I said casually.

One of the other priests leaned over a clerk's shoulder. 'Irish work,' he said.

'It looks Irish,' Alewold agreed, then looked suspiciously at me. 'You are returning it to the church?'

'Returning it?' I asked innocently.

'The plate was plainly stolen,' Alewold said, 'and you do well, Uhtred, to bring it back.'

115

'I had the plate made for you,' I said.

He turned the plate over, which took some effort for it was heavy, and once it was inverted he pointed to the scratches in the silver. 'It is old,' he said.

'I had it made in Ireland,' I said grandly, 'and doubtless it was handled roughly by the men who brought it across the sea.'

He knew I was lying. I did not care. 'There are silver-smiths in Wessex who could have made you a pyx,' one of the priests snapped.

'I thought you might want it,' I said, then leaned forward and pulled the plate out of the bishop's hands, 'but if you prefer West Saxon work,' I went on, 'then I can . . .'

'Give it back!' Alewold said and, when I made no move to obey, his voice became pleading. 'It is a beautiful thing.' He could see it in his church, or perhaps in his hall, and he wanted it. There was silence as he stared at it. If he had known that the plate existed, if I had told Mildrith of it, then he would have had a response ready, but as it was he was overwhelmed by desire for the heavy silver. A maid brought in a flagon and he waved her out of the room. She was, I noted, red-haired. 'You had the plate made,' Alewold said sceptically.

'In Dyflin,' I said.

'Is that where you went in the king's ship?' the priest who had snapped at me asked.

'We patrolled the coast,' I said, 'nothing more.'

'The value of the plate,' Alewold began, then stopped.

'Is far and above the debt Mildrith inherited,' I said. That was probably not true, but it was close to the amount, and I could see Alewold did not care. I was going to get what I wanted.

The debt was discharged. I insisted on having that written down, and written three times, and I surprised them by being able to read and so discovering that the first scrap of parchment made no mention of the church yielding their rights to the future produce of my estate, but that was corrected and I let the bishop keep one copy while I took two. 'You will not be arraigned for debt,' the bishop said as he pressed his seal into the wax of the last copy, 'but there is still the matter of Oswald's wergild.'

'I rely on your good and wise judgment, bishop,' I said, and I opened the purse hanging at my waist and took out a small lump of gold, making sure he could see there was more gold inside as I placed the small lump on the plate. 'Oswald was a thief.'

'His family will make oaths that he was not,' the priest said.

'And I will bring men who will swear he was,' I said. A trial relied heavily on oaths, but both sides would bring as many liars as they could muster, and judgment usually went to the better liars or, if both sides were equally convincing, to the side who had the sympathy of the onlookers. It was better, though, to have the sympathy of the judge. Oswald's family would have many supporters around Exanceaster, but gold is much the best argument in a law court.

And so it proved. To Mildrith's astonishment the debt was paid and Oswald's family denied two hundred shillings of wergild. I did not even bother to go to the court, relying on the persuasive power of gold, and sure enough the bishop peremptorily dismissed the demand for wergild, saying it was well known that Oswald had been a thief, and so I won. That did not make me any more popular. To the folk who lived in the Uisc's valley I was a Northumbrian interloper and, worse, it was known I was a pagan, but none dared confront me for I went nowhere beyond the estate without my men and my men went nowhere without their swords.

The harvest was in the storehouses. Now was the time for the Danes to come, when they could be sure to find food for their armies, but neither Guthrum nor Svein crossed the frontier. The winter came instead and we slaughtered the livestock, salted the meat, scraped hides and made calves' foot jelly. I listened for the sound of church bells ringing at an unusual time, for that would have been a sign that the Danes had attacked, but the bells did not ring.

Mildrith prayed that the peace would continue and I, being young and bored, prayed it would not. She prayed to the Christian god and I took Iseult to the high woods and made a sacrifice to Hoder, Odin and Thor and the gods were listening, for in the dark beneath the gallows tree, where the three spinners make our lives, a red thread was woven into my life. Fate is everything, and just after Yule the spinners brought a royal messenger to Oxton and he, in turn, brought me a summons. It seemed possible that Iseult's dream was true, and that Alfred would give me power for I was ordered to Cippanhamm to see the king. I was summoned to the Witan.

Five

Mildrith was excited by the summons. The Witan gave the king advice and her father had never been wealthy or important enough to receive such a summons, and she was overjoyed that the king wanted my presence. The witanegemot, as the meeting was called, was always held on the Feast of St Stephen, the day after Christmas, but my summons required me to be there on the twelfth day of Christmas and that gave Mildrith time to wash clothes for me. They had to be boiled and scrubbed and dried and brushed, and three women did the work and it took three days before Mildrith was satisfied that I would not disgrace her by appearing at Cippanhamm looking like a vagabond. She was not summoned, nor did she expect to accompany me, but she made a point of telling all our neighbours that I was to give counsel to the king. 'You mustn't wear that,' she told me, pointing to my Thor's hammer amulet.

'I always wear it,' I said.

'Then hide it,' she said, 'and don't be belligerent!'

'Belligerent?'

'Listen to what others say,' she said. 'Be humble. And remember to congratulate Odda the Younger.'

'For what?'

'He's to be married. Tell him I pray for them both.' She

119

was happy again, sure that by paying the church its debt I had regained Alfred's favour and her good mood was not even spoilt when I announced I would take Iseult with me. She bridled slightly at the news, then said that it was only right that Iseult should be taken to Alfred. 'If she is a queen,' Mildrith said, 'then she belongs in Alfred's court. This isn't a fit place for her.' She insisted on taking silver coins to the church in Exanceaster where she donated the money to the poor and gave thanks that I had been restored to Alfred's favour. She also thanked God for the good health of our son, Uhtred. I saw little of him, for he was still a baby and I have never had much patience for babies, but the women of Oxton constantly assured me that he was a lusty, strong boy.

We allowed two days for the journey. I took Haesten and six men as an escort for, though the shire-reeve's men patrolled the roads, there were plenty of wild places where outlaws preyed on travellers. We were in mail coats or leather tunics, with swords, spears, axes and shields. We all rode. Iseult had a small black mare I had bought for her, and I had also given her an otterskin cloak, and when we passed through villages, folk would stare at her for she rode like a man, her black hair bound up with a silver chain. They would kneel to her, as well as to me, and call out for alms. She did not take her maid for I remembered how crowded every tavern and house had been in Exanceaster when the Witan met, and I persuaded Iseult that we would be hard-pressed to find accommodation for ourselves, let alone a maid.

'What does the king want of you?' she asked as we rode up the Uisc valley. Rainwater puddled in the long furrows, gleaming in the winter sunshine, while the woods were glossy with holly leaves and bright with the berries of rowan, thorn, elder and yew.

'Aren't you supposed to tell me that?' I asked her.

She smiled. 'Seeing the future,' she said, 'is like travelling a strange road. Usually you cannot see far ahead, and when you can it is only a glimpse. And my brother doesn't give me dreams about everything.'

'Mildrith thinks the king has forgiven me,' I said.

'Has he?'

I shrugged. 'Perhaps.' I hoped so, not because I wanted Alfred's forgiveness, but because I wanted to be given command of the fleet again. I wanted to be with Leofric. I wanted the wind in my face and the sea rain on my cheek. 'It's odd, though,' I went on, 'that he didn't want me there for the whole witanegemot.'

'Maybe,' Iseult suggested, 'they discussed religious things at first?'

'He wouldn't want me there for that,' I said.

'So that's it,' she said. 'They talk about their god, but at the end they will talk of the Danes, and that is why he summoned you. He knows he needs you.'

'Or perhaps he just wants me there for the feast,' I suggested.

'The feast?'

'The Twelfth Night feast,' I explained, and that seemed to me the likeliest explanation; that Alfred had decided to forgive me and, to show he now approved of me, would let me attend the winter feast. I secretly hoped that was true, and it was a strange hope. I had been ready to kill Alfred only a few months before, yet now, though I still hated him, I wanted his approval. Such is ambition. If I could not rise with Ragnar then I would make my reputation with Alfred.

'Your road, Uhtred,' Iseult went on, 'is like a bright blade across a dark moor. I see it clearly.'

'And the woman of gold?'

She said nothing to that.

121

'Is it you?' I asked.

'The sun dimmed when I was born,' she said, 'so I am a woman of darkness and of silver, not of gold.'

'So who is she?'

'Someone far away, Uhtred, far away,' and she would say no more. Perhaps she knew no more, or perhaps she was guessing.

We reached Cippanhamm late on the eleventh day of Yule. There was still frost on the furrows and the sun was a gross red ball poised low above the tangling black branches as we came to the town's western gate. The city was full, but I was known in the Corncrake tavern where the red-headed whore called Eanflæd worked and she found us shelter in a half-collapsed cattle byre where a score of hounds had been kennelled. The hounds, she said, belonged to Huppa, Ealdorman of Thornsæta, but she reckoned the animals could survive a night or two in the yard. 'Huppa may not think so,' she said, 'but he can rot in hell.'

'He doesn't pay?' I asked her.

She spat for answer, then looked at me curiously. 'I hear Leofric's here?'

'He is?' I said, heartened by the news.

'I haven't seen him,' she said, 'but someone said he was here. In the royal hall. Maybe Burgweard brought him?' Burgweard was the new fleet commander, the one who wanted his ships to sail two by two in imitation of Christ's disciples. 'Leofric had better not be here,' Eanflæd finished.

'Why not?'

'Because he hasn't come to see me!' she said indignantly, 'that's why.' She was five or six years older than I with a broad face, a high forehead and springy hair. She was popular, so much so that she had a good deal of freedom in the tavern, that owed its profits more to her abilities than to the quality of the ale. I knew she was friendly with Leofric, but I suspected from her tone that she wanted to be more than friends. 'Who's she?' she asked, jerking her head at Iseult.

'A queen,' I said.

'That's another name for it, I suppose. How's your wife?'

'Back in Defnascir.'

'You're like all the rest, aren't you?' She shivered. 'If you're cold tonight bring the hounds back in to warm you. I'm off to work.'

We were cold, but I slept well enough and, next morning, the twelfth after Christmas, I left my six men at the Corncrake and took Iseult and Haesten to the king's buildings that lay behind their own palisade to the south of the town where the river curled about the walls. A man expected to attend the witanegemot with retainers, though not usually with a Dane and a Briton, but Iseult wanted to see Alfred and I wanted to please her. Besides, there was the great feast that evening and, though I warned her that Alfred's feasts were poor things, Iseult still wanted to be there. Haesten, with his mail coat and sword, was there to protect her, for I suspected she might not be allowed into the hall while the witanegemot debated and so might have to wait until evening for her chance to glimpse Alfred.

The gatekeeper demanded that we surrender our weapons, a thing I did with a bad grace, but no man, except the king's own household troops, could go armed in Alfred's presence. The day's talking had already begun, the gatekeeper told us, and so we hurried past the stables and past the big new royal chapel with its twin towers. A group of priests was huddled by the main door of the great hall and I recognised Beocca, my father's old priest, among them. I smiled in greeting, but his face, as he came towards us, was drawn and pale. 'You're late,' he said sharply.

'You're not pleased to see me?' I asked sarcastically.

He looked up at me. Beocca, despite his squint, red hair and palsied left hand, had grown into a stern authority. He was now a royal chaplain, confessor and a confidant to the king, and the responsibilities had carved deep lines on his face. 'I prayed,' he said, 'never to see this day.' He made the sign of the cross. 'Who's that?' he stared at Iseult.

'A queen of the Britons,' I said.

'She's what?'

'A queen. She's with me. She wants to see Alfred.'

I don't know whether he believed me, but he seemed not to care. Instead he was distracted, worried, and, because he lived in a strange world of kingly privilege and obsessive piety, I assumed his misery had been caused by some petty theological dispute. He had been Bebbanburg's mass priest when I was a child and, after my father's death, he had fled Northumberland because he could not abide living among the pagan Danes. He had found refuge in Alfred's court where he had become a friend of the king. He was also a friend to me, a man who had preserved the parchments that proved my claim to the lordship of Bebbanburg, but on that twelfth day of Yule he was anything but pleased to see me. He plucked my arm, drawing me towards the door. 'We must go in,' he said, 'and may God in his mercy protect you.'

'Protect me?'

'God is merciful,' Beocca said, 'and you must pray for that mercy,' and then the guards opened the door and we walked into the great hall. No one stopped Iseult and, indeed, there were a score of other women watching the proceedings from the edge of the hall.

There were also more than a hundred men there, though only forty or fifty comprised the witanegemot, and those thegns and senior churchmen were on chairs and benches set in a half circle in front of the dais where Alfred sat with two priests and with Ælswith, his wife, who was pregnant. Behind them, draped with a red cloth, was an altar on which stood thick candles and a heavy silver cross, while all about the walls were platforms where, in normal times, folk slept or ate to be out of the fierce draughts. This day, though, the platforms were crammed with the followers of the thegns and noblemen of the Witan and among them, of course, were a lot of priests and monks, for Alfred's court was more like a monastery than a royal hall. Beocca gestured that Iseult and Haesten should join those spectators, then he drew me towards the half circle of privileged advisers.

No one noticed my arrival. It was dark in the hall, for little of the wintry sunshine penetrated the small high windows. Braziers tried to give some warmth, but failed, succeeding only in thickening the smoke in the high rafters. There was a large central hearth, but the fire had been taken away to make room for the witanegemot's circle of stools, chairs and benches. A tall man in a blue cloak was on his feet as I approached. He was talking of the necessity of repairing bridges, and how local thegns were skimping the duty, and he suggested that the king appoint an official to survey the kingdom's roads. Another man interrupted to complain that such an appointment would encroach on the privileges of the shire ealdormen, and that started a chorus of voices, some for the proposal, most against, and two priests, seated at a small table beside Alfred's dais, tried to write down all the comments. I recognised Wulfhere, the Ealdorman of Wiltunscir, who yawned prodigiously. Close to him was Alewold, the Bishop of Exanceaster, who was swathed in furs. Still no one noticed me. Beocca had held me back, as if waiting for a lull in the proceedings before finding me a seat. Two servants brought in baskets of logs to feed the braziers, and it was then that Ælswith saw me and she leaned across and whispered in Alfred's ear. He had been paying close attention to the discussion, but now looked past his council to stare at me.

And a silence fell on that great hall. There had been a murmur of voices when men saw the king being distracted from the argument about bridges and they had all turned to look at me and then there was the silence that was broken by a priest's sneeze and a sudden odd scramble as the men closest to me, those sitting beside the cold stones of the hearth, moved to one side. They were not making way for me, but avoiding me.

Ælswith was smiling and I knew I was in trouble then. My hand instinctively went to my left side, but of course I had no sword so could not touch her hilt for luck. 'We shall talk of bridges later,' Alfred said. He stood. He wore a bronze circlet as a crown and had a fur-trimmed blue robe, matching the gown worn by his wife.

'What is happening?' I asked Beocca.

'You will be silent!' It was Odda the Younger who spoke. He was dressed in his war-glory, in shining mail covered by a black cloak, in high boots and with a red-leather sword belt from which hung his weapons, for Odda, as commander of the king's troops, was permitted to go armed in the royal hall. I looked into his eyes and saw triumph there, the same triumph that was on the Lady Ælswith's pinched face, and I knew I had not been brought to receive the king's favour, but summoned to face my enemies.

I was right. A priest was called from the dark gaggle beside the door. He was a young man with a pouchy, scowling face. He moved briskly, as if the day did not have enough hours to complete his work. He bowed to the king, then took a parchment from the table where the two clerks sat and came to stand in the centre of the Witan's circle.

'There is an urgent matter,' Alfred said, 'which, with the Witan's permission, we shall deal with now.' No one there was likely to disagree, so a low murmur offered approval of interrupting the more mundane discussions. Alfred nodded. 'Father Erkenwald will read the charges,' the king said, and took his throne again.

Charges? I was confused like a boar trapped between hounds and spears, and I seemed incapable of movement so I just stood there as Father Erkenwald unrolled the parchment and cleared his throat. 'Uhtred of Oxton,' he said, speaking in a high and precise voice, 'you are this day charged with the crime of taking a king's ship without our king's consent, and with taking that ship to the country of Cornwalum and there making war against the Britons, again without our king's consent, and this we can prove by oaths.' There was a small murmur in the hall, a murmur that was stilled when Alfred raised a thin hand. 'You are further charged,' Erkenwald went on, 'with making an alliance with the pagan called Svein, and with his help you murdered Christian folk in Cornwalum, despite those folk living in peace with our king, and this also we can prove by oaths.' He paused, and now there was complete silence in the hall. 'And you are charged,' Erkenwald's voice was lower now, as though he could scarce believe what he was reading, 'with joining the pagan Svein in an attack on our blessed king's realm by committing vile murder and impious church-robbery at Cynuit.' This time there was no murmur, but a loud outburst of indignation and Alfred made no move to check it, so Erkenwald had to raise his voice to finish the indictment. 'And this also,' he was shouting now, and men hushed to listen, 'we shall prove by oaths.' He lowered the parchment, gave me a look of pure loathing, then walked back to the edge of the dais.

'He's lying,' I snarled.

'You will have a chance to speak,' a fierce-looking churchman sitting beside Alfred said. He was in monk's robes, but over them he wore a priest's half cape richly embroidered with crosses. He had a full head of white hair and a deep, stern voice.

'Who's that?' I asked Beocca.

'The most holy Æthelred,' Beocca said softly and, seeing I did not recognise the name, 'Archbishop of Contwaraburg, of course.'

The archbishop leaned over to speak with Erkenwald. Ælswith was staring at me. She had never liked me, and now she was watching my destruction and taking a great pleasure from it. Alfred, meanwhile, was studying the roof beams as though he had never noticed them before, and I realised he intended to take no part in this trial, for trial it was. He would let other men prove my guilt, but doubtless he would pronounce sentence, and not just on me, it seemed, because the archbishop scowled. 'Is the second prisoner here?'

'He is held in the stables,' Odda the Younger said.

'He should be here,' the archbishop said indignantly. 'A man has a right to hear his accusers.'

'What other man?' I demanded.

It was Leofric, who was brought into the hall in chains, and there was no outcry against him because men perceived him as my follower. The crime was mine, Leofric had been snared by it, and now he would suffer for it, but he plainly had the sympathy of the men in the hall as he was brought to stand beside me. They knew him, he was of Wessex, while I was a Northumbrian interloper. He gave me a rueful glance as the guards led him to my side. 'Up to our arses in it,' he muttered.

'Quiet!' Beocca hissed.

'Trust me,' I said.

'Trust you?' Leofric asked bitterly.

But I had glanced at Iseult and she had given me the

smallest shake of her head, an indication, I reckoned, that she had seen the outcome of this day and it was good. 'Trust me,' I said again.

'The prisoners will be silent,' the archbishop said.

'Up to our royal arses,' Leofric said quietly.

The archbishop gestured at Father Erkenwald. 'You have oath-makers?' he asked.

'I do, lord.'

'Then let us hear the first.'

Erkenwald gestured to another priest who was standing by the door leading to the passage at the back of the hall. The door was opened and a slight figure in a dark cloak entered. I could not see his face for he wore a hood. He hurried to the front of the dais and there bowed low to the king and went on his knees to the archbishop who held out a hand so that his heavy, jewelled ring could be kissed. Only then did the man stand, push back his hood and turn to face me.

It was the Ass. Asser, the Welsh monk. He stared at me as yet another priest brought him a gospel-book on which he laid a thin hand. 'I make oath,' he said in accented English, still staring at me, 'that what I say is truth, and God so help me in that endeavour and condemn me to the eternal fires of hell if I dissemble.' He bent and kissed the gospel-book with the tenderness of a man caressing a lover.

'Bastard,' I muttered.

Asser was a good oath-maker. He spoke clearly, describing how I had come to Cornwalum in a ship that bore a beast-head on its prow and another on its stern. He told how I had agreed to help King Peredur, who was being attacked by a neighbour assisted by the pagan Svein, and how I had betrayed Peredur by allying myself with the Dane. 'Together,' Asser said, 'they made great slaughter, and I myself saw a holy priest put to death.'

'You ran like a chicken,' I said to him, 'you couldn't see a thing.'

Asser turned to the king and bowed. 'I did run, lord king. I am a brother monk, not a warrior, and when Uhtred turned that hillside red with Christian blood I did take flight. I am not proud of that, lord king, and I have earnestly sought God's forgiveness for my cowardice.'

Alfred smiled and the archbishop waved away Asser's remarks as if they were nothing. 'And when you left the slaughter,' Erkenwald asked, 'what then?'

'I watched from a hilltop,' Asser said, 'and I saw Uhtred of Oxton leave that place in the company of the pagan ship. Two ships sailing westwards.'

'They sailed westwards?' Erkenwald asked.

'To the west,' Asser confirmed.

Erkenwald glanced at me. There was silence in the hall as men leaned forward to catch each damning word. 'And what lay to the west?' Erkenwald asked.

'I cannot say,' Asser said. 'But if they did not go to the end of the world then I assume they turned about Cornwalum to go into the Sæfern Sea.'

'And you know no more?' Erkenwald asked.

'I know I helped bury the dead,' Asser said, 'and I said prayers for their souls, and I saw the smouldering embers of the burned church, but what Uhtred did when he left the place of slaughter I do not know. I only know he went westwards.'

Alfred was pointedly taking no part in the proceedings, but he plainly liked Asser for, when the Welshman's testimony was done, he beckoned him to the dais and rewarded him with a coin and a moment of private conversation. The Witan talked among themselves, sometimes glancing at me with the curiosity we give to doomed men. The Lady Ælswith, suddenly so gracious, smiled on Asser.

'You have anything to say?' Erkenwald demanded of me when Asser had been dismissed.

'I shall wait,' I said, 'till all your lies are told.'

The truth, of course, was that Asser had told the truth, and told it plainly, clearly and persuasively. The king's councillors had been impressed, just as they were impressed by Erkenwald's second oath-maker.

It was Steapa Snotor, the warrior who was never far from Odda the Younger's side. His back was straight, his shoulders square and his feral face with its stretched skin was grim. He glanced at me, bowed to the king, then laid a huge hand on the gospel-book and let Erkenwald lead him through the oath, and he swore to tell the truth on pain of hell's eternal agony, and then he lied. He lied calmly in a flat, toneless voice. He said he had been in charge of the soldiers who guarded the place at Cynuit where the new church was being built, and how two ships had come in the dawn and how warriors streamed from the ships, and how he had fought against them and killed six of them, but there were too many, far too many, and he had been forced to retreat, but he had seen the attackers slaughter the priests and he had heard the pagan leader shout his name as a boast. 'Svein, he was called.'

'And Svein brought two ships?'

Steapa paused and frowned, as though he had trouble counting to two, then nodded. 'He had two ships.'

'He led both?'

'Svein led one of the ships,' Steapa said, then he pointed a finger at me. 'And he led the other.'

The audience seemed to growl and the noise was so threatening that Alfred slapped the arm of his chair and finally stood to restore quiet. Steapa seemed unmoved. He stood, solid as an oak, and though he had not told his tale as convincingly as Brother Asser, there was something very

131

damning in his testimony. It was so matter-of-fact, so unemotionally told, so straightforward, and none of it was true.

'Uhtred led the second ship,' Erkenwald said, 'but did Uhtred join in the killing?'

'Join it?' Steapa asked. 'He led it.' He snarled those words and the men in the hall growled their anger.

Erkenwald turned to the king. 'Lord king,' he said, 'he must die.'

'And his land and property must be forfeited!' Bishop Alewold shouted in such excitement that a whirl of his spittle landed and hissed in the nearest brazier. 'Forfeited to the church!'

The men in the hall thumped their feet on the ground to show their approbation. Ælswith nodded vigorously, but the archbishop clapped his hands for silence. 'He has not spoken,' he reminded Erkenwald, then nodded at me. 'Say your piece,' he ordered curtly.

'Beg for mercy,' Beocca advised me quietly.

When you are up to your arse in shit there is only one thing to do. Attack, and so I admitted I had been at Cynuit, and that admission provoked some gasps in the hall. 'But I was not there last summer,' I went on. 'I was there in the spring, at which time I killed Ubba Lothbrokson, and there are men in this hall who saw me do it! Yet Odda the Younger claimed the credit. He took Ubba's banner, which I laid low, and he took it to his king and he claimed to have killed Ubba. Now, lest I spread the truth, which is that he is a coward and a liar, he would have me murdered by lies.' I pointed to Steapa. 'His lies.'

Steapa spat to show his scorn. Odda the Younger was looking furious, but he said nothing and some men noted it. To be called a coward and a liar is to be invited to do battle, but Odda stayed still as a stump.

132

'You cannot prove what you say,' Erkenwald said.

'I can prove I killed Ubba,' I said.

'We are not here to discuss such things,' Erkenwald said loftily, 'but to determine whether you broke the king's peace by an impious attack on Cynuit.'

'Then summon my crewmen,' I demanded. 'Bring them here, put them on oath, and ask what they did in the summer.' I waited, and Erkenwald said nothing. He glanced at the king as if seeking help, but Alfred's eyes were momentarily closed. 'Or are you in so much of a hurry to kill me,' I went on, 'that you dare not wait to hear the truth?'

'I have Steapa's sworn testimony,' Erkenwald said, as if that made any other evidence unnecessary. He was flustered.

'And you can have my oath,' I said, 'and Leofric's oath, and the oath of a crewman who is here.' I turned and beckoned Haesten who looked frightened at being summoned, but at Iseult's urging came to stand beside me. 'Put him on oath,' I demanded of Erkenwald.

Erkenwald did not know what to do, but some men in the Witan called out that I had the right to summon oath-makers and the newcomer must be heard, and so a priest brought the gospel-book to Haesten. I waved the priest away. 'He will swear on this,' I said, and took out Thor's amulet.

'He's not a Christian?' Erkenwald demanded in astonishment.

'He is a Dane,' I said.

'How can we trust the word of a Dane?' Erkenwald demanded.

'But our lord king does,' I retorted. 'He trusts the word of Guthrum to keep the peace, so why should this Dane not be trusted?'

That provoked some smiles. Many in the Witan thought Alfred far too trusting of Guthrum and I felt the sympathy in the hall move to my side, but then the archbishop intervened

133

to declare that the oath of a pagan was of no value. 'None whatsoever,' he snapped. 'He must stand down.'

'Then put Leofric under oath,' I demanded, 'and then bring our crew here and listen to their testimony.'

'And you will all lie with one tongue,' Erkenwald said, 'and what happened at Cynuit is not the only matter on which you are accused. Do you deny that you sailed in the king's ship? That you went to Cornwalum and there betrayed Peredur and killed his Christian people? Do you deny that Brother Asser told the truth?'

'But what if Peredur's queen were to tell you that Asser lies?' I asked. 'What if she were to tell you that he lies like a hound at the hearth?' Erkenwald stared at me. They all stared at me and I turned and gestured at Iseult who stepped forward, tall and delicate, the silver glinting at her neck and wrists. 'Peredur's queen,' I announced, 'whom I demand that you hear under oath, and thus hear how her husband was planning to join the Danes in an assault on Wessex.'

That was rank nonsense, of course, but it was the best I could invent at that moment, and Iseult, I knew, would swear to its truth. Quite why Svein would fight Peredur if the Briton planned to support him was a dangerously loose plank in the argument, but it did not really matter for I had confused the proceedings so much that no one was sure what to do. Erkenwald was speechless. Men stood to look at Iseult, who looked calmly back at them, and the king and the archbishop bent their heads together. Ælswith, one hand clapped to her pregnant belly, hissed advice at them. None of them wanted to summon Iseult for fear of what she would say, and Alfred, I suspect, knew that the trial, which had already become mired in lies, could only get worse.

'You're good, earsling,' Leofric muttered, 'you're very good.'

Odda the Younger looked at the king, then at his fellow

members of the Witan, and he must have known I was slithering out of his snare for he pulled Steapa to his side. He spoke to him urgently. The king was frowning, the archbishop looked perplexed, Ælswith's blotched face showed fury while Erkenwald seemed helpless. Then Steapa rescued them. 'I do not lie!' he shouted.

He seemed uncertain what to say next, but he had the hall's attention. The king gestured to him, as if inviting him to continue, and Odda the Younger whispered in the big man's ear.

'He says I lie,' Steapa said, pointing at me, 'and I say I do not, and my sword says I do not.' He stopped abruptly, having made what was probably the longest speech of his life, but it was enough. Feet drummed on the floor and men shouted that Steapa was right, which he was not, but he had reduced the whole tangled morass of lies and accusations to a trial by combat and they all liked that. The archbishop still looked troubled, but Alfred gestured for silence.

He looked at me. 'Well?' he asked. 'Steapa says his sword will support his truth. Does yours?'

I could have said no. I could have insisted on letting Iseult speak and then allowing the Witan to advise the king which side had spoken the greater truth, but I was ever rash, ever impetuous, and the invitation to fight cut through the whole entanglement. If I fought and won then Leofric and I were innocent of every charge.

I did not even think about losing. I just looked at Steapa. 'My sword,' I told him, 'says I tell the truth, and that you are a stinking bag of wind, a liar from hell, a cheat and a perjurer who deserves death.'

'Up to our arses again,' Leofric said.

Men cheered. They liked a fight to the death, and it was much better entertainment than listening to Alfred's harpist chant the psalms. Alfred hesitated, and I saw Ælswith look from me to Steapa, and she must have thought him the greater warrior for she leaned forward, touched Alfred's elbow, and whispered urgently.

And the king nodded. 'Granted,' he said. He sounded weary, as if he was dispirited by the lies and the insults. 'You will fight tomorrow. Swords and shields, nothing else.' He held up a hand to stop the cheering. 'My lord Wulfhere?'

'Sire?' Wulfhere struggled to his feet.

'You will arrange the fight. And may God grant victory to the truth.' Alfred stood, pulled his robe about him and left.

And Steapa, for the first time since I had seen him, smiled.

'You're a damned fool,' Leofric told me. He had been released from his chains and allowed to spend the evening with me. Haesten was there, as was Iseult and my men who had been brought from the town. We were lodged in the king's compound, in a cattle byre that stank of dung, but I did not notice the smell. It was Twelfth Night so there was the great feast in the king's hall, but we were left out in the cold, watched there by two of the royal guards. 'Steapa's good,' Leofric warned me.

'I'm good.'

'He's better,' Leofric said bluntly. 'He'll slaughter you.'

'He won't,' Iseult said calmly.

'Damn it, he's good!' Leofric insisted, and I believed him.

'It's that God-damned monk's fault,' I said bitterly. 'He went bleating to Alfred, didn't he?' In truth, Asser had been sent by the King of Dyfed to assure the West Saxons that Dyfed was not planning war, but Asser had taken the opportunity of his embassy to recount the tale of the *Eftwyrd* and from that it was a small jump to conclude that we had stayed with Svein while he attacked Cynuit. Alfred had no proof of our guilt, but Odda the Younger had seen a chance to destroy me and so persuaded Steapa to lie.

'Now Steapa will kill you,' Leofric grumbled, 'whatever she says.' Iseult did not bother to answer him. She was using handfuls of grubby straw to clean my mail coat. The armour had been fetched from the Corncrake tavern and given to me, but I would have to wait till morning to get my weapons, which meant they would not be newly sharpened. Steapa, because he served Odda the Younger, was one of the king's bodyguard, so he would have all night to put an edge on his sword. The royal kitchens had sent us food, though I had no appetite. 'Just take it slow in the morning,' Leofric told me.

'Slow?'

'You fight in a rage,' he said, 'and Steapa's always calm.'

'So better to get in a rage,' I said.

'That's what he wants. He'll fend you off and fend you off and wait till you're tired, then he'll finish you off. It's how he fights.'

Harald told us the same thing. Harald was the shire-reeve of Defnascir, the widower who had summoned me to the court in Exanceaster, but he had also fought alongside us at Cynuit and that makes a bond, and sometime in the dark he splashed through the rain and mud and came into the light of the small fire that lit the cattle shed without warming it. He stopped in the doorway and gazed at me reproachfully. 'Were you with Svein at Cynuit?' he asked.

'No,' I said.

'I didn't think so.' Harald came into the byre and sat by the fire. The two royal guards were at the door and he ignored them, and that was interesting. All of them served Odda, and the young ealdorman would not be pleased to hear that Harald had come to us, yet plainly Harald trusted the two guards not to tell, which suggested that there was unhappiness in Odda's ranks. Harald put a pot of ale on the floor. 'Steapa's sitting at the king's table,' he said.

'So he's eating badly,' I said.

Harald nodded, but did not smile. 'It's not much of a feast,' he admitted. He stared into the fire for a moment, then looked at me. 'How's Mildrith?'

'Well.'

'She is a dear girl,' he said, then glanced at Iseult's dark beauty before staring into the fire again. 'There will be a church service at dawn,' he said, 'and after that you and Steapa will fight.'

'Where?'

'In a field on the other side of the river,' he said, then pushed the pot of ale towards me. 'He's left-handed.'

I could not remember fighting against a man who held his sword in his left hand, but nor could I see a disadvantage in it. We would both have our shields facing the other man's shield instead of his weapon, but that would be a problem to both of us. I shrugged.

'He's used to it,' Harald explained, 'and you're not. And he wears mail down to here,' he touched his calf, 'and he has an iron strip on his left boot.'

'Because that's his vulnerable foot?'

'He plants it forward,' Harald said, 'inviting attack, then chops at your sword arm.'

'So he's a hard man to kill,' I said mildly.

'No one's done it yet,' Harald said gloomily.

'You don't like him?'

He did not answer at first, but drank ale then passed the pot to Leofric. 'I like the old man,' he said, meaning Odda the Elder. 'He's foul-tempered, but he's fair enough. But the son?' he shook his head sadly. 'I think the son is untested. Steapa? I don't dislike him, but he's like a hound. He only knows how to kill.'

I stared into the feeble fire, looking for a sign from the gods in the small flames, but none came, or none that I saw. 'He must be worried though,' Leofric said.

'Steapa?' Harald asked, 'why should he be worried?'

'Uhtred killed Ubba.'

Harald shook his head. 'Steapa doesn't think enough to be worried. He just knows he'll kill Uhtred tomorrow.'

I thought back to the fight with Ubba. He had been a great warrior, with a reputation that glowed wherever Norsemen sailed, and I had killed him, but the truth was that he had put a foot into the spilled guts of a dying man and slipped. His leg had shot sideways, he had lost his balance and I had managed to cut the tendons in his arm. I touched the hammer amulet and thought that the gods had sent me a sign after all. 'An iron strip in his boot?' I asked.

Harald nodded. 'He doesn't care how much you attack him. He knows you're coming from his left and he'll block most of your attacks with his sword. Big sword, heavy thing. But some blows will get by and he won't care. You'll waste them on iron. Heavy mail, helmet, boot, doesn't matter. It'll be like hitting an oak tree, and after a while you'll make a mistake. He'll be bruised and you'll be dead.'

He was right, I thought. Striking an armoured man with a sword rarely achieved much except to make a bruise because the edge would be stopped by mail or helmet. Mail cannot be chopped open by a sword, which was why so many men carried axes into battle, but the rules of trial by combat said the fight had to be with swords. A sword lunge would pierce mail, but Steapa was not going to make himself an easy target for a lunge. 'Is he quick?' I asked.

'Quick enough,' Harald said, then shrugged. 'Not as quick as you,' he added grudgingly, 'but he isn't slow.'

'What does the money say?' Leofric asked, though he surely knew the answer.

'No one's wagering a penny on Uhtred,' Harald said.

'You should,' I retorted.

He smiled at that, but I knew he would not take the advice. 'The big money,' he said, 'is what Odda will give Steapa when he kills you. A hundred shillings.'

'Uhtred's not worth it,' Leofric said with rough humour.

'Why does he want me dead so badly?' I wondered aloud. It could not be Mildrith, I thought, and the argument over who had killed Ubba was long in the past, yet still Odda the Younger conspired against me.

Harald paused a long time before answering. He had his bald head bowed and I thought he was in prayer, but then he looked up. 'You threaten him,' he said quietly.

'I haven't even seen him for months,' I protested, 'so how do I threaten him?'

Harald paused again, choosing his words carefully. 'The king is frequently ill,' he said after the pause, 'and who can say how long he will live? And if, God forbid, he should die soon, then the Witan will not choose his infant son to be king. They'll choose a nobleman with a reputation made on the battlefield. They'll choose a man who can stand up to the Danes.'

'Odda?' I laughed at the thought of Odda as king.

'Who else?' Harald asked. 'But if you were to stand before the Witan and swear an oath to the truth about the battle where Ubba died, they might not choose him. So you threaten him, and he fears you because of that.'

'So now he's paying Steapa to chop you to bits,' Leofric added gloomily.

Harald left. He was a decent man, honest and hard-working, and he had taken a risk by coming to see me, and I had been poor company for I did not appreciate the gesture he made. It was plain he thought I must die in the morning, and he had done his best to prepare me for the fight, but despite Iseult's confident prediction that I would live I did not sleep well. I was worried, and it was cold. The rain turned to sleet in the night and the wind whipped into the byre. By dawn the wind and sleet had stopped and instead there was a mist shrouding the buildings and icy water dripping from the mossy thatch. I made a poor breakfast of damp bread and it was while I was eating that Father Beocca came and said Alfred wished to speak with me.

I was sour. 'You mean he wants to pray with me?'

'He wants to speak with you,' Beocca insisted and, when I did not move, he stamped his lamed foot. 'It is not a request, Uhtred. It is a royal order!'

I put on my mail, not because it was time to arm for the fight, but because its leather lining offered some warmth on a cold morning. The mail was not very clean, despite Iseult's efforts. Most men wore their hair short, but I liked the Danish way of leaving it long and so I tied it behind with a lace and Iseult plucked the straw scraps from it. 'We must hurry,' Beocca said and I followed him through the mud past the great hall and the newly built church to some smaller buildings made of timber that had still not weathered grey. Alfred's father had used Cippanhamm as a hunting lodge, but Alfred was expanding it. The church had been his first new building, and he had built that even before he repaired and extended the palisade, and that was an indication of his priorities. Even now, when the nobility of Wessex was gathered just a day's march from the Danes, there seemed to be more churchmen than soldiers in the place, and that was another indication of how Alfred thought to protect his realm. 'The king is gracious,' Beocca hissed at me as we went through a door, 'so be humble.'

Beocca knocked on another door, did not wait for an answer, but pushed it open and indicated I should step inside. He did not follow me, but closed the door, leaving me in a gloomy half darkness.

A pair of beeswax candles flickered on an altar and by their light I saw two men kneeling in front of the plain wooden cross that stood between the candles. The men had their backs to me, but I recognised Alfred by his fur-trimmed blue cloak. The second man was a monk. They were both praying silently and I waited. The room was small, evidently a private chapel, and its only furniture was the draped altar and a kneeling stool on which was a closed book.

'In the name of the Father,' Alfred broke the silence.

'And of the Son,' the monk said, and he spoke English with an accent and I recognised the voice of the Ass.

'And of the Holy Ghost,' Alfred concluded, 'amen.'

'Amen,' Asser echoed, and both men stood, their faces suffused with the joy of devout Christians who have said their prayers well, and Alfred blinked as though he were surprised to see me, though he must have heard Beocca's knocking and the sound of the door opening and closing.

'I trust you slept well, Uhtred?' he said.

'I trust you did, lord.'

'The pains kept me awake,' Alfred said, touching his belly, then he went to one side of the room and hauled open a big pair of wooden shutters, flooding the chapel with a wan, misty light. The window looked onto a courtyard and I was aware of men out there. The king shivered, for it was freezing in the chapel. 'It is Saint Cedd's feast day,' he told me.

I said nothing.

'You have heard of Saint Cedd?' he asked me and, when my silence betrayed ignorance, he smiled indulgently. 'He was an East Anglian, am I not right, brother?'

'The most blessed Cedd was indeed an East Angle, lord,' Asser confirmed.

'And his mission was in Lundene,' Alfred went on, 'but he concluded his days at Lindisfarena. You must know that house, Uhtred?'

'I know it, lord,' I said. The island was a short ride from Bebbanburg and not so long before I had ridden to its monastery with Earl Ragnar and watched the monks die beneath Danish swords. 'I know it well,' I added.

'So Cedd is famous in your homeland?'

'I've not heard of him, lord.'

'I think of him as a symbol,' Alfred said, 'a man who was born in East Anglia, did his life's work in Mercia and died in Northumbria.' He brought his long, pale hands together so that the fingers embraced. 'The Saxons of England, Uhtred, gathered together before God.'

'And united in joyful prayer with the Britons,' Asser added piously.

'I beseech Almighty God for that happy outcome,' the king said, smiling at me, and by now I recognised what he was saying. He stood there, looking so humble, with no crown, no great necklace, no arm rings, nothing but a small garnet brooch holding the cloak at his neck, and he spoke of a happy outcome, but what he was really seeing was the Saxon people gathered under one king. A king of Wessex. Alfred's piety hid a monstrous ambition.

'We must learn from the saints,' Alfred told me. 'Their lives are a guide to the darkness that surrounds us, and Saint Cedd's holy example teaches that we must be united, so I am loathe to shed Saxon blood on Saint Cedd's feast day.'

'There need be no bloodshed, lord,' I said.

'I am pleased to hear it,' Alfred interjected.

'If the charges against me are retracted.'

The smile went from his face and he walked to the window and stared into the misty courtyard and I looked where he looked and saw that a small display was being mounted for my benefit. Steapa was being armoured. Two men were dropping a massive mail coat over his wide shoulders, while a third stood by with an outsized shield and a monstrous sword.

'I talked with Steapa last night,' the king said, turning from the window, 'and he told me there was a mist when Svein attacked at Cynuit. A morning mist like this one.' He waved at the whiteness sifting into the chapel.

'I wouldn't know, lord,' I said.

'So it is possible,' the king went on, 'that Steapa was mistaken when he thought he saw you.' I almost smiled. The king knew Steapa had lied, though he would not say as much. 'Father Willibald also spoke to the crew of the *Eftwyrd*,' the king went on, 'and not one of them confirmed Steapa's tale.'

The crew was still in Hamtun, so Willibald's report must have come from there and that meant the king had known I was innocent of the slaughter at Cynuit even before I was charged. 'So I was falsely arraigned?' I said harshly.

'You were accused,' the king corrected me, 'and accusations must be proven or refuted.'

'Or withdrawn.'

'I can withdraw the charges,' Alfred agreed. Steapa, outside the window, was making sure his mail coat was seated comfortably by swinging his great sword. And it was great. It was huge, a hammer of a blade. Then the king half-closed the shutter, hiding Steapa. 'I can withdraw the accusation about Cynuit,' he said, 'but I do not think Brother Asser lied to us.'

'I have a queen,' I said, 'who says he does.'

'A shadow queen,' Asser hissed, 'a pagan! A sorceress!' He looked at Alfred. 'She is evil, lord,' he said, 'a witch! *Maleficos non patieris vivere*!'

'Thou shalt not permit a witch to live,' Alfred translated for my benefit. 'That is God's commandment, Uhtred, from the holy scriptures.'

'Your answer to the truth,' I sneered, 'is to threaten a woman with death?'

Alfred flinched at that. 'Brother Asser is a good Christian,' he said vehemently, 'and he tells the truth. You went to war without my orders. You used my ship, my men, and you behaved treacherously! You are the liar, Uhtred, and you are the cheat!' He spoke angrily, but managed to control his anger. 'It is my belief,' he went on, 'that you have paid your debt to the church with goods stolen from other good Christians.'

'Not true,' I said harshly. I had paid the debt with goods stolen from a Dane.

'So resume the debt,' the king said, 'and we shall have no death on this blessed day of Saint Cedd.'

I was being offered life. Alfred waited for my response, smiling. He was sure I would accept his offer because to him it seemed reasonable. He had no love for warriors, weapons and killing. Fate decreed that he must spend his reign fighting, but it was not to his taste. He wanted to civilise Wessex, to give it piety and order, and two men fighting to the death on a winter's morning was not his idea of a well-run kingdom.

But I hated Alfred. I hated him for humiliating me at Exanceaster when he had made me wear a penitent's robe and crawl on my knees. Nor did I think of him as my king. He was a West Saxon and I was a Northumbrian, and I reckoned so long as he was king then Wessex had small chance of surviving. He believed God would protect him from the Danes, while I believed they had to be defeated by swords. I also had an idea how to defeat Steapa, just an idea, and I had no wish to take on a debt I had already paid, and I was young and I was foolish and I was arrogant and I was never able to resist a stupid impulse. 'Everything I have said is the truth,' I lied, 'and I would defend that truth with my sword.'

145

Alfred flinched from my tone. 'Are you saying Brother Asser lied?' he demanded.

'He twists truth,' I said, 'like a woman wrings a hen's neck.'

The king pulled the shutter open, showing me the mighty Steapa in his gleaming war glory. 'You really want to die?' he asked me.

'I want to fight for the truth, lord king,' I said stubbornly.

'Then you are a fool,' Alfred said, his anger showing again. 'You are a liar, a fool and a sinner.' He strode past me, pulled open the door and shouted at a servant to tell Ealdorman Wulfhere that the fight was to take place after all. 'Go,' he added to me, 'and may your soul receive its just reward.'

Wulfhere had been charged with arranging the fight, but there was a delay because the ealdorman had disappeared. The town was searched, the royal buildings were searched, but there was no sign of him until a stable slave nervously reported that Wulfhere and his men had ridden away from Cippanhamm before dawn. No one knew why, though some surmised that Wulfhere wanted no part in a trial by combat, which made little sense to me for the ealdorman had never struck me as a squeamish man. Ealdorman Huppa of Thornsæta was appointed to replace him, and so it was close to midday when my swords were brought to me and we were escorted down to the meadow that lay across the bridge which led from the town's eastern gate. A huge crowd had gathered on the river's far bank. There were cripples, beggars, jugglers, women selling pies, dozens of priests, excited children and, of course, the assembled warriors of the West Saxon nobility, all of them in Cippanhamm for the meeting of the Witan, and all eager to see Steapa Snotor show off his renowned skill.

'You're a damned fool,' Leofric said to me.

'Because I insisted on fighting?'

146

'You could have walked away.'

'And men would have called me a coward,' I said. And that too was the truth, that a man cannot step back from a fight and stay a man. We make much in this life if we are able. We make children and wealth and amass land and build halls and assemble armies and give great feasts, but only one thing survives us. Reputation. I could not walk away.

Alfred did not come to the fight. Instead, with the pregnant Ælswith and their two children, and escorted by a score of guards and as many priests and courtiers, he had ridden westwards. He was accompanying Brother Asser on the start of the monk's return journey to Dyfed, and the king was making a point that he preferred the company of the British churchman to watching two of his warriors fight like snarling hounds. But no one else in Wessex wanted to miss the battle. They were eager for it, but Huppa wanted everything to be orderly and so he insisted that the crowd push back from the damp ground beside the river to give us space. Eventually the folk were massed on a green bank overlooking the trampled grass and Huppa went to Steapa to enquire if he was ready.

He was ready. His mail shone in the weak sunlight. His helmet was glistening. His shield was a huge thing, bossed and rimmed with iron, a shield that must have weighed as much as a sack of grain and was a weapon in itself if he managed to hit me with it, but his chief weapon was his great sword that was longer and heavier than any I had seen.

Huppa, trailed by two guards, came to me. His feet squelched in the grass and I thought that the ground would prove treacherous. 'Uhtred of Oxton,' he said, 'are you ready?'

'My name,' I said, 'is Uhtred of Bebbanburg.'

147

'Are you ready?' he demanded, ignoring my correction.

'No,' I said.

A murmur went through the folk nearest to me, and the murmur spread, and after a few heartbeats the whole crowd was jeering me. They thought me a coward, and that thought was reinforced when I dropped my shield and sword and made Leofric help as I stripped off the heavy coat of mail. Odda the Younger, standing beside his champion, was laughing. 'What are you doing?' Leofric asked me.

'I hope you put money on me,' I said.

'Of course I didn't.'

'Are you refusing to fight?' Huppa asked me.

'No,' I said, and when I was stripped of my armour I took Serpent-Breath back from Leofric. Just Serpent-Breath. No helmet, no shield, just my good sword. Now I was unburdened. The ground was heavy, Steapa was armoured, but I was light and I was fast and I was ready.

'I'm ready,' I told Huppa.

He went to the meadow's centre, raised an arm, dropped it, and the crowd cheered.

I kissed the hammer around my neck, trusted my soul to the great god Thor and walked forwards.

Steapa came steadily towards me, shield up, sword held out to his left. There was no trace of concern in his eyes. He was a workman at his trade and I wondered how many men he had killed, and he must have thought my death would be easy for I had no protection, not even a shield. And so we walked towards each other until, a dozen paces from him, I ran. I ran at him, feinted right towards his sword and then broke hard to my left, still running, going past him now and I was aware of the huge blade swinging fast after me as he turned, but then I was behind him, he was still turning and I dropped to my knees, ducked, heard the blade go over my head and I was up again, lunging.

The sword pierced his mail, drew blood from just behind his left shoulder, but he was quicker than I had expected and had already checked that first great swing and was bringing the sword back and his turn pulled Serpent-Breath free. I had scratched him.

I danced back two paces. I went left again and he charged me, hoping to crush me with the weight of his shield, but I ran back to the right, fending off the sword with Serpent-Breath and the crack of the blades was like the bell of doomsday, and I lunged again, this time aiming at his waist, but he stepped back quickly. I kept going to the right, my arm jarred by the clash of the swords. I went fast, making him turn, and I feinted a lunge, brought him forward and went back to the left. The ground was boggy. I feared slipping, but speed was my weapon. I had to keep him turning, keep him swinging into empty air, and snatch what chances I could to use Serpent-Breath's point. Bleed him enough, I thought, and he would tire, but he guessed my tactics and started making short rushes to frustrate me, and each rush would be accompanied by the hiss of that huge sword. He wanted to make me parry and hoped he could break Serpent-Breath when the blades met. I feared the same. She was well made, but even the best sword can break.

He forced me back, trying to crowd me against the spectators on the bank so he could hack me to pieces in front of them. I let him drive me, then dodged to my right where my left foot slipped and I went down on that knee and the crowd, close behind me now, took in a great breath and a woman screamed because Steapa's huge sword was swinging like an axe onto my neck, only I had not slipped, merely pretended to, and I pushed off with my right foot, came out from under the blow and around his right flank, and he thrust the shield out, catching my shoulder with the rim and I knew I would have a bruise there, but I also had a heartbeat of opportunity and I darted Serpent-Breath forward and her point punctured his mail again to scrape against the ribs of his back and he roared as he turned, wrenching my blade free of his mail, but I was already going backwards.

I stopped ten paces away. He stopped too and watched me. There was a slight puzzlement on his big face now. There was still no worry there, just puzzlement. He pushed his left foot forward, as Harald had warned me, and he was hoping I would attack it and he would rely on the hidden iron strip in the boot to protect him while he thumped and hacked and bludgeoned me to death. I smiled at him and threw Serpent-Breath from my right hand into my left and held her there, and that was a new puzzle for him. Some men could fight with either hand, and perhaps I was one of them? He drew his foot back. 'Why do they call you Steapa Snotor?' I asked, 'you're not clever. You've got the brains of an addled egg.'

I was trying to enrage him and hoped that anger would make him careless, but my insult bounced off him. Instead of rushing me in fury he came slowly, watching the sword in my left hand, and the men on the hill called for him to kill me and I suddenly ran at him, broke right and he swung at me a little late, thinking I was going to go left at the last moment and I swept Serpent-Breath back and she caught his sword arm and I could feel her blade scraping through the rings of his mail, but she did not slice through them and then I was away from him and put her back into my right hand, turned, charged him and swerved away at the last moment so that his massive swing missed me by a yard.

He was still puzzled. This was like a bull-baiting and he

150

was the bull, and his problem was to get me in a place where he could use his greater strength and weight. I was the dog, and my job was to lure him, tease him and bite him until he weakened. He had thought I would come with mail and shield and we would batter each other for a few moments until my strength faded and he could drive me to the ground with massive blows and chop me to scraps with the big sword, but so far his blade had not touched me. But nor had I weakened him. My two cuts had drawn blood, but they were mere scratches. So now he came forward again, hoping to herd me back to the river. A woman screamed from the top of the bank, and I assumed she was trying to encourage him, and the screaming grew louder and I just went back faster, making Steapa lumber forward, but I had slipped away to his right and was coming back at him, making him turn, and then he suddenly stopped and stared past me and his shield went down and his sword dropped too, and all I had to do was lunge. He was there for the killing. I could thrust Serpent-Breath into his chest or throat, or ram her into his belly, but I did none of those things. Steapa was no fool at fighting and I guessed he was luring me and I did not take the bait. If I lunged, I thought, he would crush me between his shield and sword. He wanted me to think him defenceless so that I could come into range of his weapons, but instead I stopped and spread my arms, inviting him to attack me as he was inviting me to attack him.

But he ignored me. He just stared past my shoulder. And the woman's screaming was shrill now and there were men shouting, and Leofric was yelling my name, and the spectators were no longer watching us, but running in panic.

So I turned my back on Steapa and looked towards the town on its hill that was cradled by the river's bend.

And I saw that Cippanhamm was burning. Smoke was

darkening the winter sky and the horizon was filled with men, mounted men, men with swords and axes and shields and spears and banners, and more horsemen were coming from the eastern gate to thunder across the bridge.

Because all Alfred's prayers had failed and the Danes had come to Wessex.

Six

Steapa recovered his wits before I did. He stared open-mouthed at the Danes crossing the bridge and then just ran towards his master, Odda the Younger, who was shouting for his horses. The Danes were spreading out from the bridge, galloping across the meadow with drawn swords and levelled spears. Smoke poured into the low wintry clouds from the burning town. Some of the king's buildings were alight. A riderless horse, stirrups flapping, galloped across the grass, then Leofric grabbed my elbow and pulled me northwards beside the river. Most of the folk had gone south and the Danes had followed them, so north seemed to offer more safety. Iseult had my mail coat and I took it from her, leaving her to carry Wasp-Sting, and behind us the screaming rose as the Danes chopped into the panicked mass. Folk scattered. Escaping horsemen thumped past us, the hooves throwing up spadefuls of damp earth and grass with every step. I saw Odda the Younger swerve away with three other horsemen. Harald, the shire-reeve, was one of them, but I could not see Steapa and for a moment I feared the big man was looking for me. Then I forgot him as a band of Danes turned north in pursuit of Odda. 'Where are our horses?' I shouted at Leofric, who looked bemused and I remembered he had not travelled to Cippanhamm with me.

The beasts were probably still in the yard behind the Corncrake tavern, which meant they were lost.

There was a fallen willow in a stand of leafless alders by the river and we paused there for breath, hidden by the willow's trunk. I pulled on the mail coat, buckled on my swords and took my helmet and shield from Leofric. 'Where's Haesten?' I asked.

'He ran,' Leofric said curtly. So had the rest of my men. They had joined the panic and were gone southwards. Leofric pointed northwards. 'Trouble,' he said curtly. There was a score of Danes riding down our bank of the river, blocking our escape, but they were still some distance away, while the men pursuing Odda had vanished, so Leofric led us across the water meadow to a tangle of thorns, alders, nettles and ivy. At its centre was an old wattle hut, perhaps a herdsman's shelter, and though the hut had half collapsed it offered a better hiding place than the willow and so the three of us plunged into the nettles and crouched behind the rotting timbers.

A bell was ringing in the town. It sounded like the slow tolling which announced a funeral. It stopped abruptly, started again and then finally ended. A horn sounded. A dozen horsemen galloped close to our hiding place and all had black cloaks and black painted shields, the marks of Guthrum's warriors.

Guthrum. Guthrum the Unlucky. He called himself King of East Anglia, but he wanted to be King of Wessex and this was his third attempt to take the country and this time, I thought, his luck had turned. While Alfred had been celebrating the twelfth night of Yule, and while the Witan met to discuss the maintenance of bridges and the punishment of malefactors, Guthrum had marched. The army of the Danes was in Wessex, Cippanhamm had fallen, and the great men of Alfred's kingdom had been surprised, scattered or

154

slaughtered. The horn sounded again and the dozen black-cloaked horsemen turned and rode towards the sound.

'We should have known the Danes were coming,' I said angrily.

'You always said they would,' Leofric said.

'Didn't Alfred have spies at Gleawecestre?'

'He had priests praying here instead,' Leofric said bitterly, 'and he trusted Guthrum's truce.'

I touched my hammer amulet. I had taken it from a boy in Eoferwic. I had been a boy myself then, newly captured by the Danes, and my opponent had fought me in a whirl of fists and feet and I had hammered him down into the riverbank and taken his amulet. I still have it. I touch it often, reminding Thor that I live, but that day I touched it because I thought of Ragnar. The hostages would be dead, and was that why Wulfhere had ridden away at dawn? But how could he have known the Danes were coming? If Wulfhere had known then Alfred would have known and the West Saxon forces would have been ready. None of it made sense, except that Guthrum had again attacked during a truce and the last time he had broken a truce he had showed that he was willing to sacrifice the hostages held to prevent just such an attack. It seemed certain he had done it again and so Ragnar would be dead and my world was diminished.

So many dead. There were corpses in the meadow between our hiding place and the river, and still the slaughter went on. Some of the Saxons had run back towards the town, discovered the bridge was guarded and tried to escape northwards and we watched them being ridden down by the Danes. Three men tried to resist, standing in a tight group with swords ready, but a Dane gave a great whoop and charged them with his horse, and his spear went through one man's mail, crushing his chest and the other two were thrown aside by the horse's weight and immediately more Danes closed on them, swords and axes rose, and the horsemen spurred on. A girl screamed and ran in terrified circles until a Dane, long hair flying, leaned from his saddle and pulled her dress up over her head so she was blind and half naked. She staggered in the damp grass and a half-dozen Danes laughed at her, then one slapped her bare rump with his sword and another dragged her southwards, her screams muffled by the entangling dress. Iseult was shivering and I put a mail-clad arm around her shoulders.

I could have joined the Danes in the meadow. I spoke their language and, with my long hair and my arm rings, I looked like a Dane. But Haesten was somewhere in Cippanhamm and he might betray me, and Guthrum had no great love for me, and even if I survived then it would go hard with Leofric and Iseult. These Danes were in a rampant mood, flushed by their easy success and if a dozen decided they wanted Iseult then they would take her whether they thought I was a Dane or not. They were hunting in packs and so it was best to stay hidden until the frenzy had passed. Across the river, at the top of the low hill on which Cippanhamm was built, I could see the town's largest church burning. The thatched roof was whirling into the sky in great ribbons of flame and plumes of spark-riddled smoke.

'What in God's name were you doing back there?' Leofric asked me.

'Back there?' his question confused me.

'Dancing around Steapa like a gnat! He could have endured that all day!'

'I wounded him,' I said, 'twice.'

'Wounded him? Sweet Christ, he's hurt himself worse when he was shaving!'

'Doesn't matter now, does it?' I said. I guessed Steapa was dead by now. Or perhaps he had escaped. I did not know. None of us knew what was happening except that the Danes had come. And Mildrith? My son? They were far away, and presumably they would receive warning of the Danish attack, but I had no doubt that the Danes would keep going deep into Wessex and there was nothing I could do to protect Oxton. I had no horse, no men, and no chance of reaching the south coast before Guthrum's mounted soldiers.

I watched a Dane ride past with a girl across his saddle. 'What happened to that Danish girl you took home?' I asked Leofric, 'the one we captured off Wales?'

'She's still in Hamtun,' he said, 'and now that I'm not there she's probably in someone else's bed.'

'Probably? Certainly.'

'Then the bastard's welcome to her,' he said. 'She cries a lot.'

'Mildrith does that,' I said and then, after a pause, 'Eanflæd was angry with you.'

'Eanflæd? Angry with me! Why?'

'Because you didn't go to see her.'

'How could I? I was in chains.' He looked satisfied that the whore had asked after him. 'Eanflæd doesn't cry, does she?'

'Not that I've seen.'

'Good girl that. I reckon she'd like Hamtun.'

If Hamtun still existed. Had a Danish fleet come from Lundene? Was Svein attacking across the Sæfern Sea? I knew nothing except that Wessex was suffering chaos and defeat. It began to rain again, a thin winter's rain, cold and stinging. Iseult crouched lower and I sheltered her with my shield. Most of the folk who had gathered to watch the fight by the river had fled south and only a handful had come

157

our way, which meant there were fewer Danes near our hiding place, and those that were in the northern river meadows were now gathering their spoils. They stripped corpses of weapons, belts, mail, clothes, anything of value. A few Saxon men had survived, but they were being led away with the children and younger women to be sold as slaves. The old were killed. A wounded man was crawling on hands and knees and a dozen Danes tormented him like cats playing with an injured sparrow, nicking him with swords and spears, bleeding him to a slow death. Haesten was one of the tormentors. 'I always liked Haesten,' I said sadly.

'He's a Dane,' Leofric said scornfully.

'I still liked him.'

'You kept him alive,' Leofric said, 'and now he's gone back to his own. You should have killed him.' I watched as Haesten kicked the wounded man who called out in agony, begging to be killed, but the group of young men went on jabbing him, laughing, and the first ravens came. I have often wondered if ravens smell blood, for the sky can be clear of them all day, but when a man dies they come from nowhere on their shining black wings. Perhaps Odin sends them, for the ravens are his birds, and now they flapped down to start feasting on eyes and lips, the first course of every raven feast. The dogs and foxes would soon follow.

'The end of Wessex,' Leofric said sadly.

'The end of England,' I said.

'What do we do?' Iseult asked.

There was no answer from me. Ragnar must be dead, which meant I had no refuge among the Danes, and Alfred was probably dead or else a fugitive, and my duty now was to my son. He was only a baby, but he was my son and he carried my name. Bebbanburg would be his if I could take it back, and if I could not take it back then it would be his duty to recapture the stronghold, and so the name Uhtred of Bebbanburg would go on till the last weltering chaos of the dying world.

'We must get to Hamtun,' Leofric said, 'find the crew.'

Except the Danes would surely be there already? Or else on their way. They knew where the power of Wessex lay, where the great lords had their halls, where the soldiers gathered, and Guthrum would be sending men to burn and kill and so disarm the Saxons' last kingdom.

'We need food,' I said, 'food and warmth.'

'Light a fire here,' Leofric grumbled, 'and we're dead.'

So we waited. The small rain turned to sleet. Haesten and his new companions, now that their victim was dead, wandered away, leaving the meadow empty but for the corpses and their attendant ravens. And still we waited, but Iseult, who was as thin as Alfred, was shivering uncontrollably and so, in the late afternoon, I took off my helmet and unbound my hair so it hung loose.

'What are you doing?' Leofric asked.

'For the moment,' I said, 'we're Danes. Just keep your mouth shut.'

I led them towards the town. I would have preferred to wait until dark, but Iseult was too cold to wait longer, and I just hoped the Danes had calmed down. I might look like a Dane, but it was still dangerous. Haesten might see me, and if he told others how I had ambushed the Danish ship off Dyfed then I could expect nothing but a slow death. So we went nervously, stepping past bloodied bodies along the riverside path. The ravens protested as we approached, flapped indignantly into the winter willows, and returned to their feast when we had passed. There were more corpses piled by the bridge where the young folk captured for slavery were being made to dig a grave. The Danes guarding them were drunk and none challenged us as we went across the wooden span and under the gate arch that was still hung with holly and ivy in celebration of Christmas.

The fires were dying now, damped by rain or else extinguished by the Danes who were ransacking houses and churches. I stayed in the narrowest alleys, edging past a smithy, a hide-dealer's shop and a place where pots had been sold. Our boots crunched through the pottery shards. A young Dane was vomiting in the alley's entrance and he told me that Guthrum was in the royal compound where there would be a feast that night. He straightened up, gasping for breath, but was sober enough to offer me a bag of coins for Iseult. There were women screaming or sobbing in houses and their noise was making Leofric angry, but I told him to stay quiet. Two of us could not free Cippanhamm, and if the world had been turned upside down and it had been a West Saxon army capturing a Danish town it would have sounded no different. 'Alfred wouldn't allow it,' Leofric said sullenly.

'You'd do it anyway,' I said. 'You've done it.'

I wanted news, but none of the Danes in the street made any sense. They had come from Gleawecestre, leaving long before dawn, they had captured Cippanhamm and now they wanted to enjoy whatever the town offered. The big church had burned, but men were raking through the smoking embers looking for silver. For lack of anywhere else to go we climbed the hill to the Corncrake tavern where we always drank and found Eanflæd, the red-headed whore, being held on a table by two young Danes while three others, none of them more than seventeen or eighteen, took turns to rape her. Another dozen Danes were drinking peaceably enough, taking scant notice of the rape.

'You want her,' one of the young men said, 'you'll have to wait.'

'I want her now,' I said.

160

'Then you can jump in the shit-pit,' he said. He was drunk. He had a wispy beard and insolent eyes. 'You can jump in the shit-pit,' he said again, evidently liking the insult, then pointed to Iseult, 'and I'll have her while you drown.' I hit him, breaking his nose and spattering his face with blood, and while he gasped I kicked him hard between the legs. He went down, whimpering, and I hit a second man in the belly while Leofric loosed all his day's frustration in a savage attack on another. The two who had been holding Eanflæd turned on us and one of them squealed when Eanflæd grabbed his hair and hooked sharp fingernails into his eyes. Leofric's opponent was on the floor and he stamped on the boy's throat and I head-slapped my boy until I had him by the door, then I thumped another in the ribs, rescued Eanflæd's victim and broke his jaw, then went back to the lad who had threatened to rape Iseult. I ripped a silver loop from his ear, took off his one arm ring and stole his pouch that clinked with coins. I dropped the silver into Eanflæd's lap, then kicked the groaning man between the legs, did it again, and hauled him out into the street.

'Go jump in a shit-pit,' I told him, then slammed the door. The other Danes, still drinking on the tavern's far side, had watched the fight with amusement, and now gave us ironic applause.

'Bastards,' Eanflæd said, evidently talking of the men we had driven away. 'I'm sore as hell. What are you two doing here?'

'They think we're Danes,' I said.

'We need food,' Leofric said.

'They've had most of it,' Eanflæd said, jerking her head at the seated Danes, 'but there might be something left in the back.' She tied her girdle. 'Edwulf's dead.' Edwulf had owned the tavern. 'And thanks for helping me, you spavined bastards!' She shouted this at the Danes, who did

161

not understand her and just laughed at her, then she went towards the back room to find us food, but one of the men held out a hand to stop her.

'Where are you going?' he asked her in Danish.

'She's going past you,' I called.

'I want ale,' he said, 'and you? Who are you?'

'I'm the man who's going to cut your throat if you stop her fetching food,' I said.

'Quiet, quiet!' an older man said, then frowned at me. 'Don't I know you?'

'I was with Guthrum at Readingum,' I said, 'and at Werham.'

'That must be it. He's done better this time, eh?'

'He's done better,' I agreed.

The man pointed at Iseult. 'Yours?'

'Not for sale.'

'Just asking, friend, just asking.'

Eanflæd brought us stale bread, cold pork, wrinkled apples and a rock-hard cheese in which red worms writhed. The older man carried a pot of ale to our table, evidently as a peace offering, and he sat and talked with me and I learned a little more of what was happening. Guthrum had brought close to three thousand men to attack Cippanhamm. Guthrum himself was now in Alfred's hall and half his men would stay in Cippanhamm as a garrison while the rest planned to ride either south or west in the morning. 'Keep the bastards on the run, eh?' the man said, then frowned at Leofric. 'He doesn't say much.'

'He's dumb,' I said.

'I knew a man who had a dumb wife. He was ever so happy.' He looked jealously at my arm rings. 'So who do you serve?'

'Svein of the White Horse.'

'Svein? He wasn't at Readingum. Or at Werham.'

'He was in Dyflin,' I said, 'but I was with Ragnar the Older then.'

'Ah, Ragnar! Poor bastard.'

'I suppose his son's dead now?' I asked.

'What else?' the man said. 'Hostages, poor bastards.' He thought for a heartbeat then frowned again. 'What's Svein doing here? I thought he was coming by ship?'

'He is,' I said. 'We're just here to talk to Guthrum.'

'Svein sends a dumb man to talk to Guthrum?'

'He sent me to talk,' I said, 'and sent him,' I jerked a thumb at the glowering Leofric, 'to kill people who ask too many questions.'

'All right, all right!' The man held up a hand to ward off my belligerence.

We slept in the stable loft, warmed by straw, and we left before dawn, and at that moment fifty West Saxons could have retaken Cippanhamm for the Danes were drunk, sleeping, and oblivious to the world. Leofric stole a sword, axe and shield from a man snoring in the tavern, then we walked unchallenged out of the western gate. In a field outside we found over a hundred horses, guarded by two men sleeping in a thatched hut, and we could have taken all the beasts, but we had no saddles or bridles and so, reluctantly, I knew we must walk. There were four of us now, because Eanflæd had decided to come with us. She had swathed Iseult in two big cloaks, but the British girl was still shivering.

We walked west and south along a road that twisted through small hills. We were heading for Baðum, and from there I could strike south towards Defnascir and my son, but it was clear the Danes were already ahead of us. Some must have ridden this way the previous day for in the first village we reached there were no cocks crowing, no sound at all, and what I had taken for a morning mist was smoke from burned cottages. Heavier smoke showed ahead, suggesting the Danes might already have reached Baðum, a town they knew well for they had negotiated one of their truces there. Then, that afternoon, a horde of mounted Danes appeared on the road behind us and we were driven west into the hills to find a hiding place.

We wandered for a week. We found shelter in hovels. Some were deserted while others still had frightened folk, but every short winter's day was smeared with smoke as the Danes ravaged Wessex. One day we discovered a cow, trapped in its byre in an otherwise deserted homestead. The cow was with calf and bellowing with hunger, and that night we feasted on fresh meat. Next day we could not move for it was bitterly cold and a slanting rain slashed on an east wind and the trees thrashed as if in agony and the building that gave us shelter leaked and the fire choked us and Iseult just sat, eyes wide and empty, staring into the small flames.

'You want to go back to Cornwalum?' I asked her.

She seemed surprised I had spoken. It took her a few heartbeats to gather her thoughts, then she shrugged. 'What is there for me?'

'Home,' Eanflæd said.

'Uhtred is home for me.'

'Uhtred is married,' Eanflæd said harshly.

Iseult ignored that. 'Uhtred will lead men,' she said, rocking back and forth, 'hundreds of men. A bright horde. I want to see that.'

'He'll lead you into temptation, that's all he'll do,' Eanflæd said. 'Go home, girl, say your prayers and hope the Danes don't come.'

We kept trying to go southwards and we made some small progress every day, but the bitter days were short and the Danes seemed to be everywhere. Even when we travelled across countryside far from any track or path, there would be a patrol of Danes in the distance, and to avoid them we were constantly driven west. To our east was the Roman road that ran from Baðum and eventually to Exanceaster, the main thoroughfare in this part of Wessex, and I supposed the Danes were using it and sending patrols out to either side of the road, and it was those patrols that drove us ever nearer the Sæfern Sea, but there could be no safety there, for Svein would surely have come from Wales.

I also supposed that Wessex had finally fallen. We met a few folk, fugitives from their villages and hiding in the woods, but none had any news, only rumour. No one had seen any West Saxon soldiers, no one had heard about Alfred, they only saw Danes and the ever-present smoke. From time to time we would come across a ravaged village or a burned church. We would see ragged ravens flapping black and follow them to find rotting bodies. We were lost and any hope I had of reaching Oxton was long gone, and I assumed Mildrith had fled west into the hills as the folk around the Uisc always did when the Danes came. I hoped she was alive, I hoped my son lived, but what future he had was as dark as the long winter nights.

'Maybe we should make our peace,' I suggested to Leofric one night. We were in a shepherd's hut, crouched around a small fire that filled the low turf-roofed building with smoke. We had roasted a dozen mutton ribs cut from a sheep's half-eaten corpse. We were all filthy, damp and cold. 'Maybe we should find the Danes,' I said, 'and swear allegiance.'

'And be made slaves?' Leofric answered bitterly.

'We'll be warriors,' I said.

'Fighting for a Dane?' He poked the fire, throwing up a new burst of smoke. 'They can't have taken all Wessex,' he protested.

'Why not?'

'It's too big. There have to be some men fighting back. We just have to find them.'

I thought back to the long ago arguments in Lundene. Back then I had been a child with the Danes, and their leaders had argued that the best way to take Wessex was to attack its western heartland and there break its power. Others had wanted to start the assault by taking the old kingdom of Kent, the weakest part of Wessex and the part which contained the great shrine of Contwaraburg, but the boldest argument had won. They had attacked in the west and that first assault had failed, but now Guthrum had succeeded. Yet how far had he succeeded? Was Kent still Saxon? Defnascir?

'And what happens to Mildrith if you join the Danes?' Leofric asked.

'She'll have hidden,' I spoke dully and there was a silence, but I saw Eanflæd was offended and I hoped she would hold her tongue.

She did not. 'Do you care?' she challenged me.

'I care,' I said.

Eanflæd scorned that answer. 'Grown dull, has she?'

'Of course he cares,' Leofric tried to be a peacemaker.

'She's a wife,' Eanflæd retorted, still looking at me. 'Men tire of wives,' she went on and Iseult listened, her big dark eyes going from me to Eanflæd.

'What do you know of wives?' I asked.

'I was married,' Eanflæd said.

'You were?' Leofric asked, surprised.

'I was married for three years,' Eanflæd said, 'to a man who was in Wulfhere's guard. He gave me two children, then died in the battle that killed King Æthelred.'

'Two children?' Iseult asked.

'They died,' Eanflæd said harshly. 'That's what children do. They die.'

'You were happy with him?' Leofric asked, 'your husband?'

'For about three days,' she said, 'and in the next three years I learned that men are bastards.'

'All of them?' Leofric asked.

'Most.' She smiled at Leofric, then touched his knee. 'Not you.'

'And me?' I asked.

'You?' She looked at me for a heartbeat. 'I wouldn't trust you as far as I could spit,' she said, and there was real venom in her voice, leaving Leofric embarrassed and me surprised. There comes a moment in life when we see ourselves as others see us. I suppose that is part of growing up, and it is not always comfortable. Eanflæd, at that moment, regretted speaking so harshly for she tried to soften it. 'I don't know you,' she said, 'except you're Leofric's friend.'

'Uhtred is generous,' Iseult said loyally.

'Men are usually generous when they want something,' Eanflæd retorted.

'I want Bebbanburg,' I said.

'Whatever that is,' Eanflæd said, 'and to get it you'd do anything. Anything.'

There was silence. I saw a snowflake show at the half-covered door. It fluttered into the firelight and melted. 'Alfred's a good man,' Leofric broke the awkward silence.

'He tries to be good,' Eanflæd said.

'Only tries?' I asked sarcastically.

'He's like you,' she said. 'He'd kill to get what he wants, but there is a difference. He has a conscience.'

'He's frightened of the priests, you mean.'

'He's frightened of God. And we should all be that. Because one day we'll answer to God.'

'Not me,' I said.

Eanflæd sneered at that, but Leofric changed the conversation by saying it was snowing, and after a while we slept. Iseult clung to me in her sleep and she whimpered and

167

twitched as I lay awake, half dreaming, thinking of her words that I would lead a bright horde. It seemed an unlikely prophecy, indeed I reckoned her powers must have gone with her virginity, and then I slept too, waking to a world made white. The twigs and branches were edged with snow, but it was already melting, dripping into a misty dawn. When I went outside I found a tiny dead wren just beyond the door and I feared it was a grim omen.

Leofric emerged from the hut, blinking at the dawn's brilliance. 'Don't mind Eanflæd,' he said.

'I don't.'

'Her world's come to an end.'

'Then we must remake it,' I said.

'Does that mean you won't join the Danes?'

'I'm a Saxon,' I said.

Leofric half smiled at that. He undid his breeches and had a piss. 'If your friend Ragnar was alive,' he asked, watching the steam rise from his urine, 'would you still be a Saxon?'

'He's dead, isn't he?' I said bleakly, 'sacrificed to Guthrum's ambition.'

'So now you're a Saxon?'

'I'm a Saxon,' I said again, sounding more certain than I felt, for I did not know what the future held. How can we? Perhaps Iseult had told the truth and Alfred would give me power and I would lead a shining horde and have a woman of gold, but I was beginning to doubt Iseult's powers. Alfred might already be dead and his kingdom was doomed, and all I knew at that moment was that the land stretched away south to a snow-covered ridge line, and there it ended in a strange empty brightness. The skyline looked like the world's rim, poised above an abyss of pearly light. 'We'll keep going south,' I said. There was nothing else to do except walk towards the brightness.

We did. We followed a sheep track to the ridge top and

there I saw that the hills fell steeply away, dropping to the vast marshes of the sea. We had come to the great swamp, and the brightness I had seen was the winter light reflecting from the long meres and winding creeks.

'What now?' Leofric asked, and I had no answer and so we sat under the berries of a wind-bent yew and stared at the immensity of bog, water, grass and reeds. This was the vast swamp that stretched inland from the Sæfern, and if I was to reach Defnascir I either had to go around it or try to cross it. If we went around it then we would have to go to the Roman road, and that was where the Danes were, but if we tried to cross the swamp we would face other dangers. I had heard a thousand stories of men being lost in its wet tangles. It was said there were spirits there, spirits that showed at night as flickering lights, and there were paths that led only to quicksands or to drowning pools, but there were also villages in the swamp, places where folk trapped fish and eels. The people of the swamp were protected by the spirits and by the sudden surges in the tide that could drown a road in an eyeblink. Now, as the last snows melted from the reed-banks, the swamp looked like a great stretch of waterlogged land, its streams and meres swollen by the winter rains, but when the tide rose it would resemble an inland sea dotted with islands. We could see one of those islands not so far off and there was a cluster of huts on that speck of higher ground, and that would be a place to find food and warmth if we could ever reach it. Eventually we might cross the whole swamp, finding a way from island to island, but it would take far longer than a day, and we would have to find refuge at every high tide. I gazed at the long, cold stretches of water, almost black beneath the leaden clouds that came from the sea and my spirits sank for I did not know where we were going, or why, or what the future held.

It seemed to get colder as we sat, and then a light snow began drifting from the dark clouds. Just a few flakes, but enough to convince me that we had to find shelter soon. Smoke was rising from the nearest swamp village, evidence that some folk still lived there. There would be food in their hovels and a meagre warmth. 'We have to get to that island,' I said, pointing.

But the others were staring westwards to where a flock of pigeons had burst from the trees at the foot of the slope. The birds rose and flew in circles. 'Someone's there,' Leofric said.

We waited. The pigeons settled in the trees higher up the hill. 'Maybe it's a boar?' I suggested.

'Pigeons won't fly from a boar,' Leofric said. 'Boars don't startle pigeons, any more than stags do. There are folk there.'

The thought of boars and stags made me wonder what had happened to my hounds. Had Mildrith abandoned them? I had not even told her where I had hidden the remains of the plunder we had taken off the coast of Wales. I had dug a hole in a corner of my new hall and buried the gold and silver down by the post-stone, but it was not the cleverest hiding place and if there were Danes in Oxton then they were bound to delve into the edges of the hall floor, especially if a probing spear found a place where the earth had been disturbed. A flight of ducks flew overhead. The snow was falling harder, blurring the long view across the swamp.

'Priests,' Leofric said.

There were a half-dozen men off to the west. They were robed in black and had come from the trees to walk along the swamp's margin, plainly seeking a path into its tangled vastness, but there was no obvious track to the small village on its tiny island and so the priests came nearer to us, skirting the ridge's foot. One of them was carrying a long staff and, even at a distance, I could see a glint at its head and I suspected it was a bishop's staff, the kind with a heavy silver cross. Another three carried heavy sacks. 'You think there's food in those bundles?' Leofric asked wistfully.

'They're priests,' I said savagely. 'They'll be carrying silver.'

'Or books,' Eanflæd suggested. 'Priests like books.'

'It could be food,' Leofric said, though not very convincingly.

A group of three women and two children now appeared. One of the women was wearing a swathing cloak of silver fur, while another carried the smaller child. The women and children were not far behind the priests, who waited for them and then they all walked eastwards until they were beneath us and there they discovered some kind of path twisting into the marshes. Five of the priests led the women into the swamp while the sixth man, evidently younger than the others, hurried back westwards. 'Where's he going?' Leofric asked.

Another skein of ducks flighted low overhead, skimming down the slope to the long meres of the swamp. Nets, I thought. There must be nets in the swamp villages and we could trap fish and wildfowl. We could eat well for a few days. Eels, duck, fish, geese. If there were enough nets we could even trap deer by driving them into the tangling meshes.

'They're not going anywhere,' Leofric said scornfully, nodding at the priests who had stranded themselves a hundred paces out in the swamp. The path was deceptive. It had offered an apparent route to the village, but then petered out amidst a patch of reeds where the priests huddled. They did not want to come back and did not want to go forward, and so they stayed where they were, lost and cold and despairing. They looked as though they were arguing.

'We must help them,' Eanflæd said and, when I said nothing, she protested that one of the women was holding a baby. 'We have to help them!' she insisted.

I was about to retort that the last thing we needed was more hungry mouths to feed, but her harsh words in the night had persuaded me that I had to do something to show her I was not as treacherous as she evidently believed, so I stood, hefted my shield and started down the hill. The others followed, but before we were even halfway down I heard shouts from the west. The lone priest who had gone that way was now with four soldiers and they turned as horsemen came from the trees. There were six horsemen, then eight more appeared, then another ten and I realised a whole column of mounted soldiers was streaming from the dead winter trees. They had black shields and black cloaks, so they had to be Guthrum's men. One of the priests stranded in the swamp ran back along the path and I saw he had a sword and was going to help his companions.

It was a brave thing for the lone priest to do, but quite useless. The four soldiers and the single priest were surrounded now. They were standing back to back and the Danish horsemen were all around them, hacking down, and then two of the horsemen saw the priest with his sword and spurred towards him. 'Those two are ours,' I said to Leofric.

That was stupid. The four men were doomed, as was the priest if we did not intervene, but there were only two of us and, even if we killed the two horsemen, we would still face overwhelming odds, but I was driven by Eanflæd's scorn and I was tired of skulking through the winter countryside and I was angry and so I ran down the hill, careless of the noise I made as I crashed through brittle undergrowth. The lone priest had his back to the swamp now and the horsemen were charging at him as Leofric and I burst from the trees and came at them from their left side.

172

I hit the nearest horse's flank with my heavy shield. There was a scream from the horse and an explosion of wet soil, grass, snow and hooves as man and beast went down sideways. I was also on the ground, knocked there by the impact, but I recovered first and found the rider tangled with his stirrups, one leg trapped under the struggling horse and I chopped Serpent-Breath down hard. I cut into his throat, stamped on his face, chopped again, slipped in his blood, then left him and went to help Leofric who was fending off the second man who was still on horseback. The Dane's sword thumped on Leofric's shield, then he had to turn his horse to face me and Leofric's axe took the horse in the face and the beast reared, the rider slid backwards and I met his spine with Serpent-Breath's tip. Two down. The priest with the sword, not a half-dozen paces away, had not moved. He was just staring at us. 'Get back into the marsh!' I shouted at him. 'Go! Go!' Iseult and Eanflæd were with us now and they seized the priest and hurried him towards the path. It might lead nowhere, but it was better to face the remaining Danes there than on the firm ground at the hill's foot.

And those black-cloaked Danes were coming. They had slaughtered the handful of soldiers, seen their two men killed and now came for vengeance. 'Come on!' I snarled at Leofric and, taking the wounded horse by the reins, I ran onto the small twisting path.

'A horse won't help you here,' Leofric said.

The horse was nervous. Its face was wounded and the path was slippery, but I dragged it along the track until we were close to the small patch of land where the refugees huddled, and by now the Danes were also on the path, following us. They had dismounted. They could only come two abreast and, in places, only one man could use the track and in one of those places I stopped the horse and exchanged Serpent-Breath for Leofric's axe. The horse looked at me

173

with a big brown eye. 'This is for Odin,' I said, and I swung the axe into its neck, chopping down through mane and hide, and a woman screamed behind me as the blood spurted bright and high in the dull day. The horse whinnied, tried to rear and I swung again and this time the beast went down, thrashing hooves, blood and water splashing. Snow turned red as I axed it a third time, finally stilling it, and now the dying beast was an obstacle athwart the track and the Danes would have to fight across its corpse. I took Serpent-Breath back.

'We'll kill them one by one,' I told Leofric.

'For how long?' He nodded westwards and I saw more Danes coming, a whole ship's crew of mounted Danes streaming along the swamp's edge. Fifty men? Maybe more, but even so they could only use the path in ones or twos and they would have to fight over the dead horse into Serpent-Breath and Leofric's axe. He had lost his own axe, taken from him when he was brought to Cippanhamm, but he seemed to like his stolen weapon. He made the sign of the cross, touched the blade, then hefted his shield as the Danes came.

Two young men came first. They were wild and savage, wanting to make a reputation, but the first to come was stopped by Leofric's axe banging into his shield and I swept Serpent-Breath beneath the shield to slice his ankle and he fell, cursing, to tangle his companion and Leofric wrenched the wide-bladed axe free and slashed it down again. The second man stumbled on the horse, and Serpent-Breath took him under the chin, above his leather coat, and the blood ran down her blade in a sudden flood and now there were two Danish corpses added to the horseflesh barricade. I was taunting the other Danes, calling them corpse-worms, telling them I had known children who could fight better. Another man came, screaming in rage as he leaped over the horse

174

and he was checked by Leofric's shield and Serpent-Breath met his sword with a dull crack and his blade broke, and two more men were trying to get past the horse, struggling in water up to their knees and I rammed Serpent-Breath into the belly of the first, pushing her through his leather armour, left him to die, and swung right at the man trying to get through the water. Serpent-Breath's tip flicked across his face to spray blood into the thickening snowfall. I went forward, feet sinking, lunged again and he could not move in the mire and Serpent-Breath took his gullet. I was screaming with joy because the battle calm had come, the same blessed stillness I had felt at Cynuit. It is a joy, that feeling, and the only other joy to compare is that of being with a woman.

It is as though life slows. The enemy moves as if he is wading in mud, but I was kingfisher fast. There is rage, but it is a controlled rage, and there is joy, the joy that the poets celebrate when they speak of battle, and a certainty that death is not in that day's fate. My head was full of singing, a keening note, high and shrill, death's anthem. All I wanted was for more Danes to come to Serpent-Breath and it seemed to me that she took on her own life in those moments. To think was to act. A man came across the horse's flank, I thought to slice at his ankle, knew he would drop his shield and so open his upper body to an attack, and before the thought was even coherent it was done and Serpent-Breath had taken one of his eyes. She had gone down and up, was already moving to the right to counter another man trying to get around the horse, and I let him get past the stallion's bloodied head then scornfully drove him down into the water and there I stood on him, holding his head under my boot as he drowned. I screamed at the Danes, told them I was Valhalla's gatekeeper, that they had been weaned on coward's milk and that I wanted them to come to my blade.

175

I begged them to come, but six men were dead around the horse and the others were now wary.

I stood on the dead horse and spread my arms. I held the shield high to my left and the sword to my right, and my mail coat was spattered with blood and the snow fell about my wolf-crested helmet and all I knew was the young man's joy of slaughter. 'I killed Ubba Lothbrokson!' I shouted at them. 'I killed him! So come and join him! Taste his death! My sword wants you!'

'Boats,' Leofric said. I did not hear him. The man I thought I had drowned was still alive and he suddenly reared from the marsh, choking and vomiting water, and I jumped down off the horse and put my foot on his head again.

'Let him live!' A voice shouted behind me. 'I want a prisoner!'

The man tried to fight my foot, but Serpent-Breath put him down. He struggled again and I broke his spine with Serpent-Breath and he was still.

'I said I wanted a prisoner,' the voice behind protested.

'Come and die!' I shouted at the Danes.

'Boats,' Leofric said again and I glanced behind and saw three punts coming through the marsh. They were long flat boats, propelled by men with poles, and they grounded on the other side of the huddled refugees who hurried aboard. The Danes, knowing Leofric and I had to retreat if we were to gain the safety of the boats, readied for a charge and I smiled at them, inviting them.

'One boat left,' Leofric said. 'Room for us. You'll have to run like hell.'

'I'll stay here,' I shouted, but in Danish. 'I'm enjoying myself.'

Then there was a stir on the path as a man came to the front rank of the Danes and the others edged aside to give him room. He was in chain mail and had a silvered helmet

176

with a raven's wing at its crown, but as he came closer he took the helmet off and I saw the gold-tipped bone in his hair. It was Guthrum himself. The bone was one of his mother's ribs and he wore it out of love for her memory. He stared at me, his gaunt face sad, and then looked down at the men we had killed. 'I shall hunt you like a dog, Uhtred Ragnarson,' he said, 'and I shall kill you like a dog.'

'My name,' I said, 'is Uhtred Uhtredson.'

'We have to run,' Leofric hissed at me.

The snow whirled above the swamp, thick enough now so that I could hardly see the ridge top from where we had glimpsed the pigeons circling. 'You are a dead man, Uhtred,' Guthrum said.

'I never met your mother,' I called to him, 'but I would have liked to meet her.'

His face took on the reverent look that any mention of his mother always provoked. He seemed to regret that he had spoken so harshly to me for he made a conciliatory gesture. 'She was a great woman,' he said.

I smiled at him. At that moment, looking back, I could have changed sides so easily and Guthrum would have welcomed me if I had just given his mother a compliment, but I was a belligerent young man and the battle joy was on me. 'I would have spat in her ugly face,' I told Guthrum, 'and now I piss on your mother's soul, and tell you that the beasts of Niflheim are humping her rancid bones.'

He screamed with rage and they all charged, some splashing through the shallows, all desperate to reach me and avenge the terrible insult, but Leofric and I were running like hunted boars, and we charged through the reeds and into the water and hurled ourselves onto the last punt. The first two were gone, but the third had waited for us and, as we sprawled on its damp boards, the man with the pole pushed hard and the craft slid away into the black water.

The Danes tried to follow, but we were going surprisingly fast, gliding through the snowfall, and Guthrum was shouting at me and a spear was thrown, but the marshman poled again and the spear plunged harmlessly into the mud.

'I shall find you!' Guthrum shouted.

'Why should I care?' I called back. 'Your men only know how to die!' I raised Serpent-Breath and kissed her sticky blade, 'and your mother was a whore to dwarves!'

'You should have let that one man live,' a voice said behind me, 'because I wanted to question him.' The punt only contained the one passenger besides Leofric and myself, and that one man was the priest who had carried a sword and now he was sitting in the punt's flat bow, frowning at me. 'There was no need to kill that man,' he said sternly and I looked at him with such fury that he recoiled. Damn all priests, I thought. I had saved the bastard's life and all he did was reprove me, and then I saw that he was no priest at all.

It was Alfred.

The punt slid over the swamp, sometimes gliding across black water, sometimes rustling through grass or reeds. The man poling it was a bent, dark-skinned creature with a massive beard, otterskin clothes and a toothless mouth. Guthrum's Danes were far behind now, carrying their dead back to firmer ground. 'I need to know what they plan to do,' Alfred complained to me. 'The prisoner could have told us.'

He spoke more respectfully. Looking back I realised I had frightened him for the front of my mail coat was sheeted in blood and there was more blood on my face and helmet.

'They plan to finish Wessex,' I said curtly. 'You don't need a prisoner to tell you that.'

178

'Lord,' he said.

I stared at him.

'I am a king!' he insisted. 'You address a king with respect.'

'A king of what?' I asked.

'You're not hurt, lord?' Leofric asked Alfred.

'No, thank God. No.' He looked at the sword he carried. 'Thank God.' I saw he was not wearing priest's robes, but a swathing black cloak. His long face was very pale. 'Thank you, Leofric,' he said, then looked up at me and seemed to shudder. We were catching up with the other two punts and I saw that Ælswith, pregnant and swathed in a silver fox-fur cloak, was in one. Iseult and Eanflæd were also in that punt while the priests were crowded onto the other and I saw that Bishop Alewold of Exanceaster was one of them.

'What happened, lord?' Leofric asked.

Alfred sighed. He was shivering now, but he told his story. He had ridden from Cippanhamm with his family, his body-guard and a score of churchmen to accompany the monk Asser on the first part of his journey. 'We had a service of thanksgiving,' he said, 'in the church at Soppan Byrg. It's a new church,' he added earnestly to Leofric, 'and very fine. We sang psalms, said prayers, and Brother Asser went on his way rejoicing.' He made the sign of the cross. 'I pray he's safe.'

'I hope the lying bastard's dead,' I snarled.

Alfred ignored that. After the church service they had all gone to a nearby monastery for a meal, and it was while they were there that the Danes had come. The royal group had fled, finding shelter in nearby woods while the monastery burned. After that they had tried to ride east into the heart of Wessex but, like us, they had constantly been headed off by patrolling Danes. One night, sheltering in a farm, they had been surprised by Danish troops who had killed some of Alfred's guards and captured all his horses and ever since they had been wandering, as lost as us, until they came to the swamp. 'God knows what will happen now,' Alfred said.

'We fight,' I said. He just looked at me and I shrugged. 'We fight,' I said again.

Alfred stared across the swamp. 'Find a ship,' he said, but so softly that I hardly heard him. 'Find a ship and go to Frankia.' He pulled the cloak tighter around his thin body. The snow was thickening as it fell, though it melted as soon as it met the dark water. The Danes had vanished, lost in the snow behind. 'That was Guthrum?' Alfred asked me.

'That was Guthrum,' I said. 'And he knew it was you he pursued?'

'I suppose so.'

'What else would draw Guthrum here?' I asked. 'He wants you dead. Or captured.'

Yet, for the moment, we were safe. The island village had a score of damp hovels thatched with reeds and a few store-houses raised on stilts. The buildings were the colour of mud, the street was mud, the goats and the people were mud-covered, but the place, poor as it was, could provide food, shelter and a meagre warmth. The men of the village had seen the refugees and, after a discussion, decided to rescue them. I suspect they wanted to pillage us rather than save our lives, but Leofric and I looked formidable and, once the villagers understood that their king was their guest, they did their clumsy best for him and his family. One of them, in a dialect I could scarcely understand, wanted to know the king's name. He had never heard of Alfred. He knew about the Danes, but said their ships had never reached the village, or any of the other settlements in the swamp. He told us the villagers lived off deer, goats, fish, eels and wild-fowl, and they had plenty of food, though fuel was scarce.

180

Ælswith was pregnant with her third child, while her first two were in the care of nurses. There was Edward, Alfred's heir, who was three years old and sick. He coughed, and Ælswith worried about him, though Bishop Alewold insisted it was just a winter's cold. Then there was Edward's elder sister, Æthelflaed, who was now six and had a bright head of golden curls, a beguiling smile and clever eyes. Alfred adored her, and in those first days in the swamp, she was his one ray of light and hope. One night, as we sat by a small, dying fire and Æthelflaed slept with her golden head in her father's lap, he asked me about my son.

'I don't know where he is,' I said. There were only the two of us, everyone else was sleeping, and I was sitting by the door staring across the frost-bleached marsh that lay black and silver under a half-moon.

'You want to go and find him?' he asked earnestly.

'You truly want me to do that?' I asked. He looked puzzled. 'These folk are giving you shelter,' I explained, 'but they'd as soon cut your throats. They won't do that while I'm here.'

He was about to protest, then understood I probably spoke the truth. He stroked his daughter's hair. Edward coughed. He was in his mother's hut. The coughing had become worse, much worse, and we all suspected it was the whooping cough that killed small children. Alfred flinched at the sound. 'Did you fight Steapa?' he asked.

'We fought,' I said curtly, 'the Danes came, and we never finished. He was bleeding, I was not.'

'He was bleeding?'

'Ask Leofric. He was there.'

He was silent a long time, then, softly, 'I am still king.'

Of a swamp, I thought, and said nothing.

'And it is customary to call a king "lord",' he went on.

I just stared at his thin, pale face that was lit by the dying

181

fire. He looked so solemn, but also frightened, as if he were making a huge effort to hold onto the shreds of his dignity. Alfred never lacked for bravery, but he was not a warrior and he did not much like the company of warriors. In his eyes I was a brute; dangerous, uninteresting, but suddenly indispensable. He knew I was not going to call him lord, so he did not insist. 'What do you notice about this place?' he asked.

'It's wet,' I said.

'What else?'

I looked for the trap in the question and found none. 'It can only be reached by punts,' I said, 'and the Danes don't have punts. But when they do have punts it'll need more than Leofric and me to fight them off.'

'It doesn't have a church,' he said.

'I knew I liked it,' I retorted.

He ignored that. 'We know so little of our own kingdom,' he said in wonderment. 'I thought there were churches everywhere.' He closed his eyes for a few heartbeats, then looked at me plaintively. 'What should I do?'

I had told him to fight, but I could see no fight in him now, just despair. 'You can go south,' I said, thinking that was what he wanted to hear, 'go south across the sea.'

'To be another exiled Saxon king,' he said bitterly.

'We hide here,' I said, 'and when we think the Danes aren't watching, we go to the south coast and find a ship.'

'How do we hide?' he asked. 'They know we're here. And they're on both sides of the swamp.' The marshman had told us that a Danish fleet had landed at Cynuit, which lay at the swamp's western edge. That fleet, I assumed, was led by Svein and he would surely be wondering how to find Alfred. The king, I reckoned, was doomed, and his family too. If Æthelflaed was lucky she would be raised by a Danish family, as I had been, but more probably they would all be killed so that no Saxon could ever again claim the crown of Wessex. 'And the Danes will be watching the south coast,' Alfred went on.

'They will,' I agreed.

He looked out at the marsh where the night wind rippled the waters, shaking the long reflection of a winter moon. 'The Danes can't have taken all Wessex,' he said, then flinched because Edward was coughing so painfully.

'Probably not,' I agreed.

'If we could find men,' he said, then fell silent.

'What would we do with men?' I asked.

'Attack the fleet,' he said, pointing west. 'Get rid of Svein, if it is Svein at Cynuit, then hold the hills of Defnascir. Gain one victory and more men will come. We get stronger and one day we can face Guthrum.'

I thought about it. He had spoken dully, as if he did not really believe in the words he had said, but I thought they made a perverse kind of sense. There were men in Wessex, men who were leaderless, but they were men who wanted a leader, men who would fight, and perhaps we could secure the swamp, then defeat Svein, then capture Defnascir, and so, piece by piece, take back Wessex. Then I thought about it more closely and reckoned it was a dream. The Danes had won. We were fugitives.

Alfred was stroking his daughter's golden hair. 'The Danes will hunt us here, won't they?'

'Yes.'

'Can you defend us?'

'Just me and Leofric?'

'You're a warrior, aren't you? Men tell me it was really you who defeated Ubba.'

'You knew I killed Ubba?' I asked.

'Can you defend us?'

I would not be deflected. 'Did you know I won your victory at Cynuit?' I demanded.

'Yes,' he said simply.

'And my reward was to crawl to your altar? To be humiliated?' My anger made my voice too loud and Æthelflaed opened her eyes and stared at me.

'I have made mistakes,' Alfred said, 'and when this is all over, and when God returns Wessex to the West Saxons, I shall do the same. I shall put on the penitent's robe and submit myself to God.'

I wanted to kill the pious bastard then, but Æthelflaed was watching me with her big eyes. She had not moved, so her father did not know she was awake, but I did, so instead of giving my anger a loose rein I cut it off abruptly. 'You'll find that penitence helps,' I said.

He brightened at that. 'It helped you?' he asked.

'It gave me anger,' I said, 'and it taught me to hate. And anger is good. Hatred is good.'

'You don't mean that,' he said.

I half drew Serpent-Breath and little Æthelflaed's eyes grew wider. 'This kills,' I said, letting the sword slide back into its fleece-lined scabbard, 'but anger and hate are what gives it the strength to kill. Go into battle without anger and hate and you'll be dead. You need all the blades, anger and hate you can muster if we're to survive.'

'But can you do it?' he asked. 'Can you defend us here? Long enough to evade the Danes while we decide what to do?'

'Yes,' I said. I had no idea whether I spoke the truth, indeed I doubted that I did, but I had a warrior's pride so gave a warrior's answer. Æthelflaed had not taken her eyes from me. She was only six, but I swear she understood all that we talked about.

'So I give you charge of that task,' Alfred said. 'Here and now I appoint you as the defender of my family. Do you accept that responsibility?'

I was an arrogant brute. Still am. He was challenging me, of course, and he knew what he was doing even if I did not. I just bridled. 'Of course I accept it,' I said, 'yes.'

'Yes what?' he asked.

I hesitated, but he had flattered me, given me a warrior's responsibility and so I gave him what he wanted and what I had been determined not to give to him. 'Yes, lord,' I said.

He held out his hand. I knew he wanted more now. I had never meant to grant him this wish, but I had called him 'lord' and so I knelt to him and, across Æthelflaed's body, I took his hand in both mine.

'Say it,' he demanded, and he put the crucifix that hung about his neck between our hands.

'I swear to be your man,' I said, looking into his pale eyes, 'until your family is safe.'

He hesitated. I had given him the oath, but I had qualified it. I had let him know that I would not remain his man for ever, but he accepted my terms. He should have kissed me on both cheeks, but that would have disturbed Æthelflaed and so he raised my right hand and kissed the knuckles, then kissed the crucifix. 'Thank you,' he said.

The truth, of course, was that Alfred was finished, but, with the perversity and arrogance of foolish youth, I had just given him my oath and promised to fight for him.

And all, I think, because a six-year-old stared at me. And she had hair of gold.

Seven

The kingdom of Wessex was now a swamp and, for a few days, it possessed a king, a bishop, four priests, two soldiers, the king's pregnant wife, two nurses, a whore, two children, one of whom was sick, and Iseult.

Three of the four priests left the swamp first. Alfred was suffering, struck by the fever and belly pains that so often afflicted him, and he seemed incapable of rousing himself to any decision so I gathered the three youngest priests, told them they were useless mouths we could not afford to feed, and ordered them to leave the swamp and discover what was happening on dry ground. 'Find soldiers,' I told them, 'and say the king wants them to come here.' Two of the priests begged to be spared the mission, claiming they were scholars incapable of surviving the winter or of confronting the Danes or of enduring discomfort or of doing any real work, and Alewold, the Bishop of Exanceaster, supported them, saying that their joint prayers were needed to keep the king healthy and safe, so I reminded the bishop that Eanflæd was present.

'Eanflæd?' He blinked at me as though he had never heard the name.

'The whore,' I said, 'from Cippanhamm.' He still looked ignorant. 'Cippanhamm,' I went on, 'where you and she rutted in the Corncrake tavern and she says . . .'

'The priests will travel,' he said hastily.

'Of course they will,' I said, 'but they'll leave their silver here.'

'Silver?'

The priests had been carrying Alewold's hoard which included the great pyx I had given him to settle Mildrith's debts. That hoard was my next weapon. I took it all and displayed it to the marshmen. There would be silver, I said, for the food they gave us and the fuel they brought us and the punts they provided and the news they told us, news of the Danes on the swamp's far side. I wanted the marshmen on our side, and the sight of the silver encouraged them, but Bishop Alewold immediately ran to Alfred and complained that I had stolen from the church. The king was too low in spirits to care, so Ælswith, his wife, entered the fray. She was a Mercian and Alfred had married her to tighten the bonds between Wessex and Mercia, though that did little good for us now because the Danes ruled Mercia. There were plenty of Mercians who would fight for a West Saxon king, but none would risk their lives for a king reduced to a soggy realm in a tidal swamp. 'You will return the pyx!' Ælswith ordered me. She looked ragged, her greasy hair tangled, her belly swollen and her clothes filthy. 'Give it back now. This instant!'

I looked at Iseult. 'Should I?'

'No,' Iseult said.

'She has no say here!' Ælswith shrieked.

'But she's a queen,' I said, 'and you're not.' That was one cause of Ælswith's bitterness, that the West Saxons never called the king's wife a queen. She wanted to be Queen Ælswith and had to be content with less. She tried to snatch back the pyx, but I tossed it on the ground and, when she reached for it, I swung Leofric's axe. The blade chewed into

188

the big plate, mangling the silver crucifixion, and Ælswith squealed in alarm and backed away as I hacked again. It took several blows, but I finally reduced the heavy plate into shreds of mangled silver that I tossed onto the coins I had taken from the priests. 'Silver for your help!' I told the marshmen.

Ælswith spat at me, then went back to her son. Edward was three years old and it was evident now that he was dying. Alewold had claimed it was a mere winter's cold, but it was plainly worse, much worse. Every night we would listen to the coughing, an extraordinary hollow racking sound from such a small child, and all of us lay awake, dreading the next bout, flinching from the desperate, rasping sound, and when the coughing fits ended we feared they would not start again. Every silence was like the coming of death, yet somehow the small boy lived, clinging on through those cold wet days in the swamp. Bishop Alewold and the women tried all they knew. A gospel book was laid on his chest and the bishop prayed. A concoction of herbs, chicken dung and ash was pasted on his chest and the bishop prayed. Alfred travelled nowhere without his precious relics, and the toe ring of Mary Magdalen was rubbed on the child's chest and the bishop prayed, but Edward just became weaker and thinner. A woman of the swamp, who had a reputation as a healer, tried to sweat the cough from him, and when that did not work she attempted to freeze it from him, and when that did not work she tied a live fish to his chest and commanded the cough and the fever to flee to the fish, and the fish certainly died, but the boy went on coughing and the bishop prayed and Alfred, as thin as his sick son, was in despair. He knew the Danes would search for him, but so long as the child was ill he dared not move, and he certainly could not contemplate the long walk south to the coast where he might find a ship to carry him and his family into exile.

He was resigned to that fate now. He had dared to hope he might recover his kingdom, but the cold reality was more persuasive. The Danes held Wessex and Alfred was king of nothing, and his son was dying. 'It is a retribution,' he said. It was the night after the three priests had left and Alfred unburdened his soul to me and Bishop Alewold. We were outside, watching the moon silver the marsh mists, and there were tears on Alfred's face. He was not really talking to either of us, only to himself.

'God would not take a son to punish the father,' Alewold said.

'God sacrificed his own son,' Alfred said bleakly, 'and he commanded Abraham to kill Isaac.'

'He spared Isaac,' the bishop said.

'But he is not sparing Edward,' Alfred said, and flinched as the awful coughing sounded from the hut. He put his head in his hands, covering his eyes.

'Retribution for what?' I asked, and the bishop hissed in reprimand for such an indelicate question.

'Æthelwold,' Alfred said bleakly. Æthelwold was his nephew, the drunken, resentful son of the old king.

'Æthelwold could never have been king,' Alewold said. 'He is a fool!'

'If I name him king now,' Alfred said, ignoring what the bishop had said, 'perhaps God will spare Edward?'

The coughing ended. The boy was crying now, a gasping, grating, pitiful crying, and Alfred covered his ears with his hands.

'Give him to Iseult,' I said.

'A pagan!' Alewold warned Alfred, 'an adulteress!' I could see Alfred was tempted by my suggestion, but Alewold was having the better of the argument. 'If God will not cure Edward,' the bishop said, 'do you think he will let a witch succeed?'

190

'She's no witch,' I said.

'Tomorrow,' Alewold said, ignoring me, 'is Saint Agnes's Eve. A holy day, lord, a day of miracles! We shall pray to Saint Agnes and she will surely unleash God's power on the boy.' He raised his hands to the dark sky. 'Tomorrow, lord, we shall summon the strength of the angels, we shall call heaven's aid to your son and the blessed Agnes will drive the evil sickness from young Edward.'

Alfred said nothing, just stared at the swamp's pools that were edged with a thin skim of ice that seemed to glow in the wan moonlight.

'I have known the blessed Agnes perform miracles!' the bishop pressed the king, 'there was a child in Exanceaster who could not walk, but the saint gave him strength and now he runs!'

'Truly?' Alfred asked.

'With my own eyes,' the bishop said, 'I witnessed the miracle.'

Alfred was reassured. 'Tomorrow then,' he said.

I did not stay to see the power of God unleashed. Instead I took a punt and went south to a place called Æthelingæg which lay at the southern edge of the swamp and was the biggest of all the marsh settlements. I was beginning to learn the swamp. Leofric stayed with Alfred, to protect the king and his family, but I explored, discovering scores of track-ways through the watery void. The paths were called beamwegs and were made of logs that squelched underfoot, but by using them I could walk for miles. There were also rivers that twisted through the low land, and the biggest of those, the Pedredan, flowed close to Æthelingæg which was an island, much of it covered with alders in which deer and wild goats lived, but there was also a large village on the island's highest spot and the headman had built himself a great hall there. It was not a royal hall, not even as big as

191

the one I had made at Oxton, but a man could stand upright beneath its beams and the island was large enough to accommodate a small army.

A dozen beamwegs led away from Æthelingæg, but none led directly to the mainland. It would be a hard place for Guthrum to attack, because he would have to thread the swamp, but Svein, who we now knew commanded the Danes at Cynuit, at the Pedredan's mouth, would find it an easy place to approach for he could bring his ships up the river and, just north of Æthelingæg, he could turn south onto the River Thon which flowed past the island. I took the punt into the centre of the Thon and discovered, as I had feared, that it was more than deep enough to float the Dane's beast-headed ships.

I walked back to the place where the Thon flowed into the Pedredan. Across the wider river was a sudden hill, steep and high, which stood in the surrounding marshland like a giant's burial mound. It was a perfect place to make a fort, and if a bridge could be built across the Pedredan then no Danish ship could pass up river.

I walked back to the village where I discovered that the headman was a grizzled and stubborn old man called Haswold who was disinclined to help. I said I would pay good silver to have a bridge made across the Pedredan, but Haswold declared the war between Wessex and the Danes did not affect him. 'There is madness over there,' he said, waving vaguely at the eastern hills. 'There's always madness over there, but here in the swamp we mind our own business. No one minds us and we don't mind them.' He stank of fish and smoke. He wore otterskins that were greasy with fish oil and his greying beard was flecked by fish scales. He had small cunning eyes in an old cunning face, and he also had a half-dozen wives, the youngest of whom was a child who could have been his own granddaughter, and he fondled her in front of me as if her existence proved his manhood. 'I'm happy,' he said, leering at me, 'so why should I care for your happiness?'

'The Danes could end your happiness.'

'The Danes?' He laughed at that, and the laugh turned into a cough. He spat. 'If the Danes come,' he went on, 'then we go deep into the swamp and the Danes go.' He grinned at me and I wanted to kill him, but that would have done no good. There were fifty or more men in the village and I would have lasted all of a dozen heartbeats, though the man I really feared was a tall, broad-shouldered, stooping man with a puzzled look on his face. What frightened me about him was that he carried a long hunting bow. Not one of the short fowling bows that many of the marshmen possessed, but a stag killer, as tall as a man, and capable of shooting an arrow clean through a mail coat. Haswold must have sensed my fear of the bow for he summoned the man to stand beside him. The man looked confused by the summons, but obeyed. Haswold pushed a gnarled hand under the young girl's clothes then stared at me as he fumbled, laughing at what he perceived as my impotence. 'The Danes come,' he said again, 'and we go deep into the swamp and the Danes go away.' He thrust his hand deeper into the girl's goatskin dress and mauled her breasts. 'Danes can't follow us, and if they do follow us then Eofer kills them.' Eofer was the archer and, hearing his name, he looked startled, then worried. 'Eofer's my man,' Haswold boasted, 'he puts arrows where I tell him to put them.' Eofer nodded.

'Your king wants a bridge made,' I said, 'a bridge and a fort.'

'King?' Haswold stared about the village. 'I know no king. If any man is king here, 'tis me.' He cackled with laughter at that and I looked at the villagers and saw nothing but dull faces. None shared Haswold's amusement. They were not, I thought, happy under his rule and perhaps he sensed what I was thinking for he suddenly became angry, thrusting his girl-bride away. 'Leave us!' he shouted at me. 'Just go away!'

I went away, returning to the smaller island where Alfred sheltered and where Edward lay dying. It was nightfall and the bishop's prayers to Saint Agnes had failed. Eanflæd told me how Alewold had persuaded Alfred to give up one of his most precious relics, a feather from the dove that Noah had released from the ark. Alewold cut the feather into two parts, returning one part to the king, while the other was scorched on a clean pan and, when it was reduced to ash, the scraps were stirred into a cup of holy water which Ælswith forced her son to drink. He had been wrapped in lambskin, for the lamb was the symbol of Saint Agnes who had been a child martyr in Rome.

But neither feather nor lambskin had worked. If anything, Eanflæd said, the boy was worse. Alewold was praying over him now. 'He's given him the last rites,' Eanflæd said. She looked at me with tears in her eyes. 'Can Iseult help?'

'The bishop won't allow it,' I said.

'He won't allow it?' she asked indignantly. 'He's not the one who's dying!'

So Iseult was summoned, and Alfred came from the hut and Alewold, scenting heresy, came with him. Edward was coughing again, the sound terrible in the evening silence. Alfred flinched at the noise, then demanded to know if Iseult could cure his son's illness.

Iseult did not reply at once. Instead she turned and gazed across the swamp to where the moon rose above the mists. 'The moon gets bigger,' she said.

'Do you know a cure?' Alfred pleaded.

'A growing moon is good,' Iseult said dully, then turned on him. 'But there will be a price.'

194

'Whatever you want!' he said.

'Not a price for me,' she said, irritated that he had misunderstood her. 'But there's always a price. One lives? Another must die.'

'Heresy!' Alewold intervened.

I doubt Alfred understood Iseult's last three words, or did not care what she meant, he only snatched the tenuous hope that perhaps she could help. 'Can you cure my son?' he demanded.

She paused, then nodded. 'There is a way,' she said.

'What way?'

'My way.'

'Heresy!' Alewold warned again.

'Bishop!' Eanflæd said warningly, and the bishop looked abashed and fell silent.

'Now?' Alfred demanded of Iseult.

'Tomorrow night,' Iseult said. 'It takes time. There are things to do. If he lives till nightfall tomorrow I can help. You must bring him to me at moonrise.'

'Not tonight?' Alfred pleaded.

'Tomorrow,' Iseult said firmly.

'Tomorrow is the Feast of Saint Vincent,' Alfred said, as though that might help, and somehow the child survived that night and, next day, Saint Vincent's Day, Iseult went with me to the eastern shore where we gathered lichen, burdock, celandine and mistletoe. She would not let me use metal to scrape the lichen or cut the herbs, and before any was collected we had to walk three times around the plants which, because it was winter, were poor and shrivelled things. She also made me cut thorn boughs, and I was allowed to use a knife for that because the thorns were evidently not as important as the lichen or herbs. I watched the skyline as I worked, looking for any Danes, but if they patrolled the edge of the swamp none appeared that day. It was cold, a gusting wind clutching at our clothes. It took a long time to find the plants Iseult needed, but at last her pouch was full and I dragged the thorn bushes back to the island and took them into the hut where she instructed me to dig two holes in the floor. 'They must be as deep as the child is tall,' she said, 'and as far apart from each other as the length of your forearm.'

She would not tell me what the pits were for. She was subdued, very close to tears. She hung the celandine and burdock from a roof beam, then pounded the lichen and the mistletoe into a paste that she moistened with spittle and urine, and she chanted long charms in her own language over the shallow wooden bowl. It all took a long time and sometimes she just sat exhausted in the darkness beyond the hearth and rocked to and fro. 'I don't know that I can do it,' she said once.

'You can try,' I said helplessly.

'And if I fail,' she said, 'they will hate me more than ever.'

'They don't hate you,' I said.

'They think I am a sinner and a pagan,' she said, 'and they hate me.'

'So cure the child,' I said, 'and they will love you.'

I could not dig the pits as deep as she wanted, for the soil became ever wetter and, just a couple of feet down, the two holes were filling with brackish water. 'Make them wider,' Iseult ordered me, 'wide enough so the child can crouch in them.' I did as she said, and then she made me join the two holes by knocking a passage in the damp earth wall that divided them. That had to be done carefully to ensure that an arch of soil remained to leave a tunnel between the holes. 'It is wrong,' Iseult said, not talking of my excavation, but of the charm she planned to work. 'Someone will die, Uhtred. Somewhere a child will die so this one will live.'

196

'How do you know that?' I asked.

'Because my twin died when I was born,' she said, 'and I have his power. But if I use it he reaches from the dark world and takes the power back.'

Darkness fell and the boy went on coughing, though to my ears it sounded feebler now as though there was not enough life left in his small body. Alewold was praying still. Iseult crouched in the door of our hut, staring into the rain, and when Alfred came close she waved him away.

'He's dying,' the king said helplessly.

'Not yet,' Iseult said, 'not yet.'

Edward's breath rasped. We could all hear it, and we all thought every harsh breath would be his last, and still Iseult did not move, and then at last a rift showed in the rain clouds and a feeble wash of moonlight touched the marsh and she told me to fetch the boy.

Ælswith did not want Edward to go. She wanted him cured, but when I said Iseult insisted on working her charms alone, Ælswith wailed that she did not want her son to die apart from his mother. Her crying upset Edward who began to cough again. Eanflæd stroked his forehead. 'Can she do it?' she demanded of me.

'Yes,' I said and did not know if I spoke the truth.

Eanflæd took hold of Ælswith's shoulders. 'Let the boy go, my lady,' she said, 'let him go.'

'He'll die!'

'Let him go,' Eanflæd said, and Ælswith collapsed into the whore's arms and I picked up Alfred's son who felt as light as the feather that had not cured him. He was hot, yet shivering, and I wrapped him in a wool robe and carried him to Iseult.

'You can't stay here,' she told me. 'Leave him with me.'

I waited with Leofric in the dark. Iseult insisted we could not watch through the hut's entrance, but I dropped my helmet outside the door and, by crouching under the eaves I could just see a reflection of what happened inside. The small rain died and the moon grew brighter.

The boy coughed. Iseult stripped him naked and rubbed her herb paste on his chest, and then she began to chant in her own tongue, an endless chant it seemed, rhythmic, sad and so monotonous that it almost put me to sleep. Edward cried once, and the crying turned to coughing and his mother screamed from her hut that she wanted him back, and Alfred calmed her and then came to join us and I waved him down so that he would not shadow the moonlight before Iseult's door.

I peered at the helmet and saw, in the small reflected firelight, that Iseult, naked herself now, was pushing the boy into one of the pits and then, still chanting, she drew him through the earth passage. Her chanting stopped and, instead, she began to pant, then scream, then pant again. She moaned, and Alfred made the sign of the cross, and then there was silence and I could not see properly, but suddenly Iseult cried aloud, a cry of relief, as if a great pain was ended, and I dimly saw her pull the naked boy out of the second pit. She laid him on her bed and he was silent as she crammed the thorn bushes into the tunnel of earth. Then she lay beside the boy and covered herself with my large cloak.

There was silence. I waited, and waited, and still there was silence. And the silence stretched until I understood that Iseult was sleeping, and the boy was sleeping too, or else he was dead, and I picked up the helmet and went to Leofric's hut. 'Shall I fetch him?' Alfred asked nervously.

'No.'

'His mother . . .' he began.

'Must wait till morning, lord.'

'What can I tell her?'

'That her son is not coughing, lord.'

Ælswith screamed that Edward was dead, but Eanflæd and Alfred calmed her, and we all waited, and still there was silence, and in the end I fell asleep.

I woke in the dawn. It was raining as if the world was about to end, a torrential grey rain that swept in vast curtains from the Sæfern Sea, a rain that drummed on the ground and poured off the reed thatch and made streams on the small island where the little huts crouched. I went to the door of Leofric's shelter and saw Ælswith watching from her doorway. She looked desperate, like a mother about to hear that her child had died, and there was nothing but silence from Iseult's hut, and Ælswith began to weep, the terrible tears of a bereaved mother, and then there was a strange sound. At first I could not hear properly, for the seething rain was loud, but then I realised the sound was laughter. A child's laughter, and a heartbeat later Edward, still naked as an egg, and all muddy from his rebirth through the earth's passage, ran from Iseult's hut and went to his mother.

'Dear God,' Leofric said.

Iseult, when I found her, was weeping, and would not be consoled. 'I need you,' I told her harshly.

She looked up at me. 'Need me?'

'To build a bridge.'

She frowned. 'You think a bridge can be made with spells?'

'My magic this time,' I said. 'I want you healthy. I need a queen.'

She nodded. And Edward, from that day forward, thrived.

The first men came, summoned by the priests I had sent onto the mainland. They came in ones and twos, struggling

199

through the winter weather and the swamp, bringing tales of Danish raids, and when we had two days of sunshine they came in groups of six or seven so that the island became crowded. I sent them out on patrol, but ordered none to go too far west for I did not want to provoke Svein, whose men were camped beside the sea. He had not attacked us yet, which was foolish of him, for he could have brought his ships up the rivers and then struggled through the marsh, but I knew he would attack us when he was ready, and so I needed to make our defences. And for that I needed Æthelingæg.

Alfred was recovering. He was still sick, but he saw God's favour in his son's recovery and it never occurred to him that it had been pagan magic that caused the recovery. Even Ælswith was generous and, when I asked her for the loan of her silver fox-fur cloak and what few jewels she possessed, she yielded them without fuss. The fur cloak was dirty, but Eanflæd brushed and combed it.

There were over twenty men on our island now, probably enough to capture Æthelingæg from its sullen headman, but Alfred did not want the marshmen killed. They were his subjects, he said, and if the Danes attacked they might yet fight for us, which meant the large island and its village must be taken by trickery and so, a week after Edward's rebirth, I took Leofric and Iseult south to Haswold's settlement. Iseult was dressed in the silver fur and had a silver chain in her hair and a great garnet brooch at her breast. I had brushed her hair till it shone and in that winter's gloom she looked like a princess come from the bright sky.

Leofric and I, dressed in mail and helmets, did nothing except walk around Æthelingæg, but after a while a man came from Haswold and said the chieftain wished to talk with us. I think Haswold expected us to go to his stinking hut, but I demanded he come to us instead. He could have taken from us whatever he wanted, of course, for there were only the three of us and he had his men, including Eofer the archer, but Haswold had at last understood that dire things were happening in the world beyond the swamp and that those events could pierce even his watery fastness, and so he chose to talk. He came to us at the settlement's northern gate which was nothing more than a sheep hurdle propped against decaying fish traps and there, as I expected, he gazed at Iseult as though he had never seen a woman before. His small cunning eyes flickered at me and back to her. 'Who is she?' he asked.

'A companion,' I said carelessly. I turned to look at the sudden steep hill across the river where I wanted the fort made.

'Is she your wife?' Haswold asked.

'A companion,' I said again. 'I have a dozen like her,' I added.

'I will pay you for her,' Haswold said. A score of men were behind him, but only Eofer was armed with anything more dangerous than an eel spear.

I turned Iseult to face him, then I stood behind her and put my hands over her shoulders and undid the big garnet brooch. She shivered slightly and I whispered that she was safe and, when the brooch pin slid out of the heavy hide, I pulled her fur cloak apart. I showed her nakedness to Haswold and he dribbled into his fish-scaled beard and his dirty fingers twitched in his foul otterskin furs, and then I closed the cloak and let Iseult fasten the brooch. 'How much will you pay me?' I asked him.

'I can just take her,' Haswold said, jerking his head at his men.

I smiled at that. 'You could,' I said, 'but many of you will die before we die, and our ghosts will come back to kill your women and make your children scream. Have you not heard

201

that we have a witch with us? You think your weapons can fight magic?'

None of them moved.

'I have silver,' Haswold said.

'I don't need silver,' I said. 'What I want is a bridge and a fort.' I turned and pointed to the hill across the river. 'What is that hill called?'

He shrugged. 'The hill,' he said, 'just the hill.'

'It must become a fort,' I said, 'and it must have walls of logs and a gate of logs and a tower so that men can see a long way down river. And then I want a bridge leading to the fort, a bridge strong enough to stop ships.'

'You want to stop ships?' Haswold asked. He scratched his groin and shook his head. 'Can't build a bridge.'

'Why not?'

'Too deep.' That was probably true. It was low tide now and the Pedredan flowed sullenly between steep and deep mud banks. 'But I can block the river,' Haswold went on, his eyes still on Iseult.

'Block the river,' I said, 'and build a fort.'

'Give her to me,' Haswold promised, 'and you will have both.'

'Do what I want,' I said, 'and you can have her, her sisters and her cousins. All twelve of them.'

Haswold would have drained the whole swamp and built a new Jerusalem for the chance to hump Iseult, but he had not thought beyond the end of his prick. But that was far enough for me, and I have never seen work done so quickly. It was done in days. He blocked the river first and did it cleverly by making a floating barrier of logs and felled trees, complete with their tangling branches, all of them lashed together with goathide ropes. A ship's crew could eventually dismantle such a barrier, but not if they were being assailed by spears and arrows from the fort on the hill that had a wooden palisade, a flooded ditch and a flimsy tower made of alder logs bound together with leather ropes. It was all crude work, but the wall was solid enough, and I began to fear that the small fort would be finished before enough West Saxons arrived to garrison it, but the three priests were doing their job and the soldiers still came, and I put a score of them in Æthelingæg and told them to help finish the fort.

When the work was done, or nearly done, I took Iseult back to Æthelingæg and I dressed her as she had been dressed before, only this time she wore a deerskin tunic beneath the precious fur, and I stood her in the centre of the village and said Haswold could take her. He looked at me warily, then looked at her. 'She's mine?' he asked.

'All yours,' I said, and stepped away from her.

'And her sisters?' he asked greedily, 'her cousins?'

'I shall bring them tomorrow.'

He beckoned Iseult towards his hut. 'Come,' he said.

'In her country,' I said, 'it is the custom for the man to lead the woman to his bed.'

He stared at Iseult's lovely, dark-eyed face above the swathing silver cloak. I stepped further back, abandoning her, and he darted forward, reaching for her, and she brought her hands out from under the thick fur and she was holding Wasp-Sting and its blade sliced up into Haswold's belly. She gave a cry of horror and surprise as she brought the blade up, and I saw her hesitate, shocked by the effort required to pierce a man's belly and by the reality of what she had done. Then she gritted her teeth and ripped the blade hard, opening him up like a gutted carp, and he gave a strange mewing cry as he staggered back from her vengeful eyes. His intestines spilled into the mud, and I was beside her then with Serpent-Breath drawn. She was gasping, trembling. She had wanted to do it, but I doubted she would want to do it again.

'You were asked,' I snarled at the villagers, 'to fight for your king.' Haswold was on the ground, twitching, his blood soaking his otterskin clothes. He made a mewing noise again and one of his filthy hands scrabbled among his own spilt guts. 'For your king!' I repeated. 'When you are asked to fight for your king it is not a request, but a duty! Every man here is a soldier and your enemy is the Danes and if you will not fight them then you will fight against me!'

Iseult still stood beside Haswold who jerked like a dying fish. I edged her away and stabbed Serpent-Breath down to slit his throat. 'Take his head,' she told me.

'His head?'

'Strong magic.'

We mounted Haswold's head on the fort wall so that it stared towards the Danes, and in time eight more heads appeared there. They were the heads of Haswold's chief supporters, murdered by the villagers who were glad to be rid of them. Eofer, the archer, was not one of them. He was a simpleton, incapable of speaking sense, though he grunted and, from time to time, made howling noises. He could be led by a child, but when asked to use his bow he proved to have a terrible strength and uncanny accuracy. He was Æthelingæg's hunter, capable of dropping a full-grown boar at a hundred paces, and that was what his name meant; boar.

I left Leofric to command the garrison at Æthelingæg and took Iseult back to Alfred's refuge. She was silent and I thought her sunk in misery, but then she suddenly laughed. 'Look!' she pointed at the dead man's blood matted and sticky in Ælswith's fur.

She still had Wasp-Sting. That was my short sword, a sax, and it was a wicked blade in a close fight where men are so crammed together that there is no room to swing a long sword or an axe. She trailed the blade in the water, then used the hem of Ælswith's fur to scrub the diluted blood from the steel. 'It is harder than I thought,' she said, 'to kill a man.'

'It takes strength.'

'But I have his soul now.'

'Is that why you did it?'

'To give life,' she said, 'you must take it from somewhere else.' She gave me back Wasp-Sting.

Alfred was shaving when we returned. He had been growing a beard, not for a disguise, but because he had been too low in spirits to bother about his appearance, but when Iseult and I reached his refuge he was standing naked to the waist beside a big wooden tub of heated water. His chest was pathetically thin, his belly hollow, but he had washed himself, combed his hair and was now scratching at his stubble with an ancient razor he had borrowed from a marshman. His daughter Æthelflaed was holding a scrap of silver that served as a mirror. 'I am feeling better,' he told me solemnly.

'Good, lord,' I said, 'so am I.'

'Does that mean you've killed someone?'

'She did,' I jerked my head at Iseult.

He gave her a speculative look. 'My wife,' he said, dipping the razor in the water, 'was asking whether Iseult is truly a queen.'

'She was,' I said, 'but that means little in Cornwalum. She was queen of a dung-heap.'

'And she's a pagan?'

'It was a Christian kingdom,' I said. 'Didn't Brother Asser tell you that?'

'He said they were not good Christians.'

'I thought that was for God to judge.'

'Good, Uhtred, good!' He waved the razor at me, then stooped to the silver mirror and scraped at his upper lip. 'Can she foretell the future?'

'She can.'

He scraped in silence for a few heartbeats. Æthelflaed watched Iseult solemnly. 'So tell me,' Alfred said, 'does she say I will be king in Wessex again?'

'You will,' Iseult said tonelessly, surprising me.

Alfred stared at her. 'My wife,' he said, 'says that we can look for a ship now that Edward is better. Look for a ship, go to Frankia and perhaps travel on to Rome. There is a Saxon community in Rome.' He scraped the blade against his jawbone. 'They will welcome us.'

'The Danes will be defeated,' Iseult said, still tonelessly, but without a quiver of doubt in her voice.

Alfred rubbed his face. 'The example of Boethius tells me she's right,' he said.

'Boethius?' I asked, 'is he one of your warriors?'

'He was a Roman, Uhtred,' Alfred said in a tone which chided me for not knowing, 'and a Christian and a philosopher and a man rich in book-learning. Rich indeed!' He paused, contemplating the story of Boethius. 'When the pagan Alaric overran Rome,' he went on, 'and all civilisation and true religion seemed doomed, Boethius alone stood against the sinners. He suffered, but he won through, and we can take heart from him. Indeed we can.' He pointed the razor at me. 'We must never forget the example of Boethius, Uhtred, never.'

'I won't, lord,' I said, 'but do you think book-learning will get you out of here?'

'I think,' he said, 'that when the Danes are gone, I shall grow a proper beard. Thank you, my sweet,' this last was to Æthelflaed. 'Give the mirror back to Eanflæd, will you?'

Æthelflaed ran off and Alfred looked at me with some amusement. 'Does it surprise you that my wife and Eanflæd have become friends?'

'I'm glad of it, lord.'

'So am I.'

'But does your wife know Eanflæd's trade?' I asked.

'Not exactly,' he said. 'She believes Eanflæd was a cook in a tavern. Which is truth enough. So we have a fort at Æthelingæg?'

'We do. Leofric commands there and has forty-three men.'

'And we have twenty-eight here. The very hosts of Midian!' He was evidently amused. 'So we shall move there.'

'Maybe in a week or two.'

'Why wait?' he asked.

I shrugged. 'This place is deeper in the swamp. When we have more men, when we know we can hold Æthelingæg, that is the time for you to go there.'

He pulled on a grubby shirt. 'Your new fort can't stop the Danes?'

'It will slow them, lord. But they could still struggle through the marsh.' They would find it difficult, though, for Leofric was digging ditches to defend Æthelingæg's western edge.

'You're telling me Æthelingæg is more vulnerable than this place?'

'Yes, lord.'

'Which is why I must go there,' he said. 'Men can't say their king skulked in an unreachable place, can they?' He smiled at me. 'They must say he defied the Danes. That he waited where they could reach him, that he put himself into danger.'

'And his family?' I asked.

'And his family,' he said firmly. He thought for a moment. 'If they come in force they could take all the swamp, isn't that true?'

'Yes, lord.'

'So no place is safer than another. But how large a force does Svein have?'

'I don't know, lord.'

'Don't know?' It was a reproof, gentle enough, but still a reproof.

'I haven't gone close to them, lord,' I explained, 'because till now we've been too weak to resist them, and so long as they leave us undisturbed then so long do we leave them undisturbed. There's no point in kicking a wild bees' nest, not unless you're determined to get the honey.'

He nodded acceptance of that argument. 'But we need to know how many bees there are, don't we?' he said. 'So tomorrow we shall take a look at our enemy. You and me, Uhtred.'

'No, lord,' I said firmly. 'I shall go. You shouldn't risk yourself.'

'That is exactly what I need to do,' he said, 'and men must know I do it for I am the king, and why would men want a king who does not share their danger?' He waited for an answer, but I had none. 'So let's say our prayers,' he finished, 'then we shall eat.'

It was fish stew. It was always fish stew.

And next day we went to find the enemy.

There were six of us. The man who poled the punt, Iseult and I, two of the newly-arrived household troops and Alfred. I tried once again to make him stay behind, but he insisted. 'If anyone should stay,' he said, 'it is Iseult.'

'She comes,' I said.

'Evidently.' He did not argue, and we all climbed into a large punt and went westwards, and Alfred stared at the birds, thousands of birds. There were coot, moorhen, dabchicks, ducks, grebes and herons, while off to the west, white against the sullen sky, was a cloud of gulls.

The marshman slid us silent and fast through secret channels. There were times when he seemed to be taking us directly into a bank of reeds or grass, yet the shallow craft would slide through into another stretch of open water. The incoming tide rippled through the gaps, bringing fish to the hidden nets and basket traps. Beneath the gulls, far off to the west, I could see the masts of Svein's fleet, which had been dragged ashore on the coast.

Alfred saw them too. 'Why don't they join Guthrum?'

'Because Svein doesn't want to take Guthrum's orders,' I said.

'You know that?'

'He told me so.'

Alfred paused, perhaps thinking of my trial in front of the Witan. He gave me a rueful look. 'What sort of man is he?'

'Formidable.'

'So why hasn't he attacked us here?'

I had been wondering the same thing. Svein had missed a golden chance to invade the swamp and hunt Alfred down. So why had he not even tried? 'Because there's easier plunder elsewhere,' I suggested, 'and because he won't do Guthrum's bidding. They're rivals. If Svein takes Guthrum's orders then he acknowledges Guthrum as his king.'

Alfred stared at the distant masts which showed as small scratches against the sky, then I mutely pointed towards a hill that reared steeply from the western water flats and the marshman obediently went that way, and when the punt grounded we clambered through thick alders and past some sunken hovels where sullen folk in dirty otter fur watched us pass. The marshman knew no name for the place, except to call it Brant, which meant steep, and it was steep. Steep and high, offering a view southwards to where the Pedredan coiled like a great snake through the swamp's heart. And at the river's mouth, where sand and mud stretched into the Sæfern Sea, I could see the Danish ships.

They were grounded on the far bank of the Pedredan in the same place that Ubba had grounded his ships before meeting his death in battle. From there Svein could easily row to Æthelingæg, for the river was wide and deep, and he would meet no challenge until he reached the river barrier beside the fort where Leofric waited. I wanted Leofric and his garrison to have some warning if the Danes attacked, and this high hill offered a view of Svein's camp, but was far enough away so that it would not invite an attack from the enemy. 'We should make a beacon here,' I said to Alfred. A fire lit here would give Æthelingæg two or three hours' warning of a Danish attack.

He nodded, but said nothing. He stared at the distant ships, but they were too far off to count. He looked pale, and I knew he had found the climb to the summit painful, so now I urged him downhill to where the hovels leaked smoke. 'You should rest here, lord,' I told him. 'I'm going to count ships. But you should rest.'

He did not argue and I suspected his stomach pains were troubling him again. I found a hovel that was occupied by a widow and her four children, and I gave her a silver coin and said her king needed warmth and shelter for the day, and I do not think she understood who he was, but she knew the value of a shilling and so Alfred went into her house and sat by the fire. 'Give him broth,' I told the widow, whose name was Elwide, 'and let him sleep.'

She scorned that. 'Folk can't sleep while there's work!' she said. 'There are eels to skin, fish to smoke, nets to mend, traps to weave.'

'They can work,' I said, pointing to the two household troops, and I left them all to Elwide's tender mercies while Iseult and I took the punt southwards and, because the

210

Pedredan's mouth was only three or four miles away, and because Brant was such a clear landmark, I left the marshman to help skin and smoke eels.

We crossed a smaller river and then poled through a long mere broken by marram grass and by now I could see the hill on the Pedredan's far bank where we had been trapped by Ubba, and I told Iseult the story of the fight as I poled the punt across the shallows. The hull grounded twice and I had to push it into deeper water until I realised the tide was falling fast and so I tied the boat to a rotting stake, then we walked across a drying waste of mud and sea lavender towards the Pedredan. I had grounded farther from the river than I had wanted, and it was a long walk into a cold wind, but we could see all we needed once we reached the steep bank at the river's edge. The Danes could also see us. I was not in mail, but I did have my swords, and the sight of me brought men to the further shore where they hurled insults across the swirling water. I ignored them. I was counting ships and saw twenty-four beast-headed boats hauled up on the strip of ground where we had defeated Ubba the year before. Ubba's burned ships were also there, their black ribs half buried in the sand where the men capered and shouted their insults.

'How many men can you see?' I asked Iseult.

There were a few Danes in the half wrecked remnants of the monastery where Svein had killed the monks, but most were by the boats. 'Just men?' she asked.

'Forget the women and children,' I said. There were scores of women, mostly in the small village that was a little way upstream.

She did not know the English words for the bigger numbers, so she gave me her estimate by opening and closing her fingers six times. 'Sixty?' I said, and nodded. 'At most seventy. And there are twenty-four ships.' She

211

frowned, not understanding the point I made. 'Twenty-four ships,' I said, 'means an army of what? Eight hundred? Nine hundred men? So those sixty or seventy men are the ship-guards. And the others? Where are the others?' I asked the question of myself, watching as five of the Danes dragged a small boat to the river's edge. They planned to row across and capture us, but I did not intend to stay that long. 'The others,' I answered my own question, 'have gone south. They've left their women behind and gone raiding. They're burning, killing, getting rich. They're raping Defnascir.'

'They're coming,' Iseult said, watching the five men clamber into the small boat.

'You want me to kill them?'

'You can?' She looked hopeful.

'No,' I said, 'so let's go.'

We started back across the long expanse of mud and sand. It looked smooth, but there were runnels cutting through and the tide had turned and the sea was sliding back into the land with surprising speed. The sun was sinking, tangling with black clouds and the wind pushed the flood up the Sæfern and the water gurgled and shivered as it filled the small creeks. I turned to see that the five Danes had abandoned their chase and gone back to the western bank where their fires looked delicate against the evening's fading light. 'I can't see the boat,' Iseult said.

'Over there,' I said, but I was not certain I was right because the light was dimming and our punt was tied against a background of reeds, and now we were jumping from one dry spot to another, and the tide went on rising and the dry spots shrank and then we were splashing through the water and still the wind drove the tide inland.

The tides are big in the Sæfern. A man could make a house at low tide, and by high it would have vanished beneath the waves. Islands appear at low tide, islands with summits thirty feet above the water, and at the high tide they are gone, and this tide was pushed by the wind and it was coming fast and cold and Iseult began to falter so I picked her up and carried her like a child. I was struggling and the sun was behind the low western clouds and it seemed now that I was wading through an endless chill sea, but then, perhaps because the darkness was falling, or perhaps because Hoder, the blind god of the night, favoured me, I saw the punt straining against its tether.

I dropped Iseult into the boat and hauled myself over the low side. I cut the rope, then collapsed, cold and wet and frightened and let the punt drift on the tide.

'You must get back to the fire,' Iseult chided me. I wished I had brought the marshman now for I had to find a route across the swamp and it was a long, cold journey in the day's last light. Iseult crouched beside me and stared far across the waters to where a hill reared up green and steep against the eastern land. 'Eanflæd told me that hill is Avalon,' she said reverently.

'Avalon?'

'Where Arthur is buried.'

'I thought you believed he was sleeping?'

'He does sleep,' she said fervently. 'He sleeps in his grave with his warriors.' She gazed at the distant hill that seemed to glow because it had been caught by the day's last errant shaft of sunlight spearing from the west beneath the furnace of glowing clouds. 'Arthur,' she said in a whisper. 'He was the greatest king who ever lived. He had a magic sword.' She told me tales of Arthur, how he had pulled his sword from a stone, and how he had led the greatest warriors to battle, and I thought that his enemies had been us, the English Saxons, yet Avalon was now in England, and I wondered if, in a few years, the Saxons would recall their lost kings and claim they were great and all the while the

213

Danes would rule us. When the sun vanished Iseult was singing softly in her own tongue, but she told me the song was about Arthur and how he had placed a ladder against the moon and netted a swathe of stars to make a cloak for his queen, Guinevere. Her voice carried us across the twilit water, sliding between reeds, and behind us the fires of the Danish ship-guards faded in the encroaching dark and far off a dog howled and the wind sighed cold and a spattering of rain shivered the black mere.

Iseult stopped singing as Brant loomed. 'There's going to be a great fight,' she said softly and her words took me by surprise and I thought she was still thinking of Arthur and imagining that the sleeping king would erupt from his earthy bed in gouts of soil and steel. 'A fight by a hill,' she went on, 'a steep hill, and there will be a white horse and the slope will run with blood and the Danes will run from the Sais.'

The Sais were us, the Saxons. 'You dreamed this?' I asked.

'I dreamed it,' she said.

'So it is true?'

'It is fate,' she said, and I believed her, and just then the bow of the punt scraped on the island's shore.

It was pitch dark, but there were fish-smoking fires on the beach, and by their dying light we found our way to Elwide's house. It was made of alder logs thatched with reeds and I found Alfred sitting by the central hearth where he stared absently into the flames. Elwide, the two soldiers and the marshman were all skinning eels at the hut's further end where three of the widow's children were plaiting willow withies into traps and the fourth was gutting a big pike.

I crouched by the fire, wanting its warmth to bring life to my frozen legs.

Alfred blinked as though he was surprised to see me. 'The Danes?' he asked.

214

'Gone inland,' I said. 'Left sixty or seventy men as ship-guards.' I crouched by the fire, shivering, wondering if I would ever be warm again.

'There's food here,' Alfred said vaguely.

'Good,' I said, 'because we're starving.'

'No, I mean there's food in the marshes,' he said. 'Enough food to feed an army. We can raid them, Uhtred, gather men and raid them. But that isn't enough. I have been thinking. All day, I've been thinking.' He looked better now, less pained, and I suspected he had wanted time to think and had found it in this stinking hovel. 'I'm not going to run away,' he said firmly. 'I'm not going to Frankia.'

'Good,' I said, though I was so cold I was not really listening to him.

'We're going to stay here,' he said, 'raise an army, and take Wessex back.'

'Good,' I said again. I could smell burning. The hearth was surrounded by flat stones and Elwide had put a dozen oat bannocks on the stones to cook and the edges nearest the flames were blackening. I moved one of them, but Alfred frowned and gestured for me to stop for fear of distracting him. 'The problem,' he said, 'is that I cannot afford to fight a small war.'

I did not see what other war he could fight, but kept silent.

'The longer the Danes stay here,' he said, 'the firmer their grip. Men will start giving Guthrum their allegiance. I can't have that.'

'No, lord.'

'So they have to be defeated.' He spoke grimly. 'Not beaten, Uhtred, but defeated!'

I thought of Iseult's dream, but said nothing, then I thought how often Alfred had made peace with the Danes instead of fighting them, and still I said nothing.

215

'In spring,' he went on, 'they'll have new men and they'll spread through Wessex until, by summer's end, there'll be no Wessex. So we have to do two things.' He was not so much telling me as just thinking aloud. 'First,' he held out one long finger, 'we have to stop them from dispersing their armies. They have to fight us here. They have to be kept together so they can't send small bands across the country and take estates.' That made sense. Right now, from what we heard from the land beyond the swamp, the Danes were raiding all across Wessex, but they were going fast, snatching what plunder they could before other men could take it, but in a few weeks they would start looking for places to live. By keeping their attention on the swamp Alfred hoped to stop that process. 'And while they look at us,' he said, 'the fyrd must be gathered.'

I stared at him. I had supposed he would stay in the swamp until the Danes either overwhelmed us or we gained enough strength to take back a shire, and then another shire, a process of years, but his vision was much grander. He would assemble the army of Wessex under the Danish noses and take everything back at once. It was like a game of dice and he had decided to take everything he had, little as it was, and risk it all on one throw. 'We shall make them fight a great battle,' he said grimly, 'and with God's help we shall destroy them.'

There was a sudden scream. Alfred, as if startled from a reverie, looked up, but too late, because Elwide was standing over him, screaming that he had burned the oatcakes. 'I told you to watch them!' she shouted and, in her fury, she slapped the king with a skinned eel. The blow made a wet sound as it struck and had enough force to knock Alfred sideways. The two soldiers jumped up, hands going to their swords, but I waved them back as Elwide snatched the burned cakes from the stones. 'I told you to watch them!' she shrieked, and Alfred lay where he had fallen and I thought he was crying, but then I saw he was laughing. He was helpless with laughter, weeping with laughter, as happy as ever I saw him.

Because he had a plan to take back his kingdom.

Æthelingæg's garrison now had seventy-three men. Alfred moved there with his family, and sent six of Leofric's men to Brant armed with axes and orders to make a beacon. He was at his best in those days, calm and confident, the panic and despair of the first weeks of January swept away by his irrational belief that he would regain his kingdom before summer touched the land. He was immensely cheered too by the arrival of Father Beocca who came limping from the landing stage, face beaming, to fall prostrate at the king's feet. 'You live, lord!' Beocca said, clutching the king's ankles, 'God be praised, you live!'

Alfred raised him and embraced him, and both men wept and next day, a Sunday, Beocca preached a sermon which I could not help hearing because the service was held in the open air, under a clear cold sky, and Æthelingæg's island was too small to escape the priest's voice. Beocca said how David, King of Israel, had been forced to flee his enemies, how he had taken refuge in the cave of Adullam, and how God had led him back into Israel and to the defeat of his enemies. 'This is our Adullam!' Beocca said, waving his good hand at Æthelingæg's thatched roofs, 'and this is our David!' he pointed to the king, 'and God will lead us to victory!'

'It's a pity, father,' I said to Beocca afterwards, 'that you weren't this belligerent two months ago.'

'I rejoice,' he said loftily, 'to find you in the king's good graces.'

'He's discovered the value,' I said, 'of murderous bastards like me, so perhaps he'll learn to distrust the advice of snivelling bastards like you who told him the Danes could be defeated by prayer.'

He sniffed at that insult, then looked disapprovingly at Iseult. 'You have news of your wife?'

'None.'

Beocca had some news, though none of Mildrith. He had fled south in front of the invading Danes, getting as far as Dornwaraceaster in Thornsæta where he had found refuge with some monks. The Danes had come, but the monks had received warning of their approach and had hidden in an ancient fort that lay near the town. The Danes had sacked Dornwaraceaster, taking silver, coins and women, then they had moved eastwards and shortly after that Huppa, the Ealdorman of Thornsæta, had come to the town with fifty warriors. Huppa had set the monks and townspeople to mending the old Roman walls. 'The folk there are safe for the moment,' Beocca told me, 'but there is not sufficient food if the Danes return and lay siege.' Then Beocca had heard that Alfred was in the great swamps and Beocca had travelled alone, though on his last day of walking he had met six soldiers going to Alfred and so he had finished his journey with them. He brought no news of Wulfhere, but he had been told that Odda the Younger was somewhere on the upper reaches of the Uisc in an ancient fort built by the old people. Beocca had seen no Danes on his journey. 'They raid everywhere,' he said gloomily, 'but God be praised we saw none of them.'

'Is Dornwaraceaster a large place?' I asked.

'Large enough. It had three fine churches, three!'

'A market?'

'Indeed, it was prosperous before the Danes came.'

'Yet the Danes didn't stay there?'

'Nor were they at Gifle,' he said, 'and that's a goodly place.'

Guthrum had surprised Alfred, defeated the forces at Cippanhamm and driven the king into hiding, but to hold Wessex he needed to take all her walled towns, and if Beocca could walk three days across country and see no Danes then it suggested Guthrum did not have the men to hold all he had taken. He could bring more men from Mercia or East Anglia, but then those places might rise against their weakened Danish overlords, so Guthrum had to be hoping that more ships would come from Denmark. In the meantime, we learned, he had garrisons in Baðum, Readingum, Mærlebeorg and Andefera, and doubtless he held other places, and Alfred suspected, rightly as it turned out, that most of eastern Wessex was in Danish hands, but great stretches of the country were still free of the enemy. Guthrum's men were making raids into those stretches, but they did not have sufficient force to garrison towns like Wintanceaster, Gifle or Dornwaraceaster. In the early summer, Alfred knew, more ships would bring more Danes, so he had to strike before then, to which end, on the day after Beocca arrived, he summoned a council.

There were now enough men on Æthelingæg for a royal formality to prevail. I no longer found Alfred sitting outside a hut in the evening, but instead had to seek an audience with him. On the Monday of the council he gave orders that a large house was to be made into a church, and the family that lived there was evicted and some of the newly-arrived soldiers were ordered to make a great cross for the gable and to carve new windows in the walls. The council itself met in what had been Haswold's hall, and Alfred had waited till we were assembled before

219

making his entrance, and we had all stood as he came in and waited as he took one of the two chairs on the newly-made dais. Ælswith sat beside him, her pregnant belly swathed in the silver fur cloak that was still stained with Haswold's blood.

We were not allowed to sit until the Bishop of Exanceaster said a prayer, and that took time, but at last the king waved us down. There were six priests in the half circle and six warriors. I sat beside Leofric, while the other four soldiers were newly-arrived men who had served in Alfred's household troops. One of those was a grey-bearded man called Egwine who told me he had led a hundred men at Æsc's Hill and plainly thought he should now lead all the troops gathered in the swamp. I knew he had urged his case with the king and with Beocca who sat just below the dais at a rickety table on which he was trying to record what was said at the council. Beocca was having difficulties for his ink was ancient and faded, his quill kept splitting and his parchments were wide margins torn from a missal, so he was unhappy, but Alfred liked to reduce arguments to writing.

The king formally thanked the bishop for his prayer, then announced, sensibly enough, that we could not hope to deal with Guthrum until Svein was defeated. Svein was the immediate threat for, though most of his men had gone south to raid Defnascir, he still had the ships with which to enter the swamp. 'Twenty-four ships,' Alfred said, raising an eyebrow at me.

'Twenty-four, lord,' I confirmed.

'So, when his men are assembled, he can muster near a thousand men.' Alfred let that figure linger awhile. Beocca frowned as his split quill spattered ink on his tiny patch of parchment.

'But a few days ago,' Alfred went on, 'there were only seventy ship-guards at the mouth of the Pedredan.'

'Around seventy,' I said. 'There could be more we didn't see.'

'Fewer than a hundred, though?'

'I suspect so, lord.'

'So we must deal with them,' Alfred said, 'before the rest return to their ships.' There was another silence. All of us knew how weak we were. A few men arrived every day, like the half-dozen who had come with Beocca, but they came slowly, either because the news of Alfred's existence was spreading slowly, or else because the weather was cold and men do not like to travel on wet, cold days. Nor were there any thegns among the newcomers, not one. Thegns were noblemen, men of property, men who could bring scores of well-armed followers to a fight, and every shire had its thegns who ranked just below the reeve and ealdorman, who were themselves thegns. Thegns were the power of Wessex, but none had come to Æthelingæg. Some, we heard, had fled abroad, while others tried to protect their property. Alfred, I was certain, would have felt more comfortable if he had a dozen thegns about him, but instead he had me and Leofric and Egwine. 'What are our forces now?' Alfred asked us.

'We have over a hundred men,' Egwine said brightly.

'Of whom only sixty or seventy are fit to fight,' I said. There had been an outbreak of sickness, men vomiting and shivering and hardly able to control their bowels. Whenever troops gather such sickness seems to strike.

'Is that enough?' Alfred asked.

'Enough for what, lord?' Egwine was not quick-witted.

'Enough to get rid of Svein, of course,' Alfred said, and again there was silence because the question was absurd.

Then Egwine straightened his shoulders. 'More than enough, lord!'

Ælswith bestowed a smile on him.

'And how would you propose doing it?' Alfred asked.

'Take every man we have, lord,' Egwine said, 'every fit man, and attack them. Attack them!'

Beocca was not writing. He knew when he was hearing nonsense and he was not going to waste scarce ink on bad ideas.

Alfred looked at me. 'Can it be done?'

'They'll see us coming,' I said, 'they'll be ready.'

'March inland,' Egwine said, 'come from the hills.'

Again Alfred looked at me. 'That will leave Æthelingæg undefended,' I said, 'and it will take at least three days, at the end of which our men will be cold, hungry and tired, and the Danes will see us coming when we emerge from the hills, and that'll give them time to put on armour and gather weapons. And at best it will be equal numbers. At worst?' I just shrugged. After three or four days the rest of Svein's forces might have returned and our seventy or eighty men would be facing a horde.

'So how do you do it?' Alfred asked.

'We destroy their boats,' I said.

'Go on.'

'Without boats,' I said, 'they can't come up the rivers. Without boats, they're stranded.'

Alfred nodded. Beocca was scratching away again. 'So how do you destroy the boats?' the king asked.

I did not know. We could take seventy men to fight their seventy, but at the end of the fight, even if we won, we would be lucky to have twenty men still standing. Those twenty could burn the boats, of course, but I doubted we would survive that long. There were scores of Danish women at Cynuit and, if it came to a fight, they would join in and the odds were that we would be defeated. 'Fire,' Egwine said enthusiastically. 'Carry fire in punts and throw the fire from the river.'

222

'There are ship-guards,' I said tiredly, 'and they'll be throwing spears and axes, sending arrows, and you might burn one boat, but that's all.'

'Go at night,' Egwine said.

'It's almost a full moon,' I said, 'and they'll see us coming. And if the moon is clouded we won't see their fleet.'

'So how do you do it?' Alfred demanded again.

'God will send fire from heaven,' Bishop Alewold said, and no one responded.

Alfred stood. We all got to our feet. Then he pointed at me. 'You will destroy Svein's fleet,' he said, 'and I would know how you plan to do it by this evening. If you cannot do it then you,' he pointed to Egwine, 'will travel to Defnascir, find Ealdorman Odda and tell him to bring his forces to the river mouth and do the job for us.'

'Yes, lord,' Egwine said.

'By tonight,' Alfred said to me coldly, and then he walked out.

He left me angry. He had meant to leave me angry. I stalked up to the newly-made fort with Leofric and stared across the marshes to where the clouds heaped above the Sæfern. 'How are we to burn twenty-four ships?' I demanded.

'God will send fire from heaven,' Leofric said, 'of course.'

'I'd rather he sent a thousand troops.'

'Alfred won't summon Odda,' Leofric said. 'He just said that to annoy you.'

'But he's right, isn't he?' I said grudgingly. 'We have to get rid of Svein.'

'How?'

I stared at the tangled barricade that Haswold had made from felled trees. The water, instead of flowing downstream, was coming upstream because the tide was on the flood and so the ripples ran eastwards from the tangled branches.

'I remember a story,' I said, 'from when I was a small child.' I paused, trying to recall the tale which, I assume, had been told to me by Beocca. 'The Christian god divided a sea, isn't that right?'

'Moses did,' Leofric said.

'And when the enemy followed,' I said, 'they were drowned.'

'Clever,' Leofric said.

'So that's how we'll do it,' I said.

'How?'

But instead of telling him I summoned the marshmen and talked with them, and by that night I had my plan and, because it was taken from the scriptures, Alfred approved it readily. It took another day to get everything ready. We had to gather sufficient punts to carry forty men and I also needed Eofer, the simple-minded archer. He was unhappy, not understanding what I wanted, and he gibbered at us and looked terrified, but then a small girl, perhaps ten or eleven years old, took his hand and explained that he had to go hunting with us. 'He trusts you?' I asked the child.

'He's my uncle,' she said. Eofer was holding her hand and he was calm again.

'Does Eofer do what you tell him?'

She nodded, her small face serious, and I told her she must come with us to keep her uncle happy.

We left before the dawn. We were twenty marshmen, skilled with boats, twenty warriors, a simple-minded archer, a child and Iseult. Alfred, of course, did not want me to take Iseult, but I ignored him and he did not argue. Instead he watched us leave, then went to Æthelingæg's church that now boasted a newly-made cross of alder-wood nailed to its gable.

And low in the sky above the cross was the full moon. She was low and ghostly pale, and as the sun rose she faded even more, but as the ten punts drifted down the river I stared at her and said a silent prayer to Hoder because the moon is his woman and it was she who must give us victory. Because, for the first time since Guthrum had struck in a winter's dawn, the Saxons were fighting back.

Eight

Before the Pedredan reaches the sea it makes a great curve through the swamp, a curve that is almost three-quarters of a circle and on the inside of the bank where the curve begins there was another tiny settlement; just a half-dozen hovels built on stilts sunk into a slight rise in the ground. The settlement was called Palfleot, which means 'the place with the stakes', for the folk who had once lived there had staked eel and fish traps in the nearby streams, but the Danes had driven those folk away and burned their houses, so that Palfleot was now a place of charred pilings and black-ened mud. We landed there, shivering in the dawn. The tide was falling, exposing the great banks of sand and mud across which Iseult and I had struggled, while the wind was coming from the west, cold and fresh, hinting of rain, though for now there was a slanting sunlight throwing long shadows of marram grass and reeds across the marshes. Two swans flew south and I knew they were a message from the gods, but what their message was I could not tell.

The punts pushed away, abandoning us. They were now going north and east, following intricate waterways known only to the marshmen. We stayed for a while in Palfleot, doing nothing in particular, but doing it energetically so that the Danes, a long way off across the great bend in the river, would be sure to see us. We pulled down the blackened timbers and Iseult, who had acute eyesight, watched the place where the Danish ships' masts showed as scratches against the western clouds. 'There's a man up a mast,' she said after a while, and I stared, saw the man clinging to the mast top and knew we had been spotted. The tide was falling, exposing more mud and sand, and now that I was sure we had been seen we walked across the drying expanse that was cradled by the river's extravagant bend.

As we drew closer I could see more Danes in their ships' rigging. They were watching us, but would not yet be worried for they outnumbered my few forces and the river lay between us and them, but whoever commanded in the Danish camp would also be ordering his men to arm them-selves. He would want to be ready for whatever happened, but I also hoped he would be clever. I was laying a trap for him, and for the trap to work he had to do what I wanted him to do, but at first, if he was clever, he would do nothing. He knew we were impotent, separated from him by the Pedredan, and so he was content to watch as we closed on the river's bank opposite his grounded ships and then slipped and slid down the steep muddy bluff that the ebbing tide had exposed. The river swirled in front of us, grey and cold.

There were close to a hundred Danes watching now. They were on their grounded boats, shouting insults. Some were laughing, for it seemed clear to them that we had walked a long way to achieve nothing, but that was because they did not know Eofer's skills. I called the big bowman's niece to my side. 'What I want your Uncle Eofer to do,' I explained to the small girl, 'is kill some of those men.'

'Kill them?' She stared up at me with wide eyes.

'They're bad men,' I said, 'and they want to kill you.'

She nodded solemnly, then took the big man by the hand and led him to the water's edge where he sank up to his calves in the mud. It was a long way across the river and I wondered, pessimistically, if it was too far for even his massive bow, but Eofer strung the great stave and then waded into the Pedredan until he found a shallow spot which meant he could go even farther into the river and there he took an arrow from his sheaf, put it on the string and hauled it back. He made a grunting noise as he released and I watched the arrow twitch off the cord, then the fledging caught the air and the arrow soared across the stream and plunged into a group of Danes standing on the steering platform of a ship. There was a cry of anger as the arrow cut down. It did not hit any of the group, but Eofer's next arrow struck a man in his shoulder, and the Danes hurried back from their vantage point by the ship's sternpost. Eofer, who was compulsively nodding his shaggy head and making small animal noises, turned his aim to another ship. He had extraordinary strength. The distance was too great for any accuracy, but the danger of the long white-fledged arrows drove the Danes back and it was our turn to jeer at them. One of the Danes fetched a bow and tried to shoot back, but his arrow sliced into the river twenty yards short and we taunted them, laughed at them, and capered up and down as Eofer's arrows slammed into ships' timbers. Only the one man had been wounded, but we had driven them backwards and that was humiliating to them. I let Eofer loose twenty arrows, then I waded into the river and took hold of his bow. I stood in front of him so the Danes could not see what I was doing.

'Tell him not to worry,' I told the girl, and she soothed Eofer, who was frowning at me and trying to remove his bow from my grasp.

I drew a knife and that alarmed him even more. He growled at me, then plucked the bow from my hand. 'Tell him it's all right,' I told the girl, and she soothed her uncle who then let me half sever the woven hemp bowstring. I stepped away from him and pointed at a group of Danes. 'Kill them,' I said.

Eofer did not want to draw the bow. Instead he fumbled under his greasy woollen cap and produced a second bowstring, but I shook my head and the small girl persuaded him he must use the half-severed cord and so he pulled it nervously back and, just before it reached the full draw, the string snapped and the arrow span crazily into the sky to float away on the river.

The tide had turned and the water was rising. 'We go!' I shouted to my men.

It was now the Danes' turn to jeer at us. They thought we were retreating because our one bowstring had broken, and so they shouted insults as we clambered back up the muddy bluff, and then I saw two men running along the far beach and I hoped they were carrying the orders I wanted.

They were. The Danes, released from the threat of Eofer's terrible bow, were going to launch two of their smaller ships. We had stung them, laughed at them and now they would kill us.

All warriors have pride. Pride and rage and ambition are the goads to a reputation, and the Danes did not want us to think we had stung them without being punished for our temerity. They wanted to teach us a lesson. But they also wanted more. Before we left Æthelingæg I had insisted that my men be given every available coat of mail. Egwine, who had stayed behind with the king, had been reluctant to give up his precious armour, but Alfred had ordered it and so sixteen of my men were dressed in chain mail. They looked superb, like an elite group of warriors, and the Danes would win renown if they defeated such a group and captured the precious armour. Leather offers some protection, but chain mail over leather is far better and far more expensive, and by taking sixteen coats of mail to the river's edge I had given the Danes an irresistible lure.

And they snapped at it.

We were going slowly, deliberately seeming to struggle in the soft ground as we headed back towards Palfleot. The Danes were also struggling, shoving their two ships down the riverbank's thick mud, but at last the boats were launched and then, on the hurrying flood tide, the Danes did what I had hoped they would do.

They did not cross the river. If they had crossed, then they would merely have found themselves on the Pedredan's eastern bank and we would have been half a mile ahead and out of reach, so instead the commander did what he thought was the clever thing to do. He tried to cut us off. They had seen us land at Palfleot and they reckoned our boats must still be there, and so they rowed their ships up river to find those boats and destroy them.

Except our punts were not at Palfleot. They had been taken north and east, so that they were waiting for us in a reed-fringed dyke, but now was not the time to use them. Instead, as the Danes went ashore at Palfleot, we made a huddle on the sand, watching them, and they thought we were trapped, and now they were on the same side of the river as us and the two ships' crews outnumbered us by over two to one, and they had all the confidence in the world as they advanced from the burned pilings of Palfleot to kill us in the swamp.

They were doing exactly what I wanted them to do.

And we now retreated. We went back raggedly, sometimes running to open a distance between us and the confident Danes. I counted seventy-six of them and we were only thirty strong because some of my men were with the hidden punts, and the Danes knew we were dead men and they hurried across the sand and creeks, and we had to go faster, ever faster, to keep them away from us. It began to rain, the drops carried on the freshening west wind and I kept looking into the rain until at last I saw a silver bar of light glint and spill across the swamp's edge and knew the incoming tide was beginning its long fast race across the barren flats.

And still we went back, and still the Danes pursued us, but they were tiring now. A few shouted at us, daring us to stand and fight, but others had no breath to shout, just a savage intent to catch and kill us, but we were slanting eastwards now towards a line of buckthorn and reeds, and there, in a flooding creek, were our punts.

We dropped into the boats, exhausted, and the marshmen poled us back down the creek that was a tributary of the River Bru which barred the northern part of the swamp, and the flat-bottomed craft took us fast south, against the current, hurrying us past the Danes who could only watch from a quarter-mile away and do nothing to stop us, and the farther we went from them, the more isolated they looked in that wide, barren place where the rain fell and the tide seethed as it flowed into the creek beds. The wind-driven water was running deep into the swamp now, a tide made bigger by the full moon, and suddenly the Danes saw their danger and turned back towards Palfleot.

But Palfleot was a long way off, and we had already left the stream and were carrying the punts to a smaller creek, one that ran down to the Pedredan, and that stream took us to where the blackened pilings leaned against the weeping sky, and where the Danes had tied their two ships. The two craft were guarded by only four men, and we came from the punts with a savage shout and drawn swords and the four men ran. The other Danes were still out in the swamp, only now it was not a swamp, but a tidal flat and they were wading through water.

And I had two ships. We hauled the punts aboard, and then the marshmen, divided between the ships, took the oars, and I steered one and Leofric took the other, and we rowed against that big tide towards Cynuit where the Danish ships were now unguarded except for a few men and a crowd of women and children who watched the two ships come and did not know they were crewed by their enemy. They must have wondered why so few oars bit the water, but how could they imagine that forty Saxons would defeat nearly eighty Danes? And so none opposed us as we ran the ships into the bank, and there I led my warriors ashore. 'You can fight us,' I shouted at the few ship-guards left, 'or you can live.'

I was in chain mail, with my new helmet. I was a warlord. I banged Serpent-Breath against the big shield and stalked towards them. 'Fight if you want!' I shouted. 'Come and fight us!'

They did not. They were too few and so they retreated south and could only watch as we burned their ships. It took most of the day to ensure that the ships burned down to their keels, but burn they did, and their fires were a signal to the western part of Wessex that Svein had been defeated. He was not at Cynuit that day, but somewhere to the south, and as the ships burned I watched the wooded hills in fear that he would come with hundreds of men, but he was still far off and the Danes at Cynuit could do nothing to stop us. We burned twenty-three ships, including the *White Horse*, and the twenty-fourth, which was one of the two we had captured, carried us away as evening fell. We took good plunder from the Danish camp; food, rigging ropes, hides, weapons and shields.

There were a score of Danes stranded on the low island of Palfleot. The rest had died in the rising water. The survivors watched us pass, but did nothing to provoke us, and I did nothing to hurt them. We rowed on towards Æthelingæg and behind us, under a darkening sky, the water sheeted the swamp where white gulls cried above the drowned men and where, in the dusk, two swans flighted northwards, their wings like drumbeats in the sky.

The smoke of the burned boats drifted to the clouds for three days, and on the second day Egwine took the captured ship downstream with forty men and they landed on Palfleot and killed all the surviving Danes, except for six who were taken prisoner, and five of those six were stripped of their armour and lashed to stakes in the river at low tide so that they drowned slowly on the flood. Egwine lost three men in that fight, but brought back mail, shields, helmets, weapons, arm rings and one prisoner who knew nothing except that Svein had ridden towards Exanceaster. That prisoner died on the third day, the day that Alfred had prayers said in thanks to God for our victory. For now we were safe. Svein could not attack us for he had lost his ships, Guthrum had no way of penetrating the swamp and Alfred was pleased with me.

'The king is pleased with you,' Beocca told me. Two weeks before, I thought, the king would have told me that himself. He would have sat with me by the water's edge and talked, but now a court had formed and the king was hedged with priests.

'He should be pleased,' I said. I had been practising weapon-craft when Beocca sought me out. We practised every day, using stakes instead of swords, and some men grumbled that they did not need to play at fighting, and those I opposed myself and, when they had been beaten down to the mud, I told them they needed to play more and complain less.

'He's pleased with you,' Beocca said, leading me down the path beside the river, 'but he thinks you are squeamish.'

'Me! Squeamish?'

'For not going to Palfleot and finishing the job.'

'The job was finished,' I said. 'Svein can't attack us without ships.'

'But not all the Danes drowned,' Beocca said.

'Enough died,' I said. 'Do you know what they endured? The terror of trying to outrun the tide?' I thought of my own anguish in the swamp, the inexorable tide, the cold water spreading and the fear gripping the heart. 'They had no ships! Why kill stranded men?'

'Because they are pagans,' Beocca said, 'because they are loathed by God and by men, and because they are Danes.'

'And only a few weeks ago,' I said, 'you believed they would become Christians and all our swords would be beaten into ard points to plough fields.'

Beocca shrugged that off. 'So what will Svein do now?' he wanted to know.

'March around the swamp,' I said, 'and join Guthrum.'

'And Guthrum is in Cippanhamm.' We were fairly certain of that. New men were coming to the swamp and they all brought news. Much of it was rumour, but many had heard that Guthrum had strengthened Cippanhamm's walls and was wintering there. Large raiding parties still ravaged parts of Wessex, but they avoided the bigger towns in the south of the country where West Saxon garrisons had formed. There was one such garrison at Dornwaraceaster and another at Wintanceaster, and Beocca believed Alfred should go to one of those towns, but Alfred refused, reckoning that Guthrum would immediately besiege him. He would be trapped in a town, but the swamp was too big to be besieged and Guthrum could not hope to penetrate the marshes. 'You have an uncle in Mercia, don't you?' Beocca asked, changing the subject abruptly.

'Æthelred. He's my mother's brother, and an ealdorman.'

He heard the flat tone of my voice. 'You're not fond of him?'

'I hardly know him.' I had spent some weeks in his house, just long enough to quarrel with his son who was also called Æthelred.

'Is he a friend of the Danes?'

I shook my head. 'They suffer him to live and he suffers them.'

'The king has sent messengers to Mercia,' Beocca said.

I grimaced. 'If he wants them to rise against the Danes they won't. They'll get killed.'

'He'd rather they brought men south in the springtime,' Beocca said and I wondered how a few Mercian warriors were supposed to get past the Danes to join us, but said nothing. 'We look to the springtime for our salvation,' Beocca went on, 'but in the meantime the king would like someone to go to Cippanhamm.'

'A priest?' I asked sourly, 'to talk to Guthrum?'

'A soldier,' Beocca said, 'to gauge their numbers.'

'So send me,' I offered.

Beocca nodded, then limped along the riverbank where the willow fish traps had been exposed by the falling tide. 'It's so different from Northumbria,' he said wistfully.

I smiled at that. 'You miss Bebbanburg?'

'I would like to end my days at Lindisfarena,' he said. 'I would like to say my dying prayer on that island.' He turned and gazed at the eastern hills. 'The king would go to Cippanhamm himself,' he said, almost as an afterthought.

I thought I had misheard, then realised I had not. 'That's madness,' I protested.

'It's kingship,' he said.

236

'Kingship?'

'The Witan chooses the king,' Beocca said sternly, 'and the king must have the trust of the people. If Alfred goes to Cippanhamm and walks among his enemies, then folk will know he deserves to be king.'

'And if he's captured,' I said, 'then folk will know he's a dead king.'

'So you must protect him,' he said. I said nothing. It was indeed madness, but Alfred was determined to show he deserved to be king. He had, after all, usurped the throne from his nephew, and in those early years of his reign he was ever mindful of that. 'A small group will travel,' Beocca said, 'you, some other warriors, a priest and the king.'

'Why the priest?'

'To pray, of course.'

I sneered at that. 'You?'

Beocca patted his lamed leg. 'Not me. A young priest.'

'Better to send Iseult,' I said.

'No.'

'Why not? She's keeping the king healthy.' Alfred was in sudden good health, better than he had been in years, and it was all because of the medicines that Iseult made. The celandine and burdock she had gathered on the mainland had taken away the agony in his arse, while other herbs calmed the pains in his belly. He walked confidently, had bright eyes and looked strong.

'Iseult stays here,' Beocca said.

'If you want the king to live,' I said, 'send her with us.'

'She stays here,' Beocca said, 'because we want the king to live.' It took me a few heartbeats to understand what he had said, and when I did realise his meaning I turned on him with such fury that he stumbled backwards. I said nothing, for I did not trust myself to speak, or perhaps I feared that speech would turn to violence. Beocca tried to look severe, but only looked fearful. 'These are difficult times,' he said plaintively, 'and the king can only put his trust in men who serve God. In men who are bound to him by their love of Christ.'

I kicked at an eel trap, sending it spinning over the bank into the river. 'For a time,' I said, 'I almost liked Alfred. Now he's got his priests back and you're dripping poison into him.'

'He . . .' Beocca began.

I turned on him, silencing him. 'Who rescued the bastard? Who burned Svein's ships? Who, in the name of your luckless god, killed Ubba? And you still don't trust me?'

Beocca was trying to calm me now, making flapping gestures. 'I fear you are a pagan,' he said, 'and your woman is assuredly a pagan.'

'My woman healed Edward,' I snarled, 'does that mean nothing?'

'It could mean,' he said, 'that she did the devil's work.'

I was astonished into silence by that.

'The devil does his work in the land,' Beocca said earnestly, 'and it would serve the devil well if Wessex were to vanish. The devil wants the king dead. He wants his own pagan spawn all across England! There is a greater war, Uhtred. Not the fight between Saxon and Dane, but between God and the devil, between good and evil! We are part of it!'

'I've killed more Danes than you can dream of,' I told him.

'But suppose,' he said, pleading with me now, 'that your woman has been sent by the devil? That the evil one allowed her to heal Edward so that the king would trust her? And then, when the king, in all innocence, goes to spy on the enemy, she betrays him!'

'You think she would betray him?' I asked sourly, 'or do you mean I might betray him?'

238

'Your love of the Danes is well known,' Beocca said stiffly, 'and you spared the men on Palfleot.'

'So you think I can't be trusted?'

'I trust you,' he said, without conviction. 'But other men?' he waved his palsied hand in an impotent gesture. 'But if Iseult is here,' he shrugged, not ending the thought.

'So she's to be a hostage,' I said.

'A surety, rather.'

'I gave the king my oath,' I pointed out.

'And you have sworn oaths before, and you are known as a liar, and you have a wife and child, yet live with a pagan whore, and you love the Danes as you love yourself, and do you really think we can trust you?' This all came out in a bitter rush. 'I have known you, Uhtred,' he said, 'since you crawled on Bebbanburg's rush floors. I baptised you, taught you, chastised you, watched you grow, and I know you better than any man alive and I do not trust you.' Beocca stared at me belligerently. 'If the king does not return, Uhtred, then your whore will be given to the dogs.' He had delivered his message now, and he seemed to regret the force of it for he shook his head. 'The king should not go. You're right. It's a madness. It is stupidity! It is,' he paused, searching for a word, and came upon one of the worst condemnations in his vocabulary, 'it is irresponsible! But he insists, and if he goes then you must also go for you're the only man here who can pass as a Dane. But bring him back, Uhtred, bring him back, for he is dear to God and to all Saxons.'

Not to me, I thought, he was not dear to me. That night, brooding on Beocca's words, I was tempted to flee the swamp, to go away with Iseult, find a lord, give Serpent-Breath a new master, but Ragnar had been a hostage and so I had no friend among my enemies, and if I fled I would break my oath to Alfred and men would say Uhtred of

Bebbanburg could never be trusted again and so I stayed. I tried to persuade Alfred not to go to Cippanhamm. It was, as Beocca had said, irresponsible, but Alfred insisted. 'If I stay here,' he said, 'men will say I hid from the Danes. Others face them, but I hide? No. Men must see me, must know that I live, and know that I fight.' For once Ælswith and I were in agreement, and we both tried to keep him in Æthelingæg, but Alfred would not be dissuaded. He was in a strange mood, suffused with happiness, utterly confident that God was on his side, and, because his sickness had abated, he was full of energy and confidence.

He took six companions. The priest was a young man called Adelbert who carried a small harp wrapped in leather. It seemed ridiculous to take a harp to the enemy, but Adelbert was famed for his music and Alfred blithely said that we should sing God's praises while we were among the Danes. The other four were all experienced warriors who had been part of his royal guard. They were called Osferth, Wulfrith, Beorth and the last was Egwine who swore to Ælswith that he would bring the king home, which made Ælswith throw a bitter glance at me. Whatever favour I had gained by Iseult's cure of Edward had evaporated under the influence of the priests.

We dressed for war in mail and helmets, while Alfred insisted on wearing a fine blue cloak, trimmed with fur, which made him conspicuous, but he wanted folk to see a king. The best horses were selected, one for each of us and three spare mounts, and we swam them across the river, then followed log roads until we came at last to firm ground close to the island where Iseult said Arthur was buried. I had left Iseult with Eanflæd who shared quarters with Leofric.

It was February now. There had been a spell of fine weather after the burning of Svein's fleet and I had thought we should travel then, but Alfred insisted on waiting until the eighth day of February, because that was the feast of Saint Cuthman, a Saxon saint from East Anglia, and Alfred reckoned that must be a propitious day. Perhaps he was right, for the day turned out wet and bitterly cold, and we were to discover that the Danes were reluctant to leave their quarters in the worst weather. We went at dawn and by mid morning we were in the hills overlooking the swamp which was half hidden by a mist thickened by the smoke from the cooking fires of the small villages. 'Are you familiar with Saint Cuthman?' Alfred asked me cheerfully.

'No, lord.'

'He was a hermit,' Alfred said. We were riding north, keeping on the high ground with the swamp to our left. 'His mother was crippled and so he made her a wheelbarrow.'

'A wheelbarrow? What could a cripple do with a wheelbarrow?'

'No, no, no! He pushed her about in it! So she could be with him as he preached. He pushed her everywhere.'

'She must have liked that.'

'There's no written life of him that I know of,' Alfred said, 'but we must surely compose one. He could be a saint for mothers?'

'Or for wheelbarrows, lord.'

We saw our first evidence of the Danes just after midday. We were still on the high ground, but in a valley that sloped to the marshes we saw a substantial house with limewashed walls and thick thatch. Smoke came from the roof, while in a fenced apple orchard were a score of horses. No Dane would ever leave such a place unplundered, which suggested the horses belonged to them and that the farm was garrisoned. 'They're there to watch the swamp,' Alfred suggested.

241

'Probably.' I was cold. I had a thick woollen cloak, but I was still cold.

'We shall send men here,' Alfred said, 'and teach them not to steal apples.'

We stayed that night in a small village. The Danes had been there and the folk were frightened. At first, when we rode up the rutted track between the houses, they hid, thinking we were Danes, but when they heard our voices they crept out and stared at us as if we had just ridden down from the moon. Their priest was dead, killed by the pagans, so Alfred insisted that Adelbert hold a service in the burned-out remnants of the church. Alfred himself acted as precentor, accompanying his chanting with the priest's small harp. 'I learned to play as a child,' he told me. 'My stepmother insisted, but I'm not very good.'

'You're not,' I agreed, which he did not like.

'There is never enough time to practise,' he complained.

We lodged in a peasant's house. Alfred, reckoning that the Danes would have taken the harvest from wherever we visited, had laden the spare horses with smoked fish, smoked eels and oatcakes, so we provided most of the food and, after we had eaten, the peasant couple knelt to me and the woman tentatively touched the skirt of my mail coat. 'My children,' she whispered, 'there are two of them. My daughter is about seven years old and my boy is a little older. They are good children.'

'What of them?' Alfred intervened.

'The pagans took them, lord,' the woman said. She was crying. 'You can find them, lord,' she said, tugging my mail, 'you can find them and bring them back? My little ones? Please?'

I promised to try, but it was an empty promise for the children would have long gone to the slave market and, by now, would either be working on some Danish estate or, if they were pretty, sent overseas where heathen men pay good silver for Christian children.

We learned that the Danes had come to the village shortly after Twelfth Night. They had killed, captured, stolen and ridden on southwards. A few days later they had returned, going back northwards, driving a band of captives and a herd of captured horses laden with plunder. Since then the villagers had seen no Danes except for the few on the swamp's edge. Those Danes, they said, caused no trouble, perhaps because they were so few and dared not stir up the enmity of the country about them. We heard the same tale in other villages. The Danes had come, they had pillaged, then had gone back north.

But on our third day we at last saw a force of the enemy riding on the Roman road which cuts straight eastwards across the hills from Baðum. There were close to sixty of them, and they rode hard in front of dark clouds and the gathering night. 'Going back to Cippanhamm,' Alfred said. It was a foraging party, and their packhorses carried nets stuffed with hay to feed their war horses, and I remembered my childhood winter in Readingum, when the Danes first invaded Wessex, and how hard it had been to keep horses and men alive in the cold. We had cut feeble winter grass and pulled down thatch to feed our horses, which still became skeletal and weak. I have often listened to men declare that all that is needed to win a war is to assemble men and march against the enemy, but it is never that easy. Men and horses must be fed, and hunger can defeat an army much faster than spears. We watched the Danes go north, then turned aside to a half-ruined barn that offered us shelter for the night.

It began to snow that night, a relentless soft snow, silent and thick, so that by dawn the world was white under a pale blue sky. I suggested we waited till the snow had thawed

243

before we rode further, but Egwine, who came from this part of the country, said we were only two or three hours south of Cippanhamm and Alfred was impatient. 'We go,' he insisted. 'We go there, look at the town and ride away.'

So we rode north, our hooves crunching the newly fallen snow, riding through a world made new and clean. Snow clung to every twig and branch while ice skimmed the ditches and ponds. I saw a fox's trail crossing a field and thought that the spring would bring a plague of the beasts for there would have been no one to hunt them, and the lambs would die bloodily and the ewes would bleat pitifully.

We came in sight of Cippanhamm before midday, though the great pall of smoke, made by hundreds of cooking fires, had shown in the sky all morning. We stopped south of the town, just where the road emerged from a stand of oaks, and the Danes must have noticed us, but none came from the gates to see who we were. It was too cold for men to stir themselves. I could see guards on the walls, though none stayed there long, retreating to whatever warmth they could find between their short forays along the wooden ramparts. Those ramparts were bright with round shields painted blue and white and blood-red and, because Guthrum's men were there, black. 'We should count the shields,' Alfred said.

'It won't help,' I said. 'They carry two or three shields each and hang them on the walls to make it look as if they have more men.'

Alfred was shivering and I insisted we find some shelter. We turned back into the trees, following a path which led to the river and a mile or so upstream we came across a mill. The millstone had been taken away, but the building itself was whole and it was well made, with stone walls and a turf roof held up by stout rafters. There was a hearth in a room where the miller's family had lived, but I would not let Egwine light a fire in case the trickle of smoke brought curious Danes from the town. 'Wait till dark,' I said.

'We'll freeze by then,' he grumbled.

'Then you shouldn't have come,' I snapped.

'We have to get closer to the town,' Alfred said.

'You don't,' I said, 'I do.' I had seen horses paddocked to the west of the walls and I reckoned I could take our best horse and ride about the town's western edge and count every horse I saw. That would give a rough estimate of the Danish numbers, for almost every man would have a horse. Alfred wanted to come, but I shook my head. It was pointless for more than one man to go, and sensible that the one man who did go should speak Danish, so I told him I would see him back in the mill before nightfall and then I rode north. Cippanhamm was built on a hill that was almost encircled by the river, so I could not ride clear around the town, but I went as close to the walls as I dared and stared across the river and saw no horses on its farther bank which suggested that the Danes were keeping all of their beasts on the western side of the town. I went there, keeping in the snowy woods, and though the Danes must have seen me they could not be bothered to ride into the snow to chase one man, and so I was able to find the paddocks where their horses shivered. I spent the day counting. Most of the horses were in fields beside the royal compound and there were hundreds of them. By late afternoon I had estimated that there were twelve hundred, and those were only the ones I could see, and the best horses would be in the town, but my reckoning was good enough. It would give Alfred an idea of how large Guthrum's force was. Say two thousand men? And elsewhere in Wessex, in the towns the Danes had occupied, there must be another thousand. That was a strong force, but not quite strong enough to capture all the kingdom. That would have to wait until spring when reinforcements would come from Denmark or from the three conquered kingdoms of England. I rode back to the watermill as dusk fell. There was a frost and the air was still. Three rooks flew across the river as I dismounted. I reckoned one of Alfred's men could rub my horse down; all I wanted was to find some warmth and it was plain Alfred had risked lighting a fire, for smoke was pouring out of the hole in the turf roof.

They were all crouched about the small fire and I joined them, stretching my hands to the flames. 'Two thousand men,' I said, 'more or less.'

No one answered.

'Didn't you hear me?' I asked, and looked around the faces.

There were five faces. Only five.

'Where's the king?' I asked.

'He went,' Adelbert said helplessly.

'He did what?'

'He went to the town,' the priest said. He was wearing Alfred's rich blue cloak and I assumed Alfred had taken Adelbert's plain garment.

I stared at him. 'You let him go?'

'He insisted,' Egwine said.

'How could we stop him?' Adelbert pleaded. 'He's the king!'

'You hit the bastard, of course,' I snarled. 'You hold him down till the madness passes. When did he go?'

'Just after you left,' the priest said miserably, 'and he took my harp,' he added.

'And when did he say he'd be back?'

'By nightfall.'

'It is nightfall,' I said. I stood and stamped out the fire. 'You want the Danes to come and investigate the smoke?' I doubted the Danes would come, but I wanted the damned

246

fools to suffer. 'You,' I pointed to one of the four soldiers, 'rub my horse down. Feed it.'

I went back to the door. The first stars were bright and the snow glinted under a sickle moon.

'Where are you going?' Adelbert had followed me.

'To find the king, of course.'

If he lived. And if he did not, then Iseult was dead.

I had to beat on Cippanhamm's western gate, provoking a disgruntled voice from the far side demanding to know who I was.

'Why aren't you up on the ramparts?' I asked in return.

The bar was lifted and the gate opened a few inches. A face peered out, then vanished as I pushed the gate hard inwards, banging it against the suspicious guard. 'My horse went lame,' I said, 'and I've walked here.'

He recovered his balance and pushed the gate shut. 'Who are you?' he asked again.

'Messenger from Svein.'

'Svein!' He lifted the bar and dropped it into place. 'Has he caught Alfred yet?'

'I'll tell Guthrum that news before I tell you.'

'Just asking,' he said.

'Where is Guthrum?' I asked. I had no intention of going anywhere near the Danish chieftain for, after my insults to his dead mother, the best I could hope for was a swift death, and the likelihood was a very slow one.

'He's in Alfred's hall,' the man said, and pointed south. 'That side of town, so you've still farther to walk.' It never occurred to him that any messenger from Svein would never ride alone through Wessex, that such a man would come with an escort of fifty or sixty men, but he was too cold to think, and besides, with my long hair and my thick arm rings I looked like a Dane. He retreated into the house beside the gate where his comrades were clustered around a hearth and I walked on into a town made strange. Houses were missing, burned in the first fury of the Danish assault, and the large church by the market place on the hilltop was nothing but blackened beams touched white by the snow. The streets were frozen mud, and only I moved there, for the cold was keeping the Danes in the remaining houses. I could hear singing and laughter. Light leaked past shutters or glowed through smoke-holes in low roofs. I was cold and I was angry. There were men here who could recognise me, and men who might recognise Alfred, and his stupidity had put us both in danger. Would he have been mad enough to go back to his own hall? He must have guessed that was where Guthrum would be living and he would surely not risk being recognised by the Danish leader, which suggested he would be in the town rather than the royal compound.

I was walking towards Eanflæd's old tavern when I heard the roars. They were coming from the east side of town and I followed the sound which led me to the nunnery by the river wall. I had never been inside the convent, but the gate was open and the courtyard inside was lit by two vast fires which offered some warmth to the men nearest the flames. And there were at least a hundred men in the courtyard, bellowing encouragement and insults at two other men who were fighting in the mud and melted snow between the fires. They were fighting with swords and shields, and every clash of blade against blade or of blade against wood brought raucous shouts. I glanced briefly at the fighters, then searched for faces in the crowd. I was looking for Haesten, or anyone else who might recognise me, but I saw no one, though it was hard to distinguish faces in the flickering shadows. There was no sign of any nuns and I assumed they had either fled, were dead or had been taken away for the conquerors' amusement.

I slunk along the courtyard wall. I was wearing my helmet and its face-plate was an adequate disguise, but some men threw me curious glances, for it was unusual to see a helmeted man off a battlefield. In the end, seeing no one I recognised, I took the helmet off and hung it from my belt. The nunnery church had been turned into a feasting hall, but there was only a handful of drunks inside, oblivious to the noise outside. I stole half a loaf of bread from one of the drunks and took it back outside and watched the fighting.

Steapa Snotor was one of the two men. He no longer wore his mail armour, but was in a leather coat and he fought with a small shield and a long sword, but around his waist was a chain that led to the courtyard's northern side where two men held it and, whenever Steapa's opponent seemed to be in danger, they yanked on the chain to pull the huge Saxon off balance. He was being made to fight as Haesten had been fighting when I first discovered him, and doubtless Steapa's captors were making good money from fools who wanted to try their prowess against a captured warrior. Steapa's current opponent was a thin, grinning Dane who tried to dance around the huge man and slide his sword beneath the small shield, doing what I had done when I had fought Steapa, but Steapa was doggedly defending himself, parrying each blow and, when the chain allowed him, counterattacking fast. Whenever the Danes jerked him backwards the crowd jeered and once, when the men yanked the chain too hard and Steapa turned on them, only to be faced by three long spears, the crowd gave him a great cheer. He whipped back to parry the next attack, then stepped backwards, almost to the spear points, and the thin man followed fast, thinking he had Steapa at a disadvantage, but Steapa suddenly checked, slammed the shield down onto his opponent's blade and brought his left hand around, sword hilt foremost, to hit the man on the head. The Dane went down, Steapa reversed the sword to stab and the chain dragged him off his feet and the spears threatened him with death if he finished the job. The crowd liked it. He had won.

Money changed hands. Steapa sat by the fire, his grim face showing nothing, and one of the men holding the chain shouted for another opponent. 'Ten pieces of silver if you wound him! Fifty if you kill him!'

Steapa, who probably did not understand a word, just stared at the crowd, daring another man to take him on, and sure enough a half drunken brute came grinning from the crowd. Bets were made as Steapa was prodded to his feet. It was like a bull-baiting, except Steapa was being given only one opponent at a time. They would doubtless have set three or four men on him, except that the Danes who had taken him prisoner did not want him dead so long as there were still fools willing to pay to fight him.

I was sidling around the courtyard's edge, still looking at faces. 'Six pennies?' a voice said behind me and I turned to see a man grinning beside a door. It was one of a dozen similar doors, evenly spaced along the limewashed wall.

'Six pennies?' I asked, puzzled.

'Cheap,' he said, and he pushed back a small shutter on the door and invited me to look inside.

I did. A tallow candle lit the tiny room which must have been where a nun had slept, and inside was a low bed and on the bed was a naked woman who was half covered by a man who had dropped his breeches. 'He won't be long,' the man said.

I shook my head and moved away from the shutter.

'She was a nun here,' the man said. 'Nice and young? Pretty too. Screams like a pig usually.'

'No,' I said.

'Four pennies? She won't put up a fight. Not now she won't.'

I walked on, convinced I was wasting my time. Had Alfred been and gone? More likely, I thought grimly, the fool had gone back to his hall and I wondered if I dared go there, but the thought of Guthrum's revenge deterred me. The new fight had started. The Dane was crouching low, trying to cut Steapa's feet from under him, but Steapa was swatting his blows easily enough and I sidled past the men holding his chains and saw another room off to my left, a large room, perhaps where the nuns had eaten, and a glint of gold in the light of its dying fire drew me inside.

The gold was not metal. It was the gilding on the frame of a small harp that had been stamped on so hard that it broke. I looked around the shadows and saw a man lying in a heap at the far end and went to him. It was Alfred. He was barely conscious, but he was alive and, so far as I could see, unwounded, but he was plainly stunned and I dragged him to the wall and sat him up. He had no cloak and his boots were gone. I left him there, went back to the church and found a drunk to befriend. I helped him to his feet, put my arm around his shoulders and persuaded him I was taking him to his bed, then took him through the back door to the latrine yard of the nunnery where I punched him three times in the belly and twice in the face, then carried his hooded cloak and tall boots back to Alfred.

The king was conscious now. His face was bruised. He looked up at me without showing any surprise, then rubbed his chin. 'They didn't like the way I played,' he said.

'That's because the Danes like good music,' I said. 'Put these on.' I threw the boots beside him, draped him with the cloak and made him pull the hood over his face. 'You want to die?' I asked him angrily.

251

'I want to know about my enemies,' he said.

'And I found out for you,' I said. 'There are roughly two thousand of them.'

'That's what I thought,' he said, then grimaced. 'What's on this cloak?'

'Danish vomit,' I said.

He shuddered. 'Three of them attacked me,' he sounded surprised. 'They kicked and punched me.'

'I told you, the Danes like good music,' I said, helping him to his feet. 'You're lucky they didn't kill you.'

'They thought I was Danish,' he said, then spat blood that trickled from his swollen lower lip.

'Were they drunk?' I asked. 'You don't even look like a Dane.'

'I pretended I was a musician who couldn't speak,' he mouthed silently at me, then grinned bloodily, proud of his deception. I did not grin back and he sighed. 'They were very drunk, but I need to know their mood, Uhtred. Are they confident? Are they readying to attack?' He paused to wipe more blood from his lips. 'I could only find that out by coming to see them for myself. Did you see Steapa?'

'Yes.'

'I want to take him back with us.'

'Lord,' I said savagely, 'you are a fool. He's in chains. He's got half a dozen guards.'

'Daniel was in a lion's den, yet he escaped. Saint Paul was imprisoned, yet God freed him.'

'Then let God look after Steapa,' I said. 'You're coming back with me. Now.'

He bent to relieve a pain in his belly. 'They punched me in the stomach,' he said as he straightened. In the morning, I thought, he would have a rare black eye to display. He flinched as a huge cheer sounded from the courtyard and I guessed Steapa had either died or downed his last oppo-

252

nent. 'I want to see my hall,' Alfred said stubbornly.

'Why?'

'I'm a man who would look at his own home. You can come or stay.'

'Guthrum's there! You want to be recognised? You want to die?'

'Guthrum will be inside, and I just want to look at the outside.'

He would not be dissuaded and so I led him through the courtyard to the street, wondering if I should simply pick him up and carry him away, but in his obdurate mood he would probably struggle and shout until men came to find out the cause of the noise. 'I wonder what happened to the nuns,' he said as we left the nunnery.

'One of them is being whored in there for pennies,' I said.

'Oh, dear God.' He made the sign of the cross and turned back and I knew he was thinking of rescuing the woman, so I dragged him onwards. 'This is madness!' I protested.

'It is a necessary madness,' he said calmly, then stopped to lecture me. 'What does Wessex believe? It thinks I am defeated, it thinks the Danes have won, it readies itself for the spring and the coming of more Danes. So they must learn something different. They must learn that the king lives, that he walked among his enemies and that he made fools of them.'

'That he got given a bloody nose and a black eye,' I said.

'You won't tell them that,' he said, 'any more than you'll tell folk about that wretched woman who hit me with an eel. We must give men hope, Uhtred, and in the spring that hope will blossom into victory. Remember Boethius, Uhtred, remember Boethius! Never give up hope.'

He believed it. He believed that God was protecting him, that he could walk among his enemies without fear or harm, and to an extent he was right for the Danes were well supplied with ale, birch wine and mead, and most were much too drunk to care about a bruised man carrying a broken harp.

No one stopped us going into the royal compound, but there were six black-cloaked guards at the hall door and I refused to let Alfred get close to them. 'They'll take one look at your bloodied face,' I said, 'and finish what the others began.'

'Then let me at least go to the church.'

'You want to pray?' I asked sarcastically.

'Yes,' he said simply.

I tried to stop him. 'If you die here,' I said, 'then Iseult dies.'

'That wasn't my doing,' he said.

'You're the king, aren't you?'

'The bishop thought you would join the Danes,' he said. 'And others agreed.'

'I have no friends left among the Danes,' I said. 'They were your hostages and they died.'

'Then I shall pray for their pagan souls,' he said, and pulled away from me and went to the church door where he instinctively pushed the hood off his head to show respect. I snatched it back over his hair, shadowing his bruises. He did not resist, but just pushed the door open and made the sign of the cross.

The church was being used to shelter more of Guthrum's men. There were straw mattresses, heaps of chain mail, stacks of weapons and a score of men and women gathered around a newly-made hearth in the nave. They were playing dice and none took any particular interest in our arrival until someone shouted that we should shut the door.

'We're leaving,' I said to Alfred. 'You can't pray here.'

He did not answer. He was gazing reverently to where

the altar had been, and where a half-dozen horses were now tethered.

'We're leaving!' I insisted again.

And just then a voice hailed me. It was a voice full of astonishment and I saw one of the dice players stand and stare at me. A dog ran from the shadows and began to jump up and down, trying to lick me, and I saw the dog was Nihtgenga and that the man who had recognised me was Ragnar. Earl Ragnar, my friend.

Who I had thought was dead.

Nine

Ragnar embraced me. There were tears in both our eyes and for a moment neither of us could speak, though I retained enough sense to look behind me to make sure Alfred was safe. He was squatting beside the door, deep in the shadow of a bale of wool, with his cloak's hood drawn over his face. 'I thought you were dead!' I said to Ragnar.

'I hoped you would come,' he said at the same moment, and for a time we both talked and neither listened, and then Brida walked from the back of the church and I watched her, seeing a woman instead of a girl, and she laughed to see me and gave me a decorous kiss.

'Uhtred,' she said my name as a caress. We had been lovers once, though we had been little more than children then. She was Saxon, but she had chosen the Danish side to be with Ragnar. The other women in the hall were hung with silver, garnet, jet, amber and gold, but Brida wore no jewellery other than an ivory comb that held her thick black hair in a pile. 'Uhtred,' she said again.

'Why aren't you dead?' I asked Ragnar. He had been a hostage, and the hostages' lives had been forfeit the moment Guthrum crossed the frontier.

'Wulfhere liked us,' Ragnar said. He put an arm around my shoulder and drew me to the central hearth where the fire blazed. 'This is Uhtred,' he announced to the dice players, 'a Saxon, which makes him scum, of course, but he is also my friend and my brother. Ale,' he pointed to jars, 'wine. Wulfhere let us live.'

'And you let him live?'

'Of course we did! He's here. Feasting with Guthrum.'

'Wulfhere? Is he a prisoner?'

'He's an ally!' Ragnar said, thrusting a pot into my hand and pulling me down beside the fire. 'He's with us now.' He grinned at me, and I laughed for the sheer joy of finding him alive. He was a big man, golden-haired, open-faced, and as full of mischief, life and kindness as his father had been. 'Wulfhere used to talk to Brida,' Ragnar went on, 'and through her to me. We liked each other. Hard to kill a man you like.'

'You persuaded him to change sides?'

'Didn't need a great deal of persuasion,' Ragnar said. 'He could see we were going to win, and by changing sides he keeps his land, doesn't he? Are you going to drink that ale or just stare at it?'

I pretended to drink, letting some of the ale drip down my beard, and I remembered Wulfhere telling me that when the Danes came we must all make what shifts we could to survive. But Wulfhere? Alfred's cousin and the Ealdorman of Wiltunscir? He had changed sides? So how many other thegns had followed his example and now served the Danes?

'Who's that?' Brida asked. She was staring at Alfred. He was in shadow, but there was something oddly mysterious about the way he squatted alone and silent.

'A servant,' I said.

'He can come by the fire.'

'He cannot,' I said harshly. 'I'm punishing him.'

'What did you do?' Brida called to him in English. His

258

face came up and he stared at her, but the hood still shadowed him.

'Speak, you bastard,' I said, 'and I'll whip you till your
bones show.' I could just see his eyes in the hood's shadow.
'He insulted me,' I spoke in Danish again, 'and I've sworn
him to silence, and for every word he utters he receives ten
blows of the whip.'

That satisfied them. Ragnar forgot the strange hooded
servant and told me how he had persuaded Wulfhere to
send a messenger to Guthrum, promising to spare the
hostages, and how Guthrum had warned Wulfhere when
the attack would come to make sure that the ealdorman
had time to remove the hostages from Alfred's revenge. That,
I thought, was why Wulfhere had left so early on the
morning of the attack. He had known the Danes were
coming. 'You call him an ally,' I said. 'Does that make him
just a friend? Or a man who will fight for Guthrum?'

'He's an ally,' Ragnar said, 'and he's sworn to fight for
us. At least he's sworn to fight for the Saxon king.'

'The Saxon king?' I asked, confused, 'Alfred?'

'Not Alfred, no. The true king. The boy who was the
other one's son.'

Ragnar meant Æthelwold, who had been heir to Alfred's
brother, King Æthelred, and of course the Danes would want
Æthelwold. Whenever they captured a Saxon kingdom they
appointed a Saxon as king, and that gave their conquest a
cloak of legality, though the Saxon never lasted long.
Guthrum, who already called himself King of East Anglia,
wanted to be King of Wessex too, but by putting Æthelwold
on the throne he might attract other West Saxons who could
convince themselves they were fighting for the true heir.
And once the fight was over and Danish rule established
Æthelwold would be quietly killed.

'But Wulfhere will fight for you?' I persisted.

'Of course he will! If he wants to keep his land,' Ragnar said, then grimaced. 'But what fighting? We just sit here like sheep and do nothing!'

'It's winter.'

'Best time to fight. Nothing else to do.' He wanted to know where I had been since Yule and I said I had been deep inside Defnascir. He assumed I had been making sure my family was safe, and he also assumed I had now come to Cippanhamm to join him. 'You're not sworn to Alfred, are you?' he asked.

'Who knows where Alfred is?' I evaded the question.

'You were sworn to him,' he said reproachfully.

'I was sworn to him,' I said, truthfully enough, 'but only for a year, and that year has long ended.' That was no lie, I just did not tell Ragnar I had sworn myself to Alfred once again.

'So you can join me?' he asked eagerly. 'You'll give me your oath?'

I took the question lightly, though in truth it worried me. 'You want my oath?' I asked, 'just so I can sit here like a sheep doing nothing?'

'We make some raids,' Ragnar said defensively, 'and men are guarding the swamp. That's where Alfred is. In the swamps. But Svein will dig him out.' So Guthrum and his men had yet to hear that Svein's fleet was ashes beside the sea.

'So why are you just sitting here?' I asked.

'Because Guthrum won't divide his army,' Ragnar said. I half smiled at that because I remembered Ragnar's grandfather advising Guthrum never to divide an army again. Guthrum had done that at Æsc's Hill and that had been the first victory of the West Saxons over the Danes. He had done it again when he abandoned Werham to attack Exanceaster, and the part of his army that went by sea was virtually destroyed by the storm. 'I've told him,' Ragnar said, 'that we should split the army into a dozen parts. Take a dozen more towns and garrison them. All those places in southern Wessex, we should capture them, but he won't listen.'

'Guthrum holds the north and east,' I said, as if I was defending him.

'And we should have the rest! But instead we're waiting till spring in hope more men will join us. Which they will. There's land here, good land. Better than the land up north.' He seemed to have forgotten the matter of my oath. I knew he would want me to join him, but instead he talked of what happened in Northumbria, how our enemies, Kjartan and Sven, thrived in Dunholm, and how that father and son dared not leave the fortress for fear of Ragnar's revenge. They had taken his sister captive and, so far as Ragnar knew, they held her still, and Ragnar, like me, was sworn to kill them. He had no news of Bebbanburg other than that my treacherous uncle still lived and held the fortress. 'When we've finished with Wessex,' Ragnar promised me, 'we shall go north. You and I together. We'll carry swords to Dunholm.'

'Swords to Dunholm,' I said and raised my pot of ale.

I did not drink much, or if I did it seemed to have little effect. I was thinking, sitting there, that with one sentence I could finish Alfred for ever. I could betray him, I could have him dragged in front of Guthrum and then watch as he died. Guthrum would even forgive me the insults to his mother if I gave him Alfred, and thus I could finish Wessex, for without Alfred there was no man about whom the fyrd would muster. I could stay with my friend, Ragnar, I could earn more arm rings, I could make a name that would be celebrated wherever Northmen sailed their long ships, and all it would take was one sentence.

And I was so tempted that night in Cippanhamm's royal

church. There is such joy in chaos. Stow all the world's evils behind a door and tell men that they must never, ever, open the door, and it will be opened because there is pure joy in destruction. At one moment, when Ragnar was bellowing with laughter and slapping my shoulder so hard that it hurt, I felt the words form on my tongue. That is Alfred, I would have said, pointing at him, and all my world would have changed and there would have been no more England. Yet, at the last moment, when the first word was on my tongue, I choked it back. Brida was watching me, her shrewd eyes calm, and I caught her gaze and I thought of Iseult. In a year or two, I thought, Iseult would look like Brida. They had the same tense beauty, the same dark colouring and the same smouldering fire in the soul. If I spoke, I thought, Iseult would be dead, and I could not bear that. And I thought of Æthelflaed, Alfred's daughter, and knew she would be enslaved, and also knew that wherever the remnants of the Saxons gathered about their fires of exile my name would be cursed. I would be Uhtredærwe for ever, the man who destroyed a people.

'What were you about to say?' Brida asked.

'That we have never known such a hard winter in Wessex.'

She gazed at me, not believing my answer. Then she smiled. 'Tell me, Uhtred,' she spoke in English, 'if you thought Ragnar was dead then why did you come here?'

'Because I don't know where else to be,' I said.

'So you came here? To Guthrum? Whom you insulted?'

So they knew about that. I had not expected them to know and I felt a surge of fear. I said nothing.

'Guthrum wants you dead,' Brida said, speaking in Danish now.

'He doesn't mean it,' Ragnar said.

'He does mean it,' Brida insisted.

'Well I won't let him kill Uhtred,' Ragnar said. 'You're here now!' He slapped me on the back again and glared at his men as if daring any of them to betray my presence to Guthrum. None of them moved, but they were nearly all of them drunk and some already asleep.

'You're here now,' Brida said, 'yet not so long ago you were fighting for Alfred and insulting Guthrum.'

'I was on my way to Defnascir,' I said, as if that explained anything.

'Poor Uhtred,' Brida said. Her right hand fondled the black and white fur at the back of Nihtgenga's neck. 'And I thought you'd be a hero to the Saxons.'

'A hero? Why?'

'The man who killed Ubba?'

'Alfred doesn't want heroes,' I said, loudly enough for him to hear, 'only saints.'

'So tell us about Ubba!' Ragnar demanded, and so I had to describe Ubba's death, and the Danes, who love a good story of a fight, wanted every detail. I told the tale well, making Ubba into a great hero who had almost destroyed the West Saxon army, and I said he had been fighting like a god, and told how he had broken our shield wall with his great axe. I described the burning ships, their smoke drifting over the battle slaughter like a cloud from the netherworld, and I said I had found myself facing Ubba in his victory charge. That was not true, of course, and the Danes knew it was not true. I had not just found myself opposing Ubba, but had sought him out, but when a story is told it must be seasoned with modesty and the listeners, understanding that custom, murmured approval. 'I have never known such fear,' I said, and I told how we had fought, Serpent-Breath against Ubba's axe, and how he had chopped my shield into firewood, and then I described, truthfully, how he had lost his footing in the spilled guts of a dead man. The Danes about the fire sighed with disappointment. 'I cut the tendons of his arm,' I said, chopping my left hand into the crook of my right elbow to show where I had cut him, 'and then beat him down.'

'He died well?' a man asked anxiously.

'As a hero,' I said, and I told how I had put the axe back into his dying hand so that he would go to Valhalla. 'He died very well,' I finished.

'He was a warrior,' Ragnar said. He was drunk now. Not badly drunk, but tired drunk. The fire was dying, thickening the shadows at the western end of the church where Alfred sat. More stories were told, the fire died and the few candles guttered. Men were sleeping, and still I sat until Ragnar lay back and began to snore. I waited longer, letting the room go to sleep, and only then did I go back to Alfred. 'We go now,' I said. He did not argue.

No one appeared to notice as we went into the night, closing the door quietly behind us. 'Who were you talking with?' Alfred asked me.

'Earl Ragnar.'

He stopped, puzzled. 'Wasn't he one of the hostages?'

'Wulfhere let them live,' I said.

'He let them live?' he asked, astonished.

'And Wulfhere is now on Guthrum's side.' I gave him the bad news. 'He's here, in the hall. He's agreed to fight for Guthrum.'

'Here?' Alfred could scarce believe what I said. Wulfhere was his cousin, he had married Alfred's niece, he was family. 'He's here?'

'He's on Guthrum's side,' I said harshly.

He just stared at me. 'No,' he mouthed the word, rather than said it. 'And Æthelwold?' he asked.

'He's a prisoner,' I said.

'A prisoner!' he asked the question sharply, and no

wonder, for Æthelwold had no value to the Danes as a prisoner unless he had agreed to become their token king on the West Saxon throne.

'A prisoner,' I said. It was not true, of course, but I liked Æthelwold and I owed him a favour. 'He's a prisoner,' I went on, 'and there's nothing we can do about it, so let's get away from here.' I pulled him towards the town, but too late, for the church door opened and Brida came out with Nihtgenga.

She told the dog to stay at her heels as she walked towards me. Like me she was not drunk, though she must have been very cold for she wore no cloak over her plain blue woollen dress. The night was brittle with frost, but she did not shiver. 'You're going?' She spoke in English. 'You're not staying with us?'

'I have a wife and child,' I said.

She smiled at that. 'Whose names you have not mentioned all evening, Uhtred. So what happened?' I gave no answer and she just stared at me, and there was something very unsettling in her gaze. 'So what woman is with you now?' she asked.

'Someone who looks like you,' I admitted.

She laughed at that. 'And she would have you fight for Alfred?'

'She sees the future,' I said, evading the question. 'She dreams it.'

Brida stared at me. Nihtgenga whined softly and she put down a hand to calm him. 'And she sees Alfred surviving?'

'More than surviving,' I said. 'She sees him winning.' Beside me Alfred stirred and I hoped he had the sense to keep his head lowered.

'Winning?'

'She sees a green hill of dead men,' I said, 'a white horse, and Wessex living again.'

'Your woman has strange dreams,' Brida said, 'but you never answered my first question, Uhtred. If you thought Ragnar was dead, why did you come here?'

I had no ready answer so made none.

'Who did you expect to find here?' she asked.

'You?' I suggested glibly.

She shook her head, knowing I lied. 'Why did you come?' I still had no answer and Brida smiled sadly. 'If I were Alfred,' she said, 'I would send a man who spoke Danish to Cippanhamm, and that man would go back to the swamp and tell all he had seen.'

'If you think that,' I said, 'then why don't you tell them?' I nodded towards Guthrum's black-cloaked men guarding the hall door.

'Because Guthrum is a nervous fool,' she said savagely. 'Why help Guthrum? And when Guthrum fails, Ragnar will take command.'

'Why doesn't he command now?'

'Because he is like his father. He's decent. He gave his word to Guthrum and he won't break his word. And tonight he wanted you to give him an oath, but you didn't.'

'I do not want Bebbanburg to be a gift of the Danes,' I answered.

She thought about that, and understood it. 'But do you think,' she asked scornfully, 'that the West Saxons will give you Bebbanburg? It's at the other end of Britain, Uhtred, and the last Saxon king is rotting in a swamp.'

'This will give it to me,' I said, pulling back my cloak to show Serpent-Breath's hilt.

'You and Ragnar can rule the north,' she said.

'Maybe we will,' I said. 'So tell Ragnar that when this is all finished, when all is decided, I shall go north with him. I shall fight Kjartan. But in my own time.'

'I hope you live to keep that promise,' she said, then

266

leaned forward and kissed my cheek. Then, without another word, she turned and walked back to the church.

Alfred let out a breath. 'Who is Kjartan?'

'An enemy,' I said shortly. I tried to lead him away, but he stopped me.

He was staring at Brida who was nearing the church. 'That is the girl who was with you at Wintanceaster?'

'Yes.' He was talking of the time when I had first come to Wessex and Brida had been with me.

'And does Iseult truly see the future?'

'She has not been wrong yet.'

He made the sign of the cross, then let me lead him back through the town. It was quieter now, but he would not go with me to the western gate, insisting we return to the nunnery where, for a moment, we both crouched near one of the dying fires in the courtyard to get what warmth we could from the embers. Men slept in the nunnery church, but the courtyard was now deserted and quiet, and Alfred took a piece of half-burning wood and, using it as a torch, went to the row of small doors that led to the nuns' sleeping cells. One door had been fastened with two hasps and a short length of thick chain and Alfred paused there.

'Draw your sword,' he ordered me.

When Serpent-Breath was naked he unwound the chain from the hasps and pushed the door inwards. He entered cautiously, pushing the hood back from his face. He held the torch high, and in its light I saw the big man huddled on the floor.

'Steapa!' Alfred hissed.

Steapa was only pretending to be asleep and he uncoiled from the floor with wolf-like speed, lashing out at Alfred, and I rammed the sword towards his breast, but then he saw Alfred's bruised face and he froze, oblivious of the blade. 'Lord?'

267

'You're coming with us,' Alfred said.

'Lord!' Steapa fell to his knees in front of his king.

'It's cold out there,' Alfred said. It was freezing inside the cell as well. 'You can sheath your sword, Uhtred.' Steapa looked at me and seemed vaguely surprised to find I was the man he had been fighting when the Danes came. 'The two of you will be friends,' Alfred said sternly, and the big man nodded. 'And we have one other person to fetch,' Alfred said, 'so come.'

'One other person?' I asked.

'You spoke of a nun,' Alfred said.

So I had to find the nun's cell, and she was still there, lying crushed against the wall by a Dane who was snoring flabbily. The flame-light showed a small, frightened face half-hidden by the Dane's beard. His beard was black and her hair was gold, pale gold, and she was awake and, seeing us, gasped, and that woke the Dane who blinked in the flame-light and then snarled at us as he tried to throw off the thick cloaks serving as blankets. Steapa hit him and it was like the sound of a bullock being clubbed, wet and hard at the same time. The man's head snapped back and Alfred pulled the cloaks away and the nun tried to hide her nakedness. Alfred hurriedly put the cloaks back. He had been embarrassed and I had been impressed, for she was young and very beautiful and I wondered why such a woman would waste her sweetness on religion. 'You know who I am?' Alfred asked her. She shook her head. 'I am your king,' he said softly, 'and you will come with us, sister.'

Her clothes were long gone, so we swathed her in the heavy cloaks. The Dane was dead by now, his throat cut by Wasp-Sting, and I had found a pouch of coins strung around his neck on a leather thong. 'That money goes to the church,' Alfred said.

'I found it,' I said, 'and I killed him.'

'It is the money of sin,' he said patiently, 'and must be redeemed.' He smiled at the nun. 'Are there any other sisters here?' he asked.

'Only me,' she said in a small voice.

'And now you are safe, sister.' He straightened. 'We can go.'

Steapa carried the nun who was called Hild. She clung to him, whimpering, either from the cold or, more likely, from the memory of her ordeal.

We could have captured Cippanhamm that night with a hundred men. It was so bitterly cold that no guards stood on the ramparts. The gate sentries were in a house by the wall, crouched by the fire, and all the notice they took of the bar being lifted was to shout a bad-tempered question wanting to know who we were. 'Guthrum's men,' I called back, and they did not bother us further. A half-hour later we were in the watermill, reunited with Father Adelbert, Egwine and the three soldiers.

'We should give thanks to God for our deliverance,' Alfred said to Father Adelbert, who had been aghast to see the blood and bruises on the king's face. 'Say a prayer, father,' Alfred ordered.

Adelbert prayed, but I did not listen. I just crouched by the fire, thought I would never be warm again, and then slept.

It snowed all next day. Thick snow. We made a fire, careless that the Danes might see the smoke, for no Dane was going to struggle through the bitter cold and deepening snow to investigate one small, far-off trickle of grey against a grey sky.

Alfred brooded. He spoke little that day, though once he

269

frowned and asked me if it could really be true about Wulfhere. 'We didn't see him with Guthrum,' he added plaintively, desperately hoping that the ealdorman had not betrayed him.

'The hostages lived,' I said.

'Dear God,' he said, convinced by that argument, and leaned his head against the wall. He watched the snow through one of the small windows. 'He's family!' he said after a while, then fell silent again.

I fed the horses the last of the hay we had brought with us, then sharpened my swords for lack of anything else to do. Hild wept. Alfred tried to comfort her, but he was awkward and had no words, and oddly it was Steapa who calmed her. He talked to her softly, his voice a deep grumble, and when Serpent-Breath and Wasp-Sting were as sharp as I could make them, and as the snow sifted endlessly onto a silent world, I brooded like Alfred.

I thought of Ragnar wanting my oath. I thought of him wanting my allegiance.

The world began in chaos and it will end in chaos. The gods brought the world into existence, and they will end it when they fight among themselves, but in between the chaos of the world's birth and the chaos of the world's death is order, and order is made by oaths, and oaths bind us like the buckles of a harness.

I was bound to Alfred by an oath, and before I gave that oath I had wanted to bind myself to Ragnar, but now I felt affronted that he had even asked me. That was pride growing in me and changing me. I was Uhtred of Bebbanburg, slayer of Ubba, and while I would give an oath to a king I was reluctant to make an oath to an equal. The oath-giver is subservient to the man who accepts the oath. Ragnar would have said I was a friend, he would treat me like a brother, but his assumption that I would give him an oath demonstrated that he still believed I was his follower. I was a lord of Northumbria, but he was a Dane, and to a Dane all Saxons are lesser men, and so he had demanded an oath. If I gave him an oath then he would be generous, but I would be expected to show gratitude, and I could only ever hold Bebbanburg because he allowed me to hold it. I had never thought it all through before, but suddenly, on that cold day, I understood that among the Danes I was as important as my friends, and without friends I was just another landless, masterless warrior. But among the Saxons I was another Saxon, and among the Saxons I did not need another man's generosity.

'You look thoughtful, Uhtred,' Alfred interrupted my reverie.

'I was thinking, lord,' I said, 'that we need warm food.' I fed the fire, then went outside to the stream where I knocked away the skim of ice and scooped water into a pot. Steapa had followed me outside, not to talk, but to piss, and I stood behind him. 'At the witanegemot,' I said, 'you lied about Cynuit.'

He tied the scrap of rope that served as a belt and turned to look at me. 'If the Danes had not come,' he said in his growling voice, 'I would have killed you.'

I did not argue with that, for he was probably right. 'At Cynuit,' I said instead, 'when Ubba died, where were you?'

'There.'

'I didn't see you,' I said. 'I was in the thick of the battle, but I didn't see you.'

'You think I wasn't there?' he was angry.

'You were with Odda the Younger?' I asked, and he nodded. 'You were with him,' I guessed, 'because his father told you to protect him?' He nodded again. 'And Odda the Younger,' I said, 'stayed a long way from any danger. Isn't that right?'

He did not answer, but his silence told me I was right. He decided he had nothing more to say to me so started

271

back towards the mill, but I pulled on his arm to stop him. He was surprised by that. Steapa was so big and so strong and so feared that he was unused to men using force on him, and I could see the slow anger burning in him. I fed it. 'You were Odda's nursemaid,' I sneered. 'The great Steapa Snotor was a nursemaid. Other men faced and fought the Danes and you just held Odda's hand.'

He just stared at me. His face, so tight-skinned and expressionless, was like an animal's gaze, nothing there but hunger and anger and violence. He wanted to kill me, especially after I used his nickname, but I understood something more about Steapa Snotor. He was truly stupid. He would kill me if he was ordered to kill me, but without someone to instruct him he did not know what to do, so I thrust the pot of water at him. 'Carry that inside,' I told him. He hesitated. 'Don't stand there like a dumb ox!' I snapped. 'Take it! And don't spill it.' He took the pot. 'It has to go on the fire,' I told him, 'and next time we fight the Danes you'll be with me.'

'You?'

'Because we are warriors,' I said, 'and our job is to kill our enemies, not be nursemaids to weaklings.'

I collected firewood, then went inside to find Alfred staring at nothing and Steapa sitting beside Hild who now seemed to be consoling him rather than being consoled. I crumbled oatcakes and dried fish into the water and stirred the mess with a stick. It was a gruel of sorts and tasted horrible, but it was hot.

That night it stopped snowing and next morning we went home.

Alfred need not have gone to Cippanhamm. Anything he learned there he could have discovered by sending spies, but he had insisted on going himself and he came back more worried than before. He had learned some good things, that Guthrum did not have the men to subjugate all Wessex and so was waiting for reinforcements, but he had also learned that Guthrum was trying to turn the nobility of Wessex to his side. Wulfhere was sworn to the Danes, who else?

'Will the fyrd of Wiltunscir fight for Wulfhere?' he asked us.

Of course they would fight for Wulfhere. Most of the men in Wiltunscir were loyal to their lord, and if their lord ordered them to follow his banner to war then they would march. Those men who were in the parts of the shire not occupied by the Danes might go to Alfred, but the rest would do what they always did, follow their lord. And other ealdormen, seeing that Wulfhere had not lost his estates, would reckon that their own future, and their family's safety, lay with the Danes. The Danes had ever worked that way. Their armies were too small and too disorganised to defeat a great kingdom so they recruited lords of the kingdom, flattered them, even made them into kings, and only when they were secure did they turn on those Saxons and kill them.

So back in Æthelingæg Alfred did what he did best. He wrote letters. He wrote letters to all his nobility, and messengers were sent into every corner of Wessex to find ealdormen, thegns and bishops, and deliver the letters. I am alive, the scraps of parchment said, and after Easter I shall take Wessex from the pagans, and you will help me. We waited for the replies.

'You must teach me to read,' Iseult said when I told her about the letters.

'Why?'

'It is a magic,' she said.

'What magic? So you can read psalms?'

273

'Words are like breath,' she said, 'you say them and they're gone. But writing traps them. You could write down stories, poems.'

'Hild will teach you,' I said, and the nun did, scratching letters in the mud. I watched them sometimes and thought they could have been taken for sisters except one had hair black as a raven's wing and the other had hair of pale gold.

So Iseult learned her letters and I practised the men with their weapons and shields until they were too tired to curse me, and we also made a new fortress. We restored one of the beamwegs that led south to the hills at the edge of the swamp, and where that log road met dry land we made a strong fort of earth and tree-trunks. None of Guthrum's men tried to stop the work, though we saw Danes watching us from the higher hills, and by the time Guthrum understood what we were doing the fort was finished. In late February a hundred Danes came to challenge it, but they saw the thorn palisade protecting the ditch, saw the strength of the log wall behind the ditch, saw our spears thick against the sky and rode away.

Next day I took sixty men to the farm where we had seen the Danish horses. They were gone, and the farm was burned out. We rode inland, seeing no enemy. We found newborn lambs slaughtered by foxes, but no Danes, and from that day on we rode ever deeper into Wessex, carrying the message that the king lived and fought, and some days we met Danish bands, but we only fought if we outnumbered them for we could not afford to lose men.

Ælswith gave birth to a daughter whom she and Alfred called Æthelgifu. Ælswith wanted to leave the swamp. She knew that Huppa of Thornsæta was holding Dornwaraceaster for the ealdorman had replied to Alfred's letter saying that the town was secure and, as soon as Alfred demanded it, the fyrd of Thornsæta would march to his aid.

Dornwaraceaster was not so large as Cippanhamm, but it had Roman walls and Ælswith was tired of living in the marshes, tired of the endless damp, of the chill mists, and she said her newborn baby would die of the cold, and that Edward's sickness would come back, and Bishop Alewold supported her. He had a vision of a large house in Dornwaraceaster, of warm fires and priestly comfort, but Alfred refused. If he moved to Dornwaraceaster then the Danes would immediately abandon Cippanhamm and besiege Alfred and starvation would soon threaten the garrison, but in the swamp there was food. In Dornwaraceaster Alfred would be a prisoner of the Danes, but in the swamp he was free, and he wrote more letters, telling Wessex he lived, that he grew stronger and that after Easter, but before Pentecost, he would strike the pagans.

It rained that late winter. Rain and more rain. I remember standing on the muddy parapet of the new fort and watching the rain just falling and falling. Mail coats rusted, fabrics rotted and food went mouldy. Our boots fell apart and we had no men skilled in making new ones. We slid and splashed through greasy mud, our clothes were never dry, and still grey swathes of rain marched from the west. Thatch dripped, huts flooded, the world was sullen. We ate well enough, though as more men came to Æthelingæg, the food became scarcer, but no one starved and no one complained except Bishop Alewold who grimaced whenever he saw another fish stew. There were no deer left in the swamp, all had been netted and eaten, but at least we had fish, eels and wildfowl, while outside the swamp, in those areas the Danes had plundered, folk starved. We practised with our weapons, fought mock battles with staves, watched the hills, and welcomed the messengers who brought news. Burgweard, the fleet commander, wrote from Hamtun saying that the town was garrisoned by Saxons, but that

Danish ships were off the coast. 'I don't suppose he's fighting them,' Leofric remarked glumly when he heard that news.

'He doesn't say so,' I said.

'Doesn't want to get his nice ships dirty,' Leofric guessed.

'At least he still has the ships.'

A letter came from a priest in distant Kent saying that Vikings from Lundene had occupied Contwaraburg and others had settled on the Isle of Sceapig, and that the ealdorman had made his peace with the invaders. News came from Suth Seaxa of more Danish raids, but also a reassurance from Arnulf, Ealdorman of Suth Seaxa, that his fyrd would gather in the spring. He sent a gospel book to Alfred as a token of his loyalty, and for days Alfred carried the book until the rain soaked into the pages and made the ink run. Wiglaf, Ealdorman of Sumorsæte, appeared in early March and brought seventy men. He claimed to have been hiding in the hills south of Baðum and Alfred ignored the rumours which said Wiglaf had been negotiating with Guthrum. All that mattered was that the ealdorman had come to Æthelingæg and Alfred gave him command of the troops that continually rode inland to shadow the Danes and to ambush their forage parties. Not all the news was so encouraging. Wilfrith of Hamptonscir had fled across the water to Frankia, as had a score of other ealdormen and thegns.

But Odda the Younger, Ealdorman of Defnascir, was still in Wessex. He sent a priest who brought a letter reporting that the ealdorman was holding Exanceaster. 'God be praised,' the letter read, 'but there are no pagans in the town'.

'So where are they?' Alfred asked the priest. We knew that Svein, despite losing his ships, had not marched to join Guthrum, which suggested he was still skulking in Defnascir.

The priest, a young man who seemed terrified of the king,

shrugged, hesitated, then stammered that Svein was close to Exanceaster.

'Close?' the king asked.

'Nearby,' the priest managed to say.

'They besiege the town?' Alfred asked.

'No, lord.'

Alfred read the letter a second time. He always had great faith in the written word and he was trying to find some hint of the truth that had escaped him in the first reading. 'They are not in Exanceaster,' he concluded, 'but the letter does not say where they are. Nor how many they are. Nor what they're doing.'

'They are nearby, lord,' the priest said hopelessly. 'To the west, I think.'

'The west?'

'I think they're to the west.'

'What's to the west?' Alfred asked me.

'The high moor,' I said.

Alfred threw the letter down in disgust. 'Maybe you should go to Defnascir,' he told me, 'and find out what the pagans are doing.'

'Yes, lord,' I said.

'It will be a chance to discover your wife and child,' Alfred said.

There was a sting there. As the winter rains fell the priests hissed their poison into Alfred's ears and he was willing enough to hear their message, which was that the Saxons would only defeat the Danes if God willed it. And God, the priests said, wanted us to be virtuous. And Iseult was a pagan, as was I, and she and I were not married, while I had a wife, and so the accusation was whispered about the swamp that it was Iseult who stood between Alfred and victory. No one said it openly, not then, yet Iseult sensed it. Hild was her protector in those days, because Hild was a

277

nun, a Christian, and a victim of the Danes, but many thought Iseult was corrupting Hild. I pretended to be deaf to the whispers until Alfred's daughter told me of them.

Æthelflæd was almost seven and her father's favourite child. Ælswith was fonder of Edward, and in those wet winter days she worried about her son's health and the health of her newborn child, which gave Æthelflæd a deal of freedom. She would stay at her father's side much of the time, but she also wandered about Æthelingæg where she was spoiled by soldiers and villagers. She was a bright ripple of sunlight in those rain-sodden days. She had golden hair, a sweet face, blue eyes and no fear. One day I found her at the southern fort, watching a dozen Danes who had come to watch us. I told her to go back to Æthelingæg and she pretended to obey me, but an hour later, when the Danes had gone, I found her hiding in one of the turf-roofed shelters behind the wall. 'I hoped the Danes would come,' she told me.

'So they could take you away?'

'So I could watch you kill them.'

It was one of the rare days when it was not raining. There was sunshine on the green hills and I sat on the wall, took Serpent-Breath from her fleece-lined scabbard and began sharpening her two edges with a whetstone. Æthelflaed insisted on trying the whetstone and she laid the long blade on her lap and frowned in concentration as she drew the stone down the sword. 'How many Danes have you killed?' she asked.

'Enough.'

'Mama says you don't love Jesus.'

'We all love Jesus,' I said evasively.

'If you loved Jesus,' she said seriously, 'then you could kill more Danes. What's this?' She had found the deep nick in one of Serpent-Breath's edges.

'It's where she hit another sword,' I said. It had happened at Cippanhamm during my fight with Steapa and his huge sword had bitten deep into Serpent-Breath.

'I'll make her better,' she said, and worked obsessively with the whetstone, trying to smooth the nick's edges. 'Mama says Iseult is an aglæcwif.' She stumbled over the word, then grinned in triumph because she had managed to say it. I said nothing. An aglæcwif was a fiend, a monster. 'The bishop says it too,' Æthelflaed said earnestly. 'I don't like the bishop.'

'You don't?'

'He dribbles.' She tried to demonstrate and managed to spit onto Serpent-Breath. She rubbed the blade. 'Is Iseult an aglæcwif?'

'Of course not. She made Edward better.'

'Jesus did that, and Jesus sent me a baby sister.' She scowled because all her efforts had made no impression on the nick in Serpent-Breath.

'Iseult is a good woman,' I said.

'She's learning to read. I can read.'

'You can?'

'Almost. If she reads then she can be a Christian. I'd like to be an aglæcwif.'

'You would?' I asked, surprised.

For answer she growled at me and crooked a small hand so that her fingers looked like claws. Then she laughed. 'Are those Danes?' She had seen some horsemen coming from the south.

'That's Wiglaf,' I said.

'He's nice.'

I sent her back to Æthelingæg on Wiglaf's horse and I thought of what she had said and wondered, for the thousandth time, why I was among Christians who believed I was an offence to their god. They called my gods dwolgods, which meant false gods, so that made me Uhtredærwe, living with an aglæcwif and worshipping dwolgods. I flaunted it, though, always wearing my hammer amulet openly, and that night Alfred, as ever, flinched when he saw it. He had summoned me to his hall where I found him bent over a tafl board. He was playing against Beocca, who had the larger set of pieces. It seems a simple game, tafl, where one player has a king and a dozen other pieces, and the other has double the pieces, but no king, and then you move the pieces about the chequered board until one or other player has all his wooden pieces surrounded. I had no patience for it, but Alfred was fond of the game, though when I arrived he seemed to be losing and so was relieved to see me. 'I want you to go to Defnascir,' he said.

'Of course, lord.'

'I fear your king is threatened, lord,' Beocca said happily.

'Never mind,' Alfred said irritably. 'You're to go to Defnascir,' he said, turning back to me, 'but Iseult must stay here.'

I bridled at that. 'She's to be a hostage again?' I asked.

'I need her medicines,' Alfred said.

'Even though they're made by an aglæcwif?'

He gave me a sharp look. 'She is a healer,' he said, 'and that means she is God's instrument, and with God's help she will come to the truth. Besides, you must travel fast and don't need a woman for company. You will go to Defnascir and find Svein, and once you've found him you will instruct Odda the Younger to raise the fyrd. Tell him Svein must be driven from the shire, and once Odda has achieved that, he is to come here with his household troops. He commands my bodyguard, he should be here.'

'You want me to give Odda orders?' I asked, partly in surprise, partly with scorn.

'I do,' Alfred said, 'and I order you to make your peace with him.'

280

'Yes, lord,' I replied.

He heard the sarcasm in my voice. 'We are all Saxons, Uhtred, and now, more than ever, is the time to heal our wounds.'

Beocca, realising that defeating Alfred at tafl would not help the king's mood, was taking the pieces from the board. 'A house divided against itself,' he interjected, 'will be destroyed. Saint Matthew said that.'

'Praise God for that truth,' Alfred said, 'and we must be rid of Svein.' That was a greater truth. Alfred wanted to march against Guthrum after Easter, but he could scarcely do that if Svein's forces were behind him. 'You find Svein,' the king told me, 'and Steapa will accompany you.'

'Steapa!'

'He knows the country,' Alfred said, 'and I have told him he is to obey you.'

'It's best that two of you go,' Beocca said earnestly. 'Remember that Joshua sent two spies against Jericho.'

'You're delivering me to my enemies,' I said bitterly, though when I thought about it I decided that using me as a spy made sense. The Danes in Defnascir would be looking out for Alfred's scouts, but I could speak the enemy's language and could pass for one of them and so I was safer than anyone else in Alfred's force. As for Steapa, he was from Defnascir, he knew the country and he was Odda's sworn man, so he was best suited for carrying a message to the ealdorman.

And so the two of us rode south from Æthelingæg on a day of driving rain.

Steapa did not like me and I did not like him and so we had nothing to say to each other except when I suggested what path we take, and he never disagreed. We kept close to the large road, the road the Romans had made, though I went cautiously for such roads were much used by Danish bands seeking forage or plunder. This was also the route Svein must take if he marched to join Guthrum, but we saw no Danes. We saw no Saxons either. Every village and farm on the road had been pillaged and burned so that we journeyed through a land of the dead.

On the second day Steapa headed westwards. He did not explain the sudden change of direction, but doggedly pushed up into the hills and I followed him because he knew the countryside and I supposed he was taking the small paths that would lead to the high bleakness of Dærentmora. He rode urgently, his hard face grim, and I called to him once that we should take more care in case there were Danish forage parties in the small valleys, but he ignored me. Instead, almost at a gallop, he rode down into one of those small valleys until he came in sight of a farmstead.

Or what had been a farmstead. Now it was wet ashes in a green place. A deep green place where narrow pastures were shadowed by tall trees on which the very first haze of spring was just showing. Flowers were thick along the pasture edges, but there were none where the few small buildings had stood. There were only embers and the black smear of ash in mud, and Steapa, abandoning his horse, walked among the ashes. He had lost his great sword when the Danes captured him at Cippanhamm, so now he carried a huge war axe and he prodded the wide blade into the dark piles.

I rescued his horse, tied both beasts to the scorched trunk of an ash that had once grown by the farmyard, and watched him. I said nothing, for I sensed that one word would release all his fury. He crouched by the skeleton of a dog and just stared at the fire-darkened bones for a few minutes, then reached out and stroked the bared skull. There were tears on Steapa's face, or perhaps it was the rain that fell softly from low cloud.

A score of people had once lived there. A larger house had stood at the southern end of the settlement and I explored its charred remains, seeing where the Danes had dug down by the old posts to find hidden coins. Steapa watched me. He was by one of the smaller patches of charred timbers and I guessed he had grown up there, in a slave hovel. He did not want me near him, and I pointedly stayed away, wondering if I dared suggest to him that we rode on. But he began digging instead, hacking the damp red soil with his huge war axe and scooping the earth out with bare hands until he had made a shallow grave for the dog. It was a skeleton now. There were still patches of fur on the old bones, but the flesh had been eaten away so that the ribs were scattered, so this had all happened weeks before. Steapa gathered the bones and laid them tenderly in the grave.

That was when the people came. You can ride through a landscape of the dead and see no one, but they will see you. Folk hide when enemies come. They go up into the woods and they wait there, and now three men came from the trees.

'Steapa,' I said. He turned on me, furious that I had interrupted him, then saw I was pointing westwards.

He gave a roar of recognition and the three men, who were holding spears, ran towards him. They dropped their weapons and they hugged the huge man, and for a time they all spoke together, but then they calmed down and I took one aside and questioned him. The Danes had come soon after Yule, he told me. They had come suddenly, before anyone was even aware that there were pagans in Defnascir. These men had escaped because they had been felling a beech tree in a nearby wood, and they had heard the slaughter. Since then they had been living in the forests, scared of the Danes who still rode about Defnascir in search of food. They had seen no Saxons.

283

They had buried the folk of the farm in a pasture to the south, and Steapa went there and knelt in the wet grass. 'His mother died,' the man told me. He spoke English with such a strange accent that I continually had to ask him to repeat himself, but I understood those three words. 'Steapa was good to his mother,' the man said. 'He brought her money. She was no slave any more.'

'His father?'

'He died long time back. Long time.'

I thought Steapa was going to dig up his mother, so I crossed and stood in front of him. 'We have a job to do,' I said.

He looked up at me, his harsh face expressionless.

'There are Danes to kill,' I said. 'The Danes who killed folk here must be killed themselves.'

He nodded abruptly, then stood, towering over me again. He cleaned the blade of his axe and climbed into his saddle. 'There are Danes to kill,' he said and, leaving his mother in her cold grave, we went to find them.

Ten

We rode south. We went cautiously, for folk said the Danes were still seen in this part of the shire, though we saw none. Steapa was silent until, in a river meadow, we rode past a ring of stone pillars, one of the mysteries left behind by the old people. Such rings stand all across England and some are huge, though this one was a mere score of lichen-covered stones, none taller than a man, standing in a circle some fifteen paces wide. Steapa glanced at them, then astonished me by speaking. 'That's a wedding,' he said.

'A wedding?'

'They were dancing,' he growled, 'and the devil turned them to stone.'

'Why did the devil do that?' I asked cautiously.

'Because they wed on a Sunday, of course. Folk never should wed on a Sunday, never! Everyone knows that.' We rode on in silence, then, surprising me again, he began to talk about his mother and father and how they had been serfs of Odda the Elder. 'But life was good for us,' he said.

'It was?'

'Ploughing, sowing, weeding, harvest, threshing.'

'But Ealdorman Odda didn't live back there,' I said, jerking my thumb towards Steapa's destroyed homestead.

'No! Not him!' Steapa was amused I should even ask such

a question. 'He wouldn't live there, not him! Had his own big hall. Still does. But he had a steward there. Man to give us orders. He was a big man! Very tall!'

I hesitated. 'But your father was short?'

Steapa looked surprised. 'How did you know that?'

'I just guessed.'

'He was a good worker, my father.'

'Did he teach you to fight?'

'He didn't, no. No one did. I just learned myself.'

The land was less damaged the farther we went south. And that was strange, for the Danes had come this way. We knew that, for folk said the Danes were still in the southern part of the shire, but life suddenly seemed normal. We saw men spreading dung on fields, and other men ditching or hedging. There were lambs in the pastures. To the north the foxes had become fat on dead lambs, but here the shepherds and their dogs were winning that ceaseless battle.

And the Danes were in Cridianton.

A priest told us that in a village hard under a great oak-covered hill beside a stream. The priest was nervous because he had seen my long hair and arm rings and he presumed I was a Dane, and my northern accent did not persuade him otherwise, but he was reassured by Steapa. The two talked, and the priest gave his opinion that it would be a wet summer.

'It will,' Steapa agreed. 'The oak greened before the ash.'

'Always a sign,' the priest said.

'How far is Cridianton?' I broke into the conversation.

'A morning's walk, lord.'

'You've seen the Danes there?' I asked.

'I've seen them, lord, I have,' he said.

'Who leads them?'

'Don't know, lord.'

'They have a banner?' I asked.

He nodded. 'It hangs on the bishop's hall, lord. It shows a white horse.'

So it was Svein. I did not know who else it could have been, but the white horse confirmed that Svein had stayed in Defnascir rather than try to join Guthrum. I twisted in the saddle and looked at the priest's village that was unscarred by war. No thatch had been burned, no granaries emptied and the church was still standing. 'Have the Danes come here?' I asked.

'Oh yes, lord, they came. Came more than once.'

'Did they rape? Steal?'

'No, lord. But they bought some grain. Paid silver for it.'

Well-behaved Danes. That was another strange thing. 'Are they besieging Exanceaster?' I asked. That would have made a sort of sense. Cridianton was close enough to Exanceaster to give most of the Danish troops shelter while the rest invested the larger town.

'No, lord,' the priest said, 'not that I know of.'

'Then what are they doing?' I asked.

'They're just in Cridianton, lord.'

'And Odda is in Exanceaster?'

'No, lord. He's in Ocmundtun. He's with Lord Harald.'

I knew the shire-reeve's hall was in Ocmundtun that lay beneath the northern edge of the great moor. But Ocmundtun was also a long journey from Cridianton and no place to be if a man wanted to harry the Danes.

I believed the priest when he said Svein was at Cridianton, but we still rode there to see for ourselves. We used wooded, hilly tracks and came to the town at mid afternoon and saw the smoke rising from cooking fires, then saw the Danish shields hanging from the palisade. Steapa and I were hidden in the high woods and could see men guarding the gate, and other men standing watch in a pasture where forty or fifty horses were grazing on the first of the spring grass. I could see Odda the Elder's hall where I had been reunited with Mildrith after the fight at Cynuit, and I could also see a triangular Danish banner flying above the larger hall that was the bishop's home. The western gate was open, though well guarded, and despite the sentries and the shields on the wall the town looked like a place at peace, not at war. There should be Saxons on this hill, I thought, Saxons watching the enemy, ready to attack. Instead the Danes were living undisturbed. 'How far to Ocmundtun?' I asked Steapa.

'We can make it by nightfall.'

I hesitated. If Odda the Younger was at Ocmundtun then why go there? He was my enemy and sworn to my death. Alfred had given me a scrap of parchment on which he had written words commanding Odda to greet me peaceably, but what force did writing have against hatred?

'He won't kill you,' Steapa said, surprising me again. He had evidently guessed my thoughts. 'He won't kill you,' he said again.

'Why not?'

'Because I won't bide him killing you,' Steapa said and turned his horse west.

We reached Ocmundtun at dusk. It was a small town built along a river and guarded by a high spur of limestone on which a stout palisade offered a refuge if attackers came. No one was on the limestone spur now and the town, which had no walls, looked placid. There might be war in Wessex, but Ocmundtun, like Cridianton, was evidently at peace. Harald's hall was close to the fort on its hill and no one challenged us as we rode into the forecourt where servants recognised Steapa. They greeted him warily, but then a steward came from the hall door and, seeing the huge man, clapped his hands twice in a sign of delight. 'We heard you were taken by the pagans,' the steward said.

'I was.'

'They let you go?'

'My king freed me,' Steapa growled as though he resented the question. He slid from his horse and stretched. 'Alfred freed me.'

'Is Harald here?' I asked the steward.

'My lord is inside,' the steward was offended that I had not called the reeve 'lord'.

'Then so are we,' I said, and led Steapa into the hall. The steward flapped at us because custom and courtesy demanded that he seek his lord's permission for us to enter the hall, but I ignored him.

A fire burned in the central hearth and dozens of rush-lights stood on the platforms at the hall's edges. Boar spears were stacked against the wall on which hung a dozen deer-skins and a bundle of valuable pine-marten pelts. A score of men were in the hall, evidently waiting for supper, and a harpist played at the far end. A pack of hounds rushed to investigate us and Steapa beat them off as we walked to the fire to warm ourselves. 'Ale,' Steapa said to the steward.

Harald must have heard the noise of the hounds for he appeared at a door leading from the private chamber at the back of the hall. He blinked when he saw us. He had thought the two of us were enemies, then he had heard that Steapa was captured, yet here we were, side by side. The hall fell silent as he limped towards us. It was only a slight limp, the result of a spear wound in some battle that had also taken two fingers of his sword hand. 'You once chided me,' he said, 'for carrying weapons into your hall. Yet you bring weapons into mine.'

'There was no gatekeeper,' I said.

'He was having a piss, lord,' the steward explained.

'There are to be no weapons in hall,' Harald insisted.

That was customary. Men get drunk in hall and can do

enough damage to each other with the knives we use to cut meat, and drunken men with swords and axes can turn a supper table into a butcher's yard. We gave the steward our weapons, then I hauled off my mail coat and told the steward to hang it on a frame to dry, then have a servant clean its links.

Harald formally welcomed us when our weapons were gone. He said the hall was ours and that we should eat with him as honoured guests. 'I would hear your news,' he said, beckoning a servant who brought us pots of ale.

'Is Odda here?' I demanded.

'The father is, yes. Not the son.'

I swore. We had come here with a message for Ealdorman Odda, Odda the Younger, only to discover that it was the wounded father, Odda the Elder, who was in Ocmundtun. 'So where is the son?' I asked.

Harald was offended by my brusqueness, but he remained courteous. 'The ealdorman is in Exanceaster.'

'Is he besieged there?'

'No.'

'And the Danes are in Cridianton?'

'They are.'

'And are they besieged?' I knew the answer to that, but wanted to hear Harald admit it.

'No,' he said.

I let the ale pot drop. 'We come from the king,' I said. I was supposedly speaking to Harald, but I strode down the hall so that the men on the platforms could hear me. 'We come from Alfred,' I said, 'and Alfred wishes to know why there are Danes in Defnascir. We burned their ships, we slaughtered their ship-guards and we drove them from Cynuit, yet you allow them to live here? Why?'

No one answered. There were no women in the hall, for Harald was a widower who had not remarried, and so the supper guests were all his warriors or else thegns who led men of their own. Some looked at me with loathing, for my words imputed cowardice to them, while others looked down at the floor. Harald glanced at Steapa as if seeking the big man's support, but Steapa just stood by the fire, his savage face showing nothing. I turned back to stare at Harald. 'Why are there Danes in Defnascir?' I demanded.

'Because they are welcome here,' a voice said behind me.

I turned to see an old man standing in the door. White hair showed beneath the bandage that swathed his head, and he was so thin and so weak that he had to lean on the door frame for support. At first I did not recognise him, for when I had last spoken to him he had been a big man, well-built and vigorous, but Odda the Elder had taken an axe blow to the skull at Cynuit and he should have died from such a wound, yet somehow he had lived, and here he was, though now he was skeletal, pale, haggard and feeble. 'They are here,' Odda said, 'because they are welcome. As are you, Lord Uhtred, and you, Steapa.'

A woman was tending Odda the Elder. She had tried to pull him away from the door and take him back to his bed, but now she edged past him into the hall and stared at me. Then, seeing me, she did what she had done the very first time she saw me. She did what she had done when she came to marry me. She burst into tears.

It was Mildrith.

Mildrith was robed like a nun in a pale grey dress, belted with rope, over which she wore a large wooden cross. She had a close-fitting grey bonnet from which strands of her fair hair escaped. She stared at me, burst into tears, made the sign of the cross and vanished. A moment later Odda the Elder followed her, too frail to stand any longer, and the door closed.

'You are indeed welcome here,' Harald said, echoing Odda's words.

'But why are the Danes welcome here?' I asked.

Because Odda the Younger had made a truce. Harald explained it as we ate. No one in this part of Defnascir had heard how Svein's ships had been burned at Cynuit, they only knew that Svein's men, and their women and children, had marched south, burning and plundering, and Odda the Younger had taken his troops to Exanceaster and he had prepared for a siege, but instead Svein had offered to talk. The Danes, quite suddenly, had stopped raiding. Instead they had settled in Cridianton and sent an embassy to Exanceaster, and Svein and Odda had made their private peace.

'We sell them horses,' Harald said, 'and they pay well for them. Twenty shillings a stallion, fifteen a mare.'

'You sell them horses,' I said flatly.

'So they will go away,' Harald explained.

Servants threw a big birch log onto the fire. Sparks exploded outwards, scattering the hounds who lay just beyond the ring of hearth stones.

'How many men does Svein lead?' I asked.

'Many,' Harald said.

'Eight hundred?' I asked, 'nine?' Harald shrugged. 'They came in twenty-four ships,' I went on, 'only twenty-four. So how many men can he have? No more than a thousand, and we killed a few, and others must have died in the winter.'

'We think he has eight hundred,' Harald said reluctantly.

'And how many men in the fyrd? Two thousand?'

'Of which only four hundred are seasoned warriors,' Harald said. That was probably true. Most men of the fyrd are farmers, while every Dane is a sword-warrior, but Svein would never have pitted his eight hundred men against two thousand. Not because he feared losing, but because he feared that in gaining victory he would lose a hundred men. That was why he had stopped plundering and made his truce with Odda, because in southern Defnascir he could recover from his defeat at Cynuit. His men could rest, feed, make weapons and get horses. Svein was husbanding his men and making them stronger. 'It was not my choice,' Harald said defensively. 'The ealdorman ordered it.'

'And the king,' I retorted, 'ordered Odda to drive Svein out of Defnascir.'

'What do we know of the king's orders?' Harald asked bitterly, and it was my turn to give him news, to tell how Alfred had escaped Guthrum and was in the great swamp.

'And some time after Easter,' I said, 'we shall gather the shire fyrds and we shall cut Guthrum into pieces.' I stood. 'There will be no more horses sold to Svein,' I said it loudly so that every man in the big hall could hear me.

'But . . .' Harald began, then shook his head. He had doubtless been about to say that Odda the Younger, Ealdorman of Defnascir, had ordered the horses to be sold, but his voice trailed away.

'What are the king's orders?' I demanded of Steapa.

'No more horses,' he thundered.

There was silence until Harald irritably gestured at the harpist who struck a chord and began playing a melancholy tune. Someone began singing, but no one joined in and his voice trailed away. 'I must look to the sentinels,' Harald said, and he threw me an inquisitive look which I took as an invitation to join him, and so I buckled on my swords and then walked with him down Ocmundtun's long street to where three spearmen stood guard beside a wooden hut. Harald talked to them for a moment, then led me further east, away from the light of the sentinels' fire. A moon silvered the valley, lighting the empty road until the track vanished among trees. 'I have thirty fighting men,' Harald said suddenly.

He was telling me he was too weak to fight. 'How many men does Odda have in Exanceaster?' I asked.

'A hundred? Hundred and twenty?'

'The fyrd should have been raised.'

'I had no orders,' Harald said.

'Did you seek any?'

'Of course I did.' He was angry with me now. 'I told Odda we should drive Svein away, but he wouldn't listen.'

'Did he tell you the king ordered the fyrd raised?'

'No.' Harald paused, staring down the moonlit road. 'We heard nothing of Alfred, except that he'd been defeated and was hiding. And we heard the Danes were all across Wessex, and that more were gathering in Mercia.'

'Odda didn't think to attack Svein when he landed?'

'He thought to protect himself,' Harald said, 'and sent me to the Tamur.'

The Tamur was the river which divided Wessex from Cornwalum. 'The Britons are quiet?' I asked.

'Their priests are telling them not to fight us.'

'But priests or no priests,' I said, 'they'll cross the river if the Danes look like winning.'

'Aren't they winning already?' Harald asked bitterly.

'We're still free men,' I said.

He nodded at that. Behind us, in the town, a dog began howling and he turned as if the noise indicated trouble, but the howling stopped with a sharp yelp. He kicked a stone in the road. 'Svein frightens me,' he admitted suddenly.

'He's a frightening man,' I agreed.

'He's clever,' Harald said, 'clever, strong and savage.'

'A Dane,' I said drily.

294

'A ruthless man,' Harald went on.

'He is,' I agreed, 'and do you think that after you have fed him, supplied him with horses and given him shelter, he will leave you alone?'

'No,' he said, 'but Odda believes that.'

Then Odda was a fool. He was nursing a wolf cub that would tear him to shreds when it was strong enough. 'Why didn't Svein march north to join Guthrum?' I asked.

'I wouldn't know.'

But I knew. Guthrum had been in England for years now. He had tried to take Wessex before, and he had failed, but now, on the very brink of success, he had paused. Guthrum the Unlucky, he was called, and I suspected he had not changed. He was wealthy, led many men, but he was cautious. Svein, though, came from the Norsemen's settlements in Ireland and was a very different creature. He was younger than Guthrum, less wealthy than Guthrum, and led fewer men, but he was undoubtedly the better warrior. Now, bereft of his ships, he was weakened, but he had persuaded Odda the Younger to give him refuge and he gathered his strength so that when he did meet Guthrum he would not be a defeated leader in need of help, but a spear-Dane of power. Svein, I thought, was a far more dangerous man than Guthrum, and Odda the Younger was only making him more dangerous.

'Tomorrow,' I said, 'we must start raising the fyrd. Those are the king's orders.'

Harald nodded. I could not see his face in the darkness, but I sensed he was not happy, yet he was a sensible man and must have known that Svein had to be driven out of the shire. 'I shall send the messages,' he said, 'but Odda might stop the fyrd assembling. He's made his truce with Svein and he won't want me breaking it. Folk will obey him before they obey me.'

295

'And what of his father?' I asked. 'Will they obey him?'

'They will,' he said, 'but he's a sick man. You saw that. It's a miracle he lives at all.'

'Maybe because my wife nurses him?'

'Yes,' he said, and fell silent. There was something odd in the air now, something unexpressed, a discomfort. 'Your wife nurses him well,' he finished awkwardly.

'He's her godfather,' I said.

'So he is.'

'It is good to see her,' I said, not because I meant it, but because it was the proper thing to say and I could think of nothing else. 'And it will be good to see my son,' I added with more warmth.

'Your son,' Harald said flatly.

'He's here, isn't he?'

'Yes.' Harald flinched. He turned away to look at the moon and I thought he would say no more, but then he summoned his courage and looked back to me. 'Your son, Lord Uhtred,' he said, 'is in the churchyard.'

It took a few heartbeats for that to make sense, and then it did not make any sense at all, but left me confused. I touched my hammer amulet. 'In the churchyard?'

'It is not my place to tell you.'

'But you will tell me,' I said, and my voice sounded like Steapa's growl.

Harald stared at the moon-touched river, silver-white beneath the black trees. 'Your son died,' he said. He waited for my response, but I neither moved nor spoke. 'He choked to death.'

'Choked?'

'A pebble,' Harald said. 'He was just a baby. He must have picked the pebble up and swallowed it.'

'A pebble?' I asked.

'A woman was with him, but . . .' Harald's voice tailed

away. 'She tried to save him, but she could do nothing. He died.'

'On Saint Vincent's Day,' I said.

'You knew?'

'No,' I said, 'I didn't know.' But Saint Vincent's Day had been the day when Iseult drew Alfred's son, the Ætheling Edward, through the earth. And somewhere, Iseult had told me, a child must die so that the king's heir, the Ætheling, could live.

And it had been my child. Uhtred the Younger. Whom I had hardly known. Edward had been given breath and Uhtred had twitched and fought and gasped and died.

'I'm sorry,' Harald said. 'It was not my place to tell you, but you needed to know before you saw Mildrith again.'

'She hates me,' I said bleakly.

'Yes,' he said, 'she does.' He paused. 'I thought she would go mad with grief, but God has preserved her. She would like . . .'

'Like what?'

'To join the sisters at Cridianton. When the Danes leave. They have a nunnery there, a small house.'

I did not care what Mildrith did. 'And my son is buried here?'

'Under the yew tree,' he turned and pointed, 'beside the church.'

So let him stay there, I thought. Let him rest in his short grave to wait the chaos of the world's ending.

'Tomorrow,' I said, 'we raise the fyrd.'

Because there was a kingdom to save.

Priests were summoned to Harald's hall and the priests wrote the summons for the fyrd. Most thegns could not read, and many of their priests would probably struggle to decipher the few words, but the messengers would tell them what the parchments said. They were to arm their men and bring them to Ocmundtun, and the wax seal on the summons was the authority for those orders. The seal showed Odda the Elder's badge of a stag. 'It will take a week,' Harald warned me, 'for most of the fyrd to reach here, and the ealdorman will try to stop it happening at all.'

'What will he do?'

'Tell the thegns to ignore it, I suppose.'

'And Svein? What will he do?'

'Try to kill us?'

'And he has eight hundred men who can be here tomorrow,' I said.

'And I have thirty men,' Harald said bleakly.

'But we do have a fortress,' I said, pointing to the limestone ridge with its palisade.

I did not doubt that the Danes would come. By summoning the fyrd we threatened their safety, and Svein was not a man who would take a threat lightly, and so, while the messages were carried north and south, the townsfolk were told to take their valuables up to the fort beside the river. Some men were set to strengthening the palisade, others took livestock up onto the moor so the beasts could not be taken by the Danes, and Steapa went to every nearby settlement and demanded that men of fighting age go to Ocmundtun with any weapon they possessed, so that by that afternoon the fort was manned by over eighty men. Few were warriors, most had no weapons other than an axe, but from the foot of the hill they looked formidable enough. Women carried food and water to the fort, and most of the town reckoned to sleep up there, despite the rain, for fear that the Danes would come in the night.

Odda the Elder refused to go to the fort. He was too sick, he said, and too feeble, and if he was supposed to die then he would die in Harald's hall. Harald and I tried to persuade him, but he would not listen. 'Mildrith can go,' he said.

'No,' she said. She sat by Odda's bed, her hands clutched tight under the sleeves of her grey robe. She stared at me, challenge in her eyes, daring me to give her an order to abandon Odda and go to the fortress.

'I am sorry,' I said to her.

'Sorry?'

'About our son.'

'You were not a father to him,' she accused me. Her eyes glistened. 'You wanted him to be a Dane! You wanted him to be a pagan! You didn't even care for his soul!'

'I cared for him,' I said, but she ignored that. I had not sounded convincing, even to myself.

'His soul is safe,' Harald said gently. 'He is in the Lord Jesus's arms. He is happy.'

Mildrith looked at him and I saw how Harald's words had comforted her, though she still began crying. She caressed her wooden cross, then Odda the Elder reached out and patted her arm. 'If the Danes come, lord,' I said to him, 'I shall send men for you.' I turned then and went from the sickroom. I could not cope with Mildrith crying or with the thought of a dead son. Such things are difficult, much more difficult than making war, and so I buckled on my swords, picked up my shield and put on my splendid wolf-crested helmet so that, when Harald came from Odda's chamber, he checked to see me standing like a warlord by his hearth. 'If we make a big fire at the eastern end of town,' I said, 'we'll see the Danes come. It will give us time to carry Lord Odda to the fort.'

'Yes.' He looked up at the great rafters of his hall, and perhaps he was thinking that he would never see it thus again, for the Danes would come and the hall would burn. He made the sign of the cross.

'Fate is inexorable,' I told him. What else was there to say? The Danes might come, the hall might burn, but they were small things in the balance of a kingdom, and so I went to order the fire that would illuminate the eastern road, but the Danes did not come that night. It rained softly all through the darkness, so that in the morning the folk in the fort were wet, cold and unhappy. Then, in the dawn, the first men of the fyrd arrived. It might take days for the farther parts of the shire to receive their summons and to arm men and despatch them to Ocmundtun, but the nearer places sent men straight away so that by late morning there were close to three hundred beneath the fort. No more than seventy of those could be called warriors, men who had proper weapons, shields and at least a leather coat. The rest were farm labourers with hoes or sickles or axes.

Harald sent foraging parties to find grain. It was one thing to gather a force, quite another to feed it, and none of us knew how long we would have to keep the men assembled. If the Danes did not come to us, then we would have to go to them and force them from Cridianton, and for that we would need the whole fyrd of Defnascir. Odda the Younger, I thought, would never allow that to happen.

Nor did he. For, as the rain ended and the noontime prayers were said, Odda himself came to Ocmundtun and he did not come alone, but rode with sixty of his warriors in chain mail and as many Danes in their war-glory. The sun came out as they appeared from the eastern trees and it shone on mail and on spear points, on bridle chains and stirrup irons, on polished helmets and bright shield bosses. They spread into the pastures on either side of the road and advanced on Ocmundtun in a wide line, and at its centre were two standards. One, the black stag, was the banner of

Defnascir, while the other was a Danish triangle and displayed the white horse.

'There'll be no fight,' I told Harald.

'There won't?'

'Not enough of them. Svein can't afford to lose men, so he's come to talk.'

'I don't want to meet them here,' he gestured at the fort. 'We should be in the hall.'

He ordered that the best armed men should go down to the town, and there we filled the muddy street outside the hall as Odda and the Danes came from the east. The horsemen had to break their line to enter the town, making a column instead, and the column was led by three men. Odda was in the centre and he was flanked by two Danes, one of them Svein of the White Horse.

Svein looked magnificent, a silver-white warrior. He rode a white horse, wore a white woollen cloak, and his mail and boar-snouted helmet had been scrubbed with sand until they glowed silver in the watery sunlight. His shield bore a silvered boss around which a white horse had been painted. The leather of his bridle, saddle and scabbard had been bleached pale. He saw me, but showed no recognition, just looked along the line of men barring the street and seemed to dismiss them as useless. His banner of the white horse was carried by the second horseman who had the same darkened face as his master, a face hammered by sun and snow, ice and wind.

'Harald.' Odda the Younger had ridden ahead of the two Danes. He was sleek as ever, gleaming in mail, and with a black cloak draping his horse's rump. He smiled as though he welcomed the meeting. 'You have summoned the fyrd. Why?'

'Because the king commanded it,' Harald said.

Odda still smiled. He glanced at me, appeared not to notice

301

I was present, then looked to the hall door where Steapa had just appeared. The big man had been talking with Odda the Elder, and now he stared at Odda the Younger with astonishment. 'Steapa!' Odda the Younger said. 'Loyal Steapa! How good to see you!'

'You too, lord.'

'My faithful Steapa,' Odda said, plainly pleased to be reunited with his erstwhile bodyguard. 'Come here!' he commanded, and Steapa pushed past us and knelt in the mud by Odda's horse and reverently kissed his master's boot. 'Stand,' Odda said, 'stand. With you beside me, Steapa, who can hurt us?'

'No one, lord.'

'No one,' Odda repeated, then smiled at Harald. 'You said the king ordered the fyrd summoned? There is a king in Wessex?'

'There is a king in Wessex,' Harald said firmly.

'There is a king skulking in the marshes!' Odda said, loudly enough for all Harald's men to hear. 'He is the king of frogs, perhaps? A monarch of eels? What kind of king is that?'

I answered for Harald, only I answered in Danish. 'A king who ordered me to burn Svein's boats. Which I did. All but one, which I kept and still have.'

Svein took off his boar-snouted helmet and looked at me and again there was no recognition. His gaze was like that of the great serpent of death that lies at the foot of Yggdrasil. 'I burned the *White Horse*,' I told him, 'and warmed my hands on its flames.' Svein spat for answer. 'And the man beside you,' I spoke to Odda now, using English, 'is the man who burned your church at Cynuit, the man who killed the monks. The man who is cursed in heaven, in hell and in this world, yet now he is your ally?'

'Does that goat-turd speak for you?' Odda demanded of Harald.

'These men speak for me,' Harald said, indicating the warriors behind him.

'But by what right do you raise the fyrd?' Odda asked. 'I am ealdorman!'

'And who made you ealdorman?' Harald asked. He paused, but Odda gave no answer. 'The king of frogs?' Harald asked. 'The monarch of eels? If Alfred has no authority then you have lost yours with his.'

Odda was plainly surprised by Harald's defiance, and he was probably irritated by it, but he gave no sign of annoyance. He just went on smiling. 'I do believe,' he said to Harald, 'that you have misunderstood what happens in Defnascir.'

'Then explain to me,' Harald said.

'I shall,' Odda said, 'but we shall talk with ale and food.' He looked up at the sky. The brief sun was gone behind cloud and a chill wind was gusting the thatch of the street. 'And we should talk under a roof,' Odda suggested, 'before it rains again.'

There were matters to be agreed first, though that was done soon enough. The Danish horsemen would withdraw to the eastern end of the town while Harald's men would retreat to the fort. Each side could take ten men into the hall, and all of those men were to leave their weapons heaped in the street where they were to be guarded by six Danes and as many Saxons.

Harald's servants brought ale, bread, and cheese. There was no meat offered, for it was the season of Lent. Benches were placed at either side of the hearth. Svein crossed to our side of the fire as the benches were brought and at long last deigned to recognise me. 'It was really you who burned the ships?' he asked.

'Including yours.'

'The *White Horse* took a year and a day to build,' he said,

303

'and she was made of trees from which we'd hung Odin's sacrifices. She was a good ship.'

'She's all ash on the seashore now,' I said.

'Then one day I shall repay you,' he retorted, and though he spoke mildly, there was a world of threat in his voice. 'And you were wrong,' he added.

'Wrong?' I asked. 'Wrong to burn your ships?'

'There was no altar of gold at Cynuit.'

'Where you burned the monks,' I said.

'I burned them alive,' he agreed, 'and warmed my hands on their flames.' He smiled at that memory. 'You could join me again?' he suggested. 'I shall forgive you burning my ship, and you and I can fight side by side once more? I need good men. I pay well.'

'I am sworn to Alfred.'

'Ah,' he nodded. 'So be it. Enemies.' He went back to Odda's benches.

'You would see your father before we talk?' Harald asked Odda, gesturing towards the door at the hall's end.

'I shall see him,' Odda said, 'when our friendship is repaired. And you and I must be friends.' He said the last words loudly and they prompted men to sit on the benches. 'You summoned the fyrd,' he spoke to Harald, 'because Uhtred brought you orders from Alfred?'

'He did.'

'Then you did the right thing,' Odda said, 'and that is to be praised.' Svein, listening to the translation that was provided by one of his own men, stared flatly at us. 'And now you will do the right thing again,' Odda continued, 'and send the fyrd home.'

'The king has ordered otherwise,' Harald said.

'What king?' Odda asked.

'Alfred, who else?'

'But there are other kings in Wessex,' Odda said.

304

'Guthrum is King of East Anglia, and he is in Wessex, and some say Æthelwold will be crowned king before the summer.'

'Æthelwold?' Harald asked.

'You'd not heard?' Odda asked. 'Wulfhere of Wiltunscir has sided with Guthrum, and both Guthrum and Wulfhere have said Æthelwold will be King of Wessex. And why not? Is not Æthelwold the son of our last king? Should he not be king?'

Harald, uncertain, looked at me. He had not heard of Wulfhere's defection, and it was hard news for him. I nodded. 'Wulfhere is with Guthrum,' I said.

'So Æthelwold, son of Æthelred, will be king in Wessex,' Odda said, 'and Æthelwold has thousands of swords at his command. Ælfrig of Kent is with the Danes. There are Danes in Lundene, on Sceapig and on the walls of Contwaraburg. All northern Wessex is in Danish hands. There are Danes here, in Defnascir. What, tell me, is Alfred king of?'

'Of Wessex,' I said.

Odda ignored me, looking at Harald. 'Alfred has our oaths,' Harald said stubbornly.

'And I have your oath,' Odda reminded him. He sighed. 'God knows, Harald, no one was more loyal to Alfred than I. Yet he failed us! The Danes came and the Danes are here, and where is Alfred? Hiding! In a few weeks their armies will march! They will come from Mercia, from Lundene, from Kent! Their fleets will be off our coast. Armies of Danes and fleets of Vikings! What will you do then?'

Harald shifted uneasily. 'What will you do?' he retorted.

Odda gestured at Svein who, the question translated, spoke for the first time. I interpreted for Harald. Wessex is doomed, Svein said in his grating voice. By summer it will be swarming with Danes, with men newly come from the north, and the only Saxons who will live will be those men who aid the Danes now. Those who fight against the Danes, Svein said, will be dead, and their women will be whores and their children will be slaves and their homes will be lost and their names shall be forgotten like the smoke of an extinguished fire.

'And Æthelwold will be king?' I asked scornfully. 'You think we will all bow to a whoring drunkard?'

Odda shook his head. 'The Danes are generous,' he said, and he drew back his cloak and I saw that he wore six golden arm rings. 'To those who help them,' he said, 'there will be the rewards of land, wealth and honour.'

'And Æthelwold will be king?' I asked again.

Odda again gestured at Svein. The big Dane seemed bored, but he stirred himself. 'It is right,' he said, 'that Saxons should be ruled by a Saxon. We shall make a king here.'

I scorned that. They had made Saxon kings in Northumbria and in Mercia and those kings were feeble, leashed to the Danes, and then I understood what Svein meant and I laughed aloud. 'He's promised you the throne!' I accused Odda.

'I've heard more sense from a pig's fart,' Odda retorted, but I knew I was right. Æthelwold was Guthrum's candidate for the throne of Wessex, but Svein was no friend of Guthrum and would want his own Saxon as king. Odda.

'King Odda,' I said jeeringly, then spat into the fire.

Odda would have killed me for that, but we met under the terms of a truce and so he forced himself to ignore the insult. He looked at Harald. 'You have a choice, Harald,' he said, 'you can die or you can live.'

Harald was silent. He had not known about Wulfhere, and the news had appalled him. Wulfhere was the most powerful ealdorman in Wessex, and if he thought Alfred was doomed, then what was Harald to think? I could see the shire-reeve's uncertainty. His decency wanted him to declare loyalty to Alfred, but Odda had suggested that nothing but death would follow such a choice. 'I . . .' Harald began, then fell silent, unable to say what he thought for he did not know his own mind.

'The fyrd is raised,' I spoke for him, 'at the king's orders, and the king's orders are to drive the Danes from Defnascir.'

Odda spat into the fire for answer.

'Svein has been defeated,' I said. 'His ships are burned. He is like a whipped dog and you give him comfort.' Svein, when that was translated, gave me a look like the stroke of a whip. 'Svein,' I went on as though he was not present, 'must be driven back to Guthrum.'

'You have no authority here,' Odda said.

'I have Alfred's authority,' I said, 'and a written order telling you to drive Svein from your shire.'

'Alfred's orders mean nothing,' Odda said, 'and you croak like a swamp frog.' He turned to Steapa. 'You have unfinished business with Uhtred.'

Steapa looked uncertain for a heartbeat, then understood what his master meant. 'Yes, lord,' he said.

'Then finish it now.'

'Finish what now?' Harald asked.

'Your king,' Odda said the last word sarcastically, 'ordered Steapa and Uhtred to fight to the death. Yet both live! So your king's orders have not been obeyed.'

'There is a truce!' Harald protested.

'Either Uhtred stops interfering in the affairs of Defnascir,' Odda said forcefully, 'or I shall have Defnascir kill Uhtred. You want to know who is right? Alfred or me? You want to know who will be king in Wessex, Æthelwold or Alfred? Then put it to the test, Harald. Let Steapa and Uhtred finish their fight and see which man God favours. If Uhtred wins then I shall support you, and if he loses?' He smiled. He had no doubt who would win.

307

Harald stayed silent. I looked at Steapa and, as on the first time I met him, saw nothing on his face. He had promised to protect me, but that was before he had been reunited with his master. The Danes looked happy. Why should they mind two Saxons fighting? Harald, though, still hesitated, and then the weary, feeble voice sounded from the doorway at the back of the hall. 'Let them fight, Harald; let them fight.' Odda the Elder, swathed in a wolfskin blanket, stood at the door. He held a crucifix. 'Let them fight,' he said again, 'and God will guide the victor's arm.'

Harald looked at me. I nodded. I did not want to fight, but a man cannot back down from combat. What was I to do? Say that to expect God to indicate a course of action through a duel was nonsense? To appeal to Harald? To claim that everything Odda had said was wrong and that Alfred would win? If I had refused to fight I was granting the argument to Odda, and in truth he had half convinced me that Alfred was doomed, and Harald, I am sure, was wholly convinced. Yet there was more than mere pride making me fight in the hall that day. There was a belief, deep in my soul, that somehow Alfred would survive. I did not like him, I did not like his god, but I believed fate was on his side. So I nodded again, this time to Steapa. 'I do not want to fight you,' I said to him, 'but I have given an oath to Alfred, and my sword says he will win and that Danish blood will dung our fields.'

Steapa said nothing. He just flexed his huge arms, then waited as one of Odda's men went outside and returned with two swords. No shields, just swords. He had taken a pair of blades at random from the pile and he offered them to Steapa first who shook his head, indicating that I should have the choice. I closed my eyes, groped, and took the first hilt that I touched. It was a heavy sword, weighted towards its tip. A slashing weapon, not a piercing blade, and I knew I had chosen wrong.

Steapa took the other and scythed it through the air so that the blade sang. Svein, who had betrayed little emotion so far, looked impressed, while Odda the Younger smiled. 'You can put the sword down,' he told me, 'and thus yield the argument to me.'

Instead I walked to the clear space beside the hearth. I had no intention of attacking Steapa, but would let him come to me. I felt weary and resigned. Fate is inexorable.

'For my sake,' Odda the Elder spoke behind me, 'make it fast.'

'Yes, lord,' Steapa said, and he took a step towards me and then turned as fast as a striking snake and his blade whipped in a slash that took Odda the Younger's throat. The sword was not as sharp as it could have been, so that the blow drove Odda down, but it also ripped his gullet open so that blood spurted a blade's length into the air, then splashed into the fire where it hissed and bubbled. Odda was on the floor-rushes now, his legs twitching, his hands clutching at his throat that still pumped blood. He made a gargling noise, turned on his back and went into a spasm so that his heels drummed against the floor and then, just as Steapa stepped forward to finish him, he gave a last jerk and was dead.

Steapa drove the sword into the floor, leaving it quivering there. 'Alfred rescued me,' he announced to the hall. 'Alfred took me from the Danes. Alfred is my king.'

'And he has our oaths,' Odda the Elder added, 'and my son had no business making peace with the pagans.'

The Danes stepped back. Svein glanced at me, for I was still holding a sword, then he looked at the boar spears leaning against the wall, judging whether he could snatch one before I attacked him. I lowered the blade. 'We have a truce,' Harald said loudly.

'We have a truce,' I told Svein in Danish.

Svein spat on the bloody rushes, then he and his standard-bearer took another cautious backwards pace.

'But tomorrow,' Harald said, 'there will be no truce, and we shall come to kill you.'

The Danes rode from Ocmundtun. And next day they also went from Cridianton. They could have stayed if they wished. There were more than enough of them to defend Cridianton and make trouble in the shire, but Svein knew he would be besieged and, man by man, worn down until he had no force at all, and so he went north, going to join Guthrum, and I rode to Oxton. The land had never looked more beautiful, the trees were hazed with green and bullfinches were feasting on the first tight fruit buds, while anemones, stitchwort and white violets glowed in sheltered spots. Lambs ran from the buck hares in the pastures. The sun shimmered on the wide sea-reach of the Uisc and the sky was full of lark song beneath which the foxes took lambs, magpies and jays feasted on other birds' eggs, and ploughmen impaled crows at the edges of the fields to ensure a good harvest.

'There'll be butter soon,' a woman told me. She really wanted to know if I was returning to the estate, but I was not. I was saying farewell. There were slaves living there, doing their jobs, and I assured them Mildrith would appoint a steward sooner or later, then I went to the hall and I dug beside the post and found my hoard untouched. The Danes had not come to Oxton. Wirken, the sly priest of Exanmynster, heard I was at the hall and rode a donkey up to the estate. He assured me he had kept a watchful eye on the place, and doubtless he wanted a reward. 'It belongs to Mildrith now,' I told him.

'The Lady Mildrith? She lives?'

'She lives,' I said curtly, 'but her son is dead.'

'God rest his poor soul,' Wirken said, making the sign of

the cross. I was eating a scrap of ham and he looked at it hungrily, knowing I broke the rules of Lent. He said nothing, but I knew he was cursing me for a pagan.

'And the Lady Mildrith,' I went on, 'would live a chaste life now. She says she will join the sisters in Cridianton.'

'There are no sisters in Cridianton,' Wirken said. 'They're all dead. The Danes saw to that before they left.'

'Other nuns will settle there,' I said. Not that I cared, for the fate of a small nunnery was none of my business. Oxton was no longer my business. The Danes were my business, and the Danes had gone north and I would follow them.

For that was my life. That spring I was twenty-one years old and for half my life I had been with armies. I was not a farmer. I watched the slaves tearing the couch-grass from the home fields and knew the tasks of farming bored me. I was a warrior, and I had been driven from my home of Bebbanburg to the southern edge of England and I think I knew, as Wirken babbled on about how he had guarded the storehouses through the winter, that I was now going north again. Ever north. Back home.

'You lived off these storehouses all winter,' I accused the priest.

'I watched them all winter, lord.'

'And you got fat as you watched,' I said. I climbed into my saddle. Behind me were two bags, ripe with money, and they stayed there as I rode to Exanceaster and found Steapa in The Swan. Next morning, with six other warriors from Ealdorman Odda's guard, we rode north. Our way was marked by pillars of smoke, for Svein was burning and plundering as he went, but we had done what Alfred had wanted us to do. We had driven Svein back to Guthrum, so that now the two largest Danish armies were united. If Alfred had been stronger he might have left them separate and marched against each in turn, but Alfred knew he had only one chance to take back his kingdom, and that was to win one battle. He had to overwhelm all the Danes and destroy them in one blow, and his weapon was an army that existed only in his head. He had sent demands that the fyrd of Wessex would be summoned after Easter and before Pentecost, but no one knew whether it would actually appear. Perhaps we would ride from the swamp and find no one at the meeting place. Or perhaps the fyrd would come, and there would be too few men. The truth was that Alfred was too weak to fight, but to wait longer would only make him weaker. So he had to fight or lose his kingdom.

So we would fight.

Eleven

'You will have many sons,' Iseult told me. It was dark, though a half-moon was hazed by a mist. Somewhere to the north-east a dozen fires burned in the hills, evidence that a strong Danish patrol was watching the swamp. 'But I am sorry about Uhtred,' she said.

I wept for him then. I do not know why the tears had taken so long to come, but suddenly I was overwhelmed by the thought of his helplessness, his sudden smile and the pity of it all. Both my half-brothers and my half-sister had died when they were babies and I do not remember my father crying, though perhaps he did. I do remember my stepmother shrieking in grief, and how my father, disgusted by the sound, had gone hunting with his hawks and hounds.

'I saw three kingfishers yesterday,' Iseult said.

Tears were running down my cheeks, blurring the misted moon. I said nothing.

'Hild says the blue of the kingfisher's feathers is for the virgin and the red is for Christ's blood.'

'And what do you say?'

'That your son's death is my doing.'

'Wyrd bið ful aræd,' I said. Fate is fate. It cannot be changed or cheated. Alfred had insisted I marry Mildrith so I would be tied to Wessex and would put roots deep into

313

its rich soil, but I already had roots in Northumbria, roots twisted into the rock of Bebbanburg, and perhaps my son's death was a sign from the gods that I could not make a new home. Fate wanted me to go to my northern stronghold and until I reached Bebbanburg I would be a wanderer. Men fear wanderers for they have no rules. The Danes came as strangers, rootless and violent, and that, I thought, was why I was always happier in their company. Alfred could spend hours worrying about the righteousness of a law, whether it concerned the fate of orphans or the sanctity of boundary markers, and he was right to worry because folk cannot live together without law, or else every straying cow would lead to bloodshed, but the Danes hacked through the law with swords. It was easier that way, though once they had settled a land they started to make their own laws. 'It was not your fault,' I said. 'You don't command fate.'

'Hild says there is no such thing as fate,' Iseult said.

'Then Hild is wrong.'

'There is only the will of God,' Iseult said, 'and if we obey that we go to heaven.'

'And if we choose not to,' I said, 'isn't that fate?'

'That's the devil,' she said. 'We are sheep, Uhtred, and we choose our shepherd, a good one or a bad one.'

I thought Hild must have soured Iseult with Christianity, but I was wrong. It was a priest who had come to Æthelingæg while I had been in Defnascir who had filled her head with his religion. He was a British priest from Dyfed, a priest who spoke Iseult's native tongue and also knew both English and Danish. I was ready to hate him as I hated Brother Asser, but Father Pyrlig stumbled into our hut next morning booming that he had found five goose eggs and was dying of hunger. 'Dying! That's what I am, dying of starvation!' He looked pleased to see me. 'You're the famous Uhtred, eh? And Iseult tells me you hate Brother

Asser? Then you're a friend of mine. Why Abraham doesn't take Asser to his bosom I do not know, except maybe Abraham doesn't want the little bastard clinging to his bosom. I wouldn't. It would be like suckling a serpent, it would. Did I say I was hungry.'

He was twice my age and a big man, big-bellied and big-hearted. His hair stuck out in ungovernable clumps, he had a broken nose, only four teeth, and a broad smile. 'When I was a child,' he told me, 'ever such a little child, I used to eat mud. Can you believe that? Do Saxons eat mud? Of course they do, and I thought I don't want to eat mud. Mud is for toads, it is. So eventually I became a priest. And you know why? Because I never saw a hungry priest! Never! Did you ever see a hungry priest? Nor me!' All this tumbled out without any introduction, then he spoke earnestly to Iseult in her own tongue and I was sure he was pouring Christianity into her, but then he translated for me. 'I'm telling her that you can make a marvellous dish with goose eggs. Break them up, stir them well and add just a little crumbled cheese. So Defnascir is safe?'

'Unless the Danes send a fleet,' I said.

'Guthrum has that in mind,' Pyrlig said. 'He wants the Danes in Lundene to send their ships to the south coast.'

'You know that?'

'I do indeed, I do indeed! He told me! I've just spent ten days in Cippanhamm. I speak Danish, see, because I'm clever, and so I was an ambassador for my king. How about that! Me, who used to eat mud, an ambassador! Crumble the cheese finer, my love. That's right. I had to discover, you see, how much money Guthrum would pay us to bring our spearmen over the hills and start skewering Saxons. Now that's a fine ambition for a Briton, skewering Saxons, but the Danes are pagans, and God knows we can't have pagans loose in the world.'

315

'Why not?'

'It's just a fancy of mine,' he said, 'just a fancy.' He stabbed his finger into a tiny pot of butter, then licked it. 'It isn't really sour,' he told Iseult, 'not very, so stir it in.' He grinned at me. 'What happens when you put two bulls to a herd of cows?'

'One bull dies.'

'There you are! Gods are the same, which is why we don't want pagans here. We're cows and the gods are bulls.'

'So we get humped?'

He laughed. 'Theology's difficult. Anyway, God is my bull so here I am, telling the Saxons about Guthrum.'

'Did Guthrum offer you money?' I asked.

'He offered me the kingdoms of the world! He offered me gold, silver, amber and jet! He even offered me women, or boys if I had that taste, which I don't. And I didn't believe a single promise he made. Not that it mattered. The Britons aren't going to fight anyway. God doesn't want us to. No! My embassy was all a pretence. Brother Asser sent me. He wanted me to spy on the Danes, see? Then tell Alfred what I saw, so that's what I'm doing.'

'Asser sent you?'

'He wants Alfred to win. Not because he loves the Saxons, even Brother Asser isn't that curdled, but because he loves God.'

'And will Alfred win?'

'If God has anything to do with it, yes,' Pyrlig said cheerfully, then gave a shrug. 'But the Danes are strong in men. A big army! But they're not happy, I can tell you that. And they're all hungry. Not starving, mind you, but pulling their belts tighter than they'd like, and now Svein's there so there'll be even less food. Their own fault, of course. Too many men in Cippanhamm! And too many slaves! They have scores of slaves. But he's sending the slaves to Lundene, to sell them there. They need some baby eels, eh? That'll fatten them up.' The elvers were swarming into the Sæfern Sea and slithering up the shallow waterways of the swamp where they were being netted in abundance. There was no hunger in Æthelingæg, not if you gorged on elvers. 'I caught three basketfuls yesterday,' Pyrlig said happily, 'and a frog. It had a face just like Brother Asser so I gave it a blessing and threw it back. Don't just stir the eggs, girl! Beat them! I hear your son died?'

'Yes,' I answered stiffly.

'I am sorry,' he said with genuine feeling, 'I am truly sorry, for to lose a child is a desperate hard thing. I some-times think God must like children. He takes so many to him. I believe there's a garden in heaven, a green garden where children play all the time. He's got two sons of mine up there, and I tell you, the youngest must be making the angels scream. He'll be pulling the girls' hair and beating up the other boys like they were goose eggs.'

'You lost two sons?'

'But I kept three others and four daughters. Why do you think I'm never home?' He grinned at me. 'Noisy little things they are, children, and such appetites! Sweet Jesus, they'd eat a horse a day if they could! There are some folk who say priests shouldn't marry and there are times I think they're right. Do you have any bread, dearest?'

Iseult pointed to a net hanging from the roof. 'Cut the mould off,' she told me.

'I like to see a man obeying a woman,' Father Pyrlig said as I fetched the loaf.

'Why's that?' I asked.

'Because it means I'm not alone in this sorry world. Good God, but that Ælswith was weaned on gall juice, wasn't she? Got a tongue in her like a starving weasel! Poor Alfred.'

'He's happy enough.'

317

'Good God, man, that's the last thing he is! Some folk catch God like a disease, and he's one of them. He's like a cow after winter, he is.'

'He is?'

'You know when the late spring grass comes in? All green and new and rich? And you put the poor cow out to eat and she blows up like a bladder? She's nothing but shit and wind and then she gets the staggers and drops down dead if you don't take her off the grass for a while. That's Alfred. He got too much of the good green grass of God, and now he's sick on it. But he's a good man, a good man. Too thin, he is, but good. A living saint, no less. Ah, good girl, let's eat.' He scooped some of the eggs with his fingers, then passed the pot to me. 'Thank God it's Easter next week,' he said with his mouth full so that scraps of egg lodged in his huge beard, 'and then we can eat meat again. I'm wasting away without meat. You know Iseult will be baptised at Easter?'

'She told me,' I said shortly.

'And you don't approve? Just think of it as a good wash, then maybe you won't mind so much.'

I was not in Æthelingæg for Iseult's baptism, nor did I wish to be, for I knew Easter with Alfred would be nothing but prayers and psalms and priests and sermons. Instead I took Steapa and fifty men up into the hills, going towards Cippanhamm, for Alfred had ordered that the Danes were to be harried mercilessly in the next few weeks. He had decided to assemble the fyrd of Wessex close to Ascension Day, which was just six weeks away, and those were the weeks in which Guthrum would be hoping to revive his hungry horses on the spring grass, and so we rode to ambush Danish forage parties. Kill one forage party and the next must be protected by a hundred extra horsemen, and that wearies the horses even more and so requires still more

318

forage. It worked for a while, but then Guthrum began sending his foragers north into Mercia where they were not opposed.

It was a time of waiting. There were two smiths in Æthelingæg now and, though neither had all the equipment they wanted, and though fuel for their furnaces was scarce, they were making good spear points. One of my jobs was to take men to cut ash poles for the spear shafts.

Alfred was writing letters, trying to discover how many men the shires could bring to battle, and he sent priests to Frankia to persuade the thegns who had fled there to return. More spies came from Cippanhamm confirming that Svein had joined Guthrum, and that Guthrum was strengthening his horses and raising men from the Danish parts of England. He was ordering his West Saxon allies like Wulfhere to arm their men, and warning his garrisons in Wintanceaster, Readingum and Baðum that they must be ready to abandon their ramparts and march to his aid. Guthrum had his own spies and must have known Alfred was planning to assemble an army, and I dare say he welcomed that news for such an army would be Alfred's last hope and, should Guthrum destroy the fyrd, Wessex would fall never to rise again.

Æthelingæg seethed with rumour. Guthrum, it was said, had five thousand men. Ships had come from Denmark and a new army of Norsemen had sailed from Ireland. The Britons were marching. The fyrd of Mercia was on Guthrum's side, and it was said the Danes had set up a great camp at Cracgelad on the River Temes where thousands of Mercian troops, both Danish and Saxon, were assembling. The rumours of Guthrum's strength crossed the sea and Wilfrith of Hamptonscir wrote from Frankia begging Alfred to flee Wessex. 'Take ship to this coast,' he wrote, 'and save your family.'

Leofric rarely rode on patrols with us, but stayed in

Æthelingæg for he had been named commander of the king's bodyguard. He was proud of that, as he should have been, for he had been peasant-born and he could neither read nor write, and Alfred usually insisted that his commanders were literate. Eanflæd's influence was behind the appointment, for she had become a confidante of Ælswith. Alfred's wife went nowhere without Eanflæd, even in church the one-time whore sat just behind Ælswith, and when Alfred held court, Eanflæd was always there. 'The queen doesn't like you,' Eanflæd told me one rare day when I found her alone.

'She's not a queen,' I said. 'Wessex doesn't have queens.'

'She should be a queen,' she said resentfully, 'it would be right and proper.' She was carrying a heap of plants and I noticed her forearms were a pale green. 'Dyeing,' she explained brusquely, and I followed her to where a great cauldron was bubbling on a fire. She threw in the plants and began stirring the mess in the pot. 'We're making green linen,' she said.

'Green linen?'

'Alfred must have a banner,' she said indignantly. 'He can't fight without a banner.' The women were making two banners. One was the great green dragon flag of Wessex, while the other bore the cross of Christianity. 'Your Iseult's working on the cross,' Eanflæd told me.

'I know.'

'You should have been at her baptism.'

'I was killing Danes.'

'But I'm glad she's baptised. Come to her senses, she has.'

In truth, I thought, Iseult had been battered into Christianity. For weeks she had endured the rancour of Alfred's churchmen, had been accused of witchcraft and of being the devil's instrument, and it had worn her down. Then came Hild with her gentler Christianity, and Pyrlig who spoke of God in Iseult's tongue, and Iseult had been persuaded. That meant I was the only pagan left in the swamp and Eanflæd glanced pointedly at my hammer amulet. She said nothing of it, instead asking me whether I truly believed we could defeat the Danes.

'Yes,' I said confidently, though of course I did not know.

'How many men will Guthrum have?'

I knew the questions were not Eanflæd's, but Ælswith's. Alfred's wife wanted to know if her husband had any chance of survival or whether they should take the ship we had captured from Svein and sail to Frankia. 'Guthrum will lead four thousand men,' I said, 'at least.'

'At least?'

'Depends how many come from Mercia,' I said, then thought for a heartbeat, 'but I expect four thousand.'

'And Wessex?'

'The same,' I said. I was lying. With enormous luck we could assemble three thousand, but I doubted it. Two thousand? Not likely, but possible. My real fear was that Alfred would raise his banner and no one would come, or that only a few hundred men would arrive. We could lead three hundred from Æthelingæg, but what could three hundred do against Guthrum's great army?

Alfred also worried about numbers, and he sent me to Hamptonscir to discover how much of the shire was occupied by the Danes. I found them well entrenched in the north, but the south of the shire was free of them and in Hamtun, where Alfred's fleet was based, the warships were still drawn up on the beach. Burgweard, the fleet's commander, had over a hundred men in the town, all that was left of his crews, and he had them manning the palisade. He claimed he could not leave Hamtun for fear that the Danes would attack and capture the ships, but I had Alfred's scrap of parchment with his dragon seal on it, and I used it to order him to keep thirty men to protect the ships and bring the rest to Alfred.

'When?' he asked gloomily.

'When you're summoned,' I said, 'but it will be soon. And you're to raise the local fyrd too. Bring them.'

'And if the Danes come here?' he asked, 'if they come by sea?'

'Then we lose the fleet,' I said, 'and we build another.'

His fear was real enough. Danish ships were off the south coast again. For the moment, rather than attempt an invasion, they were being Vikings. They landed, raided, raped, burned, stole and went to sea again, but they were numerous enough for Alfred to worry that a whole army might land somewhere on the coast and march against him. We were harassed by that fear and by the knowledge that we were few and the enemy numerous, and that the enemy's horses were fattening on the new grass.

'Ascension Day,' Alfred announced on the day I returned from Hamtun.

That was the day we should be ready in Æthelingæg, and on the Sunday after, which was the Feast of Saint Monica, we would gather the fyrd, if there was a fyrd. Reports said the Danes were readying to march and it was plain they would launch their attack south towards Wintanceaster, the town that was the capital of Wessex, and to protect it, to bar Guthrum's road south, the fyrd would gather at Egbert's Stone. I had never heard of the place, but Leofric assured me it was an important spot, the place where King Egbert, Alfred's grandfather, had given judgements. 'It isn't one stone,' he said, 'but three.'

'Three?'

'Two big pillars and another boulder on top. The giants made it in the old days.'

And so the summons was issued. Bring every man, the parchments instructed, bring every weapon and say your prayers, for what is left of Wessex will meet at Egbert's Stone

322

to carry battle to the Danes, and no sooner was the summons sent than disaster struck. It came just a week before the fyrd was to gather.

Huppa, Ealdorman of Thornsæta, wrote that forty Danish ships were off his coast, and that he dared not lead the fyrd away from their threat. Worse, because the Danes were so numerous, he had begged Harald of Defnascir to lend him men.

That letter almost destroyed Alfred's spirits. He had clung to his dream of surprising Guthrum by raising an unexpectedly powerful army, but all his hopes were now shredding away. He had always been thin, but suddenly he looked haggard and he spent hours in the church, wrestling with God, unable to understand why the Almighty had so suddenly turned against him. And two days after the news of the Danish fleet, Svein of the White Horse led three hundred mounted men in a raid against the hills on the edge of the swamp and, because scores of men from the Sumorsæte fyrd had gathered in Æthelingæg, Svein discovered and stole their horses. We had neither the room nor the forage to keep many horses in Æthelingæg itself, and so they were pastured beyond the causeway, and I watched from the fort as Svein, riding a white horse and wearing his white-plumed helmet and white cloak, rounded up the beasts and drove them away. There was nothing I could do to stop him. I had twenty men in the fort and Svein was leading hundreds.

'Why were the horses not guarded?' Alfred wanted to know.

'They were,' Wiglaf, Ealdorman of Sumorsæte, said, 'and the guards died.' He saw Alfred's anger, but not his despair. 'We haven't seen a Dane here for weeks!' he pleaded, 'how were we to know they'd come in force?'

'How many men died?'

'Only twelve.'

'Only?' Alfred asked, wincing, 'and how many horses lost?'

'Sixty-three.'

On the night before Ascension Day Alfred walked beside the river. Beocca, faithful as a hound, followed him at a distance, wanting to offer the king God's reassurance, but instead Alfred called to me. There was a moon, and its light shadowed his cheeks and made his pale eyes look almost white. 'How many men will we have?' he asked abruptly.

I did not need to think about the answer. 'Two thousand.'

He nodded. He knew that number as well as I did.

'Maybe a few more,' I suggested.

He grunted at that. We would lead three hundred and fifty men from Æthelingæg and Wiglaf, Ealdorman of Sumorsæte, had promised a thousand, though in truth I doubted if that many would come. The fyrd of Wiltunscir had been weakened by Wulfhere's defection, but the southern part of the shire should yield five hundred men, and we could expect some from Hamptonscir, but beyond that we would depend on whatever few men made it past the Danish garrisons that now ringed the heartland of Wessex. If Defnascir and Thornsæta had sent their fyrds then we would have numbered closer to four thousand, but they were not coming.

'And Guthrum?' Alfred asked, 'how many will he have?'

'Four thousand.'

'More like five,' Alfred said. He stared at the river that was running low between the muddy banks. The water rippled about the wicker fish traps. 'So should we fight?'

'What choice do we have?'

He smiled at that. 'We have a choice, Uhtred,' he assured me. 'We can run away. We can go to Frankia. I could become a king in exile and pray that God brings me back.'

'You think God will?'

'No,' he admitted. If he ran away then he knew he would die in exile.

'So we fight,' I said.

'And on my conscience,' he said, 'I will for ever bear the weight of all those men who died in a hopeless cause. Two thousand against five thousand? How can I justify leading so few against so many?'

'You know how.'

'So I can be king?'

'So that we are not slaves in our own land,' I said.

He pondered that for a while. An owl flew low overhead, a sudden surprise of white feathers and the rush of air across stubby wings. It was an omen, I knew, but of what kind? 'Perhaps we are being punished,' Alfred said.

'For what?'

'For taking the land from the Britons?'

That seemed nonsense to me. If Alfred's god wanted to punish him for his ancestors having taken the land from the Britons, then why send the Danes? Why not send the Britons? God could resurrect Arthur and let his people have their revenge, but why send a new people to take the land? 'Do you want Wessex or not?' I asked harshly.

He said nothing for a while, then gave a sad smile. 'In my conscience,' he said, 'I can find no hope for this fight, but as a Christian I must believe we can win it. God will not let us lose.'

'Nor will this,' I said, and I slapped Serpent-Breath's hilt.

'So simple?' he asked.

'Life is simple,' I said. 'Ale, women, sword and reputation. Nothing else matters.'

He shook his head and I knew he was thinking about God and prayer and duty, but he did not argue. 'So if you were I, Uhtred,' he said, 'would you march?'

'You've already made up your mind, lord,' I said, 'so why ask me?'

He nodded. A dog barked in the village and he turned to

stare at the cottages and the hall and the church he had made with its tall alder cross. 'Tomorrow,' he said, 'you will take a hundred horsemen and patrol ahead of the army.'

'Yes, lord.'

'And when we meet the enemy,' he went on, still staring at the cross, 'you will choose fifty or sixty men from the bodyguard. The best you can find. And you will guard my banners.'

He did not say more, but nor did he need to. What he meant was that I was to take the best warriors, the most savage men, the dangerous warriors who loved battle, and I was to lead them in the place where the fight would be hardest, for an enemy loves to capture his foe's banners. It was an honour to be asked and, if the battle was lost, an almost certain death sentence. 'I shall do it gladly, lord,' I said, 'but ask a favour of you in return.'

'If I can,' he said guardedly.

'If you can,' I said, 'don't bury me. Burn my body on a pyre, and put a sword in my hand.'

He hesitated, then nodded, knowing he had agreed to a pagan funeral. 'I never told you,' he said, 'that I am sorry about your son.'

'So am I, lord.'

'But he is with God, Uhtred, he is assuredly with God.'

'So I'm told, lord, so I'm told.'

And next day we marched. Fate is inexorable, and though numbers and reason told us we could not win, we dared not lose and so we marched to Egbert's Stone.

We marched with ceremony. Twenty-three priests and eighteen monks formed our vanguard and chanted a psalm as they led Alfred's forces away from the fort guarding the southern trackway and east towards the heartland of Wessex.

They chanted in Latin so the words meant nothing to me, but Father Pyrlig had been given use of one of Alfred's horses and, dressed in a leather coat and with a great sword strapped to his side and with a stout-shafted boar spear on one shoulder, he rode alongside me and translated the words. '"God,"' he said, '"you have abandoned me, you have scattered us, you are angry with us, now turn to us again."' That sounds a reasonable request, doesn't it? You've kicked us in the face, so now give us a cuddle, eh?'

'It really means that?'

'Not the bit about kicks and cuddles. That was me.' He grinned at me. 'I do miss war. Isn't that a sin?'

'You've seen war?'

'Seen it? I was a warrior before I joined the church! Pyrlig the Fearless, they called me. I killed four Saxons in a day once. All by myself and I had nothing but a spear. And they had swords and shields, they did. Back home they made a song about me, but mind you, the Britons will sing about anything. I can sing you the song, if you like? It tells how I slaughtered three hundred and ninety-four Saxons in one day, but it's not entirely accurate.'

'So how many did you kill?'

'I told you. Four.' He laughed.

'So how did you learn English?'

'My mother was a Saxon, poor thing. She was taken in a raid on Mercia and became a slave.'

'So why did you stop being a warrior?'

'Because I found God, Uhtred. Or God found me. And I was becoming too proud. Songs about yourself go to your head and I was wickedly proud of myself, and pride is a terrible thing.'

'It's a warrior's weapon,' I said.

327

'It is indeed,' he agreed, 'and that is why it is a terrible thing, and why I pray God purges me of it.'

We were well ahead of the priests now, climbing towards the nearest hilltop to look north and east for the enemy, but the churchmen's voices followed us, their chant strong in the morning air. '"Through God we shall do bravely,"' Father Pyrlig interpreted for me, '"and God shall trample down our enemies". Now there's a blessed thought for a fine morning, Lord Uhtred!'

'The Danes are saying their own prayers, father.'

'But to what god, eh? No point in shouting at a deaf man, is there?' He curbed his horse at the hilltop and stared northwards. 'Not even a mouse stirring.'

'The Danes are watching,' I said, 'we can't see them, but they can see us.'

If they were watching then what they could see was Alfred's three hundred and fifty men riding or walking away from the swamp, and in the distance another five or six hundred men who were the fyrd from the western part of Sumorsæte who had camped to the south of the swamp and now marched to join our smaller column. Most of the men from Æthelingæg were real soldiers, trained to stand in the shield wall, but we also had fifty of the marshmen. I had wanted Eofer, the strong bowman, to come with us, but he could not fight without his niece telling him what to do and I had no intention of taking a child to war and so we had left Eofer behind. A good number of women and children were following the column, though Alfred had sent Ælswith and his children south to Scireburnan under a guard of forty men. We could hardly spare those men, but Alfred insisted his family go. Ælswith was to wait in Scireburnan and, if news came that her husband was defeated and the Danes victorious, she was to flee south to the coast and find a ship that would take her to Frankia. She was also instructed to take with her whatever books she could find in Scireburnan, for Alfred reckoned the Danes would burn every book in Wessex and so Ælswith was to rescue the gospel books and saints' lives and church fathers and histories and philosophers and thus raise her son Edward to become a learned king in exile.

Iseult was with the army, walking with Hild and with Eanflæd who had upset Ælswith by insisting on following Leofric. The women led packhorses which carried the army's shields, food and spare spears. Nearly every woman was equipped with some kind of weapon. Even Hild, a nun, wanted to take revenge on the Danes who had whored her and so carried a long, narrow-bladed knife. 'God help the Danes,' Father Pyrlig had said when he saw the women gather, 'if that lot get among them.'

He and I now trotted eastwards. I had horsemen ringing the column, riding on every crest, staying in sight of each other, and ready to signal if they saw any sign of the enemy, but there was none. We rode or marched under a spring sky, through a land bright with flowers, and the priests and monks kept up their chanting, and sometimes the men behind, who followed Alfred's two standard bearers, would start singing a battle song.

Father Pyrlig beat his hand in time to the singing, then gave me a big grin. 'I expect Iseult sings to you, doesn't she?'

'She does.'

'We Britons love to sing! I must teach her some hymns.' He saw my sour look and laughed. 'Don't worry, Uhtred, she's no Christian.'

'She isn't?' I asked, surprised.

'Well, she is, for the moment. I'm sorry you didn't come to her baptism. It was cold, that water! Fair froze me!'

'She's baptised,' I said, 'but you say she's no Christian?'

329

'She is and she isn't,' Pyrlig said with a grin. 'She is now, see, because she's among Christians. But she's still a shadow queen, and she won't forget it.'

'You believe in shadow queens?'

'Of course I do! Good God, man! She is one!' He made the sign of the cross.

'Brother Asser called her a witch,' I said, 'a sorceress.'

'Well he would, wouldn't he? He's a monk! Monks don't marry. He's terrified of women, Brother Asser, unless they're very ugly and then he bullies them. But show him a pretty young thing and he goes all addled. And of course he hates the power of women.'

'Power?'

'Not just tits, I mean. God knows tits are powerful enough, but the real thing. Power! My mother had it. She was no shadow queen, mind you, but she was a healer and a scryer.'

'She saw the future?'

He shook his head. 'She knew what was happening far off. When my father died she suddenly screamed. Screamed fit to kill herself because she knew what had happened. She was right, too. The poor man was cut down by a Saxon. But she was best as a healer. Folk came to her from miles around. It didn't matter that she was born a Saxon, they'd walk for a week to fetch the touch of her hand. Me? I got it for free! She banged me about, she did, and I dare say I deserved it, but she was a rare healer. And, of course, the priests don't like that.'

'Why not?'

'Because we priests tell folk that all power comes from God, and if it doesn't come from God then it must be evil, see? So when folk are ill the church wants them to pray and to give the priests money. Priests don't like it when they don't understand things, and they don't like folk going to the women to be healed. But what else are folk to do? My

330

mother's hand, God rest her Saxon soul, was better than any prayer! Better than the touch of the sacraments! I wouldn't stop folk going to see a healer. I'd tell them to!' He stopped talking because I raised my hand. I had seen movement on a hillside to the north, but it was only a deer. I dropped my hand and kicked the horse on. 'Now your Iseult,' Pyrlig went on, 'she's been raised with the power and she won't lose it.'

'Didn't the baptism wash it out of her?'

'Not at all! It just made her a bit colder and cleaner. Nothing wrong with a scrub once or twice a year.' He laughed. 'But she was frightened back there in the swamp. You were gone and all around were Saxons and they were spitting that she was a pagan, so what did you think she would do? She wants to be one of them, she wants folk to stop spitting at her, so she said she'd be baptised. And maybe she really is a Christian? I'd praise God for that mercy, but I'd rather praise him for making her happy.'

'You don't think she is?'

'Of course she isn't! She's in love with you!' He laughed. 'And being in love with you means living among the Saxons, doesn't it? Poor girl. She's like a beautiful young hind that finds herself living among grunting pigs.'

'What a gift for words you have,' I said.

He laughed, delighted with his insult. 'Win your war, Lord Uhtred,' he said, 'then take her away from us priests and give her lots of children. She'll be happy, and one day she'll be truly wise. That's the women's real gift, to be wise, and not many men have it.'

And my gift was to be a warrior, though there was no fighting that day. We saw no Danes, though I was certain they had seen us and that by now Guthrum would have been told that Alfred had at last come from the swamp and was marching inland. We were giving him the opportunity to destroy us, to finish Wessex, and I knew that the Danes would be readying to march on us.

We spent that night in an earthen fort built by the old people, and next morning went north and east through a hungry land. I rode ahead, going into the hills to look for the enemy, but again the world seemed empty. Rooks flew, hares danced and cuckoos called from the woods that were thick with bluebells, but there were no Danes. I rode along a high ridge, gazing northwards, and saw nothing, and when the sun was at its height I turned east. There were ten of us in my band and our guide was a man from Wiltunscir who knew the country and he led us towards the valley of the Wilig where Egbert's Stone stands.

A mile or so short of the valley we saw horsemen, but they were to the south of us and we galloped across ungrazed pastureland to find it was Alfred, escorted by Leofric, five soldiers and four priests. 'Have you been to the stone?' Alfred called out eagerly as we closed on him.

'No, lord.'

'Doubtless there are men there,' he said, disappointed that I could not bring him news.

'I didn't see any Danes either, lord.'

'It'll take them two days to organise,' he said dismissively. 'But they'll come! They'll come! And we shall beat them!' He twisted in his saddle to look at Father Beocca, who was one of the priests. 'Are you sore, father?'

'Mightily sore, lord.'

'You're no horseman, Beocca, no horseman, but it's not much farther. Not much farther, then you can rest!' Alfred was in a feverish mood. 'Rest before we fight, eh! Rest and pray, father, then pray and fight. Pray and fight!' He kicked his horse into a gallop and we pounded after him through a pink-blossomed orchard and up a slope, then across a long hilltop where the bones of dead cattle lay in the new grass.

White mayflower edged the woods at the foot of the hill and a hawk slanted away from us, sliding across the valley towards the charred remains of a barn.

'It's just across the crest, lord!' my guide shouted at me.

'What is?'

'Defereal, lord!'

Defereal was the name of the settlement in the valley of the River Wilig where Egbert's Stone waited, and Alfred now spurred his horse so that his blue cloak flapped behind him. We were all galloping, spread across the hilltop, racing to be the first over the crest to see the Saxon forces, then Father Beocca's horse stumbled. He was, as Alfred said, a bad horseman, but that was no surprise for he was both lame and palsied, and when the horse tipped forward Beocca tumbled from the saddle. I saw him rolling in the grass and turned my horse back. 'I'm not hurt,' he shouted at me, 'not hurt! Not much. Go on, Uhtred, go on!'

I caught his horse. Beocca was on his feet now, limping as fast as he could to where Alfred and the other horsemen stood in a line gazing into the valley beyond. 'We should have brought the banners,' Beocca said as I gave him his reins.

'The banners?'

'So the fyrd knows their king has come,' he said breathlessly. 'They should see his banners on the skyline, Uhtred, and know he has come. The cross and the dragon, eh? *In hoc signo*! Alfred will be the new Constantine, Uhtred, a warrior of the cross! *In hoc signo*, God be praised, God be praised, God indeed be mightily praised.'

I had no idea what he meant, and nor did I care.

For I had reached the hilltop and could stare down into the long lovely valley of the Wilig.

Which was empty.

Not a man in sight. Just the river and the willows and

the water meadows and the alders and a heron flying and the grass bending in the wind and the triple stone of Egbert on a slope above the Wilig where an army was supposed to gather. And there was not one man there. Not one single man in sight. The valley was empty.

The men we had brought from Æthelingæg straggled into the valley, and with them now was the fyrd of Sumorsæte. Together they numbered just over a thousand men, and about half were equipped to fight in the shield wall while the rest were only good for shoving the front ranks forward or for dealing with the enemy wounded or, more likely, dying.

I could not face Alfred's disappointment. He said nothing about it, but his thin face was pale and set hard as he busied himself deciding where the thousand men should camp, and where our few horses should be pastured. I rode up a high hill that lay to the north of the encampment, taking a score of men including Leofric, Steapa and Father Pyrlig. The hill was steep, though that had not stopped the old people from making one of their strange graves high on the slope. The grave was a long mound and Pyrlig made a wide detour rather than ride past it. 'Full of dragons, it is,' he explained to me.

'You've seen a dragon?' I asked.

'Would I be alive if I had? No one sees a dragon and lives!'

I turned in the saddle and stared at the mound. 'I thought folk were buried there?'

'They are! And their treasures! So the dragon guards the hoard. That's what dragons do. Bury gold and you hatch a dragon, see?'

The horses had a struggle to climb the steep slope, but

at its summit we were rewarded by a stretch of firm turf that offered views far to the north. I had climbed the hill to watch for Danes. Alfred might believe that it would be two or three days before we saw them, but I expected their scouts to be close and it was possible that a war-band might try to harass the men camping by the Wilig.

Yet I saw no one. To the north-east were great downs, sheep hills, while straight ahead was the lower ground where the cloud shadows raced across fields and over blossoming mayflower and darkened the bright green new leaves.

'So what happens now?' Leofric asked me.

'You tell me.'

'A thousand men? We can't fight the Danes with a thousand men.'

I said nothing. Far off, on the northern horizon, there were dark clouds.

'We can't even stay here!' Leofric said, 'so where do we go?'

'Back to the swamp?' Father Pyrlig suggested.

'The Danes will bring more ships,' I said, 'and eventually they'll capture the swamp. If they send a hundred ships up the rivers then the swamp is theirs.'

'Go to Defnascir,' Steapa growled.

And the same thing would happen there, I thought. We would be safe for a time in Defnascir's tangle of hills and woods, but the Danes would come and there would be a succession of little fights and bit by bit Alfred would be bled to death. And once the Danes across the sea knew that Alfred was pinned into a corner of Wessex they would bring more ships to take the good land that he could not hold. And that, I thought, was why he had been right to try and end the war in one blow, because he dared not let Wessex's weakness become known.

Except we were weak. We were a thousand men. We were pathetic. We were dreams fallen to earth, and suddenly I began to laugh. 'What is it?' Leofric asked.

'I was thinking that Alfred insisted I learn to read,' I said, 'and for what?'

He smiled, remembering. It was one of Alfred's rules that every man who commanded sizeable bodies of troops must be able to read, though it was a rule he had ignored when he made Leofric commander of his bodyguard. It seemed funny at that moment. All that effort so I could read his orders and he had never sent me one. Not one. 'Reading is useful,' Pyrlig said.

'What for?'

He thought about it. The wind gusted, flapping his hair and beard. 'You can read all those good stories in the gospel-book,' he suggested brightly, 'and the saints' lives! How about those, eh? They're full of lovely things, they are. There was Saint Donwen! Beautiful woman she was, and she gave her lover a drink that turned him into ice.'

'Why did she do that?' Leofric asked.

'Didn't want to marry him, see?' Pyrlig said, trying to cheer us up, but no one wanted to hear more about the frigid Saint Donwen so he turned and stared northwards. 'That's where they'll come from, is it?' he asked.

'Probably,' I said, and then I saw them, or thought I did. There was a movement on the far hills, something stirring in the cloud shadow and I wished Iseult was on the hilltop for she had remarkable eyesight, but she would have needed a horse to climb to that summit and there were no horses to spare for women. The Danes had thousands of horses, all the beasts they had captured from Alfred at Cippanhamm, and all the animals they had stolen across Wessex, and now I was watching a group of horsemen on that far hill. Scouts, probably, and they would have seen us. Then they were gone. It had been a glimpse, no more, and so far away that I could not be sure of what I had seen. 'Or perhaps they won't come at all,' I went on, 'perhaps they'll march around us. Capture Wintanceaster and everywhere else.'

'The bastards will come,' Leofric said grimly, and I thought he was probably right. The Danes would know we were here, they would want to destroy us, and after that all would be easy for them.

Pyrlig turned his horse as if to ride back down to the valley, then paused. 'So it's hopeless, is it?' he asked.

'They'll outnumber us four or five to one,' I said.

'Then we must fight harder!'

I smiled. 'Every Dane who comes to Britain, father,' I explained, 'is a warrior. The farmers stay in Denmark, but the wild men come here. And us? We're nearly all farmers and it takes three or four farmers to beat down a warrior.'

'You're a warrior,' he said, 'all of you! You're warriors! You all know how to fight! You can inspire men, and lead men, and kill your enemies. And God is on your side. With God on your side, who can beat you, eh? You want a sign?'

'Give me a sign,' I said.

'Then look,' he said, and pointed down to the Wilig, and I turned my horse and there, in the afternoon sun, was the miracle we had wanted. Men were coming. Men in their hundreds. Men from the east and men from the south, men streaming down from the hills, men of the West Saxon fyrd, coming at their king's command to save their country.

'Now it's only two farmers to one warrior!' Pyrlig said cheerfully.

'Up to our arseholes,' Leofric said.

But we were not alone any longer. The fyrd was gathering.

The site of the Battle of Ethandun, 878

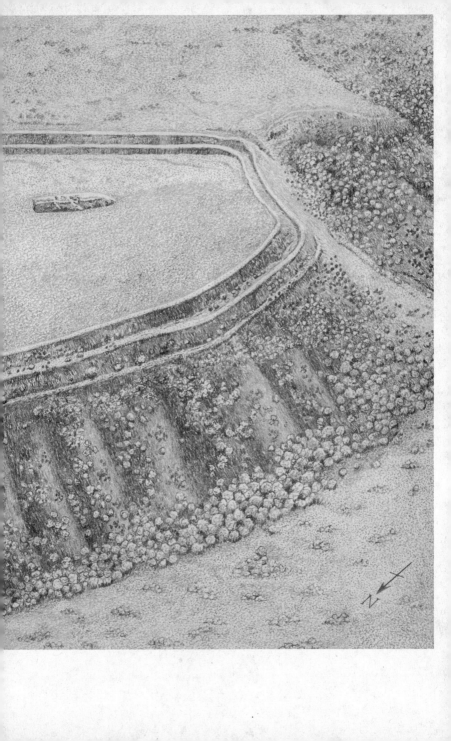

PART THREE

The Fyrd

Twelve

Most men came in large groups, led by their thegns, while others arrived in small bands, but together they swelled into an army. Arnulf, Ealdorman of Suth Seaxa, brought close to four hundred men and apologised that it could not be more, but there were Danish ships off his coast and he had been forced to leave some of his fyrd to guard the shore. The men of Wiltunscir had been summoned by Wulfhere to join Guthrum's army, but the reeve, a grim man named Osric, had scoured the southern part of the shire and over eight hundred men had ignored their ealdorman's summons and came to Alfred instead. More arrived from the distant parts of Sumorsæte to join Wiglaf's fyrd that now numbered a thousand men, while half that many came from Hamptonscir, including Burgweard's garrison in which were Eadric and Cenwulf, crewmen from the *Heahengel*, and both embraced me, and with them was Father Willibald, eager and nervous. Almost every man came on foot, weary and hungry, with their boots falling apart, but they had swords and axes and spears and shields, and by mid afternoon there were close to three thousand men in the Wilig valley and more were still coming as I rode towards the distant hill where I thought I had seen the Danish scouts.

Alfred sent me and, at the last moment, Father Pyrlig had

offered to accompany me and Alfred had looked surprised, appeared to think about it for a heartbeat, then nodded assent. 'Bring Uhtred home safe, father,' he had said stiffly.

I said nothing as we rode through the growing camp, but once we were on our own I gave Pyrlig a sour look. 'That was all arranged,' I said.

'What was?'

'You coming with me. He had your horse already saddled! So what does Alfred want?'

Pyrlig grinned. 'He wants me to talk you into becoming a Christian, of course. The king has great faith in my powers of speech.'

'I am a Christian,' I said.

'Are you now?'

'I was baptised, wasn't I? Twice, as it happens.'

'Twice! Doubly holy, eh? How come you got it twice?'

'Because my name was changed when I was a child and my stepmother thought heaven wouldn't recognise me under my old name.'

He laughed. 'So they washed the devil out of you the first time and slopped him back in the second?' I said nothing to that and Pyrlig rode in silence for a time. 'Alfred wants me to make you a good Christian,' he said after a while, 'because he wants God's blessing.'

'He thinks God will curse us because I'm fighting for him?'

Pyrlig shook his head. 'He knows, Uhtred, that the enemy are pagans. If they win then Christ is defeated. This isn't just a war over land, it's a war about God. And Alfred, poor man, is Christ's servant so he will do all he can for his master, and that means trying to turn you into a pious example of Christian humility. If he can get you onto your knees then it'll be easy to make the Danes grovel.'

I laughed, as he had meant me to. 'If it encourages Alfred,' I said, 'tell him I'm a good Christian.'

'I planned to tell him that anyway,' Pyrlig said, 'just to cheer him up, but in truth I wanted to come with you.'

'Why?'

'Because I miss this life. God, I miss it! I loved being a warrior. All that irresponsibility! I relished it. Kill and make widows, frighten children! I was good at it, and I miss it. And I was always good at scouting. We'd see you Saxons blundering away like swine and you never knew we were watching you. Don't worry, I'm not going to talk Christ into you, whatever the king wants.'

Our job was to find the Danes, if they were near. Alfred had marched to the Wilig valley to block any advance Guthrum made into the heartland of Wessex, but he still feared that the Danes might resist the lure of destroying his small army and instead march around us to take southern Wessex, which would leave us stranded and surrounded by Danish garrisons. That uncertainty meant Alfred was desperate for news of the enemy, so Pyrlig and I rode north and east up the valley until we came to where a smaller river flowed south into the Wilig and we followed that lesser stream past a large village that had been reduced to ashes. The small river passed through good farmland, but there were no cattle, no sheep and the fields were unploughed and thick with weeds. We went slowly, for the horses were tired and we were well north of our army now. The sun was low in the west, though it was early May so the days were lengthening. There were mayfly on the river and trout rising to them, and then a scuffling sound made us both pause, but it was only a pair of otter cubs scrabbling down to the water through the roots of a willow. Doves were nesting in the blackthorn, and warblers called from the riverbank, and somewhere a woodpecker drummed intermittently. We rode in silence for a while, turning away from the river to go into an orchard where wrynecks sang among the pink blossom.

Pyrlig curbed his horse under the trees and pointed at a muddy patch in the grass and I saw hoofprints sifted with fallen petals. The prints were fresh and there were a lot of them. 'Bastards were here, weren't they?' he said, 'and not so long ago.'

I looked up the valley. There was no one in sight. The hills rose steeply on either side with thick woods on their lower slopes. I had the sudden uncomfortable feeling that we were being watched, that we were blundering and the wolves were close. 'If I were a Dane,' Pyrlig spoke softly, and I suspected he shared my discomfort, 'I'd be over there,' he jerked his head to the western trees.

'Why?'

'Because when you saw them, they saw us, and that's the way to where they saw us. Does that make sense?' He laughed wryly. 'I don't know, Uhtred, I just think the bastards are over there.'

So we went east. We rode slowly, as if we did not have a care in the world, but once we were in the woods we turned north. We both searched the ground for more hoof-prints, but saw none, and the feeling of being watched had gone now, though we did wait for a long time to see if anyone was following us. There was only the wind in the trees. Yet I knew the Danes were near, just as a hall's hounds know when there are wolves in the nearby darkness. The hair on their necks stands up, they bare their teeth, they quiver.

We came to a place where the trees ended and we dismounted, tied the horses, and went to the wood's edge and just watched.

And at last we saw them.

Thirty or forty Danes were on the valley's farther side, above the woods, and they had plainly ridden to the top of the hills, looked southwards, and were now coming back.

They were scattered in a long line that was riding down into the woods. 'Scouting party,' Pyrlig said.

'They can't have seen much from that hilltop.'

'They saw us,' he said.

'I think so.'

'But they didn't attack us?' He was puzzled. 'Why not?'

'Look at me,' I said.

'I get a treat every day.'

'They thought I was a Dane,' I said. I was not in mail and had no helmet, so my long hair fell free down my leather-clad back and my arms were bright with rings. 'And they probably thought you were my performing bear,' I added.

He laughed. 'So shall we follow them?'

The only risk was crossing the valley, but if the enemy saw us they would probably still assume I was a fellow Dane, so we cantered over the open ground, then rode up into the further woods. We heard the Danes before we saw them. They were careless, talking and laughing, unaware that any Saxons were close. Pyrlig tucked his crucifix beneath his leather coat, then we waited until we were sure the last of the Danes had passed before kicking the horses uphill to find their tracks and so follow them. The shadows were lengthening, and that made me think that the Danish army must be close for the scouting party would want to reach safety before dark, but as the hilly country flattened we saw that they had no intention of joining Guthrum's forces that evening. The patrolling Danes had their own camp, and as we approached it we were nearly caught by another group of mounted scouts who rode in from the east. We heard the newcomers and swerved aside into a thicket and watched a dozen men ride by, and then we dismounted and crept through the trees to see how many enemy were in the camp.

There were perhaps a hundred and fifty Danes in a small

pasture. The first fires were being lit, suggesting they planned to spend the night where they were. 'All scouting parties,' Pyrlig suggested.

'Confident bastards,' I said. These men had been sent ahead to explore the hills, and they felt safe to camp in the open countryside, sure that no Saxon would attack them. And they were right. The West Saxon army was a long way south and we had no war-band in the area, and so the Danes would have a quiet night and, in the morning, their scouts would ride again to watch Alfred's movements.

'But if they're here,' Pyrlig suggested, 'then it means Guthrum is following them.'

'Maybe,' I said. Or perhaps Guthrum was marching well to the east or west and had sent these men to make sure that Alfred was ignorant of his movements.

'We should go back,' Pyrlig said. 'Be dark soon.'

But I had heard voices and I held up a hand to silence him, and then went to my right, keeping to the places where the undergrowth was thickest, and heard what I thought I had heard. English. 'They've got Saxons here,' I said.

'Wulfhere's men?'

Which made sense. We were in Wiltunscir and Wulfhere's men would know this country, and who better to guide the Danes as they watched Alfred?

The Saxons were coming into the wood and we stayed behind some hawthorn bushes until we heard the sound of axes. They were cutting firewood. There seemed to be about a dozen of them. Most of the men who followed Wulfhere would probably be reluctant to fight Alfred, but some would have embraced their ealdorman's new cause and doubtless those were the men who had been despatched to guide the Danish scouting parties. Wulfhere would only have sent men he could trust, fearing that less loyal men would desert to Alfred or just run away, so these Saxons were probably from

348

the ealdorman's household troops, the warriors who would profit most from being on the winner's side in the war between the Danes and the West Saxons.

'We should get back to Alfred before it's dark,' Pyrlig whispered.

But just then a voice sounded close and petulant. 'I will go tomorrow,' the voice said.

'You won't, lord,' a man answered. There was the sound of splashing and I realised one of the two men had come to the bushes for a piss and the other had followed him. 'You'll go nowhere tomorrow,' the second man went on, 'you'll stay here.'

'I just want to see them!' the petulant voice pleaded.

'You'll see them soon enough. But not tomorrow. You'll stay here with the guards.'

'You can't make me.'

'I can do what I like with you, lord. You might command here, but you take my orders all the same.' The man's voice was hard and deep. 'And my orders are that you're staying here.'

'I'll go if I want,' the first voice insisted weakly and was ignored.

Very slowly, so that the blade made no noise against the scabbard's throat, I drew Serpent-Breath. Pyrlig watched me, puzzled. 'Walk away,' I whispered to him, 'and make some noise.' He frowned in puzzlement at that, but I jerked my head and he trusted me. He stood and walked towards our horses, whistling softly, and immediately the two men followed. The one with the deep voice led. He was an old warrior, scar-faced and bulky. 'You!' he shouted, 'stop!' And just then I stepped out from behind the hawthorn and swung Serpent-Breath once and her blade cut under his beard and into his throat, and cut so deep that I felt her scrape against his spine and the blood, sudden and bright in the spring

349

dusk, sprayed across the leaf mould. The man went down like a felled ox. The second man, the petulant man, was following close behind and he was too astonished and much too scared to run away and so I seized his arm and pulled him down behind the bushes.

'You can't,' he began and I placed the flat of Serpent-Breath's bloody blade against his mouth so that he whimpered with terror.

'Not a sound,' I said to him, 'or you're dead.' Pyrlig came back then, sword drawn.

Pyrlig looked at the dead man whose breeches were still untied. He stooped to him and made the sign of the cross on his forehead. The man's death had been quick, and the capture of his companion had been quiet, and none of the woodcutters seemed to have taken alarm. Their axes went on thumping, the echoes rattling in the trees. 'We're taking this one back to Alfred,' I told Pyrlig, then I moved Serpent-Breath to my captive's throat. 'Make one sound,' I said, pressing the blade into his skin, 'and I'll gut you from your over-used gullet to your over-used crotch. Do you understand?'

He nodded.

'Because I'm doing you the favour I owe you,' I explained, and smiled nicely.

Because my captive was Æthelwold, Alfred's nephew and the would-be king of the West Saxons.

The man I had killed was named Osbergh and he had been the commander of Wulfhere's household troops. His job on the day of his death was to make certain Æthelwold got into no trouble.

Æthelwold had a talent for misfortune. By rights he

should have been the King of Wessex, though I daresay he would have been the last king for he was impetuous and foolish, and the twin solaces for having lost the throne to his uncle Alfred were ale and women. Yet he had ever wanted to be a warrior. Alfred had denied him the chance, for he dared not let Æthelwold make a name for himself on the battlefield. Æthelwold, the true king, had to be kept foolish so that no man saw in him a rival for Alfred's throne. It would have been far easier to have killed Æthelwold, but Alfred was sentimental about family. Or perhaps it was his Christian conscience. But for whatever reason, Æthelwold had been allowed to live and had rewarded his uncle's mercy by constantly making a fool of himself.

But in these last months he had been released from Alfred's leash and his thwarted ambition had been given encouragement. He dressed in mail and carried swords. He was a startling looking man, handsome and tall, and he looked the part of the warrior, though he had no warrior's soul. He had pissed himself when I put Serpent-Breath to his throat, and now that he was my captive he showed no defiance. He was submissive, frightened and glad to be led.

He told us how he had pestered Wulfhere to be allowed to fight, and when Osbergh had brought a score of men to guide the Danes in the hills, he had been given notional charge of them. 'Wulfhere said I was in command,' Æthelwold said sullenly, 'but I still had to obey Osbergh.'

'Wulfhere was a damned fool to let you go so far from him,' I said.

'I think he was tired of me,' Æthelwold admitted.

'Tired of you? You were humping his women?'

'She's only a servant! But I wanted to join the scouting parties, and Wulfhere said I could learn a lot from Osbergh.'

'You've just learned never to piss into a hawthorn bush,' I said, 'and that's worth knowing.'

351

Æthelwold was riding Pyrlig's horse and the Welsh priest was leading the beast by its reins. I had tied Æthelwold's hands. There was still a hint of light in the western sky, just enough to make our journey down the smaller river easy. I explained to Pyrlig who Æthelwold was, and the priest grinned up at him. 'So you're a prince of Wessex, eh?'

'I should be king,' Æthelwold said sullenly.

'No you shouldn't,' I said.

'My father was! And Guthrum promised to crown me.'

'And if you believed him,' I said, 'you're a damned fool. You'd be king as long as he needed you, then you'd be dead.'

'Now Alfred will kill me,' he said miserably.

'He ought to,' I said, 'but I owe you a favour.'

'You think you can persuade him to let me live?' he asked eagerly.

'You'll do the persuading,' I said. 'You'll kneel to him, and you're going to say that you've been waiting for a chance to escape the Danes, and at last you succeeded, and you got away, found us, and have come to offer him your sword.'

Æthelwold just stared at me.

'I owe you a favour,' I explained, 'and so I'm giving you life. I'll untie your hands, you go to Alfred, and you say you're joining him because that's what you've wanted to do ever since Christmas. You understand that?'

Æthelwold frowned. 'But he hates me!'

'Of course he does,' I agreed, 'but if you kneel to him and swear you never broke your allegiance to him, then what can he do? He'll embrace you, reward you and be proud of you.'

'Truly?'

'So long as you tell him where the Danes are,' Pyrlig put in.

'I can do that,' Æthelwold said, 'they're coming south from Cippanhamm. They marched this morning.'

352

'How many?'

'Five thousand.'

'Coming here?'

'They're going to wherever Alfred is. They reckon they'll have a chance to destroy him, and after that it's just a summer of women and silver.' He said the last three words plaintively and I knew he had been relishing the prospect of plundering Wessex. 'So how many men does Alfred have?' he asked.

'Three thousand,' I said.

'Sweet Jesus,' he said fearfully.

'You always wanted to be a warrior,' I said, 'and what name can you make for yourself fighting a smaller army?'

'Jesus Christ!'

The last of the light went. There was no moon, but by keeping the river on our left we knew we could not get lost and after a while we saw the glow of firelight showing over the loom of the hills and knew we were seeing Alfred's encampment. I twisted in the saddle then and thought I saw another such glow far to the north. Guthrum's army.

'If you let me go,' Æthelwold asked sulkily, 'what's to stop me going back to Guthrum?'

'Absolutely nothing,' I said, 'except the certainty that I'll hunt you down and kill you.'

He thought about that for a short while. 'You're sure my uncle will welcome me?'

Pyrlig answered for me. 'With open arms!' he said. 'It will be like the return of the prodigal son. You'll be welcomed by slaughtered calves and psalms of rejoicing. Just tell Alfred what you told us, about Guthrum marching towards us.'

We reached the Wilig and the going was easy now for the light of the campfires was much brighter. I cut Æthelwold free at the edge of the encampment, then gave him back

353

his swords. He carried two, as I did, a long one and a short sax. 'Well, my prince,' I said, 'time to grovel, eh?'

We found Alfred at the camp's centre. There was no pomp here. We did not have the animals to drag wagons loaded with tents or furniture, so Alfred was seated on a spread cloak between two fires. He looked dispirited and later I learned that he had assembled the army in the twilight and made them a speech, but the speech, even Beocca admitted, had been less than successful. 'It was more a sermon than a speech,' Beocca told me glumly. Alfred had invoked God, spoken of Saint Augustine's doctrine of a righteous war and talked about Boethius and King David, and the words had flown over the heads of the tired, hungry troops. Now Alfred sat with the leading men of the army, all of them eating stale hard bread and smoked eel. Father Adelbert, the priest who had accompanied us to Cippanhamm, was playing a lament on a small harp. A bad choice of music, I thought, then Alfred saw me and waved Adelbert to silence. 'You have news?' he asked.

For answer I stood aside and bowed to Æthelwold, gesturing him towards the king. 'Lord,' I said to Alfred, 'I bring you your nephew.'

Alfred stood. He was taken aback, especially as Æthelwold was plainly no prisoner for he wore his swords. Æthelwold looked good, indeed he looked more like a king than Alfred. He was well made and handsome, while Alfred was much too thin and his face was so haggard that he looked much older than his twenty-nine years. And of the two it was Æthelwold who knew how to behave at that moment. He unbuckled his swords and threw them with a great clatter at his uncle's feet, then he went to his knees and clasped his hands and looked up into the king's face. 'I have found you!' he said with what sounded like utter joy and conviction.

354

Alfred, bemused, did not know what to say so I stepped forward. 'We discovered him, lord,' I said, 'in the hills. He was searching for you.'

'I escaped Guthrum,' Æthelwold said, 'God be praised, I escaped the pagan.' He pushed his swords to Alfred's feet. 'My blades are yours, lord king.'

This extravagant display of loyalty gave Alfred no choice except to raise his nephew and embrace him. The men around the fires applauded, then Æthelwold gave his news, which was useful enough. Guthrum was on the march and Svein of the White Horse came with him. They knew where Alfred was and so they came, five thousand strong, to give him battle in the hills of Wiltunscir.

'When will they get here?' Alfred wanted to know.

'They should reach these hills tomorrow, lord,' Æthelwold said.

So Æthelwold was seated beside the king and given water to drink, which was hardly a fit welcome for a prodigal prince and caused him to throw me a wry glance, and it was then that I saw Harald, shire-reeve of Defnascir, among the king's companions. 'You're here?' I asked surprised.

'With five hundred men,' he said proudly.

We had expected no men from either Defnascir or Thornsæta, but Harald, the shire-reeve, had brought four hundred of his own fyrd and a hundred more from Thornsæta. 'There's enough men left to protect the coast against the pagan fleet,' he said, 'and Odda insisted we help defeat Guthrum.'

'How is Mildrith?'

'She prays for her son,' Harald said, 'and for all of us.'

There were prayers after the meal. There were always prayers when Alfred was around, and I tried to escape them, but Pyrlig made me stay. 'The king wants to talk with you,' he said.

So I waited while Bishop Alewold droned, and afterwards Alfred wanted to know whether Æthelwold had truly run away from the Danes.

'That's what he told me lord,' I said, 'and I can only say we found him.'

'He didn't run from us,' Pyrlig offered, 'and he could have done.'

'So there's good in the boy,' Alfred said.

'God be praised for that,' Pyrlig said.

Alfred paused, gazing down into the glowing embers of a campfire. 'I spoke to the army tonight,' he told us.

'I heard you did, lord,' I said.

He looked up at me sharply. 'What did you hear?'

'That you preached to them, lord.'

He flinched at that, then seemed to accept the criticism. 'What do they want to hear?' he asked.

'They want to hear,' Pyrlig answered, 'that you are ready to die for them.'

'Die?'

'Men follow, kings lead,' Pyrlig said. Alfred waited. 'They don't care about Saint Augustine,' Pyrlig went on, 'they only care that their women and children are safe, that their lands are safe, and that they'll have a future of their own. They want to know that they'll win. They want to know the Danes are going to die. They want to hear that they'll be rich on plunder.'

'Greed, revenge and selfishness?' Alfred asked.

'If you had an army of angels, lord,' Pyrlig went on, 'then a rousing speech about God and Saint Augustine would doubtless fire their ardour, but you have to fight with mere men, and there's nothing quite like greed, revenge and self-ishness to inspire mortals.'

Alfred frowned at that advice, but did not argue with it. 'So I can trust my nephew?' he asked me.

'I don't know that you can trust him,' I said, 'but nor can Guthrum. And Æthelwold did seek you out, lord, so be content with that.'

'I shall, I shall.' He bade us goodnight, going to his hard bed.

The fires in the valley were dying. 'Why didn't you tell Alfred the truth about Æthelwold?' I asked Pyrlig.

'I thought I would trust your judgement,' he said.

'You're a good man.'

'And that constantly astonishes me.'

I went to find Iseult, then slept.

Next day the whole of the northern sky was dark with cloud, while over our army, and above the hills, was sunlight.

The West Saxon army, now almost three and a half thousand strong, marched up the Wilig, then followed the smaller river that Pyrlig and I had explored the previous evening. We could see the Danish scouts on the hills, and knew they would be sending messengers back to Guthrum.

I led fifty men to one of the hilltops. We were all mounted, all armed, all with shields and helmets, and we rode ready to fight, but the Danish scouts yielded the ground. There were only a dozen of them and they rode off the hill long before we reached the summit where a host of blue butterflies flickered above the springy turf. I gazed northwards at the ominous dark sky, and watched a sparrowhawk stoop. Down the bird went, and I followed its plunging fall and suddenly saw, beneath the folded wings and reaching claws, our enemy.

Guthrum's army was coming south.

The fear came then. The shield wall is a terrible place. It is where a warrior makes his reputation, and reputation is dear to us. Reputation is honour, but to gain that honour a man must stand in the shield wall where death runs rampant. I had been in the shield wall at Cynuit and I knew the smell of death, the stink of it, the uncertainty of survival, the horror of the axes and swords and spears, and I feared it. And it was coming.

I could see it coming, for in the lowlands north of the hills, in the green ground stretching long and level towards distant Cippanhamm, was an army. The Great Army, the Danes called it, the pagan warriors of Guthrum and Svein, the wild horde of wild men from beyond the sea.

They were a dark smear on the landscape. They were coming through the fields, band after band of horsemen, spread across the country, and because their leading men were only just emerging into the sunlight it seemed as if their horde sprang from the shadowlands. Spears and helmets and mail and metal reflected the light, a myriad glints of broken sunlight that spread and multiplied as yet more men came from beneath the clouds. They were nearly all mounted.

'Jesus, Mary and Joseph,' Leofric said.

Steapa said nothing. He just glowered at them.

Osric, the shire-reeve of Wiltunscir, made the sign of the cross. 'Someone has to tell Alfred,' he said.

'I'll go,' Father Pyrlig offered.

'Tell him the pagans have crossed the Afen,' Osric said. 'Tell him they're heading towards,' he paused, trying to judge where the horde was going, 'Ethandun,' he finally said.

'Ethandun,' Pyrlig repeated the name.

'And remind him there's a fort of the old people there,' Osric said. This was his shire, his country, and he knew its hills and fields, and he sounded grim, doubtless wondering what would happen if the Danes found the old fortress and occupied it. 'God help us,' Osric said. 'They'll be in the hills tomorrow morning, tell him.'

'Tomorrow morning, at Ethandun,' Pyrlig said, then turned his horse and spurred away.

'Where's the fort?' I asked.

Osric pointed. 'You can see it.' From this distance the ancient fastness looked like nothing more than green wrinkles on a far hilltop. All across Wessex there were such forts with their massive earthen walls, and this one was built at the top of the escarpment that climbed from the lowlands, a place guarding the sudden edge of the chalk downs. 'Some of the bastards will get up there tonight,' Osric said, 'but most won't make it till morning. Let's just hope they ignore the fort.'

We had all thought that Alfred would find a place where Guthrum must attack him, a slope made for defence, a place where our smaller numbers would be helped by the difficult ground, but the sight of that distant fort was a reminder that Guthrum might adopt the same tactics. He might find a place where it would be hard for us to attack him, and Alfred would have a grim choice then. To attack would be to court disaster, while to retreat would guarantee it. Our food would be exhausted in a day or two, and if we tried to withdraw south through the hills, Guthrum would release a horde of horsemen against us. And even if the army of Wessex escaped unscathed it would be a beaten army. If Alfred brought the fyrd together, then marched it away from the enemy, men would take it for a defeat and begin to slip away to protect their homes. We had to fight, because to decline battle was a defeat.

The army camped that evening to the north of the woods where I had found Æthelwold. He was in the king's entourage now, and went with Alfred and his war-leaders to the hilltop to watch the Danish army as it closed on the

359

hills. Alfred looked a long time. 'How far away are they?' he asked.

'From here?' Osric answered. 'Four miles. From your army? Six.'

'Tomorrow, then,' Alfred said, making the sign of the cross. The northern clouds were spreading, darkening the evening, but the slanting light reflected from spears and axes at the old people's fort. It seemed Guthrum had not ignored the place after all.

We went back down to the encampment to find yet more men arriving. Not many now, just small bands, but still they came, and one such band, travel-weary and dusty, was mounted on horses and all sixteen men had chain mail and good helmets.

They were Mercians and they had ridden far to the east, crossed the Thames, then looped through Wessex, ever avoiding Danes, and so come to help Alfred. Their leader was a short young man, wide in the chest, round-faced, and with a pugnacious expression. He knelt to Alfred, then grinned at me, and I recognised my cousin, Æthelred.

My mother was a Mercian, though I never knew her, and her brother Æthelred was a power in the southern part of that country and I had spent a short time in his hall when I first fled from Northumbria. Back then I had quarrelled with my cousin, called Æthelred like his father, but he seemed to have forgotten our youthful enmity and embraced me instead. The top of his head just came up to my collar-bone. 'We've come to fight,' he told me, his voice muffled by my chest.

'You'll have a fight,' I promised him.

'Lord,' he let go of me and turned back to Alfred, 'my father would have sent more men, but he must protect his land.'

'He must,' Alfred said.

'But he sent the best he has,' Æthelred went on. He was

young and bumptious, a little strut of a youth, but his confidence pleased Alfred, as did the gleaming silver crucifix hanging over Æthelred's chain mail. 'Allow me to present Tatwine,' my cousin went on, 'the chief of my father's household troops.'

I remembered Tatwine, a barrel of a man and a real fighter, whose arms were smothered in blotchy black marks, each made with a needle and ink and representing a man killed in battle. He gave me a crooked smile. 'Still alive, lord?'

'Still alive, Tatwine.'

'Be good to fight alongside you again.'

'Good to have you here,' I said, and it was. Few men are natural-born warriors, and a man like Tatwine was worth a dozen others.

Alfred had ordered the army to assemble again. He did it partly so the men could see their own numbers and take heart from that, and he did it, too, because he knew his speech the previous night had left men confused and uninspired. He would try again. 'I wish he wouldn't,' Leofric grumbled. 'He can make sermons, but he can't make speeches.'

We gathered at the foot of a small hill. The light was fading. Alfred had planted his two banners, the dragon and the cross, on the summit of the hill, but there was a small wind so the flags stirred rather than flew. He climbed to stand between them. He was alone, dressed in a mail coat over which he wore the faded blue cloak. A group of priests began to follow him, but he waved them back to the hill's foot, then he just stared at us huddled in the meadow beneath him and for a time he said nothing and I sensed the discomfort in the ranks. They wanted fire put into their souls and expected holy water instead.

'Tomorrow!' he said suddenly. His voice was high, but it carried clearly enough. 'Tomorrow we fight! Tomorrow! The Feast of St John the Apostle!'

361

'Oh God,' Leofric grumbled next to me, 'up to our arse-holes in more saints.'

'John the Apostle was condemned to death!' Alfred said, 'he was condemned to be boiled in oil! Yet he survived the ordeal! He was plunged into the boiling oil and he lived! He came from the cauldron a stronger man! And we shall do the same.' He paused, watching us, and no one responded, we all just gazed at him, and he must have known that his homily on Saint John was not working for he made an abrupt gesture with his right hand as if he were sweeping all the saints aside. 'And tomorrow,' he went on, 'is also a day for warriors. A day to kill your enemies. A day to make the pagans wish they had never heard of Wessex!'

He paused again, and this time there were some murmurs of agreement.

'This is our land! We fight for our homes! For our wives! For our children! We fight for Wessex!'

'We do,' someone shouted.

'And not just Wessex!' Alfred's voice was stronger now. 'We have men from Mercia, men from Northumbria, men from East Anglia!' I knew of none from East Anglia and only Beocca and I were from Northumbria, but no one seemed to care. 'We are the men of England,' Alfred shouted, 'and we fight for all Saxons.'

Silence again. The men liked what they heard, but the idea of England was in Alfred's head, not theirs. He had a dream of one country, but it was too big a dream for the army in the meadow. 'And why are the Danes here?' Alfred asked. 'They want your wives for their pleasure, your children for their slaves and your homes for their own, but they do not know us!' He said the last six words slowly, spacing them out, shouting each one distinctly. 'They do not know our swords,' he went on, 'they do not know our axes, our spears, our fierceness! Tomorrow we teach them! Tomorrow we kill them! Tomorrow we hack them into pieces! Tomorrow we make the ground red with their blood and make them whimper! Tomorrow we shall make them call for our mercy!'

'None!' a man called out.

'No mercy!' Alfred shouted, and I knew he did not mean it. He would have offered every mercy to the Danes, he would have offered them the love of God and tried to reason with them, but in the last few minutes he had at last learned how to talk to warriors.

'Tomorrow,' he shouted, 'you do not fight for me! I fight for you! I fight for Wessex! I fight for your wives, for your children and your homes! Tomorrow we fight and, I swear to you on my father's grave and on my children's lives, tomorrow we shall win!'

And that started the cheering. It was not, in all honesty, a great battle speech, but it was the best Alfred ever gave and it worked. Men stamped the ground and those who carried their shields beat them with swords or spears so that the twilight was filled with a rhythmic thumping as men shouted, 'No mercy!' The sound echoed back from the hills. 'No mercy, no mercy.'

We were ready. And the Danes were ready.

That night it clouded over. The stars vanished one by one, and the thin moon was swallowed in the darkness. Sleep came hard. I sat with Iseult who was cleaning my mail while I sharpened both swords. 'You will win tomorrow,' Iseult said in a small voice.

'You dreamed that?'

She shook her head. 'The dreams don't come since I was baptised.'

'So you made it up?'

'I have to believe it,' she said.

363

The stone scraped down the blades. All around me other men were sharpening weapons. 'When this is over,' I said, 'you and I will go away. We shall make a house.'

'When this is over,' she said, 'you will go north. Ever north. Back to your home.'

'Then you'll come with me.'

'Perhaps.' She heaved the mail coat to start on a new patch, scrubbing it with a scrap of fleece to make the links shine. 'I can't see my own future. It's all dark.'

'You shall be the lady of Bebbanburg,' I said, 'and I shall dress you in furs and crown you with bright silver.'

She smiled, but I saw there were tears on her face. I took it for fear. There was plenty of that in the camp that night, especially when men noticed the glow of light showing where the Danes had lit their fires in the nearby hills. We did sleep, but I was woken long before dawn by a small rain. No one slept through it, but all stirred and pulled on war gear.

We marched in the grey light. The rain came and went, spiteful and sharp, but always at our backs. Most of us walked, using our few horses to carry shields. Osric and his men went first, for they knew the shire. Alfred had said that the men of Wiltunscir would be on the right of the battle line, and with them would be the men of Suth Seaxa. Alfred was next, leading his bodyguard that was made of all the men who had come to him in Æthelingæg, and with him was Harald and the men of Defnascir and Thornsæta. Burgweard and the men from Hamptonscir would also fight with Alfred, as would my cousin Æthelred from Mercia, while on the left would be the strong fyrd of Sumorsæte under Wiglaf. Three and a half thousand men. The women came with us. Some carried their men's weapons, others had their own.

No one spoke much. It was cold that morning, and the

rain made the grass slippery. Men were hungry and tired. We were all fearful.

Alfred had told me to collect fifty or so men to lead, but Leofric was unwilling to lose that many from his ranks, so I took them from Burgweard instead. I took the men who had fought with me in the *Heahengel* when she had been the *Fyrdraca*, and twenty-six of those men had come from Hamtun. Steapa was with us, for he had taken a perverse liking to me, and I had Father Pyrlig, who was dressed as a warrior, not a priest. We were fewer than thirty men, but as we climbed past a green-mounded grave of the old folk, Æthelwold came to us. 'Alfred said I could fight with you,' he said.

'He said that?'

'He said I'm not to leave your side.'

I smiled at that. If I wanted a man by my side it would be Eadric or Cenwulf, Steapa or Pyrlig, men I could trust to keep their shields firm. 'You're not to leave my back,' I said to Æthelwold.

'Your back?'

'And in the shield wall you stay close behind me. Ready to take my place.'

He took that as an insult, 'I want to be in the front,' he insisted.

'Have you ever fought in a shield wall?'

'You know I haven't.'

'Then you don't want to be in the front,' I said, 'and besides, if Alfred dies, who'll be king?'

'Ah.' He half smiled. 'So I stay behind you?'

'You stay behind me.'

Iseult and Hild were leading my horse. 'If we lose,' I told them, 'you both get in the saddle and ride.'

'Ride where?'

'Just ride. Take the money,' I said. My silver and treas-

365

ures, all I possessed, were in the horse's saddlebags, 'take it and ride with Hild.'

Hild smiled at that. She looked pale and her fair hair was plastered tight to her scalp by the rain. She had no hat, and was dressed in a white shift belted with rope. I was surprised that she had come with the army, thinking she would have preferred to find a convent, but she had insisted on coming. 'I want to see them dead,' she told me flatly. 'And the one called Erik I want to kill myself.' She patted the long, narrow-bladed knife hanging from her belt.

'Erik is the one who . . .' I began, then hesitated.

'The one who whored me,' she said.

'So he wasn't the one we killed that night?'

She shook her head. 'That was the steersman of Erik's ship. But I'll find Erik, and I won't go back to a convent till I see him screaming in his own blood.'

'Full of hate, she is,' Father Pyrlig told me as we followed Hild and Iseult up the hill.

'Isn't that bad in a Christian?'

Pyrlig laughed. 'Being alive is bad in a Christian! We say a person is a saint if they're good, but how few of us become saints? We're all bad! Some of us just try to be good.'

I glanced at Hild. 'She's wasted as a nun,' I said.

'You do like them thin, don't you?' Pyrlig said, amused. 'Now I like them meaty as well-fed heifers! Give me a nice dark Briton with hips like a pair of ale barrels and I'm a happy priest. Poor Hild. Thin as a ray of sunlight, she is, but I pity a Dane who crosses her path today.'

Osric's scouts came back to Alfred. They had ridden ahead and seen the Danes. The enemy was waiting, they reported, at the edge of the escarpment, where the hills were highest and where the old people's fort stood. Their banners, the scouts said, were numberless. They had also seen Danish scouts, so Guthrum and Svein must have known we were coming.

On we went, ever higher, climbing into the chalk downs, and the rain stopped, but no sun appeared for the whole sky was a turmoil of grey and black. The wind gusted from the west. We passed whole rows of graves from the ancient days and I wondered if they contained warriors who had gone to battle as we did, and I wondered if in the thousands of years to come other men would toil up these hills with swords and shields. Of warfare there is no end, and I looked into the dark sky for a sign from Thor or Odin, hoping to see a raven fly, but there were no birds. Just clouds.

And then I saw Osric's men slanting away to the right. We were in a fold of the hills and they were going around the right-hand hill and, as we reached the saddle between the two low slopes, I saw the level ground and there, ahead of me, was the enemy.

I love the Danes. There are no better men to fight with, drink with, laugh with or live with. Yet that day, as on so many others of my life, they were the enemy and they waited for me in a gigantic shield wall arrayed across the down. There were thousands of Danes, spear-Danes and sword-Danes, Danes who had come to make this land theirs, and we had come to keep it ours. 'God give us strength,' Father Pyrlig said when he saw the enemy who had begun shouting as we appeared. They clashed spears and swords against limewood shields, making a thunder on the hilltop. The ancient fort was the right wing of their army, and men were thick on the green turf walls. Many of those men had black shields and above them was a black banner, so that was where Guthrum was, while their left wing, which faced our right, was strung out on the open down and it was there I could see a triangular banner, supported by a small cross-staff, showing a white horse. So Svein commanded their left, while to the Danish right, our left, the escarpment dropped to the river plains. It was a steep drop, a tumbling hill. We could not hope to outflank the Danes on that side, for no one could fight on such a slope. We had to attack straight ahead, directly into the shield wall and against the earthen ramparts and onto the spears and the swords and the war axes of our outnumbering enemy.

I looked for Ragnar's eagle-wing banner and thought I saw it in the fort, but it was hard to be certain, for every crew of Danes flew their standard, and the small flags were crowded together and the rain had started to fall again, obscuring the symbols, but off to my right, outside the fort and close to the bigger standard of the white horse, was a Saxon flag. It was a green flag with an eagle and a cross, which meant Wulfhere was there with that part of the Wiltunscir fyrd which had followed him. There were other Saxon banners in the enemy horde. Not many, maybe a score, and I guessed that the Danes had brought men from Mercia to fight for them. All the Saxon banners were in the open ground, none was inside the fort.

We were still a long way apart, much farther than a man could shoot an arrow, and none of us could hear what the Danes were shouting. Osric's men were making our right wing as Wiglaf led his Sumorsæte fyrd off to the left. We were making a line to oppose their line, but ours would inevitably be shorter. The odds were not quite two Danes to one Saxon, but it was close. 'God help us,' Pyrlig said, touching his crucifix.

Alfred summoned his commanders, gathering them under the rain-sodden banner of the dragon. The Danish thunder went on, the clattering of thousands of weapons against shields, as the king asked his army's leaders for advice.

Arnulf of Suth Seaxa, a wiry man with a short beard and a perpetual scowl, advised attack. 'Just attack,' he said, waving at the fort. 'We'll lose some men on the walls, but we'll lose men anyway.'

'We'll lose a lot of men,' my cousin Æthelred warned. He only led a small band, but his status as the son of a Mercian ealdorman meant he had to be included in Alfred's council of war.

'We do better defending,' Osric growled. 'Give a man land to defend and he stands, so let the bastards come to us.' Harald nodded agreement.

Alfred cast a courteous eye on Wiglaf of Sumorsæte who looked surprised to be consulted. 'We shall do our duty, lord,' he said, 'do our duty whatever you decide.' Leofric and I were present, but the king did not invite our opinion so we kept silent.

Alfred gazed at the enemy, then turned back to us. 'In my experience,' he said, 'the enemy expect something of us.' He spoke pedantically, in the same tone he used when he was discussing theology with his priests. 'They want us to do certain things. What are those things?'

Wiglaf shrugged, while Arnulf and Osric looked bemused. They had both expected something fiercer from Alfred. Battle, for most of us, was a hammering rage, nothing clever, a killing orgy, but Alfred saw it as a competition of wisdom, or perhaps as a game of tafl that took cleverness to win. That, I am sure, was how he saw our two armies, as tafl pieces on their chequered board.

'Well?' he asked.

'They expect us to attack!' Osric said uncertainly.

'They expect us to attack Wulfhere,' I said.

Alfred rewarded me with a smile. 'Why Wulfhere?'

'Because he's a traitor and a bastard and a piece of whore-begotten goat-shit,' I said.

'Because we do not believe,' Alfred corrected me, 'that Wulfhere's men will fight with the same passion as the Danes. And we're right, they won't. His men will pull back from killing fellow Saxons.'

'But Svein is there,' I said.

'Which tells us?' he asked.

The others stared at him. He knew the answer, but he could never resist being a teacher, and so he waited for a response. 'It tells us,' I supplied it again, 'that they want us to attack their left, but they don't want their left to break. That's why Svein is there. He'll hold us and they'll launch an assault out of the fort to hit the flank of our attack. That breaks the right of our army and then the whole damned lot come and kill the rest of us.'

Alfred did not respond, but looked worried, suggesting that he agreed with me. The other men turned and looked at the Danes, as if some magical answer might suggest itself, but none did.

'So do as Lord Arnulf suggests,' Harald said, 'attack the fort.'

'The walls are steep,' Wiglaf warned. The Ealdorman of Sumorsæte was a man of sunny disposition, frequent laughter and casual generosity, but now, with his men arrayed opposite the fort's green ramparts, he was downcast.

'Guthrum would dearly like us to assail the fort,' the king observed.

This caused some confusion for it seemed, according to Alfred, that the Danes wanted us to attack their right just as much as they wanted us to attack their left. The Danes, meanwhile, were jeering at us for not attacking at all. One or two ran towards our lines and screamed insults, and their whole shield wall was still banging weapons in a steady, threatening rhythm. The rain made the colours of the shields darker. The colours were black and red and blue and brown and dirty yellow.

'So what do we do?' Æthelred asked plaintively.

There was silence and I realised that Alfred, though he

understood the problem, had no answer to it. Guthrum wanted us to attack and probably did not care whether we went against Svein's seasoned warriors on the left of the enemy line or against the steep, slippery ditches in front of the fort's walls. And Guthrum must also have known that we dared not retreat because his men would pursue and break us like a horde of wolves savaging a frightened flock.

'Attack their left,' I said.

Alfred nodded as though he had already come to that conclusion. 'And?' he invited me.

'Attack it with every man we've got,' I said. There were probably two thousand men outside the fort and at least half of those were Saxons. I thought we should assault them in one violent rush, and overwhelm them by numbers. Then the weakness of the Danish position would be revealed, for they were on the very lip of the escarpment and once they were forced over the edge they had nowhere to go but down the long, precipitous slope. We could have destroyed those two thousand men, then reformed our lines for the harder task of attacking the three thousand inside the fort.

'Employ all our men?' Alfred asked. 'But then Guthrum will attack our flank with every man he has.'

'Guthrum won't,' I said. 'He'll send some men to attack our flank, but he'll keep most of his troops inside the fort. He's cautious. He won't abandon the fort, and he won't risk much to save Svein. They don't like each other.'

Alfred thought about it, but I could see he did not like the gamble. He feared that while we attacked Svein the other Danes would charge from the fort and overwhelm our left. I still think he should have taken my advice, but fate is inexorable and he decided to imitate Guthrum by being cautious. 'We will attack on our right,' he said, 'and drive off Wulfhere's men, but we must be ready for their counter-stroke and so our left stays where it is.'

371

So it was decided. Osric and Arnulf, with the men of Wiltunscir and Suth Seaxa, would give battle to Svein and Wulfhere on the open land to the east of the fort, but we suspected that some Danes would come from behind the ramparts to attack Osric's flank and so Alfred would take his own bodyguard to be a bulwark against that assault. Wigulf, meanwhile, would stay where he was, which meant a third of our men were doing nothing. 'If we can defeat them,' Alfred said, 'then their remnant will retreat into the fort and we can besiege it. They have no water there, do they?'

'None,' Osric confirmed.

'So they're trapped,' Alfred said as though the whole problem was neatly resolved and the battle as good as won. He turned to Bishop Alewold. 'A prayer, bishop, if you would be so kind.'

Alewold prayed, the rain fell, the Danes went on jeering, and I knew the awful moment, the clash of the shield walls, was close. I touched Thor's hammer, then Serpent-Breath's hilt, for death was stalking us. God help me, I thought, touching the hammer again, Thor help us all, for I did not think we could win.

Thirteen

The Danes made their battle thunder and we prayed. Alewold harangued God for a long time, mostly begging him to send angels with flaming swords, and those angels would have been useful, though none appeared. It would be up to us to do the job.

We readied for battle. I took my shield and helmet from the horse that Iseult led, but first I teased out a thick hank of her black hair. 'Trust me,' I said to her, because she was nervous, and I used a small knife to cut the tress. I tied one end of the hair to Serpent-Breath's hilt and made a loop with the other end. Iseult watched. 'Why?' she asked.

'I can put the loop over my wrist,' I showed her, 'then I can't lose the sword. And your hair will bring me luck.'

Bishop Alewold was angrily demanding that the women go back. Iseult stood on tiptoe to buckle my wolf-crested helmet in place, then she pulled my head down and kissed me through the gap in the face-plate. 'I shall pray for you,' she said.

'So will I,' Hild said.

'Pray to Odin and Thor,' I urged them, then watched as they led the horse away. The women would hold the horses a quarter-mile behind our shield wall and Alfred insisted they went that far back so that no man was tempted to make a sudden dash for a horse and gallop away.

It was time to make the shield wall, and that is a cumbersome business. Some men offer to be in the front rank, but most try to be behind, and Osric and his battle-leaders were shoving and shouting as they tried to settle the men. 'God is with us!' Alfred was shouting at them. He was still mounted and rode down Osric's slowly-forming shield wall to encourage the fyrd. 'God is with us!' he shouted again, 'we cannot lose! God is with us!' The rain fell harder. Priests were walking down the lines offering blessings and adding to the rain by throwing handfuls of holy water at the shields. Osric's fyrd was mostly five ranks thick, and behind them was a scatter of men with spears. Their job, as the two sides met, was to hurl the spears over their comrades' heads, and the Danes would have similar spear-throwers readying their own weapons. 'God is with us!' Alfred shouted, 'He is on our side! Heaven watches over us! The holy saints pray for us! The angels guard us! God is with us!' His voice was already hoarse. Men touched amulets for luck, closed their eyes in silent prayer and tugged at buckles. In the front rank they obsessively touched their shields against their neighbour's shields. The right-hand edge of every man's shield was supposed to overlap the next shield so that the Danes were confronted with a solid wall of iron-reinforced limewood. The Danes would make the same wall, but they were still jeering at us, daring us to attack. A young man stumbled from the back of Osric's fyrd and vomited. Two dogs ran to eat the vomit. A spear-thrower was on his knees, shaking and praying.

Father Beocca stood beside Alfred's standards with his hands raised in prayer. I was in front of the standards with Steapa to my right and Pyrlig to my left. 'Bring fire on them, oh most holy Lord!' Beocca wailed, 'bring fire on them and strike them down! Punish them for their iniquities.' His eyes were tight closed and his face raised to the rain so that he did not see Alfred gallop back to us and push through our ranks. The king would stay mounted so he could see what happened, and Leofric and a dozen other men were also on horseback so that their shields could protect Alfred from thrown spears and axes.

'Forward!' Alfred shouted.

'Forward!' Leofric repeated the order because the king's voice was so hoarse.

No one moved. It was up to Osric and his men to begin the advance, but men are ever reluctant to go against an enemy shield wall. It helps to be drunk. I have been in battles where both sides struggled in a reeking daze of birch wine and ale, but we had little of either and our courage had to be summoned out of sober hearts and there was not much to be found on that cold wet morning.

'Forward!' Leofric shouted again, and this time Osric and his commanders took up the shout and the men of Wiltunscir shuffled a few paces forward and the Danish shields clattered into the wall and locked together and the sight of that *skjaldborg* checked the advance. That is what the Danes call their shield wall, the *skjaldborg* or shield fort. The Danes roared mockery, and two of their younger warriors strutted out of their line to taunt us and invite a duel. 'Stay in the wall!' Leofric roared.

'Ignore them!' Osric shouted.

Horsemen rode from the fort, perhaps a hundred of them, and they trotted behind the *skjaldborg* that was formed of Svein's warriors and Wulfhere's Saxons. Svein joined the horsemen. I could see his white horse, the white cloak and the white horsetail plume. The presence of the horsemen told me that Svein expected our line to break and he wanted to ride our fugitives down just as his riders had slaughtered Peredur's broken Britons at Dreyndynas. The Danes were full of confidence, and so they should have been for they outnumbered us and they were all warriors, while our ranks were filled with men more used to the plough than the sword.

'Forward!' Osric shouted. His line quivered, but did not advance more than a yard.

Rain dripped from the rim of my helmet. It ran down inside the face-plate, worked itself inside my mail coat and ran in shivers down my chest and belly.

'Strike them hard, lord!' Beocca shouted, 'slaughter them without mercy! Break them in pieces!'

Pyrlig was praying, at least I think he was praying for he was speaking in his own tongue, but I heard the word *duw* repeated over and over and I knew, from Iseult, that *duw* was the Britons' word for god. Æthelwold was behind Pyrlig. He was supposed to be behind me, but Eadric had insisted on being at my back, so Æthelwold would protect Pyrlig instead. He was chattering incessantly, trying to cover his nervousness, and I turned on him. 'Keep your shield up,' I told him.

'I know, I know.'

'You protect Pyrlig's head, understand?'

'I know!' He was irritated that I had given him the advice. 'I know,' he repeated petulantly.

'Forward! Forward!' Osric called. Like Alfred he was on horseback and he went up and down behind his line, sword drawn, and I thought he would jab the blade at his men to goad them onwards. They went a few paces and the Danish shields came up again and the limewood made a knocking sound as the *skjaldborg* was made and once again our line faltered. Svein and his horsemen were now at the very far flank, but Osric had placed a group of picked warriors there, ready to guard the open end of his line.

'For God! For Wiltunscir!' Osric shouted, 'forward!'

376

Alfred's men were on the left of Osric's fyrd where we were bent slightly back, ready to receive the expected flank attack from the fort. We went forward readily enough, but then, we were mostly warriors and knew we could not advance in front of Osric's more nervous troops. I almost stepped into a scrap of the ground where, astonishingly, three leverets lay low and quivering. I stared at them and hoped that the men behind me would avoid the little beasts and knew they would not. I do not know why hares leave their young in the open, but they do and there they lay, three sleek leverets in a hollow of the downs, doubtless the first things to die in that day of wind and rain.

'Shout at them!' Osric called. 'Tell them they're bastards! Call them sons of whores! Say they're shit from the north! Shout at them!' He knew that was one way to get men moving. The Danes were screaming at us, calling us women, saying we had no courage, and no one in our ranks was shouting back, but Osric's men started now and the wet sky was filled with the noise of weapons banging on shields and men calling insults.

I had hung Serpent-Breath on my back. In the crush of battle a sword is easier to draw over the shoulder than from the hip, and the first stroke can then be a vicious down-ward hack. I carried Wasp-Sting in my right hand. Wasp-Sting was a sax, a short-sword, a stout blade for stabbing, and in the press of men heaving against an enemy shield wall a short-sword can do more damage than a long blade. My shield, iron-rimmed, was held on my left forearm by two leather loops. The shield had a metal boss the size of a man's head, a weapon in itself. Steapa, to my right, had a long sword, not as long as the one with which he had fought me at Cippanhamm, but still a hefty blade, though in his big hand it looked almost puny. Pyrlig carried a boar spear, short and stout and with a wide blade. He was saying the same phrase over and over. '*Ein tad, yr hwn wyt yn y nefoedd, sancteiddier dy enw.*' I learned later it was the prayer Jesus had taught his disciples. Steapa was muttering that the Danes were bastards. 'Bastards,' he said, then, 'God help me, bastards.' He kept saying it. Over and over. 'Bastards, God help me, bastards.' My mouth was suddenly too dry to speak, and my stomach felt sour and my bowels loose.

'Forward! Forward!' Osric called and we shuffled on, shields touching, and we could see the enemies' faces now. We could see men's unkempt beards and yellow-toothed snarls, see their scarred cheeks, pocked skin and broken noses. My face-plate meant I could only see directly ahead. Sometimes it is better to fight without a face-plate, to see the attacks coming from the side, but in the clash of shield walls a face-plate is useful. The helmet was lined with leather. I was sweating. Arrows flicked from the Danish line. They did not have many bowmen and the arrows were scattered, but we raised shields to protect our faces. None came near me, but we were bent back from the line to watch the fort's green walls that were rimmed with men, thick with sword-Danes, and I could see Ragnar's eagle-wing banner there and I wondered what would happen if I found myself face to face with him. I could see the axes and spears and swords, the blades that sought our souls. Rain drummed on helmets and shields.

The line paused again. Osric's shield wall and Svein's *skjaldborg* were only twenty paces apart now and men could see their immediate foes, could see the face of the man they must kill or the man who would kill them. Both sides were screaming, spitting anger and insults, and the spear-throwers had their first missiles hefted.

'Keep close!' someone shouted.

'Shields touching!'

'God is with us!' Beocca called.

'Forward!' Another two paces, more of a shuffle forward than stepping.

'Bastards,' Steapa said, 'God help me, bastards.'

'Now!' Osric screamed. 'Now! Forward and kill them! Forward and kill them! Go! Go! Go!' And the men of Wiltunscir went. They let out a great war shout, as much to hearten themselves as to frighten the enemy, and suddenly, after so long, the shield wall went forward fast, men screaming, and the spears came over the Danish line and our own spears were hurled back and then came the clash, the real battle thunder as shield wall met *skjaldborg*. The shock of the collision shook our whole line so that even my troops, who were not yet engaged, staggered. I heard the first screams, the clangour of blades, the thump of metal driving into shield-wood, the grunting of men, and then I saw the Danes coming over the green ramparts, a flood of Danes charging us, intent on hacking into the flank of our attack, but that was why Alfred had put us on the left of Osric's force.

'Shields!' Leofric roared.

I hoisted my shield, touched Steapa's and Pyrlig's shields, then crouched to receive the charge. Head down, body covered by wood, legs braced, Wasp-Sting ready. Behind us and to our right Osric's men fought. I could smell blood and shit. Those are the smells of battle, then I forgot Osric's fight for the rain was in my face, and the Danes were coming at a run, no shield wall formed, just a frenzied charge intent on winning the battle in one furious assault. There were hundreds of them, and then our spear-throwers let their missiles go.

'Now!' I shouted, and we stepped one pace forward to meet the charge and my left arm was crushed into my chest as a Dane hit me, shield against shield, and he slammed an axe down and I rammed Wasp-Sting forward, past his shield, into his flank and his axe buried itself in Eadric's shield that was above my head. I twisted Wasp-Sting's blade, pulled her free and stabbed again. I could smell ale on the Dane's sour breath. His face was a grimace. He yanked his axe free. I stabbed again and twisted the sax's tip into mail or bone, I could not tell which. 'Your mother was a piece of pig-shit,' I told the Dane, and he screamed in rage and tried to bring the axe down onto my helmet, but I ducked and shoved forward, and Eadric protected me with his shield, and Wasp-Sting was red now, warm and sticky with blood, and I ripped her upwards.

Steapa was screaming incoherently, his sword slashing left and right, and the Danes avoided him. My enemy stumbled, went down onto his knees, and I hit him with the shield boss, breaking his nose and teeth, then shoved Wasp-Sting into his bloody mouth. Another man immediately took his place, but Pyrlig buried his boar spear in the newcomer's belly.

'Shields!' I shouted, and Steapa and Pyrlig instinctively lined their shields with mine. I had no idea what happened elsewhere on the hilltop. I only knew what happened within Wasp-Sting's reach.

'Back one! Back one!' Pyrlig called, and we stepped back one pace so that the next Danes, taking the place of the men we had wounded or killed, would trip over the fallen bodies of their comrades, and then we stepped forward as they came so that we met them when they were off balance. That was how to do it, the way of the warrior, and we in Alfred's immediate force were his best soldiers. The Danes had charged us wildly, not bothering to lock shields in the belief that their fury alone would overwhelm us. They had been drawn, too, by the sight of Alfred's banners and the knowledge that should those twin flags topple then the battle was as good as won, but their assault hit our shield wall like an ocean wave striking a cliff, and it shattered there. It left men on the turf and blood on the grass, and now the Danes at last made a proper shield wall and came at us more steadily.

I heard the enemy shields touching, saw the Danes' wild eyes over the round rims, saw their grimaces as they gathered their strength. Then they shouted and came to kill us.

'Now!' I shouted and we thrust forward to meet them.

The shield walls crashed together. Eadric was at my back, pressing me forward, and the art of fighting now was to keep a space between my body and my shield with a strong left arm, and then to stab under the shield with Wasp-Sting. Eadric could fight over my shoulder with his sword. I had space to my right for Steapa was left-handed which meant his shield was on his right arm, and he kept moving it away from me to give his long sword room to strike. That gap, no wider than a man's foot is long, was an invitation to the Danes, but they were scared of Steapa and none tried to burst through the small space. His height alone made him distinctive, and his skull-tight face made him fearsome. He was bellowing like a calf being gelded, half shriek and half belligerence, inviting the Danes to come and be killed. They refused. They had learned the danger of Pyrlig, Steapa and I, and they were cautious. Elsewhere along Alfred's shield wall there were men dying and screaming, swords and axes clanging like bells, but in front of me the Danes hung back and merely jabbed with spears to keep us at bay. I shouted that they were cowards, but that did not goad them onto Wasp-Sting, and I glanced left and right and saw that all along Alfred's line we were holding them. Our shield wall was strong. All that practice in Æthelingæg was proving itself, and for the Danes the fight grew ever more difficult for they were attacking us, and to reach us they had to step over the bodies of their own dead and wounded. A man does not see where he treads in battle for he is watching the enemy, and some Danes stumbled, and others slipped on the rain-slicked grass and when they were off balance we struck hard, spears and swords like snake-tongues, making more bodies to trip the enemy.

We of Alfred's household troops were good. We were steady. We were beating the Danes, but behind us, in Osric's larger force, Wessex was dying.

Because Osric's shield wall unravelled.

Wulfhere's men did it. They did not break Osric's shield wall by fighting it, but by trying to join it. Few of them wanted to fight for the Danes and, now that the battle was joined, they shouted at their countrymen that they were no enemy and wanted to change sides, and the shield wall opened to let them through, and Svein's men went for the gaps like wildcats. One after the other those gaps widened as sword-Danes burst through. They cut Wulfhere's men down from behind, they prised open Osric's ranks and spread death like a plague. Svein's Vikings were warriors among farmers, hawks among pigeons, and all of Alfred's right wing shattered. Arnulf saved the men of Suth Seaxa by leading them to the rear of our ranks, and they were safe enough there, but Osric's fyrd was broken, harried and driven away east and south.

The rain had stopped and a cold damp wind scoured the edge of the downs now. Alfred's men, reinforced by Arnulf's four hundred and a dozen or so of Osric's fugitives, stood alone as the Wiltunscir fyrd retreated. They were being driven away from us, and Svein and his horsemen were panicking them. The fyrd had been eight hundred strong, ranked firm, and now they were shattered into small groups that huddled together for protection and tried to fend off the galloping horsemen who thrust with their long spears. Bodies lay all across the turf. Some of Osric's men were wounded and crawled south as if there might be safety where the women and horses were gathered around a mounded grave of the old folk, but the horsemen turned and speared them, and the unmounted Danes were making new shield walls to attack the fugitives. We could do nothing to help, for we were still fighting Guthrum's men who had come from the fort and, though we were winning that fight, we could not turn our backs on the enemy. So we thrust and hacked and pushed, and slowly they went backwards, and then they realised that they were dying man by man, and I heard the Danish shouts to go back to the fort, and we let them go. They retreated from us, walking backwards, and when they saw we would not follow, they turned and ran to the green walls. They left a tideline of corpses, sixty or seventy Danes on the turf, and we had lost no more than twenty men. I took a silver chain off one corpse, two arm rings from another and a fine bone-handled knife with a knob of amber in its hilt from a third.

'Back!' Alfred called.

It was not till we retreated to where we had begun the fight that I realised the disaster on our right. We had been the centre of Alfred's army, but now we were its right wing, and what had been our strong right flank was splintered chaos. Many of Osric's men had retreated to where the women and horses waited, and they made a shield wall there which served to protect them, but most of the fyrd had fled farther east and was being carved into smaller and smaller groups.

Svein at last hauled his men back from the pursuit, but by then nearly all our right wing was gone. Many of those men lived, but they had been driven from the field and would be reluctant to come back and take more punishment. Osric himself had survived, and he brought the two hundred men who had retreated to the women and horses back to Alfred, but that was all he had left. Svein formed his men again, facing us, and I could see him haranguing them. 'They're coming for us,' I said.

'God will protect us,' Pyrlig said. He had blood on his face. A sword or axe had pierced his helmet and cut open his scalp so that blood was crusted thick on his left cheek.

'Where was your shield?' I demanded of Æthelwold.

'I've got it,' he said. He looked pale and frightened.

'You're supposed to protect Pyrlig's head,' I snarled at him.

'It's nothing,' Pyrlig tried to calm my anger.

Æthelwold looked as if he would protest, then suddenly jerked forward and vomited. I turned away from him. I was angry, but I was also disappointed. The bowel-loosening fear was gone, but the fighting had seemed half-hearted and ineffective. We had seen off the Danes who had attacked us, but we had not hurt them so badly that they would abandon the fight. I wanted to feel the battle-rage, the screaming joy of killing, and instead all seemed ponderous and difficult.

I had looked for Ragnar during the fight, fearing having to fight my friend, and when the Danes had gone back to the fort I saw he had been engaged further down the line. I could see him now, on the rampart, staring at us, then I looked right, expecting to see Svein lead his men in an assault on us, but instead I saw Svein galloping to the fort and I suspected he went to demand reinforcements from Guthrum.

The battle was less than an hour old, yet now it paused. Some women brought us water and mouldy bread while the wounded sought what help they could find. I wrapped a rag around Eadric's left arm where an axe blade had gone through the leather of his sleeve. 'It was aimed at you, lord,' he said, grinning at me toothlessly.

I tied the rag into place. 'Does it hurt?'

'Bit of an ache,' he said, 'but not bad. Not bad.' He flexed his arm, found it worked and picked up his shield. I looked again at Svein's men, but they seemed in no hurry to resume their attack. I saw a man tip a skin of water or ale to his mouth. Just ahead of us, among the line of dead, a man suddenly sat up. He was Danish and had plaited black hair that had been tied in knots and decorated with ribbons. I had thought he was dead, but he sat up and stared at us with a look of indignation and then, seemingly, yawned. He was looking straight at me, his mouth open, and then a flood of blood rimmed and spilled over his lower lip to soak his beard. His eyes rolled white and he fell backwards. Svein's men were still not moving. There were some eight hundred of them arrayed in their line. They were still the left wing of Guthrum's army, but that wing was much smaller now that it had been shorn of Wulfhere's men, and so I turned and pushed through our ranks to find Alfred. 'Lord!' I called, getting his attention. 'Attack those men!' I pointed to Svein's troops. They were a good two hundred paces from the fort and, for the moment at least, without their leader because Svein was still inside the ramparts. Alfred looked down on me from his saddle and I urged him to attack with every man in the centre division of our army. The Danes had the escarpment at their back and I reckoned we could tip them down that treacherous slope. Alfred listened to me, looked at Svein's men, then shook his head dumbly. Beocca was on his knees, hands spread wide and face screwed tight in an intensity of prayer.

'We can drive them off, lord,' I insisted.

'They'll come from the fort,' Alfred said, meaning that Guthrum's Danes would come to help Svein's men.

Some would, but I doubted enough would come. 'But we want them out of the fort,' I insisted. 'They're easier to kill in open ground, lord.'

Alfred just shook his head again. I think, at that moment, he was almost paralysed by the fear of doing the wrong thing, and so he chose to do nothing. He wore a plain helmet with a nasal, no other protection for his face, and he looked sickly pale. He could not see an obvious opportunity, and so he would let the enemy make the next decision.

It was Svein who made it. He brought more Danes out of the fort, three or four hundred of them. Most of Guthrum's men stayed behind the ramparts, but those men who had made the first attack on Alfred's bodyguard now streamed onto the open downland where they joined Svein's troops and made their shield wall. I could see Ragnar's banner among them.

'They're going to attack, aren't they?' Pyrlig said. The rain had washed much of the blood from his face, but the split in his helmet looked gory. 'I'm all right,' he said, seeing me glance at the damage, 'I've had worse from a row with the wife. But those bastards are coming, aren't they? They want to keep killing us from our right.'

'We can beat them, lord,' I called back to Alfred. 'Put all our men against them. All of them!'

He seemed not to hear.

'Bring Wiglaf's fyrd across, lord!' I appealed to him.

'We can't move Wiglaf,' he said indignantly.

He feared that if he moved the Sumorsæte fyrd from its place in front of the fort then Guthrum would lead all his men out to assault our left flank, but I knew Guthrum was far too cautious to do any such thing. He felt safe behind the turf ramparts and he wanted to stay safe while Svein won the battle for him. Guthrum would not move until our army was broken, then he would launch an assault. But

Alfred would not listen. He was a clever man, perhaps as clever as any man born, but he did not understand battle. He did not understand that battle is not just about numbers, it is not about moving tafl pieces, and it is not even about who has the advantage in ground, but about passion and madness and a screaming, ungovernable rage.

And so far I had felt none of those things. We in Alfred's household troops had fought well enough, but we had merely defended ourselves. We had not carried slaughter to the enemy, and it is only when you attack that you win. Now, it seemed, we were to defend ourselves again, and Alfred stirred himself to order me and my men to the right of his line. 'Leave the standards with me,' he said, 'and make sure our flank is safe.'

There was honour in that. The right end of the line was where the enemy might try to wrap around us and Alfred needed good men to hold that open flank, and so we formed a tight knot there. Far off across the down I could see the remnants of Osric's fyrd. They were watching us. Some of them, I thought, would return if they thought we were winning, but for the moment they were too full of fear to rejoin Alfred's army.

Svein rode his white horse up and down the face of his shield wall. He was shouting at his troops, encouraging them. Telling them we were weaklings who needed only one push to topple.

'And I looked,' Pyrlig said to me, 'and I saw a pale horse, and the rider's name was death.' I stared at him in astonishment. 'It's from the gospel book,' he explained sheepishly, 'and it just came to my mind.'

'Then put it out of your mind,' I said harshly, 'because our job is to kill him, not fear him.' I turned to tell Æthelwold to make certain he kept his shield up, but saw he had taken a new place in the rear rank. He was better there, I decided, so left him alone. Svein was shouting that we were lambs waiting to be slaughtered, and his men had begun beating weapons against their shields. There were just over a thousand men in Svein's ranks now, and they would be assaulting Alfred's division that numbered about the same, but the Danes still had the advantage, for every man in their shield wall was a warrior, while over half our men were from the fyrds of Defnascir, Thornsæta and Hamptonscir. If we had brought Wiglaf's fyrd to join us we could have overwhelmed Svein, but by the same token he could have swamped us if Guthrum had the courage to leave the fort. Both sides were being cautious. Neither was willing to throw everything into the battle for fear of losing everything.

Svein's horsemen were on the left flank, opposite my men. He wanted us to feel threatened by the riders, but a horse will not charge into a shield wall. It will sheer away, and I would rather face horsemen than foot-soldiers. One horse was tossing its head and I could see blood on its neck. Another horse was lying dead out where the corpses lay in the cold wind that was bringing the first ravens from the north. Black wings in a dull sky. Odin's birds.

'Come and die!' Steapa suddenly shouted. 'Come and die, you bastards! Come on!'

His shout prompted others along our line to call insults to the Danes. Svein turned, apparently surprised by our sudden defiance. His men had started forward, but stopped again, and I realised, with surprise, that they were just as fearful as we were. I had always held the Danes in awe, reckoning them the greatest fighting men under the sky. Alfred, in a moment of gloom, once told me it took four Saxons to beat one Dane, and there was a truth in that, but it was not a binding truth, and it was not true that day for there was no passion in Svein's men. There was unhappiness there, a reluctance to advance, and I reckoned that

Guthrum and Svein had quarrelled. Or perhaps the cold, damp wind had quelled everyone's ardour. 'We're going to win this battle!' I shouted, and surprised myself by shouting it.

Men looked at me, wondering if I had been sent a vision by my gods.

'We're going to win!' I was hardly aware of speaking. I had not meant to make a speech, but I made one anyway. 'They're frightened of us!' I called out, 'they're scared! Most of them are skulking in the fort because they daren't come out to face Saxon blades! And those men,' I gestured at Svein's ranks with Wasp-Sting, 'know they're going to die! They're going to die!' I took a few paces forward and spread my arms to get the Danes' attention. I held my shield out to the left and Wasp-Sting to the right. 'You're going to die!' I shouted it in Danish, loud as I could, then in English. 'You're going to die!'

And all Alfred's men took up that shout. 'You're going to die! You're going to die!'

Something odd happened then. Beocca and Pyrlig claimed that the spirit of God wafted through our army, and maybe that did happen, or else we suddenly began to believe in ourselves. We believed we could win and as the chant was shouted at the enemy we began to go forward, step by step, beating swords against shields and shouting that the enemy would die. I was ahead of my men, taunting the enemy, screaming at them, dancing as I went, and Alfred called me back to the ranks. Later, when all was done, Beocca told me that Alfred called me repeatedly, but I was capering and shouting, out ahead on the grass where the corpses lay, and I did not hear him. And Alfred's men were following me and he did not call them back though he had not ordered them forward.

'You bastards!' I screamed, 'you goat-turds! You fight like

girls!' I do not know what insults I shouted that day, only that I shouted them and that I went ahead, on my own, asking just one of them to come and fight me man to man.

Alfred never approved of those duels between the shield walls. Perhaps, sensibly, he disapproved because he knew he could not have fought one himself, but he also saw them as dangerous. When a man invites an enemy champion to a fight, man on man, he invites his own death, and if he dies he takes the heart from his own side and gives courage to the enemy, and so Alfred ever forbade us to accept Danish challenges, but on that cold wet day one man did accept my challenge.

It was Svein himself. Svein of the White Horse, and he turned the white horse and spurred towards me with his sword in his right hand. I could hear the hooves thumping, see the clods of wet turf flying behind, see the stallion's mane tossing and I could see Svein's boar-masked helmet above the rim of his shield. Man and horse coming for me, and the Danes were jeering and just then Pyrlig shouted at me. 'Uhtred! Uhtred!'

I did not turn to look at him. I was too busy sheathing Wasp-Sting and was about to pull Serpent-Breath from her scabbard, but just then Pyrlig's thick-shafted boar spear skidded beside me in the wet grass, and I understood what he was trying to tell me. I left Serpent-Breath on my shoulder and snatched up the Briton's spear just as Svein closed on me. All I could hear was the thunder of hooves, see the white cloak spreading, the bright shine of the lofted blade, the tossing horsehair plume, white eyes on the horse, teeth bared, and then Svein twitched the stallion to his left and cut the sword at me. His eyes were glitters behind the eye-pieces of his helmet as he leaned to kill me, but as his sword came I threw myself into his horse and rammed the spear into the beast's guts. I had to do it one-handed, for

I had my shield on my left arm, but the wide blade pierced hide and muscle, and I was screaming, trying to drive it deeper, and then Svein's sword struck my lifted shield like a hammer blow and his right knee struck my helmet so that I was thrown hard back to sprawl on the grass. I had let go of the spear, but it was well buried in the horse's belly and the animal was screaming and shaking, bucking and tossing, and thick blood was pouring down the spear's shaft that banged and bounced along the grass.

The horse bolted. Svein somehow stayed in the saddle. There was blood on the beast's belly. I had not hurt Svein, I had not touched him, but he was fleeing from me, or rather his white horse was bolting in pain and it ran straight at Svein's own shield wall. A horse will instinctively swerve away from a shield wall, but this horse was blinded by pain, and then, just short of the Danish shields, it half fell. It slid on the wet grass and skidded hard into the *skjaldborg*, breaking it open. Men scattered from the animal. Svein tumbled from the saddle, and then the horse somehow managed to get back on its feet, and it reared and screamed. Blood was flying from its belly, and its hooves were flailing at the Danes, and now we were charging them at the run. I was on my feet, Serpent-Breath in my right hand, and the horse was thrashing and twisting, and the Danes backed away from it, and that opened their shield wall as we hit them.

Svein was just getting to his feet as Alfred's men arrived. I did not see it, but men said Steapa's sword took Svein's head off in one blow. A blow so hard that the helmeted head flew into the air, and perhaps that was true, but what was certain was that the passion was on us now. The blinding, seething passion of battle. The blood lust, the killing rage, and the horse was doing the work for us, breaking the Danish shield wall apart so all we had to do was ram into the gaps and kill.

And so we killed. Alfred had not meant this to happen. He had expected to wait for the Danish attack and hoped we would resist it, but instead we had thrown off his leash and were doing his work, and he had the wit to send Arnulf's men out to the right because my men were among the enemy. The horsemen had tried to come around our rear, but the men of Suth Seaxa saw them off with shields and swords, then guarded the open flank as all Alfred's men from Æthelingæg, and all Harald's men from Defnascir and Thornsæta joined the slaughter. My cousin was there, with his Mercians, and he was a stout fighter. I watched him parry, stab, put down a man, take on another, kill him, and go on steadily. We were making the hilltop rich with Danish blood because we had the fury and they did not, and the men who had fled the field, Osric's men, were coming back to join the fight.

The horsemen went. I did not see them go, though their tale will be told. I was fighting, screaming, shouting at Danes to come and be killed, and Pyrlig was beside me, holding a sword now, and the whole left-hand side of Svein's shield wall had broken and its survivors were making small groups, and we attacked them. I charged one group with the shield, using its boss to slam a man back and stabbing with Serpent-Breath, feeling her break through mail and leather, and Leofric appeared from somewhere, axe swinging, and Pyrlig was ramming his sword's tip into a man's face, and for every Dane there were two Saxons and the enemy stood no chance. One man shouted for mercy and Leofric broke his helmet apart with the axe so that blood and brains oozed onto the jagged metal and I kicked the man aside and plunged Serpent-Breath into a man's groin so that he screamed like a woman in childbirth. The poets often sing of that battle, and for once they get something right when they tell of the sword joy, the blade song, the slaughter. We tore Svein's men to bloody ruin, and we did it with passion, skill and savagery. The battle-calm was on me at last and I could do no wrong. Serpent-Breath had her own life and she stole it from the Danes who tried to oppose me, but those Danes were broken and running and all the left wing of Svein's vaunted troops was defeated.

And there was suddenly no enemy near me except for the dead and injured. Alfred's nephew, Æthelwold, was jabbing his sword at one of the wounded Danes. 'Either kill him,' I snarled, 'or let him live.' The man had a broken leg and had an eye hanging down his bloody cheek and he was no danger to anyone.

'I have to kill one pagan,' Æthelwold said. He prodded the man with the sword tip and I kicked his blade aside, and would have helped the wounded man except it was then that I saw Haesten.

He was at the hill's edge, a fugitive, and I shouted his name. He turned and saw me, or saw a blood-drenched warrior in mail and a wolf-crested helmet, and he stared at me, then perhaps he recognised the helmet for he fled. 'Coward!' I shouted at him. 'You treacherous, bastard coward! You swore me an oath! I made you rich! I saved your rotten life!'

He turned then, half grinned at me and waved his left arm on which hung the splintered remnants of a shield, then he ran to what remained of the right-hand side of Svein's shield wall, and that was still in good order, its shields locked tight. There were five or six hundred men there, and they had swung back, then retreated towards the fort, but now they checked because Alfred's men, having no one left to kill, were turning on them. Haesten joined the Danish ranks, pushing through the shields, and I saw the eagle-wing banner above them and knew that Ragnar, my friend, was leading those survivors.

393

I paused. Leofric was shouting at men to form a shield wall and I knew this attack had lost its fury, but we had damaged them. We had killed Svein and a good number of his men, and the Danes were now penned back against the fort. I went to the hill's edge, following a trail of blood on the wet grass, and saw that the white horse had bolted over the down's lip and now lay, its legs grotesquely cocked in the air and its white pelt spattered with blood, a few yards down the slope.

'That was a good horse,' Pyrlig said. He had joined me on the edge of the hill. I had thought this crest was the top of the escarpment, but the land was tangled here, as though a giant had kicked the hillside with a massive boot. The ground fell away to make a steep valley that suddenly climbed to a farther crest that was the real edge of the downs, and the steep valley sloped up to the fort's eastern corner, and I wondered whether it would offer a way into the fastness. Pyrlig was still staring at the dead horse. 'You know what we say at home?' he asked me. 'We say that a good horse is worth two good women, that a good woman is worth two good hounds, and that a good hound is worth two good horses.'

'You say what?'

'Never mind,' he touched my shoulder. 'For a Saxon, Uhtred, you fight well. Like a Briton.'

I decided the valley offered no advantage over a direct assault and turned away to see that Ragnar was retreating step by step towards the fort. I knew this was the moment to attack him, to keep the battle-anger alive and the slaughter fresh, but our men were plundering the dead and the dying and none had the energy to renew the assault, and that meant we would have the harder task of killing Danes protected by a rampart. I thought of my father, killed in an attack on a wall. He had not shown much liking for me, probably because I had been a small child when he died, and now I would have to follow him into the death-trap of a well protected wall. Fate is inexorable.

Svein's banner of the white horse had been captured and a man was waving it towards the Danes. Another had Svein's helmet on the tip of a spear, and at first I thought it was Svein's head, then I saw it was only the helmet. The white horsetail plume was pink now. Father Willibald was holding his hands to heaven, saying a prayer of thanks, and that was premature, I thought, for all we had done was break Svein's men and Guthrum's troops still waited for us behind their walls. And Ragnar was there too, safe in the fort. Its walls made a semi-circle jutting into the downs, ending at the escarpment's lip. They were high walls, protected by a ditch. 'It'll be a bastard crossing those ramparts,' I said.

'Maybe we won't have to,' Pyrlig answered.

'Of course we have to.'

'Not if Alfred can talk them out of there,' Pyrlig said, and he pointed and I saw that the king, accompanied by two priests and by Osric and Harald, was approaching the fort. 'He's going to let them surrender,' Pyrlig said.

I could not believe this was the time to talk. This was the killing time, not a place for negotiations. 'They won't surrender,' I said, 'of course they won't! They still think they can beat us.'

'Alfred will try to persuade them,' Pyrlig said.

'No,' I shook my head. 'He'll offer them a truce.' I spoke angrily. 'He'll offer to take hostages. He'll preach to them. It's what he always does.' I thought about going to join him, if for nothing else to add some sourness to his reasonable suggestions, but I could not summon the effort. Three Danes had gone to talk to him, but I knew they would not accept his offer. They were not beaten, far from it. They still had more men than we did and they had the walls of the fort, and the battle was still theirs to win.

Then I heard the shouts. Shouts of anger and screams of pain, and I turned and saw that the Danish horsemen had reached our women, and the women were screaming and there was nothing we could do.

The Danish horsemen had expected to slaughter the broken remnants of Alfred's shield wall, but instead it had been Svein's men who had been broken and the riders, out on Svein's left flank, had retreated into the downs. They must have thought to circle about our army and rejoin Guthrum from the west, and on the way they had seen our women and horses and smelled easy plunder.

Yet our women had weapons, and there were a few wounded men there, and together they had resisted the horsemen. There was a brief flurry of killing, then the Danish riders, with nothing to show for their attack, rode away westwards. It had taken a few moments, nothing more, but Hild had snatched up a spear and run at a horseman, screaming hate for the horrors the Danes had inflicted on her in Cippanhamm, and Eanflæd, who saw it all, said that Hild sank the spear in a Dane's leg and the man had chopped down with his sword, and Iseult, who had gone to help Hild, had parried the blow with another sword, and a second Dane caught her from behind with an axe, and then a rush of screaming women drove the Danes away. Hild lived, but Iseult's skull had been broken open and her head almost split into two. She was dead.

'She has gone to God,' Pyrlig told me when Leofric brought us the news. I was weeping, but I did not know whether it was sorrow or anger that consumed me. I could say nothing. Pyrlig held my shoulders. 'She is with God, Uhtred.'

'Then the men who sent her there must go to hell,' I said. 'Any hell. Freeze or burn, the bastards!'

I pulled away from Pyrlig and strode towards Alfred. I saw Wulfhere then. He was a prisoner, guarded by two of Alfred's bodyguard, and he brightened when he saw me as though he thought I was a friend, but I just spat at him and walked on past.

Alfred frowned when I joined him. He was escorted by Osric and Harald, and by Father Beocca and Bishop Alewold, none of whom spoke Danish, but one of the Danes was an English-speaker. There were three of them, all strangers to me, but Beocca told me their spokesman was called Hrothgar Ericson and I knew he was one of Guthrum's chieftains. 'They attacked the women,' I told Alfred. The king just stared at me, perhaps not understanding what I had said. 'They attacked the women!' I repeated.

'He's whimpering,' the Danish interpreter spoke to his two companions, 'that the women were attacked.'

'If I whimper,' I turned on the man in fury, 'then you will scream.' I spoke in Danish. 'I shall pull your guts out of your arsehole, wrap them around your filthy neck and feed your eyeballs to my hounds. Now if you want to translate, you shrivelled bastard, translate properly, or else go back to your vomit.'

The man blinked, but said nothing. Hrothgar, resplendent in mail and silvered helmet, half smiled. 'Tell your king,' he said, 'that we might agree to withdraw to Cippanhamm, but we shall want hostages.'

I turned on Alfred. 'How many men does Guthrum still have?'

He was still unhappy that I had joined him, but he took the question seriously. 'Enough,' he said.

397

'Enough to hold Cippanhamm and a half-dozen other towns. We break them now.'

'You are welcome to try,' Hrothgar said when my words were translated.

I turned back to him. 'I killed Ubba,' I said, 'and I put Svein down, and next I shall cut Guthrum's throat and send him to his whore-mother. We'll try.'

'Uhtred.' Alfred did not know what I had said, but he had heard my tone and he tried to calm me.

'There's work to be done, lord,' I said. It was anger speaking in me, a fury at the Danes and an equal fury at Alfred, who was once again offering the enemy terms. He had done it so often. He would beat them in battle and immediately make a truce because he believed they would become Christians and live in brotherly peace. That was his desire, to live in a Christian Britain devoted to piety, but on that day I was right. Guthrum was not beaten, he still outnumbered us, and he had to be destroyed.

'Tell them,' Alfred said, 'that they can surrender to us now. Tell them they can lay down their weapons and come out of the fort.'

Hrothgar treated that proposal with the scorn it deserved. Most of Guthrum's men had yet to fight. They were far from defeated, and the green walls were high and the ditches were deep, and it was the sight of those ramparts that had prompted Alfred to speak with the enemy. He knew men must die, many men, and that was the price he had been unwilling to pay a year before when Guthrum had been trapped in Exanceaster, but it was a price that had to be paid. It was the price of Wessex.

Hrothgar had nothing more to say, so turned away. 'Tell Earl Ragnar,' I called after him, 'that I am still his brother.'

'He will doubtless see you in Valhalla one day,' Hrothgar called back, then waved a negligent hand to me. I suspected that the Danes had never intended to negotiate a truce, let alone a surrender, but when Alfred offered to talk they had accepted because it gave them time to organise their defences.

Alfred scowled at me. He was plainly annoyed that I had intervened, but before he could say anything Beocca spoke. 'What happened to the women?' he asked.

'They fought the bastards off,' I said, 'but Iseult died.'

'Iseult,' Alfred said, and then he saw the tears in my eyes and did not know what to say. He flinched, stuttered incoherently, then closed his eyes as if in prayer. 'I am glad,' he said after he had collected his thoughts, 'that she died a Christian.'

'Amen,' Beocca said.

'I would rather she was a live pagan,' I snarled, and then we went back to our army and Alfred again summoned his commanders.

There was really no choice. We had to assault the fort. Alfred talked for a time about establishing a siege, but that was not practical. We would have to sustain an army on the summit of the downs and, though Osric insisted the enemy had no springs inside the fort, neither did we have springs close by. Both armies would be thirsty, and we did not have enough men to stop Danes going down the steep embankment at night to fetch water. And if the siege lasted longer than a week, then men of the fyrd would begin to slip home to look after their fields, and Alfred would be tempted to mercy, especially if Guthrum promised to convert to Christianity.

So we urged an assault on Alfred. There could be nothing clever. Shield walls must be made and men sent against the ramparts, and Alfred knew that every man in the army must join the attack. Wiglaf and the men of Sumorsæte would attack on the left, Alfred's men in the centre, while Osric, whose fyrd had gathered again and was now reinforced by the men who had deserted from Guthrum's army, would assault on the right. 'You know how to do it,' Alfred said, though without any enthusiasm for he knew he was ordering us into a feast of death, 'put your best men in the centre, let them lead, and make the others press behind and on either side.'

No one said anything. Alfred offered a bitter smile. 'God has smiled on us so far,' he said, 'and he will not desert us.'

Yet he had deserted Iseult. Poor, fragile Iseult, shadow queen and lost soul, and I pushed into the front rank because the only thing I could do for her now was to take revenge. Steapa, as smothered in blood as I was, pushed into the rank beside me. Leofric was to my left and Pyrlig was now behind me. 'Spears and long swords,' Pyrlig advised us, 'not those short things.'

'Why not?' Leofric asked.

'You climb that steep wall,' he said, 'and all you can do is go for their ankles. Bring them down. I've done it before. You need a long reach and a good shield.'

'Jesus help us,' Leofric said. We were all fearful, for there is little in warfare as daunting as an assault on a fortress. If I had been in my senses I would have been reluctant to make that attack, but I was filled with a keening sorrow for Iseult and nothing except revenge filled my mind. 'Let's go,' I said, 'let's go.'

But we could not go. Men were collecting spears thrown in the earlier fighting, and the bowmen were being brought forward. Whenever we attacked we wanted a shower of spears to precede us, and a plague of stinging arrows to annoy the enemy, but it took time to array the spearmen and archers behind the men who would make the assault.

Then, ominously for our archers, it began to rain again. Their bows would still work, but water weakened the strings.

The sky became darker as a great belly of black cloud settled over the down and the rain started to drum on helmets. The Danes were lining the ramparts, clashing their weapons against shields as our army curled about their fastness.

'Forward!' Alfred shouted, and we went towards the ramparts, but stopped just out of bowshot. Rain beaded the rim of my shield. There was a new, bright scar in the iron there, a blade strike, but I had not been aware of the blow. The Danes mocked us. They knew what was coming, and they probably welcomed it. Ever since Guthrum had climbed the escarpment and discovered the fort he had probably imagined Alfred's men assaulting its walls and his men cutting the enemy down as we struggled up the steep banks. This was Guthrum's battle now. He had placed his rival, Svein, and his Saxon ally, Wulfhere, outside the fort, and doubtless he had hoped they could destroy a good part of our army before the assault on the ramparts, but it would not matter much to Guthrum that those men had been destroyed themselves. Now his own men would fight the battle he had always envisaged.

'In the name of God!' Alfred called, then said no more for suddenly a clap of thunder crashed, a vast sound that consumed the heavens and was so loud that some of us flinched. A crack of lightning splintered white inside the fort. The rain pelted now, a cloudburst that hammered and soaked us, and more thunder rolled away in the distance, and perhaps we thought that noise and savage light was a message from God for suddenly the whole army started forward. No one had given a command, unless Alfred's invocation was an order. We just went.

Men were shouting as they advanced. They were not calling insults, but just making a noise to give themselves courage. We did not run, but walked, because the shields had to be kept close. Then another bellow of thunder deafened us, and the rain seemed to have a new and vicious intensity. It seethed on the dead and the living, and we were close now, very close, yet the rain was so thick it was hard to see the waiting Danes. Then I saw the ditch, already flooding, and the bows sounded and the spears flew and we were splashing down the ditch's side and Danish spears were thumping into us. One stuck in my shield, fell away and I stumbled on its shaft, half sprawled in the water, then recovered and began the climb.

Not all the army tried to cross the ditch. Many men's courage faltered at the brink, but a dozen or more groups went into the attack. We were what the Danes call the *svin-fylkjas*, the swine-wedges, the elite warriors who try to pierce the *skjaldborg* like a boar trying to gouge the hunter with its tusks. But this time we not only had to gouge the *skjaldborg*, but cross the rain-flooded ditch and clamber up the bank.

We held our shields over our heads as we splashed through the ditch. Then we climbed, but the wet bank was so slippery that we constantly fell back, and the Danish spears kept coming, and someone pushed me from behind and I was crawling up the bank on my knees, the shield over my head, and Pyrlig's shield was covering my spine and I heard a thumping above me and thought it was thunder. Except the shield kept banging against my helmet and I knew a Dane was hacking at me, trying to break through the limewood to drive his axe or sword into my spine, and I crawled again, lifted the shield's lower edge and saw boots. I lunged with Serpent-Breath, tried to stand, felt a blow on my leg and fell again. Steapa was roaring beside me. There was mud in my mouth, and the rain hammered at us and I could hear the crash of blades sinking in shields and I knew we had failed, but I tried to stand again and lunged with Serpent-Breath and on my left Leofric gave a shrill cry and I saw blood streaming into the grass. The blood was instantly washed away by the rain, and another peal of thunder crashed overhead as I slithered back to the ditch.

The bank was scarred where we had tried to climb, the grass had been gouged down to the white chalk. We had failed utterly and the Danes were screaming defiance, then another rush of men splashed through the ditch and the banging of blades and shields began again. I climbed a second time, trying to dig my boots into the chalk, and my shield was raised so I did not see the Danes coming down to meet me, and the first I knew was when an axe struck the shield so hard that the boards splintered, and a second axe gave me a glancing blow on the helmet and I fell backwards and would have lost Serpent-Breath if it had not been for the loop of Iseult's hair about my wrist. Steapa managed to seize a Danish spear and pulled its owner down the bank where a half-dozen Saxons hacked and stabbed in fury so that the ditch was churning with water, blood and blades, and someone shouted for us to go again, and I saw it was Alfred, dismounted, coming to cross the ditch and I roared for my men to protect him.

Pyrlig and I managed to get in front of the king and we stayed there, protecting him as we tried to climb that blood-fouled bank a third time. Pyrlig was screaming in his native tongue, I was cursing in Danish, and somehow we got halfway up and stayed on our feet, and someone, perhaps it was Alfred, was pushing me from behind. Rain hammered us, soaked us. A peal of thunder shook the heavens and I swung Serpent-Breath, trying to hack the Danish shields aside, then swung again, and the shock of the blade striking a shield boss jarred up my arm. A Dane, all beard and wide eyes, lunged a spear at me. I lunged back with the sword, shouted Iseult's name, tried to climb and the spear-Dane slammed his spear forward again, and the blade struck my helmet's forehead and my head snapped back and another

403

Dane hit me on the side of the head and all the world went drunken and dark. My feet slid and I was half aware of falling down into the ditch-water. Someone pulled me clear and dragged me back to the ditch's far side, and there I tried to stand, but fell again.

The king. The king. He had to be protected and he had been in the ditch when I had last seen him, and I knew Alfred was no warrior. He was brave, but he did not love the slaughter as a warrior loves it. I tried to stand again, and this time succeeded, but blood squelched in my right boot and flowed over the boot-top when I put my weight on that leg. The ditch bottom was thick with dead and dying men, half drowned by the flood, but the living had fled from the ditch and the Danes were laughing at us. 'To me!' I shouted. There had to be one last effort. Steapa and Pyrlig closed on me, and Eadric was there, and I was groggy and my head was filled with a ringing sound and my arm seemed feeble, but we had to make that last effort. 'Where's the king?' I asked.

'I threw him out of the ditch,' Pyrlig said.

'Is he safe?'

'I told the priests to hold him down. Told them to hit him if he tried to go again.'

'One more attack,' I said. I did not want to make it. I did not want to clamber over the bodies in the ditch and try to climb that impossible wall, and I knew it was stupid, knew I would probably die if I went again, but we were warriors and warriors will not be beaten. It is reputation. It is pride. It is the madness of battle. I began beating Serpent-Breath against my half-broken shield, and other men took up the rhythm, and the Danes, so close, were inviting us to come and be killed, and I shouted that we were coming. 'God help us,' Steapa said.

'God help us,' Pyrlig echoed.

I did not want to go. I was frightened, but I feared being called a coward more than I feared the ramparts, and so I screamed at my men to slaughter the bastards, and then I ran. I jumped over the corpses in the ditch, lost my footing on the far side, fell on my shield and rolled aside so that no Dane could plunge a spear into my unprotected back. I hauled myself up and my helmet had skewed in the fall so that the face-plate half blinded me, and I fumbled it straight with my sword hand as I began to climb and Steapa was there, and Pyrlig was with me, and I waited for the first hard Danish blow.

It did not come. I struggled up the bank, the shield over my head, and I expected the death blow, but there was silence and I lifted the shield and thought I must have died for all I saw was the rain-filled sky. The Danes had gone. One moment they had been sneering at us, calling us women and cowards, and boasting how they would slice open our bellies and feed our guts to the ravens, and now they were gone. I clambered to the top of the wall and saw a second ditch and second wall beyond, and the Danes were scrambling up that inner rampart and I supposed that they intended to make a defence there, but instead they vanished over its top and Pyrlig grabbed my arm and pulled me on. 'They're running!' he shouted, 'by God, the bastards are running!' He had to shout to make himself heard over the rain.

'On! On!' someone shouted, and we ran into the second flooded ditch and up over the undefended inner bank and I saw Osric's men, the fyrd of Wiltunscir that had been defeated in the opening moments of the fight, had managed to cross the fort's walls. We learned later that they had gone into the valley where the white horse lay dead, and in the blinding rain they had made it to the fort's eastern corner which, because Guthrum thought it unapproachable, was only lightly defended. The rampart was lower there, hardly more than a grassy ridge on the valley's slope, and they had flooded over the wall and so got behind the other defenders.

Who now ran. If they had stayed then they would have been slaughtered to a man, so they fled across the fort's wide interior, and some were slow to realise that the battle was lost and those we trapped. I just wanted to kill for Iseult's sake, and I put two fugitives down, hacking them with Serpent-Breath with such fury that she cut through mail, leather and flesh to bite as deep as an axe. I was screaming my anger, wanting more victims, but we were too many and the trapped Danes were too few. The rain kept falling and the thunder bellowed as I looked about for enemies to kill, and then I saw one last group of them, back to back, fighting off a swarm of Saxons, and I ran towards them and suddenly saw their banner. The eagle's wing. It was Ragnar.

His men, outnumbered and overwhelmed, were dying. 'Let him live!' I shouted, 'let him live!' and three Saxons turned towards me and they saw my long hair and my arm rings bright on my mailed sleeves, and they must have thought I was a Dane for they ran at me, and I fended off the first with Serpent-Breath. The second hammered my shield with his axe, and the third circled behind me and I turned fast, scything Serpent-Breath, shouted that I was a Saxon, but they did not hear me. Then Steapa slammed into them and they scattered, and Pyrlig grabbed my arm, but I shook him off and ran towards Ragnar, who was snarling at the ring of enemies, inviting any one of them to try and kill him. His banner had fallen and his crewmen were dead, but he looked like a war god in his shining mail and with his splintered shield and his long sword and his defiant face, and then the ring began to close. I ran, shouting, and he turned towards me, thinking I had come to kill him, and he raised his sword and I brushed it aside with my shield, threw my arms around him and drove him to the turf.

Steapa and Pyrlig guarded us. They fended off the Saxons, telling them to look for other victims, and I rolled away from Ragnar, who sat up and looked at me with astonishment. I saw that his shield hand was bloody. A blade, cutting through the limewood, had sliced into his palm, hacking down between the fingers so that it looked as though he had two small hands instead of one. 'I must bind that wound,' I said.

'Uhtred,' he just said, as if he did not really believe it was me.

'I looked for you,' I told him, 'because I did not want to fight you.'

He flinched as he shook the shattered remnants of the shield away from his wounded hand. I could see Bishop Alewold running across the fort in mud-spattered robes, waving his arms and shouting that God had delivered the pagans into our hands. 'I told Guthrum to fight outside the fort,' Ragnar said. 'We would have killed you all.'

'You would,' I agreed. By staying in the fort, Guthrum had let us defeat his army piece by piece, but even so it was a miracle that the day was ours.

'You're bleeding,' Ragnar said. I had taken a spear blade in the back of my right thigh. I have the scar to this day. Pyrlig cut a strip of cloth from a dead man's jerkin and used it to bind Ragnar's hand. He wanted to bandage my thigh, but the bleeding had lessened and I managed to stand, though the pain, which I had not felt ever since the wound had been given, suddenly struck me. I touched Thor's hammer. We had won. 'They killed my woman,' I told Ragnar. He said nothing, but just stood beside me and, because my thigh was agony and I suddenly felt weak, I put an arm about his shoulders. 'Iseult, she was called,' I said, 'and my son is dead too.' I was glad it was raining or else the tears on my face would have shown. 'Where's Brida?'

'I sent her down the hill,' Ragnar told me. We were limping together towards the fort's northern ramparts.

'And you stayed?'

'Someone had to stay as a rearguard,' he said bleakly. I think he was crying too, because of the shame of the defeat. It was a battle Guthrum could not lose, yet he had.

Pyrlig and Steapa were still with me, and I could see Eadric stripping a dead Dane of his mail, but there was no sign of Leofric. I asked Pyrlig where he was, and Pyrlig gave me a pained look and shook his head.

'Dead?' I asked.

'An axe,' he said, 'in the spine.' I was numb, too numb to speak, for it did not seem possible that the indestructible Leofric was dead, but he was, and I wished I could give him a Danish funeral, a fire-funeral, so that the smoke of his corpse would rise to the halls of the gods. 'I'm sorry,' Pyrlig said.

'The price of Wessex,' I said, and then we climbed the northern ramparts, that were crowded with Alfred's soldiers.

The rain was lessening, though it still fell in great swathes across the plain below. It was as if we stood on the rim of the world, and ahead of us was an immensity of cloud and rain, while beneath us, on the long steep slope, hundreds of Danes scrambled to the foot of the escarpment where their horses had been left.

'Guthrum,' Ragnar said bitterly.

'He lives?'

'He was the first to run,' he said. 'Svein told him we should fight outside the walls,' he went on, 'but Guthrum feared defeat more than he ever wanted victory.'

A cheer sounded as Alfred's banners were carried across the captured fort to the northern ramparts. Alfred, mounted again, and with a bronze circlet about his helmet, rode with the flags. Beocca was on his knees giving thanks, while Alfred had a dazed smile and a look of disbelief, and I swear he wept as his standards were rammed into the turf at the world's edge. The dragon and the cross flew above his kingdom that had almost been lost, but had been saved so that there was still one Saxon king in England.

But Leofric was dead and Iseult was a corpse and a hard rain fell across the land we had rescued.

Wessex.

Historical Note

The Westbury white horse is cut into the chalk of the escarpment beneath Bratton Camp on the edge of the Wiltshire
Downs. From the north it can be seen for miles. The present
horse, a handsome beast, is over a hundred feet long and almost
two hundred feet high and was cut in the 1770s, making it
the oldest of Wiltshire's ten white horses, but local legend says
that it replaced a much older horse that was blazoned into the
chalk hillside after the battle of Ethandun in 878.

I should like to think that legend is true, but no histo-
rian can be certain of the location of the battle of Ethandun,
where Alfred met Guthrum's Danes, though Bratton Camp,
above the village of Edington, is the prime candidate. Bratton
Camp is an Iron Age fortress which still stands just above
the Westbury white horse. John Peddie, in his useful book,
Alfred, Warrior King, places Ethandun at Bratton Camp, and
Edgar's Stone at Kingston Deverill in the Wylye valley, and
I am persuaded by his reasoning.

There is no debate about the location of Æthelingæg. That
is now Athelney, in the Somerset Levels, near Taunton, and
if Bratton Camp is substantially unaltered since 878, the levels
are changed utterly. Today, mostly thanks to the medieval
monks who dyked and drained the land, they make a wide,
fertile plain, but in the ninth century they were a vast swamp

mingled with tidal flats, an almost impenetrable marsh into which Alfred retreated after the disaster at Chippenham.

That disaster was the result of his generosity in agreeing the truce which allowed Guthrum to leave Exeter and retreat to Gloucester in Danish-held Mercia. That truce was secured by Danish hostages, but Guthrum, just as he had broken the truce arranged at Wareham in 876, again proved untrustworthy and, immediately after Twelfth Night, attacked and captured Chippenham, thus precipitating the greatest crisis of Alfred's long reign. The king was defeated and most of his country taken by the Danes. Some great nobles, Wulfhere, the Ealdorman of Wiltshire, among them, defected to the enemy, and Alfred's kingdom was reduced to the watery wastes of the Somerset Levels. Yet in the spring, just four months after the disaster at Chippenham, Alfred assembled an army, led it to Ethandun, and there defeated Guthrum. All that happened. What, sadly, did not probably happen is the burning of the cakes. That story, how a peasant woman struck Alfred after he allowed her cakes to burn, is the most famous folk tale attached to Alfred, but its source is very late and thus very unreliable.

Alfred, Ælswith, Wulfhere, Æthelwold and Brother (later Bishop) Asser all existed, as did Guthrum. Svein is a fictional character. The great Danish enemies before Guthrum had been the three Lothbrok brothers, and the defeat of the last of them at the battle of Cynuit occurred while Alfred was at Athelney. For fictional reasons I moved that Saxon victory forward a year, and it forms the ending of *The Last Kingdom*, the novel which precedes *The Pale Horseman*, which meant I had to invent a character, Svein, and a skirmish, the burning of Svein's ships, to replace Cynuit.

The two primary sources for Alfred's reign are the Anglo-Saxon Chronicle and Bishop Asser's life of the king, and neither, alas, tells us much about how Alfred defeated

Guthrum at Ethandun. Both armies, by later standards, were small, and it is almost certain that Guthrum considerably outnumbered Alfred. The West Saxon fyrd that won Ethandun was mostly drawn from Somerset, Wiltshire and western Hampshire, suggesting that all eastern Wessex, and most of the north of the country, had been subdued by the Danes. We know the fyrd of Devonshire was intact (it had won the victory at Cynuit), as was the fyrd of Dorset, yet neither are mentioned as part of Alfred's army, suggesting that they were held back to deter a seaborne attack. The lack of the fyrds from those two powerful shires, if indeed they were absent, only confirms what a remarkable victory Alfred won.

The Saxons had been in Britain since the fifth century. By the ninth century they ruled almost all of what is now England, but then the Danes came and the Saxon kingdoms crumbled. *The Last Kingdom* tells of the defeat of Northumbria, Mercia and East Anglia, and *The Pale Horseman* describes how Wessex almost followed those northern neighbours into history's oblivion. For a few months in early 878 the idea of England, its culture and language, were reduced to a few square miles of swamp. One more defeat and there would probably never have been a political entity called England. We might have had a Daneland instead, and this novel would probably have been written in Danish. Yet Alfred survived, he won, and that is why history awarded him the honorific 'the Great'. His successors were to finish his work, they were to take back the three northern kingdoms and so, for the first time, unite the Saxon lands into one kingdom called England, but that work was begun by Alfred the Great.

Yet in 878, even after the victory at Ethandun, that must have seemed an impossible dream. It is a long way from Ethandun's white horse to the bleak moors north of Hadrian's Wall, so Uhtred and his companions must campaign again.

Also by Bernard Cornwell

The STARBUCK Chronicles
Rebel
Copperhead
Battle Flag
The Bloody Ground

The WARLORD Chronicles
The Winter King
The Enemy of God
Excalibur

By Bernard Cornwell and Susannah Kells

A Crowning Mercy
Fallen Angels

Non-Fiction

Waterloo: The History of Four Days, Three Armies
and Three Battles

THE SHARPE SERIES
(IN CHRONOLOGICAL ORDER)